THE VERY BEST OF THE BEST

ALSO BY GARDNER DOZOIS

ANTHOLOGIES

A DAY IN THE LIFE

ANOTHER WORLD

BEST SCIENCE FICTION STORIES OF THE
    YEAR #6–10

THE BEST OF ISAAC ASIMOV'S SCIENCE
    FICTION MAGAZINE

TIME-TRAVELERS FROM ISAAC ASIMOV'S
    SCIENCE FICTION MAGAZINE

TRANSCENDENTAL TALES FROM ISAAC
    ASIMOV'S SCIENCE FICTION MAGAZINE

ISAAC ASIMOV'S ALIENS

ISAAC ASIMOV'S MARS

ISAAC ASIMOV'S SF LITE

ISAAC ASIMOV'S WAR

ROADS NOT TAKEN (with Stanley Schmidt)

THE YEAR'S BEST SCIENCE FICTION, #1–35

FUTURE EARTHS: UNDER AFRICAN SKIES
    (with Mike Resnick)

FUTURE EARTHS: UNDER SOUTH AMERICAN
    SKIES (with Mike Resnick)

RIPPER! (with Susan Casper)

MODERN CLASSIC SHORT NOVELS OF
    SCIENCE FICTION

MODERN CLASSICS OF FANTASY

KILLING ME SOFTLY

DYING FOR IT

THE GOOD OLD STUFF

THE GOOD NEW STUFF

EXPLORERS

THE FURTHEST HORIZON

WORLDMAKERS

SUPERMEN

COEDITED WITH SHEILA WILLIAMS

ISAAC ASIMOV'S PLANET EARTH

ISAAC ASIMOV'S ROBOTS

ISAAC ASIMOV'S VALENTINES

ISAAC ASIMOV'S SKIN DEEP

ISAAC ASIMOV'S GHOSTS

ISAAC ASIMOV'S VAMPIRES

ISAAC ASIMOV'S MOONS

ISAAC ASIMOV'S CHRISTMAS

ISAAC ASIMOV'S CAMELOT

ISAAC ASIMOV'S WEREWOLVES

ISAAC ASIMOV'S SOLAR SYSTEM

ISAAC ASIMOV'S DETECTIVES

ISAAC ASIMOV'S CYBERDREAMS

COEDITED WITH JACK DANN

ALIENS!	SORCERERS!	DRAGONS!	HACKERS
UNICORNS!	DEMONS!	HORSES!	TIMEGATES
MAGICATS!	DOGTALES!	UNICORNS 2	CLONES
MAGICATS 2!	SEA SERPENTS!	INVADERS!	NANOTECH
BESTIARY!	DINOSAURS!	ANGELS!	IMMORTALS
MERMAIDS!	LITTLE PEOPLE!	DINOSAURS II	

FICTION

STRANGERS

THE VISIBLE MAN (COLLECTION)

NIGHTMARE BLUE
    (with George Alec Effinger)

SLOW DANCING THROUGH TIME
    (with Jack Dann, Michael Swanwick,
    Susan Casper, and Jack C. Haldeman II)

THE PEACEMAKER

GEODESIC DREAMS (collection)

NONFICTION

THE FICTION OF JAMES TIPTREE, JR.

THE VERY BEST
OF THE BEST

35 Years of the Year's Best
SCIENCE FICTION

edited by

Gardner Dozois

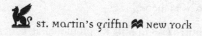 St. Martin's griffin ⚏ New York

These stories are works of fiction. All of the characters, organizations, and events portrayed in these stories are either products of the authors' imaginations or are used fictitiously.

THE VERY BEST OF THE BEST: 35 YEARS OF THE YEAR'S BEST SCIENCE FICTION. Copyright © 2019 by Gardner Dozois. All rights reserved. Printed in the United States of America. For information, address St. Martin's Press, 175 Fifth Avenue, New York, N.Y. 10010.

www.stmartins.com

The Library of Congress Cataloging-in-Publication Data is available upon request.

ISBN 978-1-250-29620-7 (trade paperback)
ISBN 978-1-250-29619-1 (hardcover)
ISBN 978-1-250-29621-4 (ebook)

Our books may be purchased in bulk for promotional, educational, or business use. Please contact your local bookseller or the Macmillan Corporate and Premium Sales Department at 1-800-221-7945, extension 5442, or by email at MacmillanSpecialMarkets@macmillan.com.

First Edition: February 2019

10 9 8 7 6 5 4 3 2 1

contents

permissions

acknowledgments

I'd like to thank all the people who have helped me assemble these volumes over the years; Susan Casper, Sean Swanwick, and Vaughne Lee Hanson for technical support; too many authors and editors to list; and thanks to my own editors, Jim Frenkel, Stuart Moore, Gordon Van Gelder, Bryan Cholfin, and, especially, Marc Resnick.

preface

The first volume of this series, *The Year's Best Science Fiction: First Annual Collection*, was published way back in 1984, a time so distant and so different that it might as well be another world, and one that would probably seem as alien as any fictional Mars to many of today's young readers. As I type these words, it's 2017, with *The Year's Best Science Fiction: Thirty-Fifth Annual Collection* about to come out. Although I already edited *The Best of the Best* in 2005 and *The Best of the Best, Volume 2: 20 Years of the Best Short Science Fiction Novels* in 2007, it seemed time for another such collection—so here it is, covering the years from 2003 to 2017, and from *The Year's Best Science Fiction: Twentieth Annual Collection* to *The Year's Best Science Fiction: Thirty-Fifth Annual Collection*.

Over the entire span of the series, from 1984 to 2017, we've reprinted more than six hundred stories, from authors from all around the world, reprinted from magazines, anthologies, electronic magazines, novella chapbooks, and podcasts. I hope that you've enjoyed and will enjoy some of them. If you do, the credit goes to the authors who wrote them, and the editors who were shrewd enough to buy them in the first place. They did the real work. All I've done, over the years, is to offer you a chance to read the stories that I myself enjoyed.

Time that is intolerant
Of the brave and innocent,
And indifferent in a week
To a beautiful physique,
Worships language and
     forgives
Everyone by whom it lives.
        —W. H. AUDEN

THE VERY BEST
OF THE BEST

the potter of Bones

ELEANOR ARNASON

Eleanor Arnason published her first novel, The Sword Smith, *in 1978, and followed it with such novels as* Daughter of the Bear King *and* To the Resurrection Station. *In 1991, she published her best-known novel, one of the strongest novels of the nineties, the critically-acclaimed* A Woman of the Iron People, *a complex and substantial novel which won the prestigious James Tiptree Jr. Memorial Award. Her short fiction has appeared in* Asimov's Science Fiction, The Magazine of Fantasy & Science Fiction, Amazing, Orbit, Xanadu, *and elsewhere. Her other books include* Ring of Swords *and* Tomb of the Fathers, *and a chapbook,* Mammoths of the Great Plains, *which includes the eponymous novella, plus an interview with her and a long essay, and a collection,* Big Mama Stories. *Her story "Stellar Harvest" was a Hugo Finalist in 2000. Her most recent books are two new collections,* Hidden Folk: Icelandic Fantasies, *and a major SF retrospective collection,* Hwarhath Stories: Transgressive Tales by Aliens. *She lives in St. Paul, Minnesota.*

Here she takes us to a strange planet sunk in its own version of a medieval past for a fascinating study of the birth of the Scientific Method . . . and also for an intricate, moving, and quietly lyrical portrait of a rebellious and sharp-minded woman born into a time she's out of synch with and a world that refuses to see what she sees all around her.

The northeast coast of the Great Southern Continent is hilly and full of inlets. These make good harbors, their waters deep and protected from the wind by steep slopes and grey stone cliffs. Dark forests top the hills. Pebble beaches edge the harbors. There are many little towns.

The climate would be tropical, except for a polar current which runs along the coast, bringing fish and rain. The local families prosper through fishing and the rich, semi-tropical forests that grow inland. Blackwood grows there, and iridescent greywood, as well as lovely ornamentals: night-blooming starflower, day-blooming skyflower and the matriarch of trees, crown-of-fire. The first two species are cut for lumber. The last three are gathered as saplings, potted and shipped to distant ports, where affluent families buy them for their courtyards.

Nowadays, of course, it's possible to raise the saplings in glass houses anywhere on the planet. But most folk still prefer trees gathered in their native forests. A plant grows better, if it's been pollinated naturally by the fabulous flying bugs of the south, watered by the misty coastal rains and dug up by a forester who's the heir to generations of diggers and potters. The most successful brands have names like "Coastal Rain" and emblems suggesting their authenticity: a forester holding a trowel, a night bug with broad furry wings floating over blossoms.

This story is about a girl born in one of these coastal towns. Her mother was a well-regarded fisherwoman, her father a sailor who'd washed up after a bad storm. Normally, a man such as this—a stranger, far from his kin—would not have been asked to impregnate any woman. But the man was clever, mannerly and had the most wonderful fur: not grey, as was usual in that part of the world, but tawny red-gold. His eyes were pale clear yellow; his ears, large and set well out from his head, gave him an entrancing appearance of alertness and intelligence. Hard to pass up looks like these! The matrons of Tulwar coveted them for their children and grandchildren.

He—a long hard journey ahead of him, with no certainty that he'd ever reach home—agreed to their proposal. A man should be obedient to the senior women in his family. If they aren't available, he should obey the matrons and matriarchs nearby. In his own country, where his looks were ordinary, he had never expected to breed. It might happen, if he'd managed some notable achievement; knowing himself, he didn't plan on it. Did he want children? Some men do. Or did he want to leave something behind him on this foreign shore, evidence that he'd existed, before venturing back on the ocean? We can't know. He mated with our heroine's mother. Before the child was born, he took a coastal trader north, leaving nothing behind except a bone necklace and Tulwar Haik.

Usually, when red and grey interbreed, the result is a child with dun fur. Maybe Haik's father wasn't the first red sailor to wash up on the Tulwar coast. It's possible that her mother had a gene for redness, which finally expressed itself, after generations of hiding. In any case, the child was red with large ears and bright green eyes. What a beauty! Her kin nicknamed her Crown-of-Fire.

When she was five, her mother died. It happened this way: the ocean current that ran along the coast shifted east, taking the Tulwar fish far out in the ocean. The Tulwar followed; and somewhere, days beyond sight of land, a storm drowned their fleet. Mothers, aunts, uncles, cousins disappeared. Nothing came home except a few pieces of wood: broken spars and oars. The people left in Tulwar Town were either young or old.

Were there no kin in the forest? A few, but the Tulwar had relied on the ocean.

Neighboring families offered to adopt the survivors. "No thank you," said the Tulwar matriarchs. "The name of this bay is Tulwar Harbor. Our houses will remain here, and we will remain in our houses."

"As you wish," the neighbors said.

Haik grew up in a half-empty town. The foresters, who provided the family's income, were mostly away. The adults present were mostly white-furred and bent: great-aunts and -uncles, who had not thought to spend their last years mending houses and caring for children. Is it any wonder that Haik grew up wild?

Not that she was bad; but she liked being alone, wandering the pebble beaches and climbing the cliffs. The cliffs were not particularly difficult to climb, being made of sedimentary stone that had eroded and collapsed. Haik walked over slopes of fallen rock or picked her way up steep ravines full of scrubby trees. It was not adventure she sought, but solitude and what might be called "nature" nowadays, if you're one of those people in love with newfangled words and ideas. Then, it was called "the five aspects" or "water, wind, cloud, leaf and stone." Though she was the daughter of sailors, supported by the forest, neither leaf nor water drew her. Instead, it was rock she studied—and the things in rock. Since the rock was sedimentary, she found fossils rather than crystals.

Obviously, she was not the first person to see shells embedded in cliffs; but the intensity of her curiosity was unusual. How had the shells gotten into the cliffs? How had they turned to stone? And why were so many of them unfamiliar?

She asked her relatives.

"They've always been there," said one great-aunt.

"A high tide, made higher by a storm," said another.

"The Goddess," a very senior male cousin told her, "whose behavior we don't question. She acts as she does for her own reasons, which are not unfolded to us."

The young Tulwar, her playmates, found the topic boring. Who could possibly care about shells made of stone? "They don't shimmer like living shells, and there's nothing edible in them. Think about living shellfish, Haik! Or fish! Or trees like the ones that support our family!"

If her kin could not answer her questions, she'd find answers herself. Haik continued her study. She was helped by the fact that the strata along the northeast coast had not buckled or been folded over. Top was new. Bottom was old. She could trace the history of the region's life by climbing up.

At first, she didn't realize this. Instead, she got a hammer and began to break out fossils, taking them to one of the town's many empty houses. There, through trial and error, she learned to clean the fossils and to open them. "Unfolding with a hammer," she called the process.

Nowadays we discourage this kind of ignorant experimentation, especially at important sites. Remember this story takes place in the distant past. There was no one on the planet able to teach Haik; and the fossils she destroyed would have been destroyed by erosion long before the science of paleontology came into existence.

She began by collecting shells, laying them out on the tables left behind when the house was abandoned. Imagine her in a shadowy room, light slanting through the shutters. The floor is thick with dust. The paintings on the walls, fish and flowering trees, are peeling. Haik—a thin red adolescent in a tunic—bends over her shells, arranging them. She has discovered one of the great pleasures of intelligent life: organization or (as we call it now) taxonomy.

This was not her invention. All people organize information. But most people organize information for which they can see an obvious use: varieties of fish and their habits, for example. Haik had discovered the pleasure of knowledge that has no evident use. Maybe, in the shadows, you should imagine an old woman with white fur, dressed in a roughly woven tunic. Her feet are bare and caked with dirt. She watches Haik with amusement.

In time, Haik noticed there was a pattern to where she found her shells. The ones on the cliff tops were familiar. She could find similar or identical shells washed up on the Tulwar beaches. But as she descended, the creatures in the stone became increasingly strange. Also, and this puzzled her, certain strata were full of bones that obviously belonged to land animals. Had the ocean advanced, then retreated, then advanced again? How old were these objects? How much time had passed since they were alive, if they had ever been alive? Some of her senior kin believed they were mineral formations that bore an odd resemblance to the remains of animals. "The world is full of repetition and similarity," they told Haik, "evidence the Goddess has little interest in originality."

Haik reserved judgment. She'd found the skeleton of a bird so perfect that she had no trouble imagining flesh and feathers over the delicate bones. The animal's wings, if wings they were, ended in clawed hands. What mineral process would create the cliff top shells, identical to living shells, and this lovely familiar-yet-unfamiliar skeleton? If the Goddess had no love for originality, how to explain the animals toward the cliff bottom, spiny and knobby, with an extraordinary number of legs? They didn't resemble anything Haik had ever seen. What did they repeat?

When she was fifteen, her relatives came to her. "Enough of this folly! We are a small lineage, barely surviving; and we all have to work. Pick a useful occupation, and we'll apprentice you."

Most of her cousins became foresters. A few became sailors, shipping out with their neighbors, since the Tulwar no longer had anything except dories. But Haik's passion in life was stone. The town had no masons, but it did have a potter.

"Our foresters need pots," said Haik. "And Rakai is getting old. Give me to her."

"A wise choice," said the great-aunts with approval. "For the first time in years, you have thought about your family's situation."

Haik went to live in the house occupied by ancient Rakai. Most of the rooms were empty, except for pots. Clay dust drifted in the air. Lumps of dropped clay spotted the floors. The old potter was never free of the material. "When I was young, I washed more," she said. "But time is running out, and I have much to do. Wash if you want. It does no harm, when a person is your age. Though you ought to remember that I may not be around to teach you in a year or two or three."

Haik did wash. She was a neat child. But she remembered Rakai's warning and studied hard. As it turned out, she enjoyed making pots. Nowadays, potters can buy their materials from a craft cooperative; and many do. But in the past every potter mined his or her own clay; and a potter like Rakai, working in a poor town, did not use rare minerals in her glazes. "These are not fine cups for rich matrons to drink from," she told Haik. "These are pots for plants. Ordinary glazes will do, and minerals we can find in our own country." Once again Haik found herself out with hammer and shovel. She liked the ordinary work of preparation, digging the clay and hammering pieces of mineral from their matrices. Grinding the minerals was fine, also, though not easy; and she loved the slick texture of wet clay, as she felt through it for grit. Somehow, though it wasn't clear to her yet, the clay—almost liquid in her fingers—was connected to the questions she had asked about stone.

The potter's wheel was frustrating. When Rakai's old fingers touched a lump of clay, it rose into a pot like a plant rising from the ground in spring, entire and perfect, with no effort that Haik could see. When Haik tried to do the same, nothing was achieved except a mess.

"I'm like a baby playing with mud!"

"Patience and practice," said old Rakai.

Haik listened, being no fool. Gradually, she learned how to shape clay and fire it in the kiln Rakai had built behind the house. Her first efforts were bad, but she kept several to store her favorite pieces of rock. One piece was red iron ore, which could be ground down to make a shiny black glaze. The rest were fossils: shells and strange marine animals and the claw-handed bird.

At this point in the story, it's important to know the meaning of the word "potter" in Haik's language. As in our language, it meant a maker of pots. In addition, it meant someone who puts things into pots. Haik was still learning to make pots. But she was already a person who put stones or bones into pots, and this is not a trivial occupation, but rather a science. Never undervalue taxonomy. The foundation of all knowledge is fact, and facts that are not organized are useless.

Several years passed. Haik learned her teacher's skill, though her work lacked Rakai's elegance.

"It's the cliffs," said the old potter. "And the stones you bring back from them. They have entered your spirit, and you are trying to reproduce them in clay. I learned from plants, which have grace and symmetry. But you—"

One of Haik's pots was on the wheel: a squat, rough-surfaced object. The handles were uneven. At first, such things had happened due to lack of skill, but she found she liked work that was a little askew. She planned a colorless, transparent glaze that would streak the jar—like water seeping down a rock face, Haik suddenly realized.

"There's no harm in this," said Rakai. "We all learn from the world around us. If you want to be a potter of stones, fine. Stones and bones, if you are right and the things you find *are* bones. Stones and bones and shells."

The old potter hobbled off. Should she break the pot, Haik wondered. Was it wrong to love the cliffs and the objects they contained? Rakai had told her no. She had the old potter's permission to be herself. On a whim Haik scratched an animal into the clay. Its head was like a hammer, with large eyes at either end—on the hammer's striking surfaces, as Haik explained it to herself. The eyes were faceted; and the long body was segmented. Each segment had a pair of legs, except for the final segment, which had two whip-like tails longer than the rest of the animal. No one she had met, not travelers to the most distant places nor the most outrageous liars, had ever described such an animal. Yet she had found its remains often, always in the cliffs' lower regions, in a kind of rock she had named "far-down dark grey."

Was this one of the Goddess's jokes? Most of the remains were damaged; only by looking carefully had she found intact examples; and no one else she knew was interested in such things. Had the Goddess built these cliffs and filled them with remains in order to fool Tulwar Haik?

Hardly likely! She looked at the drawing she'd made. The animal's body was slightly twisted, and its tails flared out on either side. It seemed alive, as if it might crawl off her pot and into Tulwar Harbor. The girl exhaled, her heart beating quickly. There was truth here. The creature she had drawn must have lived. Maybe it still lived in some distant part of the ocean. (She had found it among shells. Its home must be aquatic.) She refused to believe such a shape could come into existence through accident. She had been mixing and kneading and spinning and dropping clay for years. Nothing like this had ever appeared, except through intent. Surely it was impious to argue that the Goddess acted without thought. This marvelous world could not be the result of the Great One dropping the stuff-of-existence or squishing it aimlessly between her holy fingers. Haik refused to believe the animal was a joke. The Goddess had better things to do, and the animal was beautiful in its own strange way. Why would the Goddess, who was humorous but not usually malicious, make such an intricate and lovely lie?

Haik drew the animal on the other side of the pot, giving it a slightly different pose, then fired the pot and glazed it. The glaze, as planned, was clear and uneven, like a film of water running down the pot's dark grey fabric.

As you know, there are regions of the world where families permit sex among their members, if the relationship is distant enough. The giant families of the third continent, with fifty or a hundred thousand members, say there's nothing wrong with third or fourth or fifth cousins becoming lovers; though inbreeding is always wrong. But Haik's family did not live in such a region; and their lineage was so small and lived so closely together that no one was a distant relative.

For this reason, Haik did not experience love until she was twenty and went down the coast on a trading ship to sell pots in Tsugul.

This was an island off the coast, a famous market in those days. The harbor was on the landward side, protected from ocean storms. A town of wood and plaster buildings went down slopes to the wooden warehouses and docks. Most of the plaster had been painted yellow or pale blue. The wood, where it showed, was dark blue or red. A colorful town, thought Haik when she arrived, made even more colorful by the many plants in pots. They stood on terraces and rooftops, by doorways, on the stairway streets. A good place to sell Rakai's work and her own.

In fact, she did well, helped by a senior forester who had been sent to sell the Tulwar's other product.

"I'd never say a word against your teacher, lass," he told her. "But your pots really set off my trees. They, my trees, are so delicate and brilliant; and your pots are so rough and plain. Look!" He pointed at a young crown-of-fire, blossoming in a squat black pot. "Beauty out of ugliness! Light out of darkness! You will make a fortune for our family!"

She didn't think of the pot as ugly. On it, in relief, were shells, blurred just a bit by the iron glaze. The shells were a series, obviously related, but from different parts of the Tulwar cliffs. Midway up the cliffs, the first place she found them, the shells were a single plain coil. Rising from there, the shells became ever more spiny and intricate. This progression went in a line around the pot, till a spiked monstrosity stood next to its straightforward ancestor.

Could Haik think this? Did she already understand about evolution? Maybe not. In any case, she said nothing to her kinsman.

That evening, in a tavern, she met a sailor from Sorg, a tall thin arrogant woman, whose body had been shaved into a pattern of white fur and black skin. They talked over cups of *halin*. The woman began brushing Haik's arm, marveling at the red fur. "It goes so well with your green eyes. You're a young one. Have you ever made love with a foreigner?"

"I've never made love," said Haik.

The woman looked interested, but said, "You can't be that young."

Haik explained she'd never traveled before, not even to neighboring towns. "I've been busy learning my trade."

The Sorg woman drank more *halin*. "I like being first. Would you be interested in making love?"

Haik considered the woman, who was certainly exotic looking. "Why do you shave your fur?"

"It's hot in my home country; and we like to be distinctive. Other folk may follow each other like city-building bugs. We do not!"

Haik glanced around the room and noticed other Sorg women, all clipped and shaved in the same fashion, but she did not point out the obvious, being young and polite.

They went to the Sorg woman's ship, tied at a dock. There were other couples on the deck, all women. "We have a few men in the crew this trip," her sexual partner said. "But they're all on shore, looking for male lovers; and they won't be back till we're ready to lift anchor."

The experience was interesting, Haik thought later, though she had not imagined making love for the first time on a foreign ship, surrounded by other couples, who were not entirely quiet. She was reminded of fish, spawning in shallow water.

"Well, you seemed to enjoy that," said the Sorg woman. "Though you are a silent one."

"My kin say I'm thoughtful."

"You shouldn't be, with red fur like fire. Someone like you ought to burn."

Why? wondered Haik, then fell asleep and dreamed that she was talking with an old woman dressed in a plain, rough tunic. The woman's feet were muddy. The nails on her hands were untrimmed and long, curling over the tips of her fingers like claws. There was dirt under the nails. The old woman said, "If you were an animal, instead of a person, you would have mated with a male; and there might have been children, created not as the result of a breeding contact, but out of sexual passion. Imagine a world filled with that kind of reproduction! It is the world you live in! Only people use reason in dealing with sex. Only people breed deliberately."

She woke at dawn, remembering the dream, though it made little sense. The woman had seemed like a messenger, but her message was obvious. Haik kissed the Sorg woman goodby, pulled on her tunic and stumbled down the gangway. Around her the air was cold and damp. Her feet left prints on dew-covered wood.

She had sex with the Sorg women several more times. Then the foreign ship lifted anchor, and Haik's lover was gone, leaving only a shell necklace.

"Some other woman will have to make you burn," the lover said. "But I was the first, and I want to be remembered."

Haik thanked her for the necklace and spent a day or two walking in the island's hills. The stone here was dark red and grainy and did not appear to contain fossils. Then she and her kinsman sailed north.

After that, she made sure to go on several trips a year. If the ship was crewed by women, she began looking for lovers as soon as she was on board. Otherwise, she waited till they reached a harbor town. Sometimes she remained with a single lover. At other times, she went from one to another or joined a group. Her childhood nickname, long forgotten, came back to her, though now she was known as "Fire," rather than "Crown-of-Fire." She was a flame that burned without being burned.

"You never feel real affection," one lover told her. "This is nothing but sex for you."

Was this true? She felt affection for Rakai and her family at home and something approaching passion for her work with clay and stone. But these women?

As we know, men are more fervent and loyal lovers than women. They will organize their lives around affection. But most women are fond of their lovers and regret leaving them, as they usually must, though less often in modern times; and the departures matter less now, since travel has become so rapid. Lovers can meet fifty times a year, if they're willing to pay the airfare.

Haik enjoyed sex and her sexual partners, but left with no regrets, her spirit untouched.

"All your fire is in your sexual parts," another partner said. "Nothing burns in your mind."

When she was twenty-five her family decided to breed her. There was no way she could refuse. If the Tulwar were going to survive, every healthy female had to bear children. After discussion, the senior women approached the Tsugul, who agreed to a mating contract. What happened next Haik did not like to remember. A young man arrived from Tsugul and stayed with her family. They mated till she became pregnant, then he was sent home with gifts: fine pots mostly, made by her and Rakai.

"I won't have children in my pottery," the old woman said.

"I will give the child to one of my cousins to raise," said Haik.

She bore female twins, dun colored with bright green eyes. For a while, looking at them, she thought of raising them. But this idea came from exhaustion and relief. She was not maternal. More than children she wanted fossils and her pots.

A female cousin took them, a comfortable woman with three children of her own. "Five is always lucky," she told Haik.

It seemed to be. All five children flourished like starflower trees.

Rakai lasted till Haik was almost thirty. In her last years, the old potter became confused and wandered out of her house, looking for long-drowned relatives or clay, though she had turned clay digging over to Haik a decade before. One of these journeys took place in an early winter rain. By the time the old woman was found, she was thoroughly drenched and shaking with cold. A coughing sickness developed and carried her away. Haik inherited the pottery.

By this time, she had developed a distinctive style: solid, squat pots with strange creatures drawn on them. Sometimes, the handles were strange creatures made in molds: clawed birds or animals like flowers with thick, segmented stalks. Haik had found fossils of the animals still grasping prey. In most cases, the prey was small fish, so the creatures had been marine predators. But her customers thought they were flowers—granted, strange ones, with petals like worms. "What an imagination you have!"

The pots with molded handles were fine work, intended for small expensive plants. Most of her work was large and sturdy, without handles that could break off. Her glazes remained plain: colorless or black.

Though she was a master potter, her work known up and down the coast, she continued hunting fossils. Her old teacher's house became filled with shelves; and the shelves became filled with pieces of stone. Taking a pen, Haik wrote her name for each creature on the shelf's edge, along with the place where she'd found this particular example. Prowling through the rooms by lantern light, she saw eons of evolution and recognized what she saw. How could she fail to, once the stones were organized?

The first shelves held shells and faint impressions of things that might be seaweed. Then came animals with many limbs, then fish that looked nothing like any fish she'd ever seen. Finally came animals with four limbs, also strange. Most likely, they had lived on land.

She had a theory now. She knew that sand and clay could become solid in the right circumstances. The animals had been caught in muck at the ocean's bottom or in a sand dune on land. Through a process she did not understand, though it must be like the firing of clay in a kiln, the trapping material turned to stone. The animal vanished, most likely burnt up, though it might also have decayed. If nothing else happened, the result was an impression. If the hollow space in the stone became filled, by some liquid seeping in and leaving a deposit, the result was a solid object. Her clawed bird was an impression. Most of her shells were solid.

Was she too clever? Could no one in her age imagine such a theory?

Well, she knew about clay, about molds, about minerals suspended in water. What else is a glaze? There were people in her village who worked with mortar, which is sand that hardens. There were people in nearby villages who used the lost wax process to cast.

All the necessary information was present. But no one except Haik used it to explain the objects in the Tulwar cliffs. Why? Because her kin had barely noticed the fossils and were not curious about them, did not collect them and label them and prowl around at night, looking at the pieces of stone and thinking.

Life had changed through time. It went from the very odd to the less odd to the almost familiar. In a few places on the cliff tops were animals that still lived. So, the process that led to the creation of fossils was still happening or had stopped happening recently.

How much time had this taken? Well, the old people in her town said that species did not change; and as far as she knew, there were no traditions that said animals used to be different. Oh, a few stories about monsters that no one had seen recently. But nothing about strange shells or fish. So the time required for change was longer than the memories of people.

Think of what she had learned and imagined! A world of vast periods of time, of animals that changed, of extinction. Hah! It frightened her! Was there any reason why her people might not vanish, along with the fish and plants they knew? Their lineage was small, its existence precarious. Maybe all life was precarious.

One night she had a dream. She was standing atop the cliffs above Tulwar Town. The houses below her looked very distant, unreachable. There was nothing around her except space, stretching up and down and east over the ocean. (The forest was behind her, and she did not turn around.) Next to her stood an old woman with white fur and dirty feet. "You've come a long way," she said. "Maybe you ought to consider turning back."

"Why?" asked Haik.

"There is no point in your journey. No one is going to believe you."

"About what?"

"My creatures."

"Are you the Goddess?" asked Haik.

The woman inclined her head slightly.

"Shouldn't you look more splendid?"

"Did Rakai look splendid? She worked in clay. I work in the stuff-of-existence. I wouldn't call it clean work, and who do I need to impress?"

"Have things really died out? Or do they exist somewhere in the world?"

"I'm not going to answer your questions," the old woman said. "Figure existence out for yourself."

"Do you advise me to turn back?"

"I never give advice," the Goddess said. "I'm simply telling you that no one will believe you about time and change. Oh, one or two people. You can get some people to believe anything, but sensible people will laugh."

"Should I care?" Haik asked.

"That's the question, isn't it?" the Goddess said. "But as I've said already, I don't give advice."

Then she was gone, and Haik was falling. She woke in bed in Rakai's house. Outside her window, stars blazed and gave her no comfort.

She thought about her dream for some time, then decided to go on a voyage.

Maybe her problem was lack of sex. Her best pots went into wicker baskets, wrapped in straw, along with large plates, some plain, but most with strange creatures painted on them: her lovely bird with claws, the many-legged bugs, fish that wore plate armor instead of scales, and quadrupeds with peculiar horny heads.

When a ship arrived, going north, she took passage. It was crewed by Batanin women, so she had plenty of sex before she reached their destination. But the feeling of loneliness and fear remained. It seemed as if she stood on the edge of an abyss, with nothing around her or below her.

She got off in a harbor town inhabited by the Meskh, a good-sized family. Although they had a port, they were farmers mostly, producing grain and dried fruit for export, along with excellent *halin*.

Her pottery brought good prices in Meskh Market. By this time she was famous as the Strange Animal Potter or The Potter of Shells and Bones.

"You are here in person," her customers said. "This is wonderful! Two famous women in town at once!"

"Who is the other?" Haik asked.

"The actor Dapple. Her troop has just given a series of plays. Now, they're resting, before continuing their tour. You must meet her."

They met that night in a tavern. Haik arrived escorted by several customers, middle aged women with dark fur. At a table in the middle of the room, surrounded by dark Meskh women, was someone tall and slender, broad shouldered, her fur pale silver. Introductions were made. The actor stood. In lantern light, Haik could see the silver fur was dappled with small, dim spots. It was rare for people to keep their baby markings, but a few did.

"Hah! You're a lovely one," the actor said. "Red fur is unusual in this part of the world."

Haik sat down and told the story of her father, then how her mother died and how she had grown up in Tulwar Town. When she finally stopped, she saw the Meskh women were gone. She and Dapple sat alone at the table under the flaring lamp.

"What happened?" Haik asked.

"To the others? Most had the good sense to leave. Those who did not were removed by members of my company."

"And I didn't notice?"

"I don't believe," said Dapple, stretching, "that you are a person who notices much outside your interests. The Meskh have loaned us a house. Why don't you come there with me? We can drink more *halin* and talk more, if you wish. Though I have spent the past half an *ikun* imagining what you look like without clothing."

They went to the house, walking side by side through the dark streets. Inside, in a courtyard full of potted trees and lit by stars, they made love. Dapple pulled some blankets and pillows out of a room, so they weren't uncomfortable. "I have spent too much of my life sleeping on hard ground," the actor said. "If I can avoid discomfort, I will." Then she set to work with extraordinary skillful hands and a mouth that did not seem to belong to an ordinary woman made of flesh, but rather to some spirit out of ancient stories. The Fulfilling Every Wish Spirit, thought Haik. The Spirit of Almost Unendurable Pleasure.

The potter tried to reciprocate, though she knew it was impossible. No one, certainly not her, could equal Dapple's skill in love. But the actor made noises that indicated some satisfaction. Finally, they stopped. The actor clasped her hands in back of her head and looked at the stars. "Can you give me a pot?"

"What?" asked Haik.

"I've seen your work before this, and I would like a keepsake, something to remember you."

At last the flame felt burning. Haik sat up and looked at the long pale figure next to her. "Is this over? Do we have only this night?"

"I have engagements," Dapple said. "We've arranged our passage on a ship that leaves tomorrow. Actors don't have settled lives, Haik. Nor do we usually have permanent lovers."

As in her dream, Haik felt she was falling. But this time she didn't wake in her bed, but remained in the Meskh courtyard.

The Goddess was right. She should give up her obsession. No one cared about the objects she found in cliffs. They did care about her pottery, but she could take leave of pots for a while.

"Let me go with you," she said to Dapple.

The actor looked at her. "Are you serious?"

"I have done nothing since I was fifteen, except make pots and collect certain stones I have a fondness for. More than fifteen years! And what do I have to show? Pots and more pots! Stones and more stones! I would like to have an adventure, Dapple."

The actor laughed and said, "I've done many foolish things in my life. Now, I'll do one more. By all means, come on our journey!" Then she pulled Haik down and kissed her. What a golden tongue!

The next morning, Haik went to her ship and gathered her belongings. They fit in one basket. She never traveled with much, except her pots, and they were sold, the money in a heavy belt around her waist.

Next she went to the harbor mistress. Sitting in the woman's small house, she wrote a letter to her relatives, explaining what had happened and why she wasn't coming home.

"Are you sure this is a good idea?" the mistress said as Haik rolled the letter and put it in a message tube, then sealed the tube with wax.

"Yes." The letter was to go south on the next ship, Haik told the mistress. She gave the woman half her money to hold, till the Tulwar came to claim it.

"This is a foolish plan," the harbor mistress said.

"Have you never been in love?" Haik asked.

"Not this much in love, I'm glad to say."

Haik had started for the door. Now she stopped. The shutters on the room's windows were open. Haik was in a beam of light. Her red fur shone like fire. Her eyes were as clear and green as a cresting ocean wave. Hah! thought the harbor mistress.

"I'm thirty-two and have never been in love, until last night," Haik said. "It has come to me recently that the world is a lonely place." She slung her basket on her back and walked toward Dapple's borrowed house.

A strange woman, thought the harbor mistress.

The actors' ship left on the afternoon tide, Haik with them, standing on the deck, next to her new love.

At this point, the story needs to describe Dapple. She was forty when Haik met her, the first woman to train as an actor and the first person to assemble an acting company made of women. Her early years had been difficult; but by this time, she was successful and self-confident, a fine actor and even better playwright. Some of her writing has come forward to us, though only in a fragmentary condition. Still, the words shine like diamonds, unscratched by fate.

Dapple was her acting name. Her real name was Helwar Ahl, and her home—which she rarely visited—was Helwar Island, off the northeast corner of the Great Southern Continent. For the most part, she and her company traveled up and down the continent's eastern coast, going as far south as Ettin, where she had many friends.

They were going south now and could have taken Haik's letter, though Haik hadn't known this. In any case, their ship was a fast trader, bound for Hu and not planning to stop on the way. East they went, till the coast was a thin dark line, visible only when the ship crested a wave. The rest of the time, they were alone, except for the *peshadi* that swam in front of them and the ocean birds that followed.

The birds were familiar to Haik, but she had never seen a live *pesha* before. As the animals' sleek backs broke the water's surface, they exhaled loudly enough so Haik had no trouble hearing the sound. *Wah! Wah!* Then they dove, their long tails cutting through the water like knives. They had a second name: blue fish, which came from their hide's deep ocean color. Neither death nor tanning dimmed the hue, and *pesha* leather was a famous luxury.

"I had a pair of *pesha* boots once," said Dapple. "A wealthy matron gave them to me, because they were cracked beyond repair. I used them in plays, till they fell into pieces. You should have seen me as a warrior, strutting around in those boots!"

Years before, a dead *pesha* had washed up on a beach in Tulwar. They'd all gone to see it: this deep-sea animal their kin had hunted before the Drowning. It had been the size of a large woman, with four flippers and a tail that looked like seaweed, lying limp on the pebbles. The old men of Tulwar cut it up. Most of the women went back to work, but Haik stayed and watched. The flesh had been reddish-purple, like the flesh of land animals; the bones of the skeleton had been large and heavy. As for the famous skin, she'd felt it. Not slimy, like a fish, and with no scales, though there were scaleless fish. She knew that much, though her kin no longer went to sea.

Most interesting of all were the flippers. She begged a hind one from the old men. It was small, the hide not usable, with almost no flesh on the bones. "Take it," her senior male relatives told her. "Though nothing good is likely to come from your curiosity."

Haik carried it to her teacher's house, into a back room that Rakai never entered. Her fossils were there, along with other objects: a bird skeleton, almost complete; the skulls of various small animals; and shells from Tulwar's beaches. Laying the flipper on a table, she used a sharp knife to cut it open. Inside, hidden by blue skin and reddish-purple flesh, were five rows of long, narrow, white bones.

She had cleaned them and arranged them on the table as she'd found them in the flipper. The two outer rows were short, the thumb—could she call it that?—barely present, while the three middle rows were long and curved. Clearly, they provided a framework for the flipper. What purpose did the outer rows serve, and why had the Goddess hidden a hand inside a sea animal's flipper?

"Well," said Dapple after Haik told this story. "What's the answer to your question?"

"I don't know," said Haik, afraid to talk about her theories. What did she know for certain? A group of puzzling facts. From these she had derived a terrifying sense of time and change. Did she have the right to frighten other people, as she had been frightened?

Beside them, a *pesha* surfaced and exhaled, rolling sideways to eye them and grin with sharp white teeth.

"Rakai told me the world is full of similarities and correspondences. The Goddess is a repeater. That's what they always told me."

"And a jokester," said Dapple. "Maybe she thought it would be funny to make something that was a fish in some ways and a land animal in others."

"Maybe," Haik said in a doubtful tone. "I tanned the flipper hide and made a bag from it, but couldn't use the bag. It seemed dishonorable and wrong, as if I was using the skin from a woman's hand to keep things in. So I put the *pesha* bones in the bag and kept them on one of my shelves; and I made a pot decorated with *peshadi*. It was a failure. I didn't know how living *peshadi* moved. Now, I will be able to make the pot again."

Dapple ruffled the red fur on her shoulder. "Like fire," the actor said gently. "You burn with curiosity and a desire to get things right."

"My relatives say it will get me in trouble."

"The Goddess gave us the ability to imagine and question and judge," the actor said. "Why would she have done this, if she did not intend us to use these abilities? I question the behavior of people; you question rocks and bones. Both activities seem chulmar to me."

Then as now, *chulmar* meant to be pious and to be funny. Dapple's voice sounded amused to Haik; this made her uneasy. In Tulwar, after the Drowning, piety took the form of glumness, though the people there certainly knew the meaning of *chulmar*. They did not mean to turn their children away from enjoyment of the world, but so much had been lost; they had become afraid; and fear is the end of piety.

The ship continued south, till it was far past the Tulwar coast. During this period, Haik was preoccupied with love. Hah! It had struck her like a strong blow in battle! She could think of little except Dapple's body: the four breasts, surprisingly large for a woman who'd never borne children; the rangy limbs; the prominent nipples, the same color as the "far-down dark grey" strata at home; and the place between the actor's legs, which was a cave of pleasure. Haik could model a breast in clay, make a covered pot of it, with a nipple for the handle. But how could she replicate the hidden place? Or Dapple's mouth with its golden tongue? It could not be done, especially now, with her kiln far behind her. Better not to think of pottery.

They made love often, usually on deck, under blazing tropic stars. She was drunk with love! Love had made her crazy, and she did not care!

Five days south of Tsugul Island, the ship turned west. They came to the wide harbor at Hu, guarded by white shoals. The *peshadi* were gone by then; the birds had become more numerous. A low green coast emerged from misty rain.

Haik and Dapple were on deck. Peering forward, Haik made out the buildings of Hu Town: white and blue, with red or green roofs. Fishing boats lined the harbor docks. Their furled sails were red, white, green and yellow. "A colorful country."

"That's the south," said Dapple in agreement. As lovely as always, the actor was leaning on the ship's rail, looking happy. "People in the north call these folk barbarians, who lack refinement and a sense of nuance. But drama is not made of nuance." She raised an arm and brought it down. "It's the sword blade descending, the cry of understanding and anger and pain. I could not write the plays I write, if I didn't visit the south."

They tied up among the fishing boats, empty in mid-afternoon. The acting company went on shore, Tulwar Haik among them. She had never been this far south. The people in the streets, dressed in bright tunics and kilts, were an unfamiliar physical type: broad chested, with short thick limbs. The women were taller than women in the north, towering a full head above their male relatives. Everyone had grey fur, and Haik got many sideways glances.

"I could lose you," said Dapple with amusement.

"They're ugly," said Haik.

"They are different, dear one. When you get used to them, they will begin to look handsome."

"Have you had lovers here?"

Dapple laughed. "Many."

Their destination was an inn built around a courtyard. There were potted trees in the courtyard: skyflower and starflower and a kind Haik did not recognize, which had silver-blue leaves and frilly, bright yellow flowers. Several of the pots had been made by Rakai; one had been made by her, an early work, not bad in its way. She pointed it out to Dapple.

The innkeeper appeared, a huge woman with arms like tree limbs and four enormous breasts, barely concealed by a vest. "My favorite customer!" she cried. "Are you going to perform?"

"Most likely, yes. Haik, this is Hu Aptsi." Dapple laid a hand on Haik's red shoulder. "And this beauty is my new lover, Tulwar Haik the potter. She has given up her pots to travel with me, until we tire of each other."

"Never!" said Haik.

"Excellent work you do in Tulwar," the innkeeper said. "I have neighbors who say nothing good comes from the north. Dapple and pots and flowering trees, I say."

They went into the common room and settled around tables. A round clay hearth bulged out of one wall. Logs burned in it. The innkeeper brought a large metal bowl, filling it with fruit juices and *halin*, then heated an iron rod in the fire and put the glowing tip in the full bowl. The liquid hissed and steamed. The innkeeper served. Haik wrapped her hands around a hot cup, sniffing the aromatic steam, thinking, *I am far from home, among strangers, about to drink something for which I have no name.* She tasted the liquid. Delicious!

"It will make you drunk quickly," said Dapple in a warning tone.

Beyond the room's windows, rain fell in the courtyard, and the potted trees quivered. *I am happy,* Haik thought.

That night, as she lay in Dapple's arms, she had a dream. The old woman came to her again, this time with clean hands and feet. "Existence is made to be enjoyed. Always remember that."

"Why did you kill my mother and my other relatives?" Haik asked.

"A storm killed them. Do you think every gust of wind is my breath? Do you think it's my hand that crushes every bug and pulls every bird from the sky?"

"Why did you make things that die?"

"Why do you work in clay? Sooner or later, all your pots will break."

"I like the material."

"I like life," the Goddess said. "And change."

The next day, Haik helped the actors set up their stage in a warehouse near the docks. Rain still fell. They would not be able to perform outside. The acting company was large: ten women, all from northern towns. Five were full members of the company. Three were apprentices. One was a carpenter; one made the costumes; though both of these last could fill small parts when needed. They all worked together easily. It was Haik who was awkward and needed to be told what to do. "You will learn," said Dapple.

Midway through the morning, she disappeared. "Off to write," said the carpenter. "I could see her thinking. These southerners like rude plays, and that isn't the kind of thing we usually do, except when we're down here. You'd think they'd like hero plays; they have plenty of real heroes among them. But no, they want comedy with lots of penises."

Haik could think of nothing to say.

They ate their evening meal in the inn, a light one, since acting should never be done on a full stomach. Then they went back to the warehouse, through still-falling rain. There were lamps on the walls around the stage. The wide, dark space beyond the lamplight was full of people. The air stank of oil, damp fur and excitement.

"We know our business," said Dapple. "You keep off to the side and watch."

Haik did as told, leaning against a side wall, below a lamp that cast a yellow, flickering glow. Because she rarely thought about her appearance, she did not realize how she looked, her red fur and green eyes shining. Half the women in the audience wanted to have sex with her; half the men wished she were male. How could a woman of her age be so naive? By thinking too much and living too long in the glum family Tulwar became after the Drowning.

The play was about a *sul* with an enormous penis. Dapple played him in an animal mask. The penis, of which he was so proud, was longer than she was and limp, so it dragged on the ground. The *sul* tripped over it often, while he bragged about his masculine power and the lovers he'd had, all men of extraordinary beauty and talent. Once he was established as an irritating braggart, a *tli* appeared, played by the company's second actor. The two animals got into a betting contest, and the *tli* won the *sul's* penis, which struck the audience as funny. Getting it off was a problem, which struck the audience as even funnier. Finally, the *sul* stormed off, bereft of his male member and vowing revenge.

Now the *tli* delivered a soliloquy, while holding the huge limp object. Fine to win, the *tli* said, but he had no use for a penis this large. His own was adequate for his purposes; and the *sul* would come back with friends and weapons to reclaim the penis. This was the problem with giving into irritation. What was he to do? How could he escape the vengeance of the *sul*?

At this point, Dapple reappeared, wearing a sleek blue mask, the open mouth full of sharp white teeth. She was a *pesha*, she announced, an early version of this species. She lived in shallow water, paddling and catching fish. She wanted to move into the ocean, but her tail was too small; she needed a new one, able to drive her deep into the water or far out over the waves.

"I have just the thing," said the *tli* and showed her the *sul's* penis. "We'll sew this on your backside, and you'll swim like a fish. But in return for this gift, you must carry me to safety; and once you are able to dive deeply, I wouldn't mind having some of the treasure that's sunk in the ocean."

The *pesha* agreed, and the two animals attached the penis to the back of Dapple's costume. Than she did a dance of happiness, singing praise of the ocean and her new life.

The other actors joined them with blue and white banners, which mimicked the motion of water, through which Dapple and the *tli* escaped, dancing and singing.

When everyone was gone, and the stage was bare, Dapple returned as the *sul*, along with two more *sulin*. "Foiled!" they cried. "We can't follow. Your penis is assuredly gone, dear relative. You are not going to be socially popular in the future."

That was the end of the play, except for a final dance, done by the *tli*, surrounded by the rest of the cast, waving golden banners. These represented the treasure he had gained. As for the grateful *pesha*, she was happy in her new home, and with luck the penis would not retain any of its old qualities.

The audience stamped their feet and made hooting noises. Clearly, the play had gone over well.

Haik thought, yes, she was certain that things could turn into other things. But not, in all likelihood, a penis into a tail. And change was not a result of trickery, but time.

People came to talk with the main actors. Haik helped the carpenter and costume maker clean up.

"Ettin Taiin," said the carpenter. "I didn't know he was in town."

"Who?" asked Haik, putting the *tli* mask in a box.

"The lame man."

She looked around and saw a short fellow limping toward the stage. His fur was grey, turning silver over the shoulders and on the face. One eye was missing; he didn't bother to wear a patch over the empty socket.

"He is the foremost war captain among the Ettin," the carpenter said. "And they are the most dangerous lineage in this part of the world. Dapple calls his mother "great-aunt." If you find him scary, as I do, then you ought to meet the old lady."

There was no way for him to reach Dapple, surrounded by admirers. He greeted the carpenter and the costume maker by name, without glancing at them directly. Good manners, thought Haik.

"Is Cholkwa with you?" asked the costume maker.

"South, among the savages of the Cold Ocean Coast. I sent men with him for protection, in case the savages didn't like his comedies. May I ask about your companion, or is that rude?"

"We can hardly object to rudeness, after the play we've done," said the carpenter.

"I laughed so hard I thought I would lose control of my bladder," said the one-eyed man.

The costume maker said, "This is Tulwar Haik the potter. She's Dapple's new lover."

The man lifted his head, apparently in surprise. Haik got a glimpse of his sunken eye socket and the remaining eye, which blazed blue as a noon sky. His pupil had expanded in the dim light and lay across the eye like an iron bar. "The Potter of Strange Animals," he said.

"Yes," said Haik, surprised to be known in this distant place.

"The world is full of coincidences!" the soldier told her. "And this one is pleasant! I bought one of your pots for my mother last year. She can barely see these days, but she likes the texture of it. She especially likes to feel the animals you have used for handles. Birds with clawed hands! What an idea! How can they possibly fly?"

"I don't think they did—or do," said Haik.

"These birds exist?" asked the soldier.

Haik paused, considering. "I have found their remains."

"You don't say. The world is full of two things, then: coincidence and strangeness. Considering the Goddess, this can't be called surprising." He glanced toward Dapple. Most of the admirers had gone. "Excuse me. I want to give her news of Cholkwa. They just missed each other. His ship left two days ago; and I was planning to ride home, having stayed with him till the last *ikun*. But then I heard that Dapple had arrived."

He limped away.

"He and Cholkwa are lovers," said the carpenter. "Though the true love of Cholkwa's life is the actor Perig. Perig's old now and in poor health. He lives on

Helwar Island with Dapple's kin, who are my kin also, while Cholkwa still travels. Male actors are as promiscuous as women."

Haik finished putting away the masks. The *pesha* mask was new, she realized. The blue paint was still tacky, and the shape of the head had been changed, using cloth and glue.

"We keep blank masks," said the carpenter. "Then, when Dapple has a sudden idea, we can add new animals."

"This is something I can do," Haik said. "Shape the masks and paint them." She glanced up at the carpenter and the costume maker. "Unless the work belongs to you."

"We all do many things," said the costume maker. "If you stay with us you'll find yourself on stage."

When everything was packed up, they went back to the inn, sat in the common room and drank *halin*. The Ettin captain, who came with them, had an immense capacity. He left from time to time to urinate, but never got noticeably drunk. The idea of coincidence was stuck in his mind, and he talked about how it worked in war, sometimes to his benefit, sometimes against him.

There was the time he went to attack the Gwa and met their warband on the way, coming to attack Ettin. "We both picked the same exact route. So there we were in a mountain pass, staring at each other with mouths open. Then we fought." He spilled *halin* on the table and drew the disposition of troops. "A bad situation for both of us! Neither had an advantage, and neither had a good way to retreat. I knew I had to win and did, though I lost an eye and a brother; and enough Gwa soldiers escaped, so we could not surprise them at home. A nasty experience, caused by coincidence. Doubtless the Goddess does this to us so we won't take our plans too seriously; a good captain must always be ready to throw his ideas away."

When he finally left, walking steadily except for his limp, Dapple said, "I have sworn to myself, I will put him in a play some day. That is what a hero is really like. I'll have to make up a new story, of course. His life has not been tragic. He's never had to make difficult choices, and everything he's wanted—fame, the affection of his relatives, the love of Cholkwa—has come into his hands."

Well, thought Haik, she was certainly learning new things. The man had not seemed like a hero to her.

The next evening, they did the play a second time. The warehouse was packed, and Ettin Taiin was in the audience again. Haik watched him as he watched the play, his expression intent. Now and then, he laughed, showing white teeth. One was missing, an upper stabber. Doubtless it had been lost in battle, like his eye and his leg's agility. Haik's male relatives fought nothing except the forest predators, which were not especially dangerous. When men died in the forest, it was usually from small creatures that had a poisonous bite or sting; or they died from accidents. Old people told stories about pirates, but none had attacked the northeast coast in more than a generation. The Tulwar feared water and storms.

Now, Haik thought, she was in the south. War was continuous here; and lineages vanished from existence, the men killed, the women and children adopted. A family that lacked soldiers like Ettin Taiin would not survive.

This idea led nowhere, except to the thought that the world was full of violence, and this was hardly a new thought. In front of her, Dapple tripped over the *sul's* long dragging penis and tumbled into a somersault, which ended with her upright once again, the penis wound around her neck. The audience hooted its approval. The world was full of violence and sex, Haik thought.

Once again the captain joined them at the inn. This time he drank less and asked questions, first of the actors, then of Haik. Where exactly was her family? What did they produce besides pots?

"Are you planning to invade us?" she asked.

He looked shocked. "I am a soldier, not a bandit, young lady! I only fight with people I know. The purpose of war is to expand the size of one's family and increase the amount of land held by one's kin. That should always be done along existing borders. You push out and push out, gathering the land and the women and children immediately beyond your borders, making sure the land is always contiguous and protected—if possible—by natural barriers. Any other strategy leaves you with a territory that is not defensible."

"He's not planning to invade you," Dapple said in summary. "Your land is too far away."

"Exactly," the captain said. "Bandits and pirates use different tactics, since they want valuable objects rather than land and people. We've had both in the south and dealt with them."

"How?" asked Haik.

"The obvious way is to find where they came from, go there and kill all the men. The problem is, you have to do something with the bandit women and children. They can't be left to starve. But obviously no family wants members with bad traits."

"What do you do?"

"Adopt them but spread them among many houses, and never let any of them breed. Often, the children turn out well; and after a generation, the traits—bad or good—are gone. This, as you can imagine, is a lot of work, which is a reason to kill enough men so the bandits will think twice about returning to Ettin, but leave enough alive so the women and children are provided for."

The carpenter was right. This was a frightening man.

Dapple said, "The Tulwar are foresters. For the most part, they export lumber and flowering trees. Haik makes pots for the trees."

"Do you have children?" the captain asked Haik.

"Two daughters."

"A woman with your abilities should have more. What about brothers?"

"None."

"Male cousins?"

"Many," said Haik.

The captain glanced at Dapple. "Would it be worthwhile asking a Tulwar man to come here and impregnate one of our women? Your lover's pots are really excellent; and my mother has always liked flowers. So do I, for that matter."

"It's a small family," said Dapple. "And lives far away. A breeding contract with them would not help you politically."

"There is more to life than politics," said the captain.

"The Tulwar men aren't much for fighting," said Haik, unsure that she wanted any connection with Ettin.

"You don't mean they're cowards?"

"Of course not. They work in our wild backcountry as foresters and loggers. They used to sail the ocean, before most of my family drowned. These kinds of work require courage, but we have always gotten along with our neighbors."

"No harm in that, if you aren't ambitious." He grinned, showing his missing tooth. "We don't need to breed for ambition or violence. We have those talents in abundance. But art and beauty—" His blue eye glanced at her briefly. "These are not our gifts, though we are certainly able to appreciate both."

"Witness your appreciation of Cholkwa," said Dapple, her tone amused.

"A great comedian. and the best looking man for his age I've ever seen. But my mother and her sisters decided years ago that he should not be asked to father Ettin children. For one thing, he has never mentioned having a family. Who could the Ettin speak to, if they wanted a breeding contract? A man shouldn't make decisions like these. We do things the right way in Ettin! In any case, acting is not an entirely respectable art; who can say what qualities would appear among the Ettin, if our children were fathered by actors."

"You see why I have no children," Dapple said, then tilted her head toward the carpenter. "Though my kinswoman here has two sets of twins, because her gift is making props. We don't tell our relatives that she also acts."

"Not much," said the carpenter.

"And not well," muttered the apprentice sitting next to Haik.

The captain stayed a while longer, chatting with Dapple about his family and her most recent plays. Finally he rose. "I'm too old for these long evenings. In addition, I plan to leave for Ettin at dawn. I assume you're sending love and respect to my mother."

"Of course," said Dapple.

"And you, young lady." The one eye roved toward her. "If you come this way again, bring pots for Ettin. I'll speak to my mother about a breeding contract with Tulwar. Believe me, we are allies worth having!"

He left, and Dapple said, "I think he's imaging a male relative who looks like you, who can spend his nights with an Ettin woman and his days with Ettin Taiin."

"What a lot of hard work!" the carpenter said.

"There are no Tulwar men who look like me."

"What a sadness for Ettin Taiin!" said Dapple.

From Hu Town they went west and south, traveling with a caravan. The actors and merchants rode *tsina*, which were familiar to Haik, though she had done little riding before this. The carrying beasts were *bitalin*: great, rough quadrupeds with three sets of horns. One pair spread far to the side; one pair curled forward; and the last pair curled back. The merchants valued the animals as much as *tsina*, giving them pet names and adorning their horns with brass or iron rings. They seemed marvelous to Haik, moving not quickly, but very steadily, their shaggy bodies swaying with each step. When one was bothered by something— bugs, a scent on the wind, another *bital*—it would swing its six-horned head and groan. What a sound!

"Have you put *bitalin* in a play?" she asked Dapple.

"Not yet. What quality would they represent?"

"Reliability," said the merchant riding next to them. "Strength. Endurance. Obstinacy. Good milk."

"I will certainly consider the idea," Dapple replied.

At first the plain was green, the climate rainy. As they traveled south and west, the weather became dry, and the plain turned dun. This was not a brief journey. Haik had time to get used to riding, though the country never became ordinary to her. It was so wide! So empty!

The merchants in the caravan belonged to a single family. Both women and men were along on the journey. Of course the actors camped with the women, while the men—farther out—stood guard. In spite of this protection, Haik was uneasy. The stars overhead were no longer entirely familiar; the darkness around her seemed to go on forever; and caravan campfires seemed tiny. Far out on the plain, wild *sulin* cried. They were more savage than the domestic breeds used for hunting and guarding, Dapple told her. "And uglier, with scales covering half their bodies. Our *sulin* in the north have only a few small scaly patches left."

The *sulin* in Haik's country were entirely furry, except in the spring. Then the males lost their chest fur, revealing an area of scaly skin, dark green and glittering. If allowed to, they'd attack one another, each trying to destroy the other's chest adornment. "Biting the jewels," was the name of this behavior.

Sitting under the vast foreign sky, Haik thought about *sulin*. They were all varieties of a single animal. Everyone knew this, though it was hard to believe that Tulwar's mild-tempered, furry creatures were the same as the wild animals Dapple described. Could change go farther? Could an animal with hands become a *pesha*? And what caused change? Not trickery, as in the play. Dapple, reaching over, distracted her. Instead of evolution, she thought about love.

They reached a town next to a wide sandy river. Low bushy trees grew along the banks. The merchants made camp next to the trees, circling their wagons. Men took the animals to graze, while the women—merchants and actors—went to town.

The streets were packed dirt, the houses adobe with wood doors and beams. (Haik could see these last protruding through the walls.) The people were the same physical type as in Hu, but with grey-brown fur. A few had faint markings— not spots like Dapple, but narrow broken stripes. They dressed as all people did, in tunics or shorts and vests.

Why, thought Haik suddenly, did people come in different hues? Most wild species were a single color, with occasional freaks, usually black or white. Domestic animals came in different colors; it was obvious why; people had bred them according to different ideas of usefulness and beauty. Had people bred themselves to be grey, grey-brown, red, dun and so on? This was possible, though it seemed to Haik that most people were attracted to difference. Witness Ettin Taiin. Witness the response of the Tulwar matrons to her father.

Now to the problems of time and change, she added the problem of difference. Maybe the problem of similarity as well. If animals tended to be the same, why did difference occur? If there was a tendency toward difference, why did it become evident only sometimes? She was as red as her father. Her daughters were dun. At this point, her head began to ache; and she understood the wisdom of her senior relatives. If one began to question anything—shells in rock, the hand in a *pesha's* flipper—the questions would proliferate, till they stretched to the horizon in every direction and *why, why, why* filled the sky, like the calls of migrating birds.

"Are you all right?" asked Dapple.

"Thinking," said Haik.

At the center of the town was a square, made of packed dirt. The merchants set up a tent and laid out sample goods: dried fish from Hu, fabric made by northern weavers, boxes carved from rare kinds of wood, jewelry of silver and dark red shell. Last of all, they unfolded an especially fine piece of cloth, put it on the ground and poured out their most precious treasure: a high, white, glittering heap of salt.

Townsfolk gathered: bent matriarchs, robust matrons, slim girls and boys, even a few adult men. All were grey-brown, except the very old, who had turned white.

In general, people looked like their relatives; and everyone knew that family traits existed. Why else select breeding partners with so much care? There must be two tendencies within people, one toward similarity, the other toward difference. The same must also be true of animals. Domestic *sulin* came in different colors; by breeding, people had brought out variations that must have been in the wild animals, though never visible, except in freaks. She crouched in the shadows at the back of the merchants' tent, barely noticing the commerce in front of her, thinking difficult thoughts.

Nowadays, geneticists tell us that the variation among people was caused by drift in isolated populations, combined with the tendency of all people to modify and improve anything they can get their hands on. We have bred ourselves like *sulin* to fit in different environments and to meet different ideas of beauty.

But how could Haik know this much about the history of life? How could she know that wild animals were more varied than she had observed? There are wild *sulin* in the far northern islands as thick furred and white as the local people. There is a rare, almost extinct kind of wild *sulin* on the third continent, which is black and entirely scaly, except for a ridge of rust-brown fur along its back. She, having traveled on only one continent, was hypothesizing in the absence of adequate data. In spite of this, she caught a glimpse of how inheritance works.

How likely is this? Could a person like Haik, living in a far-back era, come so near the idea of genes?

Our ancestors were not fools! They were farmers and hunters, who observed animals closely; and they achieved technological advances—the creation through breeding of the plants that feed us and the animals we still use, though no longer exclusively, for work and travel—which we have not yet equaled, except possibly by going into space.

In addition to the usual knowledge about inheritance, Haik had the ideas she'd gained from fossils. Other folk knew that certain plants and animals could be changed by breeding; and that families had traits which could be transmitted, either for good or bad. But most life seemed immutable. Wild animals were the same from generation to generation. So were the plants of forest and plain. The Goddess liked the world to stay put, as far as most people could see. Haik knew otherwise.

Dapple came after her, saying, "We need help in setting up our stage."

That evening, in the long summer twilight, the actors performed the *pesha* comedy. Dapple had to make a speech beforehand, explaining what a *pesha* was, since they were far inland now. But the town folk knew about *sulin*, *tli* and penises; and the play went well, as had the trading of the merchants. The next day they continued west.

Haik traveled with Dapple all summer. She learned to make masks by soaking paper in glue, then applying it in layers to a wooden mask frame.

"Nothing we carry is more valuable," said the costume maker, holding a thick white sheet of paper. "Use this with respect! No other material is as light and easy to shape. But the cost, Haik, the cost!"

The *bitalin* continued to fascinate her: living animals as unfamiliar as the fossils in her cliffs! Her first mask was a *bital*. When it was dry, she painted the face tan, the six horns shiny black. The skin inside the flaring nostrils was red, as was the tongue protruding from the open mouth.

Dapple wrote a play about a solid and reliable *bital* cow, who lost her milk to a conniving *tli*. The *tli* was outwitted by other animals, friends of the *bital*. The play ended with Dapple as the cow, dancing among pots of her recovered milk, turned through the ingenuity of the *tli* into a new substance: long-lasting, delicious cheese. The play did well in towns of the western plains. By now they were in a region where the ocean was a rumor, only half-believed; but *bitalin* were known and loved.

Watching Dapple's performance, Haik asked herself another question. If there was a hand inside the *pesha's* flipper, could there be another hand in the *bital's* calloused, two-toed foot? Did every living thing contain another living thing within it, like Dapple in the *bital* costume?

What an idea!

The caravan turned east when a plant called fire-in-autumn turned color. Unknown in Tulwar, it was common on the plain, though Haik had not noticed it till now. At first, there were only a few bright dots like drops of blood fallen on a pale brown carpet. These were enough to make the merchants change direction. Day by day, the color became more evident, spreading in lines. (The plant grew through sending out runners.) Finally, the plain was crisscrossed with scarlet. At times, the caravan traveled through long, broad patches of the plant, *tsina* and *bitalin* belly-deep in redness, as if they were fording rivers of blood or fire.

When they reached the moist coastal plain, the plant became less common. The vegetation here was mostly a faded silver-brown. Rain fell, sometimes freezing; and they arrived in the merchants' home town at the start of the first winter storm. Haik saw the rolling ocean through lashes caked with snow. The pleasure of salt water! Of smelling seaweed and fish!

The merchants settled down for winter. The actors took the last ship north to Hu Town, where the innkeeper had bedrooms for them, a fire in the common room and *halin* ready for mulling.

At midwinter, Dapple went to Ettin. Haik stayed by the ocean, tired of foreigners. It had been more than half a year since she'd had clay in her hands or climbed the Tulwar cliffs in search of fossils. Now she learned that love was not enough. She walked the Hu beaches, caked with ice, and looked for shells. Most were similar to ones in Tulwar; but she found a few new kinds, including one she knew as a fossil. Did this mean other creatures—her claw-handed bird, the hammer-headed bug—were still alive somewhere? Maybe. Little was certain.

Dapple returned through a snow storm and settled down to write. The Ettin always gave her ideas. "When I'm in the south, I do comedy, because the people here prefer it. But their lives teach me how to write tragedy; and tragedy is my gift."

Haik's gift lay in the direction of clay and stone, not language. Her journey south had been interesting and passionate, but now it was time to do something. What? Hu Town had no pottery, and the rocks in the area contained no fossils. In the end, she took some of the precious paper and used it, along with metal wire, to model strange animals. The colors were a problem. She had to imagine them, using what she knew about the birds and bugs and animals of Tulwar. She made the hammer-headed bug red and black. The flower-predator was yellow and held a bright blue fish. The claw-handed bird was green.

"Well, these are certainly different," said Dapple. "Is this what you find in your cliffs?"

"The bones and shells, yes. Sometimes there is a kind of shadow of the animal in the rock. But never any colors."

Dapple picked up a tightly coiled white shell. Purple tentacles spilled out of it; and Haik had given the creature two large, round eyes of yellow glass. The eyes were a guess, derived from a living ocean creature. But Haik had seen the shadow of tentacles in stone. Dapple tilted the shell, till one of the eyes caught sunlight and blazed. Hah! It seemed alive! "Maybe I could write a play about these creatures; and you could make the masks."

Haik hesitated, then said, "I'm going home to Tulwar."

"You are?" Dapple set down the glass-eyed animal.

She needed her pottery, Haik explained, and the cliffs full of fossils, as well as time to think about this journey. "You wouldn't give up acting for love!"

"No," said Dapple. "I plan to spend next summer in the north, doing tragedies. When I'm done, I'll come to Tulwar for a visit. I want one of your pots and maybe one of these little creatures." She touched the flower-predator. "You see the world like no one else I've ever met. Hah! It is full of wonders and strangeness, when looked at by you!"

That night, lying in Dapple's arms, Haik had a dream. The old woman came to her, dirty-footed, in a ragged tunic. "What have you learned?"

"I don't know," said Haik.

"Excellent!" said the old woman. "This is the beginning of comprehension. But I'll warn you again. You may gain nothing, except comprehension and my approval, which is worth little in the towns where people dwell."

"I thought you ruled the world."

"Rule is a large, heavy word," said the old woman. "I made the world and enjoy it, but rule? Does a tree rule the shoots that rise at its base? Matriarchs may rule their families. I don't claim so much for myself."

When spring came, the company went north. Their ship stopped at Tulwar to let off Haik and take on potted trees. There were so many plants that some had to be stored on deck, lashed down against bad weather. As the ship left, it seemed like a floating grove. Dapple stood among the trees, crown-of-fire mostly, none in bloom. Haik, on the shore, watched till she could no longer see her lover or the ship. Then she walked home to Rakai's pottery. Everything was as Haik had left it, though covered with dust. She unpacked her strange animals and set them on a table. Then she got a broom and began to sweep.

After a while, her senior relatives arrived. "Did you enjoy your adventures?"

"Yes."

"Are you back to stay?"

"Maybe."

Great-aunts and uncles glanced at one another. Haik kept sweeping.

"It's good to have you back," said a senior male cousin.

"We need more pots," said an aunt.

Once the house was clean, Haik began potting: simple forms at first, with no decoration except a monochrome glaze. Then she added texture: a cord pattern at the rim, crisscross scratches on the body. The handles were twists of clay, put on carelessly. Sometimes she left her handprint like a shadow. Her glazes, applied in splashes, hid most of what she'd drawn or printed. When her shelves were full of new pots, she went to the cliffs, climbing up steep ravines and walking narrow ledges, a hammer in hand. Erosion had uncovered new fossils: bugs and fish, mostly, though she found one skull that was either a bird or a small land animal. When cleaned, it turned out to be intact and wonderfully delicate. The small teeth, still in the jaw or close to it, were like nothing she'd seen. She made a copy in grey-green clay, larger than the original, with all the teeth in place. This became the handle for a large covered pot. The body of the pot was decorated with drawings of birds and animals, all strange. The glaze was thin and colorless and cracked in firing, so it seemed as if a film of ice covered the pot.

"Who will buy that?" asked her relatives. "You can't put a tree in it, not with that cover."

"My lover Dapple," said Haik in reply. "Or the famous war captain of Ettin."

At midsummer, there was a hot period. The wind off the ocean stopped. People moved when they had to, mouths open, panting. During this time, Haik was troubled with dreams. Most made no sense. A number involved the Goddess. In one, the old woman ate an *agala*. This was a southern fruit, unknown in Tulwar, which consisted of layers wrapped around a central pit. The outermost layer was red and sweet; each layer going in was paler and more bitter, till one reached the innermost layer, bone-white and tongue-curling. Some people would unfold the fruit as if it were a present in a wrapping and eat only certain layers. Others, like Haik, bit through to the pit, enjoying the combination of sweetness and bitterness. The Goddess did as she did, Haik discovered with interest. Juice squirted out of the old woman's mouth and ran down her lower face, matting the sparse white hair. There was no more to the dream, just the Goddess eating messily.

In another dream, the old woman was with a female *bital*. The shaggy beast had two young, both covered with downy yellow fur. "They are twins," the Goddess said. "But not identical. One is larger and stronger, as you can see. That twin will live. The other will die."

"Is this surprising?" asked Haik.

The Goddess looked peeved. "I'm trying to explain how I breed!"

"Through death?" asked Haik.

"Yes." The Goddess caressed the mother animal's shaggy flank. "And beauty. That's why your father had a child in Tulwar. He was alive in spite of adversity. He was beautiful. The matrons of Tulwar looked at him and said, 'We want these qualities for our family.'

"That's why tame *sulin* are furry. People have selected for that trait, which wild *sulin* consider less important than size, sharp teeth, a crest of stiff hair along the spine, glittering patches of scales on the sides and belly, and a disposition inclined toward violence. Therefore, among wild *sulin*, these qualities grow more evident and extreme, while tame *sulin* acquire traits that enable them to live with people. The *pesha* once lived on land; the *bital* climbed among branches. In time, all life changes, shaped by beauty and death.

"Of all my creatures, only people have the ability to shape themselves and other kinds of life, using comprehension and judgment. This is the gift I have given you: to know what you are doing and what I do." The old woman touched the smaller *bital* calf. It collapsed. Haik woke.

A disturbing dream, she thought, lying in darkness. The house, as always, smelled of clay, both wet and dry. Small animals, her fellow residents, made quiet noises. She rose and dressed, going to the nearest beach. A slight breeze came off the ocean, barely moving the hot air. Combers rolled gently in, lit by the stars. Haik walked along the beach, water touching her feet now and then. The things she knew came together, interlocking; she achieved what we could call the Theory of Evolution. Hah! The Goddess thought in large ways! What a method to use in shaping life! One could not call it quick or economical, but the Goddess was—it seemed by looking at the world—inclined toward abundance; and there was little evidence that she was in a hurry.

Death made sense; without it change was impossible. Beauty made sense; without it, there couldn't be improvement or at least variety. Everything was explained, it seemed to Haik: the *pesha's* flipper, the claw-handed bird, all the animals she'd found in the Tulwar cliffs. They were not mineral formations. They had lived. Most likely, they lived no longer, except in her mind and art.

She looked at the cloudless sky. So many stars, past all counting! So much time, receding into distance! So much death! And so much beauty!

She noticed at last that she was tired, went home and went to bed. In the morning, after a bad night's sleep, the Theory of Evolution still seemed good. But there was no one to discuss it with. Her relatives had turned their backs on most of existence after the Drowning. Don't think badly of them for this. They provided potted beauty to many places; many lineages in many towns praised the Tulwar trees and pots. But their family was small, its future uncertain. They didn't have the resources to take long journeys or think about large ideas. So Haik made more pots and collected more fossils, saying nothing about her theory, till Dapple arrived late in fall. They made love passionately for several days. Then Dapple looked around at the largely empty town, guarded by dark grey cliffs. "This doesn't seem like a good place to winter, dear one. Come south with me! Bring pots, and the Ettin will make you very welcome."

"Let me think," said Haik.

"You have ten days at most," Dapple said. "A captain I know is heading south; I asked her to stop in Tulwar, in case your native town was as depressing as I expected."

Haik hit her lover lightly on the shoulder and went off to think.

She went with Dapple, taking pots, a potter's wheel and bags of clay. On the trip south—through rolling ocean, rain and snow beating against the ship—Haik told Dapple about evolution.

"Does this mean we started out as bugs?" the actor asked.

"The Goddess told me the process extended to people, though I've never found the bones of people in my cliffs."

"I've spent much of my life pretending to be one kind of animal or another. Interesting to think that animals may be inside me and in my past!"

On the same trip, Haik said, "My family wants to breed me again. There are too few of us; I'm strong and intelligent and have already had two healthy children."

"They are certainly right in doing this," said Dapple. "Have you picked a father?"

"Not yet. But they've told me this must be my last trip for a while."

"Then we'd better make the most of it," Dapple said.

There had been a family argument about the trip; and Haik had gotten permission to go only by saying she would not agree to a mating otherwise. But she didn't tell Dapple any of this. Family quarrels should be kept in the family.

They spent the winter in Hu. It was mild with little snow. Dapple wrote, and Haik made pots. Toward spring they went to Ettin, taking pots.

Ettin Taiin's mother was still alive, over a hundred and almost entirely blind with snow-white fur. But still upright, as Taiin pointed out. "I think she'll go to the crematorium upright and remain upright amid the flames."

He said this in the presence of the old lady, who smiled grimly, revealing that she'd kept almost all her teeth.

The Ettin bought all the pots Haik had, Taiin picking out one with special care. It was small and plain, with flower-predators for handles, a cover and a pure white glaze. "For my mother's ashes," the captain said quietly. "The day will come, though I dread it and make jokes about it."

Through late winter, Haik sat with the matriarch, who was obviously interested in her. They talked about pottery, their two families and the Theory of Evolution.

"I find it hard to believe we are descended from bugs and fish," Ettin Hattali said. "But your dreams have the sound of truth; and I certainly know that many of my distant ancestors were disgusting people. The Ettin have been improving, due to the wise decisions of my more recent ancestors, especially the women. Maybe if we followed this process far enough back, we'd get to bugs. Though you ought to consider the possibility that the Goddess is playing a joke on you. She does not always speak directly, and she dearly loves a joke."

"I have considered this," said Haik. "I may be a fool or crazy, but the idea seems good. It explains so much that has puzzled me."

Spring came finally. The hills of Ettin turned pale blue and orange. In the valley-fields, *bitalin* and *tsina* produced calves and foals.

"I have come to a decision," the blind old woman told Haik.

"Yes?"

"I want Ettin to interbreed with your family. To that end, I will send two junior members of my family to Tulwar with you. The lad is more like my son Taiin than any other male in the younger generation. The girl is a fine, intelligent, healthy young woman. If your senior female relatives agree, I want the boy—his name is Galhin—to impregnate you, while a Tulwar male impregnates Sai."

"It may be a wasted journey," said Haik in warning.

"Of course," said the matriarch. "They're young. They have time to spare. Dapple's family decided not to breed her, since they have plenty of children; and she is definitely odd. It's too late now. Her traits have been lost. But yours will not be; and we want the Ettin to have a share in what your line becomes."

"I will let my senior female relatives decide," said Haik.

"Of course you will," said Ettin Hattali.

The lad, as Hattali called him, turned out to be a man of 35, shoulder high to Haik and steel grey. He had two eyes and no limp. None the less, his resemblance to Taiin was remarkable: a fierce, direct man, full of good humor. Haik liked him at once. His half-sister Sai was 30, a solid woman with grey-brown fur and an excellent, even temperament. No reasonable person could dislike her.

Dapple, laughing, said, "This is Ettin in action! They live to defeat their enemies and interbreed with any family that seems likely to prove useful."

Death and beauty, Haik thought.

The four of them went east together. Haik put her potter's tools in storage at the Hu Town inn; Dapple took leave of many old friends; and the four found passage on a ship going north.

After much discussion, Haik's senior relatives agreed to the two matings, impressed by Galhin's vigor and his sister's calm solidity, by the rich gifts the Ettin kin had brought and Haik's description of the southern family.

Nowadays, with artificial insemination, we don't have to endure what happened next. But it was made tolerable to Haik by Ettin Galhin's excellent manners and the good humor with which he handled every embarrassment. He lacked, as he admitted, Taiin's extreme energy and violence. "But this is not a situation that requires my uncle's abilities; and he's really too old for mating; and it would be unkind to take him from Hattali. Who can say how long she will survive? Their love for each other has been a light for the Ettin for years. We can hardly separate them now."

The two foreigners were in Tulwar till fall. Then, both women pregnant, the Ettin departed. Haik returned to her pottery. In late spring, she bore twins, a boy and a girl. The boy died soon after birth, but the girl was large and healthy.

"She took strength from her brother in the womb," said the Tulwar matriarchs. "This happens; and the important child, the female, has survived."

Haik named the girl Ahl. She was dun like her older sisters, but her fur had more of a ruddy tint. In sunlight, her pelt shone red-gold; and her nickname became Gold.

It was two years before Dapple came back, her silver-grey fur beginning to show frost on the broad shoulders and lean upper arms. She admired the baby and the new pots, then gave information. Ettin Sai had produced a daughter, a strong child, obviously intelligent. The Ettin had named the child Haik, in hope that some of Tulwar Haik's ability would appear in their family. "They are greedy folk," said Dapple. "They want all their own strength, energy, solidity and violence. In addition, they want the beauty you make and are.

"Can you leave your daughter for a while? Come south and sell pots, while I perform my plays. Believe me, people in Hu and Ettin ask about you."

"I can," said Haik.

Gold went to a female cousin. In addition to being lovely, she had a fine disposition; and many were willing to care for her. Haik and Dapple took passage. This time, the voyage was easy, the winds mild and steady, the sky clear except for high, thin clouds called "tangled banners" and "schools of fish."

"What happened to your Theory of Evolution?" Dapple asked.

"Nothing."

"Why?"

"What could be done? Who would have believed me, if I said the world is old beyond comprehension; and many kinds of life have come into existence; and most, as far as I can determine, no longer exist?"

"It does sound unlikely," Dapple admitted.

"And impious."

"Maybe not that. The Goddess has an odd sense of humor, as almost everyone knows."

"I put strange animals on my pots and make them into toys for Gold and other children. But I will not begin an ugly family argument over religion."

You may think Haik lacked courage. Remember that she lived in an era before modern science. Yes, there were places where scholars gathered, but none in her part of the world. She'd have to travel long distances and learn a new language, then talk to strangers about concepts of time and change unfamiliar to everyone. Her proof was in the cliffs of Tulwar, which she could not take with her. Do you really think those scholars—people devoted to the study of history, mathematics, literature, chemistry and medicine—would have believed her? Hardly likely! She had children, a dear lover, a craft and friends. Why should she cast away all of this? For what? A truth no one was likely to see? Better to stay home or travel along the coast. Better to make pots on her own and love with Dapple.

They reached Hu Town in early summer. The inn's potted trees bloomed scarlet and sky-blue.

"The Potter of Strange Animals!" cried the innkeeper. "I have bought five of your pots for my trees."

Indeed the woman had. Haik wandered around the courtyard, admiring her own work. Four were the kind she'd made when she first returned from the south, decorated with scratches and glazed white or black. The fifth had an underwater scene, done in low relief. Beaked fish swam around the top. Below them, rising from the bottom of the pot, were long sinuous plants. Haik had named them "ocean whips." It was possible that they were animals; once or twice she had found shadows that might be mouths with teeth. Between the plants (or animals) were segmented bugs. The glaze was dark blue with touches of white.

"This is more recent," Haik said.

"I bought it because you are the Potter of Strange Animals. But I prefer the other pots. They set off my trees."

Who can argue with opinions about art, especially with someone who has bought five large pots?

Dapple's company was at the inn, having arrived several days before. Haik knew all of them, except the apprentices. For a while, they traveled through the little coastal towns of Hu, Tesh and Ta-tesh, performing comedies and now and then a tragedy. These last were a surprise to Haik, especially the tragedies about women. They were so subdued! Instead of tumbling and rude jokes, there were small gestures, turned heads, a few words spoken quietly. The actors wore plain robes in sober colors; their faces were unmasked; most of the time, the music came from a single flute. Its sound reminded Haik of a thread floating on moving water, coiling and uncoiling in the current.

"It's my observation that women suffer as much as men," said Dapple in explanation. "But we are expected to be solid and enduring. As a result, our suffering is quiet. I'm trying to show it in the way it happens. Hah! I am tired of loud, rude comedies! And loud, sad plays about the suffering of men!"

At last, in far southern Tesh, they turned inland, traveling without merchants. The borders between Ettin and its eastern neighbors were all quiet. The various families had been allies and breeding partners for generations; and none tolerated criminal behavior. By now, it was late summer. The plain baked under a sun like polished brass. The Ettin hills were hot and dusty. When they reached Hattali's house, it was with relief. Household women greeted them. Men took their *tsina* and the packs of props and costumes. Their rooms opened on a courtyard with two bathing pools. The water in one was colorless and cold. The other bubbled, bright green. The entire acting company stripped and climbed in. What a pleasure! Though both pools were crowded. Well, thought Haik, she'd take a slow bath later, soaking the travel aches from her muscles and bones.

When they were done and in fresh clothes, a woman came for Dapple and Haik. "Ettin Taiin wants you to join his mother."

"Of course," said Dapple.

They went through shadowy halls, silent except for birds calling in the house's eaves. They sounded like water running over stones. The woman said, "Thirty days ago, Hattali fell. She seemed unharmed, except for damage to one foot. It drags a little now. But since the fall she's been preoccupied and unwilling to do much, except sit and talk with Taiin. We fear her great strength is coming to an end."

"It can't be!" said Dapple.

"You know about old age and death. We've seen them in your plays." Saying this, the woman opened a door.

Outside was a terrace, lit by the afternoon sun. Hattali sat in a high-backed chair, leaning against the back, her eyes closed. How old she looked! How thin and frail! Her warrior son sat next to her on a stool, holding one of his mother's hands. He looked at them, laid Hattali's hand gently in her lap and rose. "Cholkwa is in the north. I'm glad to see you, Dapple."

They sat down. Hattali opened her eyes, obviously seeing nothing. "Who has come, Tai?"

"Dapple and her lover, the potter."

The old lady smiled. "One last play."

"A play, yes," said Dapple. "But not the last, I hope."

A look of irritation crossed Hattali's face. "Did the potter bring pots?"

Haik excused herself and went to find her pack. Now she understood the house's quiet. Most likely, the children had been sent out to play; and the adults—she passed a few in the halls—moved softly and gravely. A matriarch like Hattali, a woman with so much dignity, should not be bothered with noise, while deciding whether to live or die.

When Haik returned to the terrace, Hattali seemed asleep. But the old woman took the pot Haik put in her hands, feeling it with bony fingers. "What is it?"

"There's a skull on top, a replica of one I found in stone."

"It's shaped like a *tli* skull," Hattali said.

"A bit, but the teeth are different. I imagine from the teeth that the animal had scales, not hair."

Hattali exhaled and felt more. "On the sides of the pot?"

"The animal as I imagine it must have been, when alive. I found the skull first and made a pot that Dapple bought. But now I have found the entire animal, and it wasn't the way I showed it on the first pot. So I made this."

"The animals are in relief?"

"Yes."

"What do they look like, if not *tli*?"

Haik thought. "An animal about as long as my arm, four legged with a tail. Spines protrude along the back, as if the animal had a fin there like a fish. That was the thing I did not imagine: the spines. And the tail is different also, flat from side to side, like the tail of a fish."

"What color is the glaze?"

"Black, except the skull, which is white."

"Tai," said the old woman.

"Mother?"

"Is it beautiful?"

"She is the Potter of Strange Animals. The pot is strange, but well made."

"I want it for my ashes."

"You will have it," he said.

She gave her son the pot. He turned it in his blunt, strong-looking hands. Hattali turned her blind face toward Haik. "You must still believe your crazy idea, that we are descended from bugs."

"That the world is old and full of change, yes," said Haik.

"Sit down and tell me about it again."

Haik obeyed. The old woman listened as she explained about beauty, death and change.

"Well, we have certainly improved our lineage through careful breeding," said Hattali finally. "The child your kinsman fathered on Sai is a fine little girl. We hope she'll be as clever as you are, though I'm still not certain about your idea of time and change. Why didn't the Goddess simply make people? Why start with bugs?"

"She clearly likes bugs," said Haik. "The world is full of them. They are far more common than people and more varied. Maybe her plan was to create a multitude of bugs through beauty and death, and we are an accidental result of her breeding of bugs."

"Do you believe that?"

"No. She told me we have a gift no other living creature had: we know what we do. I believe this gift is not an accident. She wanted comprehension."

Haik was wrong in saying this, according to modern scientists. They believe life is entirely an accident, though evidently an accident which happens often, since life has appeared on many planets. Intelligent life is far less common, but has clearly appeared on at least two planets and may be present elsewhere in a form we do not recognize. It also is an accident, modern thinkers say. This is hard for many of us to believe; and Haik, living in the distant past, could hardly be expected to bring forward an idea so disturbing.

"Well, you certainly ought to listen to the Goddess, if she talks to you," said Hattali. "When will I hear your play, Dapple?"

"It will take a few days to prepare."

The matriarch tilted her head in acquiescence.

They left Hattali then, going back to their room. "I want you to make masks for a new play," Dapple said. "Five of your strange animals. They interest Hattali. Sit with her while you work, and tell her about your ideas. Taiin is an excellent man. None better! But her illness has got him frightened; and his fear is not helping her mood. Maybe she knows what she's doing. Maybe it is time for her to die. But I wonder if the fall has frightened her as well as her relatives. A woman like Hattali should not die from fear."

"Has she no daughters?"

"Two. Good women, but not half what she is; and she's never gotten along with either. The love of her life has always been Taiin."

He left the next morning, called to the western border. Gwa scouts had been seen. Their old enemies might have heard that Hattali was dying. What better time to attack?

"They expect that grief will break me," Taiin said, standing in the house's front court, dressed in metal and leather armor. A sword hung at his side, and a battle axe hung from a loop on his saddle. "It may, but not while there's work to be done." He swung himself onto his *tsin* easily, in spite of age and his bad leg. Once settled on the animal, he looked down at Haik and Dapple.

"She is the last of her generation. What people they were, especially the women! As solid as stone walls and towers! I have lived my entire life in their protection. Now, the walls are broken. Only one tower remains. What will I do, when Hattali is gone?"

"Defend Ettin," said Dapple.

He gathered the *tsin's* reins, grinning. "You're right, of course. Maybe, if I'm lucky, we'll capture a Gwa spy."

A moment later he was through the house's gate, moving steadily along the dusty road, his men following, armed and armored.

"You may be wondering about his last remark," Dapple said.

Haik opened her mouth to say no.

"There are men who take pleasure in raping prisoners before they kill them. Or in harming them in other ways. I have suspected Taiin is one such. Now I'm certain."

This was how he'd deal with his grief at Hattali's illness: by making someone else's end unpleasant.

"Beauty and death," Dapple said. "This is the way the Goddess has organized her world, according to you and your bones."

They spent the next several days on Ettin Hattali's terrace. The weather remained dry and sunny. Haik worked on the masks, while Dapple sat with paper and brush, sometimes writing, more often listening.

There was a folding table next to Hattali's chair. The matriarch's relatives brought out food and drink. In any ordinary circumstance, it would have been rude to eat while conversing with other people, especially guests, but the old lady had not been eating. Good health always goes in front of good manners.

At first Hattali ignored everything except water, brought in a glass goblet. This she held, turning the precious object between her bent fingers.

The first mask was the animal on Hattali's funeral pot: a long narrow head, the jaw hinged and moved with a string, the mouth full of pointed teeth. Snap! Snap!

The skin would be mottled green, Haik decided; the eyes large, round and red. There were existing animals—small hunters with scaly hides—that had triangular pupils. She would give this creature the same. The spines on the back would be a banner, supported by a harness over Dapple's shoulders. Hah! It would flutter when her lover danced! As she worked, she described the mask to Hattali.

"Have you ever found large animals?" the old woman asked.

"Not complete. But large bones, yes, and teeth that are longer than my hands. The layer they are in is high on my native cliffs and was laid down when the country was above water. They were land-dwellers, those animals, larger than anything living now, at least in the regions I've visited, and with teeth that remind me of birds' teeth, though more irregular and much larger."

"What eyesight you have!" Hattali exclaimed. "To see into the distant past! Do you really believe these creatures existed?"

"They did," said Haik firmly.

Gradually, as their conversation continued, the old lady began to eat: hard biscuits first, then pieces of fruit, then *halin* in a small, square, ceramic cup. Hattali was sitting upright now, her bony shoulders straight under an embroidered robe. Hah! She was licking her fingers! "Can you write, Haik?"

"Yes."

"I want you to write down your ideas and draw the animals you've found in stone. I'll have one of my female relatives make a copy."

"You believe me," said Haik in surprise.

"Most of what you've told me I knew already," Hattali answered. "How could any woman not know about inheritance, who has lived long enough to see traits appear and reappear in families of people, *sulin* and *tsina*? But I lacked a framework on which to string my information. This is what you've given me. The frame! The loom! Think of the patterns the Ettin will be able to weave, now that we understand what the Goddess has been doing with sex and death and time!" The old woman shifted in her chair. There was a cup of *halin* next to her on the folding table. She felt for it, grasped it and drank, then reached for a piece of fruit. "I have been wondering whether it's time for me to die. Did you notice?"

"Yes," murmured Dapple.

"The blindness is hard to endure; but life remains interesting, and my kin tell me that they still need my judgment. I can hardly refuse their pleas. But when I fell, I thought—I know this illness. It strikes woman down like a blow from a war club. When they rise, if they rise, who can say what the damage will be? Paralysis, stupor, the loss of speech or thought.

"This time the only damage was to one leg. But I may fall again. I have seen relatives, grave senior female cousins, turn into something less than animals— witless and grieving, though they do not remember the cause of their grief. Maybe, I thought, it would be better to stop eating now and die while I am still able to choose death.

"But I want your book first. Will you write it for me?"

Haik glanced at Dapple, who spoke the word "yes" in silence.

"Yes," said the potter.

The matriarch sighed and leaned back. "Good! What a marvel you are, Dapple! What a fine guest you have brought to Ettin!"

The next day Haik began her book, drawing fossils from memory. Fortunately, her memory was excellent. Her masks went to the costume maker, who finished them with the help of the apprentices. It was good work, though not equal to Haik's. One apprentice showed real promise.

The old lady was eating with zest now. The house resumed the ordinary noise of a house full of relations. Children shouted in the courtyards. Adults joked and called. Looking up once from her work, Haik saw adolescents swimming in the river below the terrace: slim naked girls, their fur sleeked by water, clearly happy.

By the time the Ettin war party returned, Taiin looking contented as he dismounted in the front courtyard, the book on evolution was done. Taiin greeted them and limped hurriedly to his mother's terrace. The old woman rose, looking far stronger than she had twenty days before.

The war captain glanced at Dapple. "Your doing?"

"Haik's."

"Ettin will buy every pot you make!" the captain said in a fierce whisper, then went to embrace his mother.

Later, he looked at Haik's book. "This renewed Hattali's interest in life? Pictures of shells and bones?"

"Ideas," said Dapple.

"Well," said Taiin, "I've never been one for thinking. Ideas belong to women, unless they're strategic or tactical. All I can be is thankful and surprised." He turned the folded pages. "Mother says we will be able to breed more carefully, thinking of distant consequences rather than immediate advantage. All this from bones!"

The actors did their play soon after this, setting their stage in the house's largest courtyard. It began with a fish that was curious about the land and crawled out of the ocean. In spite of discomfort, the fish stayed, changing into an animal with four legs and feet. Hah! The way it danced, once it had feet to dance with!

The fish's descendants, all four-footed animals, were not satisfied with their condition. They fell to arguing about what to do next. Some decided their ancestral mother had made a mistake and returned to water, becoming animals like *peshadi* and *luatin*. Others changed into birds, through a process that was not described; Haik knew too little about the evolution of birds. Other animals chose fur, with or without a mixture of scales. One animal chose judgement as well as fur.

"How ridiculous!" cried her comrades. "What use are ideas or the ability to discriminate? You can't eat a discrimination. Ideas won't keep you warm at night. Folly!" They danced away, singing praise for their fur, their teeth, their claws.

The person with fur and intelligence stood alone on the stage. "One day I will be like you," Dapple said to the audience. "No spines on my back, no long claws, no feathers, though I had these things, some of them at least, in the past. What have I gained from my choice, which my relatives have just mocked? The ability to think forward and back. I can learn about the past. Using this knowledge, I can look into the future and see the consequences of my present actions. Is this a useful gift? Decide for yourselves."

This was the play's end. The audience was silent, except for Hattali, who cried, "Excellent! Excellent!" Taking their cue from the old lady, the rest of the Ettin began to stamp and shout.

A day later, the actors were on the road. They left behind Haik's book and the new masks. Dapple said, "My play doesn't work yet, and maybe it never will. Art is about the known, rather than the unknown. How can people see themselves in unfamiliar animals?"

Haik said, "My ideas are in my head. I don't need a copy of the book."

"I will accept your gifts," said Hattali. "And send one copy of the book to another Ettin house. If anything ever happens here, we'll still have your ideas. And I will not stop eating, till I'm sure that a few of my relatives comprehend the book."

"It may take time," said Haik.

"This is more interesting than dying," Hattali said.

The story ends here. Haik went home to Tulwar and made more pots. In spite of Taiin's promise, the Ettin did not buy all her work. Instead, merchants carried it up and down the coast. Potters in other towns began to imitate her; though they, having never studied fossils, did not get the animals right. Still, it became a known style of pottery. Nowadays, in museums, it's possible to find examples of the Southern Fantastic Animal Tradition. There may even be a few of Haik's pots in museum cabinets, though no one has yet noticed their accuracy. Hardly surprising! Students of art are not usually students of paleontology.

As for Dapple, she continued to write and perform, doing animal plays in the south and heroic tragedies in the north. Her work is still famous, though only fragments remain.

The two lovers met once or twice a year, never in Tulwar. Dapple kept her original dislike of the place. Often, Haik traveled with the actor's company, taking pots if they were going to Ettin.

Finally, at age fifty, Haik said to her senior relatives, "I am leaving Tulwar."

The relatives protested.

"I have given you three children and trained five apprentices. Let them make pots for you! Enough is enough."

What could the relatives say? Plenty, as it turned out, but to no avail. Haik moved to a harbor town midway between Tulwar and Hu. The climate was mild and sunny; the low surrounding hills had interesting fossils embedded in a lovely, fine-grained, cream-yellow stone. Haik set up a new pottery. Dapple, tired of her rainy home island, joined the potter. Their house was small, with only one courtyard. A crown-of-fire tree grew there, full- sized and rooted in the ground. Every spring, it filled their rooms with a sweet aroma, then filled the courtyard with a carpet of fallen blossoms. "Beauty and death," Dapple sang as she swept the flowers up.

Imagine the two women growing old together, Dapple writing the plays that have been mostly lost, Haik making pots and collecting fossils. The creatures in those hills! If anything, they were stranger than the animals in the cliffs of Tulwar!

As far as is known, Haik never wrote her ideas down a second time. If she did, the book was lost, along with her fossils, in the centuries between her life and the rediscovery of evolution. Should she have tried harder? Would history have been changed, if she had been able to convince people other than Ettin Hattali? Let others argue this question. The purpose of this story is to be a story.

The Ettin became famous for the extreme care with which they arranged breeding contracts and for their success in all kinds of far-into-the-future planning. All through the south people said, "This is a lineage which understands cause and effect!" In modern times, they have become one of the most powerful families on the planet. Is this because of Haik's ideas? Who can say? Though they are old-fashioned in many ways, they've had little trouble dealing with new ideas. "Times change," the Ettin say. "Ideas change. We are not the same as our ancestors, nor should we be. The Goddess shows no fondness for staying put, nor for getting stuck like a cart in spring rain.

"Those willing to learn from her are likely to go forward. If they don't, at least they have shown the Great Mother respect; and she—in return—has given them a universe full of things that interest and amaze."

Rogue Farm

CHARLES STROSS

Charles Stross, fifty-three, is a full-time science fiction writer and resident of Edinburgh, Scotland. The author of seven Hugo-nominated novels and winner of three Hugo awards for best novella, Stross's works have been translated into over twelve languages. His most recent novel, Dark State, was published by Tor in January 2018; his next novel, The Labyrinth Index is due out from Tor.com and Orbit (in the UK) in October 2018. Like many writers, Stross has had a variety of careers, occupations, and job-shaped catastrophes in the past, from pharmacist (he quit after the second police stake-out) to first code monkey on the team of a successful dot-com startup (with brilliant timing he tried to change employer just as the bubble burst). Along the way he collected degrees in pharmacy and computer science, making him the world's first officially qualified cyberpunk writer (just as cyberpunk died).

Here he gives us a fast, funny, and highly inventive look at a deceptively bucolic future where nothing is quite as simple—or as harmless—as it seems . . . .

It was a bright, cool March morning: mare's tails trailed across the south-eastern sky towards the rising sun. Joe shivered slightly in the driver's seat as he twisted the starter handle on the old front-loader he used to muck out the barn. Like its owner, the ancient Massey-Fergusson had seen better days; but it had survived worse abuse than Joe routinely handed out. The diesel clattered, spat out a gob-bet of thick blue smoke, and chattered to itself dyspeptically. His mind as blank as the sky above, Joe slid the tractor into gear, raised the front scoop, and began turning it towards the open doors of the barn—just in time to see an itinerant farm coming down the road.

"Bugger," swore Joe. The tractor engine made a hideous grinding noise and died. He took a second glance, eyes wide, then climbed down from the tractor and trotted over to the kitchen door at the side of the farm house. "Maddie!" he called, forgetting the two-way radio clipped to his sweater hem. "Maddie! There's a farm coming!"

"Joe? Is that you? Where are you?" Her voice wafted vaguely from the bowels of the house.

"Where are *you*?" He yelled back.

"I'm in the bathroom."

"Bugger," he said again. "If it's the one we had round the end last month . . ."

The sound of a toilet sluiced through his worry. It was followed by a drumming of feet on the staircase, then Maddie erupted into the kitchen. "Where is it?" she demanded.

"Out front, about a quarter mile up the lane."

"Right." Hair wild and eyes angry about having her morning ablutions cut short, Maddie yanked a heavy green coat on over her shirt. "Opened the cupboard yet?"

"I was thinking you'd want to talk to it first."

"Too right I want to talk to it. If it's that one that's been lurking in the copse near Edgar's pond I got some *issues* to discuss with it." Joe shook his head at her anger and went to unlock the cupboard in the back room. "You take the shotgun and keep it off our property,"she called after him: "I'll be out in a minute."

Joe nodded to himself, then carefully picked out the twelve-gauge and a preloaded magazine. The gun's power-on self test lights flickered erratically, but it seemed to have a full charge. Slinging it, he locked the cupboard carefully and went back out into the farmyard to warn off their unwelcome visitor.

The farm squatted, buzzing and clicking to itself, in the road outside Armitage End. Joe eyed it warily from behind the wooden gate, shotgun under his arm. It was a medium-sized one, probably with half a dozen human components subsumed into it—a formidable collective. Already it was deep into farm-fugue, no longer relating very clearly to people outside its own communion of mind. Beneath its leathery black skin he could see hints of internal structure, cytocellular macro-assemblies flexing and glooping in disturbing motions. Even though it was only a young adolescent, it was already the size of an antique heavy tank, and blocked the road just as efficiently as an Apatosaurus would have. It smelled of yeast and gasoline.

Joe had an uneasy feeling that it was watching him. "Bugger it, I don't have time for this," he muttered. The stable waiting for the small herd of cloned spidercows cluttering up the north paddock was still knee-deep in manure, and the tractor seat wasn't getting any warmer while he shivered out here waiting for Maddie to come and sort this thing out. It wasn't a big herd, but it was as big as his land and his labour could manage—the big biofabricator in the shed could assemble mammalian livestock faster than he could feed them up and sell them with an honest HAND-RAISED NOT VAT-GROWN label. "What do you want with us?" he yelled up at the gently buzzing farm.

"Brains, fresh brains for baby Jesus," crooned the farm in a warm contralto, startling Joe half out of his skin. "Buy my brains!" Half a dozen disturbing cauliflower shapes poked suggestively out of the farms back then retracted again, coyly.

"Don't want no brains around here," Joe said stubbornly, his fingers whitening on the stock of the shotgun. "Don't want your kind round here, neither. Go away."

"I'm a nine-legged semi-automatic groove machine!" Crooned the farm. "I'm on my way to Jupiter on a mission for love! Won't you buy my brains?" Three curious eyes on stalks extruded from its upper glacis.

"Uh—" Joe was saved from having to dream up any more ways of saying *fuck off* by Maddie's arrival. She'd managed to sneak her old battle dress home after a stint keeping the peace in Mesopotamia twenty ago, and she'd managed to keep herself in shape enough to squeeze inside. Its left knee squealed ominously when she walked it about, which wasn't often, but it still worked well enough to manage its main task—intimidating trespassers.

"You." She raised one translucent arm, pointed at the farm. "Get off my land. *Now.*"

Taking his cue, Joe raised his shotgun and thumbed the selector to full auto. It wasn't a patch on the hardware riding Maddie's shoulders, but it underlined the point. The farm hooted: "why don't you love me?" it asked plaintively.

"*Get orf my land,*" Maddie amplified, volume cranked up so high that Joe winced. "*Ten seconds! Nine! Eight—*" Thin rings sprang out from the sides of her arms, whining with the stress of long disuse as the Gauss gun powered up.

"I'm going! I'm going!" The farm lifted itself slightly, shuffling backwards. "Don't understand. I only wanted to set you free to explore the universe. Nobody wants to buy my fresh fruit and brains. What's wrong with the world?"

They waited until the farm had retreated round the bend at the top of the hill. Maddie was the first to relax, the rings retracting back into the arms of her battle dress, which solidified from ethereal translucency to neutral olive drab as it powered down. Joe safed his shotgun. "Bastard,"he said.

"Fucking A." Maddie looked haggard. "That was a bold one." Her face was white and pinched-looking, Joe noted: her fists were clenched. She had the shakes, he realised without surprise. Tonight was going to be another major nightmare night, and no mistake.

"The fence." They'd discussed wiring up an outer wire to the CHP base load from their little methane plant, on again and off again for the past year.

"Maybe this time. Maybe." Maddie wasn't keen on the idea of frying passersby without warning, but if anything might bring her around it would be the prospect of being overrun by a bunch of rogue farms." Help me out of this and I'll cook breakfast," she said.

"Got to muck out the barn," Joe protested.

"It can wait on breakfast," Maddie said shakily. "I need you."

"Okay." Joe nodded. She was looking bad; it had been a few years since her last fatal breakdown, but when Maddie said *I need you* it was a bad idea to ignore her. That way led to backbreaking labour on the biofab and loading her backup tapes into the new body; always a messy business. He took her arm and steered her towards the back porch. They were nearly there when he paused.

"What is it?" asked Maddie.

"Haven't seen Bob for a while," he said slowly. "Sent him to let the cows into the north paddock after milking. Do you think—"

"We can check from the control room," she said tiredly. "Are you really worried . . . ?"

"With that thing blundering around? What do *you* think?"

"He's a good working dog," Maddie said uncertainly. "It won't hurt him. He'll be alright; just you page him."

After Joe helped her out of her battle dress, and after Maddie spent a good long while calming down, they breakfasted on eggs from their own hens, home-made cheese, and toasted bread made with rye from the hippie commune on the other side of the valley. The stone-floored kitchen in the dilapidated house they'd squatted and rebuilt together over the past twenty years was warm and homely. The only purchase from outside the valley was the coffee, beans from a hardy GM strain that grew like a straggling teenager's beard all along the Cumbrian hilltops. They didn't say much: Joe, because he never did, and Maddie, because there wasn't anything that she wanted to say. Silence kept her personal demons down. They'd known each other for many years, and even when there wasn't anything to say they could cope with each other's silence. The voice radio on the windowsill opposite the cast-iron stove stayed off, along with the TV set hanging on the wall next to the fridge. Breakfast was a quiet time of day.

"Dog's not answering," Joe commented over the dregs of his coffee.

"He's a good dog." Maddie glanced at the yard gate uncertainly. "You afraid he's going to run away to Jupiter?"

"He was with me in the shed." Joe picked up his plate and carried it to the sink, began running hot water onto the dishes. "After I cleaned the lines I told him to go take the herd up the paddock while I did the barn." He glanced up, looking out the window with a worried expression. The Massey-Fergusson was parked right in front of the open barn doors as if holding at bay the mountain of dung, straw, and silage that mounded up inside like an invading odious enemy, relic of a frosty winter past.

Maddie shoved him aside gently and picked up one of the walkie-talkies from the charge point on the window sill. It bleeped and chuckled at her. "Bob, come in, over." She frowned. "He's probably lost his headset again."

Joe racked the wet plates to dry. "I'll move the midden. You want to go find him?"

"I'll do that." Maddie's frown promised a talking-to in store for the dog when she caught up with him. Not that Bob would mind: words ran off him like water off a duck's back. "Cameras first." She prodded the battered TV set to life and grainy bisected views flickered across the screen, garden, yard, dutch barn, north paddock, east paddock, main field, copse. "Hmm."

She was still fiddling with the smallholding surveillance system when Joe clambered back into the driver's seat of the tractor and fired it up once more. This time there was no cough of black smoke, and as he hauled the mess of manure out of the barn and piled it into a three-metre-high midden, a quarter of a ton at a time, he almost managed to forget about the morning's unwelcome visitor. Almost.

By late morning the midden was humming with flies and producing a remarkable stench, but the barn was clean enough to flush out with a hose and broom. Joe was about to begin hauling the midden over to the fermentation tanks buried round the far side of the house when he saw Maddie coming back up the path, shaking her head. He knew at once what was wrong.

"Bob," he said, expectantly.

"Bob's fine. I left him riding shotgun on the goats." Her expression was peculiar. "But that *farm*—"

"Where?" he asked, hurrying after her.

"Sqautting in the woods down by the stream," she said tersely. "Just over our fence."

"It's not trespassing, then."

"It's put down feeder roots! Do you have any idea what that means?"

"I don't—" Joe's face wrinkled in puzzlement. "Oh."

"Yes. *oh*." She stared back at the outbuildings between their home and the woods at the bottom of their smallholding, and if looks could kill, the intruder would be dead a thousand times over. "It's going to estivate, Joe, then it's going to grow to maturity on our patch. And do you know where it said it was going to go when it finishes growing? Jupiter!"

"Bugger," Joe said faintly, as the true gravity of their situation began to sink in. "We'll have to deal with it first."

"That wasn't what I meant," Maddie finished. But Joe was already on his way out the door. She watched him crossing the yard, then shook her head. "Why am I stuck here?" she asked herself, but the cooker wasn't answering.

THE HAMLET OF Outer Cheswick lay four kilometres down the road from Armitage End, four kilometres past mostly derelict houses and broken-down barns, fields given over to weeds and walls damaged by trees. The first half of the twenty-first century had been cruel years for the British agrobusiness sector; even harsher if taken in combination with the decline in population and the consequent housing surplus. As a result, the drop-outs of the forties and fifties were able to take their pick from among the gutted shells of once fine farmhouses. They chose the best and moved in, squatted in the derelict outbuildings, planted their seeds and tended their flocks and practiced their DIY skills, until a generation later a mansion fit for a squire stood in lonely isolation alongside a decaying road where no more cars drove. Or rather, it would have taken a generation had there been any children against whose lives it could be measured; these were the latter decades of the population crash, and what a previous century would have labelled downshifter dink couples were now in the majority, far outnumbering any breeder colonies. In this aspect of their life, Joe and Maddie were boringly conventional. In other respects they weren't: Maddie's nightmares, her aversion to alcohol, and her withdrawl from society were all relics of her time in Peaceforce. As for Joe, he liked it here. Hated cities, hated the net, hated the burn of the new. Anything for a quiet life . . .

The Pig and Pizzle, on the outskirts of Outer Cheswick, was the only pub within about ten kilometres—certainly the only one within staggering distance for Joe when he'd had a skinful of mild—and it was naturally a seething den of local gossip, not least because Ole Brenda refused to allow electricity, much less bandwidth, into the premises. (This was not out of any sense of misplaced technophobia, but a side effect of Brenda's previous life as an attack hacker with the European Defense Forces.)

Joe paused at the bar. "Pint of bitter?" he asked tentatively. Brenda glanced at him and nodded, then went back to loading the antique washing machine. Presently she pulled a clean glass down from the shelf and held it under the tap.

"Hear you've got farm trouble," she said non-commitally as she worked the hand pump on the beer engine.

"Uh-huh." Joe focussed on the glass. "Where'd you hear that?"

"Never you mind." She put the glass down to give the head time to settle; "you want to talk to Arthur and Wendy-the-Rat about farms. They had one the other year."

"Happens." Joe took his pint. "Thanks, Brenda. The usual?"

"Yeah." She turned back to the washer. Joe headed over to the far corner where a pair of huge leather sofas, their arms and backs ripped and scarred by generations of Brenda's semi-feral cats, sat facing each other on either side of a cold hearth. "Art, Rats. What's up?"

"Fine, thanks." Wendy-the-Rat was well over seventy, one of those older folks who had taken the p53 chromosome hack and seemed to wither into timelessness: white dreadlocks, nose and ear studs dangling loosely from leathery holes, skin like a desert wind. Art had been her boy-toy once, back before middle age set its teeth into him. He hadn't had the hack, and looked older than she did. Together they ran a smallholding, mostly pharming vaccine chicks but also doing a brisk trade in high-nitrate fertilizer that came in on the nod and went out in sacks by moonlight.

"Heard you had a spot of bother?"

"'S true." Joe took a cautious mouthful. "Mm, good. You ever had farm trouble?"

"Maybe." Wendy looked at him askance, slitty-eyed. "What kinda trouble you got in mind"

"Got a farm collective. Says it's going to Jupiter or something. Bastard's homesteading the woods down by old Jack's stream. Listen . . . Jupiter?"

"Aye well, that's one of the destinations, sure enough." Art nodded wisely, as if he knew anything.

"Naah, that's bad." Wendy-the-Rat frowned. "Is it growing trees, do you know?"

"Trees?" Joe shook his head. "Haven't gone and looked, tell the truth. What the fuck makes people do that to themselves, anyway?"

"Who the fuck cares?" Wendy's face split in a broad grin. "Such as don't think they're human anymore, meself."

"It tried to sweet-talk us," Joe said.

"Aye, they do that," said Arthur, nodding emphatically. "Read somewhere they're the ones as think we aren't fully human. Tools an' clothes and farmyard machines, like? Sustaining a pre-post-industrial lifestyle instead of updating our genome and living off the land like God intended?"

"'Ow the hell can something with nine legs and eye stalks call itself *human*?" Joe demanded, chugging back half his pint in one angry swallow.

"It used to be, once. Maybe used to be a bunch of people." Wendy got a weird and witchy look in her eye: "'ad a boyfriend back thirty, forty years ago, joined a Lamarckian clade. Swapping genes an' all, the way you or me'd swap us underwear. Used to be a 'viromentalist back when antiglobalisation was about big corporations pissing on us all for profits. Got into gene hackery and self-sufficiency bigtime. I slung his fucking ass when he turned green and started photosynthesizing."

"Bastards," Joe muttered. It was deep green folk like that who'd killed off the agricultural-industrial complex in the early years of the century, turning large portions of the countryside into ecologically devastated wilderness gone to rack and ruin. Bad enough that they'd set millions of countryfolk out of work—but that they'd gone on to turn green, grow extra limbs and emigrate to Jupiter orbit was adding insult to injury. And having a good time in the process, by all accounts. "Din't you 'ave a farm problem, coupla years back?"

"Aye, did that," said Art. He clutched his pint mug protectively.

"It went away," Joe mused aloud.

"Yeah, well." Wendy stared at him cautiously.

"No fireworks, like." Joe caught her eye. "And no body. Huh."

"Metabolism," said Wendy, apparently coming to some kind of decision. "That's where it's at."

"Meat—" Joe, no biogeek, rolled the unfamiliar word around his mouth irritably. "I used to be a software dude before I burned, Rats. You'll have to 'splain the jargon fore using it."

"You ever wondered how those farms *get* to Jupiter?" Wendy probed.

"Well." Joe shook his head. "They, like, grow stage trees? Rocket logs? An' then they est-ee-vate and you are fucked if they do it next door 'cause when those trees go up they toast about a hundred hectares?"

"Very good," Wendy said heavily. She picked up her mug in both hands and gnawed on the rim, edgily glancing around as if hunting for police gnats. "Let's you and me take a hike."

Pausing at the bar for Ole Brenda to refill her mug, Wendy led Joe out past Spiffy Buerke—throwback in green Wellingtons and Barbour jacket—and her latest femme, out into what had once been a car park and was now a tattered wasteground out back behind the pub. It was dark, and no residual light pollution stained the sky: the Milky Way was visible overhead, along with the pea-sized red cloud of orbitals that had gradually swallowed Jupiter over the past few years. "You wired?" asked Wendy.

"No, why?"

She pulled out a fist-sized box and pushed a button on the side of it, waited for a light on its side to blink green, and nodded. "Fuckin 'polis bugs."

"Isn't that a—"

"Ask me no questions an' I'll tell you no fibs." Wendy grinned.

"Uhhuh." Joe took a deep breath: he'd guessed Wendy had some dodgy connections, and this—a portable local jammer—was proof: any police bugs within two or three metres would be blind and dumb, unable to relay their chat to the keyword-trawling subsentient coppers whose job it was to prevent consipracy-to-commit offenses before they happened. It was a relic of the internet age, when enthusiastic legislators had accidentally demolished the right of free speech in public by demanding keyword monitoring of everything within range of a network terminal—not realising that in another few decades 'network terminals' would be self-replicating bots the size of fleas and about as common as dirt. (The 'net itself had collapsed shortly thereafter, under the weight of self-replicating viral libel lawsuits, but the legacy of public surveillance remained.) "Okay. Tell me about metal, meta—"

"Metabolism." Wendy began walking towards the field behind the pub. "And stage trees. Stage trees started out as science fiction, like? Some guy called Niven—anyway. What you do is, you take a pine tree and you hack it. The xylem vessels running up the heartwood, usually they just lignify and die in a normal tree. Stage trees go one better, and before the cells die they *nitrate* the cellulose in their walls. Takes one fuckin' crazy bunch of hacked 'zymes to do it, right? And lots of energy, more energy than trees'd normally have to waste. Anyways, by the time the tree's dead it's like ninety percent nitrocellulose, plus built-in stiffeners and baffles and microstructures. It's not, like, straight explosive—it detonates cell by cell, and *some* of the xylem tubes are, eh, well, the farm grows custom-hacked fungal hyphae with a depolarizing membrane nicked from human axons down them to trigger the reaction. It's about efficient as 'at old-time Ariane or Atlas rocket. Not very, but enough."

"Uh." Joe blinked. "That meant to mean something to me?"

"Oh 'eck, Joe." Wendy shook her head. "Think I'd bend your ear if it wasn't?"

"Okay." He nodded, seriously. "What can I do?"

"Well." Wendy stopped and stared at the sky. High above them, a belt of faint light sparkled with a multitude of tiny pinpricks; a deep green wagon-train making its orbital transfer window, self-sufficient post-human Lamarckian colonists, space-adapted, embarking on the long, slow transfer to Jupiter.

"Well?" He waited expectantly.

"You're wondering where all that fertilizer's from," Wendy said eliptically.

"Fertilizer." His mind blanked for a moment.

"Nitrates."

He glanced down, saw her grinning at him. Her perfect fifth set of teeth glowed alarmingly in the greenish overspill from the light on her jammer box.

"Tha' knows it make sense," she added, then cut the jammer.

WHEN JOE FINALLY staggered home in the small hours, a thin plume of smoke was rising from Bob's kennel. Joe paused in front of the kitchen door and sniffed anxiously, then relaxed. Letting go of the door handle, he walked over to the kennel and sat down outside. Bob was most particular about his den—even his own humans didn't go in there without an invitation. So Joe waited.

A moment later there was an interrogative cough from inside. A dark, pointed snout came out, dribbling smoke from its nostrils like a particularly vulpine dragon. "Rrrrrrr?"

"'S'me."

"Uuurgh." A metallic click. "Smoke good smoke joke cough tickle funny arfarf?"

"Yeah, don't mind if I do."

The snout pulled back into the kennel; a moment later it reappeared, teeth clutching a length of hose with a mouthpiece on one end. Joe accepted it graciously, wiped off the mouthpiece, leaned against the side of the kennel, and inhaled. The weed was potent and smooth: within a few seconds the uneasy dialogue in his head was still.

"Wow, tha's a good turn-up."

"Arf-arf-ayup."

Joe felt himself relaxing. Maddie would be upstairs, snorking quietly in their decrepit bed: waiting for him, maybe. But sometimes a man just had to be alone with his dog and a good joint, doing man-and-dog stuff. Maddie understood this and left him his space. Still . . .

"'At farm been buggering around the pond?"

"Growl exclaim fuck-fuck yup! Sheep-shagger."

"If it's been at our lambs—"

"Nawwwwrr. Buggrit."

"So whassup?"

"Grrrr, Maddie yap-yap farmtalk! Sheepshagger."

"Maddie's been *talking* to it?"

"Grrr yes-yes!"

"Oh shit. Do you remember when she did her last backup?"

The dog coughed fragrant blue smoke. "Tank thump-thump full cow moo beefclone."

"Yeah, I think so too. Better muck it out tomorrow. Just in case."

"Yurrrrrp." But while Joe was wondering whether this was agreement or just a canine eructation, a lean paw stole out of the kennel mouth and yanked the hookah back inside. The resulting slobbering noises and clouds of aromatic blue smoke left Joe feeling a little queasy: so he went inside.

THE NEXT MORNING, over breakfast, Maddie was even quieter than usual. Almost meditative.

"Bob said you'd been talking to that farm," Joe commented over his eggs.

"Bob—" Maddie's expression was unreadable. "Bloody dog." She lifted the Rayburn's hot plate lid and peered at the toast browning underneath. "Talks too much."

"Did you?"

"Ayup." She turned the toast and put the lid back down on it.

"Said much?"

"It's a farm." She looked out the window. "Not a fuckin' worry in the world 'cept making its launch window for Jupiter."

"It—"

"Him. Her. They." Maddie sat down heavily in the other kitchen chair. "It's a collective. Used ta be six people. Old, young, whatether, they's decided ter go to Jupiter. One of 'em was telling me how it happened. How she'd been living like an accountant in Bradford, had a nervous breakdown. Wanted *out*. Self-sufficiency." For a moment her expression turned bleak. "Felt herself growing older but not bigger, if you follow."

"So how's turning into a bioborg an improvement?" Joe grunted, forking up the last of his scrambled eggs.

"They're still separate people: bodies are overrated, anyway. Think of the advantages: not growing older, being able to go places and survive anything, never being on your own, not bein' trapped—" Maddie sniffed. "Fuckin' toast's on fire!"

Smoke began to trickle out from under the hot plate lid. Maddie yanked the wire toasting rack out from under it and dunked it into the sink, waited for waterlogged black crumbs to float to the surface before taking it out, opening it, and loading it with fresh bread.

"Bugger," she remarked.

"You feel trapped?" Joe asked. *Again?* He wondered.

Maddie grunted evasively. "Not your fault, love. Just life."

"Life." Joe sniffed, then sneezed violently as the acrid smoke tickled his nose. "Life!"

"Horizon's closing in," she said quietly. "Need a change of horizons."

"Ayup, well, rust never sleeps, right? Got to clean out the winterstables, haven't I?" said Joe. He grinned uncertainly at her as he turned away: "got a shipment of fertilizer coming in."

IN BETWEEN MILKING the herd, feeding the sheep, mucking out the winterstables, and surruptitiously EMPing every police 'bot on the farm into the silicon afterlife, it took Joe a couple of days to get round to running up his toy on the household fabricator. It clicked and whirred to itself like a demented knitting machine as it ran up the gadgets he'd ordered—a modified crop sprayer with double-walled tanks and hoses, an air rifle with a dart loaded with a potent cocktail of tubocurarine and etorphine, and a breathing mask with its own oxygen supply.

Maddie made herself scarce, puttering around the control room but mostly disappearing during the daytime, coming back to the house after dark to crawl, exhausted, into bed. She didn't seem to be having nightmares, which was a good sign: Joe kept his questions to himself.

It took another five days for the smallholding's power field to concentrate enough juice to begin fueling up his murder weapons. During this time, Joe took the house off-net in the most deniable and surreptitiously plausible way, a bastard coincidence of squirrel-induced cable fade and a badly shielded alternator on the backhoe to do for the wireless chit-chat. He'd half expected Maddie to complain, but she didn't say anything: just spent more time away in Outer Cheswick or Lower Gruntlingthorpe or wherever she'd taken to holing up.

Finally, the tank was filled. So Joe girded his loins, donned his armour, picked up his weapons, and went to do battle with the dragon by the pond.

The woods around the pond had once been enclosed by a wooden fence, a charming copse of old-growth deciduous trees, elm and oak and beech growing uphill, smaller shrubs nestling at their ankles in a greenskirt that reached all the way to the almost-stagnant waters. A little stream fed into it during rainy months, under the feet of a weeping willow; children had played here, pretending to explore the wilderness beneath the benevolent gaze of their parental control cameras.

That had been long ago. Today the woods really *were* wild. No kids, no picnicking city folks, no cars. Badgers and wild coypu and small, frightened wallabies roamed the parching English countryside during the summer dry season. The water drew back to expose an apron of cracked mud, planted with abandoned tin cans and a supermarket trolley of precambrian vintage, its GPS tracker long since shorted out. The bones of the technological epoch, poking from the treacherous surface of a fossil mud-bath. And around the edge of the mimsy puddle, the stage-trees grew.

Joe switched on his jammer and walked in among the spear-shaped conifers. Their needles were matt black and fuzzy at the edges, fractally divided, the better to soak up all the available light: a network of tap roots and fuzzy black grasslike stuff covered the ground densely around them. Joe's breath wheezed noisily in his ears and he sweated into the airtight suit as he worked, pumping a stream of colourless, smoking liquid at the roots of each balistic trunk. The liquid fizzed and evaporated on contact: it seemed to bleach the wood where it touched. Joe carefully avoided the stream: this stuff made him uneasy. As did the trees, but liquid nitrogen was about the one thing he'd been able to think of that was guaranteed to kill the trees stone dead without igniting them. After all, they had cores that were basically made of gun cotton—highly explosive, liable to go off if you subjected them to a sudden sharp impact or the friction of a chainsaw. The tree he'd hit on creaked ominously, threatening to fall sideways, and Joe stepped round it, efficiently squirting at the remaining roots. Right into the path of a distraught farm.

"My holy garden of earthly delights! My forest of the imaginative future! My delight, my trees, my trees!" Eye stalks shot out and over, blinking down at him in horror as the farm reared up on six or seven legs and pawed the air in front of him. "Destroyer of saplings! Earth mother rapist! Bunny-strangling vivisectionist!"

"Back off," said Joe, dropping his cryogenic squirter and fumbling for his air-gun.

The farm came down with a ground-shaking thump in front of him and stretched eyes out to glare at him from both sides. They blinked, long black eyelashes fluttering across angry blue irises. "How *dare* you?" demanded the farm. "My treasured seedlings!"

"Shut the fuck up," Joe grunted, shouldering his gun. "Think I'd let you burn my holding when tha' rocket launched? Stay the *fuck* away," he added as a tentacle began to extend from the farm's back.

"My crop," it moaned quietly: "my exile! Six more years around the sun chained to this well of sorrowful gravity before next the window opens! No brains for Baby Jesus! Defenestrator! We could have been so happy together if you hadn't fucked up! Who set you up to this, Rat Lady?" It began to gather itself, muscles rippling under the leathery mantle atop its leg cluster.

So Joe shot it.

Tubocurarine is a muscle relaxant: it paralyses skeletal muscles, the kind over which human nervous systems typically exert conscious control. Etorphine is an insanely strong opiate—twelve hundred times as potent as heroin. Given time, a farm, with its alien adaptive metabolism and consciously controlled proteome might engineer a defense against the etorphine—but Joe dosed his dart with enough to stun a blue whale, and he had no intention of giving the farm enough time. It shuddered and went down on one knee as he closed in on it, a syrette raised: "why?" it asked plaintively in a voice that almost made him wish he hadn't pulled the trigger. "We could have gone together!"

"Together?" he asked. Already the eye stalks were drooping; the great lungs wheezed effortfully as it struggled to frame a reply.

"I was going to ask you," said the farm, and half its legs collapsed under it, with a thud like a baby earthquake. "Oh Joe, if only . . ."

"Joe? *Maddie?*" he demanded, nerveless fingers dropping the tranquiliser gun.

A mouth appeared in the farm's front, slurred words at him from familiar seeming lips, words about Jupiter and promises. Appalled, Joe backed away from the farm. Passing the first dead tree he dropped the nitrogen tank: then an impulse he couldn't articulate made him turn and run, back to the house, eyes almost blinded by sweat or tears. But he was too slow, and when he dropped to his knees next to the farm, pharmacopoeia clicking and whirring to itself in his arms, he found it was already dead.

"Bugger," said Joe, and he stood up, shaking his head. "*Bugger.*" He keyed his walkie-talkie: "Bob, come in, Bob!"

"Rrrrowl?"

"Momma's had another break-down. Is the tank clean, like I asked?"

"Yap!"

"Okay. I got 'er backup tapes in t'office safe. Let's get t'ank warmed up for 'er an' then shift t'tractor down 'ere to muck out this mess."

THAT AUTUMN, THE weeds grew unnaturally rich and green down in the north paddock of Armitage End.

THE LITTLE GODDESS

IAN McDONALD

British author Ian McDonald is an ambitious and daring writer with a wide range and an impressive amount of talent. His first story was published in 1982, and since then he has appeared with some frequency in Interzone, Asimov's Science Fiction, and elsewhere. In 1989 he won the Locus Best First Novel Award for his novel Desolation Road. He won the Philip K. Dick Award in 1992 for his novel King of Morning, Queen of Day. His other books include the novels Out on Blue Six and Hearts, Hands and Voices, Terminal Cafe, Sacrifice of Fools, Evolution's Shore, Kirinya, Ares Express, Brasyl, and The Dervish House, as well as three collections of his short fiction, Empire Dreams, Speaking in Tongues, and Cyberabad Days. His novel, River of Gods, was a finalist for both the Hugo Award and the Arthur C. Clarke award in 2005, and a novella drawn from it, The Little Goddess, was a finalist for the Hugo and the Nebula. He won a Hugo Award in 2007 for his novelette The Djinn's Wife, won the Theodore Sturgeon Award for his story "Tendeleo's Story," and in 2011 won the John W. Campbell Memorial Award for his novel The Dervish House. Among his most recent novels are the starting volume of a YA series, Planesrunner, and its two sequels, Be My Enemy and Empress of the Sun, along with a big retrospective collection, The Best of Ian McDonald. Born in Manchester, England, in 1960, McDonald has spent most of his life in Northern Ireland, and now lives and works in Belfast.

In the brilliant story that follows, he plunges us into a future India of dazzling complexity and cultural diversity, where the highest of high-tech exists side-by-side with the most ancient of ancient ways, and unbelievable wealth cheek-by-jowl with utter poverty, for the compelling and fascinating story of what it feels like to become a god . . . and then have to find your way in an indifferent world on the other side of divinity.

I remember the night I became a goddess.

The men collected me from the hotel at sunset. I was light-headed with hunger, for the child-assessors said I must not eat on the day of the test. I had been up since dawn, the washing and dressing and making up was a long and tiring business. My parents bathed my feet in the bidet. We had never seen such a thing before and that seemed the natural use for it. None of us had ever stayed in a hotel. We thought it most grand, though I see now that it was budget tourist chain. I remember the smell of onions cooking in *ghee* as I came down in the elevator. It smelled like the best food in the world.

I know the men must have been priests but I cannot remember if they wore formal dress. My mother cried in the lobby; my father's mouth was pulled in and he held his eyes wide, in that way that grown-ups do when they want to cry but cannot let tears be seen. There were two other girls for the test staying in the same hotel. I did not know them; they were from other villages where the *devi* could live. Their parents wept unashamedly. I could not understand it; their daughters might be goddesses.

On the street rickshaw drivers and pedestrians hooted and waved at us with our red robes and third eyes on our foreheads. The *devi*, the *devi* look! Best of all fortune! The other girls held on tight to the men's hands. I lifted my skirts and stepped into the car with the darkened windows.

They took us to the Hanumandhoka. Police and machines kept the people out of the Durbar Square. I remember staring long at the machines, with their legs like steel chickens and naked blades in their hands. The King's Own fighting machines. Then I saw the temple and its great roofs sweeping up and up and up into the red sunset and I thought for one instant its upturned eaves were bleeding.

The room was long and dim and stuffily warm. Low evening light shone in dusty rays through cracks and slits in the carved wood; so bright it almost burned. Outside you could hear the traffic and the bustle of tourists. The walls seemed thin but at the same time kilometres thick. Durbar Square was a world away. The room smelled of brassy metal. I did not recognise it then but I now know it as the smell of blood. Beneath the blood was another smell, of time piled thick as dust. One of the two women who would be my guardians if I passed the test told me the temple was five hundred years old. She was a short, round woman with a face that always seemed to be smiling but when you looked closely you saw it was not. She made us sit on the floor on red cushions while the men brought the rest of the girls. Some of them were crying already. When there were ten of us the two women left and the door was closed. We sat for a long time in the heat of the long room. Some of the girls fidgeted and chattered but I gave all my attention to the wall carvings and soon I was lost. It has always been easy for me to lose myself; in Shakya I could disappear for hours in the movement of clouds across the mountain, in the ripple of the grey river far below and the flap of the prayer banner in the wind. My parents saw it as a sign of my inborn divinity, one of thirty-two that mark girls in whom the goddess could dwell.

In the failing light I read the story of Jayaprakash Malla playing dice with the *devi* Taleju Bhawani who came to him in the shape of a red snake and left with the vow that she would only return to the Kings of Kathmandu as a virgin girl of low caste, to spite their haughtiness. I could not read its end in the darkness, but I did not need to. I was its end, or one of the other nine girls in the god-house of the *devi*.

Then the doors burst open wide and firecrackers exploded and through the rattle and smoke red demons leaped into the hall. Behind them men in crimson beat pans and clappers and bells. At once two of the girls began to cry and the two women came and took them away. But I knew the monsters were just silly men. In masks. These were not even close to demons. I have seen demons, after the rain clouds when the light comes low down the valley and all the mountains leap up as one. Stone demons, kilometres high. I have heard their voices, and their breath does not smell like onions. The silly men danced close to me, shaking their red manes and red tongues but I could see their eyes behind the painted holes and they were afraid of me.

Then the door banged open again with another crash of fireworks and more men came through the smoke. They carried baskets draped with red sheets. They set them in front of us and whipped away the coverings. Buffalo heads, so freshly struck off the blood was bright and glossy. Eyes rolled up, lolling tongues still warm, noses still wet. And the flies, swarming around the severed neck. A man pushed a basket towards me on my cushion as if it were a dish of holy food. The crashing and beating outside rose to a roar, so loud and metallic it hurt. The girl from my own Shakya village started to wail; the cry spread to another and then another, then a fourth. The other woman, the old, tall, pinched one with a skin like an old purse, came in to take them out, carefully lifting her gown so as not to trail it in the blood. The dancers whirled around like flame and the kneeling man lifted the buffalo head from the basket. He held it up in my face, eye to eye, but all I thought was that it must weigh a lot; his muscles stood out like vines, his arm shook. The flies looked like black jewels. Then there was a clap from outside and the men set down the heads and covered them up with their cloths and they left with the silly demon men whirling and leaping around them. There was one other girl left on her cushion now. I did not know her. She was of a Vajryana family from Niwar down the valley. We sat a long time, wanting to talk but not knowing if that too was part of the trial. Then the door opened a third time and two men led a white goat into the *devi* hall. They brought it right between me and the Niwari girl. I saw its wicked, slotted eye roll. One held the goat's tether, the other took a big ceremonial *kukri* from a leather sheathe. He blessed it and with one fast strong stroke sent the goat's head leaping from its body.

I almost laughed, for the goat looked so funny, its body not knowing where its head was, the head looking around for the body and then the body realising that it had no head and going down with a kick, and why was the Niwari girl screaming, couldn't she see how funny it was, or was she screaming because I saw the joke and she was jealous of that? Whatever her reason, smiling woman and weathered woman came and took her very gently away and the two men went down on their knees in the spreading blood and kissed the wooden floor. They lifted away the two parts of the goat. I wished they hadn't done that. I would have liked someone with me in the big wooden hall. But I was on my own in the heat and the dark and over the traffic I could hear the deep-voiced bells of Kathmandu start to swing and ring. Then for the last time the doors opened and there were the women, in the light.

"Why have you left me all alone?" I cried. "What have I done wrong?"

"How could you do anything wrong goddess?" said the old, wrinkled woman who, with her colleague, would become my mother and father and teacher and sister. "Now come along with us and hurry. The King is waiting."

Smiling Kumarima and Tall Kumarima (as I would now have to think of them) took a hand each and led me, skipping, from the great looming Hanuman temple. I saw that a road of white silk had been laid from the foot of the temple to a wooden palace close by. The people had been let back into the square and they pressed in on either side of the processional way, held back by the police and the King's robots. The machines held burning torches in their grasping hands. Fire glinted from their killing blades. There was great silence in the dark square.

"Your home, goddess," said Smiling Kumarima, bending low to whisper in my ear. "Walk the silk, *devi*. Do not stray off it. I have your hand, you will be safe with me."

I walked between my Kumarimas, humming a pop tune I had heard on the radio at the hotel. When I looked back I saw that I had left two sets of bloody footprints.

❄

You have no caste, no village, no home. This palace is your home, and who would wish for any other? We have made it lovely for you, for you will only leave it six times a year. Everything you need is here within these walls.

You have no mother or father. A goddess has no parents. You have no brothers or sisters. The King is your brother, the Kingdom your sister. The priests who attend on you, they are nothing. We your Kumarimas are less than nothing. Dust, dirt, a tool. You may say anything, and we must obey it.

As we have said, you will leave the palace only six times a year. You will be carried in a palanquin. Oh, it is a beautiful thing, carved wood and silk. Outside this palace you shall not touch the ground. The moment you touch the ground, you cease to be divine.

You will wear red, with your hair in a topknot and your toe- and fingernails painted. You will carry the red *tilak* of Siva on your forehead. We will help you with your preparations until they become second nature.

You will speak only within the confines of your palace, and little even then. Silence becomes the Kumari. You will not smile or show any emotion.

You will not bleed. Not a scrape, not a scratch. The power is in the blood and when the blood leaves, the *devi* leaves. On the day of your first blood, even one single drop, we will tell the priest and he will inform the King that the goddess has left. You will no longer be divine and you will leave this palace and return to your family. You will not bleed.

You have no name. You are Taleju, you are Kumari. You are the goddess.

These instructions my two Kumarimas whispered to me as we walked between kneeling priests to the King in his plumed crown of diamonds and emeralds and pearls. The King *namasted* and we sat side by side on lion thrones and long hall throbbed to the bells and drums of Durbar Square. I remember thinking that a King must bow to me but there are rules even for goddesses.

Smiling Kumarima and Tall Kumarima. I draw Tall Kumarima in my memory first, for it is right to give pre-eminence to age. She was almost as tall as a Westerner and thin as a stick in a drought. At first I was scared of her. Then I heard her voice and could never be scared of her again; her voice was kind as a singing bird. When she spoke you felt you now knew everything. Tall Kumarima lived in a small apartment above a tourist shop on the edge of Durbar Square. From her window she could see my Kumari Ghar, among the stepped towers of the *dhokas*. Her husband had died of lung cancer from pollution and cheap Indian cigarettes. Her two tall sons were grown and married with children of their own, older than me. In that time she had mothered five Kumari *Devis* before me.

Now I remember Smiling Kumarima. She was short and round and had breathing problems for which she used inhalers, blue and brown. I would hear the snake hiss of them on days when Durbar Square was golden with smog. She lived out in the new suburbs up on the western hills, a long journey even by the royal car at her service. Her children were twelve, ten, nine and seven. She was jolly and treated me like her fifth baby, the young favourite, but I felt even then that, like the demon-dancing-men, she was scared of me. Oh, it was the highest honour any woman could hope for, to be the mother of the goddess—so to speak—though you wouldn't think it to hear her neighbours in the unit, *shutting yourself away in that dreadful wooden box, and all the blood, medieval, medieval*, but they couldn't understand. Somebody had to keep the King safe against those who would turn us into another India, or worse, China; someone had to preserve the old ways of the divine kingdom. I understood early that difference between them. Smiling Kumarima was my mother out of duty. Tall Kumarima from love.

I never learned their true names. Their rhythms and cycles of shifts waxed and waned through the days and nights like the faces of the moon. Smiling Kumarima once found me looking up through the lattice of a *jali* screen at the fat moon on a rare night when the sky was clear and healthy and shouted me away, *don't be looking at that thing, it will call the blood out of you, little devi, and you will be the devi no more.*

Within the wooden walls and iron rules of my Kumari Ghar years become indistinguishable, indistinct. I think now I was five when I became Taleju Devi. The year, I believe, was 2034. But some memories break the surface, like flowers through snow.

Monsoon rain on the steep-sloped roofs, water rushing and gurgling through the gutters, and the shutter that every year blew loose and rattled in the wind. We had monsoons, then. Thunder demons in the mountains around the city, my room flash lit with lightning. Tall Kumarima came to see if I needed singing to sleep but I was not afraid. A goddess cannot fear a storm.

The day I went walking in the little garden, when Smiling Kumarima let out a cry and fell at my feet on the grass and the words to tell her to get up, not to worship me were on my lips when she held up, between thumb and forefinger, twisting and writhing and trying to find a place for its mouth to seize: a green leech.

The morning Tall Kumarima came to tell me people had asked me to show myself. At first I had thought it wonderful that people would want to come and look at me on my little *jharoka* balcony in my clothes and paint and jewels. Now I found it tiresome; all those round eyes and gaping mouths. It was a week after my tenth birthday. I remember Tall Kumarima smiled but tried not to let me see. She took me to the *jharoka* to wave to the people in the court and I saw a hundred Chinese faces upturned to me, then the high, excited voices. I waited and waited but two tourists would not go away. They were an ordinary couple, dark local faces, country clothes.

"Why are they keeping us waiting?" I asked.

"Wave to them," Tall Kumarima urged. "That is all they want." The woman saw my lifted hand first. She went weak and grabbed her husband by the arm. The man bent to her, then looked up at me. I read many emotions on that face; shock, confusion, recognition, revulsion, wonder, hope. Fear. I waved and the man tugged at his wife, *look, look up*. I remember that against all the laws, I smiled. The woman burst into tears. The man made to call out but Tall Kumarima hastened me away.

"Who were those funny people?" I asked. "They were both wearing very white shoes."

"Your mother and father," Tall Kumarima said. As she led along the Durga corridor with the usual order not to brush my free hand along the wooden walls for fear of splinters, I felt her grip tremble.

That night I dreamed the dream of my life, that is not a dream but one of my earliest experiences, knocking and knocking and knocking at the door of my remembering. This was a memory I would not admit in daylight, so it must come by night, to the secret door.

I am in the cage over a ravine. A river runs far below, milky with mud and silt, foaming cream over the boulders and slabs sheared from the mountainsides. The cable spans the river from my home to the summer grazing and I sit in the wire cage used to carry the goats across the river. At my back is the main road, always loud with trucks, the prayer banners and Kinley bottled water sign of my family's roadside teahouse. My cage still sways from my uncle's last kick. I see him, arms and legs wrapped around the wire, grinning his gap-toothed grin. His face is summer-burned brown, his hands cracked and brown from the trucks he services. Oil engrained in the creases. He wrinkles up his nose at me and unhooks a leg to kick my cage forward on its pulley-wheel. Pulley sways, cable sways, mountains, sky and river sway but I am safe my little goat-cage. I have been kicked across this ravine many times. My uncle inches forwards. Thus we cross the river, by kicks and inches.

I never see what strikes him—some thing of the brain perhaps, like the sickness Lowlanders get when they go up to the high country. But the next I look my uncle is clinging to the wire by his right arm and leg. His left arm and leg hang down, shaking like a cow with its throat cut, shaking the wire and my little cage. I am three years old and I think this is funny, a trick my uncle is doing just for me, so I shake back, bouncing my cage, bouncing my uncle up and down, up and down. Half his body will not obey him and he tries to move forward by sliding his leg along, like *this*, jerk his hand forward *quick* so he never loses grip of the wire, and all the while bouncing up and down, up and down. Now my uncle tries to shout but his words are noise and slobber because half his face is paralysed. Now I see his fingers lose their grip on the wire. Now I see him spin round and his hooked leg come free. Now he falls away, half his body reaching, half his mouth screaming. I see him fall, I see him bounce from the rocks and cartwheel, a thing I have always wished I could do. I see him go into the river and the brown water swallow him.

My older brother came out with a hook and a line and hauled me in. When my parents found I was not shrieking, not a sob or a tear or even a pout, that was when they knew I was destined to become the goddess. I was smiling in my wire cage.

I remember best the festivals, for it was only then that I left the Kumari Ghar. Dasain, at the end of summer, was the greatest. For eight days the city ran red. On the final night I lay awake listening to the voices in the square flow together into one roar, like I imagined the sea would sound, the voices of the men gambling for the luck of Lakshmi, *devi* of wealth. My father and uncles had gambled on the last night of Dasain. I remember I came down and demanded to know what all the laughing was about and they turned away from their cards and really laughed. I had not thought there could be so many coins in the world as there were on that table but it was nothing compared to Kathmandu on the eighth of Dasain. Smiling Kumarima told me it took some of the priests all year to earn back what they lost. Then came the ninth day, the great day and I sailed out from my palace for the city would worship me.

I travelled on a litter carried by forty men strapped to bamboo poles as thick as my body. They went gingerly, testing every step for the streets were slippery. Surrounded by gods and priests and *saddhus* mad with holiness, I rode on my golden throne. Closer to me than any were my Kumarimas, my two Mothers, so splendid and ornate in their red robes and headdresses and make-up they did not look like humans at all. But Tall Kumarima's voice and Smiling Kumarima's smile assured me as I rode with Hanuman and Taleju through the cheering and the music and the banners bright against the blue sky and the smell I now recognised from the night I became a goddess, the smell of blood.

That Dasain the city received me as never before. The roar of the night of

Lakshmi continued into the day. As Taleju *Devi* I was not supposed to notice anything as low as humans but out of the corners of my painted eyes I could see beyond the security robots stepping in time with my bearers, and the streets radiating out from the *stupa* of Chhetrapati were solid with bodies. They threw jets and gushes of water from plastic bottles up into the air, glittering, breaking into little rainbows, raining down on them, soaking them, but they did not care. Their faces were crazy with devotion.

Tall Kumarima saw my puzzlement and bent to whisper.

"They do *puja* for the rain. The monsoon has failed a second time, *devi*."

As I spoke, Smiling Kumarima fanned me so no one would see my lips move. "We don't like the rain," I said firmly.

"A goddess cannot do only what she likes," Tall Kumarima said. "It is a serious matter. The people have no water. The rivers are running dry."

I thought of the river that ran far down deep below the house where I was born, the water creamy and gushing and flecked with yellow foam. I saw it swallow my uncle and could not imagine it ever becoming thin, weak, hungry.

"So why do they throw water then?" I asked.

"So the *devi* will give them more," Smiling Kumarima explained. But I could not see the sense in that even for goddesses and I frowned, trying to understand how humans were and so I was looking right at him when he came at me.

He had city pale skin and hair parted on the left that flopped as he dived out of the crowd. He moved his fists to the collar of his diagonally striped shirt and people surged away from him. I saw him hook his thumbs into two loops of black string. I saw his mouth open in a great cry. Then the machine swooped and I saw a flash of silver. The young man's head flew up into the air. His mouth and eyes went round: from a cry to an oh! The King's Own machine had sheathed its blade, like a boy folding a knife, before the body, like that funny goat in the Hanumand-hoka, realised it was dead and fell to the ground. The crowd screamed and tried to get away from the headless thing. My bearers rocked, swayed, uncertain where to go, what to do. For a moment I thought they might drop me.

Smiling Kumarima let out little shrieks of horror, "Oh! Oh! Oh!" My face was spotted with blood.

"It's not hers," Tall Kumarima shouted. "It's not hers!" She moistened a hand-kerchief with a lick of saliva. She was gently wiping the young man's blood from my face when the Royal security in their dark suits and glasses arrived, beating through the crowd. They lifted me, stepped over the body and carried me to the waiting car.

"You smudged my make-up," I said to the Royal guard as the car swept away. Worshippers barely made it out of our way in the narrow alleys.

Tall Kumarima came to my room that night. The air was loud with helicopters, quartering the city for the plotters. Helicopters, and machines like the King's Own robots, that could fly and look down on Kathmandu with the eyes of a hawk. She sat on my bed and laid a little transparent blue box on the red and gold embroidered coverlet. In it were two pale pills.

"To help you sleep."

I shook my head. Tall Kumarima folded the blue box into the sleeve of her robe.

"Who was he?"

"A fundamentalist. A *karsevak*. A foolish, sad young man."

"A Hindu, but he wanted to hurt us."

"That is the madness of it, *devi*. He and his kind think our kingdom has grown too western, too far from its roots and religious truths."

"And he attacks us, the Taleju *Devi*. He would have blown up his own goddess, but the machine took his head. That is almost as strange as people throwing water to the rain."

Tall Kumarima bowed her head. She reached inside the sash of her robe and took out a second object which she set on my heavy cover with the same precise care as she had the sleeping pills. It was a light, fingerless glove, for the right hand; clinging to its back was a curl of plastic shaped like a very very tiny goat foetus.

"Do you know what this is?"

I nodded. Every devotee doing *puja* in the streets seemed to own one, right hands held up to snatch my image. A palmer.

"It sends messages into your head," I whispered.

"That is the least of what it can do, *devi*. Think of it like your *jharoka*, but this window opens onto the world beyond Durbar Square, beyond Kathmandu and Nepal. It is an aeai, an artificial intelligence, a thinking-thing, like the machines up there, but much cleverer than them. They are clever enough to fly and hunt and not much else, but this aeai can tell you anything you want to know. All you have to do is ask. And there are things you need to know, *devi*. You will not be Kumari forever. The day will come when you will leave your palace and go back to the world. I have seen them before you." She reached out to take my face between her hands, then drew back. "You are special my *devi*, but the kind of special it takes to be Kumari means you will find it hard in the world. People will call it a sickness. Worse than that, even . . ."

She banished the emotion by gently fitting the foetus-shaped receiver behind my ear. I felt the plastic move against my skin, then Tall Kumarima slipped on the glove, waved her hand in a *mudra* and I heard her voice inside my head. Glowing words appeared in the air between us, words I had been painstakingly taught to read by Tall Kumarima.

Don't let anyone find it, her dancing hand said. *Tell no one, not even Smiling Kumarima. I know you call her that, but she would not understand. She would think it was unclean, a pollution. In some ways, she is not so different from that man who tried to harm you. Let this be our secret, just you and me.*

Soon after, Smiling Kumarima came to look in on me and check for fleas but I pretended to be asleep. The glove and the foetus-thing were hidden under my pillow. I imagined them talking to me through the goose down and soft cotton, sending dreams while the helicopters and hunting robots wheeled in the night above me. When the latch on her door clicked too, I put on the glove and ear-hook and went looking for the lost rain. I found it one hundred and fifty kilometres up, through the eye of a weather aeai spinning over east India. I saw the monsoon, a coil of cloud like a cat's claw hooking up across the sea. There had been cats in the village; suspicious things lean on mice and barley. No cat was permitted in the Kumari Ghar. I looked down on my Kingdom but I could not see a city or a palace or me down here at all. I saw mountains, white mountains ridged with grey and blue ice. I was goddess of this. And the heart went out of me, because it was nothing, a tiny crust of stone on top of that huge world that hung beneath it like the full teat of a cow, rich and heavy with people and their brilliant cities and their bright nations. India, where our gods and names were born.

Within three days the police had caught the plotters and it was raining. The clouds were low over Kathmandu. The colour ran from the temples in Durbar Square but people beat tins and metal cups in the muddy streets calling praise on the Taleju *Devi*.

"What will happen to them?" I asked Tall Kumarima. "The bad men."

"They will likely be hanged," she said.

That autumn after the executions of the traitors the dissatisfaction finally poured on to the streets like sacrificial blood. Both sides claimed me: police and demonstrators. Others yet held me up as both the symbol of all that was good with our Kingdom and also everything wrong with it. Tall Kumarima tried to explain it to me but with my world mad and dangerous my attention was turned elsewhere, to the huge, old land to the south, spread out like a jewelled skirt. In such a time it was easy to be seduced by the terrifying depth of its history, by the gods and warriors who swept across it, empire after empire after empire. My Kingdom had always been fierce and free but I met the men who liberated India from the Last Empire—men like gods—and saw that liberty broken up by rivalry and intrigue and corruption into feuding states; Awadh and Bharat, The United States of Bengal, Maratha, Karnataka.

Legendary names and places. Shining cities as old as history. There aeais haunted the crowded streets like *gandhavas*. There men outnumbered women four to one. There the old distinctions were abandoned and women married as far up and men as few steps down the tree of caste as they could. I became as enthralled by their leaders and parties and politics as any of their citizens by the aeai-generated soaps they loved so dearly. My spirit was down in India in that early, hard winter when the police and King's machines restored the old order to the city beyond Durbar Square. Unrest in earth and the three heavens. One day I woke to find snow in the wooden court; the roofs of the temple of Durbar Square heavy with it, like frowning, freezing old men. I knew now that the strange weather was not my doing but the result of huge, slow changes in the climate. Smiling Kumarima came to me in my *jharoka* as I watched flakes thick and soft as ash sift down from the white sky. She knelt before me, rubbed her hands together inside the cuffs of her wide sleeves. She suffered badly in the cold and damp.

"*Devi*, are you not one of my own children to me?"

I waggled my head, not wanting to say yes.

"*Devi*, have I ever, ever given you anything but my best?"

Like her counterpart a season before, she drew a plastic pillbox from her sleeve, set it on her palm. I sat back on my chair, afraid of it as I had never been afraid of anything Tall Kumarima offered me.

"I know how happy we are all here, but change must always happen. Change in the world, like this snow—unnatural, *devi*, not right—change in our city. And we are not immune to it in here, my flower. Change will come to you, *devi*. To you, to your body. You will become a woman. If I could, I would stop it happening to you, *devi*. But I can't. No one can. What I can offer is . . . a delay. A stay. Take these. They will slow down the changes. For years, hopefully. Then we can all stay here together, *devi*." She looked up from her deferential half-bow, into my eyes. She smiled. "Have I ever wanted anything but the best for you?"

I held out my hand. Smiling Kumarima tipped the pills into my palm. I closed my fist and slipped from my carved throne. As I went to my room I could hear Smiling Kumarima chanting prayers of thanksgiving to the goddesses in the carvings. I looked at the pills in my hand. Blue seemed such a wrong colour. Then I filled my cup in my little washroom and washed them down, two gulps, down, down.

After that they came every day, two pills, blue as the Lord Krishna, appearing as miraculously on my bedside table. For some reason I never told Tall Kumarima, even when she commented on how fractious I was becoming, how strangely inattentive and absent-minded at ceremonies. I told her it was the *devis* in the walls, whispering to me. I knew enough of my specialness, that others have called my *disorder*, that that would be unquestioned. I was tired and lethargic that winter. My sense of smell grew keen to the least odour and the people in my courtyard with their stupid, beaming upturned faces infuriated me. I went for weeks without showing myself. The wooden corridors grew sharp and brassy with old blood. With the insight of demons, I can see now that my body was a chemical battlefield between my own hormones and Smiling Kumarima's puberty suppressants. It was a heavy, humid spring that year and I felt huge and bloated in the heat, a waddling bulb of fluids under my robes and waxy make-up. I started to drop the little blue pills down the commode. I had been Kumari for seven Dasains.

I had thought I would feel like I used to, but I did not. It was not unwell, like the pills had made me feel, it was sensitive, acutely conscious of my body. I would lie in my wooden bed and feel my legs growing longer. I became very very aware of my tiny nipples. The heat and humidity got worse, or so it seemed to me.

At any time I could have opened my palmer and asked it what was happening to me, but I didn't. I was scared that it might tell me it was the end of my divinity.

Tall Kumarima must have noticed that the hem of my gown no longer brushed the floorboards but it was Smiling Kumarima drew back in the corridor as we hurried towards the *darshan* hall, hesitated a moment, said, softly, smiling as always, "How you're growing, *devi*. Are you still . . . ? No, forgive me, of course . . . Must be this warm weather we're having, makes children shoot up like weeds. My own are bursting out of everything they own, nothing will fit them."

The next morning as I was dressing a tap came on my door, like the scratch of a mouse or the click of an insect.

"*Devi?*"

No insect, no mouse. I froze, palmer in hand, earhook babbling the early morning news reports from Awadh and Bharat into my head.

"We are dressing."

"Yes, *devi*, that is why I would like to come in."

I just managed to peel off the palmer and stuff it under my mattress before the heavy door swung open on its pivot.

"We have been able to dress ourselves since we were six," I retorted.

"Yes, indeed," said Smiling Kumarima, smiling. "But some of the priests have mentioned to me a little laxness in the ritual dress."

I stood in my red and gold night-robe, stretched out my arms and turned, like one of the trance-dancers I saw in the streets from my litter. Smiling Kumarima sighed.

"*Devi*, you know as well as I . . ."

I pulled my gown up over my head and stood unclothed, daring her to look, to search my body for signs of womanhood.

"See?" I challenged.

"Yes," Smiling Kumarima said, "but what is that behind your ear?"

She reached to pluck the hook. It was in my fist in a flick.

"Is that what I think it is?" Smiling Kumarima said, soft smiling bulk filling the space between the door and me. "Who gave you that?"

"It is ours," I declared in my most commanding voice but I was a naked twelve-year-old caught in wrongdoing and that commands less than dust.

"Give it to me."

I clenched my fist tighter.

"We are a goddess, you cannot command us."

"A goddess is as a goddess acts and right now, you are acting like a brat. Show me."

She was a mother, I was her child. My fingers unfolded. Smiling Kumarima recoiled as if I held a poisonous snake. To her eyes of her faith, I did.

"Pollution," she said faintly. "Spoiled, all spoiled. Her voice rose. "I know who gave you this!" Before my fingers could snap shut, she snatched the coil of plastic from my palm. She threw the earhook to the floor as if it burned her. I saw the hem of her skirt raise, I saw the heel come down, but it was my world, my oracle, my window on the beautiful. I dived to rescue the tiny plastic foetus. I remember no pain, no shock, not even Smiling Kumarima's shriek of horror and fear as her heel came down, but I will always see the tip of my right index finger burst in a spray of red blood.

The *pallav* of my yellow sari flapped in the wind as I darted through the Delhi evening crush-hour. Beating the heel of his hand off his buzzer, the driver of the little wasp-coloured *phatphat* cut in between a lumbering truck-train painted with gaudy gods and *apsaras* and a cream Government Maruti and pulled into the great *chakra* of traffic around Connaught Place. In Awadh you drive with your ears.

The roar of horns and klaxons and cycle-rickshaw bells assailed from all sides at once. It rose before the dawn birds and only fell silent well after midnight. The driver skirted a *saddhu* walking through the traffic as calmly as if he were wading through the Holy Yamuna. His body was white with sacred ash, a mourning ghost, but his Siva trident burned blood red in the low sun. I had thought Kathmandu dirty, but Delhi's golden light and incredible sunsets spoke of pollution beyond even that. Huddled in the rear seat of the auto rickshaws with Deepti, I wore smog mask and goggles to protect my delicate eye make-up. But the fold of my sari flapped over my shoulder in the evening wind and the little silver bells jingled.

There were five in our little fleet. We accelerated along the wide avenues of the British Raj, past the sprawling red buildings of old India, towards the glass spires of Awadh. Black kites circled the towers, scavengers, pickers of the dead. We turned beneath cool *neem* trees into the drive of a government bungalow. Burning torches lit us to the pillared porch. House staff in Rajput uniforms escorted us to the *shaadi* marquee.

Mamaji had arrived before any of us. She fluttered and fretted among her birds; a lick, a rub, a straightening, an admonition. "Stand up stand up, we'll have no slumping here. My girls will be the bonniest at this *shaadi*, hear me?" Shweta, her bony, mean-mouthed assistant, collected our smog-masks. "Now girls, palmers ready." We knew the drill with almost military smartness. Hand up, glove on, rings on, hook behind ear jewellery, decorously concealed by the fringed *dupattas* draped over our heads. "We are graced with Awadh's finest tonight. Crème de la crème." I barely blinked as the résumés rolled up my inner vision. "Right girls, from the left, first dozen, two minutes each then on to the next down the list. Quick smart!" Mamaji clapped her hands and we formed a line. A band struck a medley of musical numbers from *Town and Country*, the soap opera that was a national obsession in sophisticated Awadh. There we stood, twelve little wives-a-waiting while the Rajput servants hauled up the rear of the pavilion.

Applause broke around us like rain. A hundred men stood in a rough semi-circle, clapping enthusiastically, faces bright in the light from the carnival lanterns.

When I arrived in Awadh, the first thing I noticed was the people. People pushing people begging people talking people rushing past each other without a look or a word or an acknowledgement. I had thought Kathmandu held more people than a mind could imagine. I had not seen Old Delhi. The constant noise, the everyday callousness, the lack of any respect appalled me. You could vanish into that crowd of faces like a drop of rain into a tank. The second thing I noticed was that the faces were all men. It was indeed as my palmer had whispered to me. There were four men for every woman. It would never cease to amaze me, how a simple technique to predetermine a child's sex could utterly warp a nation.

Fine men good men clever men rich men, men of ambition and career and property, men of power and prospects. Men with no hope of ever marrying within their own class and caste. Men with little prospect of marrying at all. *Shaadi* had once been the word for wedding festivities, the groom on his beautiful white horse, so noble, the bride shy and lovely behind her golden veil. Then it became a name for dating agencies: *lovely wheat-complexioned Agarwal, U.S.-university MBA, seeks same civil service/military for matrimonials.* Now it was a bride-parade, a marriage-market for lonely men with large dowries. Dowries that paid a hefty commission to the Lovely Girl *Shaadi* Agency.

The Lovely Girls lined up on the left side of the Silken Wall that ran the length of the bungalow garden. The first twelve men formed up on the right. They plumped and preened in their finery but I could see they were nervous. The partition was no more than a row of saris pinned to a line strung between plastic uprights, fluttering in the rising evening wind. A token of decorum. Purdah. They were not even silk.

Reshmi was first to walk and talk the Silken Wall. She was a Yadav country girl from Uttaranchal, big-handed and big-faced. A peasant's daughter. She could cook and sew and sing, do household accounts, manage both domestic aeais and human staff. Her first prospective was a weasely man with a weak jaw in government whites and a Nehru cap. He had bad teeth. Never good. Any one of us could have told him he was wasting his *shaadi* fee, but they namasted to each other and stepped out, regulation three paces between them. At the end of the walk Reshmi would loop back to rejoin the tail of the line and meet her next prospective. On big *shaadis* like this my feet would bleed by the end of the night. Red footprints on the marble floors of Mamaji's courtyard *haveli*.

I stepped out with Ashok, a big globe of a thirty-two year-old who wheezed a little as he rolled along. He was dressed in a voluminous white *kurta*, the fashion this season though he was fourth generation Panjabi. His grooming amounted to an uncontrollable beard and oily hair that smelled of too much Dapper Deepak pomade. Even before he *namasted* I knew it was his first *shaadi*. I could see his eyeballs move as he read my résumé, seeming to hover before him. I did not need to read his to know he was a dataraja, for he talked about nothing but himself and the brilliant things he was doing; the spec of some new protein processor array, the 'ware he was breeding, the aeais he was nurturing in his stables, his trips to Europe and the United States where everyone knew his name and great people were glad to welcome him.

"Of course, Awadh's never going to ratify the Hamilton Acts—no matter how close Shrivastava Minister is to President McAuley—but if it did, if we allow ourselves that tiny counterfactual—well, it's the end of the economy: Awadh *is* IT, there are more graduates in Mehrauli than there are in the whole of California. The Americans may go out about the mockery of a human soul, but they *need* our Level 2.8s,—you know what that is? An aeai can pass as human ninety-nine percent of the time—because everybody knows no one does quantum crypto like us, so I'm not worrying about having to close up the data-haven, and even if they do, well, there's always Bharat—I cannot see the Ranas bowing down to Washington, not when twenty five percent of their forex comes out of licensing deals from *Town and Country* . . . and that's hundred percent aeai generated . . ."

He was a big affable clown of a man with wealth that would have bought my Palace in Durbar Square and every priest in it and I found myself praying to Taleju to save me from marrying such a bore. He stopped in mid-stride, so abruptly I almost tripped.

"You must keep walking," I hissed. "That is the rule."

"Wow," he said, standing stupid, eyes round in surprise. Couples piled up behind us. In my peripheral vision I could see Mamaji making urgent, threatening gestures. Get him *on*. "Oh wow. You're an ex-Kumari."

"Please, you are drawing attention to yourself." I would have tugged his arm, but that would have been an even more deadly error.

"What was it like, being a goddess?"

"I am just a woman now, like any other," I said. Ashok gave a soft harrumph, as if he had achieved a very small enlightenment, and walked on, hands clasped behind his back. He may have spoken to me once, twice before we reached the end of the Silk Wall and parted: I did not hear him, I did not hear the music, I did not even hear the eternal thunder of Delhi's traffic. The only sound in my head was the high-pitched sound between my eyes of needing to cry but knowing I could not. Fat, selfish, gabbling, Ashok had sent me back to the night I ceased to be a goddess.

Bare soles slapping the polished wood of the Kumari Ghar's corridors. Running feet, muted shouts growing ever more distant as I knelt, still unclothed for my Kumarima's inspection, looking at the blood drip from my smashed fingertip onto the painted wood floor. I remember no pain; rather, I looked at the pain from a separate place, as if the girl who felt it were another person. Far far away, Smiling Kumarima stood, held in time, hands to mouth in horror and guilt. The voices faded and the bells of Durbar Square begin to swing and toll, calling to their brothers across the city of Kathmandu until the valley rang from Bhaktapur to Trisuli Bazaar for the fall of the Kumari *Devi*.

In the space of a single night, I became human again. I was taken to the Hanumandhoka—walking this time like anyone else on the paving stones—where the priests said a final *puja*. I handed back my red robes and jewels and boxes of make-up, all neatly folded and piled. Tall Kumarima had got me human clothes. I think she had been keeping them for some time. The King did not come to say goodbye to me. I was no longer his sister. But his surgeons had put my finger back together well, though they warned that it would always feel a little numb and inflexible.

I left at dawn, while the street cleaners were washing down the stones of Durbar Square beneath the apricot sky, in a smooth-running Royal Mercedes with darkened windows. My Kumarimas made their farewells at the palace gate. Tall Kumarima hugged me briefly to her.

"Oh, there was so much more I needed to do. Well, it will have to suffice."

I felt her quivering against me, like a bird too tightly gripped in a hand. Smiling Kumarima could not look at me. I did not want her to.

As the car took me across the waking city I tried to understand how it felt to be human. I had been a goddess so long I could hardly remember feeling any other way, but it seemed so little different that I began to suspect that you are divine because people say you are. The road climbed through green suburbs, winding now, growing narrower, busy with brightly decorated buses and trucks. The houses grew leaner and meaner, to roadside hovels and *chai*-stalls and then were out of the city—the first time since I had arrived seven years before. I pressed my hands and face to the glass and looked down on Kathmandu beneath its shroud of orange smog. The car joined the long line of traffic along the narrow, rough road that clung to the valley side. Above me, mountains dotted with goatherd shelters and stone shrines flying tattered prayer banners. Below me, rushing cream-brown water. Nearly there. I wondered how far behind me on this road were those other government cars, carrying the priests sent to seek out little girls bearing the thirty-two signs of perfection. Then the car rounded the bend in the valley and I was home, Shakya, its truck halts and gas station, the shops and the temple of Padma Narteswara, the dusty trees with white rings painted around their trunks and between them the stone wall and arch where the steps led down through the terraces to my house, and in that stone-framed rectangle of sky, my parents, standing there side by side, pressing closely, shyly, against each other as I had last seen them lingering in the courtyard of the Kumari Ghar.

Mamaji was too respectable to show anything like outright anger, but she had ways of expressing her displeasure. The smallest crust of *roti* at dinner, the meanest scoop of *dhal*. New girls coming, make room make room—me to the highest, stuffiest room, furthest from the cool of the courtyard pool.

"He asked for my palmer address," I said.

"If I had a rupee for every palmer address," Mamaji said. "He was only interested in you as a novelty, dearie. Anthropology. He was never going to make a proposition. No you can forget right about him."

But my banishment to the tower was a small punishment for it lifted me above the noise and fumes of the old city. If portions were cut, small loss: the food had been dreadful every day of the almost two years I had been at the *haveli*. Through the wooden lattice, beyond the water tanks and satellite dishes and kids playing rooftop cricket, I could see the ramparts of the Red Fort, the minarets and domes of the Jami Masjid and beyond them, the glittering glass and titanium spires of New Delhi. And higher than any of them, the flocks of pigeons from the *kabooter* lofts, clay pipes bound to their legs so they fluted and sang as they swirled over Chandni Chowk. And Mamaji's worldly-wisdom made her a fool this time, for Ashok was surreptitiously messaging me, sometimes questions about when I was divine, mostly about himself and his great plans and ideas. His lilac-coloured words, floating in my inner-vision against the intricate silhouettes of my *jali* screens, were bright pleasures in those high summer days. I discovered the delight of political argument; against Ashok's breezy optimism, I set my readings of the news channels. From the opinion columns it seemed inevitable to me that Awadh, in exchange for Favoured Nation status from the United States of America, would ratify the Hamilton Acts and outlaw all aeais more intelligent than a langur monkey. I told none of our intercourse to Mamaji. She would have forbidden it, unless he made a proposal.

On an evening of pre-monsoon heat, when the boys were too tired even for cricket and the sky was an upturned brass bowl, Mamaji came to my turret on the top of the old merchant's *haveli*. Against propriety, the *jalis* were thrown open, my gauze curtains stirred in the swirls of heat rising from the alleys below.

"Still you are eating my bread." She prodded my *thali* with her foot. It was too hot for food, too hot for anything other than lying and waiting for the rain and the cool, if it came at all this year. I could hear the voices of the girls down in the courtyard as they kicked their legs in the pool. This day I would have loved to be sitting along the tiled edge with them but I was piercingly aware that I had lived in the *haveli* of the Lovely Girl *Shaadi* Agency longer than any of them. I did not want to be their Kumarima. And when the whispers along the cool marble corridors made them aware of my childhood, they would ask for small *pujas*, little miracles to help them find the right man. I no longer granted them, not because I feared that I had no power any more—that I never had—but that it went out from me and into them and that was why they got the bankers and television executives and Mercedes salesmen.

"I should have left you in that Nepalese sewer. Goddess! Hah! And me fooled into thinking you were a prize asset. Men! They may have share options and Chowpatty Beach apartments but deep down, they're as superstitious as any backcountry *yadav*."

"I'm sorry Mamaji," I said, turning my eyes away.

"Can you help it? You were only born perfect in thirty-two different ways. Now you listen, *cho chweet*. A man came to call on me."

Men always came calling, glancing up at the giggles and rustles of the Lovely Girls peeping through the *jalis* as he waited in the cool of the courtyard for Shweta to present him to Mamaji. Men with offers of marriage, men with prenuptial contracts, men with dowry down-payments. Men asking for special, private viewings. This man who had called on Mamaji had come for one of these.

"Fine young man, lovely young man, just twenty. Father's big in water. He has requested a private rendezvous, with you."

I was instantly suspicious but I had learned among the Lovely Girls of Delhi, even more than among the priests and Kumarimas of Kathmandu, to let nothing show on my painted face.

"Me? Such an honour . . . and him only twenty . . . and a good family too, so well connected."

"He is a Brahmin."

"I know I am only a Shakya . . ."

"You don't understand. He is a *Brahmin*."

There was so much more I needed to do, Tall Kumarima had said as the royal car drove away from the carved wooden gates of the Kumari Ghar. One whisper through the window would have told me everything: *the curse of the Kumari.*

Shakya hid from me. People crossed the street to find things to look at and do. Old family friends nodded nervously before remembering important business they had to be about. The *chai-dhabas* gave me free tea so I would feel uncomfortable and leave. Truckers were my friends, bus-drivers and long-haulers pulled in at the biodiesel stations. They must have wondered who was this strange twelve-year-old girl, hanging around truck-halts. I do not doubt some of them thought more. Village by village, town by town the legend spread up and down the north road. Ex-Kumari.

Then the accidents started. A boy lost half his hand in the fan belt of a Nissan engine. A teenager drank bad *rakshi* and died of alcohol poisoning. A man slipped between two passing trucks and was crushed. The talk in the *chai-dhabas* and the repair shops was once again of my uncle who fell to this death while the little goddess-to-be bounced in her wire cradle laughing and laughing and laughing.

I stopped going out. As winter took hold over the head-country of the Kathmandu valley, whole weeks passed when I did not leave my room. Days slipped away watching sleet slash past my window, the prayer banners bent almost horizontal in the wind, the wire of the cableway bouncing. Beneath it, the furious, flooding river. In that season the voices of the demons spoke loud from the mountain, telling me the most hateful things about faithless Kumaris who betray the sacred heritage of their *devi*.

On the shortest day of the year the bride buyer came through Shakya. I heard a voice I did not recognise talking over the television that burbled away day and night in the main room. I opened the door just enough to admit a voice and gleam of firelight.

"I wouldn't take the money off you. You're wasting your time here in Nepal. Everyone knows the story, and even if they pretend they don't believe, they don't act that way."

I heard my father's voice but could not make out his words. The bride buyer said,

"What might work is down south, Bharat or Awadh. They're so desperate in Delhi they'll even take Untouchables. They're a queer lot, those Indians; some of them might even like the idea of marrying a goddess, like a status thing. But I can't take her, she's too young, they'll send her straight back at the border. They've got rules. In India, would you believe? Call me when she turns fourteen."

Two days after my fourteenth birthday, the bride buyer returned to Shakya and I left with him in his Japanese SUV. I did not like his company or trust his hands, so I slept or feigned sleep while he drove down into the lowlands of the Terai. When I woke I was well over the border into my childhood land of wonder. I had thought the bride-buyer would take me to ancient, holy Varanasi, the new capital of the Bharat's dazzling Rana dynasty but the Awadhis, it seemed, were less in awe of Hindu superstitions. So we came to the vast, incoherent roaring sprawl of the two Delhis, like twin hemispheres of a brain, and to the Lovely Girl *shaadi* Agency. Where the marriageable men were not so twenty-forties sophisticated, at least in the matter of ex-devis. Where the only ones above the curse of the Kumari were those held in even greater superstitious awe: the genetically engineered children known as Brahmins.

Wisdom was theirs, health was theirs, beauty and success and status assured and a wealth that could never be devalued or wasted or gambled away, for it was worked into every twist of their DNA. The Brahmin children of India's super-elite enjoyed long life—twice that of their parents—but at a price. They were indeed the twice-born, a caste above any other, so high as to be new Untouchables. A fitting partner for a former goddess: a new god.

Gas flares from the heavy industries of Tughluq lit the western horizon. From the top of the high tower I could read New Delhi's hidden geometries, the necklaces of light around Connaught Place, the grand glowing net of the dead Raj's monumental capital, the incoherent glow of the old city to the north. The penthouse at the top of the sweeping wing-curve of Narayan Tower was glass; glass walls, glass roof, beneath me, polished obsidian that reflected the night sky. I walked with stars at my head and feet. It was a room designed to awe and intimidate. It was nothing to one who had witnessed demons strike the heads from goats, who had walked on bloody silk to her own palace. It was nothing to one dressed, as the messenger had required, in the full panoply of the goddess. Red robe, red nails, red lips, red eye of Siva painted above my own black kohled eyes, fake-gold headdress hung with costume pearls, my fingers dripped gaudy rings from the cheap jewellery sellers of Kinari Bazaar, a light chain of real gold ran from my nose stud to my ear-ring; I was once again Kumari Devi. My demons rustled inside me.

Mamaji had drilled me as we scooted from old city to new. She had swathed me in a light voile *chador*, to protect my make-up she said; in truth, to conceal me from the eyes of the street. The girls had called blessings and prayers after me as the *phatphat* scuttled out of the *haveli*'s courtyard.

"You will say nothing. If he speaks to you, you duck your head like a good Hindu girl. If anything has to be said, I will say it. You may have been a goddess but he is a Brahmin. He could buy your pissy palace a dozen times over. Above all, do not let your eyes betray you. The eyes say nothing. They taught you that at least in that Kathmandu, didn't they? Now come on *cho chweet*, let's make a match."

The glass penthouse was lit only by city-glow and concealed lamps that gave an uncomfortable blue glow. Ved Prakash Narayan sat on a *musnud*, a slab of unadorned black marble. Its simplicity spoke of wealth and power beneath any ornate jewellery. My bare feet whispered on the star-filled glass. Blue light welled up as I approached the dais. Ved Prakash Narayan was dressed in a beautifully worked long *sherwani* coat and traditional tight *churidar* pyjamas. He leaned forward into the light and it took every word of control Tall Kumarima had ever whispered to me to hold the gasp.

A ten-year-old boy sat on the throne of the Mughal Emperor.

Live twice as long, but age half as fast. The best deal Kolkata's genetic engineers could strike with four million years of human DNA. A child husband for a once-child goddess. Except this was no child. In legal standing, experience, education, taste and emotions, this was a twenty-year-old man, every way except the physical.

His feet did not touch the floor.

"Quite, quite extraordinary." His voice was a boy's. He slipped from his throne, walked around me, studying me as if I were an artefact in a museum. He was a head shorter than me. "Yes, this is indeed special. What is the settlement?"

Mamaji's voice from the door named a number. I obeyed my training and tried not to catch his eye as he stalked around me.

"Acceptable. My man will deliver the prenuptial before the end of the week. A goddess. My goddess."

Then I caught his eyes and I saw where all his missing years were. They were blue, alien blue, and colder than any of the lights of his tower-top palace.

These Brahmins are worse than any of us when it comes to social climbing, Ashok messaged me in my aerie atop the *shaadi haveli,* prison turned bridal boudoir. *Castes within castes within castes.* His words hung in the air over the hazy ramparts of the red fort before dissolving into the dashings of the musical pigeons. *Your children will be blessed.*

Until then I had not thought about the duties of a wife with a ten-year-old boy.

On a day of staggering heat I was wed to Ved Prakash Narayan in a climate-control bubble on the manicured green before Emperor Humayun's tomb. As on the night I was introduced, I was dressed as Kumari. My husband, veiled in gold, arrived perched on top of a white horse followed by a band and a dozen elephants with coloured patterns worked on their trunks. Security robots patrolled the grounds as astrologers proclaimed favourable auspices and an old-type brahmin in his red cord blessed our union. Rose petals fluttered around me, the proud father and mother distributed gems from Hyderabad to their guests, my *shaadi* sisters wept with joy and loss, Mamaji sniffed back a tear and vile old Shweta went round hoarding the free and over-flowing food from the buffet. As we were applauded and played down the receiving line, I noticed all the other sombre-faced ten-year-old boys with their beautiful, tall foreign wives. I reminded myself who was the child bride here. But none of them were goddesses.

I remember little of the grand *durbar* that followed except face after face after face, mouth after mouth after mouth opening, making noise, swallowing glass after glass after glass of French champagne. I did not drink for I did not have the taste for alcohol, though my young husband in his raja finery took it, and smoked big cigars too. As we got into the car—the *honeymoon* was another Western tradition we were adopting—I asked if anyone had remembered to inform my parents.

We flew to Mumbai on the company tilt-jet. I had never before flown in an aircraft. I pressed my hands, still hennaed with the patterns of my *mehndi,* on either side of the window as if to hold in every fleeting glimpse of Delhi falling away beneath me. It was every divine vision I had ever had looking down from my bed in the Kumari Ghar on India. This was indeed the true vehicle of a goddess. But the demons whispered as we turned in the air over the towers of New Delhi, *you will be old and withered when he is still in his prime.*

When the limousine from the airport turned on to Marine Drive and I saw the Arabian Sea glinting in the city-light, I asked my husband to stop the car so I could look and wonder. I felt tears start in my eyes and thought, *the same water in it is in you.* But the demons would not let me be: *you are married to something that is not human.*

My *honeymoon* was wonder upon wonder: our penthouse apartment with the glass walls that opened on sunset over Chowpatty Beach. The new splendid outfits we wore as we drove along the boulevards, where stars and movie-gods smiled down and blessed us in the virtual sight of our palmers. Colour, motion, noise, chatter; people and people and people. Behind it all, the wash and hush and smell of the alien sea.

Chambermaids prepared me for the wedding night. They worked with baths and balms, oils and massages, extending the now-fading henna tracery on my hands up my arms, over my small upright breasts, down the *manipuraka chakra* over my navel. They wove gold ornaments into my hair, slipped bracelets on my arms and rings on my fingers and toes, dusted and powdered my dark Nepali skin. They purified me with incense smoke and flower petals, they shrouded me in veils and silks as fine as rumours. They lengthened my lashes and kohled my eyes and shaped my nails to fine, painted points.

"What do I do, I've never even touched a man?" I asked, but they namasted and slipped away without answer. But the older—the Tall Kumarima, as I thought of her—left a small soapstone box on one of my bridal divans. Inside were two white pills.

They were good. I should have expected no less. One moment I was standing nervous and fearful on the Turkestan carpet with a soft night air that smelled of the sea stirring the translucent curtains, the next visions of the Kama Sutra, beamed into my brain through my golden earhook, swirled up around me like the pigeons over Chandni Chowk. I looked at the patterns my *shaadi* sisters had painted on the palms of my hands and they danced and coiled from my skin. The smells and perfumes of my body were alive, suffocating. It was as if my skin had been peeled back and every nerve exposed. Even the touch of the barely-moving night air was intolerable. Every car horn on Marine Drive was like molten silver dropped into my ear.

I was terribly afraid.

Then the double doors to the robing room opened and my husband entered. He was dressed as a Mughal grandee in a jewelled turban and a long-sleeved pleated red robe bowed out at the front in the manly act.

"My goddess," he said. Then he parted his robe and I saw what stood so proud.

The harness was of crimson leather intricately inlaid with fine mirror-work. It fastened around the waist and also over the shoulders, for extra security. The buckles were gold. I recall the details of the harness so clearly because I could not take more than one look at the thing it carried. Black. Massive as a horse's, but delicately upcurved. Ridged and studded. This all I remember before the room unfolded around me like the scented petals of a lotus and my senses blended as one and I was running through the apartments of the Taj Marine Hotel.

How had I ever imagined it could be different for a creature with the appetites and desires of an adult but the physical form of a ten year-old boy?

Servants and dressers approached me as I screamed incoherently, grabbing at wraps, shawls, anything to cover my shame. At some tremendous remove I remember my husband's voice calling *Goddess! My Goddess!* over and over.

"Schizophrenia is a terribly grating word," Ashok said. He twirled the stem of a red thornless rose between his fingers. "Old-school. It's dissociative disorder these days. Except there are no disorders, just adaptive behaviours. It was what you needed to cope with being a goddess. Dissociating. Disjuncting. Splitting."

Night in the gardens of the Dataraja Ashok. Water trickled in the stone canals of the *charbagh*. I could smell it, sweet and wet. A pressure curtain held the smog at bay; trees screened out Delhi's traffic. I could even see a few stars. We sat in an open *chhatri* pavilion, the marble still warm from the day. Set on silver *thalis* were medjool dates, halva—crisp with flies—folded *paan*. A security robot stepped into the lights from the Colonial bungalow, passed into shadow. But for it I might have been in the age of the rajas.

Time broken apart, whirring like *kabooter* wings. Dissociative behaviour. Mechanisms for coping. Running along the palm-lined boulevards of Mumbai, shawls clutched around my wifely finery that made me feel more naked than bare skin. I ran without heed or direction. Taxis hooted, *phatphats* veered as I dashed across crowded streets. Even if I had had money for a *phatphat*—what need had the wife of Brahmin for crude cash?—I did know where to direct it. Yet some demonic self must have known, for I found myself on the vast marble concourse of a railway station, a sole mite of stillness among the tens of thousands of hastening travellers and beggars and vendors and staff. My shawls and throws clutched around me, I looked up at the dome of red Raj stone and it was a second skull, full of the awful realisation of what I had done.

A runaway bride without even a *paisa* to her name, alone in Mumbai Chhatrapati Shivaji Terminus. A hundred trains leaving that minute for any destination but nowhere to go. People stared at me, half Nautch-courtesan, half Untouchable street-sleeper. In my shame, I remembered the hook behind my ear. *Ashok*, I wrote across the sandstone pillars and swirling ads. *Help me!*

"I don't want to be split, I don't want to be many, why can't I just be one? Be me?" I beat the heels of my hands off my forehead in frustration. "Make me well, make me right!" Shards of memory. The white-uniformed staff serving me hot *chai* in first-class private compartment of the *shatabdi* express. The robots waiting at the platform with the antique covered palanquin, to bear me through the Delhi dawn traffic to the green watered geometries of Ashok's gardens. But behind them all was one enduring image, my uncle's white fist slipping on the bouncing cable and him falling, legs pedalling air, to the creamy waters of Shakya river. Even then, I had been split. Fear and shock. Laughter and smiles. How else could anyone survive being a goddess?

Goddess. My Goddess.

Ashok could not understand. "Would you cure a singer of his talent? There is no madness, only ways of adapting. Intelligence is evolution. Some would argue that I display symptoms of mild Asperger's syndrome."

"I don't know what that means."

He twirled the rose so hard the stem snapped.

"Have you thought what you're going to do?"

I had thought of little else. The Narayans would not give up their dowry lightly. Mamaji would sweep me from her door. My village was closed to me.

"Maybe for a while, if you could . . ."

"It's not a good time . . . Who's going to have the ear of the Lok Sabha? A family building a dam that's going to guarantee their water supply for the next ten years, or a software entrepreneur with a stable of Level 2.75 aeais that the United States government thinks are the sperm of Shaitan? Family values still count in Awadh. You should know."

I heard my voice say, like a very small girl, "Where can I go?"

The bride-buyer's stories of Kumaris whom no one would marry and could not go home again ended in the woman-cages of Varanasi and Kolkata. Chinese paid rupees by the roll for an ex-Goddess.

Ashok moistened his lips with his tongue.

"I have a place in Bharat, in Varanasi. Awadh and Bharat are seldom on speaking terms."

"Oh thank you, thank you . . ." I went down on my knees before Ashok, clutched his hands between my palms. He looked away. Despite the artificial cool of the *charbagh*, he was sweating freely.

"It's not a gift. It's . . . employment. A job."

"A job, that's good, I can do that; I'm a good worker, work away at anything I will; what is it? Doesn't matter, I can do it . . ."

"There are commodities needing transport."

"What kind of commodities? Oh it doesn't mater, I can carry anything."

"Aeais." He rolled a *paan* from the silver dish. "I'm not going to wait around for Shrivastava's Krishna Cops to land in my garden with their excommunication ware."

"The Hamilton Acts," I ventured, though I did not know what they were, what most of Ashok mumbles and rants meant.

"Word is, everything above level 2.5." Ashok chewed his lower lip. His eyes widened as the *paan* curled through his skull.

"Of course, I will do anything I can to help."

"I haven't told you how I need you to transport them. Absolutely safe, secure, where no Krishna Cop can ever find them." He touched his right forefinger to his Third Eye.

I went to Kerala and had processors put into my skull. Two men did it on a converted bulk gas carrier moored outside territorial waters. They shaved my long lovely black hair, unhinged my skull and sent robots smaller than the tiniest spider spinning computers through my brain. Their position out there beyond the Keralese fast patrol boats enabled them to carry out much secret surgery, mostly for the Western military. They gave me a bungalow and an Australian girl to watch over me while my sutures fused and hormone washes speed-grew my hair back.

Protein chips; only show on the highest resolution scans but no one'll look twice at you; no one'll look twice at another shaadi *girl down hunting for a husband.*

So I sat and stared at the sea for six weeks and thought about what it would be like to drown in the middle of it, alone and lost a thousand kilometres from the nearest hand that might seize yours. A thousand kilometres north in Delhi a man in an Indian suit shook hands with a man in an American suit and announced the Special Relationship that would make Ashok an outlaw.

You know what Krishna Cops are? They hunt aeais. They hunt the people who stable them, and the people who carry them. They don't care. They're not picky. But they won't catch you. They'll never catch you.

I listened to demons in the swash and run of the big sea on the shore. Demons I now knew were other parts of myself. But I was not afraid of them. In Hinduism, demons are merely the mirrors of the gods. As with men, so with gods; it is the winners write the history. The universe would look no different had Ravana and his Rakshasas won their cosmic wars.

No one but you can carry them. No one but you has the neurological architecture. No one but you could endure another mind in there.

The Australian girl left small gifts outside my door: plastic bangles, jelly-shoes, rings and hairslides. She stole them from the shops in town. I think they were her way of saying that she wanted to know me but was afraid of what I had been, of what the things in my head would make me become. The last thing she stole was a beautiful sheer silk *dupatta* to cover my ragged hair when she took me to the airport. From beneath it I looked at the girls in business saris talking into their hands in the departure lounge and listened to the woman pilot announce the weather in Awadh. Then I looked out of the *phatphat* at the girls darting confidently through the Delhi traffic on their scooters and wondered why my life could not be like theirs.

"It's grown back well." Ashok knelt before me on my cushions in the *chhatri*. It was his sacred place, his temple. He raised his palmer-gloved hand and touched his forefinger to the *tilak* over my third eye. I could smell his breath. Onions, garlic, rancid ghee. "You may feel a little disoriented . . ."

I gasped. Senses blurred, fused, melted. I saw heard felt smelled tasted everything as one undifferentiated sensation, as gods and babies sense, wholly and purely. Sounds were coloured, light had texture, smells spoke and chimed. Then I saw myself surge up from my cushions and fall towards the hard white marble. I heard myself cry out. Ashok lunged towards me. Two Ashoks lunged towards. But it was neither of those. I saw one Ashok, with two visions, inside my head. I could not make shape or sense out of my two seeings, I could not tell which was real, which was mine, which was *me*. Universes away I heard a voice say *help me*. I saw Ashok's houseboys lift me and take me to bed. The painted ceiling, patterned with vines and shoots and flowers, billowed above me like monsoon storm clouds, then blossomed into darkness.

In the heat of the night I woke stark, staring, every sense glowing. I knew the position and velocity of each insect in my airy room that smelled of biodiesel, dust and patchouli. I was not alone. There was another under the dome of my skull. Not an awareness, a consciousness; a sense of *separateness*, a manifestation of myself. An avatar. A demon.

"Who are you?" I whispered. My voice sounded loud and full of bells, like Durbar Square. It did not answer—it could not answer, it was not a sentience—but it took me out onto the *charbagh* water garden. The stars, smudged by pollution, were a dome over me. The crescent moon lay on its back. I looked up and fell into it. *Chandra. Mangal. Budh. Guru. Shukra. Shani. Rahu. Ketu.* The planets were not points of light, balls of stone and gas; they had names, characters, loves, hatreds. The twenty-seven *Nakshatars* spun around my head. I saw their shapes and natures, the patterns of connections that bound the stars into relationships and stories and dramas as human and complex as *Town and Country.* I saw the wheel of the *rashis*, the Great Houses, arc across the sky, and the whole turning, engines within engines, endless wheels of influence and subtle communication, from the edge of the universe to the centre of the earth I stood upon. Planets, stars, constellations; the story of every human life unfolded itself above me and I could read them all. Every word.

All night I played among the stars.

In the morning, over bed-tea, I asked Ashok, "What is it?"

"A rudimentary Level 1.9. A *janampatri* aeai, does astrology, runs the permutations. It thinks it lives out there, like some kind of space monkey. It's not very smart, really. Knows about horoscopes and that's it. Now get that down you and grab your stuff. You've a train to catch"

My reserved seat was in the women's *bogie* of the high-speed *shatabdi* express. Husbands booked their wives on to it to protect them from the attentions of the male passengers who assumed every female was single and available. The few career women chose it for the same reason. My fellow passenger across the table from me was a Muslim woman in a formal business *shalwar*. She regarded me with disdain as we raced across the Ganga plain at three hundred and fifty kilometres per hour. *Little simpering wife-thing.*

You would not be so quick to judge if you knew what we really were, I thought. *We can look into your life and tell you everything that has, is and will ever happen to you, mapped out in the* chakras *of the stars.* In that night among the constellations my demon and I had flowed into each other until there was no place where we could say aeai ended and I began.

I had thought holy Varanasi would sing to me like Kathmandu, a spiritual home, a city of nine million gods and one goddess, riding through the streets in a *phatphat.* What I saw was another Indian capital of another Indian state; glass towers and diamond domes and industry parks for the big world to notice, slums and *bastis* at their feet like sewage pigs. Streets began in this millennium and ended in one three before it. Traffic and hoardings and people people people but the diesel smoke leaking in around the edges of my smog mask carried a ghost of incense.

Ashok's Varanasi agent met me in the Jantar Mantar, the great solar observatory of Jai Singh; sundials and star spheres and shadow discs like modern sculpture. She was little older than me; dressed in a cling-silk top and jeans that hung so low from her hips I could see the valley of her buttocks. I disliked her at once but she touched her palmer-glove to my forehead in the shadows around Jai Singh's astrological instruments and I felt the stars go out of me. The sky died. I had been holy again and now I was just meat. Ashok's *girli* pressed a roll of rupees into my hand. I barely looked at it. I barely heard her instructions to get something to eat, get a *kafi*, get some decent clothes. I was bereft. I found myself trudging up the steep stone steps of the great Samrat not knowing where I was who I was what I was doing halfway up a massive sundial. Half a me. Then my third eye opened and I saw the river wide and blue before me. I saw the white sands of the eastern shore and the shelters and dung fires of the *sadhus*. I saw the *ghats*, the stone river steps, curving away on either side further than the reach of my eyes. And I saw people. People washing and praying cleaning their clothes and offering *puja* and buying and selling and living and dying. People in boats and people kneeling, people waist deep in the river, people scooping up silver handfuls of water to pour over their heads. People casting handfuls of marigold flowers onto the stream, people lighting little mango-leaf *diya* lamps and setting them afloat, people bringing their dead to dip them in the sacred water. I saw the pyres of the burning *ghat*, I smelled sandalwood, charring flesh, I heard the skull burst, releasing the soul. I had heard that sound before at the Royal burning *ghats* of Pashupatinath, when the King's Mother died. A soft crack, and free. It was a comforting sound. It made me think of home.

❊

In that season I came many times to the city by the Ganga. Each time I was a different person. Accountants, counsellors, machine-soldiers, *soapi* actors, database controllers: I was the goddess of a thousand skills. The day after I saw the Krishna Cops patrolling the platforms at Delhi station with their security robots and guns that could kill both humans and aeais, Ashok began to mix up my modes of transport. I flew, I trained, I chugged overnight on overcrowded country buses, I waited in chauffeured Mercedes in long lines of brightly decorated trucks at the Awadh-Bharat border. The trucks, like the crack of an exploding skull, reminded me of my Kingdom. But at the end was always the rat-faced *girli* lifting her hand to my *tilak* and taking me apart again. In that season I was a fabric weaver, a tax accountant, a wedding planner, a *soapi* editor, an air traffic controller. She took all of them away.

And then the trip came when the Krishna Cops were waiting at the Bharat end as well. By now I knew the politics of it as well as Ashok. The Bharatis would never sign the Hamilton Acts—their multi-billion-rupee entertainment industry depended on aeais—but neither did they want to antagonise America. So, a compromise: all aeais over Level 2.8 banned, everything else licensed and Krishna

Cops patrolling the airports and railway stations. Like trying to hold back the Ganga with your fingers.

I had spotted the courier on the flight. He was two rows in front of me; young, wisp of a beard, Star-Asia youth fashion, all baggy and big. Nervous nervous nervous, all the time checking his breast pocket, checking checking checking. A small time *badmash*, a wannabe dataraja with a couple of specialist 2.75s loaded onto a palmer. I could not imagine how he had made it through Delhi airport security.

It was inevitable that the Varanasi Krishna Cops would spot him. They closed on him as we lined up at passport control. He broke. He ran. Women and children fled as he ran across the huge marble arrivals hall, trying to get to the light, the huge glass wall and the doors and the mad traffic beyond. His fists pounded at air. I heard the Krishna Cops' staccato cries. I saw them unholster their weapons. Shrieks went up. I kept my head down, shuffled forward. The immigration officer checked my papers. Another *shaadi* bride on the hunt. I hurried through, turned away towards the taxi ranks. Behind me I heard the arrivals hall fall so shockingly silent it seemed to ring like a temple bell.

I was afraid then. When I returned to Delhi it was like my fear had flown before me. The city of djinns was the city of rumours. The government had signed the Hamilton Act. Krishna Cops were sweeping house to house. Palmer files were to be monitored. Children's aeai toys were illegal. US marines were being airlifted in. Prime Minister Shrivastava was about to announce the replacement of the rupee with the dollar. A monsoon of fear and speculation and in the middle of it all was Ashok.

"One final run, then I'm out. Can you do this for me? One final run?"

The bungalow was already half-emptied. The furniture was all packed, only his processor cores remained. They were draped in dustsheets, ghosts of the creatures that had lived there. The Krishna Cops were welcome to them.

"We both go to Bharat?"

"No, that would be too dangerous. You go ahead, I'll follow when it's safe." He hesitated. Tonight, even the traffic beyond the high walls sounded different. "I need you to take more than the usual."

"How many?"

"Five."

He saw me shy back as he raised his hand to my forehead.

"Is it safe?"

"Five, and that's it done. For good."

"Is it safe?"

"It's a series of overlays, they'll share core code in common."

It was a long time since I had turned my vision inwards to the jewels Ashok had strung through my skull. Circuitry. A brain within a brain.

"Is it safe?"

I saw Ashok swallow, then bob his head: a Westerner's *yes*. I closed my eyes. Seconds later I felt the warm, dry touch of his finger to my inner eye.

We came to with the brass light of early morning shining through the *jali*. We were aware we were deeply dehydrated. We were aware that we were in need of slow-release carbohydrate. Our serotonin inhibitor levels were low. The window arch was a Mughal true arch. The protein circuits in my head were DPMA one-eight-seven-nine slash omegas, under licence from BioScan of Bangalore.

Everything we looked at gave off a rainbow of interpretations. I saw the world with the strange manias of my new guests: medic, nutritionist, architectural renderer, biochip designer, engineering aeai controlling a host of repair-shop robots. Nasatya. Vaishvanara. Maya. Brihaspati. Tvastri. My intimate demons. I was a many-headed *devi*.

All that morning, all afternoon, I fought to make sense of a world that was five worlds, five impressions. *I* fought. Fought to make us *me*. Ashok fretted, tugging at his woolly beard, pacing, trying to watch television, check his mails. At any instant Krishna Cop combat robots could come dropping over his walls. Integration would come. It had to come. I could not survive the clamour in my skull, a monsoon of interpretations. Sirens raced in the streets, far, near, far again. Every one of them fired off a different reaction from my selves.

I found Ashok sitting amongst his shrouded processors, knees pulled up to his chest, arms draped over them. He looked like a big, fat, soft boy, his Mama's favourite.

Noradrenaline pallor, mild hypoglycaemia, fatigue toxins, said Nasatya.

Yin Systems bevabyte quantum storage arrays, said Brihaspati.

I touched him on the shoulder. He jerked awake. It was full dark outside, stifling: the monsoon was already sweeping up through the United States of Bengal.

"We're ready," I said. "*I'm* ready."

Dark-scented hibiscus spilled over the porch where the Mercedes waited.

"I'll see you in a week," he said. "In Varanasi."

"In Varanasi."

He took my shoulders in his hands and kissed me lightly, on the cheek. I drew my *dupatta* over my head. Veiled, I was taken to the United Provinces Night Sleeper Service. As I lay in the first class compartment the aeais chattered away inside my head, surprised to discover each other, reflections of reflections.

The *chowkidar* brought me bed-tea on a silver tray in the morning. Dawn came up over Varanasi's sprawling slums and industrial parks. My personalised news-service aeai told me that Lok Sabha would vote on ratifying the Hamilton Accords at ten a.m. At twelve Prime Minister Shrivastava and the United States Ambassador would announce a Most Favoured Nation trade package with Awadh.

The train emptied on to the platform beneath the spun-diamond canopy I knew so well. Every second passenger, it seemed was a smuggler. If I could spot them so easily, so could the Krishna Cops. They lined the exit ramps, more than I had ever seen before. There were uniforms behind them and robots behind the uniforms. The porter carried my bag on his head; I used it to navigate the press of people pouring off the night train. *Walk straight, as your Mamaji taught you. Walk tall and proud, like you are walking the Silken Way with a rich man.* I pulled my *dupatta* over my head, for modesty. Then I saw the crowd piling up at the ramp. The Krishna Cops were scanning every passenger with palmers.

I could see the *badmashs* and smuggler-boys hanging back, moving to the rear of the mill of bodies. But there was no escape there either. Armed police backed by riot-control robots took up position at the end of the platform. Shuffle by shuffle, the press of people pushed me towards the Krishna Cops, waving their right hands like blessings over the passengers. Those things could peel back my scalp and peer into my skull. My red case bobbed ahead, guiding me to my cage.

Brihaspati showed me what they would do to the circuits in my head.

Help me! I prayed to my gods. And Maya, architect of the demons, answered me. Its memories were my memories and it remembered rendering an architectural simulation of this station long before robot construction spiders started to spin their nano-diamond web. Two visions of Varanasi station, superimposed. With one difference that might save my life. Maya's showed me the inside of things. The inside of the platform. The drain beneath the hatch between the rear of the *chai*-booth and the roof support.

I pushed through the men to the small dead space at the rear. I hesitated before I knelt beside the hatch. One surge of the crowd, one trip, one fall, and I would be crushed. The hatch was jammed shut with dirt. Nails broke, nails tore as I scrabbled it loose and heaved it up. The smell that came up from the dark square was so foul I almost vomited. I forced myself in, dropped a metre into shin-deep sludge. The rectangle of light showed me my situation. I was mired in excrement. The tunnel forced me to crawl but the end of it was promise, the end of it was a semi-circle of daylight. I buried my hands in the soft sewage. This time I did retch up my bed tea. I crept forward, trying not to choke. It was vile beyond anything I had ever experienced. But not so vile as having your skull opened and knives slice away slivers of your brain. I crawled on my hands and knees under the tracks of Varanasi Station, to the light, to the light, to the light, and out through the open conduit into the cess lagoon where pigs and rag-pickers rooted in the shoals of drying human manure.

I washed as clean as I could in the shrivelled canal. *Dhobi*-wallahs beat laundry against stone slabs. I tried to ignore Nasatya's warnings about the hideous infections I might have picked up.

I was to meet Ashok's girl on the street of *gajras*. Children sat in doorways and open shop fronts threading marigolds onto needles. The work was too cheap even for robots. Blossoms spilled from bushels and plastic cases. My *phatphat's* tyre's slipped on wet rose petals. We drove beneath a canopy of *gajra* garlands that hung from poles above the shop-fronts. Everywhere was the smell of dead, rotting flowers. The *phatphat* turned into a smaller, darker alley and into the back of a mob. The driver pressed his hand to the horn. The people reluctantly gave him way. The alcofuel engine whined. We crept forward. Open space, then a police *jawan* stepped forward to bar our way. He wore full combat armour. Brihaspati read the glints of data flickering across his visor: deployments, communications, an arrest warrant. I pulled my *dupatta* over my head and lower face as the driver talked to him. What's going on? Some *badmash*. Some dataraja.

Down the street of *gajras*, uniformed police led by a plainclothes Krishna Cop burst open a door. Their guns were drawn. In the same breath, the shutters of the *jharoka* immediately above crashed up. A figure jumped up on to the wooden rail.

Behind me, the crowd let out a vast roaring sigh. *There he is there the badmash oh look look it's a girl!*

From the folds of my *dupatta* I saw Ashok's *girli* teeter there an instant, then jump up and grab a washing line. It snapped and swung her ungently down through racks of marigold garlands into the street. She crouched a moment, saw the police, saw the crowd, saw me, then turned and ran. The *jawan* started toward here but there was another quicker, deadlier. A woman screamed as the robot bounded from the rooftop into the alley. Chrome legs pistoned, its insect head bobbed, locked on. Marigold petals flew up around the fleeing girl but everyone knew she could not escape the killing thing. One step, two step, it was behind her. I saw her glance over her shoulder as the robot unsheathed its blade.

I knew what would happen next. It had seen it before, in the petal-strewn streets of Kathmandu, as I rode my litter among my gods and Kumarimas.

The blade flashed. A great cry from the crowd. The girl's head bounded down the alley. A great jet of blood. Sacrificial blood. The headless body took one step, two.

I slipped from the *phatphat* and stole away through the transfixed crowd.

I saw the completion of the story on a news channel at a *chai-dhaba* by the tank on Scindia *ghat*. The tourists, the faithful, the vendors and funeral parties were my camouflage. I sipped *chai* from a plastic cup and watched the small screen above the bar. The sound was low but I could understand well enough from the pictures. Delhi police break up a notorious aeai smuggling ring. In a gesture of Bharati-Awadhi friendship, Varanasi Krishna cops make a series of arrests. The camera cut away before the robot struck. The final shot was of Ashok, pushed down into a Delhi police car in plastic handcuffs.

I went to sit on the lowest *ghat*. The river would still me, the river would guide me. It was of the same substance as me, divinity. Brown water swirled at my be-ringed toes. That water could wash away all earthly sin. On the far side of the holy river, tall chimneys poured yellow smoke into the sky. A tiny round-faced girl came up to me, offered me marigold *gajras* to buy. I waved her away. I saw again this river, these *ghats*, these temples and boats as I had when I lay in my wooden room in my palace in Durbar Square. I saw now the lie Tall Kumarima's palmer had fed me. I had thought India a jewelled skirt, laid out for me to wear. It was a bride-buyer with an envelope of rupees, it was walking the Silken Way until feet cracked and bled. It was a husband with the body of the child and the appetites of a man warped by his impotence. It was a saviour who had always, only wanted me for my sickness. It was a young girl's head rolling in a gutter.

Inside this still-girl's head, my demons were silent. They could see as well as I that that there would never be a home for us in Bharat, Awadh, Maratha, any nation of India.

North of Nayarangadh the road rose through wooded ridges, climbing steadily up to Mugling where it turned and clung to the side of the Trisuli's steep valley. It was my third bus in as many days. I had a routine now. Sit at the back, wrap my *dupatta* round me, look out the window. Keep my hand on my money. Say nothing.

I picked up the first bus outside Jaunpur. After emptying Ashok's account, I thought it best to leave Varanasi as inconspicuously as possible. I did not need Brihaspati to show me the hunter aeais howling after me. Of course they would have the air, rail and bus stations covered. I rode out of the Holy City on an unlicensed taxi. The driver seemed pleased with the size of the tip. The second bus took me from Gorakhpur through the *dhal* fields and banana plantations to Nautanwa on the border. I had deliberately chosen small, out-of-the-way Nautanwa, but still I bowed my head and shuffled my feet as I came up to the Sikh emigration officer behind his tin counter. I held my breath. He waved me through without even a glance at my identity card.

I walked up the gentle slope and across the border. Had I been blind, I would have known at once when I crossed into my Kingdom. The great roar that had followed me as close as my own skin fell silent so abruptly it seemed to echo. The traffic did not blare its way through all obstacles. It steered, it sought ways around pedestrians and sacred cows lolling in the middle of the road, chewing. People were polite in the bureau where I changed my Bharati rupees for Nepalese; did not press and push and try to sell me things I did not want in the shop where I bought a bag of greasy *samosas*; smiled shyly to me in the cheap hotel where I hired a room for the night. Did not demand demand demand.

I slept so deeply that it felt like a fall through endless white sheets that smelled of sky. In the morning the third bus came to take me up to Kathmandu.

The road was one vast train of trucks, winding in and out of the bluffs, looping back on itself, all the while climbing, climbing. The gears on the old bus whined. The engine strove. I loved that sound, of engines fighting gravity. It was the sound of my earliest recollection, before the child-assessors came up a road just like this to Shukya. Trains of trucks and buses in the night. I looked out at the roadside *dhabas*, the shrines of piled rocks, the tattered prayer banners bent in the wind, the cableways crossing the chocolate-creamy river far below, skinny kids kicking swaying wire cages across the high wires. So familiar, so alien to the demons that shared my skull.

The baby must have been crying for some time before the noise rose above the background hubbub of the bus. The mother was two rows ahead of me, she shushed and swung and soothed the tiny girl but the cries were becoming screams.

It was Nasatya made me get out of my seat and go to her.

"Give her to me," I said and there must have been some tone of command from the medical aeai in my voice for she passed me the baby without a thought. I pulled back the sheet in which she was wrapped. The little girl's belly was painfully bloated, her limbs floppy and waxen.

"She's started getting colic when she eats," the mother said but before she could stop me I pulled away her napkin. The stench was abominable; the shit bulky and pale.

"What are you feeding her?"

The woman held up a *roti* bread, chewed at the edges to soften it for baby. I pushed my fingers into the baby's mouth to force it open though Vaishvanara the nutritionist already knew what we would find. The tongue was blotched red, pimpled with tiny ulcers.

"This has only started since you began giving her solid food?" I said. The mother waggled her head in agreement. "This child has ceoliac disease," I pronounced. The woman put her hands to her face in horror, began to rock and wail. "Your child will be fine, you must just stop feeding her bread, anything made from any grain except rice. She cannot process the proteins in wheat and barley. Feed her rice, rice and vegetables and she will brighten up right away."

The entire bus was staring as I went back to my seat. The woman and her baby got off at Naubise. The child was still wailing, weak now from its rage, but the woman raised a hand to me. I had come to Nepal with no destination, no plan or hope, just a need to be back. But an idea was already forming

Beyond Naubise the road climbed steadily, switching back and forth over the buttresses of the mountains that embraced Kathmandu. Evening was coming on. Looking back I could see the river of headlights snaking across the mountainside. When the bus ground around another hairpin bend, I could see the same snake climb up ahead of me in red taillights. The bus laboured up a long steep climb. I could hear, everyone could hear, the noise in the engine that should not have been there. Up we crawled, to the high saddle where the watershed divided, right to the valley of Kathmandu, left to Pokhara and the High Himalaya. Slower, slower. We could all smell the burning insulation, hear the rattling.

It was not me rushed to the driver and his mate. It was the demon Trivasti.

"Stop stop at once!" I cried. "Your alternator has seized! You will burn us up."

The driver pulled into the narrow draw, up against the raw rock. On the offside, trucks passed with millimetres to spare. We got the hood up. We could see the smoke wafting from the alternator. The men shook their heads and pulled out palmers. The passengers piled to the front of the bus to stare and talk.

"No no no, give me a wrench," I ordered.

The driver stared but I shook my outstretched hand, demanding. Perhaps he remembered the crying baby. Perhaps he was thinking about how long it would take a repair truck to come up from Kathmandu. Perhaps he was thinking about how good it would be to be home with his wife and children. He slapped the monkey wrench into my hand. In less than a minute I had the belt off and the alternator disconnected.

"Your bearings have seized," I said. "It's a persistent fault on pre-2030 models. A hundred metres more and you would have burned her out. You can drive her on the battery. There's enough in it to get you down to Kathmandu."

They stared at this little girl in an Indian sari, head covered but sleeves of her *choli* rolled up and fingers greasy with biolube.

The demon returned to his place and it was clear as the darkening sky what I would do now. The driver and his mate called out to me as I walked up beside the line of vehicles to the head of the pass. We ignored them. Passing drivers sounded their multiple, musical horns, offered lifts. I walked on. I could see the top now. It was not far to the place where the three roads divided. Back to India, down to the city, up to the mountains.

There was a *chai-dhaba* at the wide, oil-stained place where vehicles turned. It was bright with neon signs for American drinks and Bharati mineral water, like something fallen from the stars. A generator chugged. A television burbled familiar, soft Nepali news. The air smelled of hot ghee and biodiesel.

The owner did not know what to make of me, strange little girl in my Indian finery. Finally he said, "Fine night."

It was. Above the smogs and soots of the valley, the air was magically clear. I could see for a lifetime in any direction. To the west the sky held a little last light. The great peaks of Manaslu and Anapurna glowed mauve against the blue.

"It is," I said, "Oh it is."

Traffic pushed slowly past, never ceasing on this high crossroads of the world. I stood in the neon flicker of the *dhaba*, looking long at the mountains and I thought, *I shall live there*. We shall live in a wooden house close to trees, with running water cold from high snow. We shall have a fire and a television for company and prayer banners flying in the wind and in time people will stop being afraid and will come up the path to our door. There are many ways to be divine. There is the big divine, of ritual and magnificence and blood and terror. Ours shall be a little divinity, of small miracles and everyday wonders. Machines mended, programmes woven, people healed, homes designed, minds and bodies fed. I shall be a little goddess. In time, the story of me will spread and people will come from all over; Nepalis and foreigners, travellers and hikers and monks. Maybe one day a man who is not afraid. That would be good. But if he does not come, that will be good also, for I shall never be alone, not with a houseful of demons.

Then I found I was running, with the surprised *chai-wallah* calling, "Hey! Hey! Hey!" after me, running down the side of the slow-moving line of traffic, banging on the doors, "Hi! Hi! Pokhara! Pokhara!," slipping and sliding over the rough gravel, towards the far, bright mountains.

Dead Men Walking

PAUL McAULEY

Born in Oxford, England, in 1955, Paul J. McAuley now makes his home in London. A professional biologist for many years, he sold his first story in 1984, and has gone on to be a frequent contributor to Interzone, *as well as to markets such as* Asimov's Science Fiction, SCI FICTION, Amazing, The Magazine of Fantasy & Science Fiction, Skylife, The Third Alternative, When the Music's Over, *and elsewhere. His first novel,* Four Hundred Billion Stars, *won the Philip K. Dick Award, and his novel* Fairyland *won both the Arthur C. Clarke Award and the John W. Campbell Award in 1996. His other books include the novels* Of the Fall, Eternal Light, *and* Pasquale's Angel, Confluence—*a major trilogy of ambitious scope and scale set ten million years in the future, comprised of the novels* Child of the River, Ancient of Days, *and* Shrine of Stars—Life on Mars, The Secret of Life, Whole Wide World, White Devils, Mind's Eye, Players, Cowboy Angels, The Quiet War, Gardens of the Sun, In the Mouth of the Whale, and Evening's Empires. *His short fiction has been collected in* The King of the Hill and Other Stories, The Invisible Country, Little Machines, *and a major retrospective collection,* A Very British History: The Best Science Fiction Stories of Paul McAuley, 1985–2011; *he is also the co-editor, with Kim Newman, of an original anthology,* In Dreams. *His most recent books are a novel,* Something Coming Through, *followed by a sequel,* Into Everywhere.*

Here he takes us to a prison in the far reaches of the solar system, to show us how some consequences of a devastating war can persist for years after the war is ostensibly over—with deadly results.

I guess this is the end. I'm in no condition to attempt the climb down, and in any case I'm running out of air. The nearest emergency shelter is only five klicks away, but it might as well be on the far side of this little moon. I'm not expecting any kind of last-minute rescue, either. No one knows I'm here, my phone and the distress beacon are out, my emergency flares went with my utility belt, and I don't think that the drones patrol this high. At least my legs have stopped hurting, although I can feel the throb of what's left of my right hand through the painkiller's haze, like the beat of distant war drums . . .

If you're the person who found my body, I doubt that you'll have time to listen to my last and only testament. You'll be too busy calling for help, securing the area, and making sure that you or any of your companions don't trample precious clues underfoot. I imagine instead that you're an investigator or civil servant sitting in an office buried deep inside some great bureaucratic hive, listening to this out of duty before consigning it to the memory hole. You'll know that my body was found near the top of the eastern wall of the great gash of Elliot Graben on Ariel, Uranus's fourth-largest moon, but I don't suppose you've ever visited the place, so I should give you an idea of what I can see.

I'm sitting with my pressure suit's backpack firmly wedged against a huge block of dirty, rock-hard ice. A little way beyond my broken legs, a cliff drops straight down for about a kilometre to the bottom of the graben's enormous trough. Its floor, resurfaced a couple of billion years ago by a flood of water-ice lava, is a level plain patched with enormous fields of semi-vacuum organisms. Orange and red, deep blacks, foxy umbers, bright yellows . . . they stretch away from me in every direction for as far as I can see, like the biggest quilt in the universe. This moon is so small and the graben is so wide that its western rim is below the horizon. Strings of suspensor lamps float high above the fields like a fleet of burning airships.

There's enough atmospheric pressure, twenty millibars of nitrogen and methane, to haze the view and give an indication of distance, of just how big this strange garden really is. It's the prison farm, of course, and every square centimetre of it was constructed by the sweat of men and women convicted by the failure of their ideals, but none of that matters to me now. I'm beyond all that up here, higher than the suspensor lamps, tucked under the eaves of the vast roof of fullerene composite and transparent halflife polymer that tents the graben. If I twist my head I can glimpse one of the giant struts that anchor the roof. Beyond it, the big, blue-green globe of Uranus floats in the black sky. The gas giant's south pole, capped with a brownish haze of photochemical smog, is pointed at the brilliant point of the sun, which hangs just above the western horizon.

Sunset's three hours off. I won't live long enough to see it. My legs are comfortably numb, but the throbbing in my hand is becoming more urgent, there's a dull ache in my chest, and every breath is an effort. I wonder if I'll live long enough to tell you my story . . .

All right. I've just taken another shot of painkiller. I had to override the suit to do it, it's a lethal dose . . .

Christos, it still hurts. It hurts to laugh.

My name is Roy Bruce. It isn't my real name. I have never had a real name. I suppose I had a number when I was decanted, but I don't know what it was. My instructors called me Dave—but they called all of us Dave, a private joke they never bothered to explain. Later, just before the war began, I took the life of the man in whose image I had been made. I took his life, his name, his identity. And after the war was over, after I evaded recall and went on the run, I had several different names, one after the other. But Roy, Roy Bruce, that's the name I've had longest. That's the name you'll find on the roster of guards. That's the name you can bury me under.

My name is Roy Bruce, and I lived in Herschel City, Ariel, for eight and a half years.

Lived. Already with the past tense . . .

My name is Roy Bruce. I'm a prison guard. The prison, TPA Facility 898, is a cluster of chambers—we call them blocks—buried in the eastern rim of Elliot Graben. Herschel City is twenty klicks beyond, a giant cylindrical shaft sunk into Ariel's icy surface, its walls covered in a vertical, shaggy green forest that grows from numerous ledges and crevices. Public buildings and little parks jut out of the forest wall like bracket fungi; homes are built in and amongst the trees. Ariel's just over a thousand kilometers in diameter and mostly ice; its gravity barely exists. The citizens of Herschel City are arboreal acrobats, swinging, climbing, sliding, flying up and down and roundabout on cableways and trapezes, nets and ropewalks.

It's a good place to live.

I have a one-room treehouse. It's not very big and plainly furnished, but you can sit on the porch of a morning, watch squirrel monkeys chase each other through the pines. I'm a member of Sweat Lodge #23. I breed singing crickets, have won several competitions with them. Mostly they're hacked to sing fragments of Mozart, nothing fancy, but my line has good sustain and excellent timbre and pitch. I hope old Willy Gup keeps it going . . . I like to hike too, and climb freestyle. I once soloed the Broken Book route in Prospero Chasma on Miranda, twenty kilometres up a vertical face, in fifteen hours. Nowhere near the record, but pretty good for someone with a terminal illness. I've already had various bouts of cancer, but retroviruses dealt with those easily enough. What's killing me— what just lost the race to kill me—is a general systematic failure something like lupus. I couldn't get any treatment for it, of course, because the doctors would find out who I really am. What I really was.

I suppose that I had a year or so left. Maybe two if I was really lucky.

It wasn't much of a life, but it was all my own.

Uranus has some twenty-odd moons, mostly captured chunks of sooty ice a few dozen kilometres in diameter. Before the Quiet War, no more than a couple of hundred people lived out here. Rugged pioneer families, hermits, a few scientists, and some kind of Hindu sect that planted huge tracts of Umbriel's sooty surface with slow-growing lichenous vacuum organisms. After the war, the Three Powers

Alliance took over the science station on Ariel, renamed it Herschel City, and built its maximum security facility in the big graben close by. The various leaders and lynchpins of the revolution, who had already spent two years being interrogated at Tycho, on Earth's Moon, were moved here to serve the rest of their life sentences of re-education and moral realignment. At first, the place was run by the Brazilian Navy, but civilian contractors were brought in after Elliot Graben was tented and the vacuum organism farms were planted. Most were ex-Service people who had settled in the Outer System after the war. I was one of them.

I had learned how to create fake identities with convincing histories during my training: my latest incarnation easily passed the security check. For eight and a half years, Roy Bruce, guard third class, cricket breeder, amateur freestyle climber, lived a quiet, anonymous life out on the fringe of the solar system. And then two guards stumbled across the body of Goether Lyle, who had been the leader of the Senate of Athens, Tethys when, along with a dozen other city states in the Outer System, it had declared independence from Earth.

I'd known Goether slightly: an intense, serious man who'd been writing some kind of philosophical thesis in his spare time. His body was found in the middle of the main highway between the facility and the farms, spread-eagled and naked, spikes hammered through hands and feet. His genitals had been cut off and stuffed in his mouth; his tongue had been pulled through the slit in his throat. He was also frozen solid—the temperature out on the floor of the graben is around minus one hundred and fifty degrees celsius, balmy compared to the surface of Ariel, but still a lot colder than the inside of any domestic freezer, so cold that the carbon dioxide given off by certain strains of vacuum organisms precipitates out of the atmosphere like hoar frost. It took six hours to thaw out his body for the autopsy, which determined that the mutilations were post mortem. He'd been strangled, and then all the other stuff had been done to him.

I was more than thirty klicks away when Goether Lyle's body was discovered, supervising a work party of ten prisoners, what we call a stick, that was harvesting a field of vacuum organisms. It's important to keep the prisoners occupied, and stoop labour out in the fields or in the processing plants leaves them too tired to plan any serious mischief. Also, export of the high-grade biochemicals which the vacuum organisms cook from methane in the thin atmosphere helps to defray the enormous cost of running the facility. So I didn't hear about the murder until I'd driven my stick back to its block at the end of the shift, and I didn't learn all the gruesome details until later that evening, at the sweat lodge.

In the vestigial gravity of worldlets like Ariel, where you can drown in a shower and water tends to slosh about uncontrollably, sweat lodges, saunas, or Turkish-style hamams are ideal ways to keep clean. You bake in steam heat, sweat the dirt out of your pores, scrape it off your skin, and exchange gossip with your neighbours and friends. Even in a little company town like Herschel City, there are lodges catering for just about every sexual orientation and religious belief. My lodge, #23, is for unattached, agnostic heterosexual males. That evening, as usual, I was sitting with a dozen or so naked men of various ages and body types in eucalyptus-scented steam. We scraped at our skin with abrasive mitts or plastered green depilatory mud on ourselves, squirted the baking stones of the hearth with water to make more steam, and talked about the murder of Goether Lyle. Mustafa Sesler, who worked in the hospital, gave us all the grisly details. There was speculation about whether it was caused by a personal beef or a turf war between gangs. Someone made the inevitable joke about it being the most thorough suicide in the history of the prison. Someone else, my friend Willy Gup, asked me if I had any idea about it.

"You had the guy in your stick last year, Roy. He have any enemies you know of?"

I gave a noncommittal answer. The mutilations described by Mustafa Sesler were straight out of my training in assassination, guerrilla tactics, and black propaganda. I was processing the awful possibility that Goether Lyle had been murdered by someone like me.

You must know by now what I am. That I am not really human. That I am a doppelganger designed by gene wizards, grown in a vat, decanted fully grown with a headful of hardwired talents and traits, trained up, and sent out to kill the person whose exact double I was, and replace him. I do not know how many doppelgangers, berserkers, suicide artists and other cloned subversives were deployed during the Quiet War, but I believe that our contribution was significant. My target was Sharwal Jah Sharja, a minor gene wizard who lived alone in the jungle in one of the tented crevasses of East of Eden, Ganymede, where he orchestrated the unceasing symphony of the city state's closed loop ecosystem. After I took his place, I began a programme of ecotage, significantly reducing the circulation of water vapour and increasing the atmospheric concentration of carbon dioxide and toxic trace gases. By the time the Quiet War kicked off, some four weeks later, the population of East of Eden was wearing breathing masks, the forests and parks were beginning to die, and most food animals and crops had died or were badly stricken, forcing the city to use biomass from vacuum organism farms to feed its citizens. A commando force of the Three Powers Alliance annexed East of Eden's farms in the first few hours of the war, and after two weeks its starving citizens agreed terms of surrender.

I was supposed to turn myself in as soon as the city had been secured, but in the middle of the formal surrender, dead-ender fanatics assassinated half the Senate and attacked the occupying force. In the subsequent confusion, the tented crevasse where I had been living was blown open to vacuum, Sharwal Jah Sharja was posted as one of the casualties, and I took the opportunity to slip away. I have successfully hidden my true identity and lived incognito amongst ordinary human beings ever since.

Why did I disobey my orders? How did I slip the bonds of my hardwired drives and instincts? It's quite simple. While I had been pretending to be Sharwal Jah Sharja, I had come to love life. I wanted to learn as much about it as I could in the brief span I'd been allotted by my designers. And so I adopted the identity of another casualty, and after the war was over and the Three Powers Alliance allowed trade and travel to resume, I left East of Eden and went out into the solar system to see what I could see.

In all my wanderings I never met any others like me, but I did find a hint that at least one of my brothers and sisters of the vat had survived the war. All of us had been imprinted with a variety of coded messages covering a vast range of possibilities, and a year after going on the run I came across one of them in a little-used passageway between two chambers of the city of Xamba, Rhea.

To anyone else it was a meaningless scrawl; to me, it was like a flash of black lightning that branded an enciphered phone number itself on my brain. The walls of the passageway were thickly scribbled with graffiti, much of it pre-war. The message could have been left there last year or last week; it could have been a trap, left by agents hunting renegades like me. I didn't have the nerve to find out. I went straight to the spaceport and bought a seat on a shuttle to Phoebe, the gateway port to the other moons of Saturn and the rest of the Outer System. Six months later, wearing the new identity of Roy Bruce, I became a guard at TPA Facility 898.

That's why, almost nine years later, I couldn't be certain that any of my brothers and sisters had survived, and I was able to convince myself that Goether Lyle had been the victim of the vicious internal politics of the prison, killed and mutilated by someone who knew about the black propaganda techniques in which we'd been trained. But that comforting fiction was blown apart the very next day, when another mutilated body was found.

The victim was a former senator of Baghdad, Enceladus, and a member of the prison gang that was intermittently at war with the gang to which Goether Lyle had belonged. A message written in blood on the ground next to the senator's body implied that he'd been murdered by Goether Lyle's cronies, but whoever had killed him must have done the deed in his cell some time between the evening count and the end of the night's lockdown, spirited his body out of the facility without being detected, and left it within the field of view of a security camera which had been hacked to show a recorded loop instead of a live feed. Members of the rival gangs lived in different blocks, had chips implanted in their skulls which constantly monitored their movements, and were under lock-down all night. If the killer was a prisoner, he would have had to bribe more than a dozen guards; it was far more likely that the senator had been killed by one of the facility's staff. And when I heard what had been done to the body, I was certain that it was the handiwork of one of my brothers or sisters. The senator had been blinded before he'd been strangled, and his lungs had been pulled through incisions in his back. It was a mutilation called the Blood Eagle, invented by the Vikings some two thousand years ago. I remembered the cold, patient voice of the instructor who had demonstrated it to us on a corpse.

Someone in the warden's office reached the same conclusion. Posted at the top of our daily orders was an announcement that a specialist team was on its way to Ariel, and emergency security measures were put in place at the spaceport. That evening Willy Gup told the sweat lodge that the warden reckoned that it was possible that the two murders were the work of the kind of vat-grown assassin used in the Quiet War.

"So if you come across anything suspicious, don't be tempted to do anything stupidly heroic, my brothers. Those things are smart and deadly and completely without any kind of human feeling. Be like me. Stay frosty, but hang back."

I felt a loathsome chill crawl through me. I knew that if Willy and the others realized that one of "those things" was sitting with them in the steamy heat of the lodge, they would fall on me at once and tear me limb from limb. And I knew that I couldn't hang back, couldn't let things run their course. No one would be able to leave Ariel for the duration of the emergency security measures, and the specialist team would search every square centimetre of the facility and Herschel City, check the records and DNA profile of every prisoner, member of staff, citizen and visitor, and release a myriad tiny drones designed to home in on anyone breathing out the combination of metabolic byproducts unique to our kind. The team would almost certainly uncover the assassin, but they would also unmask me.

Oh, I suppose that I could have hiked out to some remote location on the surface and hunkered down for the duration, but I had no idea how long the search would last. The only way I could be sure of evading it would be to force my pressure suit to put me in deep hibernation for a month or two, and how would I explain my absence when I returned? And besides, I knew that I was dying. I was already taking dangerously large daily doses of steroids to relieve the swelling of my joints and inflammation of my connective tissue caused by my pseudo-lupus. Suspended animation would slow but not stop the progress of my disease. Suppose I never woke up?

I spent a long, bleak night considering my options. By the time the city had begun to increase its ambient light level and the members of the local troop of spider monkeys were beginning to hoot softly to each other in the trees outside my little cabin, I knew what I would have to do. I knew that I would have to find the assassin before the team arrived.

My resolve hardened when I started my shift a couple of hours later and learned that there had been two more murders, and a minor riot in the prison library.

I found it laughably easy to hack into the facility's files: I had been trained well all those years ago, and the data system was old, and was easily fooled. I checked the dossiers of recently recruited staff but found nothing suspicious, and didn't have any better luck when I examined the dossiers of friends and family of prisoners, their advocates, and traders and businesspeople currently staying in Herschel City. It was possible that I had missed something—no doubt the assassin's cover story was every bit as good as the one that had served me so well for so long. But having more or less eliminated the obvious suspects, I had to consider the possibility that, just like me, the assassin had been hiding on Ariel ever since the war had ended. I had so much in common with my brothers and sisters that it would not be a wild coincidence if one of them had come to the same decision as I had, and had joined the staff of the prison. Perhaps he had finally gone insane, or perhaps the hardwired imperatives of his old mission had kicked in. Or perhaps, like me, he had discovered that he was coming to the end of his short life span, and had decided to have some fun. In the short time before the specialist team arrived, it would be impossible to check thoroughly the records of over three thousand staff members. I had reached a dead end. I decided that I needed some advice.

Everyone in Herschel City and the prison was talking about the murders. During a casual conversation with Willy Gup, I found it easy enough to ask my old friend if he had any thoughts on how someone might go about uncovering the identity of the assassin.

"Anyone with any sense would keep well clear," Willy said. "He'd keep his nose clean, he'd keep his stick in line, and he'd wait for the specialists."

"Who won't be here for a week. A full-scale war could have broken out by then."

Willy admitted that I had a point. One of the original intake of guards, a veteran who'd served in one of the Navy supply ships during the Quiet War, he had led the team that put down the trouble in the library. Three prisoners had died and eighteen had been badly injured—one had gouged out the eyes of another with her thumbs—and the incident had left him subdued and thoughtful.

After studying me for a few moments, he said, "If it was me, I wouldn't touch the files. I hear the warden is compiling a list of people who are poking around, looking for clues and so forth. He tolerates their nonsense because he desperately wants to put an end to the trouble as soon as he can, and he'll be pretty damn happy if some hack does happen to uncover the assassin. But it isn't likely, and when this thing is over you can bet he's going to come down hard on all those amateur sleuths. And it's possible the assassin is keeping tabs on the files too. Anyone who comes close to finding him could be in for a bad surprise. No, my brother, screwing around in the files is only going to get you into trouble."

I knew then that Willy had a shrewd idea of what I was about. I also knew that the warden was the least of my worries. I said, as lightly as I could, "So what would you do?"

Willy didn't answer straight away, but instead refilled his bulb from the jar of iced tea. We were sitting on the porch of his little shack, at the edge of a setback near the top of the city's shaft. Banana plants and tree ferns screened it from its neighbors; the vertical forest dropped away on either side. Willy's champion cricket, a splendid white and bronze specimen in a cage of plaited bamboo, was trilling one of Bach's Goldberg Variations.

At last, Willy passed the jar to me and said, "We're speaking purely hypothetically."

"Of course."

"You've always had a wild streak," Willy said, "I wouldn't put it past you to do something recklessly brave and dangerously stupid."

"I'm just an ordinary hack," I said.

"Who goes for long solitary hikes across the surface. Who soloed that route in Prospero Chasma and didn't bother to mention it until someone found out a couple of years later. I've known you almost nine years, Roy, and you're still a man of mystery," Willy said, and smiled. "Hey, what's that look for? All I'm saying is you have character, is all."

For a moment, my hardwired reflexes had kicked in. For a moment, I had been considering whether or not this man had blown my cover, whether or not I should kill him. I carefully manufactured a smile, and said that I hadn't realized that I seemed so odd.

"Most of us have secrets," Willy said. "That's why we're out here, my brother. We're just as much prisoners as anyone in our sticks. They don't know it, but those dumbasses blundering about in the files are trying to find a way of escaping what they are."

"And there's no way you can escape what you are," I said.

The moment had passed. My smile was a real smile now, not a mask I'd put on to hide what I really was.

Willy toasted me with his bulb of tea. "Anyone with any sense learns that eventually."

"You still haven't told me how you would catch the assassin."

"I don't intend to catch him."

"But speaking hypothetically . . ."

"For all we know, it's the warden. He can go anywhere and everywhere, and he has access to all the security systems too."

"The warden? Really?"

Willy grinned. "I'm pulling your chain. But seriously, I've done a little research about these things. They're not only stone killers: they're also real good at disguising themselves. The assassin could be any one of us. The warden, you, me, anyone. Unless this thing makes a mistake, we haven't got a hope of catching it. All we can do is what we're already doing—deploy more security drones, keep the prisoners locked down when they aren't working, and pray that that'll keep a lid on any unrest until that team arrives."

"I guess you're right," I said.

"Don't try to be a hero, my brother. Not even hypothetically."

"Absolutely not," I said.

But one of Willy's remarks had given me an idea about how to reach out to the assassin, and my mind was already racing, grappling with what I had to do.

I decided that if the assassin really was keeping an eye on the people who were hacking into the files, then he (or at least, his demon), must be lurking in the root directory of the data system. That was where I left an encrypted message explaining what I was and why I wanted to talk, attached to a demon that would attempt to trace anyone who looked at it. The demon phoned me six hours later, in the middle of the night. Someone had spotted my sign and wanted to talk.

The demon had failed to identify the person who wanted to talk, and it was infected with something, too: a simple communication program. I checked it out, excised a few lines of code that would have revealed my location, and fired it up. It connected me to a blank, two-dimensional space in which words began to appear, emerging letter by letter, traveling from right to left and fading away.

>>*you got rid of the trace function. pretty good for an old guy—if that's what you really are.*

>*they trained us well*, I typed.

>>*you think you know what i am. you think that i am like you.*

Whoever was at the other end of the program wanted to get straight down to business. That suited me, but I knew that I couldn't let him take the lead.

>*we are both children of the vat*, I typed. *that's why I reached out to you. that's why i want to help you.*

There was a pause as my correspondent thought this over.

>>*you could be a trap.*

>*the message got your attention because it is hardwired into your visual cortex, just as it is hardwired into mine.*

>>*that kind of thing is no longer the secret it once was, but let's say that i believe you . . .*

A black disc spun in the blank space for less than a second, its strobing black light flashing a string of letters and numbers, gone.

>>*do you know where that is?*

I realized that the letters and numbers burnt into my brain were a grid reference.

>*i can find it.*

>>*meet me in four hours. i have a little business to take care of first.*

It was the middle of the night; the time when the assassin did his work.

>*please don't kill anyone else until we have talked.*

My words faded. There was no reply.

The grid reference was at the precise centre of a small eroded crater sixty klicks south of the facility, an unreconstructed area in the shadow of the graben's eastern rimwall. Before I headed out, I equipped myself from the armoury and downloaded a hack into the security system so that I could move freely and unremarked. I was oddly happy, foolishly confident. It felt good to be in action again. My head was filled with a fat, contented hum as I drove a tricycle cart along an old construction road. The rendezvous point was about an hour away: I would have plenty of time to familiarize myself with the terrain and make my preparations before the assassin, if that was who I had been talking to, turned up.

I want to make it clear that my actions were in no way altruistic. The only life I wanted to save was my own. Yes, I knew that I was dying, but no one loves life more than those who have only a little of it left; no one else experiences each and every moment with such vivid immediacy. I didn't intend to throw away my life in a grand gesture. I wanted to unmask the assassin and escape the special team's inquisition.

The road ran across a flat terrain blanketed in vacuum-cemented grey-brown dust and littered with big blocks which over the eons had been eroded into soft shapes by impact cratering.

The graben's wall reared up to my left, its intricate folds and bulges like a frozen curtain. Steep cones and rounded hills of mass-wasted talus fringed its base. To my right, the land sloped away toward a glittering ribbon of fences and dykes more than a kilometer away, the boundary of the huge patchwork of fields. It was two in the morning by the clock, but the suspensor lamps were burning as brightly as they always did, and above the western horizon the sun's dim spark was almost lost in their hazy glow.

I was a couple of klicks from the rendezvous, and the road was cutting through a steep ridge that buttressed a great bulge in the wall, when the assassin struck. I glimpsed a hitch of movement high in a corner of my vision, but before I could react, a taser dart struck my cart and shorted its motor. A second later, a net slammed into me, slithering over my torso as muscular threads of myoelectric plastic tightened in constricting folds around my arms and chest. I struggled to free myself as the cart piddled to a halt, but my arms were pinned to my sides by the net and I couldn't even unfasten the safety harness. I could only sit and watch as a figure in a black pressure suit descended the steep side of the ridge in two huge bounds, reached me in two more.

It ripped out my phone, stripped away my utility belt, the gun in the pocket on the right thigh of my pressure suit and the knife in the pocket on the left thigh, then uncoupled my main air supply, punched the release of my harness and dragged me out of the low-slung seat and hauled me off the road. I was dumped on my back near a cart parked in the shadow of a house-sized block and the assassin stepped back, aiming a rail-gun at me.

The neutron camera I'd fitted inside my helmet revealed scant details of the face behind the gold-filmed mirror of my captor's visor. Its demon made an extrapolation, searched the database I'd loaded, found a match. Debra Thorn, employed as a paramedic in the facility's infirmary for the past two years, 22, unmarried, no children . . . I realized then that I'd made a serious mistake. The assassin was a doppelganger, all right, but because she was the double of someone who hadn't been an adult when the war had ended she must have been manufactured and decanted much more recently than me. She wasn't insane, and she hadn't spent years under cover. She was killing people because that was what she'd been sent here to do. Because it was her mission.

A light was winking on my head-up display—the emergency short-range, line-of-sight walkie-talkie. When I responded, an electronically distorted voice said, "Are you alone?"

"Absolutely."

"Who are you?"

I'd stripped all identifying tags from my suit before setting off, but the doppelganger who had killed Debra Thorn and taken her place was pointing a gun at my head and it seemed advisable to tell her my name. She was silent for a moment, no doubt taking a look at my file.

I said, "I'm not the doppelganger of Roy Bruce, if that's what you're thinking. The person I killed and replaced was a gene wizard by the name of Sharwal Jah Sharja."

I briefly told the assassin the story I have already told you. When I was finished, she said,

"You've really been working here for eight years?"

"Eight and a half."

I had made a very bad mistake about my captor's motives, but I must have piqued her curiosity, for otherwise I would already be dead. And even if I couldn't talk my way out of this and persuade her to spare me, I still had a couple of weapons she hadn't found. I risked a lie, said that her net had compromised my suit's thermal integrity. I told her that I was losing heat to the frozen ground; that I would freeze to death if I didn't get up.

She told me I could sit up, and to do it slowly.

As I got my feet under me, squatting on my haunches in front of her, I glanced up at the top of the ridge and made a crucial triangulation.

She said, "My instructors told me that I would live no more than a year."

"Perhaps they told you that you would burn briefly but very brightly—that's what they told me. But they lied. I expect they lied about a lot of things, but I promise to tell you only the truth. We can leave here, and go anywhere we want to."

"I have a job to finish. People to kill, riots to start."

The assassin took a long step sideways to the cart, took something the size of a basketball from the net behind its seat, bowled it towards me. It bounced slowly over the dusty ground and ended up between my legs: the severed head of an old woman, skin burnt black with cold, eyes capped by frost.

"The former leader of the parliament of Sparta, Tethys," the assassin said. "I left the body pinned to the ground in one of the fields where her friends work, with an amusing little message."

"You are trying to start a war amongst the prisoners. Perhaps the people who sent you here are hoping that the scandal will close the facility. Perhaps they think it is the only chance they'll have of freeing their comrades. Who are you working for, by the way?"

"I'll ask the questions," the assassin said.

I asked her how she would escape when she was finished. "There's a special team on the way. If you're still here when they arrive, they'll hunt you down and kill you."

"So that's why you came after me. You were frightened that this team would find you while they were hunting me."

She may have been young, but she was smart and quick.

I said, "I came because I wanted to talk to you. Because you're like me."

"Because after all these years of living amongst humans, you miss your own kind, is that it?"

Despite the electronic distortion, I could hear the sneer in the assassin's voice. I said carefully, "The people who sent you here—the people who made you—have no plans to extract you when you are finished here. They do not care if you survive your mission. They only care that it is successful. Why give your loyalty to people who consider you expendable? To people who lied to you? You have many years of life ahead of you, and it isn't as hard to disobey your orders as you might think. You've already disobeyed them, in fact, when you reached out to me. All you have to do is take one more step, and let me help you. If we work together, we'll survive this. We'll find a way to escape."

"You think you're human. You're not. You're exactly like me. A walking dead man. That's what our instructors called us, by the way: the dead. Not 'Dave.' Not anything cute. When we were being moved from one place to another, they'd shout out a warning: 'Dead men walking.'"

It is the traditional warning when a condemned person is let out of their cell. Fortunately, I've never worked in Block H, where prisoners who have murdered or tried to murder fellow inmates or guards await execution, so I've never heard or had to use it.

The assassin said, "They're right, aren't they? We're made things, so how can we be properly alive?"

"I've lived a more or less ordinary life for ten years. If you give this up and come with me, I'll show you how."

"You stole a life, just as I did. Underneath your disguise, you're a dead man, just like me."

"The life I live now is my own, not anyone else's," I said. "Give up what you are doing, and I'll show you what I mean."

"You're a dead man," the assassin said. "You're breathing the last of your air. You have less than an hour left. I'll leave you to die here, finish my work, and escape in the confusion. After that, I'm supposed to be picked up, but now I think I'll pass on that. There must be plenty of people out there who need my skills. I'll work for anyone who wants some killing done, and earn plenty of money."

"It's a nice dream," I said, "but it will never come true."

"Why shouldn't I profit from what I was made to do?"

"I've lived amongst people for more than a decade. Perhaps I don't know them as well as I should, but I do know that they are very afraid of us. Not because we're different, but because we're so very much like a part of them they don't want to acknowledge. Because we're the dark side of their nature. I've survived this long only because I have been very careful to hide what I really am. I can teach you how to do that, if you'll let me."

"It doesn't sound like much of a life to me," the assassin said.

"Don't you like being Debra Thorn?" I said.

And at the same moment I kicked off the ground, hoping that by revealing that I knew who she was I'd distracted and confused her, and won a moment's grace.

In Ariel's microgravity, my standing jump took me high above the assassin's head, up and over the edge of the ridge. As I flew up, I discharged the taser dart I'd sewn into the palm of one of my pressure suit's gloves, and the electrical charge stored in its super-conducting loop shorted out every thread of myoelectric plastic that bound my arms. I shrugged off the net as I came down and kicked off again, bounding along the ridge in headlong flight towards the bulging face of the cliff wall and a narrow chimney pinched between two folds of black, rock-hard ice.

I was halfway there when a kinetic round struck my left leg with tremendous force and broke my thigh. I tumbled headlong, caught hold a low pinnacle just before I went over the edge of the ridge. The assassin's triumphant shout was a blare of electronic noise in my ears; because she was using the line-of-sight walkie-talkie I knew that she was almost on me. I pushed up at once and scuttled towards the chimney like a crippled ape. I had almost reached my goal when a second kinetic round shattered my right knee.

My suit was ruptured at the point of impact and I felt a freezing pain as the smart fabric constricted as tightly as a tourniquet, but I was not finished. The impact of the kinetic round had knocked me head over heels into a field of ice-blocks, within striking distance of the chimney. As I half-crawled, half-swam towards it, a third round took off the top of a pitted block that might have fallen from the cliffs a billion years ago, and then I was inside the chimney, and started to climb.

The assassin had no experience of freestyle climbing. Despite my injuries I soon outdistanced her. The chimney gave out after half a kilometre, and I had no choice but to continue to climb the naked iceface. Less than a minute later, the assassin reached the end of the chimney and fired a kinetic round that smashed into the cliff a little way above me. I flattened against the iceface as a huge chunk dropped past me with dreamy slowness, then powered straight through the expanding cloud of debris, pebbles and ice grains briefly rattling on my helmet, and flopped over the edge of a narrow setback.

My left leg bent in the middle of my thigh and hurt horribly; my right leg was numb below the knee, and a thick crust of blood had frozen solid at the joint. But I had no time to tend my wounds. I sat up and ripped out the hose of the water recycling system as the assassin shot above the edge of the cliff in a graceful arc, taser in one hand, rail gun in the other. I twisted the valve, hit her with a high-pressure spray of water that struck her visor and instantly froze. I pushed off the ground with both hands (a kinetic round slammed into the dusty ice where I'd just been), collided with her in midair, clamped my glove over the diagnostic port of her backpack, and discharged my second taser dart.

The dart shorted out the electronics in the assassin's suit, and enough current passed through the port to briefly stun her. I pushed her away as we dropped towards the setback, but she managed to fire a last shot as she spun into the void beyond the edge of the setback. She was either phenomenally lucky or incredibly skillful: it took off my thumb and three fingers of my right hand.

She fell more than a kilometre. Even in the low gravity, it was more than enough to kill her, but just to make sure I dropped several blocks of ice onto her. The third smashed her visor. You'll find her body, if you haven't already, more or less directly below the spot where you found mine.

The assassin had vented most of my air supply and taken my phone and emergency beacon; the dart I'd used on her had crippled what was left of my pressure suit's life support system. The suit's insulation is pretty good, but I'm beginning to feel the bite of the cold now, my hand is growing pretty tired from using the squeeze pump to push air through the rebreather, and I'm getting a bad headache as the carbon dioxide concentration in my air supply inexorably rises. I killed the ecosystem of East of Eden by sabotaging the balance of its atmospheric gases, and now the same imbalance is killing me.

Just about the only thing still working is the dumb little chip I stuck in my helmet to record my conversation with the assassin. By now, you probably know more about her than I do. Perhaps you even know who sent her here.

I don't have much time left. Perhaps it's because the increasing carbon dioxide level is making me comfortably stupid, but I find that I don't mind dying. I told you that I confronted the assassin to save myself. I think now that I may have been wrong about that. I may have gone on the run after the Quiet War, but in my own way I have served you right up until the end of my life.

I'm going to sign off now. I want to spend my last moments remembering my freestyle climb up those twenty kilometres of sheer ice in Prospero Chasma. I want to remember how at the end I stood tired and alone at the top of a world-cleaving fault left over from a shattering collision four billion years ago, with Uranus tilted at the horizon, half-full, serene and remote, and the infinite black, starry sky above. I felt so utterly insignificant then, and yet so happy, too, without a single regret for anything at all in my silly little life.

tin marsh

michael swanwick

Michael Swanwick made his debut in 1980, and in the thirty-seven years that have followed has established himself as one of SF's most prolific and consistently excellent writers at short lengths, as well as one of the premier novelists of his generation. He has won the Theodore Sturgeon Award and the Asimov's *Readers Award poll. In 1991, his novel* Stations of the Tide *won him a Nebula Award as well, and in 1995 he won the World Fantasy Award for his story "Radio Waves." He's won the Hugo Award numerous times, for his stories "The Very Pulse of the Machine," "Scherzo with Tyrannosaur," "The Dog Said Bow-Wow," "Slow Life," and "Legions in Time." His other books include the novels* In the Drift, Vacuum Flowers, The Iron Dragon's Daughter, Jack Faust, Bones of the Earth, The Dragons of Babel, Dancing with Bears, The Iron Dragon's Mother, *and* Chasing the Phoenix. *His short fiction has been assembled in* Gravity's Angels, A Geography of Unknown Lands, Slow Dancing Through Time, Moon Dogs, Puck Aleshire's Abecedary, Tales of Old Earth, Cigar-Box Faust and Other Miniatures, Michael Swanwick's Field Guide to the Mesozoic Megafauna, The Periodic Table of SF, *and a massive retrospective collection,* The Best of Michael Swanwick. *Swanwick lives in Philadelphia with his wife, Marianne Porter. He has a website at: michaelswanwick.com and maintains a blog at floggingbabel.com*

Here he takes us to the inimical surface of a very inhospitable Venus for a deadly game of cat-and-mouse. . . .

It was hot coming down into the valley. The sun was high in the sky, a harsh white dazzle in the eternal clouds, strong enough to melt the lead out of the hills. They trudged down from the heights, carrying the drilling rig between them. A little trickle of metal, spill from a tanker bringing tin out of the mountains, glinted at the verge of the road.

A traveler coming the other way, ten feet tall and anonymous in a black muscle suit, waved at them as they passed, but even though it had been weeks since they'd seen another human being, they didn't wave back. The traveler passed them and disappeared up the road. The heat had seared the ground here black and hard. They could leave the road, if they wanted, and make almost as good time.

Patang and MacArthur had been walking for hours. They expected to walk for hours more. But then the road twisted and down at the bottom of the long decline, in the shadow of a basalt cliff, was an inn. Mostly their work kept them away from roads and inns. For almost a month they'd been living in their suits, sleeping in harness.

They looked warily at each other, mirrored visor to mirrored visor. Heat glimmered from the engines of their muscle suits. Without a word, they agreed to stop.

The inn radioed a fee schedule at their approach. They let their suits' autonomic functions negotiate for them, and carefully set the drilling rig down alongside the building.

"Put out the tarp," MacArthur said. "So it won't warp."

He went inside.

Patang deployed the gold foil tarp, then followed him in.

MacArthur was already out of his suit and seated at a cast-iron table with two cups of water in front of him when Patang cycled through the airlock. For an instant she dared hope everything was going to be all right.

Then he looked up at her.

"Ten dollars a cup." One cup was half empty. He drank the rest down in one long gulp, and closed a hairy paw around the second cup. His beard had grown since she had last seen it, and she could smell him from across the room. Presumably he could smell her too. "The bastards get you coming and going."

Patang climbed down out of her suit. She stretched out her arms as far as they would go, luxuriating in the room's openness. All that space! It was twenty feet across and windowless. There was the one table, and six iron chairs to go with it. Half a dozen cots folded up against the walls. A line of shelves offered Company goods that neither of them could afford. There were also a pay toilet and a pay shower. There was a free medical unit, but if you tried to con it out of something recreational, the Company found out and fined you accordingly.

Patang's skin prickled and itched from a month's accumulation of dried sweat. "I'm going to scratch," she said. "Don't look."

But of course MacArthur did, the pig.

Ignoring him, Patang slowly and sensuously scratched under her blouse and across her back. She took her time, digging in with her nails hard enough almost to make the skin bleed. It felt glorious.

MacArthur stared at her all the while, a starving wolf faced with a plump rabbit.

"You could have done that in your suit," he said when she was done.

"It's not the same."

"You didn't have to do that in front of—"

"*Hey!* How's about a little conversation?" Patang said loudly. So it cost a few bucks. So what?

With a click, the innkeeper came on. "Wasn't expecting any more visitors so close to the noon season," it said in a folksy synthetic voice. "What are you two prospecting for?"

"Gold, tin, lead, just about anything that'll gush up a test-hole." Patang closed her eyes, pretending she was back on Lakshmi Planum in a bar in Port Ishtar, talking with a real, live human being. "We figured most people will be working tracts in the morning and late afternoon. This way our databases are up-to-date— we won't be stepping on somebody's month-old claim."

"Very wise. The Company pays well for a strike."

"I hate those fucking things." MacArthur turned his back on the speaker and Patang both, noisily scraping his chair against the floor. She knew how badly he'd like to hurt her.

She knew that it wasn't going to happen.

The Company had three rules. The first was No Violence. The second was Protect Company Equipment. The third was Protect Yourself. They all three were enforced by neural implant.

From long experience with its prospectors, the Company had prioritized these rules, so that the first overruled the second, the second overruled the third, and the third could only be obeyed insofar as it didn't conflict with the first two. That was so a prospector couldn't decide—as had happened—that his survival depended on the death of his partner. Or, more subtly, that the other wasn't taking proper care of Company equipment, and should be eliminated.

It had taken time and experience, but the Company had finally come up with a foolproof set of algorithms. The outback was a functioning anarchy. Nobody could hurt anybody else there.

No matter how badly they needed to.

The 'plants had sounded like a good idea when Patang and MacArthur first went under contract. They'd signed up for a full sidereal day—two hundred fifty-five Earth days. Slightly longer than a Venusian year. Now, with fifty-nine days still to go, she was no longer certain that two people who hated each other as much as they did should be kept from each other's throats. Sooner or later, one of them would have to crack.

Every day she prayed that it would be MacArthur who finally yanked the escape cord, calling down upon himself the charges for a rescue ship to pull them out ahead of contract. MacArthur who went bust while she took her partial creds and skipped.

Every day he didn't. It was inhuman how much abuse he could absorb without giving in.

Only hatred could keep a man going like that.

Patang drank her water down slowly, with little slurps and sighs and lip-smackings. Knowing MacArthur loathed that, but unable to keep herself from doing it anyway.

She was almost done when he slammed his hands down on the tabletop, to either side of hers, and said, "Patang, there are some things I want to get straight between us."

"Please. Don't."

"Goddamnit, you know how I feel about that shit."

"I don't like it when you talk like that. Stop."

MacArthur ground his teeth. "No. We are going to have this out right here and now. I want you to—*what was that?*"

Patang stared blankly at her partner. Then she felt it—an uneasy vertiginous queasiness, a sense of imbalance just at the edge of perception, as if all of Venus were with infinitesimal gentleness shifting underfoot.

Then the planet roared and the floor came up to smash her in the face.

When Patang came to, everything was a jumble. The floor was canted. The shelves had collapsed, dumping silk shirts, lemon cookies, and bars of beauty soap everywhere. Their muscle suits had tumbled together, the metal arm of one caught between the legs of the other. The life support systems were still operational, thank God. The Company built them strong.

In the middle of it all, MacArthur stood motionless, grinning. A trickle of blood ran down his neck. He slowly rubbed the side of his face.

"MacArthur? Are you okay?"

A strange look was in his eyes. "By God," he said softly. "By damn."

"Innkeeper! What happened here?"

The device didn't respond. "I busted it up," MacArthur said. "It was easy."

"What?"

MacArthur walked clumsily across the floor toward her, like a sailor on an uncertain deck. "There was a cliff slump." He had a Ph.D. in extraterrestrial geology. He knew things like that. "A vein of soft basalt weakened and gave way. The inn caught a glancing blow. We're lucky to be alive."

He knelt beside her and made the OK sign with thumb and forefinger. Then he flicked the side of her nose with the forefinger.

"Ouch!" she said. Then, shocked, "Hey, you can't . . . !"

"Like hell I can't." He slapped her in the face. Hard. "Chip don't seem to work anymore."

Rage filled her. "You son of a bitch!" Patang drew back her arm to slug him. Blankness.

She came to seconds later. But it was like opening a book in the middle or stepping into an interactive an hour after it began. She had no idea what had happened or how it affected her.

MacArthur was strapping her into her muscle suit.

"Is everything okay?" she murmured. "Is something wrong?"

"I was going to kill you, Patang. But killing you isn't enough. You have to suffer first."

"What are you talking about?"

Then she remembered.

MacArthur had hit her. His chip had malfunctioned. There were no controls on him now. And he hated her. Bad enough to kill her? Oh, yes. Easily.

MacArthur snapped something off her helmet. Then he slapped the power button and the suit began to close around her. He chuckled and said, "I'll meet you outside."

Patang cycled out of the lock and then didn't know what to do. She fearfully went a distance up the road, and then hovered anxiously. She didn't exactly wait and she didn't exactly go away. She had to know what MacArthur was up to.

The lock opened, and MacArthur went around to the side of the tavern, where the drilling rig lay under its tarp. He bent down to separate the laser drill from the support struts, data boxes, and alignment devices. Then he delicately tugged the gold foil blanket back over the equipment.

He straightened, and turned toward Patang, the drill in his arms. He pointed it at her.

The words LASER HAZARD flashed on her visor.

She looked down and saw the rock at her feet blacken and smoke. "You know what would happen if I punched a hole in your shielding," MacArthur said.

She did. All the air in her suit would explode outward, while the enormous atmospheric pressure simultaneously imploded the metal casing inward. The mechanical cooling systems would fail instantly. She would be suffocated, broiled, and crushed, all in an instant.

"Turn around. Or I'll lase you a new asshole."

She obeyed.

"Here are the rules. You get a half-hour head start. Then I come for you. If you turn north or south, I'll drill you. Head west. Noonward."

"Noonward?" She booted up the geodetics. There was nothing in that direction but a couple more wrinkle ridges and, beyond them, tesserae. The tesserae were marked orange on her maps. Orange for unpromising. Prospectors had passed through them before and found nothing. "Why there?"

"Because I told you to. Because we're going to have a little fun. Because you have no choice. Understand?"

She nodded miserably.

"Go."

She walked, he followed. It was a nightmare that had somehow found its way into waking life. When Patang looked back, she could see MacArthur striding after her, small in the distance. But never small enough that she had any kind of chance to get away.

He saw her looking and stooped to pick up a boulder. He windmilled his arm and threw.

Even though MacArthur was halfway to the horizon, the boulder smashed to the ground a hundred yards ahead of her and to one side. It didn't come close to striking her, of course. That wasn't his intent.

The rock shattered when it hit. It was terrifying how strong that suit was. It filled her with rage to see MacArthur yielding all that power, and her completely helpless. "You goddamned sadist!"

No answer.

He was nuts. There *had* to be a clause in the contract covering that. Well, then . . . She set her suit on auto-walk, pulled up the indenture papers, and went looking for it. Options. Hold harmless clauses. Responsibilities of the Subcontractor—there were hundreds of those. Physical care of the Contractor's equipment.

And there it was. There it was! *In the event of medical emergency, as ultimately upheld in a court of physicians* . . . She scrolled up the submenu of qualifying conditions. The list of mental illnesses was long enough and inclusive enough that she was certain MacArthur belonged on it somewhere.

She'd lose all the equity she'd built up, of course. But, if she interpreted the contract correctly, she'd be entitled to a refund of her initial investment.

That, and her life, were good enough for her.

She slid an arm out of harness and reached up into a difficult-to-reach space behind her head. There was a safety there. She unlatched it. Then she called up a virtual keyboard, and typed out the SOS.

So simple. So easy.

DO YOU <u>REALLY</u> WANT TO SEND THIS MESSAGE? YES NO

She hit YES.

For an instant, nothing happened.

MESSAGE NOT SENT

"Shit!" She tried it again. MESSAGE NOT SENT A third time. MESSAGE NOT SENT A fourth. MESSAGE NOT SENT She ran a trouble-shooting program, and then sent the message again. MESSAGE NOT SENT

And again. And again. And again.

MESSAGE NOT SENT

MESSAGE NOT SENT

MESSAGE NOT SENT

Until the suspicion was so strong she *had* to check.

There was an inspection camera on the back of her suit's left hand. She held it up so she could examine the side of her helmet.

MacArthur had broken off the uplink antenna.

"You jerk!" She was really angry now. "You shithead! You cretin! You retard! You're nuts, you know that? Crazy. Totally whack."

No answer.

The bastard was ignoring her. He probably had his suit on auto-follow. He was probably leaning back in his harness, reading a book or watching an old movie on his visor. MacArthur did that a lot. You'd ask him a question and he wouldn't answer because he wasn't there; he was sitting front row center in the theater of his cerebellum. He probably had a tracking algorithm in the navigation system to warn him if she turned to the north or south, or started to get too far ahead of him.

Let's test that hypothesis.

She'd used the tracking algorithm often enough that she knew its specs by heart. One step sidewards in five would register immediately. One in six would not. All right, then . . . Let's see if we can get this rig turned around slowly, subtly, toward the road. She took seven strides forward, and then a half-step to the side.

LASER HAZARD

Patang hastily switched on auto-walk. So that settled that. He was watching her every step. A tracking algorithm would have written that off as a stumble. But then why didn't he speak? To make her suffer, obviously. He must be bubbling over with things to say. He must hate her almost as much as she did him.

"You son of a bitch! I'm going to *get* you, MacArthur! I'm going to turn the goddamned tables on you, and when I do—!"

It wasn't as if she were totally helpless. She had explosives. Hell, her muscle suit could throw a rock with enough energy to smash a hole right through his suit. She could—

Blankness.

She came to with the suit auto-walking down the far slope of the first wrinkle ridge. There was a buzzing in her ear. Somebody talking. MacArthur, over the short-range radio. "What?" she asked blurrily. "Were you saying something, MacArthur? I didn't quite catch that."

"You had a bad thought, didn't you?" MacArthur said gleefully. "Naughty girl! Papa spank."

LASER HAZARD

LASER HAZARD

Arrows pointed to either side. She'd been walking straight Noonward, and he'd fired on her anyway.

"Damn it, that's not <u>fair!</u>"

"Fair! Was it fair, the things you said to me? Talking. All the time talking."

"I didn't mean anything by it."

"You did! Those things . . . the things you said . . . unforgivable!"

"I was only deviling you, MacArthur," she said placatingly. It was a word from her childhood; it meant teasing, the kind of teasing a sister inflicted on a brother. "I wouldn't do it if we weren't friends."

MacArthur made a noise he might have thought was laughter. "Believe me, Patang, you and I are not friends."

The deviling had been innocent enough at the start. She'd only done it to pass the time. At what point had it passed over the edge? She hadn't always hated MacArthur. Back in Port Ishtar, he'd seemed like a pleasant companion. She'd even thought he was cute.

It hurt to think about Port Ishtar, but she couldn't help herself. It was like trying not to think about Heaven when you were roasting in Hell.

Okay, so Port Ishtar wasn't perfect. You ate flavored algae and you slept on a shelf. During the day you wore silk, because it was cheap, and you went everywhere barefoot because shoes cost money. But there were fountains that sprayed water into the air. There was live music in the restaurants, string quartets playing to the big winners, prospectors who had made a strike and were leaking wealth on the way out. If you weren't too obvious about it, you could stand nearby and listen. Gravity was light, then, and everybody was young, and the future was going to be full of money.

That was then. She was a million years older now.

LASER HAZARD

"Hey!"

"Keep walking, bitch. Keep walking or die."

This couldn't be happening.

Hours passed, and more hours, until she completely lost track of the time. They walked. Up out of the valley. Over the mountain. Down into the next valley. Because of the heat, and because the rocks were generally weak, the mountains all had gentle slopes. It was like walking up and then down a very long hill.

The land was grey and the clouds above it murky orange. These were Venus's true colors. She could have grass-green rocks and a bright blue sky if she wished— her visor would do that—but the one time she'd tried those settings, she'd quickly switched back. The falseness of it was enough to break your heart.

Better to see the bitter land and grim sky for what they were.

West, they traveled. Noonward. It was like an endless and meaningless dream.

"Hey, *Poon*tang."

"You know how I feel about that kind of language," she said wearily.

"How you feel. That's rich. How do you think I felt, some of the things you said?"

"We can make peace, MacArthur. It doesn't have to be like this."

"Ever been married, Poontang?"

"You know I haven't."

"I have. Married and divorced." She knew that already. There was very little they didn't know about each other by now. "Thing is, when a marriage breaks up, there's always one person comes to grips with it first. Goes through all the heartache and pain, feels the misery, mourns the death of the death of the relationship—and then moves on. The one who's been cheated on, usually. So the day comes when she walks out of the house and the poor schmuck is just standing there, saying, 'Wait. Can't we work this thing out?' He hasn't accepted that it's over."

"So?"

"So that's your problem, Poontang. You just haven't accepted that it's over yet."

"What? Our partnership, you mean?"

"No. Your life."

A day passed, maybe more. She slept. She awoke, still walking, with MacArthur's hateful mutter in her ear. There was no way to turn the radio off. It was Company policy. There were layers upon layers of systems and subsystems built into the walkers, all designed to protect Company investment. Sometimes his snoring would wake her up out of a sound sleep. She knew the ugly little grunt-ing noises he made when he jerked off. There were times she'd been so angry that she'd mimicked those sounds right back at him. She regretted that now.

"I had dreams," MacArthur said. "I had ambitions."

"I know you did. I did too."

"Why the hell did you have to come into my life? Why *me* and not somebody else?"

"I liked you. I thought you were funny."

"Well, the joke's on you now."

Back in Port Ishtar, MacArthur had been a lanky, clean-cut kind of guy. He was tall, and in motion you were always aware of his knees and elbows, always sure he was going to knock something over, though he never did. He had an odd, geeky kind of grace. When she'd diffidently asked him if he wanted to go part-ners, he'd picked her up and whirled her around in the air and kissed her right on the lips before setting her down again and saying, "Yes." She'd felt dizzy and happy then, and certain she'd made the right choice.

But MacArthur had been weak. The suit had broken him. All those months simmering in his own emotions, perfectly isolated and yet never alone . . . He didn't even *look* like the same person anymore. You looked at his face and all you saw were anger and those anguished eyes.

LEAVING HIGHLANDS
ENTERING TESSERAE

Patang remembered how magical the tesserae landscape had seemed in the beginning. "Complex ridged terrain," MacArthur called it, high ridges and deep groves crisscrossing each other in such profusion that the land appeared blocky from orbit, like a jumble of tiles. Crossing such terrain, you had to be constantly alert. Cliffs rose up unexpectedly, butte-high. You turned a twist in a zigzagging valley and the walls fell away and down, down, down. There was nothing remotely like it on Earth. The first time through, she'd shivered in wonder and awe.

Now she thought: Maybe I can use this. These canyons ran in and out of each other. Duck down one and run like hell. Find another and duck down it. Keep on repeating until he'd lost her.

"You honestly think you can lose me, Patang?"

She shrieked involuntarily.

"I can read your mind, Patang. I know you through and through."

It was true, and it was wrong. People weren't meant to know each other like this. It was the forced togetherness, the fact you were never for a moment alone with your own thoughts. After a while you'd heard every story your partner had to tell and shared every confidence there was to share. After a while every little thing got on your nerves.

"How about if I admit I was wrong?" she said pleadingly. "I was wrong. I admit it."

"We were both wrong. So what?"

"I'm willing to cooperate, MacArthur. Look. I've stopped so you can catch up and not have to worry about me getting away from you. Doesn't *that* convince you we're on the same side?"

LASER HAZARD

"Oh, feel free to run as fast and as far as you want, Patang. I'm confident I'll catch up with you in the end."

All right, then, she thought desperately. If that's the way you want it, asshole. Tag! You're it.

She ducked into the shadows of a canyon and ran.

The canyon twisted and, briefly, she was out of sight. MacArthur couldn't talk to her, couldn't hear her. Couldn't tell which way she went. The silence felt wonderful. It was the first privacy she'd had since she didn't know when. She only wished she could spare the attention to enjoy it more. But she had to think, and think hard. One canyon wall had slumped downward just ahead, creating a slope her walker could easily handle. Or she could keep on ahead, up the canyon.

Which way should she go?

Upslope.

She set the walker on auto-run.

Meanwhile, she studied the maps. The free satellite downloads were very good. They weren't good enough. They showed features down to three meters across, but she needed to know the land yard-by-yard. That crack–like little rille—did it split two kilometers ahead, or was there a second rille that didn't quite meet it? She couldn't tell. She'd've gladly paid for the premium service now, the caviar of info-feed detailed enough to track footprints across a dusty stretch of terrain. But with her uplink disabled, she couldn't.

Patang ducked into a rille so narrow her muscle suit's programming would have let her jump it, if she wished. It forked, and she took the right-hand branch. When the walls started closing in on them, she climbed up and out. Then she ran, looking for another rille.

Hours passed.

After a time, all that kept her going was fear. She drew her legs up into the torso of her suit and set it to auto-run. Up this canyon. Over this ridge. Twisting, turning. Scanning the land ahead, looking for options. Two directions she might go. Flip a mental coin. Choose one. Repeat the process. Keep the radio shut down so MacArthur couldn't use it to track her. Keep moving.

Keep moving.

Keep moving . . .

Was it hours that passed, or days? Patang didn't know. It might have been weeks. In times of crisis, the suit was programmed to keep her alert by artificial stimulation of her brain. It was like an electrical version of amphetamines. But, as with amphetamines, you tended to lose track of things. Things like your sense of time.

So she had no idea how long it took her to realize that it was all no use.

The problem was that the suit was so damned *heavy!* If she ran fast enough to keep her distance from MacArthur, it left a trace in the regolith obvious enough to be followed at top speed. But if she slowed down enough to place her walker's feet on bare stone when she could, and leave subtle and easy-to-miss footprints when she couldn't, he came right up behind her. And try though she might, she couldn't get far enough ahead of him to dare slow down enough to leave a trace he couldn't follow.

There was no way she could escape him.

The feeling of futility that came over her then was drab and familiar, like a shabby old coat grown colorless with age that you don't have the money to replace. Sometime, long ago, she'd crossed that line where hope ceased. She had never actually admitted to herself that she no longer believed they'd ever make that big strike—just one day woken up knowing that she was simply waiting out her contract, stubbornly trying to endure long enough to serve out her term and return to Earth no poorer than she had set out.

Which was when her deviling had turned nasty, wasn't it? It was when she had started touching herself and telling MacArthur exactly what she was doing. When she'd started describing in detail all the things she'd never do to *him*.

It was a way of getting through one more day. It was a way of faking up enough emotion to care. It was a stupid, stupid thing to do.

And this was her punishment.

But she couldn't give up. She was going to have to . . . She didn't finish that thought. If she was going to do this unnamed thing, she had to sort through the ground rules first.

The three rules were: No Violence. Protect Company Equipment. Protect Yourself. They were ranked hierarchically.

Okay, Patang thought. In order to prevent violence, I'm going to have to destroy Company property.

She waited to see if she'd pass out.

Nothing happened.

Good.

She'd come to a long ridge, steep-sided and barren and set her suit to auto-climb. As she climbed, she scanned the slope ahead, empty and rock-strewn under a permanently dazzling cover of sulfuric acid clouds. Halfway up, MacArthur emerged from the zigzagging valley below and waved jauntily.

Patang ignored him. That pile of boulders up ahead was too large. Those to the right were too small. There was a patch of loose regolith that looked promising but . . . No. In the end, she veered leftward, toward a shallow ledge that sheltered rocks that looked loose enough to be dislodged but not massive enough to do any serious damage to MacArthur's suit. All she wanted was to sweep him off his feet. He could survive a slide downslope easily enough. But could he hold onto the laser drill while doing so?

Patang didn't think so.

Okay, then. She took her suit off automatics and climbed clumsily, carefully, toward her destination. She kept her helmet up, pointed toward the top of the ridge, to avoid tipping MacArthur off to her intentions.

Slantwise across the slope, that's right. Now straight up. She glanced back and saw that she'd pulled MacArthur into her wake. He was directly beneath her. Good. All systems go.

She was up to the ledge now.

Stop. Turn around. Look down on MacArthur, surprisingly close.

If there was one thing Patang knew, after all these months, it was how easy it was to start a landslide. Lean back and brace yourself here, and start kicking. And over the rocks go and over the rocks go and—

LASER HAZARD

"Ohhhh, Patang, you are so obvious. You climb diagonally up a slope that any ordinary person would tackle straight on. You change direction halfway up. What were you planning to do, start an avalanche? What did you think that would accomplish?"

"I thought I could get the laser away from you."

"And what good would that do? I'd still have the suit. I'd still have rocks. I'd still have you at my mercy. You hadn't really thought this one through, had you?"

"No," she admitted.

"You tried to outwit me, but you didn't have the ingenuity. Isn't that right?"

"Yes."

"You were just hoping. But there isn't any hope, is there?"

"No."

He flipped one hand dismissively. "Well, keep on going. We're not done yet."

Weeping, Patang topped the ridge and started downward, into a valley shaped like a deep bowl. Glassy scarps on all sides caught whatever infrared bounced off the floor and threw it back into the valley. The temperature readings on her visor leaped. It was at least fifty degrees hotter out there than anyplace she had ever been. Hot enough that prolonged exposure would incapacitate her suit? Maybe. But there was MacArthur behind her, and the only way forward was a shallow trough leading straight down. She had no alternative.

Midway down the slope, the trough deepened. Rock walls rose up to plunge Patang into shadow. Her suit's external temperature went down, though not as much as she would've liked. Then the way grew less steep and then it flattened out. The trough ended as a bright doorway between jagged rocks.

She stepped out into the open and looked across the valley.

The ground *dazzled*.

She walked out into it. She felt weightless. Her feet floated up beneath her and her hands rose of their own accord into the air. The muscle suit's arms rose too, like a ballerina's.

A network of cracks crazed the floor of the valley, each one blazing bright as the sun. Liquid metal was just oozing up out of the ground. She'd never seen anything like it.

Patang stomped on a puddle of metal, shattering it into droplets of sunlight and setting off warning alarms in her suit. For an instant she swayed with sleepiness. But she shook it off. She snapped a stick-probe from her tool rack and jabbed it into the stuff. It measured the metal's temperature and its resistance to pressure, ran a few baby calculations, and spat out a result.

Tin.

She looked up again. There were intersecting lines of molten tin everywhere. The pattern reminded her of her childhood on the Eastern Shore, of standing at the edge of a marsh, binoculars in hand, hoping for a harrier, with the silver gleam of sun on water almost painful to the eye. This looked just like a marsh, only with tin instead of water.

A tin marsh.

For an instant, wonder flickered to life within her. How could such a thing be? What complex set of geological conditions was responsible? All she could figure was that the noontide heat was involved. As it slowly sank into the rock, the tin below expanded and pushed its way up through the cracks. Or maybe it was the rocks that expanded, squeezing out the liquid tin. In either case the effect would be very small for any given volume. She couldn't imagine how much tin there must be down there for it to be forced to the surface like this. More than she'd ever dreamed they'd find.

"We're *rich!*" she whooped. She couldn't help it. All those months, all that misery, and here it was. The payoff they'd set out to discover, the one that she'd long ago given up all hope of finding.

LASER HAZARD

LASER HAZARD

LASER HAZARD

"No! Wait! Stop!" she cried. "You don't need to do this anymore. We found it! It's here!"

Turning, she saw McArthur's big suit lumber out of shadow. It was brute strength personified, all body and no head. "What are you talking about?" he said angrily. But Patang dared think he sounded almost sane. She dared hope she could reason with him.

"It's the big one, Mac!" She hadn't called him Mac in ages. "We've got the goddamned mother lode here. All you have to do is radio in the claim. It's all over, Mac! This time tomorrow, you're going to be holding a press conference about it."

For a moment MacArthur stood silent and irresolute. Then he said, "Maybe so. But I have to kill you first."

"You turn up without me, the Company's gonna have questions. They're gonna interrogate their suit. They're gonna run a mind-probe. No, MacArthur, you can't have both. You've got to choose: money or me."

LASER HAZARD

"*Run,* you bitch!" MacArthur howled. "Run like you've got a chance to live!"

She didn't move. "Think of it, MacArthur. A nice cold bath. They chill down the water with slabs of ice, and for a little extra they'll leave the ice in. You can hear it clink."

"Shut up."

"And ice cream!" she said fervently. "A thousand different flavors of ice cream. They've got it warehoused: sherbet, gellato, water ice . . . Oh, they know what a prospector likes, all right. Beer in big, frosty mugs. Vodka so cold it's almost a slurry."

"Shut the fuck *up!*"

"You've been straight with me. You gave me a half-hour head start, just like you promised, right? Not everybody would've done that. Now I'm gonna be straight with you. I'm going to lock my suit down." She powered off the arms and legs. It would take a good minute to get them online again. "So you don't have to worry about me getting away. I'm going to just stand here, motionless and helpless, while you think about it, all right?" Then, desperation forcing her all the way into honesty, "I was wrong, MacArthur. I mean it this time. I shouldn't have done those things. Accept my apology. You can rise above it. You're a rich man now."

MacArthur roared with rage.

LASER HAZARD

LASER HAZARD

LASER HAZARD

LASER HAZARD

"Walk, damn you!" he screamed. "*Walk!*"

LASER HAZARD

LASER HAZARD

LASER HAZARD

He wasn't coming any closer. And though he kept on firing, over and over, the bolts of lased light never hit her. It was baffling. She'd given up, she wasn't running, it wasn't even possible for her to run. So why didn't he just kill her? What was stopping him?

Revelation flooded Patang then, like sudden sunlight after a long winter. So simple! So obvious! She couldn't help laughing. "You *can't* shoot me!" she cried. "The suit won't *let* you!"

It was what the tech guys called "fossil software." Before the Company acquired the ability to insert their programs into human beings, they'd programmed their tools so they couldn't be used for sabotage. People, being inventive buggers, had found ways around that programming often enough to render it obsolete. But nobody had ever bothered to dig it out of the deep levels of the machinery's code. What would be the point?

She whooped and screamed. Her suit staggered in a jittery little dance of joy. "You can't kill me, MacArthur! You can't! You can't and you know it! I can just walk right past you, and all the way to the next station, and there's nothing you can do about it."

MacArthur began to cry.

The hopper came roaring down out of the white dazzle of the sky to burn a landing practically at their feet. They clambered wearily forward and let the pilot bolt their muscle suits to the hopper's strutwork. There wasn't cabin space for them and they didn't need it.

The pilot reclaimed his seat. After his first attempts at conversation had fallen flat, he'd said no more. He had hauled out prospectors before. He knew that small talk was useless.

With a crush of acceleration their suits could only partially cushion, the hopper took off. Only three hours to Port Ishtar. The hopper twisted and Patang could see Venus rushing dizzyingly by below her. She blanked out her visor so she didn't have to look at it.

Patang tested her suit. The multiplier motors had been powered down. She was immobile.

"Hey, Patang."

"Yeah?"

"You think I'm going to go to jail? For all the shit I did to you?"

"No, MacArthur. Rich people don't go to jail. They get therapy."

"That's good," he said. "Thank you for telling me that."

"*De nada,*" she said without thinking. The jets rumbled under her back, making the suit vibrate. Two, three hours from now, they'd come down in Port Ishtar, stake their claims, collect their money, and never see each other again.

On impulse, she said, "Hey, MacArthur!"

"What?"

And for an instant she came *that close* to playing the Game one last time. Deviling him, just to hear his teeth grind. But . . .

"Nothing. Just—enjoy being rich, okay? I hope you have a good life."

"Yeah." MacArthur took a deep breath, and then let it go, as if he were releasing something painful, and said, "Yeah . . . you too."

And they soared.

good mountain

ROBERT REED

Robert Reed sold his first story in 1986 and quickly established himself as one of the most prolific of today's writers, particularly at short fiction lengths, and has managed to keep up a very high standard of quality while being prolific, something that is not at all easy to do. Reed stories count as among some of the best short work produced by anyone in the last few decades; many of his best stories have been assembled in the collections The Dragons of Springplace *and* The Cuckoo's Boys. *He won the Hugo Award in 2007 for his novella "A Billion Eves." Nor is he non-prolific as a novelist, having turned out eleven novels since the end of the eighties, including* The Lee Shore, The Hormone Jungle, Black Milk, The Remarkables, Down the Bright Way, Beyond the Veil of Stars, An Exaltation of Larks, Beneath the Gated Sky, Marrow, Sister Alice, *and* The Well of Stars, *as well as two chapbook novellas,* Mere *and* Flavors of My Genius. *Among his recent books are a chapbook novella,* Eater-of-Bone, *a novel,* The Memory of Sky, *and a collection,* The Greatship. *Reed lives with his family in Lincoln, Nebraska.*

Reed has visited the far future in his Sister Alice stories and in his sequence of stories about the Great Ship, as well as in stories such as "Whiptail" and "Marrow," but here he takes us deeper into the future than he ever has before, to a world whose origin is lost in the labyrinth of time, a world where, as a group of randomly thrown-together travelers is about to learn, everything is about to change—and not for the better.

A DOT ON OLD PAPER

"World's Edge. Approaching now . . . World's Edge!"

The worm's caretaker was an elderly fellow named Brace. Standing in the middle of the long intestinal tract, he wore a dark gray uniform, patched but scrupulously clean, soft-soled boots and a breathing mask that rode on his hip. Strong hands held an angelwood bucket filled with a thick, sour-smelling white salve. His name was embossed above his shirt pocket, preceded by his rank, which was Master. Calling out with a deep voice, Master Brace explained to the several dozen passengers, "From this station, you may find your connecting trails to Hammer and Mister Low and Green Island. If World's Edge happens to be your destination, good luck to you, and please, collect your belongings before following the signs to the security checkpoints. And if you intend to stay with this splendid worm, that means Left-of-Left will be our next stop. And Port of Krauss will be our last." The caretaker had a convincing smile and a calm, steady manner. In his presence, the innocent observer might believe that nothing was seriously wrong in the world.

"But if you do plan to stay with me," Brace continued, "you will still disembark at World's Edge, if only for the time being. My baby needs her rest and a good dinner, and she's got a few little sores that want cleaning." Then he winked at the passengers and began to walk again, totting his heavy bucket toward the stomach—up where the mockmen were quartered. "Or perhaps we'll linger here for two little whiles," the old man joked. "But I don't expect significant delays, and you shouldn't let yourselves worry."

Jopale sighed and sat back against the warm pink wall. He wasn't worried. Not through any innate bravery, but because he had been scared for so long now, there was little room left for new concerns. Or so it seemed at that particular moment. Indeed, since his last long sleep, Jopale had enjoyed a renewed sense of confidence. A guarded optimism was taking root. Calculating how far he had come, he saw that most of the world lay behind him now, while it wasn't too much of a lie to tell himself that Port of Krauss was waiting just beyond the horizon.

Jopale even managed his own convincing smile, and watching his fellow passengers, he found one other face that appeared equally optimistic.

A young woman, built small and just a little short of pretty, was sitting directly across from him. She must have come onboard during his last sleep. Maybe at Which-Way, he reasoned. There was a fine university in that ancient city. Perhaps she was a student heading home, now that every school was officially closed. Her bags were few and small. A heavy book filled her tiny lap. Her breathing mask looked as if it had never been used, while a powerful torch rode on her other hip. Her clothes were comfortable if somewhat heavy—wool dyed green with thick leather pads on the knees and elbows. Bare black toes wiggled against a traveling blanket. Her leather boots had tough rubber soles, which was why she didn't wear them inside the worm. She looked ready for a long journey into cold darkness. But where could a young woman be going, and smiling about her prospects too?

There was one logical conclusion: Jopale caught the woman's gaze, nodded and offered a friendly wink. "Are you like me, miss?" he inquired. "Are you traveling to Port of Krauss?"

She hesitated, glancing at the other passengers. Then she shook her head. "I'm not, no," she told him.

Jopale thought he understood.

"But you're traveling through Krauss," he persisted. "On your way to some other destination, perhaps?"

He was thinking about the New Isles.

But she shook her head, a little embarrassed perhaps, but also taking some pleasure from his confusion.

No one else was speaking just then, and the intestine of a worm was a very quiet place. It was easy to eavesdrop and to be heard whenever you spoke. In quick succession, three young men offered possible destinations, picking little cities set on the auxiliary trails—each man plainly wishing that this woman's destination was his own.

"No," she told them. "No. And I'm sorry, but no."

Other passengers began to play the silly game, and to her credit, the woman remained cheerful and patient, responding immediately to each erroneous guess. Then the great worm began to shake around them, its muscular body twisting as it pulled off onto one of the side trails. Suddenly there was good reason to hurry the game along. The young men were leaving here; didn't they deserve a useful hint or two?

"All right," she said reasonably. "I'll remain on this trail until I'm done." Then she closed her book with a heavy thump, grinning as she imagined her final destination.

"Left-of-Left?" somebody shouted.

"We've already guessed that," another passenger complained.

"Where else is there?"

"Does anybody have a map?"

Jopale stood up. When their worm was young and quite small, holes had been cut through its fleshy sides, avoiding the major muscle groups. Each hole was fitted with progressively larger rubber plugs, and finally a small plastic window that looked as if it was carved from a cold fog. Through one of those windows, Jopale could see the tall buildings of the city and their long shadows, plus the high clear sky that was as close to night as anything he had ever known. What a journey this had been, and it wasn't even finished yet. Not for the first time, Jopale wished he had kept a journal. Then when there was time—once he was living on the New Isles, perhaps—he would write a thorough account of every awful thing that had happened, as well as his final triumphs.

A dozen travelers were now examining their maps, calling out the names of tiny places and abandoned cities. There was a time when people lived in the Tanglelands and points beyond, but that had been years ago. Only the oldest maps bothered to show those one-time destinations. A young man, very tall and shockingly thin, was standing close to the woman—too close, in Jopale's mind—and he carefully listed a string of places that existed nowhere but on a sheet of yellowed paper and faded ink that he held up the window's light.

"Yes," said the woman, just once.

But the tall man didn't notice. He kept reading off names, pushing his finger along the black worm trail, and the woman was saying, "No, no, no," again, smiling pleasantly at his foolishness.

But Jopale had noticed.

"Go back," he said.

The tall man looked at him, bothered by the interruption.

Then a stocky old woman reached up high, hitting the fellow between the shoulder blades. "The girl said, 'Yes'. Didn't you hear?"

Another woman said, "Read backwards."

The tall man was too flustered to do anything now.

So Jopale took the map for himself, and in the dim light, he made his best guess. "What about Good Mountain?"

Once more, the girl said, "Yes."

"What kind of name is that?" the tall man asked, reclaiming his map, taking the trouble to fold it up neatly. "What does that word mean? 'Mountain'? I've never heard it before."

But the game was finished. Suddenly the old caretaker had returned, carrying an empty bucket with one bony hand. "This is the station at World's Edge," Master Brace called out.

The worm had come to a stop.

"My baby needs to breathe and to eat her fill," he reminded everyone. "So please, you must disembark. With your luggage, and with your tickets." Then a look of mischief came into the weathered face, and he added, "But if you will, please leave your hopes behind. I'd like to claim a few of them for myself."

A few passengers laughed at his bleak humor. But most just shook their heads and growled to themselves, or they quietly spat on the smooth pink floor.

The young woman was picking up her book and bags and her heavy boots, a joyous smile setting her apart from everyone else.

About her destination—the enigmatic Good Mountain—she said nothing at all.

A MOUTHFUL OF HISTORY

Every homeland was once new land, small and thin, pushed about by the willful winds. But the ground where Jopale grew up was still relatively young, and for much of its life, it had been a free-drifting body.

Jopale felt an easy pride toward his native wood—dense and fine-grained and very dark, almost black in its deep reaches, with a thick cuticle and the pleasant odor of sin-spice when sliced apart with steel saws. The wood's appearance and its telltale genetics made it the offspring of Graytell and Sweetsap lineages. According to the oldest nautical maps, an island matching that description first collided with the Continent near what was today Port of Krauss. But it didn't linger for long. In those ancient times, the Continent turned like a gigantic if extraordinarily slow wheel, deep-water roots helping to hold its green face under the eternal sunshine. This tiny unnamed body clung to the wheel's outer edge until it passed into the polar waters, and then it vanished from every record, probably drifting off into the cold gloom.

Unable to grow, the island shrank. Hungry, it drank dry its sap reservoirs. It could have brushed up against the Continent again, perhaps several more times, but some current or chance storm always pushed it away again. Then it wandered, lost on the dark face of the world. The evidence remained today inside its body. Its oldest wood was full of scars and purple-black knots—a catalog of relentless abuse brought on by miserly times. Not even a flicker of sunlight fell on its bleached surface. Starving, the island digested its deep-water roots and every vein of starch. Saprophytes thrived on its surface and giant worms gnawed their way through its depths. But each of those enemies was a blessing too. The tallest branches of the saprophytes caught the occasional breeze, helping the increasingly frail island drift across the quiet water. And the worms ate so much of the island that it floated easily, buoyed up by the air-filled caverns.

Finally the near-corpse was pushed into the storm belt, and the storms blew just so, carrying it out under the motionless sun. There the island turned a dark vibrant green again, dropping new roots that pulled minerals out of the nearly bottomless ocean—roots that flexed and rippled to help hold the island in the bright sunshine. And that's when new wood was built, and rivers of sugary sap, and a multitude of colonists began to find their way to its shores, including Jopale's distant ancestors.

Twelve hundred years ago, the island again collided with the Continent. But this time it struck the eastern shore, as far from Port of Krauss as possible. Its leeward edge pushed into the Plain of Perfect Deeds while another free-drifting island barged in behind, pinning it in place. Two more islands arrived over the next several years. Small bodies like those often splintered between shifting masses, or they were tilted up on end, shattering when their wood couldn't absorb the strain. Or sometimes they were shoved beneath the ancient Continent, rotting to form black muck and anaerobic gases. But Jopale's homeland proved both durable and extremely fortunate. Its wood was twisted into a series of fantastic ridges and deep valleys, but it outlasted each of the islands that came after it, its body finding a permanent nook where it could sit inside the world's Great Mother.

By the time Jopale was born, his land was far from open water. The sun wobbled in the sky but never climbed too high overhead or dropped near any horizon. By then, more islands and two lesser continents had coalesced with the Continent, and the once-elegant wheel had become an ungainly oval. Most of the world's dayside face was covered with a single unbroken lid too cumbersome to be turned. Competing wood had pushed the weakest lands deep beneath the Ocean, and like the keel of a great boat, those corpses held the Continent in one stubborn alignment, only the strongest currents and the most persistent winds able to force the oval toward the east or the west.

When Jopale was a young boy, disaster struck. The trade winds strengthened abruptly, and in a single year the Continent drifted west almost one thousand kilometers. Cities and entire homelands were plunged into darkness. Millions of free citizens saw their crops die and their homelands starve. The only rational response was to move away, living as immigrants on other lands, or as refugees, or in a few cases—like Port of Krauss—remaining where they were, in the darkness, making the very best of the tragedy.

To a young boy, the disaster seemed like enormous good fun. There was excitement in the air, a delicious sense of danger walking on the world. Strange new children arrived with their peculiar families, living in tiny homes given to them by charities and charitable guilds. Jopale got to know a few of those people, at least well enough to hear their stories about endless night and the flickering of nameless stars. But he still couldn't appreciate the fact that his own life was precarious now. Jopale was a bright child, but conventional. And he had a conventional family who promised him that the trade winds would soon weaken and the Continent would push its way back to its natural location. What was dead now would live again, those trusted voices argued. The dark lands would grow again. And because he was young and naturally optimistic, Jopale convinced himself that he would live to enjoy that glorious rebirth.

But the boy grew into a rather less optimistic young man, and the young man became a respectable and ordinary teacher of literature. During the average cycle, between one quiet sleep and the next, Jopale wouldn't once imagine that anything important about his world could ever change.

He was in his house, sleeping unaware, when a moderate quake split the land beneath him.

Early-warning sensors recorded the event, and Jopale happened to read about the quake in the morning newsbook. But no expert mentioned any special danger. The Continent was always shifting and cracking. Drowned islands would shatter, and bubbles of compressed gas were constantly pushing toward the surface. There was no compelling reason for worry, and so he ate his normal first-meal and rode his two-wheel over the ridge to work—a small landowners' school set on softer, paler ground just beyond his homeland—and there he taught the classics to his indifferent students, sat through a long department meeting, and then returned home again. Alone in his quiet house, he ate his last-meal and read until drowsy, and then he slipped his sleep-hood over his head and curling up in bed.

His house was small and relatively new, set in a corner of his parent's original farm. Jopale's property was part of a long prosperous valley. But since he was no farmer, he rented most of the ground to neighbors who raised crops and kept four-foots—milking varieties that were made into stew meat and bone meal once they grew old. The neighbors also kept scramblers for their sweet meat, and they used teams of mockmen to work the land and its animals, lending every waking moment a busy, industrious quality.

Jopale rose with the next cycle and went to work, as he did with the cycle after that, and the cycles that followed.

His homeland was blackish-green beneath its transparent cuticle of hard wax. The rough walls of the valley were covered with parasites and epiphytes that sprang from crevices and wormholes. There were even a few wild animals, though not as many as when he was a boy. With each passing year, people were more common, the forests more carefully tended, and like every inhabited part in the world, his home was becoming domesticated, efficient and ordinary.

For twenty cycles, Jopale went about his life without worry, unaware that the first quake was followed by a series of little events—rumbles and slow, undetectable shifts that let gas and black seawater intrude into the gap between his one-time island and the buried coastline. Nobody knew the danger; there was nobody to blame afterwards. Indeed, only a few dozen people were killed in the incident, which meant that it was barely noticed beyond Jopale's horizon.

He woke early that last morning and slipped quietly from his house. A neighbor woman was still sleeping in his bed. She had arrived at his doorstep at the end of the last cycle, a little drunk and in the mood for sex. Jopale enjoyed her companionship, on occasion, but he felt no obligation to be with her when she woke. That's why he dressed in a hurry and rode off to school. Nobody knew that the seawater and its poisons had traveled so close to the surface. But in the time it takes a lover's heart to beat twice, the pressurized water found itself inside a sap well, nothing above but an open shaft and the sky.

The resulting geyser was a spectacle; every survivor said so. Presumably the doomed were even more impressed, watching the tower of saltwater and foam soar high overhead, dislodged chunks of wood falling around them, and an endless thunder shaking the world as huge quantities of gas—methane laced with hydrogen sulfide—bubbled free.

Suffocation was the standard death, for people and everything else.

The entire valley was killed within minutes. But the high ridges trapped the poisons, keeping the carnage contained. Even before Jopale heard the news, the disaster was finished. By the time he rode home again, crews of mockmen dressed in diving suits had capped the geyser. Engineers were busy drawing up plans for permanent repairs. And it was safe enough that a grieving survivor could walk to the ridge above, holding a perfumed rag against his face as he stared down at the fate of the world.

Water covered the valley floor—a stagnant gray lake already growing warm in the brilliant sunlight. The forested slopes had either drowned or been bleached by the suffocating gases. From his vantage point, Jopale couldn't see his house. But the land beneath the sea was still alive—still a vibrant blackish-green. Pumps would have to be set up, and osmotic filters, and then everything else could be saved. But if the work happened too slowly, too much salt would seep through the cuticle, causing the land to sicken and die. Then the valley would become a single enormous sore, attacked by fungi and giant worms. If nature was allowed its freedom, this tiny portion of the Continent would rot through, and the sea would come up again, spreading along the ancient fault lines, untold volumes of gas bubbling up into the rapidly sickening air.

People had to save the valley.

Why shouldn't they? A rational part of Jopale knew what was at stake—what almost every long-term prediction said was inevitable. But he couldn't shake his selfish need to enjoy the next cycle and the rest of his life. This ground had always been a part of him. Why wouldn't he want it saved? Let other people lose their little places. Let the Continent die everywhere but here. That's what he told himself as he walked down the path, the perfumed rag pressed against his nose and mouth, a self-possessed optimism flourishing for those next few steps.

Where the gases hadn't reached, epiphytes still flourished. Each tree stood apart from its neighbors, like the hair on the head of an elderly mockman. That made for a tall open forest, which in turn allowed the land to receive its share of sunlight. A flock of day-yabbers watched him from the high branches, leathery wings folded close, bright blue eyes alarmed by nothing except his presence. Giant forest roaches danced from crevice to crevice. Wild scramblers hid in nests of hair and woven branches, calling out at him with soft mournful voices. Then the path bent and dropped, and everything changed. More yabbers lay dead beneath their perches, and countless silverfish and juvenile worms had crawled up out of their holes before dying. A giant golden gyretree—one of Jopale's favorite specimens— was already turning black at its base. But the air was breathable again, the wind having blown away the highest poisons. Jopale wished he had his breathing mask, but he had left it inside his house, floating in a cupboard somewhere close to his dead lover. That woman had always been good company. But in death, she had grown unreal, abstract and distant. Walking around a next turn in the trail, Jopale found himself imagining her funeral and what delicate role he might play. And that was when he saw the wild scramblers that had fled the rising gas, but not fast enough. They belonged to one of the ground-dwelling species; he wasn't sure which. They had short hairy bodies and long limbs and little hands that reached out for nothing. Crests of bright blue fur topped the otherwise naked faces. The gases had stolen away their oxygen, then their lives. Already they were beginning to swell and turn black, lending them a strange, unfamiliar appearance; and when Jopale looked into their miserable little faces, he felt a sharp, unbearable fear.

In death more than life, those scramblers resembled human beings.

Here was the moment when everything changed for this scholarly gentleman— this creature of tradition and habit, of optimism and indifference. Gazing into those smoky green eyes and the wide mouths choked by their fat purple tongues, he saw his own future. That he didn't love the dead woman was important: If they were married and had children, and if his family had died today, Jopale would have felt an unrelenting attachment to this tiny corner of the world. In their honor, he would have ignored the urge to run away, remaining even as the land splintered and bled poisons and turned to dust and dead water.

But escape was what he wanted. The urge was sudden and irresistible. And later, when he examined what was possible, Jopale discovered only one solution that gave him any confidence.

If he sold his parent's land to his surviving neighbors and relatives, and if he bled his savings blue . . . then he could abandon the only home he had ever known, and forsake the sun, as well as abandoning all of those foolish little scramblers who couldn't see past their next little while . . .

WORLD'S EDGE

The great worm had come to a stop, but its muscles continued to shiver, long ripples traveling the length of the body, its misery made all the more obvious by a deep low moan that Jopale didn't hear so much as he felt it in his bones.

World's Edge: In some past eon, the city stood on the Continent's shoreline, nothing beyond but darkening skies and bottomless water. For generations, this great port had served as a home for fishermen, and more importantly, for the brave souls who journeyed onto the trackless sea hunting giant rust-fins and the copper eels and vicious many-mouths. Fortunes were made from every carcass brought home—great masses of inedible meat and iron-rich bone pushed into furnaces and burned away, leaving nothing behind but a few dozen kilos of precious metal. But new islands were always being born, oftentimes half a world away, and they grew as they wandered, eventually slamming into this coastline and sticking fast. Removed from its livelihood, the once great city fell into hard times. Most of the neighboring towns vanished completely. But World's Edge managed to survive, clinging to its outmoded name, and when times and the world's growing population demanded it, the city blossomed again, new industries and a relentless sense of commerce producing a metropolis where two million people could live out their busy, unexceptional lives.

Birth and growth, followed by death and rebirth—no story told by Man was as important as this.

Then the Continent suddenly drifted west, and again, World's Edge wore the perfect name.

Jopale considered the ironies as he carried his bags to the front of the intestine, then out through an artificial sphincter fitted into the worm's side. From there, it was a short climb to the station's high wooden platform. A bright sign flashed from the top of the greeting arch, displaying the present atmospheric readings, following by the cheery promise, "No hazards, none foreseen." The sun hovered just above the eastern horizon, stratospheric clouds and low pollution obscuring only a portion of its fierce glare. Squinting, Jopale faced the sun. At least two large balloons were visible in the sky, suspended on long ropes, spotters busily watching the land for geysers or more subtle ruptures. Behind him, long shadows stretched toward lands rendered unfit for normal life. Not that nothing and no one could live out there . . . but still, Jopale felt as if he was standing on the brink of a profound desolation, and that image struck him in some innate, profoundly emotional fashion . . .

The caretakers walked on top of their friend and along the concave, heavily greased trail, examining the worm's gray skin and poking its long tired muscles, sometimes using electric wands but mostly employing nothing but their bare hands. The worm's reflexes were slow. The old caretaker said as much to the younger workers. "She's gone too far with too many in her empty bellies," Master Brace complained, gesturing at the milling passengers. "She needs half a cycle at least, and all she can eat."

Jopale realized their delay would be longer than he had anticipated. Pulling two tickets from his traveler's belt, he carefully read the deeply legal language. If he didn't reach Port of Krauss within another fifteen cycles, the worm's owners would refund half of the value of the first ticket. But that was an inconsequential gesture, all things considered. Because the second ticket promised him a small cabin onboard a methane-fueled ship that would leave for the New Isles two cycles later. Punctuality was his responsibility. If he was late, the ticket was worthless. And Jopale would be trapped in the Port with every other refugee, shepherding the last of his money while absorbing news from around the world, hoping that the coming nightmare would take its time and he could eventually purchase a new berth on some later, unpromised vessel.

What good would fear do him now? Or rage?

"No good at all," he said with a stiff voice, turning his back to the sun.

The station was a strangely quiet place. The only other worms were small or plainly ill, and even those specimens were pointed west, aimed at the darkness, as if waiting for the order to flee. Besides caretakers, the only human workers were soldiers. Older men, mostly. Disciplined and probably without families—exactly the sort of people to be trusted in the worst of times. Two soldiers stood farther up the worm, guarding the sphincter leading into the stomach. Mockmen waited in the darkness. Each creature had its owner's name tattooed on its forearms and back. Humans had to come forward to claim what was theirs, and even then, the soldiers questioned them with suspicious voices—as if somebody might try to steal one of these creatures now.

The mysterious young woman was standing with the other passengers, her book in one arm, eyes pointed in the general direction of the unloading.

"Which is yours?" Jopale asked.

She didn't seem to hear the question. Then he realized that her gaze reached past the mockmen, bright tan eyes staring at the night lands, her mind probably traveling on to her destination.

"Good Mountain, is it?" Jopale asked.

"I'm sorry, no." She was answering his first question, smiling in his general direction. "I don't own any of these creatures."

Jopale had brought a mockman from home, to help with his bags and his life, as well as giving him this ready excuse to stand where he was, chatting with this young woman.

With a quiet, gentlemanly voice, he offered his name.

She nodded and said, "Yes. Good Mountain."

They had found a pattern. He would ask some little question, and she would answer his former question.

"The word 'mountain'," he said. "Do you know what it means?"

She smiled now, glancing at his face. "Do you?"

He allowed himself the pleasure of a wise nod. "It is an ancient word," he answered. "The oldest texts employ it. But even by then, the word had fallen into a rotten disuse."

"Really?"

"We have words for ridges and hills. With great clarity, we can describe the color and quality of any ground. But from what we can determine, using our oldest sources, 'mountain' implies a titanic uplifting of something much harder than any wood. Harder and more durable, and a true mountain rises high enough to puncture the sky. At least according to some expert interpretations."

She laughed, very softly. "I know."

"Do you?"

"That's why they picked the name," she explained.

Jopale didn't understand, and his expression must have said as much.

"Of course, there's no actual mountain there," she admitted. "It's just a flat plain shoved high by a set of faults and buoyant substrates. But there was a time, long ago, when the Continent pushed in from every side, and an entire island was buried. Buried and carried a long ways under the sea."

The woman liked to explain things. Was she a teacher?

"Interesting," Jopale offered, though he wasn't convinced that it was.

"That island is like a mountain in reverse, you see. It extends a long ways below the waterline. Like a fist sticking out from the bottom of the Continent, reaching deeper into our ocean than any other feature we know of."

"I see," he muttered.

But why she would call it, "Our ocean"? How many oceans were there?

"That's why the science station was built there," she explained. "'A good mountain to do research.' That what my colleagues used to joke."

"What kind of research?" he asked.

"Land distortions and water cycles, mostly. And various experts who work with that submerged ground."

He said, "Really?" with a false enthusiasm.

The woman nodded, returning to her distant stare.

"Is that your specialty?" he asked, trying to read the binding of her book. "Prehistoric islands?"

"Oh, no." She passed the heavy book to her other arm.

"Then what do you do?"

It was an exceptionally reasonable question, but she was a peculiar creature. Smiling as if nothing had ever been funnier, she said, "Do-ane." She wasn't quite looking at his face, telling him, "That is my name."

He didn't have a ready response.

"You told me yours. I assumed you wanted to know mine."

"Thank you," Jopale muttered.

"I'm sorry, but I can't say anything else."

He nodded and shrugged. And then his mockman emerged from the stomach: A mature female with big blue eyes riding high on her broad stoic face. Jopale had recently purchased her from a cousin, replacing the mockmen he had lost when the valley flooded. For her species, she was smart and adaptable. By any standard, she was loyal, and in countless domestic tasks, she was helpful. And like every passenger from the worm's stomach, she smelled of acid and other unpleasant secretions. But at least this creature didn't want to play word games, or dance silly secrets before his eyes.

Jopale spoke to one of the soldiers, proving his ownership to everyone's satisfaction.

"My bags," he ordered.

The creature snatched each by its rope handle.

"This way," he said. Then with a minimal nod, he excused himself from Doane, pushing through the station, searching for some place where the noble refugee might eat a fit meal.

PARANOIA

Dining halls next to worm stations were rarely elegant. World's Edge was an exception: Using the local wood, artisans had carved long blocks into a series of omega-shaped beams, each a little different from the others, all linked like ribs to form a single long room. Woven gyre-tree branches created a porous roof. Heavy planks had been bleached white and laid out for a floor, each fastened to the foundation with solid pins made of dense black knot-wood. The tables and chairs were brightly colored, orange and gold predominating, everything made from slick new plastics—one of those expensive programs underwritten by some well-meaning government agency, public moneys helping lock away a few breaths of methane into this more permanent form. The usual indoor epiphytes clung to the overhead beams—vigorous plants with dark leaves that thrived in the artificial light, their finger-like roots drinking nothing but the travelers' nervous breathing. Jopale noticed a familiar figure planted at one end of a busy table, accompanied by two mockmen that sat backwards on turned-around chairs, eating their rations off their laps—a common custom in many places.

"May I join you?" asked Jopale.

"Please." The man was tall even when he was sitting, and unlike practically everyone else in the place, he wasn't eating. His old map was opened up before him, and with long fingers and sharpened nails, he measured and remeasured the distances between here and Port of Krauss.

Jopale set down his platter and handed his mockman two fresh rations of syrup-and-roach. The big female settled on the floor, legs crossed, hands and mind focused on the screw-style lids on both wooden jars.

Unsure what to say, Jopale said nothing. But silence proved uncomfortable, which was why he eventually picked the most obvious topic. "So why are you going to Port of Krauss?"

The thin man glanced up for a moment, apparently startled.

"You are going there, aren't you?"

"No."

"I'm sorry then," said Jopale. "I just assumed—"

"My trip doesn't end there," the thin man continued. "I have business, of a kind . . . business in another place . . ."

"The New Isles?"

Surprise turned to pleasure. "Are you going there too?"

Jopale nodded.

"Well, good. I knew there had to be others. Wonderful!"

Somehow that revelation didn't bring comfort. Jopale had the impression that his companion was difficult, and the idea of traveling with him across the rest of the Continent and then out over the Ocean felt daunting, if not out and out unpleasant.

"I need somebody to keep my confidence up," the tall man proclaimed.

What did confidence have to do with anything?

"My name is Rit."

"Jopale."

Rit didn't seem to hear him. Glancing over his shoulder, he observed, "There aren't any people working in the kitchen. Did you notice?"

Only mockmen were cooking and washing dishes. There wasn't even an overseer walking among them, keeping order.

"I don't know if I could make myself go to work," Jopale admitted. "All that's happening, even if it's far from here—"

"Not that far away," Rit interrupted.

"What? Has the news changed?"

"Aren't things awful enough as they are?" The tall man shuddered, then steered clear of that dangerous subject. He licked his lips and stared down at the big map, fingers stretched wide. Then with a tight voice, he asked the lines and tiny dots, "You do believe in the Isles, don't you?"

"Why wouldn't I?"

The narrow face twisted. "But have you ever seen the Isles? Or do you know anyone who's actually visited them?"

Jopale had never considered the possibility. "What do you mean? How could they not exist?" He immediately reached for the only book in his personal satchel—a leather-bound, professionally printed volume full of photographs and exhaustive explanations. With his voice rising, he said, "I haven't heard anything like that. Not even the rumor of a rumor."

Rit shook his head and began to fold up his map, saying to no one in particular, "I'm sorry. I have these panics. Always have."

The man was insane, or nearly so.

"It's just that in times like these . . ." Rit took a moment to compose himself. "When disaster reigns, deceitful souls prosper. Have you noticed? Criminals rise up like worms inside dead wood. They come from below to hurt good people, for profit and for fun."

There was an obvious, ominous counter to that logic. "We've never seen times as bad as these," Jopale said.

That observation earned a terrified but respectful look from his companion. "I suppose that's so."

"Why go to so much trouble to mislead us? With the worst happening, in far off places now and maybe here soon . . . even a despicable thief knows he wouldn't have enough time to enjoy his money . . ."

"Unless he doesn't believe he will die." Rit leaned across the table, putting his bony face close to Jopale's face. "Most people still don't appreciate their mortality. They read about the deaths of strangers. Places they don't know are poisoned or burning. But until their lungs are sick and their skin is cooking, they think their chances are exceptionally good."

There were stubborn souls in the world, yes. Jopale knew a history teacher—a brilliant man by any measure—who had openly mocked him. "Nothing ever changes in the world," the colleague had claimed. "The Continent will shatter here and there, and some old islands will be destroyed. But others islands will survive, along with the people riding them. That is the irrefutable lesson of our past, Jopale. Our world is tough, our species is lucky, and both will survive every onslaught."

Jopale nodded for a moment, as if accepting that remembered lecture. Then with an honest conviction, he reminded Rit, "There are easier and much cheaper ways to fool people. And steal a fortune in the process, I might add."

His companion gave a grudging nod.

"I am like you," Jopale continued, knowing that he wasn't anything like this crazy fellow. "I've had some suspicions, yes. I wanted to know: Were the New Isles really as strong and smartly designed as their builders claim them to be? So I made inquiries before committing my money. And yes, the New Isles do exist. They were built at the Port of Krauss, at the main shipyard. The last Isle was launched just a year ago, and it's still being towed to its final destination. I even spoke to workers at the Port, using a radiophone. And while they couldn't promise that the Isles were located in safe places, or that I had an open berth waiting for me and my mockman, they were definite about one issue: They had done their best work, fabricating the largest, strongest ships humans had ever known."

Jopale glanced at the cover of his book. From the bluffs overlooking the unlit ocean, someone had taken a photograph showing a wide vessel built from tough old wood. Some of the strongest, most enduring land in the world had been cut free of the Continent and floated into position, then carved into a cumbersome but durable ensemble of hulls and empty chambers. And to make the Isle even stronger, a fortune in refined metals had been fashioned into cables and struts and long nails that were fixed throughout the Isle's body. Metal was what Port of Krauss was famous for—the rare elements that could be filtered from the cold dark seawater. With the best alloys in the world, insulated tanks were built, and they were filled with methane and dangled far beneath each Isle, using the sea's own pressure and cold to help keep the gas liquefied. That gas would eventually power lights and hydroponics, with enough energy in reserve to tear the seawater apart . . . to carve hydrogen from the precious oxygen, allowing everyone to breathe without any cumbersome masks.

With the surety of a good teacher, Jopale dismissed Rit's concerns. "These are genuine sanctuaries, and my new home is waiting for me. I just have to get there now. And I feel quite sure that I will."

Saying those words, he believed them.

Rit seemed to take it all to heart. He put away his map and found his own copy of the member's handbook, opening it to one of his favorite pages.

Finally, Jopale began to eat his meal. He had purchased two scrambler hands, fried but not too greasy, and a whitish lump of sweetcake and cultured algae in a salty soup, all washed down with a tall bottle of fermented sap imported from the Earlands. The drink was the most expensive item on the limited menu, and it was the most appreciated. The hard kick of the liquor was already working on his mood when his companion spoke again, using a sorry little voice to ask, "But what if?"

"What if what?" Jopale responded testily.

"What if these thieves and con artists did believe this world was coming to an end? And by promising berths to us and maybe a million others like us, they earned enough money to finance their own salvation."

Jopale grimaced, breathing through his teeth.

"What if a New Isle is waiting, but not for us?" Rit persisted.

Jopale felt a smile emerge on its own. Then with a bitter laugh, he told his traveling companion, "Well then. Then we aren't in any worse shape than the rest of the world. Now are we?"

ON AGAIN

Jopale had always excelled at school, including respectable grades earned in each of the three sciences. But he never achieved a profound understanding of genetics or selective forces. He learned what was absolutely necessary, relying on his clear memory when it came to the standard exams. Introductory classes demanded little else, while the high-level courses—those rarefied environments where professors wanted more than disgorged fact and holy equations—had never been in his future.

But one lesson Jopale took from science was this: Mockmen were wondrous creatures, pliable and creative by every genetic measure.

A glance around the station proved that truism. Most of the mockmen were big creatures, two or three times larger than a grown human. They had been bred for compliance and power when necessary and a minimal metabolism to help reduce the food bills. Yet some of these creatures were small and slender as a child. And a few of the kitchen workers were quicker than any human being—a blessing in this hurly-burly business. What's more, no two of them could be confused for each other, even though they might be siblings or a parent and grown child. All had an oval face and a protruding chin beneath a small, seemingly inadequate mouth. Yet each face was unique. Jopale's own girl had descended from giants that lived for generations on his family farm—a generalist by design and by training, her head topped with beastly red hair, a dramatic chin hanging from the parabolic jaw, and blue inhuman eyes gazing out at a world full of motion and incomprehensible purpose. If the creature had a voice, she would have commanded a vocabulary of several hundred easy words. But of course the larynx was pierced when she was a baby, leaving her able to communicate only with simple gestures and vaguely human expressions. A creature of habit and duty, his mockman was too simple to understand the dire state of the world—an ignorance that Jopale couldn't help but envy, at least now and again.

"Everything with a spine arose from a common ancestor," he had learned long ago. His biology professor—an ancient woman blessed with her own sturdy backbone—explained to the class, "A single creature must have been the originator of us all. On some ancient continent, long dead and rotted away, this precursor to humans ran about on two legs, climbing up into the saprophytes and epiphytes, grabbing what food it could with its primitive hands."

"Like a scrambler?" a student had asked.

Jopale didn't ask the question, thankfully. The professor reacted with a click of the tongue and a sorry shake of her head. "Hardly," she replied. "Scramblers are as far removed from our founding species as we are. As the mockmen are. Flying yabbers, copper eels, plus everything else you can name . . . all of these species would look at that vanished organism as being its very distant ancestor. That is, if simple beasts could ever think in such abstract terms."

"But where did the first vertebrates come from?" another student inquired. "From the sea? Or from some earlier continent?"

"Nobody knows," the professor replied. Then with the surety of age, she added, "And nobody will ever discover that unnecessary answer. Since there's no way to study the matter any farther than it has been studied by now."

Jopale had been sitting in the station for several hours, changing position as the plastic chair pushed against his rump. At that moment, he happened to be thinking about his biology teacher, long dead, and about the nature of surety. And to stave off boredom, he was studying the astonishing diversity of false humans who sat and walked among those who were real.

Suddenly a short, homely mockman entered the dining hall. It was female, dressed in the stiff uniform of a station worker. And like with a few of her species, some quirk of genetics had swollen her skull, giving her a genuine forehead under a cap of thick black hair. That forehead was remarkable enough. But then the newcomer opened her mouth, revealing a clear and exceptionally strong voice.

"The westbound worm is rested and ready," she sang out, the clarity of each word taking travelers by surprise. "Leave by way of the door behind me, sirs and madams. If you have a ticket. You must have a ticket. The westbound worm is fed and eager. She will be leaving shortly, my friends."

Most of the room stood up.

"That wasn't as long as I feared." An elderly woman wearing elegant clothes and amber gems was smiling at her good fortune. "I was ready to sit for quite a while longer," she admitted to her companion.

A handsome man, perhaps half her age, muttered, "I wonder why this is."

The rich woman had to laugh at him. "It's because we are special, darling. What more reason do you need?"

Jopale was among the last to reach the open doorway. Soldiers were waiting, carefully examining each ticket and every piece of identification. Meanwhile, the uniformed mockman stood beside the long line, smiling happily. Why did that creature make him feel so uneasy? Was it her face? Her voice? No, what bothered Jopale was the way she stared at the other faces, black eyes settling only on those who were human.

"Good journey," she said to Jopale.

Then to Rit, who was directly behind him, she said, "You are in trustworthy hands, sir. No need to worry."

She could read the man's fear.

A one-in-a-million creature, thought Jopale. Or there was another explanation, and far more sordid too. Glancing over his shoulder, he wondered if she could be a hybrid—a quirk of biology that wasn't destroyed at birth, but instead was fed and trained for this halfway demanding task. Nothing like her would ever happen in his homeland. It wasn't allowed. But World's Edge was a different part of the world, and Jopale's long journey had taught him many lessons, including that every place had its own culture, and cultures were defined by odd little customs understandable only to themselves.

"This way, this way!" the old caretaker cried out.

Jopale showed the soldiers what they wanted to see, his own mockman standing silently to his right.

Master Brace was at the end of the long platform, shouting for the passengers and waving both arms. Even at a distance, his face betrayed a look of genuine concern. Something bad must have happened. But their giant worm lay motionless on the greased trail, apparently sleeping. Its intestine was still jammed full of half-digested food. The worm's bloated shape said as much, and looking through the plastic windows, Jopale saw a rich dark mixture of masticated wood pulp and sweet knuckle-roots, happy muscles pressing the feast into new positions, the elastic walls working on the stubborn chunks and bubbles.

The passengers were being led up toward the stomach.

Jopale was disgusted, but compliant. The wealthy woman who talked about being special was now first to complain. Shaking an accusing finger at the caretaker, she said, "I did not pay for an acid-bath."

The caretaker had discarded his charm. He looked tired and perhaps a little scared, not to mention short of patience. "Her stomach isn't hungry anymore," he said with a loud, slow voice. "And it's thoroughly buffered, madam. You'll be comfortable enough inside there, I promise."

"But my mockmen—"

"Will ride above, in the open air." Brace gestured impatiently. The pilothouse was fixed on top of the long blind head, and behind it were ropes and straps and simple chairs. With a loud voice, Brace told every passenger, "If we waited for my baby to empty her bowels, we'd remain here until the next cycle. Which might be just as well. But word just came up from One-Time—"

An earlier stop, two cycles to the east.

"A new fissure has broken open there. The situation is dicey. And since there's room enough inside the stomach, I'm sure you can see . . . this is the best answer to our many problems . . . !"

The passengers turned together, gazing toward the east. While everyone was busily filling his own belly, the bright face of the sun had been covered over. Distant clouds seemed thicker than natural, and blacker, and the clouds were rising up like a great angry wall, towering over the green land that these people had only recently journeyed across.

A purposeful panic took hold of the crowd.

Jopale claimed his belongings from his mockman and ordered her to climb on top of the worm. Then he passed through the cramped sphincter and into the stomach, sniffing the air as an afterthought, pleased to find it fresh enough and even a little scented. The shaggy pink floor was a little damp but not truly wet. Worm stomachs were shorter than the duodenum, and most of the floor had been claimed. A simple latrine stood in back. Do-ane sat alone in the middle of the remaining space, hiking boots beside her. She showed Jopale a polite smile, nothing more. Where else could he go? Nowhere. Claiming the empty stomach to her right, he threw open his traveling blanket and inflated his pillow. Setting the pillow on the highest portion of his floor, he tried to ignore her. Then Rit knelt on the other side of the young woman, carefully laying out his blanket, preparing his fragile nerves for the next leg of this very long journey.

Jopale was terrified, genuinely terrified, right up until the moment when the alarms were sounded.

The sharp wailing of sirens began in the distance, diluted and distorted by the worm's body. Then the station's sirens joined in, and the floor rolled ominously. Was it a quake, or was the worm waking? Probably both reasons, he decided. Then the stomach sphincter closed, choking off the worst of the noise, and the giant creature gulped air into its long lungs and into its empty belly, needing little prompting to begin squirming against the trail's slick surface. Rolling muscle and the long powerful tail created a sound unlike any other in nature. Jopale was reminded of a thick fluid being forced down a very narrow drain. Slowly, slowly, the creature built its momentum, the trail's oils eliminating most of the friction, allowing its bulk to gradually become something swift and relentless.

Passengers held their air masks in their hands, waiting for instructions or the telltale stink of a gas cloud. Because there had to be gas somewhere close. A quake wasn't reason enough to sound the city's alarms. Yet curiously, in the midst of this obvious emergency, Jopale felt much calmer. He knew he had to remain vigilant and clear-headed. And gas was only an inconvenience to a man with the proper equipment. Standing beside one of the few stomach windows, he watched the station vanish behind them, replaced by broad government buildings and assorted shops, and then suddenly, by countless homes stacked three deep and set beside narrow, shade-drenched streets. A few mockmen were walking with purposeful shuffles; otherwise no one appeared in the open. Most of the homes were shuttered and sealed. If poisons were boiling up from below, private detectors would smell them, and people would huddle inside their little safe rooms, breathing filtered air or oxygen from bottles, or breathing nothing but the increasingly stale air. An awful experience, Jopale knew. There was no more helpless feeling in the world. Yet his overriding emotion now was a tremendous, almost giddy relief.

He had escaped again, just in time.

Do-ane joined him. The window was quite tiny, not designed for looking outside, but instead to let in sunlight and allow the caretakers to monitor the mockmen who normally rode here. Do-ane stood on her toes to look outside. She seemed prettier when she was nervous, and rather more appealing. In her hand was the most sophisticated gas-gauge that Jopale had ever seen. In a whisper, she said, "Hydrogen sulfide."

His own confidence fell to pieces. Methane was awful—suffocating and flammable—but the putrid hydrogen sulfide gas was far worse. There were places beneath the Continent where the dissolved oxygen had been exhausted. The living wood and dark currents couldn't freshen that water any more. And different types of rot took hold there, anaerobic bacteria creating a sour poison that could kill within minutes.

The city kept sliding past.

"Is that a body?" she asked suddenly.

What might be a mockman was lying on its side, tucked against the foundation of a long house. Or was it just trash dressed in a blanket? Jopale wasn't sure, and then they had passed both the body and the street. With his own quiet voice, he said, "It was nothing."

"It was human," Do-ane said.

"A sleeping mockman," he offered. "Or a dead one, maybe. But that means nothing. Disease or age, or boys out damaging property, maybe."

"Do you think so?" Do-ane asked hopefully.

"Oh, yes," he said. And because it felt good, he again said that word. "Yes." Then he added with his most reasonable tone, "If the gas was that terrible, the streets would be jammed with suffocating bodies."

She looked at him, desperate to believe those sordid words.

Suddenly Jopale couldn't remember why the young woman had bothered him. He smiled and she did the same, and with that, they leaned against the living wall, watching the city fall away and the countryside reemerge. Tall epiphytes spread their leaves to the waning light. Rain showers were soaking the land to the south. Maybe those clouds would drift north; that would lessen the chances of a fire, at least for a little while. Right? Meanwhile, Do-ane's sensor continued to record the fluctuating levels of sulfides, plus the usual methane and ethane that were pulled inside whenever the worm belched and swallowed more air. But none of the toxins reached a suffocating level, and except for a foul taste in the back of the mouth, they remained unnoticed by the other passengers.

Finally the sun merged with the horizon and the numbers began to fall again, working their way back toward levels that were normal enough, at least over the last few years.

Jopale sat on his blanket, enjoying his good fortune.

Then for no clear reason, he thought about the hybrid woman back at the station—the black-haired creature with the big lovely voice—and it occurred to him that unlike the human soldiers, she'd had no air mask riding upon her hip.

Had she survived?

And why, in the face of everything, did he seem to care?

PLANS OF ESCAPE

At the school where Jopale taught, the conclusion of each term meant a party thrown for the faculty and staff. Liquor was involved, and school politics, and during that final gathering, some extraordinarily raw emotions. Radiophone broadcasts had just reported a cluster of villages in the distant north destroyed by an eruption of poisons. Sober voices were repeating rumors—false rumors, as it happened—that the local engineers and mockmen crews couldn't stop the enormous jets of methane. The party soon divided itself into two camps: Some wanted to embrace their doom, while others clung to any excuse for hope. Jopale found himself on the fringes of the argument, unsure which stance to take. Then a colleague wandered past, his cup drained and his mind intoxicated. Listening to a few declarations of terror, the normally timid fellow found a buoyant courage. "The situation is not that dangerous," he declared. "Believe me, we can seal up holes ten times worse than what I've heard described in these stories!"

The optimists happily embraced those defiant words.

But the teacher shrugged off their praise. "You're as silly as the rest of them," he declared. "And at least as ignorant, too."

"What do you know?" someone asked.

"More than anybody else here, I can tell you that." Then the drunken man scanned the room. Searching for an escape route? No, he wanted the big bowl set on the central table—a leather bowl where sweet punch and fermented gigberries created a small pond. "Look here," he called out. "I'll show you exactly what I mean."

His audience gathered at the table, maintaining a skeptical silence.

Using the thick decorative leaves of a hush-woad, the teacher began covering the pond's surface. And while he worked, he lectured about the wooden Continent and the bottomless Ocean and how things like rot and methane were the inevitable end products in a very ancient cycle.

Jopale understood it all, or he thought he did.

Then a third teacher—the most accomplished science instructor on their staff—cleared his throat before mentioning, "This isn't your professional area, you know."

"My area?" The lecturer with the leaves asked, "What is my area? Remind me now."

"Maps," the scientist said, that single word wrapped inside a smug and blatantly dismissive tone.

Anger showed on the colleague's face. But he didn't lose his temper. He just shook his head for a moment and set another layer of leaves on the pond. Then with a quiet, brittle voice, he said, "Jopale."

"Yes?"

"What do you know about the Man-and-Sky texts?"

Jopale had read excerpts in college. But even in these modest academic circles, it was best to appear well trained. "I studied them for a semester," he replied with a careful tone. "What about them?"

"How old are they?"

"No one knows."

"But judging by the different dead languages, we can assume they're probably several different ages . . . a mishmash of writings from a series of unnamed authors. Yes?"

Jopale offered a nod.

His colleague took a deep breath. "Scholars believe the Man-and-Sky offers at least three descriptions of the world, possibly four. Or five. Or even six. What's certain is that each description is not that much different from our world. There is a large continent and a motionless sun. Only the names of every location have been changed, and the peoples use different languages, and sometimes the animals and vegetation are not quite recognizable."

Like bored students, the teachers began to mutter among themselves.

The lecturer placed a hand upon the floating leaves. "My area . . . my intellectual passion . . . is too complicated for ordinary minds. I'll grant you that. Thousands upon thousands of islands coalesce into a single body, each island fighting with its stubborn neighbors to remain on the Ocean's surface, basking in the brightest possible sunshine. It makes for a grand, glorious puzzle that would baffle most of you . . ."

Feeling the insult, his audience fell silent.

"The Man-and-Sky texts give us the best maps of those earlier continents. And they offer some of the most compelling accounts of how the old continents fell to pieces." The geographer picked a pale yellow straw off the table, his mouth pressed into a wide, painful smile. "You probably don't know this. Those lost continents were barely half the size of ours. There is no evidence—none—that the islands in the past have ever managed to cover the entire day-face of our world. Which makes what is happening now into a singular event. An elaborate collision of random events, and perhaps selective forces too."

"What about selective forces?" the scientist grumbled.

"Which islands prosper?" their colleague asked. "The strong ones, of course. And those that remain on the surface for the longest time. Those that can resist the poisons in the bad times, and those that will endure the longest, darkest famines." Then he shrugged, adding, "In earlier cycles, the wood beneath us would have been dead long ago. The collapses would have come sooner; the tragedies would have been smaller. But this time—in our time—the islands have descended from a few durable lineages. And what's more, every other force at play in the world has pushed us to the worst stage imaginable."

Even in his blackest moods, Jopale didn't want to believe that.

"We don't know how much methane is under our toes," the lecturer admitted. "But even the median guesses are awful."

A small, sorry voice said, "The entire world could suffocate."

Jopale had offered those words.

"Oh, but it's far worse than that!" His colleague stuck the long straw into his mouth, then slipped the other end into a small wooden flask hidden in his coat pocket. He sucked up the liquid and covered the straw's upper end with his thumb, lifting the leaves until he could see the open punch, then he set the bottom of the straw against the sweet drink. "Of course I mean this as an illustration," he mentioned. Then he winked at the scientist, saying, "I know, I know. There's no genuine consensus among the experts. Or should I say specialists? Since there is, if you think about it, an important difference between those two words . . ."

"Don't," Jopale cautioned.

But the man struck a long match, making a yellow flame. Then winking at his audience, he said, "Of course, the Continent might collapse slowly, over many generations. A little gas here, a lot of gas there. People die, but not too many of us. And maybe we will marshal the necessary resources. Cut holes to the Ocean below and let out the bubbles in manageable little breaths. Or pump pure oxygen down under our feet, freshening the cold dead water." He waved the flame in front of his eyes. "Perhaps humans can do whatever it takes, and our atmosphere isn't destroyed when the hydrocarbons eat up our precious free oxygen."

"You're drunk," the scientist complained.

"Wonderfully drunk, yes." Then the teacher of city names and island positions laughed, and he lowered the flame.

Everyone stared at the leaf-covered punch.

Jopale assumed that the liquid from the vial was pure alcohol. But his colleague had decided to make a more effective demonstration of his argument, which was why he used a collection of long-chain hydrocarbons purchased from an industrial source—a highly flammable concoction that made a soft but impressive wooshing sound as it set the leaves on fire, and then the drunken man's hand, and a moment later, his astonished, pain-wracked face.

THE EVENING AIR

Left-of-Left was the next official stop—a safe station where the hard-pressed worm could catch its breath and empty its swollen bowels. Most of the passengers had fallen asleep by then. The only light inside the crowded stomach came from a bioluminescent culture hung on an acid-etched brass hook. Do-ane hadn't bothered with a sleeping hood, curled up on her blanket, hands sweetly tucked between her pillow and face. Rit didn't seem able to relax, sitting up occasionally to adjust his hood or take another white melatonin pill. Only Jopale didn't feel tired—an illusion brought on by too much nervous energy—and that was why he stepped outdoors, using this brief pause to check on his mockman's health, breathe the open air, and absorb the depressing sights.

The station was empty and dark. Information displays had been turned off, while the offices and cafeteria had their doors locked. Master Brace was standing alone on the platform, watching his colleagues use electric wands to stimulate the worm's anus. Jopale approached, then hesitated. Was the old caretaker crying? But Brace sensed his audience. Suddenly wiping his eyes with a sleeve, he turned to the lone passenger, habit or perhaps some unflagging sense of duty helping him create a magnificent, heartening smile.

"A gloomy darkness, but a very pleasant climate," he remarked. "Don't you think so, sir?"

Jopale nodded.

"I've stood here at least a hundred times, sir."

"With our worm?"

"Oh, yes." Men like Brace often spent their professional lives caring for the same worm, learning its talents and peculiarities; and since worms were creatures of relentless habit, they were rarely asked to change routes or schedules.

"Pleasant," the old man said again.

Tall clouds stood on the eastern horizon, obscuring the last hints of sunlight. From a distance, the clouds resembled a thick purplish-red tower that was either extraordinarily lovely or extraordinarily terrible.

Jopale asked if the clouds were made from smoke or water.

Master Brace shrugged his shoulders. "We won't be staying long, sir," was all he said.

Left-of-Left was a small city, and judging by the spacious warehouses standing beside the various worm trails, it had been exceptionally prosperous. Great slabs of freshly cut wood waited beside the widest worm trails, mounted on sleds ready to be towed east by giant freight worms. But there was only one other worm in the station besides theirs, and it had dragged itself between two buildings and died, its pale carcass beginning to swell as it rotted from within.

"This wood—?" Jopale began.

"The finest in the world," the caretaker offered. "This ground is dense and durable—a sweet grain, and almost perfectly free of knots. It has been in demand, for centuries now. And when the Continent shifted east, the local miners adapted quickly." Brace gestured toward the south. "They poisoned the best of their wood with arsenic salts. Even if their land starved, they weren't going to allow any worm infestations. Beautiful planks were still coming out of this place . . . but you certainly don't want to breathe the sawdust, I can tell you."

Sprawling homes stood north of the station, yards sprinkled with tall poles. Gas-jet lights were strung high overhead—a cheat to bring light to a place without sunshine. But not one of the torches was burning now, and none of the windows on any house showed the barest hint of life.

Even the lowliest mockmen were missing.

"Because everybody left," the caretaker explained. "They went off . . . I don't quite know . . . maybe forty cycles ago? They were still here on my last trip through. Nobody warned me. But they were quiet while I was here, which was unusual for them. Very chatty folk, most of the time. Which makes me believe that they'd come to their decision already."

Their worm began to shake now. Intestines contracted and the long body grew longer, the creature beginning to clear its bowels. The stink of the process was horrific, yet it bothered no one but the lone passenger.

Jopale turned his face away. "What decision was that?" he asked, one hand thrown across his mouth and nose.

"These people had their escape prepared," the caretaker replied. "Probably years ago. A lot of these little communities . . . out here in the dark . . . they have schemes. Sanctuaries, special ground."

"Is that so?"

"Oh, yes," Brace replied, as if this was common knowledge. "People living in the night know what disaster means. They have experience and common sense. Like Left-of-Left here. One lady told me, with a confidential voice, that her family had built themselves a fireproof shelter and surrounded it with a deep moat. When the air soured, they would breathe bottled oxygen. And if the fires came, they'd flood the moat with water and spray it over their heads."

Jopale almost responded.

But the caretaker saw doubt in his face. "Oh, I know, sir. I realize. That doesn't sound workable. This would be no ordinary fire, and this dense ground is sure to burn hot and long. If that miserable time should come." He laughed amiably for a moment, then added, "She was definitely lying to me. I know that now, and maybe I knew it then. You see . . . I would normally remain here for a cycle or two. We like to give this worm a long sleep and a chance to fatten up, and that local woman would let me share her bed. A wonderful lady, and a good friend, and she wanted me to know that she had arrangements made. But she didn't tell me enough so that I could find her. Which is reasonable, and I shouldn't be hurt. Wherever these people have gone, they don't have extra room for their occasional lovers."

Jopale didn't know what to say, so he remained silent.

Then the caretaker turned back to his colleagues, and with a sharp, accusing tone, he called out, "Leave those turds on the trail. You hear me?"

A young woman was standing in the worm-greased trail. Spiked boots kept her from falling, and she held a special stick used to shove the foul wastes to the side. "But the regulations—" she began.

"Regulations?" the old man interrupted. Forgetting about Jopale, he stepped to the edge of the platform, throwing out a few curses before reminding his crew, "Our first concern is our own worm. Our second concern is our passengers. And we are not wasting any time rolling crap out of the way of worms and people who are not going to be coming.

"Do you hear what I'm saying to you?"

A LAST MOMENT PLEA

Friends and colleagues were remarkably supportive of Jopale's decision to leave home. Most offered polite words, while a few posed the most obvious questions. "Where did you learn about the New Isles?" they asked. He had come across an article in a small journal that catered to the wealthy. For a fee, he was able to purchase an introductory book filled with photographs and useful descriptions. "And they had space available?" people wondered. "At this late date?" But a New Isle was being built every few years—the process guaranteed to continue until the disaster came or the danger passed. So yes, there was space enough for him. "But how does a teacher afford it?" they pressed. "How could you afford it?" Jopale offered a shrug and shy smile, mentioning his substantial inheritance. He always made that confession warily, expecting others to be openly jealous or envious or even noticeably bitter. But people absorbed the news with surprise and resignation. Which was a little disappointing, curiously enough. It would have made Jopale feel more secure about his solution—more optimistic by a long measure—if what he was doing caused pointed hatred in the people that he was prepared to leave behind.

Acquaintances and fellow teachers always seemed to have their own escape routes planned—hopeful schemes wrapped around the local civil protection service or private bunkers. And there was some good reason for hope: Throughout the district, old worm holes were being sealed and stocked with provisions. If the fires came, locals would hunker in the dark, sipping bottled air, while the ground above was saturated with pure water and complex foams guaranteed to shoulder all but the most catastrophic heat.

The problem was that if the fires came, the heat would turn catastrophic. The worst fires to date were in the south, not far from the polar zone. Epiphyte forests were being consumed in an instant. The normally inflammable cuticle boiled away soon after that. Then the deep living wood caught fire and burned off, allowing drowned, half-rotted islands free to spring to the surface, bringing up fresh methane that only caused the fires to grow larger. After that, the soggiest, most rotten wood was soon baked to a crisp and set on fire, and despite an army of mockmen and brave firefighters, that circular zone of total destruction was spreading outwards, eating a kilometer with every cycle, engulfing abandoned villages and useless farms in a roaring, irresistible maelstrom.

Yet Jopale's friends put on hopeful, brave faces. "We'll get the upper hand soon," they claimed, sounding as if they were fighting on the front lines. "And we'll beat the next twenty blazes too. You just wait and see."

But nothing happened quickly in the world. Cycle after cycle, the southern fire continued to spread, and new ones exploded to life in other distant places. The steady, irresistible disaster gave everyone time enough to doubt his most cherished beliefs. That's when people found themselves admitting to their very lousy prospects, particularly in conversation with their oldest friends.

"I keep telling people that I'm staying," announced one of Jopale's neighbors. A bachelor like Jopale, bright and well-read, he admitted, "I'm always saying that the fires will be put out, or they'll miss us. But when it comes down to it, do you know what I'll do? Run. Run east to the Ocean, just like you're running west. If I can slip past the provincial guards and disappear into the chaos . . ."

"Maybe," Jopale replied, unsure what that would accomplish.

But the fellow had written himself into an interesting story. "All those last islands that merged with the Continent? Well, I've heard their citizens are burying explosives inside the old fault lines. And when the time comes, they'll set off the biggest blasts in history."

Again, Jopale said, "Maybe."

He didn't want to attack the man's dream. But doubt must have crept into his face, because his friend bristled, asking, "What's wrong?"

Jopale was no expert. But in every account he had read, those giant fires were accompanied by fabulously strong winds. The winds blew toward the flames, feeding them the oxygen critical to their survival. You could shatter the old fractures from end to end, chiseling the islands free of the doomed Continent; but those enormous masses of wood and scared humanity would still have to move into the open water, pressing against that roaring gale.

"Well then," the friend responded. "They'll think of that. Probably they'll blow their way free long before the fire comes."

And release any methane trapped under their feet, starting their own deadly blaze. But this time, Jopale found the tact to say, "That's reasonable, sure." Then he added, "I don't know much about technical matters."

"Keep that in mind, Jopale." Shaking a finger, the old friend said, "You don't know much about anything."

True enough.

Jopale's relatives surprised him with their calm, stubborn dismissal of his New Isles plan. Uncles and older cousins thought he was a fool for surrendering to popular despair. Poisons and fires would kill distant strangers and burn up portions of the world. But not their good ground, no. They couldn't imagine their lucky island being changed in any lasting fashion. At the very worst, forests and farms would burn up, which would bring a famine that would quickly silence the extra mouths in the world. But that would be a blessing and a grand opportunity, they maintained. To his considerable astonishment, Jopale learned that his family had been preparing for years: Secret lockers were stuffed full of dried scramblers and wooden tubs jammed with pickled fruit, plus enough roach cakes and syrup to keep the most useful mockmen alive. There would be a few hard years, they agreed. Only the prepared would survive to the end. But that's what they intended to do. Survive at all costs. Then life would settle back into its comfortable, profitable, and entirely natural routine.

"Stay with us," they pleaded, but not too hard. Perhaps they'd decided that Jopale was one of those extra mouths.

One old aunt assured him, "You will go insane in the darkness. Starlight has that effect on people, you know."

That wasn't true. Humans were adaptable, and besides, the New Isles were lit up with blue-white lights very much like sunshine. Yet his response was deflected with a cold pleasure. "You *will* go insane," his aunt repeated. "Don't for two moments think otherwise, my boy."

Then a pair of young cousins—a twin brother and sister—explained what was plainly obvious to them. "When the time comes," they said, "the Spirit of Man will rise from the Ocean's center to save all of the good people."

It was an old faith, half-remembered and twisted to fit the times.

"Only true believers will be spared," they promised. "How about you, Jopale? Will you join us with the reborn?"

"Never," he responded, amazed by his sudden anger. His cousins were probably no more mistaken about the future than those with well-stocked bunkers. But he found himself panting, telling them, "That's a stupid creed, and you can't make me buy into it."

"Then you will die horribly," they told him, speaking with one voice. "And that's precisely what you deserve, Jopale."

But people rarely got what they deserved; wasn't that the central lesson of the modern world?

With his critical possessions packed and his precious tickets and papers in easy reach, Jopale walked to the nearest worm station, accompanied by his only remaining mockman. No well-wishers were waiting to send him off. Thank goodness. He and a few other travelers stood on the open platform, looking off to the east. The huge gray worm appeared on schedule, sliding in on the side trail and stopping before them, deep wet breaths making the entire station shake. Travelers formed a line, ready to prove themselves to the waiting soldiers. Then a single voice called out, "Jopale." It was a woman's voice, vaguely familiar. Jopale looked over his shoulder. He had grown up with this woman—a natural beauty who hadn't spoken ten words to him in the last ten years—but there she stood, dressed to travel and smiling only at him.

Jopale assumed she was heading west, perhaps even to the New Isles.

But no, she explained that she didn't have any ticket. She'd heard about his plans and simply come here to speak with him now.

"Please," she implored, touching her wide mouth, then running a hand across her long, elegant scalp.

He stepped out of line.

"This is difficult," she admitted. Then with a deep, soul-wrenching sigh, she added, "I wish I'd done what you've done."

But she hadn't, of course.

"If I stay here, I'll die here," she told him and every other person in earshot. "But I'll ask you, Jopale: Is there any way I could travel with you?"

There wasn't. No. "All the berths on the New Isles are taken by now. I'm quite sure. And I'm bringing only what I'm allowed to bring. Even with these little bags here, I'm pressing against my limits."

The woman wrapped her arms around her perfect chest, shivering as if chilled. Then quietly, through a clenched mouth, she said, "But there is a way."

"What?"

Standing beside Jopale was his red-haired mockman. The beautiful woman glanced up at the gigantic creature. Then with a stiff, somewhat angry voice, she said, "Leave it behind. Take me instead."

Did Jopale hear that correctly?

"I'll ride inside the worm's stomach with the mockmen," she promised. "And I'll carry your luggage for you too."

"No," he said.

"I'll even eat mockman rations—"

"No."

The woman began to cry, tears rolling down her lovely, pain-wracked face. "I'll do whatever you wish, Jopale. I'll even relinquish my legal rights, and you can beat me if I'm slow—"

"Stop it," he cried out.

"Please, Jopale! Please?"

Then a soldier stepped up, asking to see their papers. What could Jopale do?

He was startled, off-balance. This unexpected idea hadn't had time enough to take root in his head. The woman could never survive the life she was begging for. Besides, he had never lived without a mockman on his right side. And if he ever needed new money, this was a valuable creature on any market.

Jopale's only rational choice was to turn away from the woman, saying nothing else. He silently handed his identification to the armed man and then his precious ticket to an elderly fellow wearing the gray uniform of a worm caretaker.

"Master Brace" was written over the chest pocket.

"All the way to the Port of Krauss, sir?" asked the old fellow.

"Yes, I am."

Offering a wink and jolly laugh, Brace said, "Well, sir. You and I should get to know each other by the end of the line, sir. I should think."

"IT IS COMING"

The sky was cloudless and absolutely dark, save for a single point of soft yellow light—one of the Four Sisters slowly dancing about the hidden sun. The distant stars were too faint to be seen through the thick window—a few hundred specks that only scientists had bothered to name and map. Stars meant very little to Jopale. What captured his mind was soft country beneath: The Tanglelands. Relentless pressures had crumbled this wood, exposing every old seam and any line of weakness. Long ridges and single hills had been erected through a series of unending quakes. As a result, the trail was far from a straight line, and the climb as well as fatigue kept slowing the worm's progress. But there were no fresh breaks or blockages on the trail, at least so far. The waking passengers seemed thrilled to be alive, or at least they pretended to share a renewed confidence. And of course everyone wanted at least a glimpse of the tall saprophytes that grew beside the trail, watching the exotic forest passing by for a moment or two, then returning to their blankets and more familiar distractions.

Jopale had never seen country like this, save in picture books.

He mentioned his interest to Do-ane, and she responded as he hoped. "I've seen the Tanglelands," she admitted. "Several times now. But I still think they're lovely. Just wonderful."

The girl had a buoyant, joyful attitude when she wanted to.

Jopale stood beside her, watching the pale, many-hued light pouring out of the dense foliage. Sometimes he asked about a particularly bright or massive tree. Do-ane would warn that she didn't know her fungi as well as she would like. But every time, she named the species. Then when the rest of the passengers had settled on the stomach's floor, leaving them alone, she quietly asked her new student, "Do you know why this country is so rich?"

"The old islands are broken into hundreds of pieces," he offered. "Plenty of fresh surfaces ready to rot away."

"That's part of it," she allowed. "But as much as anything, it's because of the moisture. Three large islands were compressed and splintered to make the

Tanglelands, and each one had tremendous reserves of fresh water underground. Which the saprophytes need as much as they need food, of course."

He nodded amiably.

"And besides, rain likes hilly country," she continued. "Given its choice, a storm will drop its wealth on broken ground."

"How about your Good Mountain? Is it very wet . . . ?"

She shook her head. "Not particularly. That country is very flat and very boring. And beneath the surface, the wood is exceptionally dry."

"Why?"

"Because the island on the surface can't reach the Ocean anymore." Do-ane put one tiny hand beneath the other, as an illustration. "I think I mentioned: There's a second island resting under it, thick and solid, blocking almost every root."

"That's your Mountain? The underneath island?"

She hesitated, making some kind of delicate calculation. Then she looked out the window again, saying, "No," in the tone people use when they want to say a good deal more.

Jopale waited. Then he said, "Tell me more."

She squinted, saying nothing.

"About your undersea mountain," he coaxed. "What do you do down there?"

"Research," she allowed.

"In biology?" he asked. And when she didn't responded, he offered a mild lie. "I was once an avid biology student. Some years ago now."

Do-ane glanced at the passengers. Rit was sleeping. None of the others were paying attention to the two of them. Yet the young woman whispered so softly that Jopale could barely hear her words. "No," she said. "It's not really biology that I'm studying, no."

"Not really?" he pushed.

She wasn't supposed to speak, but she also wanted to explain herself. With a slender smile, she said, "I can't."

"I don't mean to interrogate," he lied.

The young woman's life was wrapped around her work. It showed in her face, her manners. In her anxious, joyful silence.

"Forget it," he muttered. An enormous fungus stood beside the trail—a pillar topped with fruiting bodies that bled a bright purple light. It was a common species whose name he had already forgotten. Staring at that apparition of rot and death, Jopale remarked with the coldest possible voice, "It's not as if the world is going to end soon."

"But it won't end," Do-ane said.

He gave a little sniff, and that's when he discovered that he was crying. It was the sort of manipulative gesture Jopale might have attempted and would have failed at. But his tears were as honest as anything he had ever done, a fabulous pain hiding inside him, any excuse good enough to make it surge into public view.

"This disaster has happened before," the young woman promised.

"So I've heard."

"But it's true. A new continent always grows on the sunlit face of the world. The water below is always choked of its free oxygen. Old wood compresses and shatters, and the methane rises up through the fissures and holes."

"What about wildfires?" he asked.

"There have been big fires before." She smiled to herself, betraying a deep fascination, as if describing an enjoyable novel full of fictional tragedies. Then she added, "These world-consuming fires have come seventeen other times."

Not sixteen times, or fifty thousand.

Jopale invested several long minutes contemplating her precision. Then he asked, "How do you know that? An exact number?"

"I can't," she said.

"You can't tell me?"

"No."

He stared at her face, letting his own anger bubble up. "This place where you're going," he started to ask. "This peculiar mountain . . . ?"

"Yes?"

"Your colleagues, those scientists who discovered the feature . . . I don't think they used the old word 'mountain' because it reaches in any particular direction. Toward the sky or toward the world's core, either."

Do-ane avoided his weepy eyes.

"My guess? The object was named for its composition. That's another quality inherent in the word. The mythical mountain is supposed to be harder and far more enduring than any wood. Am I right?"

The young woman was standing on her stocking feet, staring through the window again. The Tanglelands were beginning to thin out and turn flat, stretches of empty dead ground between the occasional giant fungi. Now the brightest stars were visible through the window, twinkling and jumping as the worm slid along. Do-ane was standing close enough to Jopale to touch him, and she was taking quick shallow breaths, her face growing brighter even as the empty land around them turned blacker.

Jopale held his breath.

Then very quietly, his companion said, "The great fire," and touched the plastic of the window with the tips of two fingers.

Do-ane announced, "It is coming . . . !"

THE HEART OF THINGS

When a worm like theirs was a baby, it was abused in the most awful ways—or so it might seem to somebody who didn't concern himself with the rough necessities of the world. Stolen from its mother, the newborn creature was cut through in several places and the wounds were kept open until they became permanent holes, ready for the first in a series of increasingly large sphincters. Then its diet was strictly controlled while professional handlers assessed its tendencies and potential uses. Intelligent and mild-tempered worms were given over to passenger duties. Many of the candidates didn't survive the conditioning of their digestive tracts or the additional surgeries. Among the alterations, inflatable bladders were inserted into the region directly behind the head, producing a series of permanent cavities where individual caretakers could live, each fitting with a rubber doorway leading into a narrow, astonishingly dry esophagus.

Jopale stood beneath a glow-light, shouting Brace's name. A voice called back to him. A few moments later, the old caretaker stepped from inside one of the little rooms, wiping his sleepy face while asking what was wrong.

With words and manic gestures, Jopale explained the situation.

For an instant, the caretaker didn't believe him. The weathered face looked doubtful, and the pursed lips seemed ready to downplay what he was being told. But then one of the worm's drivers ran down the narrow esophagus, shouting the same essential news.

"Where are we now?" the caretaker asked her.

The woman offered a number and letter designation that might as well have been in another language.

But the old man instantly absorbed the knowledge. "We'll stop at Kings Crossing," he ordered. "The station's gone, but the ground is up on the last ridge. We'll be able to see how bad things are. And any good news too."

Jopale couldn't imagine anything good.

Then the caretaker turned to him, saying, "Sir," with a firm tone. "I need to know. Have the other passengers noticed?"

"Just one. The girl—"

The caretaker hesitated for a moment. Then he said, "Say nothing. I'll see if I can raise some voices on the radiophone, get the latest news . . . and then I'll walk through the belly and offer a few words . . ."

Brace's voice fell away. What kind of encouragement could he offer anyone now?

There was tense silence, then a deep slow rumbling. The sound that came and then came again, making the great throat shiver.

"What is that?" Jopale had to ask.

"That would be the worm's heart," the caretaker offered. He tilted his head and held his breath, listening carefully. "And you can hear her lungs working too. Which is why we live up here, sir. So we can keep tabs on our baby."

Jopale nodded.

Then the caretaker touched the rough pink wall, and the driver did the same, both using that pause to fight back their own tears.

Do-ane had abandoned the window, sitting alone on her blanket, using her electric torch to read her book. Everyone else was sitting too, including Rit. The old map was unfolded before him. Glancing up, he said nothing to Jopale. Then he looked down again, asking the map, "What's wrong?"

"Nothing," Jopale lied, as a reflex.

The tall man glanced at Do-ane, and with the heightened senses of a paranoid, he announced, "Something is wrong."

She started to look at the window, then stopped herself.

But Rit noticed. He decided to take his own look, pulling his long legs under his body, taking a deep breath, and another. But there wasn't enough courage inside him to stand. His legs stretched out again, and a long hand wiped his mouth dry, and then he carefully fixed his eyes on the old map, nourishing his own faltering sense of ignorance.

"Did you tell?" Do-ane whispered, closing the book on her thumb.

Jopale nodded.

She stared at his face, his eyes. Something about her expression was new—a hard stare meant to reach down to his soul, seemingly. Then she made her decision, whatever that might be. Opening the book again, she flipped through pages until she found what she wanted. Placing her back to Rit, she pushed the book toward Jopale and handed him her torch, giving his face one last study, just to convince herself that her feelings were right.

The page was blank.

No, it unfolded. Jopale found a corner bent up by use, and he lifted the slick paper and gave the book a quarter turn, an elaborate drawing showing what looked to be the configuration for some type of worm.

"Is it—?" he began.

"The mountain," she interrupted, fingers held to her mouth.

Rit seemed to notice nothing. No one was paying attention to the two of them. The wealthy old woman who had complained at World's End was making her male companion look out the window. But she only wanted to know what was approaching, and he only looked ahead, reporting with a matter-of-fact voice, "There's some long slope. And that's all I can tell."

Was the mountain a worm? Jopale wondered.

He returned to the diagram, finding a scale that gave him a sense of size. But surely there was a mistake here. Even if the scale were wrong by a factor of ten, this worm would be larger than a dozen rust-fins set in a row. And if the scale were right, then the mountain would dwarf a hundred and twenty full-grown rust-fins . . . making it larger than most cities, wouldn't it . . . ?

He looked up. "Is it alive?" he whispered.

Do-ane had no simple answer for that. She shrugged and said, "It isn't now," in a soft voice. And then even softer, she said, "Look again."

He was no expert about worms. But he knew enough to tell that the mountain shared little with the creatures he had grown up with. Its mouth was enormous but without true jaws, forming a perfect circle from which every tooth had been removed. The throat was straight and wide, and then like a funnel, it collapsed on itself, becoming too tiny to show on this diagram. The anus was an equally tiny opening at the very tip of the tail. And between mouth and anus was a digestive tract that filled only a portion of the worm's enormous body.

"What are these?" he asked.

She touched the lines and the spaces within them, saying, "Chambers. Cavities. Rooms, of a kind."

He didn't understand. "How could a creature survive this much surgery?" he asked. And when she didn't answer, he looked up, realizing, "But this isn't any species of worm, is it?"

She mouthed the word, "No."

"It is a machine," he muttered.

She tilted her head, as if to say, "Maybe."

"Or is it alive?"

"Not now, no. Not anymore. We think."

The worm carrying them was attacking the last long slope, slowing as it crawled higher. Another person stood to look outside. But he was on the north side of the worm, and from that angle, nothing was visible behind them.

"The tail and some of the mid-section cavities are flooded," Do-ane told him.

Those were drawn with blue ink.

He asked, "Is the tail the deepest part?"

She nodded.

"And the mouth?"

"Buried inside a fossil island," she reported.

"Choked while eating its lunch?" He meant it as a joke, forcing himself to laugh.

But Do-ane just shook her head. "We don't know what it ate in life," she reported. "But this organism, this machine . . . whatever it was . . . it probably required more energy than you could ever pull out of wood pulp and stolen sap."

Jopale closed the book and turned it in his hands, examining the binding. But there was nothing to read except a cryptic "Notes" followed by a date from several years earlier.

"What I am," Do-ane began.

He reopened the book and unfolded the diagram again. "What are you?"

"In the sciences, I have no specialty." She smiled, proud to say it. "I belong to a special project. A confidential research project, you see. My colleagues and I are trained in every discipline. The hope is . . . was . . . that we could piece together what this thing might be . . ."

"It's metal," Jopale guessed.

"Within its body," she said, "we have found more iron and copper and zinc than all of the peoples of the world have gathered. Plus there's gold and silver, and elements too unusual to have common names."

Jopale wanted to turn through the pages, but he still couldn't make sense of this one.

"Yet the body is composed mostly of other substances," she continued. "Plastics and compounds that look plastic. Ceramic materials. And lining the mouth and what seems to be the power plant . . . well, there are things too strong to cut samples from, which means we can't even test them in any useful fashion . . ."

"And what are you?" he asked again.

"One member of a large, secret team trying to make sense of this." She showed him a grim smile, adding, "I'm just a novice still. Some of us have worked forty years on this project."

"And have you learned anything?"

A hopeful expression passed across her face. But again, they had reached a juncture where Do-ane didn't want to say anything more. Jopale sensed that she'd already told him too much. That they were pushing into codes and laws that had to be obeyed, even when Catastrophe walked across their world.

Again, their worm was slowing.

Passengers noticed, and in a moment, they grew uneasy.

"Where?" Jopale asked.

Do-ane ran a finger over the giant mouth. "What are you asking?"

"Its origin," he said. "Do you know that much?"

"Guess," she whispered.

He could see only two possibilities. "It comes from the world's center," he offered. "There are metals down there. I remember that much from school. Deep inside the world, the temperatures and chemistries are too strange for us to even imagine."

"What's the second possibility?"

He remembered what she had said earlier. "Our ocean," she mentioned, as if there could be more than one. Then he pointed at the sky.

"In my little profession," she sighed, "those are the two islands of opinion. I'm one of the other-world people, and I believe that this object is a kind of ship meant to cross from star to star."

Jopale closed the book and pushed it back to her.

By then, their worm had pulled to a stop, and the passengers were looking at each other, plainly wondering what was happening. But Master Brace was absent, probably still listening to the radiophone. Which was why Jopale took it upon himself to stand and say to the others, "This is Kings Crossing."

Rit pulled the map to his face, asking, "Why here?"

Like any good caretaker, Jopale managed to smile. But he couldn't maintain the lie past that point. Shaking his head and looking at the warm damp floor, he reminded everyone, "We're alive still." And then he started marching toward the still-closed sphincter.

FIRE

The night air was cool and dry, and it blew softly toward the east—a breeze at this moment, but gaining strength and urgency with the passage of time. Years ago, a tidy little city had grown up on this ridge, but then the sun vanished, and the city had died. Homes and shops quickly became piles of anonymous rubble. But the worm station must have survived for more years. The facility was only recently stripped of its metal, but otherwise it had been left intact. Only a few saprophytic weeds were rooted in the softest planks, while the damp faces of the main building were painted with a rough fungus. Regardless of color, every surface glowed with a steady red light. Jopale read "Kings Crossing" on the greeting arch, painted in a flowing script that was popular back when he was a child. Behind him, the other passengers were slowly stepping onto the platform, talking in breathless whispers. He didn't hear their words so much as he listened to the terror in their voices, and Jopale did nothing for the moment but stare at the planks beneath his feet and at his own trembling hands. Then when he felt ready—when no other choice seemed left for him—he forced himself to breathe and turn around, staring wide-eyed at the burning world.

Jopale once toured a factory where precious iron was melted inside furnaces built from equally precious ceramic bricks. He remembered watching the red-hot liquid being poured into thin syrupy ribbons that were quickly attacked by the artisans in charge. He decided that this wildfire possessed the same fierce, unworldly glow. It was crimson and brilliant enough to make eyes tear up, and it seemed as if some wickedly powerful artist, inspired by his malevolent urges, must have pulled molten metal across the entire eastern horizon.

Every passenger had left the confines of the worm. Most of the caretakers were busy breaking into a nearby warehouse, presumably under orders to claim any useful supplies. "How far away is that?" a young fellow asked. Jopale couldn't gauge distances, but others gladly threw out numbers. Optimists claimed the fire was just a few kilometers behind them, and it was really quite small. While Rit admitted that the flames were enormous, but trying to be positive, he thought they might be as far away as World's Edge.

"Oh, it's closer than that," the old caretaker called out. "As we stand here, Left-of-Left is being incinerated."

With a haughty tone, Rit asked, "And you know that how?"

Swollen eyes studied the horizon. Master Brace had been crying again. But he had dried his face before joining the others, and he managed to keep his voice steady and clear. "I was listening to broadcasts, where I could find them. From spotters near the fire lines, mostly."

Every face was sorry and scared.

"That quake we felt? As we were crawling out of World's Edge?" Brace shook his head, telling them, "That was an old seam south and east of the city. It split wide, along a hundred kilometer line. I didn't know this till now . . . but so much gas came from that rupture, emergency crews didn't have time to dress. They were killed, mostly. And the methane kept bubbling out. For a full cycle, it was mixing with the air. Then something . . . a person, or maybe lightning from a thunderstorm . . . made the spark that set the whole damn mess on fire."

"What happened to the city?" Jopale asked.

Brace glanced at him for a moment, then stared at the planks. "I talked to a spotter. She's riding her balloon east of World's Edge. The city's gone now, she says. Including the ground it was sitting on. From where she is, she sees open water where millions of people should be . . ."

"Open water?" Rit asked. "Does that mean the fire is going out?"

Brace hesitated.

Do-ane said, "No." The woman looked tiny and exceptionally young, her boots back on her feet but still needing to be buttoned. Clearing her throat, she explained, "If too much methane saturates the atmosphere, and the local oxygen is exhausted or pushed aside . . . there can't be any fire . . ."

Jopale closed his eyes, seeing the beautiful station and the black-haired woman with that lovely, lost voice.

Brace nodded, saying, "There's two fire lines now. One's racing east, the other west. In the middle, the water's bubbling up so hard, huge chunks of rotten wood are being flung up in the air. So the methane . . . it's still coming, yes sir. And the spotter told me that our fire . . . the one that's chasing us . . . it just now reached to the fringes of the Tanglelands . . . and then I lost her signal . . ."

Some people wept; others appeared too numb or tired to react at all.

Two drivers were standing near the worm's head. One of them suddenly called out a few words, her voice barely legible.

The other caretakers had vanished inside an unlit warehouse.

Master Brace turned to the drivers. "The full dose, yes," he shouted. "Under the vestigial arm."

"But the flames don't look that tall," said the wealthy woman. She shook her head, refusing to accept their awful prospects. To her companion, she said, "Perhaps the fire's just burning off the forests."

Her young man muttered a few agreeable words.

But Do-ane said, "No, you're confused. It's the smoke that fools you."

"Pardon me, miss?"

"That land is definitely burning," she said. "Huge volumes of green wood are being turned to smoke and ash, which help hide the tops of the flames. And of course that scorching heat will lift everything." She pointed at the sky, asking, "Can you see what I see?"

Jopale hadn't noticed. But the eastern half of the sky had no stars, a dense black lid set over the dying world. Flood this landscape with daylight, and half of the heavens would be choked beneath a foul mass of boiling, poisonous clouds.

"Are you certain?" the old woman asked doubtfully. "What do you know about any of this?"

Do-ane hesitated.

"The girl's a scientist," Rit interjected. "She understands everything that's happening to us."

"Is that so, miss?"

Do-ane glanced at Jopale, eyes narrowed, as if blaming him for making public what she had told him in the strictest confidence.

But he hadn't said one word.

"She and her friend here thought that I was napping," Rit confessed. "But I wasn't. I heard every word they said."

Do-ane looked embarrassed, shrinking a little bit, and her tiny hands nervously wrestled with one another.

Jopale tried to find a reply—gentle words to help deflate the palpable tension. But then a hard prolonged shock came through the ground, everybody's legs bending, and the land beneath them fell several meters in one steady, terrifying moment.

When the falling sensation ended, the old woman asked Do-ane, "Would you explain that, dear? What just happened?"

"This ridge," Do-ane began, opening her hands again. "We're standing on the last slab of the Tanglelands. It's the largest slab, and it reaches back to the east, deep underwater, ending up under Left-of-Left." Like a teacher, she used hands to help explain. "As the ground above is burned away, and as methane rushes to the open surface, this land's foundation is being torn loose."

As if to prove her words, the ridge shook again.

Jopale looked over his shoulder, but Master Brace had slipped away. He was standing besides the worm, he and the two drivers busily manipulating a leather sack filled with some kind of dense liquid. The sack was connected to a hose, and the hose fitted into a needle large enough to push through two grown men. The trio was having trouble with the work, and noticing Jopale, the caretaker cried out, "Sir, would you help us? Just for a moment. She knows we're up to something, and she isn't cooperating."

The others glanced at Jopale, surprised he would be called, and perhaps a little impressed.

The worm had stopped against the trail's closer edge. But there were still a few steps of greased ground to cross. Generations of worms had laid down this thick impermeable oil—the same white gunk that its wild counterparts used to lubricate their enormous tunnels. On soft-soled shoes, Jopale let himself slide down to the creature. He hadn't touched a worm since he was a boy, and he didn't relish touching one now. He could smell oil and worm sweat—a rich mingling of distinct odors—and he looked up at the vestigial limb, crooked and thin and held flat against the huge gray body.

"Take this extra wand, sir," said Brace. "Like I'm doing. Just stroke her belly, if you will."

The rubber wand ended with a metal electrode, batteries strapped to a spice-wood handle. The drivers had set a tall ladder beside the worm, spikes driven through the oil and into the ground. The woman driver climbed quickly and her colleague followed—a boyish fellow carrying the enormous needle as if it was a spear. The ladder was topped by a narrow platform. The woman grabbed the limb and pulled hard, and Brace ran his wand back and forth against the worm's slick belly, small blue flashes producing what must be a pleasurable tingle.

The woman forced the limb to extend.

"Why there?" Jopale asked, mimicking the old man's motions.

"It's a good blood-rich site," he said quickly, as if speaking one long word. "And besides, there's no time to open the usual veins."

The other passengers had come to watch and listen. Except for Do-ane, who drifted to the far end of the platform, studying her magnificent fire.

"Is this a drug?" Jopale wanted to know.

"I like the word 'medicine'," the caretaker admitted. Patting the sack, he said, "We keep this stuff for drivers more than for the worm. Of course, there's enough in this sack to kill a thousand people. But what it is—"

Somebody cursed, and a second voice shouted, "Watch out!"

The long needle fell between Jopale and Brace, landing flat on the oil.

"It's a stimulant, sir." The caretaker picked up the needle, and with a quick voice explained, "It will make our girl faster, and she won't need sleep, and it may well kill her. But of course, we don't have any choice now."

"I suppose—"

"Two more favors, sir. Please?"

"Yes."

"Take the needle up. All right?" Then he asked for a second favor, promising, "It should help quite a lot."

Jopale had never enjoyed heights, but he didn't hesitate. There were twenty rungs to manage, and the breeze seemed to grow stronger as he climbed higher. Over his shoulder, he saw the rest of the crew returning from the warehouse, nothing worth stealing in their hands. Then Jopale was standing on the narrow platform, and the driver had the vestigial limb extended as far as she could, and her assistant took the needle with both hands, starting to jab its tip into the exposed flesh while shouting, "Now!"

A tiny pump began to sing.

"The hand, sir," Brace called out. "Please, sir."

The worm's arm was tiny compared to its enormous body, but it was far longer than any human limb. Perched on the end of it were three fingers fused into a knobby extrusion and a stiff little finger beside it. And there was a thumb too. Not every worm possessed thumbs; Jopale had read that odd fact once or twice. And more unusual, this particular thumb could move, at least well enough to curl around his hands as he clasped hold of the worm. Then he squeezed its hand as tight as he could, trying to make certain that his grip was noticed, letting the great beast feel a little more ease, at least until the medicine found its home.

WORMS

Then they were moving again. The pace felt swift, but the worm was sliding down a considerable slope. Without landmarks, the casual eye had trouble discerning their true speed. But later, when they were crossing a flat empty plain, Jopale was sure they were making swift progress. Wandering up into the throat again, he listened to the hard swift beating of the heart, and he was sure that whatever else, the creature's body was expending a fabulous amount of energy.

Returning to the stomach, he found every passenger gathered around Do-ane. "Show us that book of yours," Rit was saying. "Show us your machine."

"We're very interested," said the rich woman's companion. Then with a wink, he asked, "What harm would it do?"

People were scared and miserable and desperate for any distraction.

Jopale sat next to Do-ane.

She seemed to consider the possibilities. Then she said, "Here," and opened the book to a fresh page—a page showing photographs of giant chambers and smooth-walled tunnels. Holding her torch above, she explained what she had already told Jopale, and a little more. "We think these were living quarters. It's hard to realize how big everything . . . but this is a colleague of mine, here, standing in the background . . ."

The scientist was little more than a dot on the grayish landscape.

"If this machine was a ship that traveled between the stars, as some believe . . . as I believe . . . then its engines would have produced an acceleration, and this would have been the floor." She pulled a fond finger over the image. "This was taken ten years ago. Do you see the dirt in the corner?"

Some people nodded, but those in the back could see nothing.

Do-ane turned the page. The next image was a large black-and-white photograph showing a skull and ribs and a very long backbone that had curled up in death. The earlier colleague was present again, standing on the giant skull. And again, he was still little more than a dot on this bizarre landscape.

"That's a dead worm," Jopale whispered.

Do-ane glanced at him, then at the others.

"This machine came from another star," Rit said, repeating her verdict.

"Yes," she said.

"A spaceship, you're saying?"

"It seems obvious—"

"And that's where our worms came from too?" The tall man was kneeling on the other side of her, his expression doubtful but focused. "They came from this spaceship of yours?"

Do-ane said, "Yes."

Then she said, "No."

"Which is it?" Rit demanded.

The young woman sighed. And then a second time, she sighed. Finally she looked up, telling everyone, "Suppose that we built a starship, and we went out hunting for a new home. Even a machine as powerful as this needs a great deal of time to cross from one sun to the next. And if that new sun didn't happen to have an inviting world, we'd have to travel farther. And if that next sun didn't offer a home, then we would have to travel farther still. And if we could never find a planet like our old home, at some point, wouldn't we have to make due with the best world that was in reach?"

Jopale tried to study the worm's skeleton.

"I don't know any of this as fact," she said. "But we've learned this much. This starship's crew was nothing like us. Not like people, or anything simply organic." She ran a finger along the edge of the fossil skull. "What looks like bone is not. It's ceramic and very tough, ancient beyond anything we can measure. And what organs we find aren't livers or hearts or lungs. They're machines, and we can't even begin to decipher how they might have functioned when they were slipped inside a living body."

Rit started to make a comment, then thought better of it.

"These creatures were built from metals and ceramics, plus rare earth elements that exist to us only in the tiniest amounts. Scarce beyond measure. But if you look deeper into the galaxy, into the spiral arms, you see suns with more metals than our sun has. And presumably, the worlds circling them are built from similar bones."

She breathed, breathed again.

"Our sun, you see . . . it is very large and bright, and it is metal-poor and rather young. By many measures, it won't live long at all. Less than a billion years, which is a short time in the universe." She lifted her torch higher, allowing more people to see the bizarre skeleton. "I don't know any of this for sure. I'm telling you a story, and maybe it's all wrong. But what I think happened . . . what many of my colleagues, the true geniuses in this endeavor, feel is self-evident . . . is that this starship journeyed all the way to our world and could go no farther. It landed on the Ocean and tasted the water, tasted the air, and its crew took what they had in reach. Metals were scarce, as were silicon and all the other heavy elements. But at least they could borrow the oldest genetics inside their own bodies. To build a full functioning ecosystem, they wove a thousand new species. Humans. Mockmen. Copper-eels and many-mouths. Plus all the little scramblers. And they used the other species that were brought with them. We've found spores and dead seeds on the ship, so we're sure that our ancestors brought plants with them. They devised giant plants that could thrive on the Ocean's surface, roots reaching deep to bring up the scarce minerals. And think of our forest roaches, too. We have found little versions of them dead in the ship's darkest corners, hiding in the cracks. Incredible as it sounds, perhaps they rode here as pests."

"But where are the human bones?" Jopale asked.

She looked at him, her face sad for a brief moment, but then drifting into a cautious amusement.

"I mean the crew that piloted this starship," Jopale continued. "What finally happened to them?"

Judging by the murmurs, others had made the same obvious assumption.

Do-ane shook her head. Then she said, "No," with a grim finality. "Think if you can in these terms: You fly from star to star. Your body is as much a machine as it is flesh. And everything you need comes to you with the help of your loyal machinery. With that kind of freedom, you can acquire any shape that you wish. Which is why you might allow your limbs to grow smaller with the eons, and why you perhaps would decide, finally, to let yourself become a worm.

"Assuming that we began as human beings, of course. Or something that resembles humans, back on that other world of ours.

"This lost, unnamable home."

GOOD MOUNTAIN

Caretakers began to hurry through the stomach, in twos and threes, carrying buckets of salve and sacks of buffering agents back into the now-empty intestines. Jopale guessed what this meant, and he felt sure when another pair of caretakers arrived, hurriedly dismantling the latrine and its privacy curtain. But where would the worm's next meal come from, and how much time would they spend waiting for her to eat her fill?

Capping the nearly filled latrine, the caretakers began wrestling it towards the esophagus. That was when Jopale decided to confront them, and that was when Master Brace finally reappeared.

The old caretaker wore a grimacing smile. He tried to wink at Jopale, and then he noticed Do-ane sitting among the passengers, flipping from page to page in her enormous book.

"Are we stopping now?" Jopale asked.

Brace nodded. With a distracted voice, he said, "There's an emergency locker up ahead. Always stocked with knuckle-roots and barrels of sap. Or at least it's supposed to be stocked."

His voice fell away.

"How long will this take?" Jopale wanted to know.

Brace heard something in his tone. Speaking with absolute surety, he admitted, "My girl needs food. Badly. If we don't give her sugar, we won't make it off this wasteland. Fire or not."

Jopale nodded. "All right. I see."

"Good Mountain," said the caretaker. "That's where we're stopping."

A dozen faces looked up.

Realizing that he had been noticed, Brace straightened his back and took a deep breath. Then without hesitation, he said, "Everyone will disembark. The feeding will be done as fast as possible. And from this point, everyone rides on top of the worm. Up where the mockmen are sitting now."

The old woman bristled. "But where will my mockmen ride?"

"They will not, madam." With squared shoulders, the caretaker faced the spoiled creature, explaining to her and to everyone, "This is an emergency situation, if ever there was. And I'm using the powers of my office, madam. Do not try to stop me."

The woman shrank a little bit.

But her companion, smelling his duty, climbed to his feet. "We can't just leave these creatures behind," he argued.

Brace smiled. Then he laughed, quietly and with considerable relish. And he opened his arms while gesturing at the surrounding stomach, admitting, "Oh, I don't intend to leave them. Not at all."

There was no station at Good Mountain, abandoned or otherwise. There wasn't even an auxiliary trail for a worm to pull to one side. But the foundations for homes were visible, plus markings lain out to define a network of streets. The only signs of recent habitation were the promised locker—an underground facility little bigger than a worm's stomach—and standing to the north, a beacon tower built of wood and capped with an enormous bone-lined bowl. A reservoir of fats and cured sap was burning slowly, yellow flames swirling with the wind. In other times, this would have been the brightest light for a hundred kilometers—a navigation point to help any lost souls. But the firestorm to the east made the fire seem quite weak. Against that rushing, sizzling wall of scorching fire and vaporized wood, everything about the world seemed small and feeble.

The wind was blowing harder now, and with it came a chill from the west, causing Jopale to shiver.

Caretakers worked frantically, breaking open the locker, rolling barrel after barrel onto the trail directly in front of the worm. And other caretakers ordered the mockmen off the worm's back, gathering them together on the dusty, dry ground, loud voices warning them not to take another step.

Jopale thought he could hear the firestorm, even though it was still ten or twenty kilometers behind them.

It sounded like water, oddly enough. Like a strong current flowing over a brink, then falling fast.

Do-ane appeared suddenly, almost close enough to touch him. Her boots were buttoned. Her book was cradled under one arm. She studied his face for a moment. Then she regarded the firestorm with the same speculative intensity. And finally, she said to Jopale, "Come with me."

He wasn't surprised. For a long while now, he had imagined this invitation and his response. But what startled him was his own reaction, feeling decidedly unsure about what to do.

"My colleagues are there now," she continued, pointing at the still-distant tower. "Behind the beacon is a little hut, and there's a shaft and elevator that will drop us all the way to the starship—"

"What about me?" Rit interrupted.

Do-ane gave him a moment's glance. She seemed unprepared for his entirely natural question.

"Your starship is huge," Rit reminded her. "Huge and empty. Don't you think your friends would welcome me, too?"

She tried to speak.

Then the old wealthy woman stepped forwards. "There isn't much time, miss. Where's this sanctuary of yours—?"

"Beyond that tower," Rit offered.

"Thank you." Then to her companion, she said, "Help me, will you dear? I'm not sure I can manage such a long walk."

Her young man was holding their essential bags, a faint smile showing as he stared off to the north. With an agreeable tone, he said, "I'm sure you'll do fine." Then he winked, adding, "Start right away. As fast as you can." And with the strength of youth, he ran off into the ruddy gloom, dropping his bags and hers in his wake.

Other passengers began to follow him.

"Well," the old woman muttered. Then with a shuffling gait, she tried to keep up.

Rit glared at Do-ane. Appalled by the circumstances, he asked, "So just how big is this elevator? And how fast? And will it take all of us at once?"

She tried to answer, but her voice kept failing her.

Rit looked back at the worm, then focused on the tower.

"Where are you going?" Master Brace hollered. He was still up near the worm's mouth, but moving toward them as fast as he could manage. "What are you people doing? What in the hell are you thinking?"

Do-ane saw him coming. Then she threw down everything but her precious book, and glancing at Jopale one last time, she turned and sprinted across the empty plain.

Rit considered Jopale, plainly doubting his good sense and sanity. Then he was gone too, his long stride letting him catch up to Do-ane, then the old woman, leaving both of them behind.

"Sir," said Brace, staggering up next to Jopale.

He would say his good-byes; then he would run too. Jopale had made up his mind, or so he believed.

"Don't," was the caretaker's advice.

"Don't what?" Jopale asked.

Brace took him by the shoulder. Panting from his run, he said, "I like you, sir. And I honestly meant to warn you before now."

"Warn me?"

"And then . . . then I saw the girl talking to everybody, and I didn't think . . . I couldn't imagine . . . that all of you would actually believe her—"

"What is this?" Jopale cried out.

"She's ridden my worm in the past, sir." Brace looked across the plain. The fire to the east was tall enough and bright enough to illuminate each of the fleeing passengers. Tiny now. Frantic little shapes soon to be lost against that great expanse of dead dry wood.

"I know she's ridden this way," Jopale said. "Of course she has. She comes here to study the secret mountain."

Brace shook his head.

"No, sir," he said.

Then he looked Jopale in the eyes, saying, "She does this. She has that book of hers, and she befriends a man . . . usually an older man . . . convincing him that everything she says is real. Then she steps off at this place and invites him to join her adventure, and of course any man would happily walk off with a pretty young thing like that.

"But she is insane, sir. I am sure.

"On my worm, she has ridden west at least five times now. And three times, she has set off a flare to make us stop here and pick her up on our eastbound leg." He gulped the cool air. "That's what people do in this country when there is no station, sir." Offering a grim smile, he added, "But sometimes we haven't brought her, and it's her men who set off the flares. We've rescued several gentlemen of your age and bearing, and they're always angry. 'She showed me this big book,' they'll say. They'll say, 'I was going to explore an ancient starship and look at the bones of gods.'"

Jopale wrapped his arms around his chest, moaning softly.

"That girl is quite crazy, sir. And that's all she is." Brace placed a comforting hand upon Jopale's shoulder. "She takes her men walking in the darkness. She keeps telling them that their destination is just a little farther now. But there's nothing to find out there. Even the most foolish man figures that out. And do you know what she does? At some point, she'll turn and tell him, 'You are the problem. You don't believe, so of course we can't find it.'

"Then those fellows return here and continue their journey west. And she wanders for a little while, then comes and waits here for the next eastbound worm. Somehow she always has money. Her life is spent riding worms and reading her book, and when she forgets that nothing on those pages is real, she comes back this way again. And that's all that she does in her life, from what I can tell."

Jopale was confused, and he had never been so angry. But somehow none of this was a perfect surprise.

"I should have said something," Brace admitted. "In my baby's stomach, when I saw her talking to everybody . . ."

"Should we chase after them?" Jopale asked.

But the caretaker could only shake his head, telling him, "There isn't time, sir. And honestly, I don't think we could make those people listen to reason now. They're chasing the only hope they've got left."

"But we should try to do what's right," Jopale maintained. "Perhaps we can convince one or two of them to turn back—"

"Sir," Brace interrupted.

Then the old fellow laughed at him.

"I don't know if you've noticed this, sir. But there is an exceptionally good chance that we ourselves won't be alive for much longer."

Again, Jopale heard the soft watery rumbling of the fire.

"Yes. Of course . . ."

TOWARD PORT OF KRAUSS

Brace began walking toward the worm's head.

The worm was slowly crawling forward, gulping down the big sweet barrels as she moved. Farther ahead, several dozen mockmen were being coaxed down onto the trail. At a distance, they looked entirely human. They seemed small and plainly scared, clinging to one another while their bare feet slipped on the white grease.

Jopale caught Brace, and before he lost his own scarce courage, he made an enormous request.

"I know it's asking a lot," he admitted.

"That won't make much difference," the old man said, offering a dark little laugh. Then he paused and cupped his hands around his mouth, shouting new orders into the wind.

The red-haired female was separated from the other mockmen.

Jopale rejoined his companion, and the two of them grabbed his bags and then a rope ladder, climbing onto the worm's wide back.

Without prompting, the mockman claimed one of the low chairs, facing forward, her long legs stretched out before her. If the creature was grateful, it didn't show on her stoic face. Either she was too stupid to understand what he had done, or she was perceptive enough to despise him for saving only her, leaving her friends to their gruesome fate.

The worm's bare flesh was warm to the touch. Jopale sat directly behind his mockman, letting her bulk block the wind. He could feel the great spine shifting beneath his rump. Facing backwards, he didn't watch the rest of the feeding, and save for a few muddled screams, he heard nothing. Then the worm began to accelerate, drugs and this one meal lending her phenomenal energy. And after a little while, when they were racing across the empty landscape, Master Brace came and sat beside him.

"But the book," Jopale began.

"It certainly looks real enough," the old man replied, guessing his mind. "And maybe it is genuine. Maybe she stole it from a true scientist who actually knows where the starship is buried. Or maybe it's an ancient manuscript, and there was once a starship . . . but the ship sank to the core ages ago, and some curious fluke has placed it in her strange hands."

"Or she invented everything," Jopale allowed.

"Perhaps." Watching the firestorm, Brace nodded. "Perhaps the girl heard a story about space flight and lost worlds, and she has a talent that lets her draw elaborate diagrams and play games with cameras. And these times are what made her insane. The terrors and wild hopes tell her that everything she can dream up is real. Perhaps."

Or she was perfectly rational, Jopale thought, and the starship really *was* waiting out there. Somewhere. While Brace was the creature whose sanity had been discarded along the way, his mind lying to both of them, forcing them to stay onboard his treasured worm.

"But the name," Jopale muttered.

"Sir?"

"'Good Mountain'. She told me why the scientists used that old word. And honestly, I can't think of another reason for placing that noble name on this ridiculous place?"

"First of all, sir—"

"Call me Jopale, please."

"Jopale. Yes." Brace held both of his hands against the worm's skin, listening to the great body. "First of all, I know this country well. If there were a project here, a research station of any size, it would not be a secret from me. And I can tell you frankly, Jopale . . . except for that one strange girl and her misguided men, nobody comes to this wasted space . . ."

A small quake rolled beneath them.

When it passed, Brace suggested, "We might be in luck here, sir. Do-ane may have told you: There's a dead island under this ground. There's a lot of wood sitting between us and the methane. So when the fire gets off the Tanglelands, it should slow down. At least for a little while. This wood's going to burn, sure, but not as fast as that damned gas does."

Jopale tried to feel encouraged. Then he repeated the words, "'First of all.'"

"Sir?"

"You said, 'First of all.' What's second of all?"

Master Brace nodded in a thoughtful fashion, then said, "You know, my mother was a caretaker on a worm exactly like this one. And her father was a driver on a freighter worm that crawled along this same trail, bringing the new iron back from Port of Krauss. It was that grandfather who told me that even when there was sunlight here, this was an awful place to live. Flat like this. Sapless. Hard to farm, and hard on the soul. But some greedy fellow bought this land for nothing, then sold pieces of it to people in more crowded parts of the world. He named his ground 'Good Mountain' because he thought the old word sounded strong and lasting. But of course, all he wanted was to lure fools into his trap . . ."

Jopale reached back over his head, burying one of his hands into the mockman's thick hair. Then he pushed with his legs, feeling a consuming need to be closer to her, grinding his spine hard up against her spine.

"It's just one old word," Brace was saying. With his face lit up by the endless fire, he said, "And I don't know if you've noticed this, sir. But words . . . what they are . . . they're just sounds and scribbles. It's *people* who give them meaning. Without us, the poor things wouldn't have any life at all."

And they pressed on, rushing toward the promised Ocean, with the End of the World following close behind.

where the golden apples grow

KAGE BAKER

One of the most prolific new writers to appear in the late nineties, the late Kage Baker made her first sale in 1997, with "Noble Mold," the first of her long sequence of sly and compelling stories of the adventures and misadventures of the time-traveling agents of the Company. Her Company novels include In the Garden of Iden, Sky Coyote, Mendoza in Hollywood, The Graveyard Game, The Life of the World to Come, The Machine's Child, Sons of Heaven, *and* Not Less Than Gods. *Her other books include fantasy novels* The Anvil of the World, The House of the Stag, *and* The Bird on the River, *science fiction novel* The Empress of Mars, *YA novel* The Hotel Under the Sand, *and* Or Else My Lady Keeps the Key, *about some of the real pirates of the Caribbean. Her many stories were collected in* Black Projects, White Knights, Mother Aegypt and Other Stories, The Children of the Company, Dark Mondays, *and* Gods and Pawns. *Her posthumously published books include* Neil Gwynne's Scarlet Spy, Neil Gwynne's On Land and Sea *(with Kathleen Barholomew), and a collection,* In the Company of Thieves. *Baker died, tragically young, in 2010.*

Here she takes us to a newly colonized frontier Mars, still wild and dangerous, for a taut adventure that demonstrates that the grass is always greener on the other side of the fence—no matter which side of the fence you're looking over.

I

He was the third boy born on Mars.

He was twelve years old now and had spent most of his life in the cab of a freighter. His name was Bill.

Bill lived with his dad, Billy Townsend. Billy Townsend was a Hauler. He made the long runs up and down Mars, to Depot North and Depot South, bringing ice back from the ends of the world. Bill had always gone along on the runs, from the time he'd been packed into the shotgun seat like a little duffel bag to now, when he sat hunched in the far corner of the cab with his Gamebuke, ignoring his dad's loud and cheerful conversation.

There was no other place for him to be. The freighter was the only home he had ever known. His dad called her *Beautiful Evelyn.*

As far as Bill knew, his mum had passed on. That was one of the answers his dad had given him, and it might be true; there were a lot of things to die from on Mars, with all the cold and dry and blowing grit, and so little air to breathe. But it was just as likely she had gone back to Earth, to judge from other things his dad had said. Bill tried not to think about her, either way.

He didn't like his life very much. Most of it was either boring—the long, long runs to the Depots, with nothing to look at but the monitor screens showing miles of red rocky plain—or scary, like the times they'd had to run through bad storms, or when *Beautiful Evelyn* had broken down in the middle of nowhere.

Better were the times they'd pull into Mons Olympus. The city on the mountain had a lot to see and do (although Bill's dad usually went straight to the Empress of Mars Tavern and stayed there); there were plenty of places to eat, and shops, and a big public data terminal where Bill could download school programs into his Buke. But what Bill liked most about Mons Olympus was that he could look down through its dome and see the Long Acres.

The Long Acres weren't at all like the city, and Bill dreamed of living there. Instead of endless cold red plains, the Long Acres had warm expanses of green life, and actual canals of water for crop irrigation, stretching out for kilometers under vizio tunnels. Bill had heard that from space, it was supposed to look like green lines crossing the lowlands of the planet.

People stayed put in the Long Acres. Families lived down there and worked the land. Bill liked that idea.

His favorite time to look down the mountain was at twilight. Then the lights were just coming on, shining through the vizio panels, and the green fields were empty; Bill liked to imagine families sitting down to dinner together, a dad and a mum and kids in their home, safe in one place from one year to the next. He imagined that they saved their money, instead of going on spending sprees when they hit town, like Bill's dad did. They never forgot things, like birthdays. They never made promises and forgot to keep them.

"Payyyydayyyy!" Billy said happily, beating out a rhythm on the console wheel as he drove. "Gonna spend my money free! Yeah! We'll have us a good time, eh, mate?"

"I need to buy socks," said Bill.

"Whatever you want, bookworm. Socks, boots, buy out the whole shop."

"I just need socks," said Bill. They were on the last stretch of the High Road, rocketing along under the glittering stars, and ahead of them he could see the high-up bright lights of Mons Olympus on the monitor. Its main dome was luminous with colors from the neon signs inside; even the outlying Tubes were lit up, from all the psuit-lights of the people going to and fro. It looked like pictures he had seen of circus tents on Earth. Bill shut down his Gamebuke and slid it into the front pocket of his psuit, and carefully zipped the pocket shut.

"Time to put your mask on, Dad," he said. If Billy wasn't reminded, he tended to just take a gulp of air, jump from the cab and sprint for the Tube airlocks, and one or twice he had tripped and fallen, and nearly killed himself before he'd got his mask on.

"Sure thing," said Billy, fumbling for the mask. He had managed to get it on his face unassisted by the time *Beautiful Evelyn* roared into the freighter barn and backed into the Unload bay. Father and son climbed from the cab and walked away together toward the Tube, stiff-legged after all those hours on the road.

At this moment, walking side by side, they really did look like father and son. Bill had Billy's shock of wild hair that stuck up above the mask, and though he was small for a Mars-born kid, he was lean and rangy like Billy. Once they stepped through the airlocks and into the Tube, they pushed up their masks, and then they looked different; for Billy had bright crazy eyes in a lean wind-red face, and a lot of wild red beard. Bill's eyes were dark, and there was nothing crazy about him.

"Payday, payday, got money on my mind," sang Billy as they walked up the hill toward the freight office. "Bam! I'm gonna start with a big plate of Scramble with gravy, and then *two* slices of duff, and then it's hello Ares Amber Lager. What'll you do, kiddo?"

"I'm going to buy socks," said Bill patiently. "Then I guess I'll go to the public terminal. I need my next lesson plan, remember?"

"Yeah, right." Billy nodded, but Bill could tell he wasn't paying attention.

Bill went into the freight office with his dad, and waited in the lobby while Billy went in to present their chits. As he waited, he took out his Buke and thumbed it on, and accessed their bank account. He watched the screen until it flashed and updated, and checked the bank balance against what he thought it should be; the amount was correct.

He sighed and relaxed. For a long while last year, the paycheck had been short every month; money taken out by the civil court to pay off a fine Billy had incurred for beating up another guy. Billy was easygoing and never started fights, even when he drank, but he had a long reach and no sense of fear, so he tended to win them. The other Haulers never minded a good fight; this one time, though, the other guy had been a farmer from the MAC, and he had sued Billy.

Billy came out of the office now whistling, with the look in his eyes that meant he wanted to go have fun.

"Come on, bookworm, the night's young!" he said. Bill fell into step beside him as they went on up the Tube, and out to Commerce Square.

Commerce Square was the biggest single structure on the planet. Five square miles of breathable air! The steel beams soared in an unsupported arch, holding up Permavizio panes through which the stars and moons shone down. Beneath it rose the domes of houses and shops, and the spiky towers of the Edgar Allan Poe Memorial Center for the Performing Arts. It was built in an Old Earth style called *Gothic*. Bill had learned that just last term.

"Right!" Billy stretched. "I'm off to the Empress! Where you going?

"To buy socks, remember?" said Bill.

"Okay," said Billy. "See you round, then." He wandered off into the crowd.

Bill sighed. He went off to the general store.

You could get almost anything at Prashant's; this was the only one on Mars and it had been here a whole year now, but Bill still caught his breath when he stepped inside. Row upon row of shiny things in brilliant colors! Cases of fruit juice, electronics, furniture, tools, clothing, tinned delicacies—and all of it imported from Earth. A whole aisle of download stations selling music, movies, books and games. Bill, packet of cotton socks in hand, approached the aisle furtively.

Should he download more music? It wasn't as though Billy would ever notice or care, but the downloads were expensive. All the same . . .

Bill saw that Earth Hand had a new album out, and that decided him. He plugged in his Buke and ordered the album, and twenty minutes later was sneaking out of the store, feeling guilty. He went next to the public terminal and downloaded his lesson plan; that, at least, was free. Then he walked on up the long steep street, under the flashing red and green and blue signs for the posh hotels. His hands were cold, but rather than put his gloves back on he simply jammed his fists in his suit pockets.

At the top of the street was the Empress of Mars. It was a big place, a vast echoing tavern with a boarding house and restaurant opening off one side and a bath-house opening off the other. All the Haulers came here. Mother, who ran the place, didn't mind Haulers. They weren't welcome in the fancy new places, which had rules about noise and gambling and fighting, but they were always welcome at the *Empress*.

Bill stepped through the airlock and looked around. It was dark and noisy in the tavern, with only a muted golden glow over the bar and little colored lights in the booths. It smelled like spilled beer and frying food, and the smell of the food made Bill's mouth water. Haulers sat or stood everywhere, and so did construction workers, and they were all eating and drinking and talking at the top of their lungs.

But where was Billy? Not in his usual place at the bar. Had he decided to go for a bath first? Bill edged his way through the crush to the bathhouse door, which was already so clouded with steam he couldn't see in. He opened the door and peered at the row of psuits hung up behind the attendant, but Billy's psuit wasn't one of them.

"Young Bill?" said someone, touching him on the shoulder. He turned and saw Mother herself, a solid little middle-aged lady who spoke with a thick Pan-Celtic accent. She wore a lot of jewelery; she was the richest lady on Mars, and owned most of Mons Olympus. "What do you need, my dear?"

"Where's my dad?" Bill shouted, to be heard above the din.

"Hasn't come in yet," Mother replied. "What, was he to meet you here?"

Bill felt the familiar stomach ache he got whenever Billy went missing. Mother, looking into his eyes, patted his arm.

"Like as not just stopped to talk to somebody, I'm sure. He's friendly, our Billy, eh? Would start a conversation with any stone in the road, if he thought he recognized it. Now, you come and sit in the warm, my dear, and have some supper. Soygold strip with gravy and sprouts, that's your favorite, yes? And we've barley-sugar duff for afters. Let's get you some tea . . ."

Bill let her settle him in a corner booth and bring him a mug of tea. It was delicious, salty-sweet and spicy, and the warmth of the mug felt good on his hands; but it didn't unclench the knot in his stomach. He sipped tea and watched the airlock opening and closing. He tried raising Billy on the psuit comm, but Billy seemed to have forgotten to turn it on. Where was his dad?

II

He was the second boy born on Mars, and he was six years old.

In MAC years, that is.

The Martian year was twenty-four months long, but most of the people in Mons Olympus and the Areco administrative center had simply stuck to reckoning time in twelve-month-long Earth years. That way, every other year, Christmas fell in the Martian summer, and those years were called Australian years. A lot of people on Mars had emigrated from Australia, so it suited them fine.

When the Martian Agricultural Collective had arrived on Mars, though, they'd decided to do things differently. After all (they said), it was a new world; they were breaking with Earth and her traditions forever. So they set up a calendar with twenty-four months. The twelve new months were named Stothart, Engels, Hardie, Bax, Blatchford, Pollitt, Mieville, Attlee, Bentham, Besant, Hobsbawm and Quelch.

When a boy had been born to Mr. and Mrs. Marlon Thurkettle on the fifth day of the new month of Blatchford, they named their son in honor of the month. His friends, such of them as he had, called him Blatt.

He disliked his name because he thought it sounded stupid, but he *really* disliked Blatt, because it led to another nickname that was even worse: Cockroach.

Martian cockroaches were of the order *Blattidae*, and they had adapted very nicely to all the harsh conditions that had made it such a struggle for humans to settle Mars. In fact, they had mutated, and now averaged six inches in length and could survive outside the Tubes. Fortunately they made good fertilizer when ground up, so the Collective had placed a bounty of three Martian Pence on each insect. MAC children hunted them with hammers and earned pocket money that way. They knew all about cockroaches, and so Blatchford wasn't even two before Hardie Stubbs started calling him Cockroach. All the other children thought it was the funniest thing they'd ever heard.

He called himself Ford.

He lived with his parents and his brothers and sisters, crowded all together in an allotment shelter. He downloaded lesson programs and studied whenever he'd finished his chores for the day, but now that he was as tall as his dad and his brother Sam, his dad had begun to mutter that he'd had all the schooling he needed.

There was a lot of work for an able-bodied young man to do, after all: milking the cows, mucking out their stalls, spreading muck along the rows of sugar beets and soybeans. There was cleaning the canals, repairing the vizio panels that kept out the Martian climate, working in the methane plant. There was work from before the dim sun rose every morning until after the little dim moons rose at night. The work didn't stop for holidays, and it didn't stop if you got sick or got old or had an accident and were hurt.

The work had to be done, because if the MAC worked hard enough, they could turn Mars into another Earth; only one without injustice, corruption, or poverty. Every MAC child was supposed to dream of that wonderful day, and do his or her part to make it arrive.

But Ford liked to steal out of the shelter at night, and look up through the vizio at the foot of Mons Olympus, where its city shone out across the long miles of darkness. That was where he wanted to be! It was full of lights. The high-beam lights of the big freighters rocketed along the High Road toward it, roaring out of the dark and cold, and if you watched you could see them coming and going from the city all night. They came back from the far poles of the world, and went out there again.

The Haulers drove them. The Haulers were the men and women who rode the High Road through the storms, through the harsh dry places nobody else dared to go, but they went because they were brave. Ford had heard lots of stories about them. Ford's dad said Haulers were all scum, and half of them were criminals. They got drunk, they fought, they made huge sums in hazard pay and gambled it away or spent it on rich food. They had adventures. Ford thought he'd like to have an adventure someday.

As he grew up, though, he began to realize that this wasn't very likely to happen.

"Will you be taking Blatchford?" asked his mum, as she shaved his head.

Ford nearly jumped up in his seat, he was so startled. But the habit of long years kept him still, and he only peered desperately into the mirror to see his dad's face before the reply. *Yes please, yes please, yes please!*

His dad hesitated a moment, distracted from bad temper.

"I suppose so," he said. "Time he saw for himself what it's like up there."

"I'll pack you another lunch, then," said his mum. She wiped the razor and dried Ford's scalp with the towel. "There you go, dear. Your turn, Baxine."

Ford got up as his little sister slid into his place, and turned to face his dad. He was all on fire with questions he wanted to ask, but he knew it wasn't a good idea to make much noise when his dad was in a bad mood. He sidled up to his older brother Sam, who was sitting by the door looking sullen.

"Never been up there," he said. "What's it like, eh?"

Sam smiled a little.

"You'll see. There's this place called the Blue Room, right? Everything's blue in there, with holos of the Sea of Earth, and lakes too. I remember lakes! And they play sounds from Earth like rain—"

"You shut your face," said his dad. "You ought to be ashamed of yourself, talking like that to a kid."

Sam turned a venomous look on their dad.

"Don't start," said their mum, sounding more tired than angry. "Just go and do what you've got to do."

Ford sat quietly beside Sam until it was time to go, when they all three pulled on their stocking caps and facemasks, slid on their packs, and went skulking up the Tube.

They skulked because visiting Mons Olympus was frowned upon. There was no need to go up there, or so the Council said; everything a good member of the Collective might need could be found in the MAC store, and if it couldn't, then you probably didn't need it, and certainly shouldn't want it.

The problem was that the MAC store didn't carry boots in Sam's size. Ford's dad had tried to order them, but there was endless paperwork to fill out, and the store clerk had looked at Sam as though it was his fault for having such big feet, as though a *good* member of the Collective would have sawed off a few toes to make himself fit the boots the MAC store stocked.

But Prashant's up in Mons Olympus carried all sizes, so every time Sam wore out a pair of boots, that was where Ford's dad had to go.

As though to make up for the shame of it, he lectured Ford the whole way up the mountain, while Sam stalked along beside them in resentful silence.

"This'll be an education for you, Blatchford, yes indeed. You'll get to see thieves and drunks and fat cats living off the sweat of others. Everything we left Earth to get away from! Shops full of vanities to make you weak. Eating places full of poisons. It's a right cesspool, that's what it is."

"What'll happen to it when we turn Mars into a paradise?" asked Ford.

"Oh, it'll be gone by then," said his dad. "It'll collapse under its own rotting weight, you mark my words."

"I reckon I'll have to go home to Earth to buy boots then, won't I?" muttered Sam.

"Shut up, you ungrateful lout," said his dad.

They came out under the old Settlement dome, where the Areco offices and the MAC store were, as well as the spaceport and the Ephesian Church. This was the farthest Ford had ever been from home, and up until today the most exotic place he had ever seen. There was a faint sweet incense wafting out from the Church, and the sound of chanting. Ford's dad hurried them past the Ephesian Tea Room with a disdainful sniff, ignoring the signs that invited wayfarers in for a hot meal and edifying brochures about the Goddess.

"Ignorance and superstition, that is," he told Ford. "Another thing we left behind when we came here, but you can see it's still putting out its tentacles, trying to control the minds of the people."

He almost ran them past the MAC store, and they were panting for breath as they ducked up the Tube that led to Mons Olympus.

Ford stared around. The Tube here was much wider, and much better maintained, than where it ran by his parents' allotment. The vizio used was a more expensive kind, for one thing: it was almost as transparent as water. Ford could now see clearly across the mountainside, the wide cinnamon-colored waste of rocks and sand. He gazed up at Mons Olympus, struck with awe at its sheer looming size. He turned and looked back on the lowlands, and for the first time saw the green expanse of the Long Acres that had been his whole world until now, stretching out in domed lines to the horizon. He walked backwards a while, gaping, until he stumbled and his dad caught him.

"It's hard to look away from, isn't it?" said his dad. "Don't worry. We'll be going home soon enough."

"Soon enough," Sam echoed in a melancholy sort of way.

Once past the airlock from the spaceport, the Tube became crowded, with suited strangers pushing past them, dragging baggage, or walking slow and staring as hard as Ford was staring: he realized they must be immigrants from Earth, getting their first glimpse of a new world.

But Ford got his new world when he stepped through the last airlock and looked into Commerce Square.

"Oh . . ." he said.

Even by daylight, it glittered and shone. Along the main street was a double line of actual *trees*, like on Earth; there was a green and park-like place immediately to the left, where real flowers grew. Ford thought he recognized roses, from the images in his lessons. Their scent hung in the air like music. There were other good smells, from spicy foods cooking in a dozen little stalls and wagons along the Square, and big stores breathing out a perfume of expensive wares.

And there were *people*! More people, and more kinds of people, than Ford had even known existed. There were Sherpa contract laborers and Incan construction workers, speaking to one another in languages Ford couldn't understand. There were hawkers selling souvenirs and cheap nanoprocessors from handcarts. There were Ephesian missionaries talking earnestly to thin people in ragged clothes.

There were Haulers—Ford knew them at once, big men and women in their psuits, and their heads were covered in long hair and the men had beards. Some had tattooed faces. All had bloodshot eyes. They talked loudly and laughed a lot, and they looked as though they didn't care what anyone thought of them at all. Ford's dad scowled at them.

"Bloody lunatics," he told Ford. "Most of 'em were in Hospital on Earth, did you know that, Blatchford? Certifiable. The only ones Areco could find who were reckless enough for that kind of work. Exploitation, I call it."

Sam muttered something. Their dad turned on him.

"What did you say, Samuel?" he demanded.

"I said we're at the shop, all right?" said Sam, pointing at the neon sign.

Ford gasped as they went in, as the warmed air and flowery scent wrapped around him. It was nothing like the MAC store, which had rows of empty shelves, and what merchandise was there, was dusty; everything here looked clean and new. He didn't even know what most of it was for. Sleek, pretty people smiled from behind the counters.

He smiled back at them, until he passed a counter and came face to face with three men skulking along—skinny scarecrows with shaven heads, with canal mud on their boots. He blushed scarlet to realize he was looking into a mirror. Was *he* that gawky person between his dad and Sam? Did his ears really stick out like that? Ford pulled his cap down, so mortified he wanted to run all the way back down the mountain.

But he kept his eyes on the back of his dad's coat instead, following until they came to the Footwear Department. There he was diverted by the hundreds and hundreds of shoes on the walls, apparently floating in space, turning so he could see them better. They were every color there was, and they were clearly never designed to be worn while shoveling muck out of the cowsheds.

He came close and peered at them, as his dad and Sam argued with one of the beautiful people, until he saw the big-eyed boy staring back at him from beyond the dancing shoes. Another mirror; did he really have his mouth hanging open like that? And, oh, look at his nose, pinched red by the cold, and look at those watery blue eyes all rimmed in red, and those gangling big hands with the red chapped knuckles!

Ford turned around, wishing he could escape from himself. There were his dad and Sam, and they looked just like him, except his dad was old. Was he, Ford, going to look just like that, when he was somebody's dad? How mean and small his dad looked, trying to sound posh as he talked to the clerk:

"Look, we don't want this fancy trim and we don't want your shiny brass, thank you *very* much, we just want plain decent waders the lad can do a day's honest work in! Now, you can understand that much, can't you?"

"I like the brass buckles, Dad," said Sam.

"Well, you don't need 'em—they're only a vanity," said their dad. Sam shut his mouth like a box.

Ford stood by, cringing inside, as more boots were brought, until at last a pair was found that was plain and cheap enough to suit their dad. More embarrassment followed then, as their dad pulled out a wad of MAC scrip and tried to pay with it, before remembering that scrip could only be used at the MAC store. Worse still, he then pulled out a wrinkly handful of Martian paper money. Both Ford and Sam saw the sales clerks exchange looks; what kind of people didn't have credit accounts? Sam tried to save face by being sarcastic.

"We're all in the Stone Age down the hill, you know," he said loudly, accepting the wrapped boots and tucking them under his arm. "I reckon we'll get around to having banks one of these centuries."

"Banks are corrupt institutions," said their dad like a shot, rounding on him. "How'd you get so tall without learning anything, eh? What have I told—"

"Sam?" A girl's voice stopped him. Ford turned in astonishment and saw one of the beautiful clerks hurrying toward them, smiling as though she meant it. "Sam, where were you last week? We missed you at the party—I wanted to show you my new . . ." She faltered to a stop, looking from Sam to their dad and Ford. Ford felt his heart jump when she looked at him. She had silver-gold hair, and wore makeup, and smelled sweet.

"I . . . er . . . Is this your family? How nice to meet you—" she began lamely, but their dad cut her off.

"Who's *this* painted cobweb, then?" he demanded of Sam. Sam's face turned red.

"Don't you talk that way about her! Her name is Galadriel, and—it so happens we're dating, not that it's any of your business."

"You're *what*?" Outraged, their dad clenched his knobby fists. "So you've been sneaking up here at night to live the high life, have you? No wonder you're no bloody use in the mornings! MAC girls not good enough for you? Fat lot of use a little mannequin like that's going to be when you settle down! Can she drive a tractor, eh?"

Sam threw down the boots. "Got a wire for you, Dad," he shouted. "I'm not settling down on Mars! I *hate* Mars, I've hated it since the day you dragged me up here, and the *minute* I come of age, I'm off back to Earth! Get it?"

Sam leaving? Ford felt a double shock, of sadness and betrayal. Who'd tell him stories if Sam left?

"You self-centered great twerp!" their dad shouted back. "Of all the ungrateful—when the MAC's fed you and clothed you all these years—just going to walk out on your duty, are you?"

Galadriel was backing away into the crowd, looking as though she wished she were invisible, and Ford wished he could be invisible too. People all over the store had stopped what they were doing to turn and stare.

"I never asked to join the MAC, you know," said Sam. "Nobody's ever given a thought to what *I* wanted at all!"

"That's because there are a few more important things in the world than what one snotty-nosed brat wants for himself!"

"Well, I'm telling you now, Dad—if you think I'm going to live my life doing the same boring thing every day until I get old like you, you're sadly mistaken!"

"Am I then?" Their dad jumped up and grabbed Sam by the ear, wringing tight. "I'll sort you out—"

Sam, grimacing in pain, socked their dad. Ford bit his knuckles, terrified. Their dad staggered back, his eyes wide and furious.

"Right, that's it! You're no son of mine, do you hear me? You're disowned! The Collective doesn't need a lazy, backsliding traitor like you!"

"Don't you call me a traitor!" said Sam. He put his head down and ran at their dad, and their dad jumped up and butted heads with him. Sam's nose gushed blood. They fell to the ground, punching each other. Sam was sobbing in anger.

Ford backed away from them. He was frightened and miserable, but there was a third emotion beginning to float up into his consciousness: a certain sense of wonder. Could Sam really stop being his father's son? Was it really possible just to become somebody else, to drop all the obligations and duties of your old life and step into a new life? Who would he, Ford, be, if he had the chance to be somebody else?

Did he *have* to be that red-nosed farm boy with muddy boots?

People were gathering around, watching the fight with amusement and disgust. Someone shouted, "You can't take the MAC anyplace nice, can you?" Ford's ears burned with humiliation.

Then someone else shouted, "Here come Mother's Boys!"

Startled, Ford looked up and saw several big men in Security uniforms making their way through the crowd. Security!

The police are a bunch of brutes, his dad had told him. *They like nothing better than to beat the daylights out of the likes of you and me, son!*

Ford's nerve broke. He turned and fled, weaving and dodging his way through the crowd until he got outside the shop, and then he ran for his life.

He had no idea where he was going, but he soon found himself in a street that wasn't nearly as elegant as the promenade. It was an industrial district, dirty and shabby, with factory workers and energy plant techs hurrying to and fro. If the promenade with its gardens was the fancy case of Mons Olympus, this was its circuit board, where the real works were. Feeling less out of place, Ford slowed to a walk and caught his breath. He wandered on, staring around him.

He watched for a long moment through the open door of a machine shop, where a pair of mechanics were repairing a quaddy. Their welding tools shot out fiery-bright stars that bounced harmlessly to the ground. There were two other men watching too, though as the minutes dragged by they began watching Ford instead. Finally they stepped close to him, smiling.

"Hey, Collective. You play cards?" said one of them.

"No," said Ford.

"That's okay," said the other. "This is an easy game." He opened his coat and Ford saw that he had a kind of box strapped to his chest. It had the word NEBU-LIZER painted on it, but when the man pressed a button, the front of the box swung down and open like a tray. The other man pulled a handful of cards from his back pocket.

"Here we go," he said. "Just three cards. Ace, deuce, Queen of Diamonds. See 'em? I'm going to shuffle them and lay them out, one, two, three." He laid them out face down on the tray. "See? Now, which one's the queen? Can you find her?"

Ford couldn't believe what a dumb game this was. Only three cards? He turned over the queen.

"Boy, it's hard to fool *you*," said the man with the tray. "You've got natural luck, kid. Want to go again?" The other man had already swept the three cards up and was shuffling them.

"Okay," said Ford.

"Got any money? Want to place a bet?"

"I don't have any money," said Ford.

"No money? That's too bad," said the man with the tray, closing it up at once. "A lucky guy like you, you could win big. But they don't get rich down there in the Collective, do they? Same dull work every day of your life, and nothing to show for it when it's all over. That's what I hear."

Ford nodded sadly. It wasn't just Sam, he realized; everybody laughed at the MAC.

"What would you say to a chance at something better, eh?" said the man with the cards. In one smooth movement he made the cards vanish and produced instead a text plaquette. Its case was grubby and cracked, but the screen was bright with a lot of very small words.

"Know what I have here? This is a deal that'll set you up as a diamond prospector. Think of that! You could make more with one lucky strike than you'd make working the Long Acres the whole rest of your life. Now, I know what you're going to say—you don't have any tools and you don't have any training. But, you know what you *have* got? You're *young*. You're in good shape, and you can take the weather Outside.

"So here's the deal: Mr. Agar has the tools and the training, but he ain't young. You agree to go to work for him, and he'll provide what you need. You pay him off out of your first big diamond strike, and then you're in business for yourself. Easiest way to get rich there is! And all you have to do is put your thumbprint right there. What do you say?" He held out the plaquette to Ford.

Ford blinked at it. He had heard stories of the people who dug red diamonds out of the clay—why, Mons Olympus had been founded by a lady who'd got rich like that! He was reaching for the plaquette when a voice spoke close to his ear.

"Can you read, kid?"

Ford turned around. A Hauler was looking over his shoulder, smiling.

"Well—I read a little—"

"Get lost!" said the man with the plaquette, looking angry.

"I can't read," the Hauler went on, "but I know these guys. They're with Agar Steelworks. You know what they're trying to get you to thumb? That's a contract that'll legally bind you to work in Agar's iron mines for fifteen years."

"Like you'd know, jackass!" said the man with the plaquette, slipping it out of sight. He brought out a short length of iron bar and waved it at the Hauler meaningfully. The Hauler's red eyes sparkled.

"You want to fight?" he said, smacking his fists together. "Yeah! You think I'm afraid of you? You lousy little street-corner hustler! C'mere!"

The man took a swipe at him with the bar, and the Hauler dodged it and grabbed it out of his hand. The other two broke and ran, vanishing down an alley. The Hauler grinned after them, tossing the bar into the street.

"Freakin' kidnappers," he said to Ford. "You're, what, twelve? I have a kid your age."

"Thank you," Ford stammered.

"That's okay. You want to watch out for Human Resourcers, though, kid. They work that con on a lot of MAC boys like you. Diamond prospectors! Nobody but Mother ever got rich that way." The Hauler yawned and stretched. "You head off to the nearest Security post and report 'em now, okay?"

"I can't," said Ford, and to his horror he felt himself starting to shake. "I—they—there was this fight, and—Security guys came and—I have to hide."

"You in trouble?" The Hauler leaned down and looked at Ford closely. "Fighting? Mother's Boys don't allow no fighting, that's for sure. You need a place to hide? Maybe get out of town until it all blows over?" He gave Ford a conspiratorial wink.

"Yes, please," said Ford.

"You come along with me, then. I got a safe place," said the Hauler. Without looking back to see if Ford was following him, he turned and loped off up the street. Ford ran after him.

"Please, who are you?"

The Hauler glanced over his shoulder. "Billy Townsend," he said. "But don't tell me who you are. Safer that way, right?"

"Right," said Ford, falling into step beside him. He looked up at his rescuer. Billy was tall and gangly, and lurched a little when he walked, but he looked as though he wasn't the least bit worried what people thought of him. His face and dreadlocked hair and beard were all red, the funny bricky red that came from years of going Outside and having the red dust get everywhere, until it became so deeply engrained water wouldn't wash it off. There were scars all over his face and hands, too. On the back of his psuit someone had painted white words in a circle.

"What's it say on your back?" Ford asked him.

"Says *Bipolar Boys and Girls*," said Billy. "On account of we go Up and Down there, see? And because we're nutcases, half of us."

"What's it like in the ice mines?"

"Cold," said Billy, chuckling. "Get your face mask on, now. Here we go! Here's our *Beautiful Evelyn*."

They stepped out through the airlock, and the cold bit into Ford. He gulped for air and followed Billy into a vast echoing building like a hangar. It was the car barn for the ice processing plant. Just now it was deserted, but over by the loading chute sat a freighter. Ford caught his breath.

He had never seen one up close before, and it was bigger than he had imagined. Seventy-five meters long, set high on big knobbed ball tires. Its steel tank had been scoured to a dull gleam by the wind and sand. At one end was a complication of hatches and lenses and machinery that Ford supposed must be the driver's cab. Billy reached up one long arm and grabbed a lever. The foremost hatch hissed, swung open and a row of steps clanked down into place.

"There you go," said Billy. "Climb on up! Nobody'll think to look for you in there. I'll be back later. Make yourself at home."

Ford scrambled up eagerly. He looked around as the hatch squeezed shut behind him, and air rushed back in. He pulled down his mask.

He was in a tiny room with a pair of bunks built into one side. The only light came from a dim panel set in the ceiling. There was nothing else in the room, except for a locker under the lower bunk and three doors in the wall opposite. It was disappointingly plain and spotless.

Ford opened the first door and beheld the tiniest lavatory he had ever seen, so compact he couldn't imagine how to use it. He tried the second door and found a kitchen built along similar lines, more a series of shelves than a room. The third door opened into a much larger space. He crawled through and found himself in the driver's cab.

Timidly, he edged his way farther in and sat down at the console. He looked up at the instrument panels, at the big screens that ran all around the inside of the cab. They were blank and blind now, but what would it be like to sit here when the freighter was roaring along the High Road?

On the panel above the console was a little figurine, glued in place. It was a cheap-looking thing, of cast red stone like the souvenirs he had seen for sale on the handcarts in Commerce Square. It represented a lady, leaning forward as though she were running, or perhaps flying. The sculptor had given her hair that streamed back in an imaginary wind. She was grinning crazily, as the Haulers all did. She had only one eye, of red cut glass; Ford guessed the matching one had fallen off. He looked on the floor of the cab, but didn't see it.

Ford grinned too, and, because no one was there to see him, he put his hands on the wheel. "Brrrrroooom," he whispered, and looked up at the screens as though to check on his location. He felt a little stupid.

But in every one of the screens, his reflection was smiling back at him. Ford couldn't remember when he'd been so happy.

III

Bill's dinner had gone cold, though he stuffed a forkful in his mouth every now and then when he noticed Mother watching him. He couldn't keep his eyes away from the door much. *Where was Billy?*

He might have gotten in a fight, and Mother's Boys might have hauled him off to the Security Station; if that were the case, sooner or later Mother would come over to Bill with an apologetic cough and say something like, "Your dad's just had a bit of an argument, dear, and I think you'd best doss down here tonight until he, er, wakes up. We'll let him out tomorrow." And Bill would feel his face burning with shame, as he always did when that happened.

Or Billy might have met someone he knew, and forgotten about the time . . . or he might have gone for a drink somewhere else . . . or . . .

Bill was so busy imagining all the places Billy might be that he got quite a shock when Billy walked through the airlock. Before Billy had spotted him and started making his way across the room, the cramping worry had turned to anger.

"Where were you?" Bill shouted. "You were supposed to be here!"

"I had stuff to do," said Billy vaguely, sliding into the booth. He waved at Mother, who acknowledged him with a nod and sent one of her daughters over to take his order. Bill looked him over suspiciously. No cuts or bruises on his face, nothing broken on his psuit. Not fighting, then. Maybe he had met a girl. Bill relaxed just a little, but his anger kept smoldering.

When Billy's beer had been brought, Bill said:

"I wondered where you were. How come you had the comm turned off?"

"Is it off?" Billy groped for the switch in his shoulder. "Oh. Wow. Sorry, kiddo. Must have happened when I took my mask off."

He had a sip of beer. Bill gritted his teeth. He could tell that, as far as Billy was concerned, the incident was over. It had just been a mistake, right? What was the point of getting mad about it? Never mind that Bill had been scared and alone . . .

Bill exhaled forcefully and shoveled down his congealing dinner.

"I got my socks," he said loudly.

"That's nice," said Billy. Lifting his glass for another sip, his attention was taken by the holo playing above the bar. He stared across at it. Bill turned around in his seat to look. There was the image of one of Mother's Boys, a sergeant from his uniform, staring into the foremost camera as he made some kind of announcement. His lips moved in silence, though, with whatever he was saying drowned out by the laughter and the shouting in the bar.

Bill looked quickly back at Billy. Why was he watching the police report? Had he been in some kind of incident after all? Billy snorted with laughter, watching, and then pressed his lips shut to hide a smile. Why was he doing that?

Bill looked back at the holo, more certain than ever that Billy was in trouble, but now saw holofootage of two guys fighting. Was either one of them Billy? No; Bill felt his anger damp down again as he realized it was only a couple of MAC colonists, kicking and punching each other. Bill was appalled; he hadn't thought the Collective ever did stupid stuff like that.

Then there was a closeup shot of a skinny boy, with a shaven head—MAC, Bill supposed. He shrugged and turned his attention back to his plate.

Billy's food was brought and he dug into it with gusto.

"Think we'll head out again tonight," he said casually.

"But we just got back in!" Bill said, startled.

"Yeah. Well . . ." Billy sliced off a bit of Grilled Strip, put it in his mouth and chewed carefully before going on. "There's . . . mm . . . this big bonus right now for CO_2, see? MAC's getting a crop of something or other in the ground and they've placed like this humongous order for it. So we can earn like double what we just deposited if I get a second trip in before the end of the month."

Bill didn't know what to say. It was the sort of thing he nagged at his dad to do, saving more money; usually Billy spent it as fast as he had it. Bill looked at him with narrowed eyes, wondering if he had gotten into trouble after all. But he just shrugged again and said, "Okay."

"Hey, Mona?" Billy waved at the nearest of Mother's daughters. "Takeaway order too, okay, sweetheart? Soygold nuggets and sprouts. And a bottle of batch."

"Why are we getting takeaway?" Bill asked him.

"Er . . ." Billy looked innocent. "I'm just way hungry, is all. Think I'll want a snack later. I'll be driving all night."

"But you drove for twelve hours today!" Bill protested. "Aren't you ever going to sleep?"

"Sleep is for wusses," said Billy. "I'll just pop a Freddie."

Bill scowled. Freddies were little red pills that kept you awake and jittery for days. Haulers took them sometimes when they needed to be on the road for long runs without stopping. It was stupid to take them all the time, because they could kill you, and Bill threw them away whenever he found any in the cab. Billy must have stopped to buy some more. So *that* was where he'd been.

Night had fallen by the time they left the *Empress* and headed back down the hill. Cold penetrated down through the Permavizio; Bill shivered, and his psuit's thermostat turned itself up. There were still people in the streets, though fewer of them, and some of the lights had been turned out. Usually by this time, when they were in off the road, Bill would be soaking in a stone tub full of hot water, and looking forward to a good night's sleep someplace warm for a change. The thought made him grumpy as they came round the corner into the airlock.

"Masks on, Dad," Bill said automatically. Billy nodded, shifting the stoneware bucket of takeaway to his other hand as he reached for his mask. They went out to *Beautiful Evelyn*.

Bill was climbing up to open the cab when Billy grabbed him and pulled him back.

"Hang on," he said, and reached up and knocked on the hatch. "Yo, kid! Mask up, we're coming in!"

"What?" Bill staggered back, staring at Billy. "Who's in there?"

Billy didn't answer, but Bill heard a high-pitched voice calling "okay" from inside the cab, and Billy swung the hatch open and climbed up. Bill scrambled after him. The hatch sealed behind them and the air whooshed back. Bill pulled off his mask as the lights came on to reveal a boy, pulling off his own mask. They stared at each other, blinking.

Billy held out the bucket of takeaway. "Here you go, kid. Hot dinner!"

"Oh! Thank you," said the other, as Bill recognized him for the MAC boy from the holofootage he'd watched.

"What's *he* doing here?" he demanded.

"Just, you know, sort of laying low," said Billy. "Got in a little trouble and needs to go off someplace until things cool down. Thought we could take him out on the run with us, right? No worries." He stepped sidelong into the cab and threw himself into the console seat, where he proceeded to start up *Beautiful Evelyn's* drives.

"But—but—" said Bill.

"Er . . . Hi," said the other boy, avoiding his eyes. He was taller than Bill but looked younger, with big wide eyes and ears that stuck out. His shaven head made him look even more like a baby.

"Who're you?" said Bill.

"I'm, ah—" said the other boy, just as Billy roared from the cab:

"No names! No names! The less we know, the less they can beat out of us!" And he whooped with laughter. The noise of the drives powering up drowned out anything else he might have said. Bill clenched his fists and stepped close to Ford, glaring up into his eyes.

"What's going on? What'd my dad do?"

"Nothing!" Ford took a step backward.

"Well then, what'd *you* do? You must have done something, because you were on the holo. I saw you! You were fighting, huh?"

Ford gulped. His eyes got even wider and he said, "Er—yeah. Yeah, I punched out these guys. Who were trying to trick me into working in the mines for them. And, uh, I ran because, because the Security Fascists were going to beat the day-lights out of me. So Billy let me hide in here. What's your name?"

"Bill," he replied. "You're with the MAC, aren't you? What were you fighting for?"

"Well—the other guys started it," said Ford. He looked with interest at the take-away. "This smells good. It was really nice of your dad to bring it for me. Is there anywhere I can sit down to eat?"

"In there," said Bill in disgust, pointing into the cab.

"Thank you. You want some?" Ford held out the bucket timidly.

"No," said Bill. "I want to go to sleep. Go on, clear out of here!"

"Okay," said Ford, edging into the cab. "It's nice meeting you, Billy."

"Bill!" said Bill, and slammed the door in his face.

Muttering to himself, he dimmed down the lights and lay down in his bunk. He threw the switch that inflated the mattress, and its contours puffed out around him, cradling him snugly as the freighter began to move. He didn't know why he was so angry, but somehow finding Ford here had been the last straw.

He closed his eyes and tried to send himself to sleep in the way he always had, by imagining he was going down the Tube to the long Acres, step by step, into green, warm, quiet places. Tonight, though, he kept seeing the two MAC colonists from the holo, whaling away at each other like a couple of clowns while the city people looked on and laughed.

Ford, clutching his dinner, sat down in the cab and looked around. With all the screens lit up there was plenty of light by which to eat.

"Is it okay if I sit in here?" he asked Billy, who waved expansively.

"Sure, kid. Don't mind li'l Bill. He's cranky sometimes."

Ford opened the bucket and looked inside. "Do you have any forks?"

"Yeah. Somewhere. Try the seat pocket."

Ford groped into the pocket and found a ceramic fork that was, perhaps, clean. He was too hungry to care whether it was or not, and ate quickly. He wasn't sure what he was eating, but it tasted wonderful.

As he ate, he looked up at the screens. Some had just figures on them, data from the drives and external sensors. Four of them had images from the freighter's cameras, mounted front and rear, right and left. There was no windscreen— even Ford knew that an Earth-style glass windscreen would be scoured opaque by even one trip through the storms of sand and grit along the High Road, unless a forcefield was projected in front of it, and big forcefields were expensive, and unlikely to deflect blowing rocks anyhow. Easier and cheaper to fix four little force-fields over the camera lenses.

The foremost screen fascinated him. He saw the High Road itself, rolling out endlessly to the unseen night horizon under the stars. It ran between two lines of big rocks, levered into place over the years by Haulers to make it easier to find the straightest shot to the pole.

Every now and then Ford caught a glimpse of carving on some of the boulders as they flashed by—words, or figures. Some of them had what looked like tape wrapped around them, streaming out in the night wind.

"Are those . . ." Ford sought to remember his lessons about Earth roads. "Are those road signs? With, er, kilometer numbers and all?"

"What, on the boulders? Nope. They're shrines," said Billy.

"What's a shrine?"

"Place where somebody died," said Billy. "Or where somebody should have died, but didn't, because Marswife saved their butts." He reached out and tapped the little red lady on the console.

Ford thought about that. He looked at the figurine. "So . . . she's like, that Goddess the Ephesians are always on about?"

"No!" Billy grinned. "Not our Marswife. She was just this Sheila, see? Somebody from Earth who came up here like the rest of us, and she was crazy. Same as us. She thought Mars, was, like, her husband or something. And there was this big storm and she went out into it, without a mask. And they say she didn't die! Mars got her and changed her into something else so she could live Outside. That's what they say, anyway."

"Like, she mutated?" Ford stared at the little figure.

"I guess so."

"But really she died, huh?"

"Well, you'd think so," Billy said, looking at him sidelong. "Except that there are guys who swear they've seen her. She lives on the wind. She's red like the sand and her eye is a ruby, and if you're lost sometimes you'll see a red light way off, which is her eye, see? And if you follow it, you'll get home again safe. And I *know* that's true, because it happened to me."

"Really?"

Billy held up one hand, palm out. "No lie. It was right out by Two-Fifty-K. There was a storm swept through so big, it was able to pick up the road markers and toss 'em around, see? And *Beautiful Evelyn* got thrown like she was a feather by the gusts, and my nav system went out. It was just me and li'l Bill, and he was only a baby then, and I found myself so far off the road I had no clue, *no clue*, where I was, and I was sure we were going to die out there. But I saw that red light and I figured, that's somebody who knows where they are, anyway. I set off after it. Hour later the light blinks out and there's Two-Fifty-K Station right in front of me on the screen, but there's no red lights anyplace."

"Whoa," said Ford, wondering what Two-Fifty-K station was.

"There's other stories about her, too. Guys who see her riding the storm, and when she's there they know to make for a bunker, because there's a Strawberry coming."

"What's a Strawberry?"

"It's this kind of cyclone. Big *big* storm full of sand and rocks. Big red cone dancing across the ground. One took out that temple the Ephesians built, when they first got up here, and tore open half the Tubes. They don't come up Tharsis way much, but when they do—" Billy shook his head. "People die, man. Some of your people died, that time. You never heard that story?"

"No," said Ford, "But we're not supposed to talk about bad stuff after it happens."

"Really?" Billy looked askance.

"Because we can't afford to be afraid of the past," said Ford, half-quoting what he remembered from every Council Meeting he'd ever been dragged to. "Because fear will make us weak, but working fearlessly for the future will make us strong." He chanted the last line, unconsciously imitating his dad's intonation.

"Huh," said Billy. "I guess that's a good idea. You can't go through life being scared of everything. That's what I tell Bill."

Ford looked into the takeaway bucket, surprised that he had eaten his way to the bottom so quickly.

"It's good to hear stories, though," he said. "Sam, that's my brother, he gets into trouble for telling stories."

"Heh! Little white lies?"

"No," Ford said, "Real stories. Like about Earth. He remembers Earth. He says everything was wonderful there. He wants to go back."

"Back?" Billy looked across at him, startled. "But kids can't go back. I guess if he was old enough when he came up, maybe he might make it. I hear it's tough, though, going back down. The gravity's intense."

"Would you go back?"

Billy shook his head. "All I remember of Earth is the insides of rooms. Who needs that? Nobody up here to tell me what to do, man. I can just point myself at the horizon and go, and *go*, as far and as fast as I want. Zoom! I can think what I want, I can feel what I want, and you know what? The sand and the rocks don't care. The horizon don't care. The wind don't care.

"That's why they call this *space*. No, no way I'd ever go back."

Ford looked up at the screens, and remembered the nights he had watched for the long light-beams coming in from the darkness. It had given him an aching feeling for as long as he could remember, and now he understood why.

He had wanted *space*.

IV

They drove all night, and at some point Billy's stories of storms and fights and near-escapes from death turned into confusion, with Sam there somehow, and a room that ran blue with water. Then abruptly Ford was sitting up, staring around at the inside of the cab.

"Where are we?" he asked. The foremost screen showed a spooky gray distance, the High Road rolling ahead between its boulders to . . . what? A pale void full of roaming shadows.

"Almost to Five-Hundred-K Station," said Billy, from where he hunched over the wheel. "Stop pretty soon."

"Can Security follow us out here?"

Billy just laughed and shook his head. "No worries, kiddo. There's no law out here but Mars's."

The door into the living space opened abruptly, and Bill looked in at them.

"Morning, li'l Bill!"

"Good morning," said Bill in a surly voice. "You never stopped once all night. Are you ever going to pull us off somewhere so you can sleep?"

"At Five-Hundred-K," Billy promised. "How about you fix a bite of scran, eh?"

Bill did not reply. He stepped back out of sight and a moment later Ford felt the warmth in the air that meant that water was steaming. He could almost taste it, and realized that he was desperately thirsty. He crawled from his seat and followed the vapor back to where Bill had opened the kitchen and was shoving a block of something under heating coils.

"Are you fixing tea?"

"Yeah," said Bill, with a jerk of his thumb at the tall can that steamed above a heat element.

"Can I have a cup, when it's ready?"

Bill frowned, but he got three mugs from a drawer.

"Do you fight much, in the Collective?" he asked. Ford blinked in surprise.

"No," he said. "It wasn't me fighting, actually. It was just my dad and my brother. They hate each other. But my mum won't let them fight in the house. Sam said he was deserting us and my dad went off on him about it. I ran when the Security came."

"Oh," said Bill. He seemed to become a little less hostile, but he said: "Well, that was pretty bloody stupid. They'd only have taken you to Mother's until your dad sobered up. You'd be safe home by now."

Ford shrugged.

"So, what's your name, really?"

"Ford."

"Like that guy in *The Hitchhiker's Guide to the Galaxy?*" Bill smiled for the first time.

"What's that?"

"It's a book I listen to all the time. Drowns out Billy singing." Bill's smile went away again. The tea can beeped to signal it was hot enough, and Bill turned and pulled it out. He poured dark bubbling stuff into the three mugs, and, reaching in a cold-drawer, took out a slab of something yellow on a dish. He spooned out three lumps of it, one into each mug, and presented one to Ford.

"Whoa." Ford stared into his mug. "That's not sugar."

"It's butter," said Bill, as though that were obvious. He had a gulp of tea, and, not wanting to seem picky, Ford took a gulp too. It wasn't as nasty as he had expected. In fact, it wasn't nasty at all. Bill, watching his face, said:

"You've never had this before?"

Ford shook his head.

"But you guys are the ones who make the butter up here," said Bill. "This is MAC butter. What do you drink, if you don't drink this?"

"Just . . . batch, and tea with sugar sometimes," said Ford, wondering why this should matter. He had another gulp of the tea. It tasted even better this time.

"And the sugar comes from the sugar beets you grow?" Bill persisted.

"I guess so," said Ford. "I never thought about it."

"What's it like, living down there?"

"What's it like?" Ford stared at him. Why in the world would anybody be curious about the Long Acres? "I don't know. I muck out cow sheds. It's boring, mostly."

"How could it be *boring*?" Bill demanded. "It's so beautiful down there! Are you crazy?"

"No," said Ford, taking a step backward. "But if you think a big shovelful of cowshite and mega-roaches is beautiful, *you're* crazy."

Billy shouted something from the front of the cab and a second later *Beautiful Evelyn* swerved around. Both boys staggered a little at the shift in momentum, glaring at each other, and righted themselves as forward motion ceased.

"We're at Five-Hundred-K Station," Bill guessed. There was another beep. He turned automatically to pull the oven drawer open as Billy came staggering back into the living area.

"Mons Olympus to Five-Hundred-K in one night," he chortled. "That is some righteous driving! Where's the tea?"

They crowded together in the cramped space, sipping tea and eating something brown and bubbly that Ford couldn't identify. Afterward Billy climbed into his bunk with a groan, and yanked the cord that inflated his mattress.

"I am so ready for some horizontal. You guys go up front and talk about stuff, okay?"

"Whatever," said Bill, picking up his Gamebuke and stalking out. Billy, utterly failing to notice the withering scorn to which he had just been subjected, smiled and waved sleepily at Ford. Ford smiled back, but his smile faded as he turned, shut the door behind him, and followed Bill, whom he had decided was a nasty little know-it-all.

Bill was sitting in one corner, staring into the screen of his Gamebuke. He had put on a pair of earshells and was listening to something fairly loud. He ignored Ford, who sat and looked up at the screens in puzzlement.

"Is this the station?" he asked, forgetting that Bill couldn't hear him. He had expected a domed settlement, but all he could see was a wide place by the side of the road, circled by boulders that appeared to have been whitewashed.

Bill didn't answer him. Ford looked at him in annoyance. He studied the controls on the inside of the hatch. When he thought he knew which one opened it, he slipped his mask on. Then he leaned over and punched Bill in the shoulder.

"Mask up," he yelled. "I'm going out."

Bill had his mask on before Ford had finished speaking, and Ford saw his eyes going wide with alarm as he activated the hatch. It sprang open; Ford turned and slid into a blast of freezing air.

He hit the ground harder than he expected to, and almost fell. Gasping, hugging himself against a cold so intense it burned, he stared in astonishment at the dawn.

There was no ceiling. There were no walls. There was nothing around the freighter, as far as the limits of his vision, but limitless space, limitless sky of the palest, chilliest blue he had ever seen, stretching down to a limitless red plain of sand and rock. He turned, and kept turning: no domes, no Tubes, nothing but the wide open world in every direction.

And here was a red light appearing on the horizon, red as blood or rubies, so bright a red it dazzled his eyes, and he wondered for a moment if it was the eye of Marswife. Long purple shadows sprang from the boulders and stretched back toward his boots. He realized he was looking at the rising sun.

So this is where the lights were going to, he said to himself, *all those nights they were going away into the dark. They were coming out here. This is the most wonderful thing I have ever seen.*

Somehow he had fallen into the place he had always wanted to be.

But the cold was eating into his bones, and he realized that if he kept on standing there he'd freeze solid in his happy dream. He set off toward the nearest boulder, fumbling with the fastening of his pants.

Someone grabbed his shoulder and spun him around.

"You *idiot!*" Bill shouted at him. "Don't you know what happens if you try to pee out here?"

From the horror on Bill's face, even behind the mask, Ford realized that he'd better get back in the cab as fast as he could.

When they were safely inside and the seals had locked, when Bill had finished yelling at him, Ford still sat shivering with more than cold.

"You mean it boils and *then* it explodes?" he said.

"You are such an idiot!" Bill repeated in disbelief.

"How was I supposed to know?" Ford said. "I've never been Outside before! We use the reclamation conduits at home—"

"This isn't the Long Acres, dumbbell. This is the middle of frozen Nowhere and it'll kill you in two seconds, okay?"

"Well, where can you go?"

"In the lavatory!"

"But I didn't want to wake up your dad."

"He'll sleep through anything," said Bill. "Trust me."

Red with humiliation, Ford crawled into the back and after several tries figured out how to operate the toilet, as Billy snored away oblivious. Afterward he crawled back up front, carefully closed the door and said:

"Er . . . so, where does somebody have their bath?"

Bill, who had turned his Gamebuke on again, did not look up as he said:

"At the Empress."

"No, I mean . . . when somebody has a bath *out here,* where do they have it?"

Bill lifted his eyes. He looked perplexed.

"What are you on about? Nobody bathes out here."

"You mean, you only wash when you're at the Empress?"

Now it was Bill's turn to flush with embarrassment.

"Yeah."

Ford tried to keep his dismay from showing, but he wasn't very good at hiding his feelings. "You mean I can't have a bath until we get back?"

"No. You can't. I guess people wash themselves every day in the Long Acres, huh?" said Bill angrily.

Ford nodded. "We have to. It stinks too bad if we don't. Because there's, er, manure and algae and, er, the methane plant, and . . . we work hard and sweat a lot. So we shave and wash every day, see?"

"Is *that* why the MAC haven't got any hair?"

"Yeah," said Ford. He added, "Plus my dad says hair is a vanity. Means being a showoff, being flash."

"I know what it means," said Bill. He was silent a moment, and then said:

"Well, you won't be sweating much out here. Freezing is more like it. So you'll have to cope until we get back to the Empress. It'll only be two weeks."

Two weeks? Ford thought of what his dad and mum would say to him when he turned up again, after being missing for so long. His mouth dried, his heart pounded. He wondered desperately what kind of lie he might tell to get himself out of trouble. Maybe that he'd been kidnapped? It had almost really happened. Kidnapped and taken to work in the iron mines, right, and . . . somehow escaped, and . . .

Billy retreated to his Gamebuke again, as Ford sat there trying to imagine what he might say. The stories became wilder, more unbelievable, as they grew more elaborate; and gradually he found himself drifting away from purposeful lies altogether, dreamily wondering what it might be like if he never went back to face the music at all.

After all, Sam was going to do it; Sam was clever and funny and brave, and he was walking away from the Collective to a new life. Why couldn't Ford have a new life too? What if he became a Hauler, like Billy, and lived out the rest of his life up here where there were no limits to the world? Blatchford the MAC boy would vanish and he could be just Ford, himself, not part of anything. *Free.*

V

It took them most of a week to get to Depot South. Ford enjoyed every minute of it, even getting used to the idea of postponing his bath for two weeks. Mostly he rode up front with Billy, as Bill stayed in the back sulking. Billy told him stories as they rocketed along, and taught him the basics of driving the freighter; it was harder than driving a tractor but not by as much as Ford would have thought.

"Look at you, holding our *Evelyn* on the road!" said Billy, chuckling. "You are one strong kid, for your age. Li'l Bill can't drive her at all yet."

"I'm a better navigator than you are!" yelled Bill from the back, in tones of outrage.

"He is, actually," said Billy. "Best navigator I ever saw. Half the time I have to get him to figure coordinates for me. You ever get lost in a storm or anything, you'll wish you had li'l Bill there with you." He looked carefully into the back to see if Bill was watching, and then unzipped a pouch in his psuit and took out a small bottle. Quickly he shook two tiny red pills into his palm and popped them into his mouth.

"What're those?" Ford asked.

"Freddie Stay-awakes," said Billy in a low voice. "Just getting ready for another night shift. We're going to set a new record for getting to the Depot, man."

"We don't have to hurry or anything," said Ford. "Really."

"Yeah, we do," said Billy, looking uncomfortable for the first time since Ford had known him. "Fun's fun, and everything, but . . . your people must be kind of wondering where you are, you know? I mean, it was a good idea to get you away from Mother's Boys and all, but we don't want people thinking you're dead, huh?"

"I guess not," said Ford. He looked sadly up at the monitor, at the wide-open world. The thought of going back into the Tubes, into the reeking dark of the cowsheds and the muddy trenches, made him despair.

Depot South loomed ahead of them at last, a low rise of ice above the plain. At first, Ford was disappointed; he had expected a gleaming white mountain, but Billy explained that the glacier was sanded all over with red dust from the windstorms. As the hours went by and they drew closer, Ford saw a low-lying mist of white, from which the glacier rose like an island. Later, two smaller islands seemed to rise from it as well, one on either side of the road.

"There's old Jack and Jim!" cried Billy. "We're almost there, when we see Jack and Jim."

Ford watched them with interest. As they drew near, he laughed; for they looked like a pair of bearded giants hacked out of the red stone. One was sitting up, peering from blind hollow eyes and holding what appeared to be a mug clutched to his stomach. The other reclined, with his big hands folded peacefully on his chest.

"How'd they get there?" he exclaimed, delighted.

"The glacier deposited them," said Bill, who had come out of the back to see.

"No! No! You have to tell him the story," said Billy gleefully. "See, Jack and Jim were these two Haulers, come up from Australia. So they liked their beer cold, see? *Really* cold.

"So they go into the Empress, and Mother, she says, Welcome, my dears, have a drop of good cheer, warm buttery beer won't cost you dear. But Jack and Jim, both he and him, they liked their beer cold. Really cold!

"Says one to the other, like brother to brother, there must be a place in this here space where a cobber can swill a nice bit of chill, if he likes his beer cold. Really *cold*.

"So they bought them a keg, and off they legged it for the Pole, the pole, where it's nice and cold, and they chopped out a hole in the ice-wall so, and that keg they stowed in the ice, cobber, ever so nice. And it got cold. *Really* cold.

"So they drank it down and another round and another one still and they drank until they set and they sot and they clean forgot, where the white mists creep they fell asleep, and they got cold. Really cold.

"In fact they froze, from nose to toes, and there they are to this very day, and the moral is, don't die that way! 'Cause what's right for Oz ain't right on Moz, 'cause up here it's *cold*. Really cold!"

Billy laughed like a loon, pounding his fist on the console. Bill just rolled his eyes.

"They're only a couple of boulders," he said.

"But you used to love that song," said Billy plaintively.

"When I was three, maybe," said Bill, turning and going into the back. "You'd better get him out one of your extra psuits. He won't fit in any of mine."

"He used to sing it with me," said Billy to Ford, looking crestfallen.

They pulled into Depot South, and once again Ford expected to see buildings, but there were none; only a confused impression of tumbled rock on the monitor. He looked up at it as Billy helped him into a psuit.

"Is it colder out there?" he asked.

"Yeah," said Bill, getting down three helmets from a locker. "You're at the South Pole, dummy."

"Aw, now, he's never been there, has he?" said Billy, adjusting the fit of the suit for Ford. "That feel okay?"

"I guess it—whoa!" said Ford, for once the fastenings had been sealed up the suit seemed to flex, like a hand closing around him, and though it felt warm and snug it was still a slightly creepy sensation. "What's it doing?"

"Just kind of programming itself so it gets to know you," Billy explained, accepting a helmet from Bill. "That's how it keeps you alive, see? Just settles in real close and puts a couple of sensors places you don't notice. Anything goes wrong, it'll try to fix you, and if it can't, it'll flash lights at you so you know."

"Like that?" Ford pointed at the little red light flashing on Billy's psuit readout panel. Billy looked down at it.

"Oh. No, that's just a short circuit or glitch or something. It's been doing that all the time lately when nothing's wrong."

"Some people take their suits into the shop when they need repair, you know," said Bill, putting on his own helmet. "Just an idea, Dad. Hope it's not too radical for you."

As Billy helped him seal up his helmet, Ford looked at Bill and thought: *You're a mean little twit. I'd give anything if my dad was like yours.*

But when they stepped Outside, he forgot about Bill and even about Billy. He barely noticed the cold, though it was so intense it took his breath away and the psuit helpfully turned up its thermostat for him. Depot South had all his attention.

They were surrounded on three sides by towering walls, cloudy white swirled through with colors like an Ice Pop, green and blue blue blue and lavender, all scarred and rough, faceted and broken. Underneath his feet was a confusion of crushed and broken rock, pea-sized gravel to cobbles, ice mixed with grit and stone, and a roiling mist swirled about his ankles.

Here and there were carvings in the ice wall, roughly gouged and hacked: HAULERS RULE OK and BARSOOM BRUCE GOT HERE ALIVE, and one that simply said THANKS MARSWIFE, over a niche that had been scraped from the ice where somebody had left a little figurine like the one on *Beautiful Evelyn*'s console. There were figures carved too; on a section of green ice, Ford noticed a four-armed giant with tusks.

Behind him, he became aware of a clatter as Billy and Bill opened a panel in the freighter's side and drew out something between them. He turned to see Billy hoisting a laser-saw, and heard the *hummzap* as it was turned on.

"Okay!" said Billy, his voice coming tinnily over the speaker. "Let's go cut some ice!"

He went up to the nearest wall, hefted the laser, and disappeared in a cloud of white steam. A moment later, a great chunk of ice came hurtling out of the steam, and bounced and rolled to Bill's feet. He picked it up, as another block bounded out.

"Grab that," said Bill. "If we don't start loading this stuff, Dad will be up to his neck in ice."

Ford obeyed, and followed Bill around to the rear of the freighter, where a sort of escalator ramp had been lowered, and watched as Bill dropped the block to the ramp. It traveled swiftly up the ramp to a hopper at the top of *Beautiful Evelyn*'s tank, where it vanished with a grinding roar, throwing up a rainbowed shatter of ice-shards and vapor against the sunlight. Fascinated, Ford set his block on the ramp and watched as the same thing happened.

"What's it doing?"

"Making carbon dioxide snowcones, what do you think?" said Bill. "And we take the whole lot back to Settlement Base, and sell it to the MAC."

"You do?" Ford was astonished. "What do we need it for?"

"Hel-LO, terraforming, remember?" said Bill. "Making Mars green like Earth? What the MAC was brought up here to do?"

He turned and trudged back around the side of the freighter, and Ford walked after him thinking: *I'll bet you wouldn't hold that nose so high up in the air if I bashed it with my forehead.*

But he said nothing, and for the next hour they worked steadily as machines, going back and forth with ice blocks to the ramp. The tank was nearly full when they heard the drone of icecutting stop.

"That's not enough, Dad," Bill called, and nobody answered. He turned and ran. Ford walked around the side of the freighter and saw him kneeling beside Billy, who had fallen and lay with the white mist curling over his body.

Ford gasped and ran to them. The whole front of Billy's psuit was lit with blinking colors, dancing over a readout panel that had activated. Bill was bending close, waving away the mist to peer at it. Ford leaned down and saw Billy's face slack within the helmet, his eyes staring and blank.

"What's wrong with him?" said Ford.

"He's had a blowout," said Bill flatly.

"What's a blowout?"

"Blood vessel goes *bang*. Happens sometimes to people who go Outside a lot." Bill rested his hand on his father's chest. He felt something in one of the sealed pouches; he opened it, and drew out the bottle of Freddie Stay-awakes. After staring at it for a long moment, his face contorted. He hurled the bottle at the ice-wall, where it popped open and scattered red pills like beads of blood.

"I knew it! I knew he'd do this! I knew this would happen someday!" he shouted. Ford felt like crying, but he fought it back and said:

"Is he going to die?"

"What do you think?" said Bill. "We're at the bloody South Pole! We're a week away from the infirmary!"

"But—could we maybe keep him alive until we get back?"

Bill turned to him, and a little of the incandescent rage faded from his eyes. "We might," he said. "The psuit's doing what it can. We have some emergency medical stuff. You don't understand, though. His brain's turning to goo in there."

"Maybe it isn't," said Ford. "Please! We have to try."

"He'll die anyway," said Bill, but he got Billy under the shoulders and tried to lift him. Ford came around and took his place, lifting Billy easily; Bill grabbed his father's legs, and between them they hoisted Billy up and carried him into the cab.

There they settled him in his bunk, and Bill fumbled in a drawer for a medical kit. He drew out three sealed bags of colored liquid with tubes leading from one end and hooks on the other. The tubes he plugged into ports in the arm of Billy's psuit; the hooks fitted into loops on the underside of the upper bunk, so the bags hung suspended above Billy.

"Should we get his helmet off him?" Ford asked. Bill just shook his head. He turned and stalked out of the compartment. Ford took a last look at Billy, with the glittering lights on his chest and his dead eyes staring, and followed Bill.

"What do we do now?"

"We get the laser," said Bill. "We can't leave it. It cost a month's pay."

VI

The freighter was a lot harder to handle now, full of ice, than it had been on the way out when Billy had let him drive. It took all Ford's strength to back her around and get her on the road again, and even so the console beeped a warning as they trundled out through Jack and Jim, for he nearly swerved and clipped one of the giants. At last he was able to steer straight between the boulders and get up a little speed.

"We really can't, er, send a distress signal or anything?" he asked Bill. Bill sat hunched at his end of the cab, staring at the monitors.

"Nobody'll hear us," he said bitterly, "There's half a planet between Mons Olympus and us. Did you notice any relay towers on the way out here?"

"No."

"That's because there aren't any. Why should Areco build any? Nobody comes out here except Haulers, and who cares if Haulers die? We do this work because nobody else wants to do it, because it's too dangerous. But Haulers are a bunch of idiots; *they* don't care if they get killed."

"They're not idiots, they're brave!" said Ford. Bill looked at him with contempt. Neither of them said anything for a long while after that.

By the time it was beginning to get dark, Ford was aching in every muscle of his body from the sheer effort of keeping the freighter on the road. The approaching darkness was not as fearful as he'd thought it might be, because for several miles now someone had daubed the lines of boulders with photoreflective paint, and they lit up nicely in the freighter's high-beams. But *Beautiful Evelyn* seemed to want to veer to the left, and Ford wondered if there was something wrong with her steering system until he saw drifts of sand flying straight across the road in front of her, like stealthy ghosts.

"I think the wind's rising," he said.

"You think, genius?" Bill pointed to a readout on the console.

"What's it mean?"

"It means we're probably driving right into a storm," said Bill, and then they heard a shrill piping alarm from the back. Bill scrambled aft; Ford held the freighter on the road. *Please don't let that be Billy dying! Please, Marswife, if you're out there, help us!*

Bill returned and crawled into his seat. "The air pressure's dropping in here. The psuit needed somebody to okay turning it up a notch."

"Why's the air pressure dropping?"

Bill sounded weary. "Because this is going to be a really bad storm. You'd better pull over and anchor us."

"But we have to get your dad to an infirmary!"

"Did you think we were going to drive for a whole week without sleeping?" Bill said. "We don't have any Freddies now. We have to sit out the storm no matter what happens. Five-Fifty-K is coming up soon. Maybe we can make it that far."

It was in fact twelve kilometers away, and the light faded steadily as they roared along. Ford could hear the wind howling now. He remembered a story Billy had told him, about people seeing dead Haulers in their high-beams, wraiths signaling for help at the scenes of long-ago breakdowns. The whirling sand looked uncannily like figures with streaming hair, diving in front of the freighter as though waving insubstantial arms. He was grateful when the half-circle of rocks that was Five-Fifty-K Station appeared in her lights at last, and she seemed eager to swerve away from the road.

Bill punched in the anchoring protocol, and *Beautiful Evelyn* gave a lurch and dropped abruptly, as though she were sitting down. Ford cut the power; the drives fell silent. They sat there side by side in the silence that was filled up steadily by the whine of blowing sand, and a patter of blown gravel that might have sounded to them like rain, if they had ever heard rain.

"What do we do now?" said Ford.

"We wait it out," said Bill.

They went into the back to check on Billy—no change—and heated something frozen and ate it, barely registering what it was. Then they went back into the cab and sat, in their opposite corners.

"So we really are on our own?" said Ford at last. "Areco won't send Security looking for us?"

"Areco doesn't send Mother's Boys anyplace," said Bill, staring into the dark. "Mother hired 'em."

"Who's Mother, anyway?"

"The lady who found the diamond and got rich," said Bill. "And bought Mons Olympus, and everybody thought she was crazy, because it was just this big volcano where nobody could grow anything. Only, she had a well drilled into a magma pocket and built a power station. And she leased lots to a bunch of people from Earth and that's why Mons Olympus makes way more money than Areco and the MAC."

"The MAC isn't supposed to make money," said Ford. "We're supposed to turn Mars into a paradise. Our contract says Areco is going to give it to us for our own, once we've done it."

"Well, you can bet Areco isn't going to come rescue us," said Bill. "Nobody looks out for Haulers except other Haulers. And their idea of help would be giving Dad a big funeral and getting stinking drunk afterward."

"Oh," said Ford. Bill gave him an odd look.

"People in the MAC look out for each other, though, don't they?"

"Yeah," said Ford wretchedly. "There's always somebody watching what you do. Always somebody there to tell you why what you want to do is wrong. Council meetings go on for hours because everybody has to say something or it isn't fair, but they all say the same thing anyway. Blah blah blah. I *hate* it there," he said, surprising himself by how intensely he felt.

"What's it supposed to be like, when Mars is a paradise?"

Ford looked at Bill to see if he was being mocking, but he wasn't smiling.

"Well, it'll be like . . . there'll be no corruption or oppression. And stuff. They say water will fall out of the sky, and nobody will ever have to wear a mask again." Ford slumped forward and put his head on his knees. "I used to imagine it'd be . . . I don't know. Full of lights."

"People would be safe, if Mars could be made like that," said Bill in a thoughtful voice. "Terraformed. Another Earth. No more big empty spaces."

"I *like* big empty spaces," said Ford. "Why does Mars have to be just like Earth anyway? Why can't things stay the way they are?"

"You *like* this?" Bill swung his arm up at the monitors, which showed only the howling night and a blur of sand. "'Cause you can have it. I hate it! Tons of big nothing waiting to kill us, all my whole life! And Dad just laughed at it, but he isn't laughing now, huh? You know what's really sick? If he dies—if we get back alive—I'll be better off."

"Oh, shut up," said Ford.

"But I *will*," said Bill, with a certain wonderment. "Lots better off. I can sell this freighter—and Dad paid into the Hauler's Club, so there'd be some money coming in there—and . . . wow, I could afford a *good* education. Maybe University level. I'll be able to have everything I've always wanted, and I'll never have to come out here again."

"How can you talk like that?" Ford yelled. "You selfish pig! You're talking about your own dad dying! You don't even care, do you? Your dad's the bravest guy I ever met!"

"He got himself killed, after everything I told him. He was stupid," said Bill.

"He isn't even dead yet!" Ford, infuriated, swung at him. Bill ducked backward, away from his flailing fists, and got his legs up on the seat and kicked Ford. Ford fell sideways, but scrambled up on his knees and kept coming, trying to back Bill into the corner. Bill dodged and hit him hard, and then again and again, until Ford got so close he couldn't get his arms up all the way. Ford, sobbing with anger, punched as hard as he could in the cramped space, but Bill was a much better fighter for all that he was so small.

By the time they had hurt each other enough to stop, both of them had bloody noses and Ford had the beginning of a black eye. Swearing, they retreated into their separate corners of the cab, and glared at each other until the droning hiss of the wind and the pattering of gravel on the tank lulled them to sleep.

VII

When they woke, hours later, it was dead quiet.

Ford woke groaning, partly because his face was so sore and partly because he had a stiff neck from sleeping curled up on the seat. He sat up and looked around blearily.

He realized that he couldn't hear anything. He looked up at the monitors and realized that he couldn't see anything, either; the screens were black. Frightened, he leaned over and shook Bill awake. Bill woke instantly, staring around.

"The power's gone out!" Ford said.

"No, it hasn't. We'd be dead," said Bill. He punched a few buttons on the console and peered intently at figures that appeared on the readout. Then he looked up at the monitors. "What's that?" He pointed at the monitor for the rear of the freighter, where there was a sliver of image along the top. Just a grayish triangle of light, shifting a little along its lower edge, just like . . .

"Sand," said Bill. "We're buried. The storm blew a dune over us."

"What do we do now?" said Ford, shivering, and the psuit thought he was cold and warmed up comfortingly.

"Maybe we can blow it away," said Bill. "Some, anyway." He switched on the drives and there was a shudder and a jolt that ran the whole length of the freighter. With a *whoosh, Beautiful Evelyn* rose a few inches. The rear monitor lit up with an image of sand cascading past it; some light showed on her left-hand monitor too.

"Okay!" said Bill, shutting her down again. "We're not going to die. Not here, anyway. We can dig out. Get a helmet on."

They went aft to get helmets—Billy still stared at nothing, though his psuit blinked at them reassuringly—and, when they had helmeted up, Bill reached past Ford to activate the hatch. It made a dull muffled sound, but would not open. He had to try three more times before it consented to open out about a hand's width. Sand spilled into the cab, followed by daylight.

Bill swore and climbed up on the seat, pushing the hatch outward. "Get up here and help me!"

Ford scrambled up beside him and set his shoulder to the hatch. A lot more sand fell in, but they were able to push it open far enough for Bill to grab the edge and pull himself up, and worm his way out. Ford climbed after, and in a moment was standing with Bill on the top of the dune that covered the freighter.

Bill swore quietly. Ford didn't blame him.

They stood on a mountain of red sand and looked out on a plain of red sand, endless, smooth to the wide horizon, and the low early sun threw their shadows far out behind them. The sky had a flat metallic glare; the wind wailed high and mournful.

"Where's the road?" cried Ford

"Buried under there," said Bill, pointing down the slope in front of them. "It happens sometimes. Come on." He turned and started down the slope. Ford stumbled after him, slipped, and fell, rolling ignominiously to the bottom. He picked himself up, feeling stupid, but Bill hadn't noticed; he was digging with his hands, scooping away sand from the freighter.

Ford waded in to help him. He reached up to brush sand from the tank, but at his touch the sand puckered out in a funny starred pattern. Startled, he drew his hand back. Cautiously he reached out a fingertip to the tank; the instant he touched it, a rayed star of sand formed once again.

"Hey, look at this!" Giggling, he drew his finger along the tank, and the star spread and followed it.

"It's magnetic," said Bill. "Happens sometimes, when the wind's been bad. My dad said it's all the iron in the sand. It fries electronics. Hard to clean off, too."

Ford brushed experimentally at the tank, but the sand stuck as though it were a dense syrup.

"This'll take us forever," he said.

"Not if we get to the tool chest," said Bill. "We can scrape off most of it."

They worked together and after ten minutes had cleared a panel in the freighter's undercarriage; Bill pried it open and pulled out a couple of big shovels, and after that the work went more quickly.

"Wowie. Sand spades. All we need is buckets and we could make sand castles, huh?" said Ford, grinning sheepishly.

"What's that mean?"

"It's something kids do on Earth. Sam says, before we emigrated, our dad and mum took him to this place called Blackpool. There was all this blue water, see, washing in over the sand. He had a bucket and spade and he made sand castles. So here we are in the biggest Blackpool in the universe, with the biggest sand spades, yeah? Only there's no water."

"How could you make castles out of sand?" Bill said, scowling as he worked. "They'd just fall in on you."

"I don't know. I think you'd have to get the sand wet."

"But why would anybody get sand wet?"

"I don't know. I don't think people do it on purpose; I think it just happens. There's all this water on Earth, see, and it gets on things. That's what Sam says."

Bill shook his head grimly and kept digging. They cleared the freighter's rear wheels, and Ford said:

"Why do you reckon the water's blue on Earth? It's only green or brown up here."

"It's not blue," said Bill.

"Yes, it is," said Ford. "Sam has holos of it. I've seen 'em. It's bluer than the sky. Blue as blue paint."

"Water isn't any color really," said Bill. "It just looks blue. Something about the air."

Ford scowled and went around to the other side of the freighter, where he dug out great shovelfuls of sand and muttered, "It *is* blue. They wouldn't have that Blue Room if it wasn't blue. All the songs and stories say it's blue. So there, you little know-it-all."

He had forgotten that Bill could hear him on the psuit comm, so he was quite startled when Bill's voice sounded inside his helmet:

"Songs and stories? Right. Go stick your head in a dune, moron."

Ford just gritted his teeth and kept shoveling.

It took them a long while to clear the freighter, because they only made real progress once the wind fell a little. Eventually, though, they were able to climb back into the cab and start up *Beautiful Evelyn*'s drives. She blasted her way free of the dune and Ford strained to steer her up, over and down across the rippled slope below.

"Okay! Where's the road?" he said.

"There," said Bill, pointing. "Don't you even know directions? We anchored at right angles to the road. It's still there, even if we can't see it. Just take her straight that way."

Ford obeyed. They rumbled off.

They drove for five hours, over sand and then over rocky sand and at last over a cobbled plain, and there was no sign of the double row of boulders that should have been there if they had been on the High Road.

Bill, who had been watching the readouts, grew more and more pale and silent. "We need to stop," he said at last. "Something's wrong."

"We aren't on the High Road anymore, are we?" said Ford sadly.

"No. We're lost."

"What happened?"

"The storm must have screwed up the nav system," said Bill. "All that magnetic crap spraying around."

"Can we fix it?"

"I can reset it," said Bill. "But I can't recalibrate it, because I don't know where we are. So it wouldn't do us any good."

"But your dad said you were this great navigator!" said Ford.

Bill looked at his boots. "I'm not. He just thought I was."

"Well, isn't that great?" said Ford. "And here you thought *I* was such an idiot. What do we do now, Professor?"

"Shut up," said Bill. "Just shut up. We're supposed to go north, okay? And the sun rises in the east and sets in the west. So as long as we keep the setting sun on our left, we're going mostly in the right direction."

"What happens at night?"

"If the sky's clear of dust clouds, maybe we can steer by the stars."

Ford brightened up at that. "I used to watch the stars a lot," he said. "And we ought to be able to see the mountain after a while, right?"

"Mons Olympus? Yeah."

"Okay then!" Ford accelerated again, and *Beautiful Evelyn* plunged forward. "We can do this! Billy wouldn't be scared if he was lost, would he?"

"No," admitted Bill.

"No, because he'd just point himself at the horizon and he'd just *go*, zoom, and he wouldn't worry about it."

"He never worried about anything," said Bill, though not as though he thought that was especially smart.

"Well, it's dumb to worry," said Ford, with a slightly rising note of hysteria in his voice. "You live or you die, right? The main thing, is . . . is . . . to be really *alive* before you die. I could have lived my whole life walking around in the Tubes and never, ever seen stuff like I've seen since I ran away. All this sky. All that sand. The ice and the mist and the different colors and everything! So maybe I don't get to be old like Hardie Stubbs's granddad. Who wants to be all shriveled up and coughing anyway?"

"Don't be stupid," said Bill. "I'd give anything to be down in the Long Acres right now, and I wouldn't care what work I had to do. And you wish you were there too."

"No, I don't!" Ford shouted. "You know what I'm going to do? As soon as we get back, I'll go see my dad and I'll say: 'Dad, I'm leaving the MAC.' Sam did it and so can I. Only I'm not going back to Earth. Mars is *my* place! And I'm going to be a Hauler, and stay Outside all the rest of my life!"

Bill stared at him.

"You're crazy," he said. "You think your dad will just let you go?"

"No," said Ford. "He'll grab my ear and about pull it off. It doesn't matter. Once I'm nine, the MAC says I have a right to pick whatever job I want."

"Once you're *nine*?"

Ford turned red. "In MAC years. We have one for every two Earth years."

"So . . . you're how old now?" Bill began to grin. "Six?"

"Yeah," said Ford. "And you can just shut up, okay?"

"Okay," said Bill, but his grin widened.

VIII

They drove all the rest of that day, but when night fell they were so tired they agreed to pull over to sleep. Ford stretched out in the cab and Bill went back to crawl into the bunk above Billy, who lay there still, staring and unresponsive as a waxwork.

He was still alive when morning came. Bill was changing his tube-bags when Ford came edging in, yawning.

"You wait and see," said Ford, in an attempt to be comforting. "He'll be fine if we can get him to the infirmary. Eric Chetwynd's dad fell off a tractor and fractured his skull, and *he* was in this coma, see, for days, but then they did surgery on him and he was opening his eyes and talking and everything. And your dad hasn't even got any broken bones."

"It's not the same," said Bill morosely. "Never mind. Let's get going. Sun's on our right until noon, got it?"

They drove on. Ford's muscles ached less now; he was beginning to feel more confident with *Beautiful Evelyn*. He watched the horizon and imagined Mons Olympus rising there, inevitable, the red queen on the vast chessboard of the plain. She *would* come into view soon. She had to. And someday, when he had a freighter of his own and drove this route all the time, a little thing like going off course wouldn't bother him at all. He'd know every sand hill and rock outcropping like the palm of his hand.

He thought about getting a tattoo on his face. Deciding what it ought to look like occupied his thoughts for the next couple of hours, as Bill sat silent across from him, staring at the monitors and twisting his hands together in his lap.

Then:

"Something's moving!" said Bill, pointing at the backup cam monitor.

Ford spotted it: something gleaming, sunlight striking off a vehicle far back in their dust-wake.

"Yowie! It's another Hauler!" he said. "Billy's saved!"

He slowed *Beautiful Evelyn* and turned her around, so the plume of dust whirled away and they could see the other vehicle more clearly.

"It's not a Hauler," said Bill. "It's just a cab. Who is that? That's nobody I know."

"Who cares?" said Ford, pounding on the console in his glee. "They'll know how to get back to the road!"

"Not if they're lost too," said Bill. The stranger was barreling toward them quite deliberately and they could see it clearly now: a freighter's cab with no tank attached, just the tang of the hookup sticking out behind, looking strange as some tiny insect with an immense head. It pulled up alongside them. Bill hit the comm switch and cried, "Who's that?"

There was a silence. Then a voice crackled through the speakers, distorted and harsh: "Who's that crying who's that? Sounds like a youngster."

Ford leaned over and shouted, "Please, we're lost! Can you show us how to get back to the road?"

Another silence, and then:

"Two little boys? What're you doing out here, then? Daddy had a mishap, did he?"

Bill gave Ford a furious look. Ford wondered why, but said:

"Yes, sir! We need to get him to the infirmary, and our nav system went out in the storm! Can you help us?"

"Why, sure I can," said the voice, and it sounded as though the speaker was smiling. "Mask up now, kids, and step Outside. Let's talk close-up, eh?"

"You jackass," muttered Bill, but he pulled on his mask.

When they slid down out of the cab they saw that the stranger had painted his cab with the logo CELTIC POWER and pictures of what had been celtic knots and four-leafed clovers, though they were half scoured away. The hatch swung up and a man climbed out, a big man in a psuit also painted in green and yellow patterns. He looked them over and grinned within his mask.

"Well, hello there, kids," he said. "Gwill Griffin, at your service. Diamond prospector by trade. What's the story?"

"Bill's dad had a blowout," said Ford. "And we were trying to get him back, but we've lost the road. Can you help us, please?"

"A blowout?" The man raised his eyebrows. "Now, that's an awful thing. Let's have a look at him."

"You don't need—" began Bill, but Mr. Griffin had already vaulted up into *Beautiful Evelyn*'s cab. Bill and Ford scrambled after him. By the time they had got in he was already in the back, leaning down to peer at Billy.

"Dear, dear, he's certainly in trouble," he said. "Yes, you'd better get him back to Mons Olympus, and no mistake." He looked around the inside of the cab. "Nice rig he's got here, though, isn't it? And a nice full tank of CO_2, I take it?"

"Yeah," said Ford. "It happened right as we were finishing up. Do you know how to, er, recalibrate nav systems?"

"No trouble at all," said Mr. Griffin, shoving past them and into the seat at the console. Bill watched him closely as he punched it up and set in new figures. "Poor little lads, lost on your own Outside. You're lucky I found you, you know. The road's just five kilometers east of here, but you might have wandered around forever without finding it."

"I knew we had to be close," said Ford, though he did not feel quite the sense of relief he might have, and wondered why.

"Yes; terrible things can happen out here. I saw your rig in the middle of nowhere, zigzagging along, and I said to myself: 'Goddess save me, that must be Freeze-Dried Dave!' I've seen some strange things out here in my time, I can tell you."

"Who's Freeze-Dried Dave?" asked Ford.

"Him? The Demon Hauler of Mare Cimmerium?" Mr. Griffin turned to him, pushing his mask up. He was beardless and freckled, though he wore a wide mustache, and was not as old as Ford had thought him to be at first.

"Nobody knows who Freeze-Dried Dave was; just some poor soul who was up here in the early days, and they say he died at the console whilst on a run, see?

And his cab's system took over and went on Autopilot. They think it veered off the road in a storm and just kept rovering on, and every time the battery'd wear out it'd sit somewhere until another storm scoured the dust off the solar cells. Then it'd just start itself up again."

Ford realized what was making him uneasy. The man sounded like an actor in a holo, like somebody who was speaking lines for an effect.

"Some prospectors found it clean out in the middle of nowhere, and went up to it and got the hatch to open. There was Freeze-Dried Dave still sitting inside her, shriveled up like; but no sooner had they set foot to the ladder than she roared to life and took off, scattering 'em like bowling pins. And what do you think she did then? Only swerved around and came back at 'em, that's what she did, and mashed one into the sand while the others ran for their lives.

"*They* made it home to tell the tale. There's many a Hauler since then who's seen her, thundering along on her own business off the road, with that dead man rattling around inside. Some say it's Dave's ghost driving her, trying to find his way back to Settlement Base. Some say it's the freighter herself, that her system's gone mad with sorrow and wants to kill anyone gets close enough, so they don't take her Dave away. You'll never find a prospector like me who'll go anywhere near her. Why, it's bad luck even to see her." He winked broadly at Ford.

"We need to get my dad to the infirmary," said Bill, clearing his throat. "Thanks for helping us. Let's go, okay?"

"Right," said Mr. Griffin, masking up again. "Only you'd best let me do a point-check on your freighter first, don't you think? That was quite a storm; could be all sorts of things gummed up you don't know about. Wouldn't want to have a breakdown out here, eh?"

"No, sir," said Ford. Mr. Griffin jumped down from the cab. Bill was preparing to jump after him, but he held up his hand.

"Now, I'll tell you what we'll do," he said. "You lads sit in there and watch the console. I'm going to test the tread relays; that's the surest thing will go wrong after a storm, with all those little magnetic particles getting everywhere and persuading the relays to do things they shouldn't. Could cause all your wheels to lock on one side, and you don't want that to happen at speed! You'd roll and kill yourselves for sure. I'll just open the panel and run a quick diagnostic; you can give me a shout when the green lights go on."

"Okay," said Bill, and climbed back in and closed the hatch. As soon as it was closed, he swore, and kept swearing. Ford stared at him.

"What are you on about?" he demanded. "We're safe now."

"No, we bloody aren't," said Bill. "Gwill Griffin, my butt. I know who that guy is. His name's Art Finlay. He was one of Mother's Boys. She fired him last year. He liked to go into the holding cell and slap guys around. He thought nobody was looking, but the cameras caught him. So all that old-diamond-prospector-with-his-tall-tales stuff was so much crap. So's the PanCeltic accent; he emigrated up here from some place in the Americas on Earth."

"So he's a phony?" Ford thought of the inexplicably creepy feeling the stranger had given him.

"Yeah. He's a phony," said Bill, and reached over to switch on the comm unit. "How are those relays?" he said.

"Look fine," was the crackly answer. "Your daddy took care of this rig, sure enough. Look at the console, now, lads; tell me when the green lights go on."

They stared at the panel, and in a moment: "They're on," chorused Bill and Ford.

"Then you're home and dry."

"Thanks! We're going to go on now, okay?" said Bill.

"You do that. I'll just follow along behind to be sure you get home safe, eh?"

"Okay," said Bill, and shut off the comm. "Get going!" he told Ford. "Five kilometers due east. We ought to be able to see it once we get over that rise. Let's leave this guy way behind us."

Ford started her up again, and *Beautiful Evelyn* rolled forward. She picked up speed and he charged her at the hill, feeling a wonderful sense of freedom as she zoomed upward. Bill cut into his reverie by yelling:

"The camera's been changed!"

"Huh?"

"Look," said Bill, pointing up at the left-hand monitor. It was no longer showing *Beautiful Evelyn's* port side and a slice of ground, as it had been; now there was only a view of the northern horizon. "He moved the lens. Move it back!"

"I don't know how!" Ford leaned in, flustered, as Bill jumped up and reached past him to stab at the controls that would align the camera lenses. *Beautiful Evelyn's* side came back into view.

"She looks all right," said Ford. "And, hey! There's the High Road! Hooray!"

"No, she doesn't look all right!" said Bill. "Look! He left the relay panel open! How come the telltale warning isn't lit?"

"I don't know," said Ford.

"Of course *you* don't know, you flaming idiot," said Bill, shrill with anger. "And here he comes!"

Ford looked up at the backup cam and saw Mr. Griffin's cab advancing behind the freighter; then the image switched to the left hand camera, as it moved up on *Beautiful Evelyn's* port side. It drew level with the open panel. They watched in horror as the cab's hatch swung down. They saw Mr. Griffin, masked up, leaning out.

"He's going to do something to the panel!" shrieked Bill.

"Oh, no, he won't," said Ford, more angry than he had ever been in his life. Without a second's hesitation, he steered *Beautiful Evelyn* sharply to the left. She more than sideswiped Mr. Griffin; with a terrific crash, she sent his cab spinning away, rolling over and over, and they saw him go flying out of it. *Beautiful Evelyn* lurched and sagged. They rumbled to a stop. They sat for a moment, shaking.

"We have to go see," said Bill. "Something's wrong."

They masked up and went Outside.

IX

Beautiful Evelyn's foremost left tire had exploded. There was a thick crust of poly-ceramic around the wheel, but nothing else. It must have sent pieces flying in all directions when it burst. Ford gaped at it while Bill ran down to the open panel. Ford heard a lot of swearing. He turned and saw Bill tearing something loose, and holding it up.

"Duct tape," said Bill. "He put a piece of duct tape over the warning sensor."

"Did he damage the, whatzis, the relays?" Ford looked in concern at the open panel, with no idea what he was seeing inside.

"No. You nailed him in time. But if he'd bashed them with something once we'd come up to speed, we'd have flipped over, just like he said. Then all he'd have had to do was move in and pick over the wreck. Help himself to the tank. Tell anybody who asked questions a story about some 'poor little dead lads' he'd found out here." Bill looked over at the dust rising from the wreck of Griffin's cab.

He bent and picked up a good-sized rock.

Ford followed his gaze.

"You think he's still alive?" he said, shuddering.

"Maybe," said Bill. "Get a rock. Let's go find out."

But he wasn't alive. They found him where he'd fallen, nine meters from his cab.

His mask had come off.

"Oh," said Ford, backing away. "Oh—"

He turned hastily and doubled up, vomiting into his mask. Turning, he ran for the freighter. Scrambling in and closing the hatch, he groped his way to the lavatory and pulled his mask off. He vomited again, under Billy's blank gaze.

He had cleaned himself up a little and stopped crying by the time he heard Bill coming back.

"Can you mask up?" Bill asked him, over the commlink.

"Yeah—" said Ford, his voice breaking on another sob. Hating himself, he pulled the mask on and heard the hatch open. Bill climbed in.

"We might be okay," said Bill. "I had a look at his rig. Same size tires as ours. Maybe we can change one out."

"Okay," said Ford. Bill looked at him.

"Are you going to be all right? You're green."

"I killed a guy," said Ford.

"He was trying to kill us," said Bill. "He deserved what he got."

"I know," said Ford, beginning to shiver again. "It's just—the way it *looked*. The face. Oh, man. I'm going to see it when I close my eyes at night, for the rest of my life."

"I know," said Bill, sounding tired. "That was how I felt, the first time I saw somebody die like that."

"Does it happen a lot?"

"To Haulers? Yeah. Mostly to new guys." Bill stood up. "Come on. Blow your nose and let's go see if we can change the tire."

Walking out to the wreck, Ford began to giggle weakly.

"We really blew *his* nose for him, huh?"

The cab had come to rest upright. Its hatch had been torn away, and the inside was a litter of tumbled trash and spilled coffee that had already frozen. Ford made a step of his hands so Bill could climb up and in.

"I don't see any lug nuts," Ford said, looking at the nearest tire. "How do we get them off?"

"They're not like tractor tires," said Bill crossly, punching buttons on the console. "Crap. All the electronics are fried. There's supposed to be an emergency release, though. Ours is under the console, because it's a Mitsubishi. This is a Toutatis. Let me look around in here . . ."

Ford glanced over his shoulder in the direction in which the dead man lay. He looked back hurriedly and gave an experimental tug at the tire. It felt as immovable as a ten-ton boulder. He reached in and got his arms around it, and pulled as hard as he could.

"I think maybe this is it," said Bill, from inside the cab. "Stand clear, okay?"

Ford let go hastily and tried to scramble away, but the tire shot off the axle as though it had been fired from a cannon.

It caught him in the stomach. He was thrown backward two meters, and fell sprawling on the ground, too winded to groan.

"Dumbass," said Bill, looking down. He jumped from the cab and pushed the tire off Ford. "I *said* stand clear. Why doesn't anybody ever listen to me?"

Ford rolled over, thinking he might have to throw up again. He got painfully to his hands and knees. Bill was already rolling the tire toward *Beautiful Evelyn*, so Ford struggled to his feet and followed.

He held the tire upright, standing well clear of the axle when Bill fired off the burst one. It shot all the way over to the wreck. Then Bill got back down, and, together, they lifted the tire up and slammed it into place. They drove down to the road, between two boulders, and turned north again.

"Look, you need to get over it," said Bill, who had been watching Ford. "It's not like you meant to kill him."

"It's not that," said Ford, who was gray-faced and sweating. "My stomach really hurts, is all."

Bill leaned close and looked at him.

"Your psuit says something's wrong," he said.

"It does?" Ford looked down at himself. How had he missed that flashing yellow light? "It's like it's shrinking or something. It's so tight I can almost not breathe."

"We have to stop," said Bill.

"Okay," said Ford. *Beautiful Evelyn* coasted to a stop and sat there in the middle of the road, as Bill climbed over and stared intently at the diagnostic panel on the front of Ford's psuit. He went pale, but all he said was:

"Let's trade places."

"But you can't drive her," Ford protested.

"If we're on the straightaway and there's no wind, I can sort of drive," said Bill. He dove into the back, as Ford crawled sideways into his seat, and came out a moment later with one of the little tube-bags. "Stick your arm up like *this*, okay?"

Ford obeyed, and watched as Bill plugged the tube into the psuit's port. "So that'll make me feel better?"

"Yeah, it ought to." Bill swung himself into the console seat and sent *Beautiful Evelyn* trundling on.

"Good." Ford sighed. "What's wrong with me?"

"Psuit says you've ruptured something," said Bill, staring at the monitor. He accelerated.

"Oh. Well, that's not too bad," said Ford, blinking. "Jimmy Linton got a rupture and he's okay. Better than okay, actually. The medic said he couldn't work with a shovel anymore. So . . . they made him official secretary for the Council, see? All he has to do is record stuff at meetings and post notices."

"Really."

"So if I have a rupture, maybe my dad won't take it so hard that I want to be a Hauler. Since that way I get out of working in the methane plant and the cow sheds. Maybe."

Bill gave him an incredulous look.

"All this, and you still want to be a Hauler?"

"Of course I do!"

Bill just shook his head.

They drove in a dead calm, at least compared to the weather before. Far off across the plains they saw dust devils here and there, twirling lazily. The farther north they drove, the clearer the air was, the brighter the light of the sun, shining on standing outcroppings of rock the color of rust, or milk chocolate, or tangerines, or new pennies.

"This is so great," said Ford, slurring his words as he spoke. "This is more beautiful than anything. Isn't the world a big place?"

"I guess so," said Bill.

"It's *our* place,' said Ford. "They can all go back to Earth, but we never will. We're Martians."

"Yeah."

"Did you see, I have hair growing in?" Ford swung his hand up to pat his scalp. "Red like Mars."

"Don't move your arm around, okay? You'll rip the tube out."

"Sorry."

"That's all right. Maybe you should mask up, you know? You could probably use the oxygen."

"Sure . . ." Ford dragged his mask into place

After a while, he smiled and said: "I know who I am."

He murmured to himself for a while, muffled behind the mask. The next time Bill glanced over at him, he was unconscious.

And Bill was all alone.

Billy wasn't there to be yelled at, or blamed for anything. He might never be there again. He couldn't be argued with, he couldn't be shamed or ignored or made to feel anything Bill wanted him to feel. Not if he was dead.

But he'd been like that when he'd been alive, too, hadn't he?

The cold straight road stretched out across the cold flat plain, and there was no mercy out here, no right or wrong, no lies. There was only this giant machine hurtling along, which took all Bill's strength to keep on the road.

If he couldn't do it, he'd die.

Bill realized, with a certain shock, how much of his life he'd wanted an audience. Someone else to be a witness to how scared and angry he was, to agree with him on how bad a father Billy had been.

What had he thought? That someday he'd stand up in some kind of giant courtroom, letting the whole world know how unfair everything had been from the day he'd been born?

Out here, he knew the truth.

There was no vast cosmic court of justice that would turn Billy into the kind of father Bill had wanted him to be. There was no Marswife to swoop down from the dust clouds and guide a lost boy home. The red world didn't care if he sulked; it would casually kill him, if it caught him Outside.

And he had always known it.

Then what was the point of being angry about it all the time?

What was the point of white-knuckled fists and a knotted-up stomach if things would never change?

His anger would never force anybody to fix the world for him.

But . . .

There were people who tried to fix the world for themselves. Maybe he could fix his world, just the narrow slice of it that was his.

He watched the monitors, watched the wind driving sand across the barren stony plain, the emptiness that he had hated ever since he could remember. What would it take to make him love it, the way Billy or Ford loved it?

He imagined water falling from the sky, bubbling up from under the frozen rock. Maybe it would be blue water. It would splash and steam, the way it did in the bathhouse. Running, gurgling water to drown the dust and irrigate the red sand.

And green would come. He couldn't get a mental image of vizio acres over the whole world, tenting in greenness even up here; that was crazy. But the green might creep out on its own, if there was enough water. Wiry little desert plants at first, maybe, and then . . . Bill tried to remember the names of plants from his lesson plans. Sagebrush, right. Sequoias. Clover. Edelweiss. Apples. A memory came back to him, a nursery rhyme he'd had on his Buke once: *I should like to rise and go, where the golden apples grow* . . .

He blurred his vision a little and saw himself soaring past green rows that went out forever, that arched over and made warm shade and shelter from the wind. Another memory floated up, a picture from a lesson plan, and his dream caught it and slapped it into place: cows grazing in a green meadow, out under a sky full of white clouds, clouds of water, not dust.

And, in the most sheltered places, there would be people. Families. Houses lit warm at night, with the lights winking through the green leaves. Just as he had always imagined. One of them would be his house. He'd live there with his family.

Nobody would give him a house, or a family, or a safe world to live in, of course. Ever. They didn't exist. But . . .

Bill wrapped it all around himself anyway, to keep out the cold and the fear, and he drove on.

At some point—hours or days later, he never knew—his strength gave out and he couldn't hold *Beautiful Evelyn* on the road anymore. She drifted gently to the side, clipping the boulders as she came, and rumbled to a halt just inside Thousand-K Station.

Bill lay along the seat where he had fallen, too tired and in too much pain to move. Ford still sat, propped up in his corner, most of his face hidden by his mask. Bill couldn't tell if he was still alive.

He closed his eyes and went down, and down, into the green rows.

He was awakened by thumping on the cab, and shouting, and was bolt upright with his mask on before he had time to realize that he wasn't dreaming. He crawled across the seat and threw the release switches. The hatch swung down, and red light streamed in out of a black night. There stood Old Brick, granddaddy of the Haulers, with his long beard streaming sideways in the gale and at least three other Haulers behind him. His eyes widened behind his mask as he took in Bill and Ford. He reached up and turned up the volume on his psuit.

"CONVOY! WE GOT KIDS HERE! LOOKS LIKE TOWNSEND'S RIG!"

X

Bill was all right after a couple of days, even though he had to have stuff fed into his arm while he slept. He was still foggy-headed when Mother came and sat by his bed, and very gently told him about Billy.

Bill mustn't worry, she said; she would find Billy a warm corner in the *Empress*, with all the food and drink he wanted the rest of his days, and surely Bill would come talk to him sometimes? For Billy was ever so proud of Young Bill, as everyone knew. And perhaps take him on little walks round the Tubes, so he could see Outside now and again? For Billy had so loved the High Road.

Ford wasn't all right. He had to have surgery for a ruptured spleen, and almost bled to death once they'd cut his psuit off him.

He still hadn't regained consciousness when Bill, wrapped in an outsize bath-robe, shuffled down to the infirmary's intensive care unit to see him. *See him* was all Bill could do; pale as an egg, Ford lay in the center of a mass of tubes and plastic tenting. The only parts of him that weren't white were his hair, which was growing in red as Martian sand, and the greenish bruise where Bill had punched him in the eye.

Bill sat there staring at the floor tiles, until he became aware that someone else had entered the room. He looked up.

He knew the man in front of him must be Ford's father; his eyes were the same watery blue, and his ears stuck out the same way. He wore patched denim and muddy boots, and a stocking cap pulled down almost low enough to hide the ban-dage over his left eyebrow. There was a little white stubble along the line of his jaw, like a light frost.

He looked at Ford, and the watery eyes brimmed over with tears. He glanced uncertainly at Bill. He looked down, lined up the toes of his boots against a seam in the tile.

"You'd be that Hauler's boy, then?" he said. "I have to thank you, on behalf of my Blatchford."

"Blatchford," repeated Bill, dumfounded until he realized whom the old man meant. "Oh."

"That woman explained everything to me," said Ford's dad. "Wasn't my Blatch-ford's fault. Poor boy. Don't blame him for running off scared. Your dad did a good thing, taking him in like that. I'm sorry about your dad."

"Me, too," said Bill. "But For—Blatchford'll be all right."

"I know he will," said Ford's dad, looking yearningly at his son. "He's a strong boy, my Blatchford. Not like his brother. You can raise somebody up his whole life and do your best to teach him what's right, and—and overnight, he can just turn into a stranger on you.

"My Sam did that. I should have seen it coming, him walking out on us. He never was any good, really. A weakling.

"Not like my little Blatchford. Never a word of complaint out of *him*, or whin-ing after vanities. *He* knows who he is. He'll make the Collective proud one day."

Bill swallowed hard. He knew that Ford would never make the Collective proud; Ford would be off on the High Road as soon as he could, in love with the wide horizon, and the old man's angry heart would break again.

The weight of everything that had happened seemed to come crashing down on Bill at once. He couldn't remember when he'd felt so miserable.

"Would you tell me something, sir?" he said. "What does it take to join the MAC?"

"Hm?" Ford's dad turned.

"What do you have to do?"

Ford's dad looked at him speculatively. He cleared his throat. "It isn't what you do. It's what you *are*, young man."

He came and sat down beside Bill, and threw back his shoulders.

"You have to be the kind of person who believes a better world is worth working for. You can't be weak, or afraid, or greedy for things for yourself. You have to know that the only thing that matters is making that better world, and making it for everyone, not just for you.

"You may not even get to see it come into existence, because making the world right is hard work. It'll take all your strength and all your bravery, and maybe you'll be left at the end with nothing but knowing that you did your duty.

"But that'll be enough for you."

His voice was thin and harsh; he sounded as though he was reciting a lecture he'd memorized. But his eyes shone like Ford's had, when Ford had looked out on the open sky for the first time.

"Well—I'm going to study agriculture," said Bill. "And I thought, maybe, when I pass my levels, I'd like to join the MAC. I want that world you talk about. It's all I've ever wanted."

"Good on you, son," said Ford's dad, nodding solemnly. "You study hard, and I'm sure you'd be welcome to join us. You're the sort of young man we need in the MAC. And it does my heart good to know my Blatchford's got a friend like you. Gives me hope for the future, to think we'll have two heroes like you working in our cause!"

He shook Bill's hand, and then the nurse looked in at them and said that visiting hours were over. Ford's dad went away, down the hill. Bill walked slowly back to his room.

He didn't climb back into bed. He sat down in a chair in the corner, and looked out through Settlement Dome at the cold red desert, at the far double line of boulders where the High Road ran off into places Billy would never see again. He began to cry, silently, tears burning as they ran down his face.

He didn't know whether he was crying for Billy, or for Ford's dad.

The world was ending. The world was beginning.

The Sledge-Maker's Daughter

Alastair Reynolds

A professional scientist with a Ph.D. in astronomy, Alastair Reynolds worked for the European Space Agency in the Netherlands for a number of years but has recently moved back to his native Wales to become a full-time writer. His first novel, Revelation Space, was widely hailed as one of the major SF books of the year; it was quickly followed by Chasm City, Redemption Ark, Absolution Gap, Century Rain, and Pushing Ice, all big sprawling Space Operas that were big sellers as well, establishing Reynolds as one of the best and most popular new SF writers to enter the field in many years. His other books include a novella collection, Diamond Dogs, Turquoise Days, and a chapbook novella, The Six Directions of Space, as well as three collections, Galactic North, Zima Blue and Other Stories, and Deep Navigation. His other novels include The Prefect, House of Suns, Terminal World, Blue Remembered Earth, On the Steel Breeze, Terminal World, Slow Bullets, and Sleepover, and a Doctor Who novel, Harvest of Time.

Reynolds's work is known for its grand scope, sweep, and scale (in one story, "Galactic North," a spaceship sets out in pursuit of another in a stern chase that takes thousands of years of time and hundreds of thousands of light-years to complete; in another, "Thousandth Night," ultrarich immortals embark on a plan that will call for the physical rearrangement of all the stars in the galaxy.) Here he takes us somewhat closer to home, in a distressed civilization that's been set back hundreds of years by war and disaster, for a study of a young girl with an all-too-common problem who finds an extremely unique solution for it.

She stopped in sight of Twenty Arch Bridge, laying down her bags to rest her hands from the weight of two hog's heads and forty pence worth of beeswax candles. While she paused, Kathrin adjusted the drawstring on her hat, tilting the brim to shade her forehead from the sun. Though the air was still cool, there was a fierce new quality to the light that brought out her freckles.

Kathrin moved to continue, but a tightness in her throat made her hesitate. She had been keeping the bridge from her thoughts until this moment, but now the fact of it could not be ignored. Unless she crossed it she would face the long trudge to New Bridge, a diversion that would keep her on the road until long after sunset.

"Sledge-maker's daughter!" called a rough voice from across the road.

Kathrin turned sharply at the sound. An aproned man stood in a doorway, smearing his hands dry. He had a monkeylike face, tanned a deep liverish red, with white sideboards and a gleaming pink tonsure.

"Brendan Lynch's daughter, isn't it?"

She nodded meekly, but bit her lip rather than answer.

"Thought so. Hardly one to forget a pretty face, me." The man beckoned her to the doorway of his shop. "Come here, lass. I've something for your father."

"Sir?"

"I was hoping to visit him last week, but work kept me here." He cocked his head at the painted wooden trademark hanging above the doorway. "Peter Rigby, the wheelwright. Kathrin, isn't it?"

"I need to be getting along, sir . . ."

"And your father needs good wood, of which I've plenty. Come inside for a moment, instead of standing there like a starved thing." He called over his shoulder, telling his wife to put the water on the fire.

Reluctantly Kathrin gathered her bags and followed Peter into his workshop. She blinked against the dusty air and removed her hat. Sawdust carpeted the floor, fine and golden in places, crisp and coiled in others, while a heady concoction of resins and glues filled the air. Pots simmered on fires. Wood was being steamed into curves, or straightened where it was curved. Many sharp tools gleamed on one wall, some of them fashioned with blades of skydrift. Wheels, mostly awaiting spokes or iron tyres, rested against another. Had the wheels been sledges, it could have been her father's workshop, when he had been busier.

Peter showed Kathrin to an empty stool next to one of his benches. "Sit down here and take the weight off your feet. Mary can make you some bread and cheese. Or bread and ham if you'd rather."

"That's kind sir, but Widow Grayling normally gives me something to eat, when I reach her house."

Peter raised a white eyebrow. He stood by the bench with his thumbs tucked into the belt of his apron, his belly jutting out as if he was quietly proud of it. "I didn't know you visited the witch."

"She will have her two hog's heads, once a month, and her candles. She only buys them from the Shield, not the Town. She pays for the hogs a year in advance, twenty-four whole pounds."

"And you're not scared by her?"

"I've no cause to be."

"There's some that would disagree with you."

Remembering something her father had told her, Kathrin said, "There are folk who say the Sheriff can fly, or that there was once a bridge that winked at travelers like an eye, or a road of iron that reached all the way to London. My father says there's no reason for anyone to be scared of Widow Grayling."

"Not afraid she'll turn you into a toad, then?"

"She cures people, not put spells on them."

"When she's in the mood for it. From what I've heard she's just as likely to turn the sick and needy away."

"If she helps some people, isn't that better than nothing at all?"

"I suppose." She could tell Peter didn't agree, but he wasn't cross with her for arguing. "What does your father make of you visiting the witch, anyway?"

"He doesn't mind."

"No?" Peter asked, interestedly.

"When he was small, my dad cut his arm on a piece of skydrift that he found in the snow. He went to Widow Grayling and she made his arm better again by tying an eel around it. She didn't take any payment except the skydrift."

"Does your father still believe an eel can heal a wound?"

"He says he'll believe anything if it gets the job done."

"Wise man, that Brendan, a man after my own heart. Which reminds me." Peter ambled to another bench, pausing to stir one of his bubbling pots before gathering a bundle of sawn-off wooden sticks. He set them down in front of Kathrin on a scrap of cloth. "Off cuts," he explained. "But good seasoned beech, which'll never warp. No use to me, but I am sure your father will find use for them. Tell him that there's more, if he wishes to collect it."

"I haven't got any money for wood."

"I'd take none. Your father was always generous to me, when I was going through lean times." Peter scratched behind his ear. "Only fair, the way I see it."

"Thank you," Kathrin said doubtfully. "But I don't think I can carry the wood all the way home."

"Not with two hog's heads as well. But you can drop by when you've given the heads to Widow Grayling."

"Only I won't be coming back over the river," Kathrin said. "After I've crossed Twenty Arch Bridge, I'll go back along the south quayside and take the ferry at Jarrow."

Peter looked puzzled. "Why line the ferryman's pocket when you can cross the bridge for nowt?"

Kathrin shrugged easily. "I've got to visit someone on the Jarrow road, to settle an account."

"Then you'd better take the wood now, I suppose," Peter said.

Mary bustled in, carrying a small wooden tray laden with bread and ham. She was as plump and red as her husband, only shorter. Picking up the entire gist of the conversation in an instant, she said, "Don't be an oaf, Peter. The girl cannot carry all that wood *and* her bags. If she will not come back this way, she must pass a message onto her father. Tell him that there's wood here if he wants it." She shook her head sympathetically at Kathrin. "What does he think you are, a pack mule?"

"I'll tell my father about the wood," she said.

"Seasoned beech," Peter said emphatically. "Remember that."

"I will."

Mary encouraged her to take some of the bread and meat, despite Kathrin again mentioning that she expected to be fed at Widow Grayling's. "Take it anyway," Mary said. "You never know how hungry you might get on the way home. Are you sure about not coming back this way?"

"I'd best not," Kathrin said.

After an awkward lull, Peter said, "There is something else I meant to tell your father. Could you let him know that I've no need of a new sledge this year, after all?"

"Peter," Mary said. "You promised."

"I said that I should *probably* need one. I was wrong in that." Peter looked exasperated. "The fault lies in Brendan, not me! If he did not make such good and solid sledges, then perhaps I should need another by now."

"I shall tell him," Kathrin said.

"Is your father keeping busy?" Mary asked.

"Aye," Kathrin answered, hoping the wheelwright's wife wouldn't push her on the point.

"Of course he will still be busy," Peter said, helping himself to some of the bread. "People don't stop needing sledges, just because the Great Winter loosens its hold on us. Any more than they stopped needing wheels when the winter was at its coldest. It's still cold for half the year!"

Kathrin opened her mouth to speak. She meant to tell Peter that he could pass the message on to her father directly, for he was working not five minutes' walk from the wheelwright's shop. Peter clearly had no knowledge that her father had left the village, leaving his workshop empty during these warming months. But she realized that her father would be ashamed if the wheelwright were to learn of his present trade. It was best that nothing be said.

"Kathrin?" Peter asked.

"I should be getting on. Thank you for the food, and the offer of the wood."

"You pass our regards onto your father," Mary said.

"I shall."

"God go with you. Watch out for the jangling men."

"I will," Kathrin replied, because that was what you were supposed to say.

"Before you go," Peter said suddenly, as if a point had just occurred to him. "Let me tell you something. You say there are people who believe the Sheriff can fly, as if that was a foolish thing, like the iron road and the winking bridge. I cannot speak of the other things, but when I was boy I met someone who had seen the Sheriff's flying machine. My grandfather often spoke of it. A whirling thing, like a windmill made of tin. He had seen it when he was a boy, carrying the Sheriff and his men above the land faster than any bird."

"If the Sheriff could fly then, why does he need a horse and carriage now?"

"Because the flying machine crashed down to Earth, and no tradesman could persuade it to fly again. It was a thing of the old world, before the Great Winter. Perhaps the winking bridge and the iron road were also things of the old world.

We mock too easily, as if we understood everything of our world where our fore-bears understood nothing."

"But if I should believe in certain things," Kathrin said, "should I not also be-lieve in others? If the Sheriff can fly, then can a jangling man not steal me from my bed at night?"

"The jangling men are a story to stop children misbehaving," Peter said with-eringly. "How old are you now?"

"Sixteen," Kathrin answered.

"I am speaking of something that was seen, in daylight, not made up to frighten bairns."

"But people say they have seen jangling men. They have seen men made of tin and gears, like the inside of a clock."

"Some people were frightened too much when they were small," Peter said, with a dismissive shake. "No more than that. But the Sheriff is real, and he was once able to fly. That's God's truth."

Her hands were hurting again by the time she reached Twenty Arch Bridge. She tugged down the sleeves of her sweater, using them as mittens. Rooks and jack-daws wheeled and cawed overhead. Seagulls feasted on waste floating in the nar-row races between the bridge's feet, or pecked at vile leavings on the road that had been missed by the night soil gatherers. A boy laughed as Kathrin nearly tripped on the labyrinth of criss-crossing ruts that had been etched by years of wagon wheels entering and leaving the bridge. She hissed a curse back at the boy, but now the wagons served her purpose. She skulked near a doorway until a heavy cart came rumbling along, top-heavy with beer barrels from the Blue Star Brew-ery, drawn by four snorting dray-horses, a bored-looking drayman at the reins, huddled so down deep into his leather coat that it seemed as if the Great Winter still had its icy hand on the country.

Kathrin started walking as the cart lumbered past her, using it as a screen. Be-tween the stacked beer barrels she could see the top level of the scaffolding that was shoring up the other side of the arch, visible since no house or parapet stood on that part of the bridge. A dozen or so workers—including a couple of aproned foremen—were standing on the scaffolding, looking down at the work going on below. Some of them had plumb lines; one of them even had a little black rod that shone a fierce red spot wherever he wanted something moved. Of Garret, the reason she wished to cross the bridge only once if she could help it, there was nothing to be seen. Kathrin hoped that he was under the side of the bridge, hec-toring the workers. She felt sure that her father was down there too, being told what to do and biting his tongue against answering back. He put up with being shouted at, he put up with being forced to treat wood with crude disrespect, because it was all he could do to earn enough money to feed and shelter himself and his daughter. And he never, ever, looked Garret Kinnear in the eye.

Kathrin felt her mood easing as the dray ambled across the bridge, nearing the slight rise over the narrow middle arches. The repair work, where Garret was most likely to be, was now well behind her. She judged her progress by the passage of alehouses. She had passed the newly painted Bridge Inn and the shuttered gloom of the Lord's Confessor. Fiddle music spilled from the open doorway of the Dancing Panda: an old folk song with nonsense lyrics about *sickly sausage rolls*.

Ahead lay the Winged Man, its sign containing a strange painting of a foreboding figure rising from a hilltop. If she passed the Winged Man, she felt she would be safe.

Then the dray hit a jutting cobblestone and rightmost front wheel snapped free of its axle. The wheel wobbled off on its own. The cart tipped to the side, spilling beer barrels onto the ground. Kathrin stepped nimbly aside as one of the barrels ruptured and sent its fizzing, piss-colored contents across the roadway. The horses snorted and strained. The drayman spat out a greasy wad of chewing tobacco and started down from his chair, his face a mask of impassive resignation, as if this was the kind of thing that could be expected to happen once a day. Kathrin heard him whisper something in the ear of one of the horses, in beast-tongue, which calmed the animal.

Kathrin knew that she had no choice but to continue. Yet she had no sooner resumed her pace—moving faster now, the bags swaying awkwardly—than she saw Garret Kinnear. He was just stepping out of the Winged Man's doorway.

He smiled. "You in a hurry or something?"

Kathrin tightened her grip on the bags, as if she was going to use them as weapons. She decided not to say anything, not to openly acknowledge his presence, even though their eyes had met for an electric instant.

"Getting to be a big strong girl now, Kathrin Lynch."

She carried on walking, each step taking an eternity. How foolish she had been, to take Twenty Arch Bridge when it would only have cost her another hour to take the further crossing. She should not have allowed Peter to delay her with his good intentions.

"You want some help with them bags of yours?"

Out of the corner of her eye she saw him move out of the doorway, tugging his mud-stained trousers higher onto his hip. Garret Kinnear was snake thin, all skin and bone, but much stronger than he looked. He wiped a hand across his sharp beardless chin. He had long black hair, the greasy gray color of dishwater.

"Go away," she hissed, hating herself in the same instant.

"Just making conversation," he said.

Kathrin quickened her pace, glancing nervously around. All of a sudden the bridge appeared deserted. The shops and houses she had yet to pass were all shuttered and silent. There was still a commotion going on by the dray, but no one there was paying any attention to what was happening further along the bridge.

"Leave me alone," Kathrin said.

He was walking almost alongside her now, between Kathrin and the road. "Now what kind of way to talk is that, Kathrin Lynch? Especially after my offer to help you with them bags. What have you got in them, anyways?"

"Nothing that's any business of yours."

"I could be the judge of that." Before she could do anything, he'd snatched the bag from her left hand. He peered into its dark depths, frowning. "You came all the way from Jarrow Ferry with this?"

"Give me back the bag."

She reached for the bag, tried to grab it back, but he held it out of her reach, grinning cruelly.

"That's mine."

"How much would a pig's head be worth?"

"You tell me. There's only one pig around here."

They'd passed the mill next to the Winged Man. There was a gap between the mill and the six-story house next to it, where some improbably narrow property must once have existed. Garret turned down the alley, still carrying Kathrin's bag. He reached the parapet at the edge of the bridge and looked over the side. He rummaged in the bag and drew out the pig's head. Kathrin hesitated at the entrance to the narrow alley, watching as Garret held the head out over the roiling water.

"You can have your pig back. Just come a wee bit closer."

"So you can do what you did last time?"

"I don't remember any complaints." He let the head fall, then caught it again, Kathrin's heart in her throat.

"You know I couldn't complain."

"Not much to ask for a pig's head, is it?" With his free hand, he fumbled open his trousers, tugging out the pale worm of his cock. "You did it before, and it didn't kill you. Why not now? I won't trouble you again."

She watched his cock stiffen. "You said that last time."

"Aye, but this time I mean it. Come over here, Kathrin. Be a good girl now and you'll have your pig back."

Kathrin looked back over her shoulder. No one was going to disturb them. The dray had blocked all the traffic behind it, and nothing was coming over the bridge from the south.

"Please," she said.

"Just this once," Garret said. "And make your mind up fast, girl. This pig's getting awfully heavy in my hand."

Kathrin stood in the widow's candlelit kitchen—it only had one tiny, dusty window—while the old woman turned her bent back to attend to the coals burning in her black metal stove. She poked and prodded the fire until it hissed back like a cat. "You came all the way from Jarrow Ferry?" she asked.

"Aye," Kathrin said. The room smelled smoky.

"That's too far for anyone, let alone a sixteen-year-old lass. I should have a word with your father. I heard he was working on Twenty Arch Bridge."

Kathrin shifted uncomfortably. "I don't mind walking. The weather's all right."

"So they say. All the same, the evenings are still cold, and there are types about you wouldn't care to meet on your own, miles from Jarrow."

"I'll be back before it gets dark," Kathrin said, with more optimism than she felt. Not if she went out of her way to avoid Garret Kinnear she wouldn't. He knew the route she'd normally take back home, and the alternatives would mean a much longer journey.

"You sure about that?"

"I have no one else to visit. I can start home now." Kathrin offered her one remaining bag, as Widow Grayling turned from the fire, brushing her hands on her apron.

"Put it on the table, will you?"

Kathrin put the bag down. "One pig's head, and twenty candles, just as you wanted," she said brightly.

Widow Grayling hobbled over to the table, supporting herself with a stick, eyeing Kathrin as she opened the bag and took out the solitary head. She weighed it in her hand then set it down on the table, the head facing Kathrin in such a way that its beady black eyes and smiling snout suggested amused complicity.

"It's a good head," the widow said. "But there were meant to be two of them."

"Can you manage with just the one, until I visit again? I'll have three for you next time."

"I'll manage if I must. Was there a problem with the butcher in the Shield?"

Kathrin had considered feigning ignorance, saying that she did not recall how only one head had come to be in her bags. But she knew Widow Grayling too well for that.

"Do you mind if I sit down?"

"Of course." The widow hobbled around the table to one of the rickety stools and dragged it out. "Are you all right, girl?"

Kathrin lowered herself onto the stool.

"The other bag was taken from me," she answered quietly.

"By who?"

"Someone on the bridge."

"Children?"

"A man."

Widow Grayling nodded slowly, as if Kathrin's answer had only confirmed some deep-seated suspicion she had harbored for many years. "Thomas Kinnear's boy, was it?"

"How could you know?"

"Because I've lived long enough to form ready opinions of people. Garret Kinnear is filth. But there's no one that'll touch him, because they're scared of his father. Even the Sheriff tugs his forelock to Thomas Kinnear. Did he rape you?"

"No. But he wanted me to do something nearly as bad."

"And did he make you?"

Kathrin looked away.

"Not this time."

Widow Grayling closed her eyes. She reached across the table and took one of Kathrin's hands, squeezing it between her own. "When was it?"

"Three months ago, when there was still snow on the ground. I had to cross the bridge on my own. It was later than usual, and there weren't any people around. I knew about Garret already, but I'd managed to keep away from him. I thought I was going to be lucky." Kathrin turned back to face her companion. "He caught me and took me into one of the mills. The wheels were turning, but there was nobody inside except me and Garret. I struggled, but then he put his finger to my lips and told me to shush."

"Because of your father."

"If I made trouble, if I did not do what he wanted, Garret would tell his father some lie about mine. He would say that he caught him sleeping on the job, or drunk, or stealing nails."

"Garret promised you that?"

"He said, life's hard enough for a sledge-maker's daughter when no one wants sledges. He said it would only be harder if my father lost his work."

"In that respect he was probably right," the widow said resignedly. "It was brave of you to hold your silence, Kathrin. But the problem hasn't gone away, has it? You cannot avoid Garret forever."

"I can take the other bridge."

"That'll make no difference, now that he has his eye on you."

Kathrin looked down at her hands. "Then he's won already."

"No, he just thinks that he has." Without warning the widow stood from her chair. "How long have we known each other, would you say?"

"Since I was small."

"And in all that time, have I come to seem any older to you?"

"You've always seemed the same to me, Widow Lynch."

"An old woman. The witch on the hill."

"There are good witches and bad witches," Kathrin pointed out.

"And there are mad old women who don't belong in either category. Wait a moment."

Widow Grayling stooped under the impossibly low doorway into the next room. Kathrin heard a scrape of wood on wood, as of a drawer being opened. She heard rummaging sounds. Widow Grayling returned with something in her hands, wrapped in red cotton. Whatever it was, she put it down on the table. By the noise it made Kathrin judged that it was an item of some weight and solidity.

"I was just like you once. I grew up not far from Ferry, in the darkest, coldest years of the Great Winter."

"How long ago?"

"The Sheriff then was William the Questioner. You won't have heard of him." Widow Grayling sat down in the same seat she'd been using before and quickly exposed the contents of the red cotton bundle.

Kathrin wasn't quite sure what she was looking at. There was a thick and un-ornamented bracelet, made of some dull grey metal like pewter. Next to the bracelet was something like the handle of a broken sword: a grip, with a criss-crossed pattern on it, with a curved guard reaching from one end of the hilt to the other. It was fashioned from the same dull grey metal.

"Pick it up," the widow said. "Feel it."

Kathrin reached out tentatively and closed her finger around the criss-crossed hilt. It felt cold and hard and not quite the right shape for her hand. She lifted it from the table, feeling its weight.

"What is it, widow?"

"It's yours. It's a thing that has been in my possession for a very long while, but now it must change hands."

Kathrin didn't know quite what to say. A gift was a gift, but neither she nor her father would have any use for this ugly broken thing, save for its value to a scrap man.

"What happened to the sword?" she asked.

"There was never a sword. The thing you are holding is the entire object."

"Then I don't understand what it is for."

"You shall, in time. I'm about to place a hard burden on your shoulders. I have often thought that you were the right one, but I wished to wait until you were older, stronger. But what has happened today cannot be ignored. I am old and weakening. It would be a mistake to wait another year."

"I still don't understand."

"Take the bracelet. Put it on your wrist."

Kathrin did as she was told. The bracelet opened on a heavy hinge, like a manacle. When she locked it together, the join was nearly invisible. It was a cunning thing, to be sure. But it still felt as heavy and dead and useless as the broken sword.

Kathrin tried to keep a composed face, while all the while suspecting that the widow was as mad as people had always said.

"Thank you," she said, with as much sincerity as she could muster.

"Now listen to what I have to say. You walked across the bridge today. Doubtless you passed the inn known as the Winged Man."

"It was where Garret caught up with me."

"Did it ever occur to you to wonder where the name of the tavern comes from?"

"My dad told me once. He said the tavern was named after a metal statue that used to stand on a hill to the south, on the Durham road."

"And did your father explain the origin of this statue?"

"He said some people reckoned it had been up there since before the Great Winter. Other people said an old sheriff had put it up. Some other people . . ." But Kathrin trailed off.

"Yes?"

"It's silly, but they said a real Winged Man had come down, out of the sky."

"And did your father place any credence in that story?"

"Not really," Kathrin said.

"He was right not to. The statue was indeed older than the Great Winter, when they tore it down. It was not put up to honor the sheriff, or commemorate the arrival of a Winged Man." Now the widow looked at her intently. "But a Winged Man *did* come down. I know what happened, Kathrin; I saw the statue with my own eyes, before the Winged Man fell. I was there."

Kathrin shifted. She was growing uncomfortable in the widow's presence.

"My dad said people reckoned the Winged Man came down hundreds of years ago."

"It did."

"Then you can't have been there, Widow Grayling."

"Because if I had been, I should be dead by now? You're right. By all that is natural, I should be. I was born three hundred years ago, Kathrin. I've been a widow for more than two hundred of those years, though not always under this name. I've moved from house to house, village to village, as soon as people start suspecting what I am. I found the Winged Man when I was sixteen years old, just like you."

Kathrin smiled tightly. "I want to believe you."

"You will, shortly. I already told you that this was the coldest time of the Great Winter. The sun was a cold gray disk, as if it was made of ice itself. For years the river hardly thawed at all. The Frost Fair stayed almost all year round. It was nothing like the miserable little gatherings you have known. This was ten times bigger, a whole city built on the frozen river. It had streets and avenues, its own quarters. There were tents and stalls, with skaters and sledges everywhere. There'd be races, jousting competitions, fireworks, mystery players, even printing presses to make newspapers and souvenirs just for the Frost Fair. People came from miles around to see it, Kathrin; from as far away as Carlisle or York."

"Didn't they get bored with it, if it was always there?"

"It was always changing, though. Every few months there was something different. You would travel fifty miles to see a new wonder if enough people started talking about it. And there was no shortage of wonders, even if they were not always quite what you had imagined when you set off on your journey. Things fell from the sky more often in those days. A living thing like the Winged Man was still a rarity, but other things came down regularly enough. People would spy where they fell and try to get there first. Usually all they'd find would be bits of hot metal, all warped and runny like melted sugar."

"Skydrift," Kathrin said. "Metal that's no use to anyone, except barbers and butchers."

"Only because we can't make fires hot enough to make that metal smelt down like iron or copper. Once, we could. But if you could find a small piece with an edge, there was *nothing* it couldn't cut through. A surgeon's best knife will always be skydrift."

"Some people think the metal belongs to the jangling men, and that anyone who touches it will be cursed."

"And I'm sure the sheriff does nothing to persuade them otherwise. Do you think the jangling men care what happens to their metal?"

"I don't think they care, because I don't think they exist."

"I was once of the same opinion. Then something happened to make me change my mind."

"This being when you found the Winged Man, I take it."

"Before even that. I would have been thirteen, I suppose. It was in the back of a tent in the Frost Fair. There was a case holding a hand made of metal, found among skydrift near Wallsend."

"A rider's gauntlet."

"I don't think so. It was broken off at the wrist, but you could tell that it used to belong to something that was also made of metal. There were metal bones and muscles in it. No cogs or springs, like in a clock or tin toy. This was something finer, more ingenious. I don't believe any man could have made it. But it cannot just be the jangling men who drop things from the sky, or fall out of it."

"Why not?" Kathrin asked, in the spirit of someone going along with a game.

"Because it was said that the sheriff's men once found a head of skin and bone, all burned up, but which still had a pair of spectacles on it. The glass in them was dark like coal, but when the sheriff wore them, he could see at night like a wolf. Another time, his men found a shred of garment that kept changing color, depending on what it was lying against. You could hardly see it then. Not enough to make a suit, but you could imagine how useful that would have been to the sheriff's spies."

"They'd have wanted to get to the Winged Man first."

Widow Grayling nodded. "It was just luck that I got to him first. I was on the Durham road, riding a mule, when he fell from the sky. Now, the law said that they would spike your head on the bridge if you touched something that fell on the Sheriff's land, especially skydrift. But everyone knew that the Sheriff could only travel so fast, even when he had his flying machine. It was a risk worth taking, so I took it, and I found the Winged Man, and he was still alive."

"Was he really a man?"

"He was a creature of flesh and blood, not a jangling man, but he was not like any man I had seen before. He was smashed and bent, like a toy that had been trodden on. When I found him he was covered in armor, hot enough to turn the snow to water and make the water hiss and bubble under him. I could only see his face. A kind of golden mask had come off, lying next to him. There were bars across his mask, like the head of the Angel on the tavern sign. The rest of him was covered in metal, jointed in a clever fashion. It was silver in places and black in others, where it had been scorched. His arms were metal wings, as wide across as the road itself if they had not been snapped back on themselves. Instead of legs he just had a long tail, with a kind of fluke at the end of it. I crept closer, watching the sky all around me for the sheriff's whirling machine. I was fearful at first, but when I saw the Winged Man's face I only wanted to do what I could for him. And he was dying. I knew it, because I'd seen the same look on the faces of men hanging from the sheriff's killing poles."

"Did you talk to him?"

"I asked him if he wanted some water. At first he just looked at me, his eyes pale as the sky, his lips opening and closing like a fish that has just been landed. Then he said 'water will not help me.' Just those five words, in a dialect I didn't know. Then I asked him if there was anything else I could do to help him, all the while glancing over my shoulder in case anyone should come upon us. But the road was empty and the sky was clear. It took a long time for him to answer me again."

"What did he say?"

"He said 'thank you, but there is nothing you can do for me.' Then I asked him if he was an angel. He smiled, ever so slightly. 'No,' he said. 'Not an angel, really. But I am a flier.' I asked him if there was a difference. He smiled again before answering me. 'Perhaps not, after all this time. Do you know of fliers, girl? Do any of you still remember the war?'"

"What did you tell him?"

"The truth. I said I knew nothing of a war, unless he spoke of the Battle of the Stadium of Light, which had only happened twenty years earlier. He looked sad, then, as if he had hoped for a different answer. I asked him if he was a kind of soldier. He said that he was. 'Fliers are warriors,' he said. 'Men like me are fighting a great war, on your behalf, against an enemy you do not even remember.'"

"What enemy?"

"The jangling men. They exist, but not in the way we imagine them. They don't crawl in through bedroom windows at night, clacking tin-bodied things with skull faces and clockwork keys whirring from their backs. But they're real enough."

"Why would such things exist?"

"They'd been made to do the work of men on the other side of the sky, where men cannot breathe because the air is so thin. They made the jangling men canny enough that they could work without being told *exactly* what to do. But that already made them slyer than foxes. The jangling men coveted our world for themselves. That was before the Great Winter came in. The flier said that men like him—special soldiers, born and bred to fight the jangling men—were all that was holding them back."

"And he told you they were fighting a war, above the sky?"

Something pained Widow Grayling. "All the years since haven't made it any easier to understand what the flier told me. He said that, just as there may be holes in a old piece of timber, one that has been eaten through by woodworm, so there may be holes in the sky itself. He said that his wings were not really to help him fly, but to help him navigate those tunnels in the sky, just as the wheels of a cart find their way into the ruts on a road."

"I don't understand. How can there be holes in the sky, when the air is already too thin to breathe?"

"He said that the fliers and the jangling men make these holes, just as armies may dig a shifting network of trenches and tunnels as part of a long campaign. It requires strength to dig a hole and more strength to shore it up when it has already been dug. In an army, it would be the muscle of men and horses and whatever machines still work. But the flier was talking about a different kind of strength altogether." The widow paused, then stared into Kathrin's eyes with a look of foreboding. "He told me where it came from, you see. And ever since then, I have seen the world with different eyes. It is a hard burden, Kathrin. But someone must bear it."

Without thinking, Kathrin said, "Tell me."

"Are you sure?"

"Yes. I want to know."

"That bracelet has been on your wrist for a few minutes now. Does it feel any different?"

"No," Kathrin said automatically, but as soon as she'd spoken, as soon as she'd moved her arm, she knew that it was not the case. The bracelet still looked the same, it still looked like a lump of cold dead metal, but it seemed to hang less heavily against her skin than when she'd first put it on.

"The flier gave it to me," Widow Grayling said, observing Kathrin's reaction. "He told me how to open his armor and find the bracelet. I asked why. He said it was because I had offered him water. He was giving me something in return for that kindness. He said that the bracelet would keep me healthy, make me strong in other ways, and that if anyone else was to wear it, it would cure them of many ailments. He said that it was against the common law of his people to give such a gift to one such as I, but he chose to do it anyway. I opened his armor, as he told me, and I found his arm, bound by iron straps to the inside of his wing, and broken like the wing itself. On the end of his arm was this bracelet."

"If the bracelet had the power of healing, why was the Winged Man dying?"

"He said that there were certain afflictions it could not cure. He had been touched by the poisonous ichor of a jangling man, and the bracelet could do nothing for him now."

"I still do not believe in magic," Kathrin said carefully.

"Certain magics are real, though. The magic that makes a machine fly, or a man see in the dark. The bracelet feels lighter, because part of it has entered you. It is in your blood now, in your marrow, just as the jangling man's ichor was in the flier's. You felt nothing, and you will continue to feel nothing. But so long as you wear the bracelet, you will age much slower than anyone else. For centuries, no sickness or infirmity will touch you."

Kathrin stroked the bracelet. "I do not believe this."

"I would not expect to you. In a year or two, you will feel no change in yourself. But in five years, or in ten, people will start to remark upon your uncommon youthfulness. For a while, you will glory in it. Then you will feel admiration turn slowly to envy and then to hate, and it will start to feel like a curse. Like me, you will need to move on and take another name. This will be the pattern of your life, while your wear the flier's charm."

Kathrin looked at the palms of her hand. It might have been imagination, but the lines where the handles had cut into her were paler and less sensitive to the touch.

"Is this how you heal people?" she asked.

"You're as wise as I always guessed you were, Kathrin Lynch. Should you come upon someone who is ill, you need only place the bracelet around their wrist for a whole day and—unless they have the jangling man's ichor in them—they will be cured."

"What of the other things? When my father hurt his arm, he said you tied an eel around his arm."

Her words made the widow smile. "I probably did. I could just as well have smeared pigeon dung on it instead, or made him wear a necklace of worms, for all the difference it would have made. Your father's arm would have mended itself on its own, Kathrin. The cut was deep, but clean. It did not need the bracelet to heal, and your father was neither stupid nor feverish. But he did have the loose tongue of all small boys. He would have seen the bracelet, and spoken of it."

"Then you did nothing."

"Your father believed that I did something. That was enough to ease the pain in his arm and perhaps allow it to heal faster than it would otherwise have done."

"But you turn people away."

"If they are seriously ill, but neither feverish nor unconscious, I cannot let them see the bracelet. There is no other way, Kathrin. Some must die, so that the brace-let's secret is protected."

"This is the burden?" Kathrin asked doubtfully.

"No, this is the reward for carrying the burden. The burden is knowledge."

Again, Kathrin said, "Tell me."

"This is what the flier told me. The Great Winter fell across our world because the sun itself grew colder and paler. There was a reason for that. The armies of the celestial war were mining its fire, using the furnace of the sun itself to dig and shore up those seams in the sky. How they did this is beyond my comprehension, and perhaps even that of the flier himself. But he did make one thing clear. So long as the Great Winter held, the celestial war must still be raging. And that would mean that the jangling men had not yet won."

"But the Thaw . . ." Kathrin began.

"Yes, you see it now. The snow melts from the land. Rivers flow, crops grow again. The people rejoice, they grow stronger and happier, skins darken, the Frost Fairs fade into memory. But they do not understand what it really means."

Kathrin hardly dared ask. "Which side is winning, or has already won?"

"I don't know; that's the terrible part of it. But when the flier spoke to me, I sensed an awful hopelessness, as if he knew things were not going to go the way of his people."

"I'm frightened now."

"You should be. But someone needs to know, Kathrin, and the bracelet is los-ing its power to keep me out of the grave. Not because there is anything wrong with it, I think—it heals as well as it has ever done—but because it has decided that my time has grown sufficient, just as it will eventually decide the same thing with you."

Kathrin touched the other object, the thing that looked like a sword's handle. "What is this?"

"The flier's weapon. His hand was holding it from inside the wing. It poked through the outside of the wing like the claw of a bat. The flier showed me how to remove it. It is yours as well."

She had touched it already, but this time Kathrin felt a sudden tingle as her fingers wrapped around the hilt. She let go suddenly, gasping as if she had reached for a stick and picked up an adder, squirming and slippery and venomous.

"Yes, you feel its power," Widow Grayling said admiringly. "It works for no one unless they carry the bracelet."

"I can't take it."

"Better you have it, than let that power go to waste. If the jangling men come, then at least someone will have a means to hurt them. Until then, there are other uses for it."

Without touching the hilt, Kathrin slipped the weapon into her pocket where it lay as heavy and solid as a pebble.

"Did you ever use it?"

"Once."

"What did you do?"

She caught a secretive smile on Widow Grayling's face. "I took something precious from William the Questioner. Banished him to the ground like the rest of us. I meant to kill him, but he was not riding in the machine when I brought it down."

Kathrin laughed. Had she not felt the power of the weapon, she might have dismissed the widow's story as the ramblings of an old woman. But she had no reason in the world to doubt her companion.

"You could have killed the sheriff later, when he came to inspect the killing poles."

"I nearly did. But something always stayed my hand. Then the sheriff was replaced by another man, and he in turn by another. Sheriffs came and went. Some were evil men, but not all of them. Some were only as hard and cruel as their office demanded. I never used the weapon again, Kathrin. I sensed that its power was not limitless, that it must be used sparingly, against the time when it became really necessary. But to use it in defence, against a smaller target . . . that would be a different matter, I think."

Kathrin thought she understood.

"I need to be getting back home," she said, trying to sound as if they had discussed nothing except the matter of the widow's next delivery of provisions. "I am sorry about the other head."

"There is no need to apologize. It was not your doing."

"What will happen to you now, widow?"

"I'll fade, slowly and gracefully. Perhaps I will see things through to the next winter. But I don't expect to see another thaw."

"Please. Take the bracelet back."

"Kathrin, listen. It will make no difference to me now, whether you take it or not."

"I'm not old enough for this. I'm only a girl from the Shield, a sledge-maker's daughter."

"What do you think I was, when I found the flier? We were the same. I've seen your strength and courage."

"I wasn't strong today."

"Yet you took the bridge, when you knew Garret would be on it. I have no doubt, Kathrin."

She stood. "If I had not lost the other head . . . if Garret had not caught me . . . would you have given me these things?"

"I was minded to do it. If not today, it would have happened next time. But let us give Garret due credit. He helped me make up my mind."

"He's still out there," Kathrin said.

"But he will know you will not be taking the bridge to get back home, even though that would save you paying the toll at Jarrow Ferry. He will content himself to wait until you cross his path again."

Kathrin collected her one remaining bag and moved to the door.

"Yes."

"I will see you again, in a month. Give my regards to your father."

"I will."

Widow Grayling opened the door. The sky was darkening to the east, in the direction of Jarrow Ferry. The dusk stars would appear shortly, and it would be dark within the hour. The crows were still wheeling, but more languidly now, preparing to roost. Though the Great Winter was easing, the evenings seemed as cold as ever, as if night was the final stronghold, the place where the winter had retreated when the inevitability of its defeat became apparent. Kathrin knew that she would be shivering long before she reached the tollgate at the crossing, miles down the river. She tugged down her hat in readiness for the journey and stepped onto the broken road in front of the widow's cottage.

"You will take care now, Kathrin. Watch out for the janglies."

"I will, Widow Grayling."

The door closed behind her. She heard a bolt slide into place.

She was alone.

Kathrin set off, following the path she had used to climb up from the river. If it was arduous in daylight, it was steep and treacherous at dusk. As she descended she could see Twenty Arch Bridge from above, a thread of light across the shadowed ribbon of the river. Candles were being lit in the inns and houses that lined the bridge, tallow torches burning along the parapets. There was still light at the north end, where the sagging arch was being repaired. The obstruction caused by the dray had been cleared, and traffic was moving normally from bank to bank. She heard the calls of men and women, the barked orders of foremen, the braying of drunkards and slatterns, the regular creak and splash of the mill wheels turning under the arches.

Presently she reached a fork in the path and paused. To the right lay the quickest route down to the quayside road to Jarrow Ferry. To the left lay the easiest descent down to the bridge, the path that she had already climbed. Until that moment, her resolve had been clear. She would take the ferry, as she always did, as she was expected to do.

But now she reached a hand into her pocket and closed her fingers around the flier's weapon. The shiver of contact was less shocking this time. The object already felt a part of her, as if she had carried it for years.

She drew it out. It gleamed in twilight, shining where it had appeared dull before. Even if the widow had not told her of its nature, there would have been no doubt now. The object spoke its nature through her skin and bones, whispering to her on a level beneath language. It told her what it could do and how she could make it obey her. It told her to be careful of the power she now carried in her hand. She must scruple to use it wisely, for nothing like it now existed in the world.

It was the power to smash walls. Power to smash bridges and towers and flying machines. Power to smash jangling men.

Power to smash ordinary men, if that was what she desired.

She had to know.

The last handful of crows gyred overhead. She raised the weapon to them and felt a sudden dizzying apprehension of their number and distance and position, each crow feeling distinct from its brethren, as if she could almost name them.

She selected one laggard bird. All the others faded from her attention, like players removing themselves from a stage. She came to know that last bird intimately. She could feel its wingbeats cutting the cold air. She could feel the soft thatch of its feathers, and the lacelike scaffolding of bone underneath. Within the cage of its chest she felt the tiny strong pulse of its heart, and she knew that she could make that heart freeze just by willing it.

The weapon seemed to urge her to do it. She came close. She came frighteningly close.

But the bird had done nothing to wrong her, and she spared it. She had no need to take a life to test this new gift, at least not an innocent one. The crow rejoined its brethren, something skittish and hurried in its flight, as if it had felt that coldness closing around its heart.

Kathrin returned the weapon to her pocket. She looked at the bridge again, measuring it once more with clinical eyes, eyes that were older and sadder this time, because she knew something that the people on the bridge could never know.

"I'm ready," she said, aloud, into the night, for whoever might be listening.

Then resumed her descent.

glory

GREG EGAN

*Australian writer Greg Egan was one of the big new names to emerge in
SF in the nineties and is probably one of the most significant talents to
enter the field in the last several decades. Already one of the most widely
known of all Australian genre writers, Egan may well be the best new
"hard science" writer to enter the field since Greg Bear, and is still growing
in range, power, and sophistication. In the last few years, he has become a
frequent contributor to* Interzone *and* Asimov's Science Fiction, *and has
made sales as well to* Pulphouse, Analog, Aurealis, Eidolon, *and elsewhere;
many of his stories have also appeared in various Best of the Year series,
and he was on the Hugo Final Ballot in 1995 for his story "Cocoon," which
won the Ditmar Award and the* Asimov's *Readers Award. He won the
Hugo Award in 1999 for his novella "Oceanic." His first novel,* Quarantine, *appeared in 1992; his second novel,* Permutation City, *won the
John W. Campbell Memorial Award in 1994. His other books include the
novels* Distress, Diaspora, Oceanic, Teranesia, Zendegi, *and* Schild's
Ladder, *and four collections of his short fiction,* Axiomatic, Luminous,
Our Lady of Chernobyl, *and* Crystal Nights and Other Stories. *His*
Orthogonal *trilogy consists of* The Clockwork Rocket, The Eternal
Flame, *and* The Arrows of Time. *He has a website at www.netspace.netau
/^gregegan.*

*Egan has pictured galaxy-spanning civilizations in stories such as "Bor-
der Guards" and "Riding the Crocodile." Here he sweeps us along with
scientists who are willing to go to enormous lengths (including changing
their species!) and travel across the galaxy to investigate a scientific
mystery—one that inimical forces don't want them to solve.*

I

An ingot of metallic hydrogen gleamed in the starlight, a narrow cylinder half a
meter long with a mass of about a kilogram. To the naked eye, it was a dense, solid
object, but its lattice of tiny nuclei immersed in an insubstantial fog of electrons
was one part matter to two hundred trillion parts empty space. A short distance
away was a second ingot, apparently identical to the first, but composed of anti-
hydrogen.

A sequence of finely tuned gamma rays flooded into both cylinders. The protons that absorbed them in the first ingot spat out positrons and were transformed into neutrons, breaking their bonds to the electron cloud that glued them in place. In the second ingot, antiprotons became antineutrons.

A further sequence of pulses herded the neutrons together and forged them into clusters; the antineutrons were similarly rearranged. Both kinds of cluster were unstable, but in order to fall apart, they first had to pass through a quantum state that would have strongly absorbed a component of the gamma rays constantly raining down on them. Left to themselves, the probability of them being in this state would have increased rapidly, but each time they measurably failed to absorb the gamma rays, the probability fell back to zero. The quantum Zeno effect endlessly reset the clock, holding the decay in check.

The next series of pulses began shifting the clusters into the space that had separated the original ingots. First neutrons, then antineutrons, were sculpted together in alternating layers. Though the clusters were ultimately unstable, while they persisted they were inert, sequestering their constituents and preventing them from annihilating their counterparts. The end point of this process of nuclear sculpting was a sliver of compressed matter and antimatter, sandwiched together into a needle one micron wide.

The gamma ray lasers shut down, the Zeno effect withdrew its prohibitions. For the time it took a beam of light to cross a neutron, the needle sat motionless in space. Then it began to burn, and it began to move.

The needle was structured like a meticulously crafted firework, and its outer layers ignited first. No external casing could have channeled this blast, but the pattern of tensions woven into the needle's construction favored one direction for the debris to be expelled. Particles streamed backward; the needle moved forward. The shock of acceleration could not have been borne by anything built from atomic-scale matter, but the pressure bearing down on the core of the needle prolonged its life, delaying the inevitable.

Layer after layer burned itself away, blasting the dwindling remnant forward ever faster. By the time the needle had shrunk to a tenth of its original size, it was moving at ninety-eight percent of light speed; to a bystander, this could scarcely have been improved upon, but from the needle's perspective, there was still room to slash its journey's duration by orders of magnitude.

When just one thousandth of the needle remained, its time, compared to the neighboring stars, was passing five hundred times more slowly. Still the layers kept burning, the protective clusters unraveling as the pressure on them was released. The needle could only reach close enough to light speed to slow down time as much as it required if it could sacrifice a large enough proportion of its remaining mass. The core of the needle could only survive for a few trillionths of a second, while its journey would take two hundred million seconds as judged by the stars. The proportions had been carefully matched, though: out of the two kilograms of matter and antimatter that had been woven together at the launch, only a few million neutrons were needed as the final payload.

By one measure, seven years passed. For the needle, its last trillionths of a second unwound, its final layers of fuel blew away, and at the moment its core was ready to explode, it reached its destination, plunging from the near-vacuum of space straight into the heart of a star.

Even here, the density of matter was insufficient to stabilize the core, yet far too high to allow it to pass unhindered. The core was torn apart. But it did not go quietly, and the shock waves it carved through the fusing plasma endured for a million kilometers: all the way through to the cooler outer layers on the opposite side of the star. These shock waves were shaped by the payload that had formed them, and though the initial pattern imprinted on them by the disintegrating cluster of neutrons was enlarged and blurred by its journey, on an atomic scale it remained sharply defined. Like a mold stamped into the seething plasma, it encouraged ionized molecular fragments to slip into the troughs and furrows that matched their shape, and then brought them together to react in ways that the plasma's random collisions would never have allowed. In effect, the shock waves formed a web of catalysts, carefully laid out in both time and space, briefly transforming a small corner of the star into a chemical factory operating on a nanometer scale.

The products of this factory sprayed out of the star, riding the last traces of the shock wave's momentum: a few nanograms of elaborate, carbon-rich molecules, sheathed in a protective fullerene weave. Traveling at seven hundred kilometers per second, a fraction below the velocity needed to escape from the star completely, they climbed out of its gravity well, slowing as they ascended.

Four years passed, but the molecules were stable against the ravages of space. By the time they'd traveled a billion kilometers, they had almost come to a halt, and they would have fallen back to die in the fires of the star that had forged them if their journey had not been timed so that the star's third planet, a gas giant, was waiting to urge them forward. As they fell toward it, the giant's third moon moved across their path. Eleven years after the needle's launch, its molecular offspring rained down on to the methane snow.

The tiny heat of their impact was not enough to damage them, but it melted a microscopic puddle in the snow. Surrounded by food, the molecular seeds began to grow. Within hours, the area was teeming with nanomachines, some mining the snow and the minerals beneath it, others assembling the bounty into an intricate structure, a rectangular panel a couple of meters wide.

From across the light years, an elaborate sequence of gamma ray pulses fell upon the panel. These pulses were the needle's true payload, the passengers for whom it had merely prepared the way, transmitted in its wake four years after its launch. The panel decoded and stored the data, and the army of nanomachines set to work again, this time following a far more elaborate blueprint. The miners were forced to look further afield to find all the elements that were needed, while the assemblers labored to reach their goal through a sequence of intermediate stages, carefully designed to protect the final product from the vagaries of the local chemistry and climate.

After three months' work, two small fusion-powered spacecraft sat in the snow. Each one held a single occupant, waking for the first time in their freshly minted bodies, yet endowed with memories of an earlier life.

Joan switched on her communications console. Anne appeared on the screen, three short pairs of arms folded across her thorax in a posture of calm repose. They had both worn virtual bodies with the same anatomy before, but this was the first time they had become Noudah in the flesh.

"We're here. Everything worked," Joan marveled. The language she spoke was not her own, but the structure of her new brain and body made it second nature.

Anne said, "Now comes the hard part."

"Yes." Joan looked out from the spacecraft's cockpit. In the distance, a fissured blue-gray plateau of water ice rose above the snow. Nearby, the nanomachines were busy disassembling the gamma ray receiver. When they had erased all traces of their handiwork, they would wander off into the snow and catalyze their own destruction.

Joan had visited dozens of planet-bound cultures in the past, taking on different bodies and languages as necessary, but those cultures had all been plugged in to the Amalgam, the meta-civilization that spanned the galactic disk. However far from home she'd been, the means to return to familiar places had always been close at hand. The Noudah had only just mastered interplanetary flight, and they had no idea that the Amalgam existed. The closest node in the Amalgam's network was seven light years away, and even that was out of bounds to her and Anne now: they had agreed not to risk disclosing its location to the Noudah, so any transmission they sent could only be directed to a decoy node that they'd set up more than twenty light years away.

"It will be worth it," Joan said.

Anne's Noudah face was immobile, but chromatophores sent a wave of violet and gold sweeping across her skin in an expression of cautious optimism. "We'll see." She tipped her head to the left, a gesture preceding a friendly departure.

Joan tipped her own head in response, as if she'd been doing so all her life. "Be careful, my friend," she said.

"You too."

Anne's ship ascended so high on its chemical thrusters that it shrank to a speck before igniting its fusion engine and streaking away in a blaze of light. Joan felt a pang of loneliness; there was no predicting when they would be reunited.

Her ship's software was primitive; the whole machine had been scrupulously matched to the Noudah's level of technology. Joan knew how to fly it herself if necessary, and on a whim she switched off the autopilot and manually activated the ascent thrusters. The control panel was crowded, but having six hands helped.

II

The world the Noudah called home was the closest of the system's five planets to their sun. The average temperature was one hundred and twenty degrees Celsius, but the high atmospheric pressure allowed liquid water to exist across the entire surface. The chemistry and dynamics of the planet's crust had led to a relatively flat terrain, with a patchwork of dozens of disconnected seas but no globe-spanning ocean. From space, these seas appeared as silvery mirrors, bordered by a violet and brown tarnish of vegetation.

The Noudah were already leaving their most electromagnetically promiscuous phase of communications behind, but the short-lived oasis of Amalgam-level technology on Baneth, the gas giant's moon, had had no trouble eavesdropping on their chatter and preparing an updated cultural briefing which had been spliced into Joan's brain.

The planet was still divided into the same eleven political units as it had been fourteen years before, the time of the last broadcasts that had reached the node before Joan's departure. Tira and Ghahar, the two dominant nations in terms of territory, economic activity, and military power, also occupied the vast majority of significant Niah archaeological sites.

Joan had expected that they'd be noticed as soon as they left Baneth—the exhaust from their fusion engines glowed like the sun—but their departure had triggered no obvious response, and now that they were coasting they'd be far harder to spot. As Anne drew closer to the home world, she sent a message to Tira's traffic control center. Joan tuned in to the exchange.

"I come in peace from another star," Anne said. "I seek permission to land."

There was a delay of several seconds more than the light-speed lag, then a terse response. "Please identify yourself and state your location."

Anne transmitted her coordinates and flight plan.

"We confirm your location, please identify yourself."

"My name is Anne. I come from another star."

There was a long pause, then a different voice answered. "If you are from Ghahar, please explain your intentions."

"I am not from Ghahar."

"Why should I believe that? Show yourself."

"I've taken the same shape as your people, in the hope of living among you for a while." Anne opened a video channel and showed them her unremarkable Noudah face. "But there's a signal being transmitted from these coordinates that might persuade you that I'm telling the truth." She gave the location of the decoy node, twenty light years away, and specified a frequency. The signal coming from the node contained an image of the very same face.

This time, the silence stretched out for several minutes. It would take a while for the Tirans to confirm the true distance of the radio source.

"You do not have permission to land. Please enter this orbit, and we will rendezvous and board your ship."

Parameters for the orbit came through on the data channel. Anne said, "As you wish."

Minutes later, Joan's instruments picked up three fusion ships being launched from Tiran bases. When Anne reached the prescribed orbit, Joan listened anxiously to the instructions the Tirans issued. Their tone sounded wary, but they were entitled to treat this stranger with caution, all the more so if they believed Anne's claim.

Joan was accustomed to a very different kind of reception, but then the members of the Amalgam had spent hundreds of millennia establishing a framework of trust. They also benefited from a milieu in which most kinds of force had been rendered ineffectual; when everyone had backups of themselves scattered around the galaxy, it required a vastly disproportionate effort to inconvenience someone, let alone kill them. By any reasonable measure, honesty and cooperation yielded far richer rewards than subterfuge and slaughter.

Nonetheless, each individual culture had its roots in a biological heritage that gave rise to behavior governed more by ancient urges than contemporary realities, and even when they mastered the technology to choose their own nature, the precise set of traits they preserved was up to them. In the worst case, a species still saddled with inappropriate drives but empowered by advanced technology could wreak havoc. The Noudah deserved to be treated with courtesy and respect, but they did not yet belong in the Amalgam.

The Tirans' own exchanges were not on open channels, so once they had entered Anne's ship, Joan could only guess what was happening. She waited until two of the ships had returned to the surface, then sent her own message to Ghahar's traffic control.

"I come in peace from another star. I seek permission to land."

III

The Ghahari allowed Joan to fly her ship straight down to the surface. She wasn't sure if this was because they were more trusting, or if they were afraid that the Tirans might try to interfere if she lingered in orbit.

The landing site was a bare plain of chocolate colored sand. The air shimmered in the heat, the distortions intensified by the thickness of the atmosphere, making the horizon waver as if seen through molten glass. Joan waited in the cockpit as three trucks approached; they all came to a halt some twenty meters away. A voice over the radio instructed her to leave the ship; she complied, and after she'd stood in the open for a minute, a lone Noudah left one of the trucks and walked toward her.

"I'm Pirit," she said. "Welcome to Ghahar." Her gestures were courteous but restrained.

"I'm Joan. Thank you for your hospitality."

"Your impersonation of our biology is impeccable." There was a trace of skepticism in Pirit's tone; Joan had pointed the Ghahari to her own portrait being broadcast from the decoy node, but she had to admit that in the context her lack of exotic technology and traits would make it harder to accept the implications of that transmission.

"In my culture, it's a matter of courtesy to imitate one's hosts as closely as possible."

Pirit hesitated, as if pondering whether to debate the merits of such a custom, but then rather than quibbling over the niceties of interspecies etiquette she chose to confront the real issue head on. "If you're a Tiran spy, or a defector, the sooner you admit that the better."

"That's very sensible advice, but I'm neither."

The Noudah wore no clothing as such, but Pirit had a belt with a number of pouches. She took a hand-held scanner from one and ran it over Joan's body. Joan's briefing suggested that it was probably only checking for metal, volatile explosives and radiation; the technology to image her body or search for pathogens would not be so portable. In any case, she was a healthy, unarmed Noudah down to the molecular level.

Pirit escorted her to one of the trucks, and invited her to recline in a section at the back. Another Noudah drove while Pirit watched over Joan. They soon arrived at a small complex of buildings a couple of kilometers from where the ship had touched down. The walls, roofs, and floors of the buildings were all made from the local sand, cemented with an adhesive that the Noudah secreted from their own bodies.

Inside, Joan was given a thorough medical examination, including three kinds of full-body scan. The Noudah who examined her treated her with a kind of detached efficiency devoid of any pleasantries; she wasn't sure if that was their standard bedside manner, or a kind of glazed shock at having been told of her claimed origins.

Pirit took her to an adjoining room and offered her a couch. The Noudah anatomy did not allow for sitting, but they liked to recline.

Pirit remained standing. "How did you come here?" she asked.

"You've seen my ship. I flew it from Baneth."

"And how did you reach Baneth?"

"I'm not free to discuss that," Joan replied cheerfully.

"Not free?" Pirit's face clouded with silver, as if she was genuinely perplexed.

Joan said, "You understand me perfectly. Please don't tell me there's nothing *you're* not free to discuss with me."

"You certainly didn't fly that ship twenty light years."

"No, I certainly didn't."

Pirit hesitated. "Did you come through the Cataract?" The Cataract was a black hole, a remote partner to the Noudah's sun; they orbited each other at a distance of about eighty billion kilometers. The name came from its telescopic appearance: a dark circle ringed by a distortion in the background of stars, like some kind of visual aberration. The Tirans and Ghahari were in a race to be the first to visit this extraordinary neighbor, but as yet neither of them were quite up to the task.

"*Through* the Cataract? I think your scientists have already proven that black holes aren't shortcuts to anywhere."

"Our scientists aren't always right."

"Neither are ours," Joan admitted, "but all the evidence points in one direction: black holes aren't doorways, they're shredding machines."

"So you traveled the whole twenty light years?"

"More than that," Joan said truthfully, "from my original home. I've spent half my life traveling."

"Faster than light?" Pirit suggested hopefully.

"No. That's impossible."

They circled around the question a dozen more times, before Pirit finally changed her tune from *how* to *why?*

"I'm a xenomathematician," Joan said. "I've come here in the hope of collaborating with your archaeologists in their study of Niah artifacts."

Pirit was stunned. "What do you know about the Niah?"

"Not as much as I'd like to." Joan gestured at her Noudah body. "As I'm sure you've already surmised, we've listened to your broadcasts for some time, so we know pretty much what an ordinary Noudah knows. That includes the basic facts about the Niah. Historically, they've been referred to as your ancestors, though the latest studies suggest that you and they really just have an earlier common ancestor. They died out about a million years ago, but there's evidence that they might have had a sophisticated culture for as long as three million years. There's no indication that they ever developed space flight. Basically, once they achieved material comfort, they seem to have devoted themselves to various artforms, including mathematics."

"So you've traveled twenty light years just to look at Niah tablets?" Pirit was incredulous.

"Any culture that spent three million years doing mathematics must have something to teach us."

"Really?" Pirit's face became blue with disgust. "In the ten thousand years since we discovered the wheel, we've already reached halfway to the Cataract. They wasted their time on useless abstractions."

Joan said, "I come from a culture of spacefarers myself, so I respect your achievements. But I don't think anyone really knows what the Niah achieved. I'd like to find out, with the help of your people."

Pirit was silent for a while. "What if we say no?"

"Then I'll leave empty-handed."

"What if we insist that you remain with us?"

"Then I'll die here, empty-handed." On her command, this body would expire in an instant; she could not be held and tortured.

Pirit said angrily, "You must be willing to trade *something* for the privilege you're demanding!"

"Requesting, not demanding," Joan insisted gently. "And what I'm willing to offer is my own culture's perspective on Niah mathematics. If you ask your archaeologists and mathematicians, I'm sure they'll tell you that there are many things written in the Niah tablets that they don't yet understand. My colleague and I"—neither of them had mentioned Anne before, but Joan was sure that Pirit knew all about her—"simply want to shed as much light as we can on this subject."

Pirit said bitterly, "You won't even tell us how you came to our world. Why should we trust you to share whatever you discover about the Niah?"

"Interstellar travel is no great mystery," Joan countered. "You know all the basic science already; making it work is just a matter of persistence. If you're left to develop your own technology, you might even come up with better methods than we have."

"So we're expected to be patient, to discover these things for ourselves . . . but you can't wait a few centuries for us to decipher the Niah artifacts?"

Joan said bluntly, "The present Noudah culture, both here and in Tira, seems to hold the Niah in contempt. Dozens of partially excavated sites containing Niah artifacts are under threat from irrigation projects and other developments. That's the reason we couldn't wait. We needed to come here and offer our assistance, before the last traces of the Niah disappeared forever."

Pirit did not reply, but Joan hoped she knew what her interrogator was thinking: *Nobody would cross twenty light years for a few worthless scribblings. Perhaps we've underestimated the Niah. Perhaps our ancestors have left us a great secret, a great legacy. And perhaps the fastest—perhaps the only—way to uncover it is to give this impertinent, irritating alien exactly what she wants.*

IV

The sun was rising ahead of them as they reached the top of the hill. Sando turned to Joan, and his face became green with pleasure. "Look behind you," he said.

Joan did as he asked. The valley below was hidden in fog, and it had settled so evenly that she could see their shadows in the dawn light, stretched out across the top of the fog layer. Around the shadow of her head was a circular halo like a small rainbow.

"We call it the Niah's light," Sando said. "In the old days, people used to say that the halo proved that the Niah blood was strong in you."

Joan said, "The only trouble with that hypothesis being that *you* see it around *your* head . . . and I see it around mine." On Earth, the phenomenon was known as a "glory." The particles of fog were scattering the sunlight back toward them, turning it one hundred and eighty degrees. To look at the shadow of your own head was to face directly away from the sun, so the halo always appeared around the observer's shadow.

"I suppose you're the final proof that Niah blood has nothing to do with it," Sando mused.

"That's assuming I'm telling you the truth, and I really can see it around my own head."

"And assuming," Sando added, "that the Niah really did stay at home, and didn't wander around the galaxy spreading their progeny."

They came over the top of the hill and looked down into the adjoining riverine valley. The sparse brown grass of the hillside gave way to a lush violet growth closer to the water. Joan's arrival had delayed the flooding of the valley, but even alien interest in the Niah had only bought the archaeologists an extra year. The dam was part of a long-planned agricultural development, and however tantalizing the possibility that Joan might reveal some priceless insight hidden among the Niah's "useless abstractions," that vague promise could only compete with more tangible considerations for a limited time.

Part of the hill had fallen away in a landslide a few centuries before, revealing more than a dozen beautifully preserved strata. When Joan and Sando reached the excavation site, Rali and Surat were already at work, clearing away soft sedimentary rock from a layer that Sando had dated as belonging to the Niah's "twilight" period.

Pirit had insisted that only Sando, the senior archaeologist, be told about Joan's true nature; Joan refused to lie to anyone, but had agreed to tell her colleagues only that she was a mathematician and that she was not permitted to discuss her past. At first, this had made them guarded and resentful, no doubt because they assumed that she was some kind of spy sent by the authorities to watch over them. Later, it had dawned on them that she was genuinely interested in their work, and that the absurd restrictions on her topics of conversation were not of her own choosing. Nothing about the Noudah's language or appearance correlated strongly with their recent division into nations—with no oceans to cross, and a long history of migration, they were more or less geographically homogeneous—but Joan's odd name and occasional *faux pas* could still be ascribed to some mysterious exoticism. Rali and Surat seemed content to assume that she was a defector from one of the smaller nations, and that her history could not be made explicit for obscure political reasons.

"There are more tablets here, very close to the surface," Rali announced excitedly. "The acoustics are unmistakable." Ideally, they would have excavated the entire hillside, but they did not have the time or the labor, so they were using acoustic tomography to identify likely deposits of accessible Niah writing, and then concentrating their efforts on those spots.

The Niah had probably had several ephemeral forms of written communication, but when they found something worth publishing, it stayed published: they carved their symbols into a ceramic that made diamond seem like tissue paper. It was almost unheard of for the tablets to be broken, but they were small, and multitablet works were sometimes widely dispersed. Niah technology could probably have carved three million years' worth of knowledge on to the head of a pin—they seemed not to have invented nanomachines, but they were into high quality bulk materials and precision engineering—but for whatever reason they had chosen legibility to the naked eye above other considerations.

Joan made herself useful, taking acoustic readings further along the slope, while Sando watched over his students as they came closer to the buried Niah artifacts. She had learned not to hover around expectantly when a discovery was imminent; she was treated far more warmly if she waited to be summoned. The tomography unit was almost foolproof, using satellite navigation to track its position and software to analyze the signals it gathered; all it really needed was someone to drag it along the rock face at a suitable pace.

Through the corner of her eye, Joan noticed her shadow on the rocks flicker and grow complicated. She looked up to see three dazzling beads of light flying west out of the sun. She might have assumed that the fusion ships were doing something useful, but the media was full of talk of "military exercises," which meant the Tirans and the Ghahari engaging in expensive, belligerent gestures in orbit, trying to convince each other of their superior skills, technology, or sheer strength of numbers. For people with no real differences apart from a few centuries of recent history, they could puff up their minor political disputes into matters of the utmost solemnity. It might almost have been funny, if the idiots hadn't incinerated hundreds of thousands of each other's citizens every few decades, not to mention playing callous and often deadly games with the lives of the inhabitants of smaller nations.

"Jown! Jown! Come and look at this!" Surat called to her. Joan switched off the tomography unit and jogged toward the archaeologists, suddenly conscious of her body's strangeness. Her legs were stumpy but strong, and her balance as she ran came not from arms and shoulders but from the swish of her muscular tail.

"It's a significant mathematical result," Rali informed her proudly when she reached them. He'd pressure-washed the sandstone away from the near-indestructible ceramic of the tablet, and it was only a matter of holding the surface at the right angle to the light to see the etched writing stand out as crisply and starkly as it would have a million years before.

Rali was not a mathematician, and he was not offering his own opinion on the theorem the tablet stated; the Niah themselves had a clear set of typographical conventions which they used to distinguish between everything from minor lemmas to the most celebrated theorems. The size and decorations of the symbols labeling the theorem attested to its value in the Niah's eyes.

Joan read the theorem carefully. The proof was not included on the same tablet, but the Niah had a way of expressing their results that made you believe them as soon as you read them; in this case the definitions of the terms needed to state the theorem were so beautifully chosen that the result seemed almost inevitable.

The theorem itself was expressed as a commuting hypercube, one of the Niah's favorite forms. You could think of a square with four different sets of mathematical objects associated with each of its corners, and a way of mapping one set into another associated with each edge of the square. If the maps commuted, then going across the top of the square, then down, had exactly the same effect as going down the left edge of the square, then across: either way, you mapped each element from the top-left set into the same element of the bottom-right set. A similar kind of result might hold for sets and maps that could naturally be placed at the corners and edges of a cube, or a hypercube of any dimension. It was also possible for the square faces in these structures to stand for relationships that held between the maps between sets, and for cubes to describe relationships between those relationships, and so on.

That a theorem took this form didn't guarantee its importance; it was easy to cook up trivial examples of sets and maps that commuted. The Niah didn't carve trivia into their timeless ceramic, though, and this theorem was no exception. The seven-dimensional commuting hypercube established a dazzlingly elegant correspondence between seven distinct, major branches of Niah mathematics, intertwining their most important concepts into a unified whole. It was a result Joan had never seen before: no mathematician anywhere in the Amalgam, or in any ancestral culture she had studied, had reached the same insight.

She explained as much of this as she could to the three archaeologists; they couldn't take in all the details, but their faces became orange with fascination when she sketched what she thought the result would have meant to the Niah themselves.

"This isn't quite the Big Crunch," she joked, "but it must have made them think they were getting closer." *The Big Crunch* was her nickname for the mythical result that the Niah had aspired to reach: a unification of every field of mathematics that they considered significant. To find such a thing would not have meant the end of mathematics—it would not have subsumed every last conceivable, interesting mathematical truth—but it would certainly have marked a point of closure for the Niah's own style of investigation.

"I'm sure they found it," Surat insisted. "They reached the Big Crunch, then they had nothing more to live for."

Rali was scathing. "So the whole culture committed collective suicide?"

"Not actively, no," Surat replied. "But it was the search that had kept them going."

"Entire cultures don't lose the will to live," Rali said. "They get wiped out by external forces: disease, invasion, changes in climate."

"The Niah survived for three million years," Surat countered. "They had the means to weather all of those forces. Unless they were wiped out by alien invaders with vastly superior technology." She turned to Joan. "What do you think?"

"About aliens destroying the Niah?"

"I was joking about the aliens. But what about the mathematics? What if they found the Big Crunch?"

"There's more to life than mathematics," Joan said. "But not much more."

Sando said, "And there's more to this find than one tablet. If we get back to work, we might have the proof in our hands before sunset."

V

Joan briefed Halzoun by video link while Sando prepared the evening meal. Halzoun was the mathematician Pirit had appointed to supervise her, but apparently his day job was far too important to allow him to travel. Joan was grateful; Halzoun was the most tedious Noudah she had encountered. He could understand the Niah's work when she explained it to him, but he seemed to have no interest in it for its own sake. He spent most of their conversations trying to catch her out in some deception or contradiction, and the rest pressing her to imagine military or commercial applications of the Niah's gloriously useless insights. Sometimes she played along with this infantile fantasy, hinting at potential superweapons based on exotic physics that might come tumbling out of the vacuum, if only one possessed the right Niah theorems to coax them into existence.

Sando was her minder too, but at least he was more subtle about it. Pirit had insisted that she stay in his shelter, rather than sharing Rali and Surat's; Joan didn't mind, because with Sando she didn't have the stress of having to keep quiet about everything. Privacy and modesty were non-issues for the Noudah, and Joan had become Noudah enough not to care herself. Nor was there any danger of their proximity leading to a sexual bond; the Noudah had a complex system of bio-chemical cues that meant desire only arose in couples with a suitable mixture of genetic differences and similarities. She would have had to search a crowded Nou-dah city for a week to find someone to lust after, though at least it would have been guaranteed to be mutual.

After they'd eaten, Sando said, "You should be happy. That was our best find yet."

"I am happy." Joan made a conscious effort to exhibit a viridian tinge. "It was the first new result I've seen on this planet. It was the reason I came here, the reason I traveled so far."

"Something's wrong, though, I think."

"I wish I could have shared the news with my friend," Joan admitted. Pirit claimed to be negotiating with the Tirans to allow Anne to communicate with her, but Joan was not convinced that she was genuinely trying. She was sure that she would have relished the thought of listening in on a conversation between the two of them—while forcing them to speak Noudah, of course—in the hope that they'd slip up and reveal something useful, but at the same time she would have had to face the fact that the Tirans would be listening too. What an excruciating dilemma.

"You should have brought a communications link with you," Sando suggested. "A home-style one, I mean. Nothing we could eavesdrop on."

"We couldn't do that," Joan said.

He pondered this. "You really are afraid of us, aren't you? You think the small-est technological trinket will be enough to send us straight to the stars, and then you'll have a horde of rampaging barbarians to deal with."

"We know how to deal with barbarians," Joan said coolly.

Sando's face grew dark with mirth. "Now *I'm* afraid."

"I just wish I knew what was happening to her," Joan said. "What she was doing, how they were treating her."

"Probably much the same as we're treating you," Sando suggested. "We're really not that different." He thought for a moment. "There was something I wanted to show you." He brought over his portable console, and summoned up an article from a Tiran journal. "See what a borderless world we live in," he joked.

The article was entitled "Seekers and Spreaders: What We Must Learn from the Niah." Sando said, "This might give you some idea of how they're thinking over there. Jaqad is an academic archaeologist, but she's also very close to the people in power."

Joan read from the console while Sando made repairs to their shelter, secret-ing a molasses-like substance from a gland at the tip of his tail and spreading it over the cracks in the walls.

There were two main routes a culture could take, Jaqad argued, once it satisfied its basic material needs. One was to think and study: to stand back and observe, to seek knowledge and insight from the world around it. The other was to invest its energy in entrenching its good fortune.

The Niah had learned a great deal in three million years, but in the end it had not been enough to save them. Exactly what had killed them was still a matter of speculation, but it was hard to believe that if they had colonized other worlds they would have vanished on all of them. "Had the Niah been Spreaders," Jaqad wrote, "we might expect a visit from them, or them from us, sometime in the coming centuries."

The Noudah, in contrast, were determined Spreaders. Once they had the means, they would plant colonies across the galaxy. They would, Jaqad was sure, create new biospheres, reengineer stars, and even alter space and time to guarantee their survival. The growth of their empire would come first; any knowledge that failed to serve that purpose would be a mere distraction. "In any competition between Seekers and Spreaders, it is a Law of History that the Spreaders must win out in the end. Seekers, such as the Niah, might hog resources and block the way, but in the long run their own nature will be their downfall."

Joan stopped reading. "When you look out into the galaxy with your telescopes," she asked Sando, "how many *reengineered stars* do you see?"

"Would we recognize them?"

"Yes. Natural stellar processes aren't that complicated; your scientists already know everything there is to know about the subject."

"I'll take your word for that. So . . . you're saying Jaqad is wrong? The Niah themselves never left this world, but the galaxy already belongs to creatures more like them than like us?"

"It's not Noudah versus Niah," Joan said. "It's a matter of how a culture's perspective changes with time. Once a species conquers disease, modifies their biology, and spreads even a short distance beyond their home world, they usually start to relax a bit. The territorial imperative isn't some timeless Law of History; it belongs to a certain phase."

"What if it persists, though? Into a later phase?"

"That can cause friction," Joan admitted.

"Nevertheless, no Spreaders have conquered the galaxy?"

"Not yet."

Sando went back to his repairs; Joan read the rest of the article. She'd thought she'd already grasped the lesson demanded by the subtitle, but it turned out that Jaqad had something more specific in mind.

"Having argued this way, how can I defend my own field of study from the very same charges as I have brought against the Niah? Having grasped the essential character of this doomed race, why should we waste our time and resources studying them further?

"The answer is simple. We still do not know exactly how and why the Niah died, but when we do, that could turn out to be the most important discovery in history. When we finally leave our world behind, we should not expect to find only other Spreaders to compete with us, as honorable opponents in battle. There will be Seekers as well, blocking the way: tired, old races squatting uselessly on their hoards of knowledge and wealth.

"Time will defeat them in the end, but we already waited three million years to be born; we should have no patience to wait again. If we can learn how the Niah died, that will be our key, that will be our weapon. If we know the Seekers' weakness, we can find a way to hasten their demise."

VI

The proof of the Niah's theorem turned out to be buried deep in the hillside, but over the following days they extracted it all.

It was as beautiful and satisfying as Joan could have wished, merging six earlier, simpler theorems while extending the techniques used in their proofs. She could even see hints at how the same methods might be stretched further to yield still stronger results. "The Big Crunch" had always been a slightly mocking, irreverent term, but now she was struck anew by how little justice it did to the real trend that had fascinated the Niah. It was not a matter of everything in mathematics collapsing in on itself, with one branch turning out to have been merely a recapitulation of another under a different guise. Rather, the principle was that every sufficiently beautiful mathematical system was rich enough to mirror *in part*—and sometimes in a complex and distorted fashion—every other sufficiently beautiful system. Nothing became sterile and redundant, nothing proved to have been a waste of time, but everything was shown to be magnificently intertwined.

After briefing Halzoun, Joan used the satellite dish to transmit the theorem and its proof to the decoy node. That had been the deal with Pirit: anything she learned from the Niah belonged to the whole galaxy, as long as she explained it to her hosts first.

The archaeologists moved across the hillside, hunting for more artifacts in the same layer of sediment. Joan was eager to see what else the same group of Niah might have published. One possible eight-dimensional hypercube was hovering in her mind; if she'd sat down and thought about it for a few decades she might have worked out the details herself, but the Niah did what they did so well that it would have seemed crass to try to follow clumsily in their footsteps when their own immaculately polished results might simply be lying in the ground, waiting to be uncovered.

A month after the discovery, Joan was woken by the sound of an intruder moving through the shelter. She knew it wasn't Sando; even as she slept an ancient part of her Noudah brain was listening to his heartbeat. The stranger's heart was too quiet to hear, which required great discipline, but the shelter's flexible adhesive made the floor emit a characteristic squeak beneath even the gentlest footsteps. As she rose from her couch she heard Sando waking, and she turned in his direction.

Bright torchlight on his face dazzled her for a moment. The intruder held two knives to Sando's respiration membranes; a deep enough cut there would mean choking to death, in excruciating pain. The nanomachines that had built Joan's body had wired extensive skills in unarmed combat into her brain, and one scenario involving a feigned escape attempt followed by a sideways flick of her powerful tail was already playing out in the back of her mind, but as yet she could see no way to guarantee that Sando came through it all unharmed.

She said, "What do you want?"

The intruder remained in darkness. "Tell me about the ship that brought you to Baneth."

"Why?"

"Because it would be a shame to shred your colleague here, just when his work was going so well." Sando refused to show any emotion on his face, but the blank pallor itself was as stark an expression of fear as anything Joan could imagine.

She said, "There's a coherent state that can be prepared for a quark-gluon plasma in which virtual black holes catalyze baryon decay. In effect, you can turn all of your fuel's rest mass into photons, yielding the most efficient exhaust stream possible." She recited a long list of technical details. The claimed baryon decay process didn't actually exist, but the pseudo-physics underpinning it was mathematically consistent, and could not be ruled out by anything the Noudah had yet observed. She and Anne had prepared an entire fictitious science and technology, and even a fictitious history of their culture, precisely for emergencies like this; they could spout red herrings for a decade if necessary, and never get caught out contradicting themselves.

"That wasn't so hard, was it?" the intruder gloated.

"What now?"

"You're going to take a trip with me. If you do this nicely, nobody needs to get hurt."

Something moved in the shadows, and the intruder screamed in pain. Joan leaped forward and knocked one of the knives out of his hand with her tail; the other knife grazed Sando's membrane, but a second tail whipped out of the darkness and intervened. As the intruder fell backward, the beam of his torch revealed Surat and Rali tensed beside him, and a pick buried deep in his side.

Joan's rush of combat hormones suddenly faded, and she let out a long, deep wail of anguish. Sando was unscathed, but a stream of dark liquid was pumping out of the intruder's wound.

Surat was annoyed. "Stop blubbing, and help us tie up this Tiran cousin-fucker."

"Tie him up? You've killed him!"

"Don't be stupid, that's just sheath fluid." Joan recalled her Noudah anatomy; sheath fluid was like oil in a hydraulic machine. You could lose it all and it would cost you most of the strength in your limbs and tail, but you wouldn't die, and your body would make more eventually.

Rali found some cable and they trussed up the intruder. Sando was shaken, but he seemed to be recovering. He took Joan aside. "I'm going to have to call Pirit."

"I understand. But what will she do to these two?" She wasn't sure exactly how much Rali and Surat had heard, but it was certain to have been more than Pirit wanted them to know.

"Don't worry about that, I can protect them."

Just before dawn someone sent by Pirit arrived in a truck to take the intruder away. Sando declared a rest day, and Rali and Surat went back to their shelter to sleep. Joan went for a walk along the hillside; she didn't feel like sleeping.

Sando caught up with her. He said, "I told them you'd been working on a military research project, and you were exiled here for some political misdemeanor."

"And they believed you?"

"All they heard was half of a conversation full of incomprehensible physics. All they know is that someone thought you were worth kidnapping."

Joan said, "I'm sorry about what happened."

Sando hesitated. "What did you expect?"

Joan was stung. "One of us went to Tira, one of us came here. We thought that would keep everyone happy!"

"We're Spreaders," said Sando. "Give us one of anything, and we want two. Especially if our enemy has the other one. Did you really think you could come here, do a bit of fossicking, and then simply fly away without changing a thing?"

"Your culture has always believed there were other civilizations in the galaxy. Our existence hardly came as a shock."

Sando's face became yellow, an expression of almost parental reproach. "Believing in something in the abstract is not the same as having it dangled in front of you. We were never going to have an existential crisis at finding out that we're not unique; the Niah might be related to us, but they were still alien enough to get us used to the idea. But did you really think we were just going to relax and accept your refusal to share your technology? That one of you went to the Tirans only makes it worse for the Ghahari, and vice versa. Both governments are going absolutely crazy, each one terrified that the other has found a way to make its alien talk."

Joan stopped walking. "The war games, the border skirmishes? You're blaming all of that on Anne and me?"

Sando's body sagged wearily. "To be honest, I don't know all the details. And if it's any consolation, I'm sure we would have found another reason if you hadn't come along."

Joan said, "Maybe I should leave." She was tired of these people, tired of her body, tired of being cut off from civilization. She had rescued one beautiful Niah theorem and sent it out into the Amalgam. Wasn't that enough?

"It's up to you," Sando replied. "But you might as well stay until they flood the valley. Another year isn't going to change anything. What you've done to this world has already been done. For us, there's no going back."

VII

Joan stayed with the archaeologists as they moved across the hillside. They found tablets bearing Niah drawings and poetry, which no doubt had their virtues but to Joan seemed bland and opaque. Sando and his students relished these discoveries as much as the theorems; to them, the Niah culture was a vast jigsaw puzzle, and any clue that filled in the details of their history was as good as any other.

Sando would have told Pirit everything he'd heard from Joan the night the intruder came, so she was surprised that she hadn't been summoned for a fresh interrogation to flesh out the details. Perhaps the Ghahari physicists were still digesting her elaborate gobbledygook, trying to decide if it made sense. In her more cynical moments she wondered if the intruder might have been Ghahari himself, sent by Pirit to exploit her friendship with Sando. Perhaps Sando had even been in on it, and Rali and Surat as well. The possibility made her feel as if she was living in a fabricated world, a scape in which nothing was real and nobody could be trusted. The only thing she was certain that the Ghaharis could not have faked was the Niah artifacts. The mathematics verified itself; everything else was subject to doubt and paranoia.

Summer came, burning away the morning fogs. The Noudah's idea of heat was very different from Joan's previous perceptions, but even the body she now wore found the midday sun oppressive. She willed herself to be patient. There was still a chance that the Niah had taken a few more steps toward their grand vision of a unified mathematics, and carved their final discoveries into the form that would outlive them by a million years.

When the lone fusion ship appeared high in the afternoon sky, Joan resolved to ignore it. She glanced up once, but she kept dragging the tomography unit across the ground. She was sick of thinking about Tiran-Ghahari politics. They had played their childish games for centuries; she would not take the blame for this latest outbreak of provocation.

Usually the ships flew by, disappearing within minutes, showing off their power and speed. This one lingered, weaving back and forth across the sky like some dazzling insect performing an elaborate mating dance. Joan's second shadow darted around her feet, hammering a strangely familiar rhythm into her brain.

She looked up, disbelieving. The motion of the ship was following the syntax of a gestural language she had learned on another planet, in another body, a dozen lifetimes ago. The only other person on this world who could know that language was Anne.

She glanced toward the archaeologists a hundred meters away, but they seemed to be paying no attention to the ship. She switched off the tomography unit and stared into the sky. *I'm listening, my friend. What's happening? Did they give you back your ship? Have you had enough of this world, and decided to go home?*

Anne told the story in shorthand, compressed and elliptic. The Tirans had found a tablet bearing a theorem: the last of the Niah's discoveries, the pinnacle of their achievements. Her minders had not let her study it, but they had contrived a situation making it easy for her to steal it, and to steal this ship. They had wanted her to take it and run, in the hope that she would lead them to something they valued far more than any ancient mathematics: an advanced spacecraft, or some magical stargate at the edge of the system.

But Anne wasn't fleeing anywhere. She was high above Ghahar, reading the tablet, and now she would paint what she read across the sky for Joan to see.

Sando approached. "We're in danger, we have to move."

"Danger? That's my friend up there! She's not going to shoot a missile at us!"

"Your friend?" Sando seemed confused. As he spoke, three more ships came into view, lower and brighter than the first. "I've been told that the Tirans are going to strike the valley, to bury the Niah sites. We need to get over the hill and indoors, to get some protection from the blast."

"Why would the Tirans attack the Niah sites? That makes no sense to me."

Sando said, "Nor me, but I don't have time to argue."

The three ships were menacing Anne's, pursuing her, trying to drive her away. Joan had no idea if they were Ghahari defending their territory, or Tirans harassing her in the hope that she would flee and reveal the nonexistent shortcut to the stars, but Anne was staying put, still weaving the same gestural language into her maneuvers even as she dodged her pursuers, spelling out the Niah's glorious finale.

Joan said, "You go. I have to see this." She tensed, ready to fight him if necessary.

Sando took something from his tool belt and peppered her side with holes. Joan gasped with pain and crumpled to the ground as the sheath fluid poured out of her.

Rali and Surat helped carry her to the shelter. Joan caught glimpses of the fiery ballet in the sky, but not enough to make sense of it, let alone reconstruct it.

They put her on her couch inside the shelter. Sando bandaged her side and gave her water to sip. He said, "I'm sorry I had to do that, but if anything had happened to you I would have been held responsible."

Surat kept ducking outside to check on the "battle," then reporting excitedly on the state of play. "The Tiran's still up there, they can't get rid of it. I don't know why they haven't shot it down yet."

Because the Tirans were the ones pursuing Anne, and they didn't want her dead. But for how long would the Ghahari tolerate this violation?

Anne's efforts could not be allowed to come to nothing. Joan struggled to recall the constellations she'd last seen in the night sky. At the node they'd departed from, powerful telescopes were constantly trained on the Noudah's home world. Anne's ship was easily bright enough, its gestures wide enough, to be resolved from seven light years away—if the planet itself wasn't blocking the view, if the node was above the horizon.

The shelter was windowless, but Joan saw the ground outside the doorway brighten for an instant. The flash was silent; no missile had struck the valley, the explosion had taken place high above the atmosphere.

Surat went outside. When she returned she said quietly, "All clear. They got it."

Joan put all her effort into spitting out a handful of words. "I want to see what happened."

Sando hesitated, then motioned to the others to help him pick up the couch and carry it outside.

A shell of glowing plasma was still visible, drifting across the sky as it expanded, a ring of light growing steadily fainter until it vanished into the afternoon glare.

Anne was dead in this embodiment, but her backup would wake and go on to new adventures. Joan could at least tell her the story of her local death: of virtuoso flying and a spectacular end.

She'd recovered her bearings now, and she recalled the position of the stars. The node was still hours away from rising. The Amalgam was full of powerful telescopes, but no others would be aimed at this obscure planet, and no plea to redirect them could outrace the light they would need to capture in order to bring the Niah's final theorem back to life.

VIII

Sando wanted to send her away for medical supervision, but Joan insisted on remaining at the site.

"The fewer officials who get to know about this incident, the fewer problems it makes for you," she reasoned.

"As long as you don't get sick and die," he replied.

"I'm not going to die." Her wounds had not become infected, and her strength was returning rapidly.

They compromised. Sando hired someone to drive up from the nearest town to look after her while he was out at the excavation. Daya had basic medical training and didn't ask awkward questions; he seemed happy to tend to Joan's needs, and then lie outside daydreaming the rest of the time.

There was still a chance, Joan thought, that the Niah had carved the theorem on a multitude of tablets and scattered them all over the planet. There was also a chance that the Tirans had made copies of the tablet before letting Anne abscond with it. The question, though, was whether she had the slightest prospect of getting her hands on these duplicates.

Anne might have made some kind of copy herself, but she hadn't mentioned it in the prologue to her aerobatic rendition of the theorem. If she'd had any time to spare, she wouldn't have limited herself to an audience of one: she would have waited until the node had risen over Ghahar.

On her second night as an invalid, Joan dreamed that she saw Anne standing on the hill looking back into the fog-shrouded valley, her shadow haloed by the Niah light.

When she woke, she knew what she had to do.

When Sando left, she asked Daya to bring her the console that controlled the satellite dish. She had enough strength in her arms now to operate it, and Daya showed no interest in what she did. That was naive, of course: whether or not Daya was spying on her, Pirit would know exactly where the signal was sent. So be it. Seven light years was still far beyond the Noudah's reach; the whole node could be disassembled and erased long before they came close.

No message could outrace light directly, but there were more ways for light to reach the node than the direct path, the fastest one. Every black hole had its glory, twisting light around it in a tight, close orbit and flinging it back out again.

Seventy-four hours after the original image was lost to them, the telescopes at the node could still turn to the Cataract and scour the distorted, compressed image of the sky at the rim of the hole's black disk to catch a replay of Anne's ballet.

Joan composed the message and entered the coordinates of the node. *You didn't die for nothing, my friend. When you wake and see this, you'll be proud of us both.*

She hesitated, her hand hovering above the send key. The Tirans had wanted Anne to flee, to show them the way to the stars, but had they really been indifferent to the loot they'd let her carry? The theorem had come at the end of the Niah's three-million-year reign. To witness this beautiful truth would not destroy the Amalgam, but might it not weaken it? If the Seekers' thirst for knowledge was slaked, their sense of purpose corroded, might not the most crucial strand of the culture fall into a twilight of its own? There was no shortcut to the stars, but the Noudah had been goaded by their alien visitors, and the technology would come to them soon enough.

The Amalgam had been goaded, too: the theorem she'd already transmitted would send a wave of excitement around the galaxy, strengthening the Seekers, encouraging them to complete the unification by their own efforts. The Big Crunch might be inevitable, but at least she could delay it, and hope that the robustness and diversity of the Amalgam would carry them through it, and beyond.

She erased the message and wrote a new one, addressed to her backup via the decoy node. It would have been nice to upload all her memories, but the Noudah were ruthless, and she wasn't prepared to stay any longer and risk being used by them. This sketch, this postcard, would have to be enough.

When the transmission was complete, she left a note for Sando in the console's memory.

Daya called out to her, "Jown? Do you need anything?"

"No. I'm going to sleep for a while."

finisterra

DAVID MOLES

David Moles is a past finalist for the Hugo Award, the World Fantasy Award, and the John W. Campbell Award for Best New Writer, as well as the winner of the 2008 Theodore Sturgeon Memorial Award. His work has appeared in Strange Horizons, Asimov's Science Fiction, The Magazine of Fantasy & Science Fiction, *and various anthologies. He lives in California with his family.*

In the vivid and fast-paced story that follows, he takes us to a world of living, floating islands in the sky, to teach us the uncomfortable lesson that you're never safe from predation, no matter how big you are. Or from your own past, either.

1. ENCANTADA

Bianca Nazario stands at the end of the world.

The firmament above is as blue as the summer skies of her childhood, mirrored in the waters of *la caldera*; but where the skies she remembers were bounded by mountains, here on Sky there is no real horizon, only a line of white cloud. The white line shades into a diffuse grayish fog that, as Bianca looks down, grows progressively murkier, until the sky directly below is thoroughly dark and opaque.

She remembers what Dinh told her about the ways Sky could kill her. With a large enough parachute, Bianca imagines, she could fall for hours, drifting through the layered clouds, before finding her end in heat or pressure or the jaws of some monstrous denizen of the deep air.

If this should go wrong, Bianca cannot imagine a better way to die.

Bianca works her way out a few hundred meters along the base of one of Encantada's ventral fins, stopping when the dry red dirt beneath her feet begins to give way to scarred gray flesh. She takes a last look around: at the pall of smoke obscuring the *zaratán's* tree-lined dorsal ridge, at the fin she stands on, curving out and down to its delicate-looking tip, kilometers away. Then she knots her scarf around her skirted ankles and shrugs into the paraballoon harness, still warm from the bungalow's fabricators. As the harness tightens itself around her, she takes a deep breath, filling her lungs. The wind from the burning camp smells of wood smoke and pine resin, enough to overwhelm the taint of blood from the killing ground.

Blessed Virgin, she prays, be my witness: this is no suicide.

This is a prayer for a miracle.
She leans forward.
She falls.

2. THE FLYING ARCHIPELAGO

The boat-like anemopter that Valadez had sent for them had a cruising speed of just less than the speed of sound, which in this part of Sky's atmosphere meant about nine hundred kilometers per hour. The speed, Bianca thought, might have been calculated to bring home the true size of Sky, the impossible immensity of it. It had taken the better part of their first day's travel for the anemopter's point of departure, the ten-kilometer, billion-ton vacuum balloon *Transient Meridian*, to drop from sight—the dwindling golden droplet disappearing, not over the horizon, but into the haze. From that Bianca estimated that the bowl of clouds visible through the subtle blurring of the anemopter's static fields covered an area about the size of North America.

She heard a plastic clattering on the deck behind her, and turned to see one of the anemopter's crew, a globular, brown-furred alien with a collection of arms like furry snakes, each arm tipped with a mouth or a round and curious eye. The *firija* were low-gravity creatures; the ones Bianca had seen on her passage from Earth had tumbled joyously through the *Caliph of Baghdad*'s inner ring spaces like so many radially symmetrical monkeys. The three aboard the anemopter, in Sky's heavier gravity, had to make do with spindly-legged walking machines, and there was a droop in their arms that was both comical and melancholy.

"Come forward," this one told Bianca in fractured Arabic, its voice like a Peruvian pipe ensemble. She thought it was the one that called itself Ismaíl. "Make see archipelago."

She followed it forward to the anemopter's rounded prow. The naturalist, Erasmus Fry, was already there, resting his elbows on the rail, looking down.

"Pictures don't do them justice, do they?" he said.

Bianca went to the rail and followed the naturalist's gaze. She did her best to maintain a certain stiff formality around Fry; from their first meeting aboard *Transient Meridian* she'd had the idea that it might not be good to let him get too familiar. But when she saw what Fry was looking at, the mask slipped for a moment, and she couldn't help a sharp, quick intake of breath.

Fry chuckled. "To stand on the back of one," he said, "to stand in a valley and look up at the hills and know that the ground under your feet is supported by the bones of a living creature—there's nothing else like it." He shook his head.

At this altitude they were above all but the highest-flying of the thousands of beasts that made up Septentrionalis Archipelago. Bianca's eyes tried to make the herd (or flock, or school) of *zaratanes* into other things: a chain of islands, yes, if she concentrated on the colors, the greens and browns of forests and plains, the grays and whites of the snowy highlands; a fleet of ships, perhaps, if she instead focused on the individual shapes, the keel ridges, the long, translucent fins, ribbed like Chinese sails.

The *zaratanes* of the archipelago were more different from one another than the members of a flock of birds or a pod of whales, but still there was a symmetry, a regularity of form, the basic anatomical plan—equal parts fish and mountain—repeated throughout, in fractal detail from the great old shape of Zaratán Finisterra, a hundred kilometers along the dorsal ridge, down to the merely hill-sized bodies of the nameless younger beasts. When she took in the archipelago as a whole, it was impossible for Bianca not to see the *zaratanes* as living things.

"Nothing else like it," Fry repeated.

Bianca turned reluctantly from the view, and looked at Fry. The naturalist spoke Spanish with a flawless Miami accent, courtesy, he'd said, of a Consilium language module. Bianca was finding it hard to judge the ages of *extrañados*, particularly the men, but in Fry's case she thought he might be ten years older than Bianca's own forty, and unwilling to admit it—or ten years younger, and in the habit of treating himself very badly. On her journey here she'd met cyborgs and foreigners and artificial intelligences and several sorts of alien—some familiar, at least from media coverage of the *hajj*, and some strange—but it was the *extrañados* that bothered her the most. It was hard to come to terms with the idea of humans born off Earth, humans who had never been to Earth or even seen it; humans who, many of them, had no interest in it.

"Why did you leave here, Mr. Fry?" she asked.

Fry laughed. "Because I didn't want to spend the rest of my life out *here*." With a hand, he swept the horizon. "Stuck on some godforsaken floating island for years on end, with no one but researchers and feral refugees to talk to, nowhere to go for fun but some slum of a balloon station, nothing but a thousand kilometers of air between you and Hell?" He laughed again. "You'd leave, too, Nazario, believe me."

"Maybe I would," Bianca said. "But you're back."

"I'm here for the money," Fry said. "Just like you."

Bianca smiled, and said nothing.

"You know," Fry said after a little while, "they have to kill the *zaratanes* to take them out of here." He looked at Bianca and smiled, in a way that was probably meant to be ghoulish. "There's no atmosphere ship big enough to lift a *zaratán* in one piece—even a small one. The poachers deflate them—gut them—flatten them out and roll them up. And even then, they throw out almost everything but the skin and bones."

"Strange," Bianca mused. Her mask was back in place. "There was a packet of material on the *zaratanes* with my contract; I watched most of it on the voyage. According to the packet, the Consilium considers the *zaratanes* a protected species."

Fry looked uneasy, and now it was Bianca's turn to chuckle.

"Don't worry, Mr. Fry," she said. "I may not know exactly what it is Mr. Valadez is paying me to do, but I've never had any illusion that it was legal."

Behind her, the *firija* made a fluting noise that might have been laughter.

3. THE STEEL BIRD

When Bianca was a girl, the mosque of Punta Aguila was the most prominent feature in the view from her fourth-floor window, a sixteenth-century structure of tensegrity cables and soaring catenary curves, its spreading white wings vaguely—but only vaguely—recalling the bird that gave the city its name. The automation that controlled the tension of the cables and adjusted the mosque's wings to match the shifting winds was hidden within the cables themselves, and was very old. Once, after the hurricane in the time of Bianca's grandfather, it had needed adjusting, and the old men of the *ayuntamiento* had been forced to send for *extrañado* technicians, at an expense so great that the *jizyah* of Bianca's time was still paying for it.

But Bianca rarely thought of that. Instead she would spend long hours surreptitiously sketching those white wings, calculating the weight of the structure and the tension of the cables, wondering what it would take to make the steel bird fly.

Bianca's father could probably have told her, but she never dared to ask. Raúl Nazario de Arenas was an aeronautical engineer, like the seven generations before him, and flight was the Nazarios' fortune; fully a third of the aircraft that plied the skies over the Rio Pícaro were types designed by Raúl or his father or his wife's father, on contract to the great *moro* trading and manufacturing families that were Punta Aguila's truly wealthy.

Because he worked for other men, and because he was a Christian, Raúl Nazario would never be as wealthy as the men who employed him, but his profession was an ancient and honorable one, providing his family with a more than comfortable living. If Raúl Nazario de Arenas thought of the mosque at all, it was only to mutter about the *jizyah* from time to time—but never loudly, because the Nazarios, like the other Christians of Punta Aguila, however valued, however ancient their roots, knew that they lived there only on sufferance.

But Bianca would sketch the aircraft, too, the swift gliders and lumbering flying boats and stately dirigibles, and these drawings she did not have to hide; in fact for many years her father would encourage her, explaining this and that aspect of their construction, gently correcting errors of proportion and balance in Bianca's drawings; would let her listen in while he taught the family profession to her brothers, Jesús the older, Pablo the younger.

This lasted until shortly before Bianca's *quinceañera*, when Jesús changed his name to Walíd and married a *moro*'s daughter, and Bianca's mother delivered a lecture concerning the difference between what was proper for a child and what was proper for a young Christian woman with hopes of one day making a good marriage.

It was only a handful of years later that Bianca's father died, leaving a teenaged Pablo at the helm of his engineering business; and only Bianca's invisible assistance and the pity of a few old clients had kept contracts and money coming into the Nazario household.

By the time Pablo was old enough to think he could run the business himself, old enough to marry the daughter of a musical instrument maker from Tierra Ceniza, their mother was dead, Bianca was thirty, and even if her dowry had been half her father's business, there was not a Christian man in Rio Pícaro who wanted it, or her.

And then one day Pablo told her about the *extrañado* contract that had been brought to the *ayuntamiento*, a contract that the *ayuntamiento* and the Guild had together forbidden the Christian engineers of Punta Aguila to bid on—a contract for a Spanish-speaking aeronautical engineer to travel a very long way from Rio Pícaro and be paid a very large sum of money indeed.

Three months later Bianca was in Quito, boarding an elevator car. In her valise was a bootleg copy of her father's engineering system, and a contract with the factor of a starship called the *Caliph of Baghdad*, for passage to Sky.

4. THE KILLING GROUND

The anemopter's destination was a *zaratán* called Encantada, smaller than the giant Finisterra but still nearly forty kilometers from nose to tail, and eight thousand meters from gray-white keel to forested crest. From a distance of a hundred kilometers, Encantada was like a forested mountain rising from a desert plain, the clear air under its keel as dreamlike as a mirage. On her pocket system, Bianca called up pictures from Sky's network of the alpine ecology that covered the hills and valleys of Encantada's flanks: hardy grasses and small warm-blooded creatures and tall evergreens with spreading branches, reminding her of the pines and redwoods in the mountains west of Rio Pícaro.

For the last century or so Encantada had been keeping company with Zaratán Finisterra, holding its position above the larger beast's eastern flank. No one, apparently, knew the reason, and Fry—who, he being the expert, Bianca had expected to at least have a theory—didn't even seem to be interested in the question.

"They're beasts, Nazario," he said. "They don't do things for reasons. We only call them animals and not plants because they bleed when we cut them."

They were passing over Finisterra's southern slopes. Looking down, Bianca saw brighter, warmer greens, more shades than she could count, more than she had known existed, the green threaded through with bright ribbons of silver water. She saw the anemopter's shadow, a dark oblong that rode the slopes and ridges, ringed by brightness—the faint reflection of Sky's sun behind them.

And just before the shadow entered the larger darkness that was the shadow of Encantada, Bianca watched it ride over something else: a flat green space carved out of the jungle, a suspiciously geometric collection of shapes that could only be buildings, the smudge of chimney smoke.

"Fry—" she started to say.

Then the village, if that's what it was, was gone, hidden behind the next ridge.

"What?" said Fry.

"I saw—I thought I saw—"

"People?" asked Fry. "You probably did."

"But I thought Sky didn't have any native sentients. Who are they?"

"Humans, mostly," Fry said. "Savages. Refugees. Drug farmers. Five generations of escaped criminals, and their kids, and *their* kids." The naturalist shrugged. "Once in a while, if the Consilium's looking for somebody in particular, the wardens might stage a raid, just for show. The rest of the time, the wardens fly their dope, screw their women . . . and otherwise leave them alone."

"But where do they come from?" Bianca asked.

"Everywhere," Fry said with another shrug. "Humans have been in this part of space for a long, long time. This is one of those places people end up, you know? People with nowhere else to go. People who can't fall any farther."

Bianca shook her head, and said nothing.

The poachers' camp, on Encantada's eastern slope, was invisible until they were almost upon it, hidden from the wardens' satellite eyes by layers of projected camouflage. Close up, the illusion seemed flat, its artificiality obvious, but it was still not until the anemopter passed through the projection that the camp itself could be seen: a clear-cut swath a kilometer wide and three times as long, stretching from the lower slopes of Encantada's dorsal ridge down to the edge of the *zaratán*'s cliff-like flank. Near the edge, at one corner, there was a small cluster of prefabricated bungalows; but at first it seemed to Bianca that most of the space was wasted.

Then she saw the red churned into the brown mud of the cleared strip, saw the way the shape of the terrain suggested the imprint of a gigantic, elongated body.

The open space was for killing.

"Sky is very poor, Miss Nazario," said Valadez, over his shoulder.

The poacher boss looked to be about fifty, stocky, his hair still black and his olive skin well-tanned but pocked with tiny scars. His Spanish was a dialect Bianca had never heard before, strange and lush, its vowels rich, its *h*s breathy as Bianca's *j*s, its *j*s warm and liquid as the *y*s of an Argentine. When he said *fuck your mother*—and already, in the hour or so Bianca had been in the camp, she had heard him say it several times, though never yet to her—the *madre* came out *madri*.

About half of the poachers were human, but Valadez seemed to be the only one who spoke Spanish natively; the rest used Sky's dialect of bazaar Arabic. Valadez spoke that as well, better than Bianca did, but she had the sense that he learned it late in life. If he had a first name, he was keeping it to himself.

"There are things on Sky that people want," Valadez went on. "But the *people* of Sky have nothing of interest to anybody. The companies that mine the deep air pay some royalties. But mostly what people live on here is Consilium handouts."

The four of them—Bianca, Fry, and the *firija*, Ismaíl, who as well as being an anemopter pilot seemed to be Valadez' servant or business partner or bodyguard, or perhaps all three—were climbing the ridge above the poachers' camp. Below them workers, some human, some *firija*, a handful of other species, were setting up equipment: mobile machines that looked like they belonged on a construction site, pipes and cylindrical tanks reminiscent of a brewery or a refinery.

"I'm changing that, Miss Nazario." Valadez glanced over his shoulder at Bianca. "Off-world, there are people—like Ismaíl's people here"—he waved at the *firija*—"who like the idea of living on a floating island, and have the money to pay for one." He swept an arm, taking in the camp, the busy teams of workers. "With that money, I take boys out of the shantytowns of Sky's balloon stations and elevator gondolas. I give them tools, and teach them to kill beasts.

"To stop me—since they can't be bothered to do it themselves—the Consilium takes the same boys, gives them guns, and teaches them to kill men."

The poacher stopped and turned to face Bianca, jamming his hands into the pockets of his coat.

"Tell me, Miss Nazario—is one worse than the other?"

"I'm not here to judge you, Mr. Valadez," said Bianca. "I'm here to do a job."

Valadez smiled. "So you are."

He turned and continued up the slope. Bianca and the *firija* followed, Fry trailing behind. The path switchbacked through unfamiliar trees, dark, stunted, waxy-needled; these gave way to taller varieties, including some that Bianca would have sworn were ordinary pines and firs. She breathed deeply, enjoying the alpine breeze after the crowds-and-machines reek of *Transient Meridian's* teeming slums, the canned air of ships and anemopters.

"It smells just like home," she remarked. "Why is that?"

No once answered.

The ridge leveled off, and they came out into a cleared space, overlooking the camp. Spread out below them Bianca could see the airfield, the globular tanks and pipes of the poachers' little industrial plant, the bungalows in the distance—and, in between, the red-brown earth of the killing ground, stretching out to the cliff-edge and the bases of the nearest translucent fins.

"This is a good spot," Valadez declared. "Should be a good view from up here."

"A view of what?" said Fry.

The poacher didn't answer. He waved to Ismaíl, and the *firija* took a small folding stool out of a pocket, snapping it into shape with a flick of sinuous arms and setting it down behind him. Valadez sat.

And after a moment, the answer to Fry's question came up over the edge.

Bianca had not thought hardly at all about the killing of a *zaratán*, and when she had thought of it she had imagined something like the harpooning of a whale in ancient times, the great beast fleeing, pursued by the tiny harassing shapes of boats, gored by harpoons, sounding again and again, all the strength bleeding out of the beast until there was nothing left for it to do but wallow gasping on the surface and expire, noble and tragic. Now Bianca realized that for all their great size, the *zaratanes* were far weaker than any whale, far less able to fight or to escape or even—she sincerely hoped—to understand what was happening to them.

There was nothing noble about the way the nameless *zaratán* died. Anemopters landed men and aliens with drilling tools at the base of each hundred-meter fin, to bore through soil and scale and living flesh and cut the connecting nerves that controlled them. This took about fifteen minutes, and to Bianca there seemed to be something obscene in the way the paralyzed fins hung there afterwards, life-less and limp. Thus crippled, the beast was pushed and pulled by aerial tugs— awkward machines, stubby and cylindrical, converted from the stationkeeping engines of vacuum balloons like *Transient Meridian*—into position over Encan-tada's killing ground. Then the drilling teams moved in again, to the places marked for them ahead of time by seismic sensors and ultrasound, cutting this time through bone as well as flesh, to find the *zaratán's* brain.

When the charges the drilling teams had planted went off, a ripple went through the *zaratán's* body, a slow-motion convulsion that took nearly a minute to travel down the body's long axis, as the news of death passed from synapse to synapse; and Bianca saw flocks of birds started from the trees along the *zaratán's* back as if by an earthquake, which in a way she supposed this was. The carcass immediately began to pitch downward, the nose dropping—the result, Bianca re-alized, of sphincters relaxing one by one, all along the *zaratán's* length, venting hydrogen from the ballonets.

Then the forward edge of the keel fin hit the ground and crumpled, and the whole length of the dead beast, a hundred thousand tons of it, crashed down into the field; and even at that distance Bianca could hear the cracking of gargantuan bones.

She shivered, and glanced at her pocket system. The whole process, she was amazed to see, had taken less than half an hour.

"That's this trip paid for, whatever else happens," said Valadez. He turned to Bianca. "Mostly, though, I thought you should see this. Have you guessed yet what it is I'm paying you to do, Miss Nazario?"

Bianca shook her head. "Clearly you don't need an aeronautical engineer to do what you've just done." She looked down at the killing ground, where men and aliens and machines were already climbing over the *zaratán's* carcass, uproot-ing trees, peeling back skin and soil in great strips like bleeding boulevards. A wind had come up, blowing from the killing ground across the camp, bringing with it a smell that Bianca associated with butcher shops.

An engineering problem, she reminded herself, as she turned her back on the scene and faced Valadez. That's all this is.

"How are you going to get it out of here?" she asked.

"Cargo-lifter," said Valadez. "The *Lupita Jeréz*. A supply ship, diverted from one of the balloon stations."

The alien, Ismaíl, said: "Like fly anemopter make transatmospheric." The same fluting voice and broken Arabic. "Lifter plenty payload mass limit, but fly got make have packaging. Packaging for got make platform have stable." On the word *pack-aging* the *firija's* arms made an expressive gesture, like rolling something up into a bundle and tying it.

Bianca nodded hesitantly, hoping she understood. "And so you can only take the small ones," she said. "Right? Because there's only one place on Sky you'll find a stable platform that size: on the back of another *zaratán*."

"You have the problem in a nutshell, Miss Nazario," said Valadez. "Now, how would you solve it? How would you bag, say, Encantada here? How would you bag Finisterra?"

Fry said: "You want to take one *alive?*" His face was even more pale than usual, and Bianca noticed that he, too, had turned his back to the killing ground.

Valadez was still looking at Bianca, expectantly.

"He doesn't want it alive, Mr. Fry," she said, watching the poacher expectantly. "He wants it dead—but intact. You could take even Finisterra apart, and lift it piece by piece, but you'd need a thousand cargo-lifters to do it."

Valadez smiled.

"I've got another ship," he said. "Built for deep mining, outfitted as a mobile elevator station. Counterweighted. The ship itself isn't rated for atmosphere, but if you can get one of the big ones to the edge of space, we'll lower the skyhook, catch the beast, and catapult it into orbit. The buyer's arranged an FTL tug to take it from there."

Bianca made herself look back at the killing ground. The workers were freeing the bones, lifting them with aerial cranes and feeding them into the plant; for cleaning and preservation, she supposed. She turned back to Valadez.

"We should be able to do that, if the *zaratán*'s body will stand up to the low pressure," she said. "But why go to all this trouble? I've seen the balloon stations. I've seen what you people can do with materials. How hard can it be to make an imitation *zaratán?*"

Valadez glanced at Ismaíl. The walker was facing the killing ground, but two of the alien's many eyes were watching the sky—and two more were watching Valadez. The poacher looked back at Bianca.

"An imitation's one thing, Miss Nazario; the real thing is something else. And worth a lot more, to the right buyer." He looked away again; not at Ismaíl this time, but up the slope, through the trees. "Besides," he added, "in this case I've got my own reasons."

"Ship come," Ismaíl announced.

Bianca looked and saw more of the *firija*'s eyes turning upward. She followed their gaze, and at first saw only empty sky. Then the air around the descending *Lupita Jeréz* boiled into contrails, outlining the invisible ovoid shape of the ship's lifting fields.

"Time to get to work," said Valadez.

Bianca glanced toward the killing ground. A pink fog was rising to cover the work of the flensing crews.

The air was full of blood.

5. THE AERONAUTS

Valadez's workers cleaned the nameless *zaratán*'s bones one by one; they tanned the hide, and rolled it into bundles for loading aboard the *Lupita Jeréz*. That job, grotesque though it was, was the cleanest part of the work. What occupied most of the workers was the disposal of the unwanted parts, a much dirtier and more arduous job. Exotic internal organs the size of houses; tendons like braided, knotted bridge cables; ballonets large enough, each of them, to lift an ordinary dirigible; and hectares and hectares of pale, dead flesh. The poachers piled up the mess with earth-moving machines and shoveled it off the edge of the killing ground, a rain of offal falling into the clouds in a mist of blood, manna for the ecology of the deep air. They sprayed the killing ground with antiseptics, and the cool air helped to slow decay a little, but by the fourth day the butcher-shop smell had nonetheless given way to something worse.

Bianca's bungalow was one of the farthest out, only a few dozen meters from Encantada's edge, where the wind blew in from the open eastern sky, and she could turn her back on the slaughter to look out into clear air, dotted with the small, distant shapes of younger *zaratanes*. Even here, though, a kilometer and more upwind of the killing ground, the air carried a taint of spoiled meat. The sky was full of insects and scavenger birds, and there were always vermin underfoot.

Bianca spent most of her time indoors, where the air was filtered and the wet industrial sounds of the work muted. The bungalow was outfitted with all the mechanisms the *extrañados* used to make themselves comfortable, but while in the course of her journey Bianca had learned to operate these, she made little use of them. Besides her traveling chest—a gift from her older brother's wife, which served as armoire, desk, dresser and drafting table—the only furnishings were a woven carpet in the Lagos Grandes style, a hard little bed, and a single wooden chair, not very different from the ones in her room in Punta Aguila. Though those had been handmade, and these were simulations provided by the bungalow's machines.

The rest of the room was given over to the projected spaces of Bianca's engineering work. The tools Valadez had given her were slick and fast and factory-fresh, the state of somebody's art, somewhere; but what Bianca mostly found herself using was her pocket system's crippled copy of the Nazario family automation.

The system Bianca's father used to use, to calculate stresses in fabric and metal and wood, to model the flow of air over wings and the variation of pressure and temperature through gasbags, was six centuries old, a slow, patient, reliable thing that dated from before the founding of the London Caliphate. It had aged along with the family, grown used to their quirks and to the strange demands of aviation in Rio Pícaro. Bianca's version of it, limited though it was, at least didn't balk at control surfaces supported by muscle and bone, at curves not aerodynamically smooth but fractally complex with grasses and trees at hanging vines. If the *zaratanes* had been machines, they would have been marvels of engineering, with their internal networks of gasbags and ballonets, their reservoir-sized ballast bladders full of collected rainwater, their great delicate fins. The *zaratanes* were beyond the poachers' systems' stubborn, narrow-minded comprehension; for all their speed and flash, the systems sulked like spoiled children whenever Bianca tried to use them to do something their designers had not expected her to do.

Which she was doing, all the time. She was working out how to draw up Leviathan with a hook.

"Miss Nazario."

Bianca started. She had yet to grow used to these *extrañado* telephones that never rang, but only spoke to her out of the air, or perhaps out of her own head.

"Mr. Valadez," she said, after a moment.

"Whatever you're doing, drop it," said Valadez's voice. "You and Fry. I'm sending a 'mopter for you."

"I'm working," said Bianca. "I don't know what Fry's doing."

"This *is* work," said Valadez. "Five minutes."

A change in the quality of the silence told Bianca that Valadez had hung up. She sighed; then stood, stretched, and started to braid her hair.

The anemopter brought them up over the dorsal ridge, passing between two of the great translucent fins. At this altitude, Encantada's body was clear of vegetation; Bianca looked down on hectares of wind-blasted gray hide, dusted lightly with snow. They passed within a few hundred meters of one of the huge spars that anchored the aft fin's leading edge: a kilometers-high pillar of flesh, teardrop in cross-section and at least a hundred meters thick. The trailing edge of the next fin, by contrast, flashed by in an instant, and Bianca had only a brief impression of a silk-supple membrane, veined with red, clear as dirty glass.

"What do you think he wants?" Fry asked.

"I don't know." She nodded her head toward the *firija* behind them at the steering console. "Did you ask the pilot?"

"I tried," Fry said. "Doesn't speak Arabic."

Bianca shrugged. "I suppose we'll find out soon enough."

Then they were coming down again, down the western slope. In front of Bianca was the dorsal ridge of Zaratán Finisterra. Twenty kilometers away and blue with haze, it nonetheless rose until it seemed to cover a third of the sky.

Bianca looked out at it, wondering again what kept Encantada and Finisterra so close; but then the view was taken away, and they were coming down between the trees, into a shady, ivy-filled creekbed somewhere not far from Encantada's western edge. There was another anemopter already there, and a pair of aerial tugs—and a whitish mass that dwarfed all of these, sheets and ribbons of pale material hanging from the branches and draped over the ivy, folds of it damming the little stream.

With an audible splash, the anemopter set down, the ramps lowered, and Bianca stepped off, into cold, ankle-deep water that made her glad of her knee-high boots. Fry followed, gingerly.

"You!" called Valadez, pointing at Fry from the deck of the other anemopter. "Come here. Miss Nazario—I'd like you to have a look at that balloon."

"Balloon?"

Valadez gestured impatiently downstream, and suddenly Bianca saw the white material for the shredded, deflated gasbag it was; and saw, too, that there was a basket attached to it, lying on its side, partially submerged in the middle of the stream. Ismaíl was standing over it, waving.

Bianca splashed over to the basket. It actually *was* a basket, two meters across and a meter and a half high, woven from strips of something like bamboo or rattan. The gasbag—this was obvious, once Bianca saw it up close—had been made from one of the ballonets of a *zaratán*, a *zaratán* younger and smaller even than the one Bianca had seen killed; it had been tanned, but inexpertly, and by someone without access to the sort of industrial equipment the poachers used.

Bianca wondered about the way the gasbag was torn up. The tissues of the *zaratánes*, she knew, were very strong. A hydrogen explosion?

"Make want fly got very bad," Ismaíl commented, as Bianca came around to the open side of the basket.

"They certainly did," she said.

In the basket there were only some wool blankets and some empty leather waterbags, probably used both for drinking water and for ballast. The lines used to control the vent flaps were all tangled together, and tangled, too, with the lines that secured the gasbag to the basket, but Bianca could guess how they had worked. No stove. It seemed to have been a pure hydrogen balloon; and why not, she thought, with all the hydrogen anyone could want free from the nearest *zaratán*'s vent valves?

"Where did it come from?" she asked.

Ismaíl rippled his arms in a way that Bianca guessed was meant to be an imitation of a human shrug. One of his eyes glanced downstream.

Bianca fingered the material of the basket: tough, woody fiber. Tropical, from a climate warmer than Encantada's. She followed Ismaíl's glance. The trees hid the western horizon, but she knew, if she could see beyond them, what would be there.

Aloud, she said: "Finisterra."

She splashed back to the anemopters. Valadez's hatch was open.

"I'm telling you," Fry was saying, "I don't know her!"

"Fuck off, Fry," Valadez said as Bianca stepped into the cabin. "Look at her ID."

The *her* in question was a young woman with short black hair and sallow skin, wearing tan off-world cottons like Fry's under a colorful homespun *serape*; and at first Bianca was not sure the woman was alive, because the man next to her on Valadez's floor, also in homespun, was clearly dead, his eyes half-lidded, his olive skin gone muddy gray.

The contents of their pockets were spread out on a low table. As Bianca was taking in the scene, Fry bent down and picked up a Consilium-style ID tag.

"'Edith Dinh,'" he read. He tossed the tag back and looked at Valadez. "So?"

"'Edith Dinh, *Consilium Ethnological Service*,'" Valadez growled. "Issued Shawwal '43. *You* were here with the *Ecological* Service from Rajab '42 to Muharram '46. Look again!"

Fry turned away.

"All right!" he said. "Maybe—maybe I met her once or twice."

"So," said Valadez. "Now we're getting somewhere. Who the hell is she? And what's she doing *here*?"

"She's . . ." Fry glanced at the woman and then quickly looked away. "I don't know. I think she was a population biologist or something. There was a group working with the, you know, the natives—"

"There aren't any natives on Sky," said Valadez. He prodded the dead man with the toe of his boot. "You mean these *cabrones*?"

Fry nodded. "They had this 'sustainable development' program going—farming, forestry. Teaching them how to live on Finisterra without killing it."

Valadez looked skeptical. "If the Consilium wanted to stop them from killing Finisterra, why didn't they just send in the wardens?"

"Interdepartmental politics. The *zaratanes* were EcoServ's responsibility; the n . . . I mean, the *inhabitants* were EthServ's." Fry shrugged. "You know the wardens. They'd have taken bribes from anyone who could afford it, and shot the rest."

"Damn right I know the wardens." Valadez scowled. "So instead EthServ sent in these do-gooders to teach them to make balloons?"

Fry shook his head. "I don't know anything about that."

"Miss Nazario? Tell me about that balloon."

"It's a hydrogen balloon, I think. Probably filled from some *zaratán*'s external vents." She shrugged. "It looks like the sort of thing I'd expect someone living out here to build, if that's what you mean."

Valadez nodded.

"But," Bianca added, "I can't tell you why it crashed."

Valadez snorted. "I don't need you to tell me that," he said. "It crashed because we shot it down." Pitching his voice for the anemopter's communication system, he called out: "Ismaíl!"

Bianca tried to keep the shock from showing on her face, and after a moment, she had regained her composure. *You knew they were criminals when you took their money*, she told herself.

The *firija*'s eyes came around the edge of the doorway.

"Yes?"

"Tell the tug crews to pack that thing up," said Valadez. "Every piece, every scrap. Pack it up and drop it into clear air."

The alien's walking machine clambered into the cabin. Its legs bent briefly, making a little bob like a curtsey.

"Yes." Ismaíl gestured at the bodies of the dead man and the unconscious woman. Several of the *firija*'s eyes met Valadez's. "These two what do?" he asked.

"Them, too," said Valadez. "Lash them into the basket."

The *firija* made another bob, and started to bend down to pick them up.

Bianca looked down at the two bodies, both of them, the dead man and the unconscious woman, looking small and thin and vulnerable. She glanced at Fry, whose eyes were fixed on the floor, his lips pressed together in a thin line.

Then she looked over at Valadez, who was methodically sweeping the balloonists' effects into a pile, as if neither Bianca nor Fry was present.

"No," she said; and Ismaíl stopped, and straightened up.

"What?" said Valadez.

"No," Bianca repeated.

"You want her bringing the wardens down on us?" Valadez demanded.

"That's murder, Mr. Valadez," Bianca said. "I won't be a party to it."

The poacher's eyes narrowed. He gestured at the dead man.

"You're already an accessory," he said.

"After the fact," Bianca replied evenly. She kept her eyes on Valadez.

The poacher looked at the ceiling. "Fuck your mother," he muttered. He looked down at the two bodies, and at Ismaíl, and then over at Bianca. He sighed, heavily.

"All right," he said to the *firija*. "Take the live one back to the camp. Secure a bungalow, one of the ones out by the edge"—he glanced at Bianca—"and lock her in it. Okay?"

"Okay," said Ismaíl. "Dead one what do?"

Valadez looked at Bianca again. "The dead one," he said, "goes in the basket."

Bianca looked at the dead man again, wondering what bravery or madness had brought him aboard that fragile balloon, and wondering what he would have thought if he had known that the voyage would end this way, with his body tumbling down into the deep air. She supposed he must have known there was a chance of it.

After a moment, she nodded, once.

"Right," said Valadez. "Now get back to work, damn it."

6. THE CITY OF THE DEAD

The anemopter that brought Bianca and Fry over the ridge took them back. Fry was silent, hunched, his elbows on his knees, staring at nothing. What fear or guilt was going through his mind, Bianca couldn't guess.

After a little while she stopped watching him. She thought about the Finisterran balloon, so simple, so fragile, making her father's wood-and-silk craft look as sophisticated as the Lupita Jeréz. She took out her pocket system, sketched a simple globe and basket, then erased them.

Make want fly very bad, Ismaíl the *firija* had said. Why?

Bianca undid the erasure, bringing her sketch back. She drew the spherical balloon out into a blunt torpedo, round at the nose, tapering to a point behind. Added fins. An arrangement of pulleys and levers, allowing them to be controlled from the basket. A propeller, powered by—she had to think for a little while—by an alcohol-fueled engine, carved from *zaratán* bones . . .

The anemopter was landing. Bianca sighed and again erased the design. Why?

The *firija* guard outside Edith Dinh's bungalow didn't seem to speak Arabic or Spanish, or in fact any human language at all. Bianca wondered if the choice was deliberate, the guard chosen by Valadez as a way of keeping a kind of solitary confinement.

Or was the guard Valadez's choice at all? she wondered suddenly, and shivered, looking at the meter-long weapon cradled in the alien's furred arms.

Then she squared her shoulders and approached the bungalow. Wordlessly, she waved the valise she was carrying, as if by it her reason for being there were made customary and obvious.

The alien said something in its own fluting language—whether a reply to her, or a request for instructions from some unseen listener, Bianca couldn't tell. Either those instructions were to let her pass, though, or by being seen in Valadez's company she had acquired some sort of reflected authority; because the *firija* lifted its weapon and, as the bungalow's outer door slid open, motioned for her to enter. The inner door was already open.

"¿*Hóla*?" Bianca called out, tentatively, and immediately felt like an idiot.

But the answer came:

"*Aqui*."

The interior layout of the bungalow was the same as Bianca's. The voice came from the sitting room, and Bianca found Dinh there, still wearing the clothes she had on when they found her, sitting with her knees drawn up, staring out the east window into the sky. The east was dark with rain clouds, and far below, Bianca could see flashes of lightning.

"*Salaam aleikum*," said Bianca, taking refuge in the formality of the Arabic.

"*Aleikum as-salaam*," Dinh replied. She glanced briefly at Bianca and looked away; then looked back again. In a Spanish that was somewhere between Valadez's strange accent and the mechanical fluency of Fry's language module, she said: "You're not from Finisterra."

"No," said Bianca, giving up on the Arabic. "I'm from Rio Pícaro—from Earth. My name is Nazario, Bianca Nazario y Arenas."

"Edith Dinh."

Dinh stood up. There was an awkward moment, where Bianca was not sure whether to bow or curtsey or give Dinh her hand. She settled for proffering the valise.

"I brought you some things," she said. "Clothes, toiletries."

Dinh looked surprised. "Thanks," she said, taking the valise and looking inside.

"Are they feeding you? I could bring you some food."

"The kitchen still works," said Dinh. She held up a white packet. "And these?"

"Sanitary napkins," said Bianca.

"Sanitary . . . ?" Color rose to Dinh's face. "Oh. That's all right. I've got implants." She dropped the packet back in the valise and closed it.

Bianca looked away, feeling her own cheeks blush in turn. Damned *extrañados*, she thought. "I'd better—" be going, she started to say.

"Please—" said Dinh.

The older woman and the younger stood there for a moment, looking at each other, and Bianca suddenly wondered what impulse had brought her here, whether curiosity or Christian charity or simply a moment of loneliness, weakness. Of course she'd had to stop Valadez from killing the girl, but this was clearly a mistake.

"Sit," Dinh said. "Let me get you something. Tea. Coffee."

"I—All right." Bianca sat, slowly, perching on the edge of one of the too-soft *extrañado* couches. "Coffee," she said.

The coffee was very dark, and sweeter than Bianca liked it, flavored with something like condensed milk. She was glad to have it, regardless, glad to have something to look at and something to occupy her hands.

"You don't look like a poacher," Dinh said.

"I'm an aeronautical engineer," Bianca said. "I'm doing some work for them." She looked down at her coffee, took a sip, and looked up. "What about you? Fry said you're a biologist of some kind. What were you doing in that balloon?"

She couldn't tell whether the mention of Fry's name had registered, but Dinh's mouth went thin. She glanced out the west window.

Bianca followed her glance and saw the guard, slumped in its walker, watching the two women with one eye each. She wondered again whether Valadez was really running things, and then whether the *firija*'s ignorance of human language was real or feigned—and whether, even if it *was* real, someone less ignorant might be watching and listening, unseen.

Then she shook her head and looked back at Dinh, waiting.

"Finisterra's falling," Dinh said eventually. "Dying, maybe. It's too big; it's losing lift. It's fallen more than fifty meters in the last year alone."

"That doesn't make sense," Bianca said. "The lift-to-weight ratio of an aerostat depends on the ratio of volume to surface area. A larger *zaratán* should be *more* efficient, not less. And even if it *does* lose lift, it should only fall until it reaches a new equilibrium."

"It's not a *machine*," Dinh said. "It's a living creature."

Bianca shrugged. "Maybe it's old age, then," she said. "Everything has to die sometime."

"Not like this," Dinh said. She set down her coffee and turned to face Bianca fully. "Look. We don't know who built Sky, or how long ago, but it's obviously artificial. A gas giant with a nitrogen-oxygen atmosphere? That *doesn't happen*. And the Earthlike biology—the *zaratanes* are DNA-based, did you know that? The whole place is astronomically unlikely; if the Phenomenological Service had its way, they'd just quarantine the entire system, and damn Sky and everybody on it.

"The archipelago ecology is as artificial as everything else. Whoever designed it must have been very good; post-human, probably, maybe even post-singularity. It's a robust equilibrium, full of feedback mechanisms, ways to correct itself. But we, us ordinary humans and human-equivalents, we've"—she made a helpless gesture—"*fucked it up*. You know why Encantada's stayed here so long? Breeding, that's why . . . or maybe 'pollination' would be a better way to put it . . ."

She looked over at Bianca.

"The death of an old *zaratán* like Finisterra should be balanced by the birth of dozens, hundreds. But you, those bastards you work for, you've killed them all."

Bianca let the implication of complicity slide. "All right, then," she said. "Let's hear your plan."

"What?"

"Your *plan*," Bianca repeated. "For Finisterra. How are you going to save it?"

Dinh stared at her for a moment, then shook her head. "I can't," she said. She stood up, and went to the east window. Beyond the sheet of rain that now poured down the window the sky was deep mauve shading to indigo, relieved only by the lightning that sparked in the deep and played across the fins of the distant *zaratanes* of the archipelago's outer reaches. Dinh put her palm flat against the diamond pane.

"I *can't* save Finisterra," she said quietly. "I just want to stop you *hijos de puta* from doing this again."

Now Bianca was stung. "*Hija de puta*, yourself," she said. "You're killing them, too. Killing them and making balloons out of them, how is that better?"

Dinh turned back. "One *zaratán* the size of the one they're slaughtering out there right now would keep the Finisterrans in balloons for a hundred years," she said. "The only way to save the archipelago is to make the *zaratanes* more valuable alive than dead—and the only value a live *zaratán* has, on Sky, is as living space."

"You're trying to get the Finisterrans to colonize the other *zaratanes*?" Bianca asked. "But why should they? What's in it for them?"

"I told you," Dinh said. "Finisterra's dying." She looked out the window, down into the depths of the storm, both hands pressed against the glass. "Do you know how falling into Sky kills you, Bianca? First, there's the pressure. On the slopes of Finisterra, where the people live, it's a little more than a thousand millibars. Five kilometers down, under Finisterra's keel, it's double that. At two thousand millibars you can still breathe the air. At three thousand nitrogen narcosis sets in—'rapture of the deep,' they used to call it. At four thousand, the partial pressure of oxygen alone is enough to make your lungs bleed."

She stepped away from the window and looked at Bianca.

"But you'll never live to suffer that," she said, "because of the heat. Every thousand meters the average temperature rises six or seven degrees. Here it's about fifteen. Under Finisterra's keel it's closer to fifty. Twenty kilometers down, the air is hot enough to boil water."

Bianca met her gaze steadily. "I can think of worse ways to die," she said.

"There are seventeen thousand people on Finisterra," said Dinh. "Men, women, children, old people. There's a town—they call it the Lost City, *la ciudad perdida*. Some of the families on Finisterra can trace their roots back six generations." She gave a little laugh, with no humor in it. "They should call it *la ciudad muerta*. They're the walking dead, all seventeen thousand of them. Even though no one's alive on Finisterra today who will live to see it die. Already the crops are starting to fail. Already more old men and old women die every summer, as the summers get hotter and drier. The children of the children who are born today will have to move up into the hills as it starts to get too hot to grow crops on the lower slopes; but the soil isn't as rich up there, so many of those crops will fail, too. And *their* children's children . . . won't live to be old enough to have children of their own."

"Surely someone will rescue them before then," Bianca said.

"Who?" Dinh asked. "The Consilium? Where would they put them? The vacuum balloons and the elevator stations are already overcrowded. As far as the rest of Sky is concerned, the Finisterrans are 'malcontents' and 'criminal elements.' Who's going to take them in?"

"Then Valadez is doing them a favor," Bianca said.

Dinh started. "*Emmanuel Valadez* is running your operation?"

"It's *not my* operation," Bianca said, trying to keep her voice level. "And I didn't ask his first name."

Dinh fell into the window seat. "Of course it would be," she said. "Who else would they . . ." She trailed off, looking out the west window, toward the killing ground.

Then, suddenly, she turned back to Bianca.

"What do you mean, *doing them a favor*?" she said.

"Finisterra," Bianca said. "He's poaching Finisterra."

Dinh stared at her. "My God, Bianca! What about the people?"

"What about them?" asked Bianca. "They'd be better off somewhere else—you said that yourself."

"And what makes you think Valadez will evacuate them?"

"He's a *thief*, not a mass murderer."

Dinh gave her a withering look. "He *is* a murderer, Bianca. His father was a warden, his mother was the wife of the *alcalde* of Ciudad Perdida. He killed his own stepfather, two uncles, and three brothers. They were going to execute him—throw him over the edge—but a warden airboat picked him up. He spent two years with them, then killed his sergeant and three other wardens, stole their ship and sold it for a ticket off-world. He's probably the most wanted man on Sky."

She shook her head and, unexpectedly, gave Bianca a small smile.

"You didn't know any of that when you took the job, did you?"

Her voice was full of pity. It showed on her face as well, and suddenly Bianca couldn't stand to look at it. She got up and went to the east window. The rain was lighter now, the lightning less frequent.

She thought back to her simulations, her plans for lifting Finisterra up into the waiting embrace of the skyhook: the gasbags swelling, the *zaratán* lifting, first slowly and then with increasing speed toward the upper reaches of Sky's atmosphere. But now her inner vision was not the ghost-shape of a projection but a living image—trees cracking in the cold, water freezing, blood boiling from the ground in a million, million tiny hemorrhages.

She saw her mother's house in Punta Aguila—her sister-in-law's house, now: saw its windows rimed with frost, the trees in the courtyard gone brown and sere. She saw the Mercado de los Maculados beneath a blackening sky, the awnings whipped away by a thin wind, ice-cold, bone-dry.

He killed that Finisterran balloonist, she thought. He was ready to kill Dinh. He's capable of murder.

Then she shook her head.

Killing one person, or two, to cover up a crime, was murder, she thought.

Killing seventeen thousand people by deliberate asphyxiation—men, women, and children—wasn't murder, it was genocide.

She took her cup of coffee from the table, took a sip and put it down again.

"Thank you for the coffee," she said, and turned to go.

"How can you just let him do this?" Dinh demanded. "How can you *help him do this?*"

Bianca turned on her. Dinh was on her feet; her fists were clenched, and she was shaking. Bianca stared her down, her face as cold and blank as she could make it. She waited until Dinh turned away, throwing herself into a chair, staring out the window.

"I saved your life," Bianca told her. "That was more than I needed to do. Even if I *did* believe that Valadez meant to kill every person on Finisterra, *which I don't*, that wouldn't make it my problem."

Dinh turned farther away.

"Listen to me," Bianca said, "because I'm only going to explain this once."

She waited until Dinh, involuntarily, turned back to face her.

"This job is my one chance," Bianca said. "*This job* is what I'm here to do. I'm not here to save the world. Saving the world is a luxury for spoiled *extrañado* children like you and Fry. It's a luxury I don't have."

She went to the door, and knocked on the window to signal the *firija* guard.

"I'll get you out of here if I can," she added, over her shoulder. "But that's all I can do. I'm sorry."

Dinh hadn't moved.

As the *firija* opened the door, Bianca heard Dinh stir.

"*Erasmus* Fry?" she asked. "The naturalist?"

"That's right." Bianca glanced back, and saw Dinh looking out the window again.

"I'd like to see him," Dinh said.

"I'll let him know," said Bianca.

The guard closed the door behind her.

7. THE FACE IN THE MIRROR

There was still lightning playing along Encantada's dorsal ridge, but here on the eastern edge the storm had passed. A clean, electric smell was in the air, relief from the stink of the killing ground. Bianca returned to her own bungalow through a rain that had died to sprinkles.

She called Fry.

"What is it?" he asked.

"Miss Dinh," Bianca said. "She wants to see you."

There was silence on the other end. Then:

"You told her I was here?"

"Sorry," Bianca said, insincerely. "It just slipped out."

More silence.

"You knew her better than you told Valadez, didn't you," she said.

She heard Fry sigh. "Yes."

"She seemed upset," Bianca said. "You should go see her."

Fry sighed again, but said nothing.

"I've got work to do," Bianca said. "I'll talk to you later."

She ended the call.

She was supposed to make a presentation tomorrow, to Valadez and some of the poachers' crew bosses, talking about what they would be doing to Finisterra. It was mostly done; the outline was straightforward, and the visuals could be auto-generated from the design files. She opened the projection file, and poked at it for a little while, but found it hard to concentrate.

Suddenly to Bianca her clothes smelled of death, of Dinh's dead companion and the slaughtered *zaratán* and the death she'd spared Dinh from and the eventual deaths of all the marooned Finisterrans. She stripped them off and threw them in the recycler; bathed, washed her hair, changed into a nightgown.

They should call it la ciudad muerta.

Even though no one who's alive on Finisterra today will live to see it die.

She turned off the light, Dinh's words echoing in her head, and tried to sleep. But she couldn't; she couldn't stop thinking. Thinking about what it felt like to be forced to live on, when all you had to look forward to was death.

She knew that feeling very well.

What Bianca had on Pablo's wife, Mélia, the instrument-maker's daughter, was ten years of age, and a surreptitious technical education. What Mélia had on Bianca was a keen sense of territory, and the experience of growing up in a house full of sisters. Bianca continued to live in the house after Mélia moved in, even though it was Mélia's house now, and continued, without credit, to help her brother with the work that came in. But she retreated over the years, step by step, until the line was drawn at the door of the fourth-floor room that had been hers ever since she was a girl, and buried herself in her blueprints and her calculations, and tried to pretend she didn't know what was happening.

And then there was the day she met her *other* sister-in-law. Her *moro* sister-in-law. In the Mercado de los Maculados, where the aliens and the *extrañados* came to sell their trinkets and their medicines; a dispensation from the *ayuntamiento* had recently opened it to Christians.

Zahra al-Halim, a successful architect, took Bianca to her home, where Bianca ate caramels and drank blackberry tea and saw her older brother for the first time in more than twenty years, and tried very hard to call him Walíd and not Jesús. Here was a world—Bianca sensed; her brother and his wife were very discreet—that could be hers, too, if she wanted it. But like Jesús/Walíd, she would have to give up her old world to have it. Even if she remained a Christian she would never see the inside of a church again. And she would still never be accepted by the engineers' guild.

She went back to the Nazario house that evening, ignoring the barbed questions from Mélia about how she had spent her day; she went back to her room, with its blueprints and its models, and the furnishings she'd had all her life. She tried for a little while to work, but was unable to muster the concentration she needed to interface with the system.

Instead she found herself looking into the mirror.

And looking into the mirror Bianca focused not on the fragile trapped shapes of the flying machines tacked to the wall behind her, spread out and pinned down like so many chloroformed butterflies, but on her own tired face, the stray wisps of dry, brittle hair, the lines that years of captivity had made across her forehead and around her eyes. And, meeting those eyes, it seemed to Bianca that she was looking not into the mirror but down through the years of her future, a long, straight, narrow corridor without doors or branches, and that the eyes she was meeting at the end of it were the eyes of Death, Bianca's own, *su propria Muerte*, personal, personified.

Bianca got out of bed, turning on the lights. She picked up her pocket system. She wondered if she should call the wardens.

Instead she un-erased, yet again, the sketch she'd made earlier of the simple alcohol-powered dirigible. She used the Nazario family automation to fill it out with diagrams and renderings, lists of materials, building instructions, maintenance and pre-flight checklists.

It wasn't much, but it was better than Dinh's balloon.

Now she needed a way for Dinh to get it to the Finisterrans.

For that—thinking as she did so that there was some justice in it—she turned back to the system Valadez had given her. This was the sort of work the *extrañado* automation had been made for, no constraints other than those imposed by function, every trick of exotic technology available to be used. It was a matter of minutes for Bianca to sketch out her design; an hour or so to refine it, to trim away the unnecessary pieces until what remained was small enough to fit in the valise she'd left with Dinh. The only difficult part was getting the design automation to talk to the bungalow's fabricator, which was meant for clothes and furniture and domestic utensils. Eventually she had to use her pocket system to go out on Sky's local net—hoping as she did so that Valadez didn't have anyone monitoring her— and spend her own funds to contract the conversion out to a consulting service, somewhere out on one of the elevator gondolas.

Eventually she got it done, though. The fabricator spit out a neat package, which Bianca stuffed under the bed. Tomorrow she could get the valise back and smuggle the package to Dinh, along with the dirigible designs.

But first she had a presentation to make to Valadez. She wondered what motivated him. Nothing so simple as money—she was sure of that, even if she had trouble believing he was the monster Dinh had painted him to be. Was it revenge he was after? Revenge on his family, revenge on his homeland?

That struck Bianca a little too close to home.

She sighed, and turned out the lights.

8. THE PROFESSIONALS

By morning the storm had passed and the sky was blue again, but the inside of Valadez' bungalow was dark, to display the presenters' projections to better advantage. Chairs for Valadez and the human crew bosses were arranged in a rough semicircle; with them were the aliens whose anatomy permitted them to sit down. Ismaíl and the other *firija* stood in the back, their curled arms and the spindly legs of their machines making their silhouettes look, to Bianca, incongruously like those of potted plants.

Then the fronds stirred, suddenly menacing, and Bianca shivered. Who was really in charge?

No time to worry about that now. She straightened up and took out her pocket system.

"In a moment," she began, pitching her voice to carry to the back of the room, "Mr. Fry will be going over the *zaratán*'s metabolic processes, and our plans to stimulate the internal production of hydrogen. What I'm going to be talking about is the engineering work required to make that extra hydrogen do what we need it to do."

Bianca's pocket system projected the shape of a hundred-kilometer *zaratán*, not Finisterra or any other particular individual but rather an archetype, a sort of Platonic ideal. Points of pink light brightened all across the projected *zaratán*'s back, each indicating the position of a sphincter that would have to be cut out and replaced with a mechanical valve.

"Our primary concern during the preparation phase has to be these external vents. However, we also need to consider the internal trim and ballast valves . . ."

As she went on, outlining the implants and grafts, surgeries and mutilations needed to turn a living *zaratán* into an animatronic corpse, a part of her was amazed at her own presumption, amazed at the strong, confident, professional tone she was taking.

It was almost as if she were a real engineer.

The presentation came to a close. Bianca drew in a deep breath, trying to maintain her veneer of professionalism. This part wasn't in her outline.

"And then, finally, there is the matter of evacuation," she said.

In the back of the room, Ismaíl stirred. "Evacuation?" he asked—the first word anyone had uttered through the whole presentation.

Bianca cleared her throat. Red stars appeared along the imaginary *zaratán*'s southeastern edge, approximating the locations of Ciudad Perdida and the smaller Finisterran villages.

"Finisterra has a population of between fifteen and twenty thousand, most of them concentrated in these settlements here," she began. "Using a ship the size of the *Lupita Jeréz*, it should take roughly—"

"Not your problem, Miss Nazario." Valadez waved a hand. "In any case, there won't be any evacuations."

Bianca looked at him, appalled, and it must have shown on her face, because Valadez laughed.

"Don't look at me like that, Miss Nazario. We'll set up field domes over Ciudad Perdida and the central pueblos, to tide them over till we get them where they're going. If they keep their heads they should be fine." He laughed again. "Fucking hell," he said, shaking his head. "What did you think this was about? You didn't think we were going to kill twenty thousand people, did you?"

Bianca didn't answer. She shut the projection off and sat down, putting her pocket system away. Her heart was racing.

"Right," said Valadez. "Nice presentation, Miss Nazario. Mr. Fry?"

Fry stood up. "Okay," he said. "Let me—" He patted his pockets. "I, ah, I think I must have left my system in my bungalow."

Valadez sighed.

"We'll wait," he said.

The dark room was silent. Bianca tried to take slow, deep breaths. Mother of God, she thought, thank you for not letting me do anything stupid.

In the next moment she doubted herself. Dinh had been so sure. How could Bianca know whether Valadez was telling the truth?

There was no way to know, she decided. She'd just have to wait and see.

Fry came back in, breathless.

"Ah, it wasn't—"

The voice that interrupted him was loud enough that at first it was hardly recognizable as a voice; it was only a wall of sound, seeming to come from the air itself, echoing and reechoing endlessly across the camp.

"THIS IS AN ILLEGAL ENCAMPMENT," it said, in bazaar Arabic. "ALL PERSONNEL IN THE ENCAMPMENT WILL ASSEMBLE ON OPEN GROUND AND SURRENDER TO THE PARK WARDENS IN AN ORDERLY FASHION. ANY PERSONS CARRYING WEAPONS WILL BE PRESUMED TO BE RESISTING ARREST AND WILL BE DEALT WITH ACCORDINGLY. ANY VEHICLE ATTEMPTING TO LEAVE THE ENCAMPMENT WILL BE DESTROYED. YOU HAVE FIVE MINUTES TO COMPLY."

The announcement repeated itself: first in the fluting language of the *firija*, then in Miami Spanish, then as a series of projected alien glyphs, logograms and semagrams. Then the Arabic started again.

"Fuck your mother," said Valadez grimly.

All around Bianca, poachers were gathering weapons. In the back of the room, the *firija* were having what looked like an argument, arms waving, voices raised in a hooting, atonal cacophony.

"*What do we do?*" Fry shouted, over the wardens' announcement.

"Get out of here," said Valadez.

"Make fight!" said Ismaíl, turning several eyes from the *firija* discussion.

"Isn't that *resisting arrest?*" asked Bianca.

Valadez laughed harshly. "Not shooting back isn't going to save you," he said. "The wardens aren't the Phenomenological Service. They're not civilized Caliphate cops. *Killed while resisting arrest* is what they're all about. Believe me—I used to be one."

Taking a surprisingly small gun from inside his jacket, he kicked open the door and was gone.

Around the *Lupita Jeréz* was a milling knot of people, human and otherwise, some hurrying to finish the loading, others simply fighting to get aboard.

Something large and dark, and fast, passed over the camp, and there was a white flash from the cargo-lifter, and screams.

In the wake of the dark thing came a sudden sensation of heaviness, as if the flank of Encantada were the deck of a ship riding a rogue wave, leaping up beneath Bianca's feet. Her knees buckled and she was thrown to the ground, pressed into the grass by twice, three times her normal weight.

The feeling passed as quickly as the wardens' dark vehicle, and Ismaíl, whose walker had kept its footing, helped Bianca up.

"What was *that*?" Bianca demanded, bruises making her wince as she tried to brush the dirt and grass from her skirts.

"Antigravity ship," Ismaíl said. "Same principle like starship wave propagation drive."

"*Antigravity*?" Bianca stared after the ship, but it was already gone, over Encantada's dorsal ridge. "If you *coños* have antigravity, then why in God's name have we been sitting here playing with catapults and balloons?"

"Make very expensive," said Ismaíl. "Minus two suns exotic mass, same like starship." The *firija* waved two of its free eyes. "Why do? Plenty got cheap way to fly."

Bianca realized that despite the remarks Valadez had made on the poverty of Sky, she had been thinking of all *extrañados* and aliens—with their ships and machines, their familiar way with sciences that in Rio Pícaro were barely more than a whisper of forbidden things hidden behind the walls of the rich *moros'* palaces—as wealthy, and powerful, and free. Now, feeling like a fool for not having understood sooner, she realized that between the power of the Consilium and people like Valadez there was a gap as wide as, if not wider than, the gap between those rich *moros* and the most petty Ali Baba in the back streets of Punta Aguila.

She glanced toward the airfield. Aerial tugs were lifting off; anemopters were blurring into motion. But as she watched, one of the tugs opened up into a ball of green fire. An anemopter made it as far as the killing ground before being hit by something that made its static fields crawl briefly with purple lightnings and then collapse, as the craft's material body crashed down in an explosion of earth.

And all the while the wardens' recorded voice was everywhere and nowhere, repeating its list of instructions and demands.

"Not any more, we don't," Bianca said to Ismaíl. "We'd better run."

The *firija* raised its gun. "First got kill prisoner."

"*What?*"

But Ismaíl was already moving, the mechanical legs of the walker sure-footed on the broken ground, taking long, swift strides, no longer comical but frighteningly full of purpose.

Bianca struggled after the *firija*, but quickly fell behind. The surface of the killing ground was rutted and scarred, torn by the earth-moving equipment used to push the offal of the gutted *zaratanes* over the edge. Bianca supposed grasses had covered it once, but now there was only mud and old blood. Only the certainty that going back would be as bad as going forward kept Bianca moving, slipping and stumbling in reeking muck that was sometimes ankle-deep.

By the time she got to Dinh's bungalow, Ismaíl was already gone. The door was ajar.

Maybe the wardens rescued her, Bianca thought; but she couldn't make herself believe it.

She went inside, moving slowly.

"Edith?"

No answer; not that Bianca had really expected any.

She found her in the kitchen, face down, feet toward the door as if she had been shot while trying to run, or hide. From three meters away Bianca could see the neat, black, fist-sized hole in the small of Dinh's back. She felt no need to get closer.

Fry's pocket system was on the floor in the living room, as Bianca had known it would be.

"You should have waited," Bianca said to the empty room. "You should have trusted me."

She found her valise in Dinh's bedroom, and emptied the contents onto the bed. Dinh did not seem to have touched any of them.

Bianca's eyes stung with tears. She glanced again at Fry's system. He'd left it on purpose, Bianca realized; she'd underestimated him. Perhaps he had been a better person than she herself, all along.

She looked one more time at the body lying on the kitchen floor.

"No, you shouldn't," she said then. "You shouldn't have trusted me at all."

Then she went back to her own bungalow and took the package out from under the bed.

9. FINISTERRA

A hundred meters, two hundred, five hundred—Bianca falls, the wind whipping at her clothes, and the hanging vegetation that covers Encantada's flanks is a green-brown blur, going gray as it thins, as the *zaratán*'s body curves away from her. She blinks away the tears brought on by the rushing wind, and tries to focus on the monitor panel of the harness. The wind speed indicator is the only one that makes sense; the others—altitude, attitude, rate of descent—are cycling through nonsense in three languages, baffled by the instruments' inability to find solid ground anywhere below.

Then Bianca falls out of Encantada's shadow into the sun, and before she can consciously form the thought her hand has grasped the emergency handle of the harness and pulled, convulsively; and the glassy fabric of the paraballoon is billowing out above her, rippling like water, and the harness is tugging at her, gently but firmly, smart threads reeling themselves quickly out and then slowly in again on their tiny spinnerets.

After a moment, she catches her breath. She is no longer falling, but flying.

She wipes the tears from her eyes. To the west, the slopes of Finisterra are bright and impossibly detailed in the low-angle sunlight, a million trees casting a million tiny shadows through the morning's rapidly dissipating mist.

She looks up, out through the nearly invisible curve of the paraballoon, and sees that Encantada is burning. She watches it for a long time.

The air grows warmer, and more damp, too. With a start, Bianca realizes she is falling below Finisterra's edge. When she designed the paraballoon, Bianca intended for Dinh to fall as far as she safely could, dropping deep into Sky's atmosphere before firing up the reverse Maxwell pumps, to heat the air in the balloon and lift her back to Finisterra; but it does not look as if there is any danger of pursuit now, from either the poachers or the wardens. Bianca starts the pumps, and the paraballoon slows, then begins to ascend.

As the prevailing wind carries her inland, over a riot of tropical green, and in the distance Bianca sees the smoke rising from the chimneys of Ciudad Perdida, Bianca glances up again at the burning shape of Encantada, and wonders whether she'll ever know if Valadez was telling the truth.

Abruptly the jungle below her opens up, and Bianca is flying over cultivated fields, and people are looking up at her in wonder.

Bianca looks out into the eastern sky, dotted with distant *zaratanes*. There is a vision in her mind, a vision that she thinks maybe Edith Dinh saw: the skies of Sky more crowded than the skies over Rio Pícaro, Septentrionalis Archipelago alive with the bright shapes of dirigibles and gliders, those nameless *zaratanes* out there no longer uncharted shoals but comforting and familiar landmarks.

She cuts the power to the pumps and opens the parachute valve at the top of the balloon. This isn't what she wanted, when she set out from home; but she is still a Nazario, and still an engineer. As she drops, children are already running toward her across the field.

A small miracle, but perhaps it is enough.

the illustrated Biography of Lord Grimm

DARYL GREGORY

Daryl Gregory's latest work includes the novel Spoonbenders *and the novella* We Are All Completely Fine, *which won the World Fantasy and Shirley Jackson awards. His five other novels include the hard SF book* Afterparty *and the zombie tale* Raising Stony Mayhall. *His stories are collected in* Unpossible and Other Stories.*

Here he takes us to an embattled country where a strange, almost surreal war is being fought—one, however, with very real consequences for the people who live there.

T he 22nd Invasion of Trovenia began with a streak of scarlet against a gray sky fast as the flick of a paintbrush. The red blur zipped across the length of the island, moving west to east, and shot out to sea. The sonic boom a moment later scattered the birds that wheeled above the fish processing plant and sent them squealing and plummeting.

Elena said, "Was that—it was, wasn't it?"

"You've never seen a U-Man, Elena?" Jürgo said.

"Not in person." At nineteen, Elena Pendareva was the youngest of the crew by at least two decades, and the only female. She and the other five members of the heavy plate-welding unit were perched 110 meters in the air, taking their lunch upon the great steel shoulder of the Slaybot Prime. The giant robot, latest in a long series of ultimate weapons, was unfinished, its unpainted skin speckled with bird shit, its chest turrets empty, the open dome of its head covered only by a tarp.

It had been Jürgo's idea to ride up the gantry for lunch. They had plenty of time: for the fifth day in a row, steel plate for the Slaybot's skin had failed to arrive from the foundry, and the welding crew had nothing to do but clean their equipment and play cards until the guards let them go home.

It was a good day for a picnic. An unseasonably warm spring wind blew in from the docks, carrying the smell of the sea only slightly tainted by odors of diesel fuel and fish guts. From the giant's shoulder the crew looked down on the entire capital, from the port and industrial sector below them, to the old city in the west and the rows of gray apartment buildings rising up beyond. The only structures higher than their perch were Castle Grimm's black spires, carved out of the sides of Mount Kriegstahl, and the peak of the mountain itself.

"You know what you must do, Elena," Verner said with mock sincerity. He was the oldest in the group, a veteran mechaneer whose body was more metal than flesh. "Your first übermensch, you must make a wish."

Elena said, "Is 'Oh shit,' a wish?"

Verner pivoted on his rubber-tipped stump to follow her gaze. The figure in red had turned about over the eastern sea, and was streaking back toward the island. Sunlight glinted on something long and metallic in its hands.

The UM dove straight toward them.

There was nowhere to hide. The crew sat on a naked shelf of metal between the gantry and the sheer profile of the robot's head. Elena threw herself flat and spread her arms on the metal surface, willing herself to stick.

Nobody else moved. Maybe because they were old men, or maybe because they were all veterans, former zoomandos and mechaneers and castle guards. They'd seen dozens of U-Men, fought them even. Elena didn't know if they were unafraid or simply too old to care much for their skin.

The UM shot past with a whoosh, making the steel shiver beneath her. She looked up in time to take in a flash of metal, a crimson cape, black boots—and then the figure crashed *through* the wall of Castle Grimm. Masonry and dust exploded into the air.

"Lunch break," Jürgo said in his Estonian accent, "is over."

Toolboxes slammed, paper sacks took to the wind. Elena got to her feet. Jürgo picked up his lunch pail with one clawed foot, spread his patchy, soot-stained wings, and leaned over the side, considering. His arms and neck were skinny as always, but in the past few years he'd grown a beer gut.

Elena said, "Jürgo, can you still fly?"

"Of course," he said. He hooked his pail to his belt and backed away from the edge. "However, I don't believe I'm authorized for this air space."

The rest of the crew had already crowded into the gantry elevator. Elena and Jürgo pressed inside and the cage began to slowly descend, rattling and shrieking.

"What's it about this time, you think?" Verner said, clockwork lungs wheezing. "Old Rivet Head kidnap one of their women?" Only the oldest veterans could get away with insulting Lord Grimm in mixed company. Verner had survived at least four invasions that she knew of. His loyalty to Trovenia was assumed to go beyond patriotism into something like ownership.

Guntis, a gray, pebble-skinned amphibian of Latvian descent, said, "I fought this girlie with a sword once, Energy Lady—"

"*Power Woman*," Elena said in English. She'd read the *Illustrated Biography of Lord Grimm* to her little brother dozens of times before he learned to read it himself. The Lord's most significant adversaries were all listed in the appendix, in multiple languages.

"That's the one, *Par-wer Woh-man*," Guntis said, imitating her. "She had enormous—"

"Abilities," Jürgo said pointedly. Jürgo had been a friend of Elena's father, and often played the protective uncle.

"I think he meant to say 'tits,'" Elena said. Several of the men laughed.

"No! Jürgo is right," Guntis said. "They were more than breasts. They had *abilities*. I think one of them spoke to me."

The elevator clanged down on the concrete pad and the crew followed Jürgo into the long shed of the 3000 line. The factory floor was emptying. Workers pulled on coats, joking and laughing as if it were a holiday.

Jürgo pulled aside a man and asked him what was going on. "The guards have run away!" the man said happily. "Off to fight the übermensch!"

"So what's it going to be, boss?" Guntis said. "Stay or go?"

Jürgo scratched at the cement floor, thinking. Half-assembled Slaybot 3000s, five-meter-tall cousins to the colossal Prime, dangled from hooks all along the assembly line, wires spilling from their chests, legs missing. The factory was well behind its quota for the month. As well as for the quarter, year, and five-year mark. Circuit boards and batteries were in particularly short supply, but tools and equipment vanished daily. Especially scarce were acetylene tanks, a home-heating accessory for the very cold, the very stupid, or both.

Jürgo finally shook his feathered head and said, "Nothing we can do here. Let's go home and hide under our beds."

"And in our bottles," Verner said.

Elena waved good-bye and walked toward the women's changing rooms to empty her locker.

A block from her apartment she heard Mr. Bojars singing out, "Guh-RATE day for sausa-JEZ! Izza GREAT day for SAW-sages!" The mechaneer veteran was parked at his permanent spot at the corner of Glorious Victory Street and Infinite Progress Avenue, in the shadow of the statue of Grimm Triumphant. He saw her crossing the intersection and shouted, "My beautiful Elena! A fat bratwurst to go with that bread, maybe. Perfect for a celebration!"

"No thank you, Mr. Bojars." She hoisted the bag of groceries onto her hip and shuffled the welder's helmet to her other arm. "You know we've been invaded, don't you?"

The man laughed heartily. "The trap is sprung! The crab is in the basket!" He wore the same clothes he wore every day, a black nylon ski hat and a green, grease-stained parka decorated at the breast with three medals from his years in the motorized cavalry. The coat hung down to cover where his flesh ended and his motorcycle body began.

"Don't you worry about Lord Grimm," he said. "He can handle any American muscle-head stupid enough to enter his lair. Especially the Red Meteor."

"It was Most Excellent Man," Elena said, using the Trovenian translation of his name. "I saw the Staff of Mightiness in his hand, or whatever he calls it."

"Even better! The man's an idiot. A U-Moron."

"He's defeated Lord Grimm several times," Elena said. "So I hear."

"And Lord Grimm has been declared dead a dozen times! You can't believe the underground newspapers, Elena. You're not reading that trash are you?"

"You know I'm not political, Mr. Bojars."

"Good for you. This Excellent Man, let me tell you something about—yes sir? Great day for a sausage." He turned his attention to the customer and Elena quickly wished him luck and slipped away before he could begin another story.

The small lobby of her apartment building smelled like burnt plastic and cooking grease. She climbed the cement stairs to the third floor. As usual the door to her apartment was wide open, as was the door to Mr. Fishman's apartment across the hall. Staticky television laughter and applause carried down the hallway: It sounded like *Mr. Sascha's Celebrity Polka Fun-Time*. Not even an invasion could pre-empt Mr. Sascha.

She knocked on the frame of his door. "Mr. Fishman," she called loudly. He'd never revealed his real name. "Mr. Fishman, would you like to come to dinner tonight?"

There was no answer except for the blast of the television. She walked into the dim hallway and leaned around the corner. The living room was dark except for the glow of the TV. The little set was propped up on a wooden chair at the edge of a large cast iron bathtub, the light from its screen reflecting off the smooth surface of the water. "Mr. Fishman? Did you hear me?" She walked across the room, shoes crinkling on the plastic tarp that covered the floor, and switched off the TV.

The surface of the water shimmied. A lumpy head rose up out of the water, followed by a pair of dark eyes, a flap of nose, and a wide carp mouth.

"I was watching that," the zooman said.

"Some day you're going to pull that thing into the tub and electrocute yourself," Elena said.

He exhaled, making a rude noise through rubbery lips.

"We're having dinner," Elena said. She turned on a lamp. Long ago Mr. Fishman had pushed all the furniture to the edge of the room to make room for his easels. She didn't see any new canvases upon them, but there was an empty liquor bottle on the floor next to the tub. "Would you like to join us?"

He eyed the bag in her arms. "That wouldn't be, umm, fresh catch?"

"It is, as a matter of fact."

"I suppose I could stop by." His head sank below the surface.

In Elena's own apartment, Grandmother Zita smoked and rocked in front of the window, while Mattias, nine years old, sat at the table with his shoe box of colored pencils and several gray pages crammed with drawings. "Elena, did you hear?" Matti asked. "A U-Man flew over the island! They canceled school!"

"It's nothing to be happy about," Elena said. She rubbed the top of her brother's head. The page showed a robot of Matti's own design marching toward a hyper-muscled man in a red cape. In the background was a huge, lumpy monster with triangle eyes—an escaped MoG, she supposed.

"The last time the U-men came," Grandmother Zita said, "more than robots lost their heads. This family knows that better than most. When your mother—"

"Let's not talk politics, Grandmother." She kissed the old woman on the cheek, then reached past her to crank open the window—she'd told the woman to let in some air when she smoked in front of Matti, to no avail. Outside, sirens wailed.

Elena had been only eleven years old during the last invasion. She'd slept through most of it, and when she woke to sirens that morning the apartment was cold and the lights didn't work. Her parents were government geneticists—there was no other kind—and often were called away at odd hours. Her mother had left her a note asking her to feed Baby Matti and please stay indoors. Elena made oatmeal, the first of many breakfasts she would make for her little brother. Only after her parents failed to come home did she realize that the note was a kind of battlefield promotion to adulthood: impossible to refuse because there was no one left to accept her refusal.

Mr. Fishman, in his blue bathrobe and striped pajama pants, arrived a half hour later, his great webbed feet slapping the floor. He sat at the table and argued with Grandmother Zita about which of the twenty-one previous invasions was most violent. There was a time in the 1960s and seventies when their little country seemed to be under attack every other month. Matti listened raptly.

Elena had just brought the fried whitefish to the table when the thumping march playing on the radio suddenly cut off. An announcer said, "Please stand by for an important message from His Royal Majesty, the Guardian of our Shores, the Scourge of Fascism, Professor General of the Royal Academy of Sciences, the Savior of Trovenia—"

Mr. Fishman pointed at Matti. "Boy, get my television!" Matti dashed to the man's apartment and Elena cleared a spot on the table.

After Mr. Fishman fiddled with the antenna the screen suddenly cleared, showing a large room decorated in Early 1400s: stone floors, flickering torches, and dulled tapestries on the walls. The only piece of furniture was a huge oaken chair reinforced at the joints with plates and rivets.

A figure appeared at the far end of the room and strode toward the camera.

"He's still alive then," Grandmother said. Lord Grimm didn't appear on live television more than once or twice a year.

Matti said, "Oh, look at him."

Lord Grimm wore the traditional black and green cape of Trovenian nobility, which contrasted nicely with the polished suit of armor. His faceplate, hawk-nosed and heavily riveted, suggested simultaneously the prow of a battleship and the beak of the Baltic albatross, the Trovenian national bird.

Elena had to admit he cut a dramatic figure. She almost felt sorry for people in other countries whose leaders all looked like postal inspectors. You could no more imagine those timid, pinch-faced bureaucrats leading troops into battle than you could imagine Lord Grimm ice skating.

"Sons and daughters of Trovenia," the leader intoned. His deep voice was charged with metallic echoes. "We have been invaded."

"We knew that already," Grandmother said, and Mr. Fishman shushed her.

"Once again, an American superpower has violated our sovereignty. With typical, misguided arrogance, a so-called übermensch has trespassed upon our borders, destroy our property . . ." The litany of crimes went on for some time.

"Look! The U-Man!" Matti said.

On screen, castle guards carried in a red-clad figure and dumped him in the huge chair. His head lolled. Lord Grimm lifted the prisoner's chin to show his bloody face to the camera. One eye was half open, the other swelled shut. "As you can see, he is completely powerless."

Mr. Fishman grunted in disappointment.

"What?" Matti asked.

"Again with the captives, and the taunting," Grandmother said.

"Why not? They invaded us!"

Mr. Fishman grimaced, and his gills flapped shut.

"If Lord Grimm simply beat up Most Excellent Man and sent him packing, that would be one thing," Grandmother said. "Or even if he just promised to stop doing what he was doing for a couple of months until they forgot about him, then—"

"Then we'd all go back to our business," Mr. Fishman said.

Grandmother said, "But no, he's got to keep him captive. Now it's going to be just like 1972."

"And seventy-five," Mr. Fishman said. He sawed into his whitefish. "And eighty-three."

Elena snapped off the television. "Matti, go pack your school bag with clothes. Now."

"What? Why?"

"We're spending the night in the basement. You too, Grandmother."

"But I haven't finished my supper!"

"I'll wrap it up for you. Mr. Fishman, I can help you down the stairs if you like."

"Pah," he said. "I'm going back to bed. Wake me when the war's over."

A dozen or so residents of the building had gotten the same idea. For several hours the group sat on boxes and old furniture in the damp basement under stuttering fluorescent lights, listening to the distant roar of jets, the rumble of mechaneer tanks, and the bass-drum stomps of Slaybot 3000s marching into position.

Grandmother Zita had claimed the best seat in the room, a ripped vinyl armchair. Matti had fallen asleep across her lap, still clutching the *Illustrated Biography of Lord Grimm*. The boy was so comfortable with her. Zita wasn't even a relative, but she'd watched over the boy since he was a toddler and so became his grandmother—another wartime employment opportunity. Elena slipped the book from under Matti's arms and bent to put it into his school bag.

Zita lit another cigarette. "How do you suppose it really started?" she said.

"What, the war?" Elena asked.

"No, the first time." She nodded at Matti's book. "Hating the Americans, okay, no problem. But why the scary mask, the cape?"

Elena pretended to sort out the contents of the bag.

"What possesses a person to do that?" Zita said, undeterred. "Wake up one day and say, Today I will put a bucket over my head. Today I declare war on all U-Men. Today I become, what's the English . . ."

"Grandmother, please," Elena said, keeping her voice low.

"A *supervillain*," Zita said.

A couple of the nearest people looked away in embarrassment. Mr. Rimkis, an old man from the fourth floor, glared at Grandmother down the length of his gray-bristled snout. He was a veteran with one long tusk and the other snapped off at the base. He claimed to have suffered the injury fighting the U-Men, though others said he'd lost the tusk in combat with vodka and gravity: The Battle of the Pub Stairs.

"*He* is the hero," Mr. Rimkis said. "Not these imperialists in long underwear. They invaded his country, attacked his family, maimed him and left him with—"

"Oh please," Grandmother said. "Every villain believes himself to be a hero."

The last few words were nearly drowned out by the sudden wail of an air raid siren. Matti jerked awake and Zita automatically put a hand to his sweat-dampened forehead. The residents stared up at the ceiling. Soon there was a chorus of sirens.

They've come, Elena thought, as everyone knew they would, to rescue their comrade.

From somewhere in the distance came a steady *thump*, *thump* that vibrated the ground and made the basement's bare cinderblock walls chuff dust into the air. Each explosion seemed louder and closer. Between the explosions, slaybot auto cannons whined and chattered.

Someone said, "Everybody just remain calm—"

The floor seemed to jump beneath their feet. Elena lost her balance and smacked into the cement on her side. At the same moment she was deafened by a noise louder than her ears could process.

The lights had gone out. Elena rolled over, eyes straining, but she couldn't make out Grandmother or Matti or anyone. She shouted but barely heard her own voice above the ringing in her ears.

Someone behind her switched on an electric torch and flicked it around the room. Most of the basement seemed to have filled with rubble.

Elena crawled toward where she thought Grandmother's chair had been and was stopped by a pile of cement and splintered wood. She called Matti's name and began to push the debris out of the way.

Someone grabbed her foot, and then Matti fell into her, hugged her fiercely. Somehow he'd been thrown behind her, over her. She called for a light, but the torch was aimed now at a pair of men attempting to clear the stairway. Elena took Matti's hand and led him cautiously toward the light. Pebbles fell on them; the building seemed to shift and groan. Somewhere a woman cried out, her voice muffled.

"Grandmother Zita," Matti said.

Elena was grateful that she could hear him. "I'll come back for Grandmother," she said, though she didn't know for sure if it had been Zita's voice. "First you."

The two men had cleared a passage to the outside. One of them boosted the other to where he could crawl out. The freed man then reached back and Elena lifted Matti to him. The boy's jacket snagged on a length of rebar, and the boy yelped. After what seemed like minutes of tugging and shouting the coat finally ripped free.

"Stay there, Mattias!" Elena called. "Don't move!" She turned to assist the next person in line to climb out, an old woman from the sixth floor. She carried an enormous wicker basket which she refused to relinquish. Elena promised repeatedly that the basket would be the first thing to come out after her. The others in the basement began to shout at the old woman, which only made her grip the handle more fiercely. Elena was considering prying her fingers from it when a yellow flash illuminated the passage. People outside screamed.

Elena scrambled up and out without being conscious of how she managed it. The streetlights had gone out but the gray sky flickered with strange lights. A small crowd of dazed citizens sat or sprawled across the rubble-strewn street, as if a bomb had gone off. The man who'd pulled Matti out of the basement sat on the ground, holding his hands to his face and moaning.

The sky was full of flying men.

Searchlights panned from a dozen points around the city, and clouds pulsed with exotic energies. In that spasmodic light dozens of tiny figures darted: caped invaders, squadrons of Royal Air Dragoons riding pinpricks of fire, winged zoo-mandos, glowing U-Men leaving iridescent fairy trails. Beams of energy flicked from horizon to horizon; soldiers ignited and dropped like dollops of burning wax.

Elena looked around wildly for her brother. Rubble was everywhere. The front of her apartment building had been sheared off, exposing bedrooms and bathrooms. Protruding girders bent toward the ground like tongues.

Finally she saw the boy. He sat on the ground, staring at the sky. Elena ran to him, calling his name. He looked in her direction. His eyes were wide, unseeing.

She knelt down in front of him.

"I looked straight at him," Matti said. "He flew right over our heads. He was so bright. So bright."

There was something wrong with Matti's face. In the inconstant light she could only tell that his skin was darker than it should have been.

"Take my hand," Elena said. "Can you stand up? Good. Good. How do you feel?"

"My face feels hot," he said. Then, "Is Grandmother out yet?"

Elena didn't answer. She led him around the piles of debris. Once she had to yank him sideways and he yelped. "Something in our way," she said. A half-buried figure lay with one arm and one leg jutting into the street. The body would have been unrecognizable if not for the blue-striped pajamas and the webbing between the toes of the bare foot.

Matti wrenched his hand from her grip. "Where are we going? You have to tell me where we're going."

She had no idea. She'd thought they'd be safe in the basement. She'd thought it would be like the invasions everyone talked about, a handful of U-Men—a *super team*—storming the castle. No one told her there could be an army of them. The entire city had become the battleground.

"Out of the city," she said. "Into the country."

"But Grandmother—"

"I promise I'll come back for Grandmother Zita," she said.

"And my book," he said. "It's still in the basement."

All along Infinite Progress Avenue, families spilled out of buildings carrying bundles of clothes and plastic jugs, pushing wheelchairs and shopping carts loaded with canned food, TV sets, photo albums. Elena grabbed tight to Matti's arm and joined the exodus north.

After an hour they'd covered only ten blocks. The street had narrowed as they left the residential district, condensing the stream of people into a herd, then a single shuffling animal. Explosions and gunfire continued to sound from behind them and the sky still flashed with parti-colored lightning, but hardly anyone glanced back.

The surrounding bodies provided Elena and Matti with some protection against the cold, though frigid channels of night air randomly opened through the crowd. Matti's vision still hadn't returned; he saw nothing but the yellow light of the U-Man. He told her his skin still felt hot, but he trembled as if he were cold. Once he stopped suddenly and threw up into the street. The crowd behind bumped into them, forcing them to keep moving.

One of their fellow refugees gave Matti a blanket. He pulled it onto his shoulders like a cape but it kept slipping as he walked, tripping him up. The boy hadn't cried since they'd started walking, hadn't complained—he'd even stopped asking about Grandmother Zita—but Elena still couldn't stop herself from being annoyed at him. He stumbled again and she yanked the blanket from him. "For God's sake, Mattias," she said. "If you can't hold onto it—" She drew up short. The black-coated women in front of them had suddenly stopped.

Shouts went up from somewhere ahead, and then the crowd surged backward. Elena recognized the escalating whine of an auto-cannon coming up to speed.

Elena pulled Matti up onto her chest and he yelped in surprise or pain. The boy was heavy and awkward; she locked her hands under his butt and shoved toward the crowd's edge, aiming for the mouth of an alley. The crowd buffeted her, knocked her off course. She came up hard against the plate glass window of a shop.

A Slaybot 3000 lumbered through the crowd, knocking people aside. Its gun arm, a huge thing like a barrel of steel pipes, jerked from figure to figure, targeting automatically. A uniformed technician sat in the jumpseat on the robot's back, gesturing frantically and shouting, "Out of the way! Out of the way!" It was impossible to tell whether he'd lost control or was deliberately marching through the crowd.

The mass of figures had almost certainly overwhelmed the robot's vision and recognition processors. The 3000 model, like its predecessors, had difficulty tell-ing friend from foe even in the spare environment of the factory QA room.

The gun arm pivoted toward her: six black mouths. Then the carousel began to spin and the six barrels blurred, became one vast maw.

Elena felt her gut go cold. She would have sunk to the ground—she wanted desperately to disappear—but the mob held her upright, pinned. She twisted to place at least part of her body between the robot and Matti. The glass at her shoul-der trembled, began to bow.

For a moment she saw both sides of the glass. Inside the dimly lit shop were two rows of blank white faces, a choir of eyeless women regarding her. And in the window's reflection she saw her own face, and above that, a streak of light like a falling star. The UM flew toward them from the west, moving incredibly fast.

The robot's gun fired even as it flicked upward to acquire the new target.

The glass shattered. The mass of people on the street beside her seemed to disintegrate into blood and cloth tatters. A moment later she registered the sound of the gun, a thunderous *ba-rap*! The crowd pulsed away from her, releasing its pressure, and she collapsed to the ground.

The slaybot broke into a clumsy stomping run, its gun ripping at the air.

Matti had rolled away from her. Elena touched his shoulder, turned him over. His eyes were open, but unmoving, glassy.

The air seemed to freeze. She couldn't breathe, couldn't move her hand from him.

He blinked. Then he began to scream.

Elena got to her knees. Her left hand was bloody and freckled with glass; her fingers glistened. Each movement triggered the prick of a thousand tiny needles. Matti screamed and screamed.

"It's okay, it's okay," she said. "I'm right here."

She talked to him for almost a minute before he calmed down enough to hear her and stop screaming.

The window was gone, the shop door blown open. The window case was filled with foam heads on posts, some with wigs askew, others tipped over and bald. She got Matti to take her hand—her good hand—and led him through the doorway. She was thankful that he could not see the things they stepped over.

Inside the scene was remarkably similar. Arms and legs of all sizes hung from straps on the walls. Trays of dentures sat out on the countertops. A score of heads sported hairstyles old-fashioned even by Trovenian standards. There were several such shops across the city. Decent business in a land of amputees.

Elena's face had begun to burn. She walked Matti through the dark, kicking aside prosthetic limbs, and found a tiny bathroom at the back of the shop. She pulled on the chain to the fluorescent light and was surprised when it flickered to life.

This was her first good look at Matti's face. The skin was bright red, puffy and raw looking—a second-degree burn at least.

She guided the boy to the sink and helped him drink from the tap. It was the only thing she could think of to do for him. Then she helped him sit on the floor just outside the bathroom door.

She could no longer avoid looking in the mirror.

The shattering glass had turned half of her face into a speckled red mask. She ran her hands under the water, not daring to scrub, and then splashed water on her face. She dabbed at her cheek and jaw with the tail of her shirt but the blood continued to weep through a peppering of cuts. She looked like a cartoon in Matti's Lord Grimm book, the coloring accomplished by tiny dots.

She reached into her jacket and took out the leather work gloves she'd stuffed there when she emptied her locker. She pulled one onto her wounded hand, stifling the urge to shout.

"Hello?" Matti said.

She turned, alarmed. Matti wasn't talking to her. His face was turned toward the hallway.

Elena stepped out. A few feet away were the base of a set of stairs that led up into the back of the building. A man stood at the first landing, pointing an ancient rifle at the boy. His jaw was flesh-toned plastic, held in place by an arrangement of leather straps and mechanical springs. A woman with outrageously golden hair stood higher on the stairs, leaning around the corner to look over the man's shoulder.

The man's jaw clacked and he gestured with the gun. "Go. Get along," he said. The syllables were distorted.

"They're hurt," the wigged woman said.

The man did not quite shake his head. Of course they're hurt, he seemed to say. Everyone's hurt. It's the national condition.

"We didn't mean to break in," Elena said. She held up her hands. "We're going." She glanced back into the showroom. Outside the smashed window, the street was still packed, and no one seemed to be moving.

"The bridge is out," the man said. He meant the Prince's Bridge, the only paved bridge that crossed the river. No wonder then that the crowd was moving so slowly.

"They're taking the wounded to the mill," the woman said. "Then trying to get them out of the city by the foot bridges."

"What mill?" Elena asked.

The wigged woman wouldn't take them herself, but she gave directions. "Go out the back," she said.

The millrace had dried out and the mill had been abandoned fifty years ago, but its musty, barn-like interior still smelled of grain. Its rooms were already crowded with injured soldiers and citizens.

Elena found a spot for Matti on a bench inside the building and told him not to move. She went from room to room asking if anyone had aspirin, antibiotic cream, anything to help the boy. She soon stopped asking. There didn't seem to be any doctors or nurses at the mill, only wounded people helping the more severely wounded, and no medicines to be found. This wasn't a medical clinic, or even a triage center. It was a way station.

She came back to find that Matti had fallen asleep on the gray-furred shoulder of a veteran zoomando. She told the man that if the boy woke up she would be outside helping unload the wounded. Every few minutes another farm truck pulled up and bleeding men and women stepped out or were passed down on litters. The emptied trucks rumbled south back into the heart city.

The conversation in the mill traded in rumor and wild speculation. But what report could be disbelieved when it came to the U-Men? Fifty of them were attacking, or a hundred. Lord Grimm was both dead and still fighting on the battlements. The MoGs had escaped from the mines in the confusion.

Like everyone else Elena quickly grew deaf to gunfire, explosions, crackling energy beams. Only when something erupted particularly close—a nearby building bursting into flame, or a terrordactyl careening out of control overhead—did the workers look up or pause in their conversation.

At some point a woman in the red smock of the Gene Corps noticed that Elena's cheek had started bleeding again. "It's a wonder you didn't lose an eye," the scientist said, and gave her a wad of torn-up cloth to press to her face. "You need to get that cleaned up or it will scar."

Elena thanked her curtly and walked outside. The air was cold but felt good on her skin.

She was still dabbing at her face when she heard the sputter of engines. An old mechaneer cavalryman, painted head to wheels in mud, rolled into the north end of the yard, followed by two of his wheeled brethren. Each of them was towing a narrow cart padded with blankets.

The lead mechaneer didn't notice Elena at first, or perhaps noticed her but didn't recognize her. He suddenly said, "My beautiful Elena!" and puttered forward, dragging the squeaking cart after him. He put on a smile but couldn't hold it.

"Not so beautiful, Mr. Bojars."

The old man surveyed her face with alarm. "But you are all right?" he asked. "Is Mattias—?"

"I'm fine. Matti is inside. He's sick. I think he . . . ." She shook her head. "I see you've lost your sausage oven."

"A temporary substitution only, my dear." The surviving members of his old unit had reunited, he told her matter-of-factly, to do what they could. In the hours since the Prince's Bridge had been knocked out they'd been ferrying wounded across the river. A field hospital had been set up at the northern barracks of the city guard. The only ways across the river were the footbridges and a few muddy low spots in the river. "We have no weapons," Mr. Bojars said, "but we can still drive like demons."

Volunteers were already carrying out the people chosen to evacuate next, four men and two women who seemed barely alive. Each cart could carry only two persons at a time, laid head to foot. Elena helped secure them.

"Mr. Bojars, does the hospital have anything for radiation poisoning?"

"Radiation?" He looked shocked. "I don't know, I suppose . . .

One of the mechaneers waved to Mr. Bojars, and the two-wheeled men began to roll out.

Elena said, "Mr. Bojars—"

"Get him," he replied.

Elena ran into mill, dodging pallets and bodies. She scooped up the sleeping boy, ignoring the pain in her hand, and carried him back outside. She could feel his body trembling in her arms.

"I can't find my book," Matti said. He sounded feverish. "I think I lost it."

"Matti, you're going with Mr. Bojars," Elena said. "He's going to take you someplace safe."

He seemed to wake up. He looked around, but it was obvious he still couldn't see. "Elena, no! We have to get Grandmother!"

"Matti, listen to me. You're going across the river to the hospital. They have medicine. In the morning I'll come get you."

"She's still in the basement. She's still there. You promised you would—"

"Yes, I promise!" Elena said. "Now go with Mr. Bojars."

"Matti, my boy, we shall have such a ride!" the mechaneer said with forced good humor. He opened his big green parka and held out his arms.

Matti released his grip on Elena. Mr. Bojars set the boy on the broad gas tank in front of him, then zipped up the jacket so that only Matti's head was visible. "Now we look like a cybernetic kangaroo, hey Mattias?"

"I'll be there in the morning," Elena said. She kissed Matti's forehead, then kissed the old man's cheek. He smelled of grilled onions and diesel. "I can't thank you enough," she said.

Mr. Bojars circled an arm around Matti and revved his engine. "A kiss from you, my dear, is payment enough."

She watched them go. A few minutes later another truck arrived in the yard and she fell in line to help carry in the wounded. When the new arrivals were all inside and the stained litters had all been returned to the truck, Elena stayed out in the yard. The truck drivers, a pair of women in coveralls, leaned against the hood. The truck's two-way radio played ocean noise: whooshing static mixed with high, panicked pleas like the cries of seagulls. The larger of the women took a last drag on her cigarette, tossed it into the yard, and then both of them climbed into the cab. A minute later the vehicle started and began to move.

"Shit," Elena said. She jogged after the truck for a few steps, then broke into a full run. She caught up to it as it reached the road. With her good hand she hauled herself up into the open bed.

The driver slowed and leaned out her window. "We're leaving now!" she shouted. "Going back in!"

"So go!" Elena said.

The driver shook her head. The truck lurched into second gear and rumbled south.

As they rolled into the city proper it was impossible for Elena to tell where they would find the front line of the battle, or if there was a front line at all. Damage seemed to be distributed randomly. The truck would roll through a sleepy side street that was completely untouched, and twenty yards away the buildings would be cracked open, their contents shaken into the street.

The drivers seemed to possess some sixth sense for knowing where the injured were waiting. The truck would slow and men and women would emerge from the dark and hobble toward the headlights of the truck, or call for a litter. Some people stood at street corners and waved them down as if flagging a bus. Elena helped the drivers lift the wounded into the back, and sometimes had to force them to leave their belongings.

"Small boats," the largest driver said over and over. A Trovenian saying: In a storm, all boats are too small.

Eventually she found herself crouched next to a burned dragoon who was half-welded to his jet pack. She held his hand, thinking that might give him something to feel besides the pain, but he only moaned and muttered to himself, seemingly oblivious to her presence.

The truck slammed to a stop, sending everyone sliding and crashing into each other. Through the slats Elena glimpsed a great slab of blue, some huge, organic shape. A leg. A giant's leg. The U-Man had to be bigger than an apartment building. Gunfire clattered, and a voice like a fog horn shouted something in English.

The truck lurched into reverse, engine whining, and Elena fell forward onto her hands. Someone in the truck bed cried, "Does he see us? Does he see us?"

The truck backed to the intersection and turned hard. The occupants shouted as they collapsed into each other yet again. Half a block more the truck braked to a more gradual stop and the drivers hopped out. "Is everyone okay?" they asked.

The dragoon beside Elena laughed.

She stood up and looked around. They were in the residential district, only a few blocks from her apartment. She made her way to the gate of the truck and hopped down. She said to the driver, "I'm not going back with you."

The woman nodded, not needing or wanting an explanation.

Elena walked slowly between the hulking buildings. The pain in her hand, her face, all seemed to be returning.

She emerged into a large open space. She realized she'd been mistaken about where the truck had stopped—this park was nowhere she recognized. The ground in front of her had been turned to glass.

The sky to the east glowed. For a moment she thought it was another super-powered UM. But no, only the dawn. Below the dark bulk of Mount Kriegstahl stood the familiar silhouette of the Slaybot Prime bolted to its gantry. The air battle had moved there, above the factories and docks. Or maybe no battle at all. There seemed to be only a few flyers in the air now. The planes and TDs had disappeared. Perhaps the only ones left were U-Men.

Power bolts zipped through the air. They were firing at the Prime.

A great metal arm dropped away from its shoulder socket and dangled by thick cables. Another flash of energy severed them. The arm fell away in seeming slow motion, and the sound of the impact reached her a moment later. The übermenschen were carving the damn thing up.

She almost laughed. The Slaybot Prime was as mobile and dangerous as the

Statue of Liberty. Were they actually afraid of the thing? Was that why an army of them had shown up for an ordinary hostage rescue?

My God, she thought, the morons had actually believed Lord Grimm's boasting.

She walked west, and the rising sun turned the glazed surface in front of her into a mirror. She knew now that she wasn't lost. The scorched buildings surrounding the open space were too familiar. But she kept walking. After a while she noticed that the ground was strangely warm beneath her feet. Hot even.

She looked back the way she'd come, then decided the distance was shorter ahead. She was too tired to run outright but managed a shuffling trot. Reckoning by rough triangulation from the nearest buildings she decided she was passing over Mr. Bojars's favorite spot, the corner of Glorious Victory Street and Infinite Progress Avenue. Her own apartment building should have loomed directly in front of her.

After all she'd seen tonight she couldn't doubt that there were beings with the power to melt a city block to slag. But she didn't know what strange ability, or even stranger whim, allowed them to casually trowel it into a quartz skating rink.

She heard another boom behind her. The Slaybot Prime was headless now. The southern gantry peeled away, and then the body itself began to lean. Elena had been inside the thing; the chest assembly alone was as big as a cathedral.

The Slaybot Prime slowly bowed, deeper, deeper, until it tumbled off the pillars of its legs. Dust leaped into the sky where it fell. The tremor moved under Elena, sending cracks snaking across the glass.

The collapse of the Prime seemed to signal the end of the fighting. The sounds of the energy blasts ceased. Figures flew in from all points of the city and coalesced above the industrial sector. In less than a minute there were dozens and dozens of them, small and dark as blackcap geese. Then she realized that the flock of übermenschen was flying toward her.

Elena glanced to her left, then right. She was as exposed as a pea on a plate. The glass plain ended fifty or sixty meters away at a line of rubble. She turned and ran.

She listened to the hiss of breath in her throat and the smack of her heavy boots against the crystalline surface. She was surprised at every moment that she did not crash through.

Elongated shadows shuddered onto the mirrored ground ahead of her. She ran faster, arms swinging. The glass abruptly ended in a jagged lip. She leaped, landed on broken ground, and stumbled onto hands and knees. Finally she looked up.

Racing toward her with the sun behind them, the U-Men were nothing but silhouettes—shapes that suggested capes and helmets; swords, hammers, and staffs; bows and shields. Even the energy beings, clothed in shimmering auras, seemed strangely desaturated by the morning light.

Without looking away from the sky she found a chunk of masonry on the ground in front of her. Then she stood and climbed onto a tilting slab of concrete.

When the mass of U-Men was directly above her she heaved with all her might.

Useless. At its peak the gray chunk fell laughably short of the nearest figure. It clattered to the ground somewhere out of sight.

Elena screamed, tensed for—longing for—a searing blast of light, a thunderbolt. Nothing came. The U-Men vanished over the roof of the next apartment building, heading out to sea.

Weeks after the invasion, the factory remained closed. Workers began to congregate there anyway. Some mornings they pushed around brooms or cleared debris, but mostly they played cards, exchanged stories of the invasion, and speculated on rumors. Lord Grimm had not been seen since the attack. Everyone agreed that the Savior of Trovenia had been dead too many times to doubt his eventual resurrection.

When Elena finally returned, eighteen days after the invasion, she found Verner and Guntis playing chess beside the left boot of the Slaybot Prime. The other huge components of the robot's body were scattered across two miles of the industrial sector like the buildings of a new city.

The men greeted her warmly. Verner, the ancient mechaneer, frankly noted the still-red cuts that cross-hatched the side of her face, but didn't ask how she'd acquired them. If Trovenians told the story of every scar there'd be no end to the talking.

Elena asked about Jürgo and both men frowned. Guntis said that the birdman had taken to the air during the fight. As for the other two members of the heavy plate-welding unit, no news.

"I was sorry to hear about your brother," Verner said.

"Yes," Elena said. "Well."

She walked back to the women's changing rooms, and when she didn't find what she was looking for, visited the men's. One cinderblock wall had caved in, but the lockers still stood in orderly rows. She found the locker bearing Jürgo's name on a duct tape label. The door was padlocked shut. It took her a half hour to find a cutting rig with oxygen and acetylene cylinders that weren't empty, but only minutes to wheel the rig to the changing rooms and burn off the lock.

She pulled open the door. Jürgo's old-fashioned, rectangle-eyed welding helmet hung from a hook, staring at her. She thought of Grandmother Zita. *What possesses a person to put a bucket on their head?*

The inside of the locker door was decorated with a column of faded photographs. In one of them a young Jürgo, naked from the waist up, stared into the camera with a concerned squint. His new wings were unfurled behind him. Elena's mother and father, dressed in their red Gene Corps jackets, stood on either side of him. Elena unpeeled the yellowed tape and put the picture in her breast pocket, then unhooked the helmet and closed the door.

She walked back to the old men, pulling the cart behind her. "Are we working today or what?" she asked.

Guntis looked up from the chess board with amusement in his huge wet eyes. "So you are the boss now, eh, Elena?"

Verner, however, said nothing. He seemed to recognize that she was not quite the person she had been. Damaged components had been stripped away, replaced by cruder, yet sturdier approximations. He was old enough to have seen the process repeated many times.

Elena reached into the pockets of her coat and pulled on her leather work gloves. Then she wheeled the cart over to the toe of the boot and straightened the hoses with a flick of her arm.

"Tell us your orders, Your Highness," Guntis said.

"First we tear apart the weapons," she said. She thumbed the blast trigger and blue flame roared from the nozzle of the cutting torch. "Then we build better ones."

She slid the helmet onto her head, flipped down the mask, and bent to work.

utriusque cosmi

ROBERT CHARLES WILSON

Robert Charles Wilson made his first sale in 1974, to Analog, but little more was heard from him until the late eighties, when he began to publish a string of ingenious and well-crafted novels and stories that have since established him among the top ranks of the writers who came to prominence in the last two decades of the twentieth century. His first novel, A Hidden Place, *appeared in 1986. He won the John W. Campbell Memorial Award for his novel* The Chronoliths, *the Philip K. Dick Award for his novel* Mysterium, *and the Aurora Award for his story "The Perseids." In 2006, he won the Hugo Award for his acclaimed novel* Spin. *His other books include the novels* Memory Wire, Gypsies, The Divide, The Harvest, A Bridge of Years, Darwinia, Blind Lake, Bios, Axis, Julian, Axis, Vortex, *and a collection of his short work,* The Perseids and Other Stories.*

Here he tells the compelling story of a young woman faced with the most significant choice she will ever make in her life—after which, nothing will ever be the same.

Diving back into the universe (now that the universe is a finished object, boxed and ribboned from bang to bounce), Carlotta calculates ever-finer loci on the frozen ordinates of spacetime until at last she reaches a trailer park outside the town of Commanche Drop, Arizona. Bodiless, no more than a breath of imprecision in the Feynman geography of certain virtual particles, thus powerless to affect the material world, she passes unimpeded through a sheet-aluminum wall and hovers over a mattress on which a young woman sleeps uneasily.

The young woman is her own ancient self, the primordial Carlotta Boudaine, dewed with sweat in the hot night air, her legs caught up in a spindled cotton sheet. The bedroom's small window is cranked open, and in the breezeless distance a coyote wails.

Well, look at me, Carlotta marvels: skinny girl in panties and a halter, sixteen years old—no older than a gnat's breath—taking shallow little sleep-breaths in the moonlit dark. Poor child can't even see her own ghost. Ah, but she will, Carlotta thinks—she *must*.

The familiar words echo in her mind as she inspects her dreaming body, buried in its tomb of years, eons, kalpas. *When it's time to leave, leave. Don't be afraid. Don't wait. Don't get caught. Just go. Go fast.*

Her ancient beloved poem. Her perennial mantra. The words, in fact, that saved her life.

She needs to share those words with herself, to make the circle complete. Everything she knows about the nature of the physical universe suggests that the task is impossible. Maybe so . . . but it won't be for lack of trying.

Patiently, slowly, soundlessly, Carlotta begins to speak.

Here's the story of the Fleet, girl, and how I got raptured up into it. It's all about the future—a bigger one than you believe in—so brace yourself.

It has a thousand names and more, but we'll just call it the Fleet. When I first encountered it, the Fleet was scattered from the core of the galaxy all through its spiraled tentacles of suns, and it had been there for millions of years, going about its business, though nobody on this planet knew anything about it. I guess every now and then a Fleet ship must have fallen to Earth, but it would have been indistinguishable from any common meteorite by the time it passed through the atmosphere: a chunk of carbonaceous chondrite smaller than a human fist, from which all evidence of ordered matter had been erased by fire—and such losses, which happened everywhere and often, made no discernable difference to the Fleet as a whole. All Fleet data (that is to say, all *mind*) was shared, distributed, fractal. Vessels were born and vessels were destroyed; but the Fleet persisted down countless eons, confident of its own immortality.

Oh, I know you don't understand the big words, child! It's not important for you to hear them—not *these* words—it's only important for me to *say* them. Why? Because a few billion years ago tomorrow, I carried your ignorance out of this very trailer, carried it down to the Interstate and hitched west with nothing in my backpack but a bottle of water, a half-dozen Tootsie Rolls, and a wad of twenty-dollar bills stolen out of Dan-O's old ditty bag. That night (tomorrow night: mark it) I slept under an overpass all by myself, woke up cold and hungry long before dawn, and looked up past a concrete arch crusted with bird shit into a sky so thick with falling stars it made me think of a dark skin bee-stung with fire. Some of the Fleet vectored too close to the atmosphere that night, no doubt, but I didn't understand that (any more than *you* do, girl)—I just thought it was a big flock of shooting stars, pretty but meaningless. And, after a while, I slept some more. And come sunrise, I waited for the morning traffic so I could catch another ride . . . but the only cars that came by were all weaving or speeding, as if the whole world was driving home from a drunken party.

"They won't stop," a voice behind me said. "Those folks already made their decisions, Carlotta. Whether they want to live or die, I mean. Same decision you have to make."

I whirled around, sick-startled, and that was when I first laid eyes on dear Erasmus.

Let me tell you right off that Erasmus wasn't a human being. Erasmus just then was a knot of shiny metal angles about the size of a microwave oven, hovering in mid-air, with a pair of eyes like the polished tourmaline they sell at those road-side souvenir shops. He didn't *have* to look that way—it was some old avatar he used because he figured that it would impress me. But I didn't know that then. I was only surprised, if that's not too mild a word, and too shocked to be truly frightened.

"The world won't last much longer," Erasmus said in a low and mournful voice. "You can stay here, or you can come with me. But choose quick, Carlotta, because the mantle's come unstable and the continents are starting to slip."

I half believed that I was still asleep and dreaming. I didn't know what that meant, about the mantle, though I guessed he was talking about the end of the world. Some quality of his voice (which reminded me of that actor Morgan Free-man) made me trust him despite how weird and impossible the whole conversation was. Plus, I had a confirming sense that *something* was going bad *somewhere*, partly because of the scant traffic (a Toyota zoomed past, clocking speeds it had never been built for, the driver a hunched blur behind the wheel), partly because of the ugly green cloud that just then billowed up over a row of rat-toothed moun-tains on the horizon. Also the sudden hot breeze. And the smell of distant burn-ing. And the sound of what might have been thunder, or something worse.

"Go with you where?"

"To the stars, Carlotta! But you'll have to leave your body behind."

I didn't like the part about leaving my body behind. But what choice did I have, except the one he'd offered me? Stay or go. Simple as that.

It was a ride—just not the kind I'd been expecting.

There was a tremor in the earth, like the devil knocking at the soles of my shoes. "Okay," I said, "whatever," as white dust bloomed up from the desert and was taken by the frantic wind.

Don't be afraid. Don't wait. Don't get caught. Just go. Go fast.

Without those words in my head, I swear, girl, I would have died that day. Billions did.

She slows down the passage of time so she can fit this odd but somehow neces-sary monologue into the space between one or two of the younger Carlotta's breaths. Of course, she has no real voice in which to speak. The past is static, im-perturbable in its endless sleep; molecules of air on their fixed trajectories can't be manipulated from the shadowy place where she now exists. Wake up with the dawn, girl, she says, steal the money you'll never spend—it doesn't matter; the important thing is to *leave*. It's time.

When it's time to leave, leave. Of all the memories she carried out of her earthly life, this is the most vivid: waking to discover a ghostly presence in her darkened room, a white-robed woman giving her the advice she needs at the moment she needs it. Suddenly Carlotta wants to scream the words: *When it's time to leave—*

But she can't vibrate even a single mote of the ancient air, and the younger Carlotta sleeps on.

Next to the bed is a thrift-shop night table scarred with cigarette burns. On the table is a child's night-light, faded cut-outs of SpongeBob SquarePants pasted on the paper shade. Next to that, hidden under a splayed copy of *People* magazine, is the bottle of barbiturates Carlotta stole from Dan-O's ditty-bag this afternoon, the same khaki bag in which (she couldn't help but notice) Dan-O keeps his cash, a change of clothes, a fake driver's license, and a blue steel automatic pistol.

Young Carlotta detects no ghostly presence . . . nor is her sleep disturbed by the sound of Dan-O's angry voice and her mother's sudden gasp, two rooms away. Apparently, Dan-O is awake and sober. Apparently, Dan-O has discovered the theft. That's a complication.

But Carlotta won't allow herself to be hurried.

The hardest thing about joining the Fleet was giving up the idea that I had a body, that my body had a real place to be.

But that's what everybody believed at first, that we were still whole and normal—everybody rescued from Earth, I mean. Everybody who said "Yes" to Erasmus—and Erasmus, in one form or another, had appeared to every human being on the planet in the moments before the end of the world. Two and a half billion of us accepted the offer of rescue. The rest chose to stay put and died when the Earth's continents dissolved into molten magma.

Of course, that created problems for the survivors. Children without parents, parents without children, lovers separated for eternity. It was as sad and tragic as any other incomplete rescue, except on a planetary scale. When we left the Earth, we all just sort of reappeared on a grassy plain as flat as Kansas and wider than the horizon, under a blue faux sky, each of us with an Erasmus at his shoulder and all of us wailing or sobbing or demanding explanations.

The plain wasn't "real," of course, not the way I was accustomed to things being real. It was a virtual place, and all of us were wearing virtual bodies, though we didn't understand that fact immediately. We kept on being what we expected ourselves to be—we even wore the clothes we'd worn when we were raptured up. I remember looking down at the pair of greasy second-hand Reeboks I'd found at the Commanche Drop Goodwill store, thinking: in Heaven? *Really?*

"Is there any place you'd rather be?" Erasmus asked with a maddening and clearly inhuman patience. "Anyone you need to find?"

"Yeah, I'd rather be in New Zealand," I said, which was really just a hysterical joke. All I knew about New Zealand was that I'd seen a show about it on PBS, the only channel we got since the cable company cut us off.

"Any particular part of New Zealand?"

"What? Well—okay, a beach, I guess."

I had never been to a real beach, a beach on the ocean.

"Alone, or in the company of others?"

"Seriously?" All around me people were sobbing or gibbering in (mostly) foreign languages. Pretty soon, fights would start to break out. You can't put a couple of billion human beings so close together under circumstances like that and expect any other result. But the crowd was already thinning, as people accepted similar offers from their own Fleet avatars.

"Alone," I said. "Except for you."

And quick as that, there I was: Eve without Adam, standing on a lonesome stretch of white beach.

After a while, the astonishment faded to a tolerable dazzle. I took off my shoes and tested the sand. The sand was pleasantly sun-warm. Saltwater swirled up between my toes as a wave washed in from the coral-blue sea.

Then I felt dizzy and had to sit down.

"Would you like to sleep?" Erasmus asked, hovering over me like a gem-studded party balloon. "I can help you sleep, Carlotta, if you'd like. It might make the transition easier if you get some rest, to begin with."

"You can answer some fucking *questions*, is what you can *do*!" I said.

He settled down on the sand beside me, the mutant offspring of a dragonfly and a beach ball. "Okay, shoot," he said.

It's a read-only universe, Carlotta thinks. The Old Ones have said as much, so it must be true. And yet, she knows, she *remembers*, that the younger Carlotta will surely wake and find her here: a ghostly presence, speaking wisdom.

But how can she make herself perceptible to this sleeping child? The senses are so stubbornly material, electrochemical data cascading into vastly complex neural networks . . . is it possible she could intervene in some way at the borderland of quanta and perception? For a moment, Carlotta chooses to look at her younger self with different eyes, sampling the fine gradients of molecular magnetic fields. The child's skin and skull grow faint and then transparent as Carlotta shrinks her point of view and wanders briefly through the carnival of her own animal mind, the buzzing innerscape where skeins of dream merge and separate like fractal soap-bubbles. If she could manipulate even a single boson—influence the charge at some critical synaptic junction, say—

But she can't. The past simply doesn't have a handle on it. There's no uncertainty here anymore, no alternate outcomes. To influence the past would be to *change* the past, and, by definition, that's impossible.

The shouting from the next room grows suddenly louder and more vicious, and Carlotta senses her younger self moving from sleep toward an awakening, too soon.

Of course, I figured it out eventually, with Erasmus's help. Oh, girl, I won't bore you with the story of those first few years—they bored *me*, heaven knows.

Of course "heaven" is exactly where we weren't. Lots of folks were inclined to see it that way—assumed they must have died and been delivered to whatever afterlife they happened to believe in. Which was actually not *too* far off the mark: but, of course, God had nothing to do with it. The Fleet was a real-world business, and ours wasn't the first sentient species it had raptured up. Lots of planets got destroyed, Erasmus said, and the Fleet didn't always get to them in time to salvage the population, hard as they tried—we were *lucky*, sort of.

So I asked him what it was that caused all these planets to blow up.

"We don't know, Carlotta. We call it the Invisible Enemy. It doesn't leave a signature, whatever it is. But it systematically seeks out worlds with flourishing civilizations and marks them for destruction." He added, "It doesn't like the Fleet much, either. There are parts of the galaxy where we don't go—because if we *do* go there, we don't come back."

At the time, I wasn't even sure what a "galaxy" was, so I dropped the subject, except to ask him if I could see what it looked like—the destruction of the Earth, I meant. At first, Erasmus didn't want to show me; but after a lot of coaxing, he turned himself into a sort of floating TV screen and displayed a view "looking back from above the plane of the solar ecliptic," words which meant nothing to me.

What I saw was . . . well, no more little blue planet, basically.

More like a ball of boiling red snot.

"What about my mother? What about Dan-O?"

I didn't have to explain who these people were. The Fleet had sucked up all kinds of data about human civilization, I don't know how. Erasmus paused as if he was consulting some invisible Rolodex. Then he said, "They aren't with us."

"You mean they're dead?"

"Yes. Abby and Dan-O are dead."

But the news didn't surprise me. It was almost as if I'd known it all along, as if I had had a vision of their deaths, a dark vision to go along with that ghostly visit the night before, the woman in a white dress telling me *go fast*.

Abby Boudaine and Dan-O, dead. And me raptured up to robot heaven. Well, well.

"Are you sure you wouldn't like to sleep now?"

"Maybe for a while," I told him.

Dan-O's a big man, and he's working himself up to a major tantrum. Even now, Carlotta feels repugnance at the sound of his voice, that gnarl of angry consonants. Next, Dan-O throws something solid, maybe a clock, against the wall. The clock goes to pieces, noisily. Carlotta's mother cries out in response, and the sound of her wailing seems to last weeks.

"It's not good," Erasmus told me much later, "to be so much alone."

Well, I told him, I *wasn't* alone—he was with me, wasn't he? And he was pretty good company, for an alien machine. But that was a dodge. What he *meant* was that I ought to hook up with somebody human.

I told him I didn't care if I never set eyes on another human being ever again. What had the human race ever done for *me*?

He frowned—that is, he performed a particular contortion of his exposed surfaces that I had learned to interpret as disapproval. "That's entropic talk, Carlotta. Honestly, I'm worried about you."

"What could happen to me?" Here on this beach where nothing ever *really* happens, I did not add.

"You could go crazy. You could sink into despair. Worse, you could die."

"I could *die*? I thought I was immortal now."

"Who told you that? True, you're no longer *living*, in the strictly material sense. You're a metastable nested loop embedded in the Fleet's collective mentation. But everything's mortal, Carlotta. Anything can die."

I couldn't die of disease or falling off a cliff, he explained, but my "nested loop" was subject to a kind of slow erosion and stewing in my own lonely juices for too long was liable to bring on the decay that much faster.

And, admittedly, after a month on this beach, swimming and sleeping too much and eating the food Erasmus conjured up whenever I was hungry (though I didn't really need to eat), watching recovered soap operas on his bellyvision screen or reading celebrity magazines (also embedded in the Fleet's collective memory) that would never get any fresher or produce another issue, and just being basically miserable as all hell, I thought maybe he was right.

"You cry out in your sleep," Erasmus said. "You have bad dreams."

"The world ended. Maybe I'm depressed. You think meeting people would help with that?"

"Actually," he said, "you have a remarkable talent for being alone. You're sturdier than most. But that won't save you, in the long run."

So I tried to take his advice. I scouted out some other survivors. Turned out, it was interesting what some people had done in their new incarnations as Fleet-data. The Erasmuses had made it easy for like-minded folks to find each other and to create environments to suit them. The most successful of these cliques, as they were sometimes called, were the least passive ones: the ones with a purpose. Purpose kept people lively. Passive cliques tended to fade into indifference pretty quickly, and the purely hedonistic ones soon collapsed into dense orgasmic singularities; but if you were curious about the world, and hung out with similarly curious friends, there was a lot to keep you thinking.

None of those cliques suited me in the long run, though. Oh, I made some friends, and I learned a few things. I learned how to access the Fleet's archival data, for instance—a trick you had to be careful with. If you did it right, you could think about a subject as if you were doing a Google search, all the relevant information popping up in your mind's eye just as if it had been there all along. Do it too often or too enthusiastically, though, and you ran the risk of getting lost in the overload—you might develop a "memory" so big and all-inclusive that it absorbed you into its own endless flow.

(It was an eerie thing to watch when it happened. For a while, I hung out with a clique that was exploring the history of the non-human civilizations that had been raptured up by the Fleet in eons past . . . until the leader of the group, a Jordanian college kid by the name of Nuri, dived down too far and literally fogged out. He got this look of intense concentration on his face, and, moments later, his body turned to wisps and eddies of fluid air and faded like fog in the sunlight. Made me shiver. And I had liked Nuri—I missed him when he was gone.)

But by sharing the effort, we managed to safely learn some interesting things. (Things the Erasmuses could have just *told* us, I suppose; but we didn't know the right questions to ask.) Here's a big for-instance: although every species was mortal after it was raptured up—every species eventually fogged out much the way poor Nuri had—there were actually a few very long-term survivors. By that, I mean individuals who had outlived their peers, who had found a way to preserve a sense of identity in the face of the Fleet's hypercomplex data torrent.

We asked our Erasmuses if we could meet one of these long-term survivors.

Erasmus said no, that was impossible. The Elders, as he called them, didn't live on our timescale. The way they had preserved themselves was by dropping out of realtime.

Apparently, it wasn't necessary to "exist" continuously from one moment to the next. You could ask the Fleet to turn you off for a day or a week, then turn you on again. Any moment of active perception was called a *saccade*, and you could space your saccades as far apart as you liked. Want to live a thousand years? Do it by living one second out of every million that passes. Of course, it wouldn't *feel* like a thousand years, subjectively; but a thousand years would flow by before you aged much. That's basically what the Elders were doing.

We could do the same, Erasmus said, if we wanted. But there was a price tag attached to it. "Timesliding" would carry us incomprehensibly far into a future nobody could predict. We were under continual attack by the Invisible Enemy, and it was possible that the Fleet might lose so much cohesion that we could no longer be sustained as stable virtualities. We wouldn't get a long life out of it, and we might well be committing a kind of unwitting suicide.

"You don't really go anywhere," Erasmus summed up. "In effect, you just go fast. I can't honestly recommend it."

"Did I ask for your advice? I mean, what *are* you, after all? Just some little fragment of the Fleet mind charged with looking after Carlotta Boudaine. A cybernetic babysitter."

I swear to you, he looked *hurt*. And I heard the injury in his voice.

"I'm the part of the Fleet that cares about you, Carlotta."

Most of my clique backed down at that point. Most people aren't cut out to be timesliders. But I was more tempted than ever. "You can't tell me what to do, Erasmus."

"I'll come with you, then," he said. "If you don't mind."

It hadn't occurred to me that he might *not* come along. It was a scary idea. But I didn't let that anxiety show.

"Sure, I guess that'd be all right," I said.

Enemies out there too, the elder Carlotta observes. A whole skyful of them. As above, so below. Just like in that old drawing—what was it called? *Utriusque cosmi.* Funny what a person remembers. Girl, do you hear your mother crying?

The young Carlotta stirs uneasily in her tangled sheet.

Both Carlottas know their mother's history. Only the elder Carlotta can think about it without embarrassment and rage. Oh, it's an old story. Her mother's name is Abby. Abby Boudaine dropped out of high school pregnant, left some dreary home in South Carolina to go west with a twenty-year-old boyfriend who abandoned her outside Albuquerque. She gave birth in a California emergency ward and nursed Carlotta in a basement room in the home of a retired couple, who sheltered her in exchange for housework until Carlotta's constant wailing got on their nerves. After that, Abby hooked up with a guy who worked for a utility company and grew weed in his attic for pin money. The hookup lasted a few years, and might have lasted longer, except that Abby had a weakness for what the law called "substances," and couldn't restrain herself in an environment where coke and methamphetamine circulated more or less freely. A couple of times, Carlotta was bounced around between foster homes while Abby Boudaine did court-mandated dry-outs or simply binged. Eventually, Abby picked up ten-year-old Carlotta from one of these periodic suburban exiles and drove her over the state border into Arizona, jumping bail. "We'll never be apart again," her mother told her, in the strained voice that meant she was a little bit high or hoping to be. "Never again!" Blessing or curse? Carlotta wasn't sure which. "You'll never leave me, baby. You're my one and only."

Not such an unusual story, the elder Carlotta thinks, though her younger self, she knows, feels uniquely singled out for persecution.

Well, child, Carlotta thinks, try living as a distributed entity on a Fleet that's being eaten by invisible monsters, *then* see what it feels like.

But she knows the answer to that. It feels much the same.

"Now you *steal* from me?" Dan-O's voice drills through the wall like a rusty auger. Young Carlotta stirs and whimpers. Any moment now, she'll open her eyes, and then what? Although this is the fixed past, it feels suddenly unpredictable, unfamiliar, dangerous.

Erasmus came with me when I went timesliding, and I appreciated that, even before I understood what a sacrifice it was for him.

Early on, I asked him about the Fleet and how it came to exist. The answer to that question was lost to entropy, he said. He had never known a time without a Fleet—he couldn't have, because Erasmus *was* the Fleet, or at least a sovereign fraction of it.

"As we understand it," he told me, "the Fleet evolved from networks of self-replicating data-collecting machine intelligences, no doubt originally created by some organic species, for the purpose of exploring interstellar space. Evidence suggests that we're only a little younger than the universe itself."

The Fleet had outlived its creators. "Biological intelligence is unstable over the long term," Erasmus said, a little smugly. "But out of that original compulsion to acquire and share data, we evolved and refined our own collective purpose."

"That's why you hoover up doomed civilizations? So you can catalogue and study them?"

"So they won't be *forgotten*, Carlotta. That's the greatest evil in the universe— the entropic decay of organized information. Forgetfulness. We despise it."

"Worse than the Invisible Enemy?"

"The Enemy is evil to the degree to which it abets entropic decay."

"Why does it want to do that?"

"We don't know. We don't even understand what the Enemy *is*, in physical terms. It seems to operate outside of the material universe. If it consists of matter, that matter is non-baryonic and impossible to detect. It pervades parts of the galaxy—though not *all* parts—like an insubstantial gas. When the Fleet passes through volumes of space heavily infested by the Enemy, our loss-rate soars. And as these infested volumes of space expand, they encompass and destroy life-bearing worlds."

"The Enemy's growing, though. And the Fleet isn't."

I had learned to recognize Erasmus's distress, not just because he was slowly adopting somewhat more human features. "The Fleet is my home, Carlotta. More than that. It's my body, my heart."

What he didn't say was that by joining me in the act of surfing time, he would be isolating himself from the realtime network that had birthed and sustained him. In realtime, Erasmus was a fraction of something reassuringly immense. But in slide-time, he'd be as alone as an Erasmus could get.

And yet, he came with me, when I made my decision. He was *my* Erasmus as much as he was the Fleet's, and he came with me. What would you call that, girl? Friendship? At least. I came to call it love.

The younger Carlotta has stolen those pills (the ones hidden under her smudged copy of *People*) for a reason. To help her sleep, was what she told herself. But she didn't really have trouble sleeping. No: if she was honest, she'd have to say the pills were an escape hatch. Swallow enough of them, and it's, hey, fuck you, world! Less work than the highway, an alternative she was also considering.

More shouting erupts in the next room. A real roust-up, bruises to come. Then, worse, Dan-O's voice goes all small and jagged. That's a truly bad omen, Carlotta knows. Like the smell of ozone that floods the air in advance of a lightning strike, just before the voltage ramps up and the current starts to flow.

Erasmus built a special virtuality for him and me to time-trip in. Basically, it was a big comfy room with a wall-sized window overlooking the Milky Way.

The billions of tiny dense components that made up the Fleet swarmed at velocities slower than the speed of light, but timesliding made it all seem faster— scarily so. Like running the whole universe in fast-forward, knowing you can't go back. During the first few months of our expanded Now, we soared a long way out of the spiral arm that contained the abandoned Sun. The particular sub-swarm of the Fleet that hosted my sense of self was on a long elliptical orbit around the supermassive black hole at the galaxy's core, and from this end of the ellipse, over the passing days, we watched the Milky Way drop out from under us like a cloud of luminous pearls.

When I wasn't in that room, I went off to visit other timesliders, and some of them visited me there. We were a self-selected group of radical roamers with a thing for risk, and we got to know one another pretty well. Oh, girl, I wish I could tell you all the friends I made among that tribe of self-selected exiles! Many of them human, not all: I met a few of the so-called Elders of other species and managed to communicate with them on a friendly basis. Does that sound strange to you? I guess it is. Surpassing strange. I thought so too, at first. But these were people (mostly people) and things (but things can be people too) that I mostly liked and often loved, and they loved me back. Yes, they did. Whatever quirk of personality made us timesliders drew us together against all the speedy dark outside our virtual walls. Plus—well, we were survivors. It took not much more than a month to outlive all the remaining remnant of humanity. Even our ghosts were gone, in other words, unless you counted *us* as ghosts.

Erasmus was a little bit jealous of the friends I made. He had given up a lot for me, and maybe I ought to have appreciated him more for it. Unlike us formerly biological persons, though, Erasmus maintained a tentative link with realtime. He had crafted protocols to keep himself current on changes in the Fleet's symbolsets and core mentation. That way, he could update us on what the Fleet was doing—new species raptured up from dying worlds and so forth. None of these newcomers lasted long, though, from our lofty perspective, and I once asked Erasmus why the Fleet even bothered with such ephemeral creatures as (for instance) human beings. He said that every species was doomed in the long run, but that didn't make it okay to kill people—or to abandon them when they might be rescued. That instinct was what made the Fleet a moral entity, something more than just a collection of self-replicating machines.

And it made *him* more than a nested loop of complex calculations. In the end, Carlotta, I came to love Erasmus best of all.

Meanwhile the years and stars scattered in our wake like dust—a thousand years, a hundred thousand, a million, more, and the galaxy turned like a great white wheel. We all made peace with the notion that we were the last of our kind, whatever "kind" we represented.

If you could hear me, girl, I guess you might ask what I found in that deep well of strangeness that made the water worth drinking. Well, I found friends, as I said—isn't that enough? And I found lovers. Even Erasmus began to adopt a human avatar, so we could touch each other in the human way.

I found, in plain words, a *home*, Carlotta, however peculiar in its nature—a *real* home, for the first time in my life.

Which is why I was so scared when it started to fall apart.

In the next room, Abby isn't taking Dan-O's anger lying down. It's nearly the perfect storm tonight—Dan-O's temper and Abby's sense of violated dignity both rising at the same ferocious pitch, rising toward some unthinkable crescendo.

But her mother's outrage is fragile, and Dan-O is frankly dangerous. The young Carlotta had known that about him from the get-go, from the first time her mother came home with this man on her arm: knew it from his indifferent eyes and his mechanical smile; knew it from the prison tattoos he didn't bother to disguise and the boastfulness with which he papered over some hole in his essential self. Knew it from the meth-lab stink that burned off him like a chemical perfume. Knew it from the company he kept, from the shitty little deals with furtive men arranged in Carlotta's mother's home because his own rental bungalow was littered with incriminating cans of industrial solvent. Knew it most of all by the way he fed Abby Boudaine crystal meth in measured doses, to keep her wanting it, and by the way Abby began to sign over her weekly Walmart paycheck to him like a dutiful servant, back when she was working checkout.

Dan-O is tall, wiry, and strong despite his vices. The elder Carlotta can hear enough to understand that Dan-O is blaming Abby for the theft of the barbiturates—an intolerable sin, in Dan-O's book. Followed by Abby's heated denials and the sound of Dan-O's fists striking flesh. All this discovered, not remembered: the young Carlotta sleeps on, though she's obviously about to wake; the critical moment is coming fast. And Carlotta thinks of what she saw when she raided Dan-O's ditty bag, the blue metal barrel with a black gnurled grip, a thing she had stared at, hefted, but ultimately disdained.

We dropped back down the curve of that elliptic, girl, and suddenly the Fleet began to vanish like drops of water on a hot griddle. Erasmus saw it first, because of what he was, and he set up a display so I could see it too: Fleet-swarms set as ghostly dots against a schema of the galaxy, the ghost-dots dimming perilously and some of them blinking out altogether. It was a graph of a massacre. "Can't anyone stop it?" I asked.

"They would if they could," he said, putting an arm (now that he had grown a pair of arms) around me. "They will if they can, Carlotta."

"Can *we* help?"

"We are helping, in a way. Existing the way we do means they don't have to use much mentation to sustain us. To the Fleet, we're code that runs a calculation for a few seconds out of every year. Not a heavy burden to carry."

Which was important, because the Fleet could only sustain so much computation, the upper limit being set by the finite number of linked nodes. And that number was diminishing as Fleet vessels were devoured wholesale.

"Last I checked," Erasmus said (which would have been about a thousand years ago, realtime), "the Fleet theorized that the Enemy is made of dark matter."

(Strange stuff that hovers around galaxies, invisibly—it doesn't matter, girl; take my word for it; you'll understand it one day.) "They're not material objects so much as *processes*—parasitical protocols played out in dark matter clouds. Apparently, they can manipulate quantum events we don't even see."

"So we can't defend ourselves against them?"

"Not yet. No. And you and I might have more company soon, Carlotta. As long-timers, I mean."

That was because the Fleet continued to rapture up dying civilizations, nearly more than their shrinking numbers could contain. One solution was to shunt survivors into the Long Now along with us, in order to free up computation for battlefield maneuvers and such.

"Could get crowded," he warned.

"If a lot of strangers need to go Long," I said . . .

He gave me a carefully neutral look. "Finish the thought."

"Well . . . can't we just . . . go Longer?"

Fire a pistol in a tin box like this ratty trailer and the sound is ridiculously loud. Like being spanked on the ear with a two-by-four. It's the pistol shot that finally wakes the young Carlotta. Her eyelids fly open like window shades on a haunted house.

This isn't how the elder Carlotta remembers it. *Gunshot?* No, there was no *gunshot*: she just came awake and saw the ghost—

And no ghost, either. Carlotta tries desperately to speak to her younger self, wills herself to succeed, and fails yet again. So who fired that shot, and where did the bullet go, and why can't she *remember* any of this?

The shouting in the next room has yielded up a silence. The silence becomes an eternity. Then Carlotta hears the sound of footsteps—she can't tell whose—approaching her bedroom door.

In the end, almost every conscious function of the Fleet went Long, just to survive the attrition of the war with the dark-matter beings. The next loop through the galactic core pared us down to a fraction of what we used to be. When I got raptured up, the Fleet was a distributed cloud of baseball-sized objects running quantum computations on the state of their own dense constituent atoms—*millions and millions* of such objects, all linked together in a nested hierarchy. By the time we orbited back up our ellipsis, you could have counted us in the thousands, and our remaining links were carefully narrowbanded to give us maximum stealth.

So us wild timesliders chose to go Longer.

Just like last time, Erasmus warned me that it might be a suicidal act. If the Fleet was lost, we would be lost along with it . . . our subjective lives could end within days or hours. If, on the other hand, the Fleet survived and got back to reproducing itself, well, we might live on indefinitely—even drop back into real-time if we chose to do so. "Can you accept the risk?" he asked.

"Can *you*?"

He had grown a face by then. I suppose he knew me well enough to calculate what features I'd find pleasing. But it wasn't his ridiculous fake humanity I loved. What I loved was what went on behind those still-gemlike tourmaline eyes—the person he had become by sharing my mortality. "I accepted that risk a long time ago," he said.

"You and me both, Erasmus."

So we held on to each other and just—*went fast*.

Hard to explain what made that time-dive so vertiginous, but imagine centuries flying past like so much dust in a windstorm! It messed up our sense of *place*, first of all. Used to be we had a point of view light-years wide and deep . . . now all those loops merged into one continuous cycle; we grew as large as the Milky Way itself, with Andromeda bearing down on us like a silver armada. I held Erasmus in my arms, watching wide-eyed while he updated himself on the progress of the war and whispered new discoveries into my ear.

The Fleet had worked up new defenses, he said, and the carnage had slowed; but our numbers were still dwindling.

I asked him if we were dying.

He said he didn't know. Then he looked alarmed and held me tighter. "Oh, Carlotta . . ."

"What?" I stared into his eyes, which had gone faraway and strange. "*What is it?* Erasmus, tell me!"

"The Enemy," he said in numbed amazement.

"What about them?"

"*I know what they are.*"

The bedroom door opens.

The elder Carlotta doesn't remember the bedroom door opening. None of this is as she remembers it should be. The young Carlotta cringes against the backboard of the bed, so terrified she can barely draw breath. *Bless you, girl, I'd hold your hand if I could!*

What comes through the door is just Abby Boudaine. Abby in a cheap white nightgown. But Abby's eyes are yellow-rimmed and feral, and her nightgown is spattered with blood.

See, the thing is this. All communication is limited by the speed of light. But if you spread your saccades over time, that speed-limit kind of expands. Slow as we were, light seemed to cross galactic space in a matter of moments. Single thoughts consumed centuries. We felt the supermassive black hole at the center of the galaxy beating like a ponderous heart. We heard whispers from nearby galaxies, incomprehensibly faint but undeniably manufactured. Yes, girl, we were *that* slow.

But the Enemy was even slower.

"Long ago," Erasmus told me, channeling this information from the Fleet's own dying collectivity, "long ago, the Enemy learned to parasitize dark matter . . . to use it as a computational substrate . . . to evolve *within* it . . ."

"*How* long ago?"

His voice was full of awe. "Longer than you have words for, Carlotta. They're older than the universe itself."

Make any sense to you? I doubt it would. But here's the thing about our universe: it oscillates. It *breathes*, I mean, like a big old lung, expanding and shrinking and expanding again. When it shrinks, it wants to turn into a singularity, but it can't do that, because there's a limit to how much mass a quantum of volume can hold without busting. So it all bangs up again, until it can't accommodate any more emptiness. Back and forth, over and over. Perhaps, *ad infinitum*.

Trouble is, no information can get past those hot chaotic contractions. Every bang makes a fresh universe, blank as a chalkboard in an empty schoolhouse . . .

Or so we thought.

But dark matter has a peculiar relationship with gravity and mass, Erasmus said; so when the Enemy learned to colonize it, they found ways to propagate themselves from one universe to the next. They could survive *the end of all things material*, in other words, and they had already done so—many times!

The Enemy was genuinely immortal, if that word has any meaning. The Enemy conducted its affairs not just across galactic space, but across the voids that separate galaxies, clusters of galaxies, superclusters. . . . slow as molasses, they were, but vast as all things, and as pervasive as gravity, and very powerful.

"So what have they got against the Fleet, if they're so big and almighty? Why are they killing us?"

Erasmus smiled then, and the smile was full of pain and melancholy and an awful understanding. "But they're not *killing* us, Carlotta. They're rapturing us up."

One time in school, when she was trying unsuccessfully to come to grips with *The Merchant of Venice*, Carlotta had opened a book about Elizabethan drama to a copy of an old drawing called *Utriusque Cosmi*. It was supposed to represent the whole cosmos, the way people thought of it back in Shakespeare's time, all layered and orderly: stars and angels on top, hell beneath, and a naked guy stretched foursquare between divinity and damnation. Made no sense to her at all. Some antique craziness. She thinks of that drawing now, for no accountable reason. *But it doesn't stop at the angels, girl. I learned that lesson. Even angels have angels, and devils dance on the backs of lesser devils.*

Her mother in her bloodstained nightgown hovers in the doorway of Carlotta's bedroom. Her unblinking gaze strafes the room until it fixes at last on her daughter. Abby Boudaine might be standing right here, Carlotta thinks, but those eyes are looking out from someplace deeper and more distant and far more frightening.

The blood fairly drenches her. But it isn't Abby's blood.

"Oh, Carlotta," Abby says. Then she clears her throat, the way she does when she has to make an important phone call or speak to someone she fears. "Carlotta . . ."

And Carlotta (the invisible Carlotta, the Carlotta who dropped down from that place where the angels dice with eternity) understands what Abby is about to say, recognizes at last the awesome circularity, not a paradox at all. She pronounces the words silently as Abby makes them real: "Carlotta. Listen to me, girl. I don't guess you understand any of this. I'm so sorry. I'm sorry for many things. But listen now. When it's time to leave, you leave. Don't be afraid, and don't get caught. Just go. Go *fast*."

Then she turns and leaves her daughter cowering in the darkened room.

Beyond the bedroom window, the coyotes are still complaining to the moon. The sound of their hooting fills up the young Carlotta's awareness until it seems to speak directly to the heart of her.

Then comes the second and final gunshot.

I have only seen the Enemy briefly, and by that time, I had stopped thinking of them as the Enemy.

Can't describe them too well. Words really do fail me. And by that time, might as well admit it, I was not myself a thing I would once have recognized as human. Just say that Erasmus and I and the remaining timesliders were taken up into the Enemy's embrace along with all the rest of the Fleet—all the memories we had deemed lost to entropy or warfare were preserved there. The virtualities the Enemies had developed across whole kalpas of time were labyrinthine, welcoming, strange beyond belief. Did I roam in those mysterious glades? Yes I did, girl, and Erasmus by my side, for many long (subjective) years, and we became—well, larger than I can say.

And the galaxies aged and flew away from one another until they were swallowed up in manifolds of cosmic emptiness, connected solely by the gentle and inexorable thread of gravity. Stars winked out, girl; galaxies merged and filled with dead and dying stars; atoms decayed to their last stable forms. But the fabric of space can tolerate just so much emptiness. It isn't infinitely elastic. Even vacuum ages. After some trillions and trillions of years, therefore, the expansion became a contraction.

During that time, I occasionally sensed or saw the Enemy—but I have to call them something else: say, *the Great Old Ones*, pardon my pomposity—who had constructed the dark matter virtualities in which I now lived. They weren't people at all. Never were. They passed through our adopted worlds like storm clouds, black and majestic and full of subtle and inscrutable lightnings. I couldn't speak to them, even then; as large and old as I had become, I was only a fraction of what they were.

I wanted to ask them why they had destroyed the Earth, why so many people had to be wiped out of existence or salvaged by the evolved benevolence of the Fleet. But Erasmus, who delved into these questions more deeply than I was able to, said the Great Old Ones couldn't perceive anything as tiny or ephemeral as a rocky planet like the Earth. The Earth and all the many planets like her had been destroyed, not by any willful calculation, but by autonomic impulses evolved over the course of many cosmic conflations—impulses as imperceptible and involuntary to the Old Ones as the functioning of your liver is to *you*, girl.

The logic of it is this: Life-bearing worlds generate civilizations that eventually begin playing with dark matter, posing a potential threat to the continuity of the Old Ones. Some number of these intrusions can be tolerated and contained—like the Fleet, they were often an enriching presence—but too many of them would endanger the stability of the system. It's as if we were germs, girl, wiped out by a giant's immune system. They couldn't *see* us, except as a somatic threat. Simple as that.

But they could see the *Fleet*. The Fleet was just big enough and durable enough to register on the senses of the Old Ones. And the Old Ones weren't malevolent: they perceived the Fleet much the way the Fleet had once perceived *us*, as something primitive but alive and thinking and worth the trouble of salvation.

So they raptured up the Fleet (and similar Fleet-like entities in countless other galaxies), thus preserving us against the blind oscillations of cosmic entropy.

(Nice of them, I suppose. But if I ever grow large enough or live long enough to confront an Old One face to face, I mean to lodge a complaint. Hell *yes* we were small—people are some of the smallest thought-bearing creatures in the cosmos, and I think we all kind of knew that even before the end of the world . . . *you* did, surely. But pain is pain and grief is grief. It might be inevitable, it might even be built into the nature of things; but it isn't *good*, and it ought not to be tolerated, if there's a choice.)

Which I guess is why I'm here watching you squinch your eyes shut while the sound of that second gunshot fades into the air.

Watching you process a nightmare into a vision.

Watching you build a pearl around a grain of bloody truth.

Watching you *go fast*.

The bodiless Carlotta hovers a while longer in the fixed and changeless corridors of the past.

Eventually, the long night ends. Raw red sunlight finds the window.

Last dawn this small world will ever see, as it happens; but the young Carlotta doesn't know that yet.

Now that the universe has finished its current iteration, all its history is stored in transdimensional metaspace like a book on a shelf—it can't be changed. Truly so. I guess I know that now, girl. Memory plays tricks that history corrects.

And I guess that's why the Old Ones let me have access to these events, as we hover on the brink of a new creation.

I know some of the questions you'd ask me if you could. You might say, *Where are you really?* And I'd say, *I'm at the end of all things, which is really just another beginning.* I'm walking in a great garden of dark matter, while all things known and baryonic spiral up the ladder of unification energies to a fiery new dawn. I have grown so large, girl, that I can fly down history like a bird over a prairie field. But I cannot remake what has already been made. That is one power I do not possess.

I watch you get out of bed. I watch you dress. Blue jeans with tattered hems, a man's lumberjack shirt, those thrift-shop Reeboks. I watch you go to the kitchen and fill your vinyl Bratz backpack with bottled water and Tootsie Rolls, which is all the cuisine your meth-addled mother has left in the cupboards.

Then I watch you tiptoe into Abby's bedroom. I confess I don't remember this part, girl. I suppose it didn't fit my fantasy about a benevolent ghost. But here you are, your face fixed in a willed indifference, stepping over Dan-O's corpse. Dan-O bled a lot after Abby Boudaine blew a hole in his chest, and the carpet is a sticky rust-colored pond.

I watch you pull Dan-O's ditty bag from where it lies half under the bed. On the bed, Abby appears to sleep. The pistol is still in her hand. The hand with the pistol in it rests beside her head. Her head is damaged in ways the young Carlotta can't stand to look at. Eyes down, girl. That's it.

I watch you pull a roll of bills from the bag and stuff it into your pack. Won't need that money where you're going! But it's a wise move, taking it. Commendable forethought.

Now go.

I have to go too. I feel Erasmus waiting for me, feel the tug of his love and loyalty, gentle and inevitable as gravity. He used to be a machine older than the dirt under your feet, Carlotta Boudaine, but he became a man—*my* man, I'm proud to say. He needs me, because it's no easy thing crossing over from one universe to the next. There's always work to do, isn't that the truth?

But right now, you go. You leave those murderous pills on the nightstand, find that highway. Don't be afraid. Don't wait. Don't get caught. Just go. Go fast. And excuse me while I take my own advice.

Events preceding the Helvetican Renaissance

John Kessel

Critically acclaimed author John Kessel is the author of two new novels,
The Moon and the Other *and* Pride and Prometheus. *His other novels
are* Good News from Outer Space *and* Corrupting Dr. Nice, *and in
collaboration with James Patrick Kelly,* Freedom Beach. *His short story
collections are* Meeting in Infinity, The Pure Product, The Baum Plan
for Financial Independence and Other Stories *and* The Collected Kessel.
*His fiction has twice received the Nebula Award, in addition to the Theodore
Sturgeon Memorial Award, the Locus Award, and the James Tiptree Jr. Memorial Award. His play* Faustfeathers *won the Paul Green Playwright's Prize,
and his story "A Clean Escape" was adapted as an episode of the 2006
ABC-TV series* Masters of Science Fiction. *In 2009 his* Pride and Prometheus *received both the Nebula and the Shirley Jackson Awards.*

*With Kelly, he has edited several anthologies of stories re-visioning
contemporary short speculative fiction, including* Digital Rapture: The
Singularity Anthology *(2012) and* Kafkaesque *(2011).*

*Kessel has taught American literature and fiction writing at North Carolina State University since 1982, helped found the NCSU MFA program
in creative writing, and served twice as its director. He lives with his wife,
the novelist Therese Anne Fowler, in Raleigh.*

*In the story that follows, Kessel spins a traditional action-packed space
adventure, with some inventive and individual touches that are very much
his own.*

When my mind cleared, I found myself in the street. A god spoke to me then:
*The boulevard to the spaceport runs straight up the mountain. And you must run
straight up the boulevard.*

The air was full of wily spirits, and moving fast in the Imperial City was a crime.
But what is man to disobey the voice of a god? So I ran. The pavement vibrated

with the thunder of the great engines of the Caslonian Empire. Behind me the curators of the Imperial Archives must by now have discovered the mare's nest I had made of their defenses, and perhaps had already realized that something was missing.

Above the plateau the sky was streaked with clouds, through which shot violet gravity beams carrying ships down from and up to planetary orbit. Just outside the gate to the spaceport a family in rags—husband, wife, two children—used a net of knotted cords to catch fish from the sewers. Ignoring them, prosperous citizens in embroidered robes passed among the shops of the port bazaar, purchasing duty-free wares, recharging their concubines, seeking a meal before departure. *Slower, now.*

I slowed my pace. I became indistinguishable from them, moving smoothly among the travelers.

To the Caslonian eye, I was calm, self-possessed; within me, rage and joy contended. I had in my possession the means to redeem my people. I tried not to think, only to act, but now that my mind was rekindled, it raced. Certainly it would go better for me if I left the planet before anyone understood what I had stolen. Yet I was very hungry, and the aroma of food from the restaurants along the way enticed me. It would be foolishness itself to stop here.

Enter the restaurant, I was told. So I stepped into the most elegant of the establishments.

The maître d' greeted me. "Would the master like a table, or would he prefer to dine at the bar?"

"The bar," I said

"Step this way." There was no hint of the illicit about his manner, though something about it implied indulgence. He was proud to offer me this experience that few could afford.

He seated me at the circular bar of polished rosewood. Before me, and the few others seated there, the chef grilled meats on a heated metal slab. Waving his arms in the air like a dancer, he tossed flanks of meat between two force knives, letting them drop to the griddle, flipping them dexterously upward again in what was as much performance as preparation. The energy blades of the knives sliced through the meat without resistance, the sides of these same blades batting them like paddles. An aroma of burning hydrocarbons wafted on the air.

An attractive young man displayed for me a list of virtualities that represented the "cuts" offered by the establishment, including subliminal tastes. The "cuts" referred to the portions of the animal's musculature from which the slabs of meat had been sliced. My mouth watered.

He took my order, and I sipped a cocktail of bitters and Belanova.

While I waited, I scanned the restaurant. The fundamental goal of our order is to vindicate divine justice in allowing evil to exist. At a small nearby table, a young woman leaned beside a child, probably her daughter, and encouraged her to eat. The child's beautiful face was the picture of innocence as she tentatively tasted a scrap of pink flesh. The mother was very beautiful. I wondered if this was her first youth.

The chef finished his performance, to the mild applause of the other patrons. The young man placed my steak before me. The chef turned off the blades and laid them aside, then ducked down a trap door to the oubliette where the slaves were kept. As soon as he was out of sight, a god told me, *Steal a knife.*

While the diners were distracted by their meals, I reached over the counter, took one of the force blades, and slid it into my boot. Then I ate. The taste was extraordinary. Every cell of my body vibrated with excitement and shame. My senses reeling, it took me a long time to finish.

A slender man in a dark robe sat next to me. "That smells good," he said. "Is that genuine animal flesh?"

"Does it matter to you?"

"Ah, brother, calm yourself. I'm not challenging your taste."

"I'm pleased to hear it."

"But I am challenging your identity." He parted the robe—his tunic bore the sigil of Port Security. "Your passport, please."

I exposed the inside of my wrist for him. A scanlid slid over his left eye and he examined the marks beneath my skin. "Very good," he said. He drew a blaster from the folds of his cassock. "We seldom see such excellent forgeries. Stand up, and come with me."

I stood. He took my elbow in a firm grip, the bell of the blaster against my side. No one in the restaurant noticed. He walked me outside, down the crowded bazaar. "You see, brother, that there is no escape from consciousness. The minute it returns, you are vulnerable. All your prayer is to no avail."

This is the arrogance of the Caslonian. They treat us as non-sentients, and they believe in nothing. Yet as I prayed, I heard no word.

I turned to him. "You may wish the absence of the gods, but you are mistaken. The gods are everywhere present." As I spoke the plosive "p" of "present," I popped the cap from my upper right molar and blew the moondust it contained into his face.

The agent fell writhing to the pavement. I ran off through the people, dodging collisions. My ship was on the private field at the end of the bazaar. Before I had gotten half way there, an alarm began sounding. People looked up in bewilderment, stopping in their tracks. The walls of buildings and stalls blinked into multiple images of me. Voices spoke from the air: "This man is a fugitive from the state. Apprehend him."

I would not make it to the ship unaided, so I turned on my perceptual overdrive. Instantly, everything slowed. The voices of the people and the sounds of the port dropped an octave. They moved as if in slow motion. I moved, to myself, as if in slow motion as well—my body could in no way keep pace with my racing nervous system—but to the people moving at normal speed, my reflexes were lighting fast. Up to the limit of my physiology—and my joints had been reinforced to take the additional stress, my muscles could handle the additional lactic acid for a time—I could move at twice the speed of a normal human. I could function for perhaps ten minutes in this state before I collapsed.

The first person to accost me—a sturdy middle-aged man—I seized by the arm.

I twisted it behind his back and shoved him into the second who took up the command. As I dodged through the crowd up the concourse, it began to drizzle. I felt as if I could slip between the raindrops. I pulled the force blade from my boot and sliced the ear from the next man who tried to stop me. His comic expression of dismay still lingers in my mind. Glancing behind, I saw the agent in black, face swollen with pustules from the moondust, running toward me.

I was near the field. In the boarding shed, attendants were folding the low-status passengers and sliding them into dispatch pouches, to be carried onto a ship and stowed in drawers for their passage. Directly before me, I saw the woman and child I had noticed in the restaurant. The mother had out a parasol and was holding it over the girl to keep the rain off her. Not slowing, I snatched the little girl and carried her off. The child yelped, the mother screamed. I held the blade to the girl's neck. "Make way!" I shouted to the security men at the field's entrance. They fell back.

"Halt!" came the call from behind me. The booth beside the gate was seared with a blaster bolt. I swerved, turned, and, my back to the gate, held the girl before me.

The agent in black, followed by two security women, jerked to a stop. "You mustn't hurt her," the agent said.

"Oh? And why is that?"

"It's against everything your order believes."

Master Darius had steeled me for this dilemma before sending me on my mission. He told me, "You will encounter such situations, Adlan. When they arise, you must resolve the complications."

"You are right!" I called to my pursuers, and threw the child at them.

The agent caught her, while the other two aimed and fired. One of the beams grazed my shoulder. But by then I was already through the gate and onto the tarmac.

A port security robot hurled a flame grenade. I rolled through the flames. My ship rested in the maintenance pit, cradled in the violet anti-grav beam. I slid down the ramp into the open airlock, hit the emergency close, and climbed to the controls. Klaxons wailed outside. I bypassed all the launch protocols and released the beam. The ship shot upward like an apple seed flicked by a fingernail; as soon as it had hit the stratosphere, I fired the engines and blasted through the scraps of the upper atmosphere into space.

The orbital security forces were too slow, and I made my escape.

I AWOKE BATTERED, bruised, and exhausted in the pilot's chair. The smell of my burned shoulder reminded me of the steak I had eaten in the port bazaar. The stress of accelerating nerve impulses had left every joint in my body aching. My arms were blue with contusions, and I was as enfeebled as an old man.

The screens showed me to be in an untraveled quarter of the system's cometary cloud; my ship had cloaked itself in ice so that on any detector I would simply be another bit of debris among billions. I dragged myself from the chair and down to the galley, where I warmed some broth and gave myself an injection of cellular repair mites. Then I fell into my bunk and slept.

My second waking was relatively free of pain. I recharged my tooth and ate again. I kneeled before the shrine and bowed my head in prayer, letting peace flow down my spine and relax all the muscles of my back. I listened for the voices of the gods.

I was reared by my mother on Bembo. My mother was an extraordinarily beautiful girl. One day, Akvan, looking down on her, was so moved by lust that he took the form of a vagabond and raped her by the side of the road. Nine months later I was born.

The goddess Peri became so jealous that she laid a curse on my mother, who turned into a lawyer. And so we moved to Helvetica. There, in the shabby city of Urushana, in the waterfront district along the river, she took up her practice, defending criminals and earning a little *baksheesh* greasing the relations between the Imperial Caslonian government and the corrupt local officials. Mother's ambition for me was to go to an off-planet university, but for me the work of a student was like pushing a very large rock up a very steep hill. I got into fights; I pursued women of questionable virtue. Having exhausted my prospects in the city, I entered the native constabulary, where I was re-engineered for accelerated combat. But my propensity for violence saw me cashiered out of the service within six months. Hoping to get a grip on my passions, I made the pilgrimage to the monastery of the Pujmanian Order. There I petitioned for admission as a novice, and, to my great surprise, was accepted.

It was no doubt the work of Master Darius, who took an interest in me from my first days on the plateau. Perhaps it was my divine heritage, which had placed those voices in my head. Perhaps it was my checkered career to that date. The Master taught me to distinguish between those impulses that were the work of my savage nature, and those that were the voices of the gods. It is not an easy path. I fasted, I worked in the gardens, I practiced the martial arts, I cleaned the cesspool, I sewed new clothes and mended old, I tended the orchards. I became an expert tailor, and sewed many of the finest kosodes worn by the masters on feast days. In addition, Master Darius held special sessions with me, putting me into a trance during which, I was later told by my fellow novices, I continued to act normally for days, only to awake with no memories of my actions.

And so I was sent on my mission. Because I had learned how not to think, I could not be detected by the spirits who guarded the Imperial Archives.

Five plays, immensely old, collectively titled *The Abandonment*, are all that document the rebirth of humanity after its long extinction. The foundational cycle consists of *The Archer's Fall, Stochik's Revenge, The Burning Tree, Close the Senses, Shut the Doors,* and the mystical fifth, *The Magic Tortoise*. No one knows who wrote them. It is believed they were composed within the first thirty years after the human race was recreated by the gods. Besides being the most revered cultural artifacts of humanity, these plays are also the sacred texts of the universal religion, and claimed as the fundamental political documents by all planetary governments. They are preserved only in a single copy. No recording has ever been made of their performance. The actors chosen to present the plays in the foundational festivals on all the worlds do not study and learn them; through a process similar to the one Master Darius taught me to confuse the spirits, the actors *become* the characters. Once the performance is done, it passes from their minds.

These foundational plays, of inestimable value, existed now only in my mind. I destroyed the crystal containing them in the archives. Without these plays, the heart of Caslon had been ripped away. If the populace knew of their loss, there would be despair and riot.

And once Master Darius announced that the Order held the only copy in our possession, it would only be a matter of time before the Empire would be obliged to free our world.

Three days after my escape from Caslon, I set course for Helvetica. Using an evanescent wormhole, I would emerge within the planet's inner ring. The ship, still encased in ice, would look like one of the fragments that formed the ring. From there I would reconnoiter, find my opportunity to leave orbit, and land. But because the ring stood far down in the gravitation well of the planet, it was a tricky maneuver.

Too tricky. Upon emergence in the Helvetican ring, my ship collided with one of the few nickel-iron meteoroids in the belt, disabling my engines. Within twenty minutes, Caslonian hunter-killers grappled with the hull. My one advantage was that by now they knew that I possessed the plays, and therefore they could not afford to blast me out of the sky. I could kill them, but they could not harm me. But I had no doubt that once they caught me, they would rip my mind to shreds seeking the plays.

I had only minutes—the hull door would not hold long. I abandoned the control room and retreated to the engine compartment. The place was a mess, barely holding pressure after the meteoroid collision, oxygen cylinders scattered about and the air acrid with the scent of burned wiring. I opened the cat's closet, three meters tall and two wide. From a locker I yanked two piezofiber suits. I turned them on, checked their readouts—they were fully charged—and threw them into the closet. It was cramped in there with tools and boxes of supplies. Sitting on one of the crates, I pulled up my shirt, exposing my bruised ribs. The aluminum light of the closet turned my skin sickly white. Using a microtome, I cut an incision in my belly below my lowest rib. There was little blood. I reached into the cut, found the nine-dimensional pouch, and drew it out between my index and middle fingers. I sprayed false skin over the wound. As I did, the artificial gravity cut off, and the lights went out.

I slipped on my night vision eyelids, read the directions on the pouch, ripped it open, removed the soldier and unfolded it. The body expanded, became fully three dimensional, and, in a minute, was floating naked before me. My first surprise: it was a woman. Dark skinned, slender, her body was very beautiful. I leaned over her, covered her mouth with mine, and blew air into her lungs. She jerked convulsively and drew a shuddering breath, then stopped. Her eyelids fluttered, then opened.

"Wake up!" I said, drawing on my piezosuit. I slipped the force blade into the boot, strapped on the belt with blaster and supplies, shrugged into the backpack. "Put on this suit! No time to waste."

She took in my face, the surroundings. From beyond the locker door I heard the sounds of the commandos entering the engine room.

"I am Brother Adlan," I whispered urgently. "You are a soldier of the Republican Guard?" As I spoke I helped her into the skinsuit.

"Lieutenant Nahid Esfandiar. What's happening?"

"We are in orbit over Helvetica, under attack by Caslonian commandos. We need to break out of here."

"What weapons have we?"

I handed her a blaster. "They will have accelerated perceptions. Can you speed yours?"

Her glance passed over me, measuring me for a fool. "Done already." She sealed her suit and flipped down the faceplate on her helmet.

I did not pay attention to her, because as she spoke, a god spoke to me. *Three men beyond this door.* In my mind I saw the engine room, and the three soldiers who were preparing to rip open the closet.

I touched my helmet to hers and whispered to Nahid, "There are three of them outside. The leader is directly across from the door. He has a common blaster, on stun. To the immediate right, a meter away, one of the commandos has a pulse rifle. The third, about to set the charge, has a pneumatic projector, probably with sleep gas. When they blow the door, I'll go high, you low. Three meters to the cross corridor, down one level and across starboard to the escape pod."

Just then, the door to the closet was ripped open, and through it came a blast of sleep gas. But we were locked into our suits, helmets sealed. Our blaster beams, pink in the darkness, crossed as they emerged from the gloom of the closet. We dove through the doorway in zero-G, bouncing off the bulkheads, blasters flaring. The commandos were just where the gods had told me they would be. I cut down one before we even cleared the doorway. Though they moved as quickly as we did, they were trying not to kill me, and the fact that there were two of us now took them by surprise.

Nahid fired past my ear, taking out another. We ducked through the hatch and up the companionway. Two more commandos came from the control room at the end of the corridor; I was able to slice one of them before he could fire, but the other's stunner numbed my thigh. Nahid torched his head and grabbed me by the arm, hurling me around the corner into the cross passageway.

Two more commandos guarded the hatchway to the escape pod. Nahid fired at them, killing one and wounding the other in a single shot. But instead of heading for the pod she jerked me the other way, toward the umbilical to the Caslonian ship.

"What are you doing?" I protested.

"Shut up," she said. "They can hear us." Halfway across the umbilical, Nahid stopped, braced herself against one wall, raised her blaster, and, without hesitation, blew a hole in the wall opposite. The air rushed out. A klaxon sounded the pressure breach, another commando appeared at the junction of the umbilical and the Caslonian ship—I burned him down—and we slipped through the gap into the space between the two ships. She grabbed my arm and pulled me around the hull of my own vessel.

I realized what she intended. Grabbing chunks of ice, we pulled ourselves over the horizon of my ship until we reached the outside hatch of the escape pod. I punched in the access code. We entered the pod and while Nahid sealed the hatch, I powered up and blasted us free of the ship before we had even buckled in.

The pod shot toward the upper atmosphere. The commandos guarding the inner hatch were ejected into the vacuum behind us. Retro fire slammed us into our seats. I caught a glimpse of bodies floating in the chaos we'd left behind before proton beams lanced out from the Caslonian raider, clipping the pod and sending us into a spin.

"You couldn't manage this without me?" Nahid asked.

"No sarcasm, please." I fought to steady the pod so the heat shields were oriented for atmosphere entry.

We hit the upper atmosphere. For twenty minutes we were buffeted by the jet stream, and it got hot in the tiny capsule. I became very aware of Nahid's scent, sweat and a trace of rosewater; she must have put on perfume before she was folded into the packet that had been implanted in me. Her eyes moved slowly over the interior of the pod.

"What is the date?" she asked.

"The nineteenth of Cunegonda," I told her. The pod bounced violently and drops of sweat flew from my forehead. Three red lights flared on the board, but I could do nothing about them.

"What year?"

I saw that it would not be possible to keep many truths from her. "You have been suspended in nine-space for sixty years."

The pod lurched again, a piece of the ablative shield tearing away. She sat motionless, taking in the loss of her entire life.

A snatch of verse came to my lips, unbidden:

"Our life is but a trifle
A child's toy abandoned by the road
When we are called home."

"Very poetic," she said. "Are we going to ride this pod all the way down? They probably have us on locator from orbit, and will vaporize it the minute it hits. I'd rather not be called home just now."

"We'll eject at ten kilometers. Here's your chute."

When the heat of the reentry had abated and we hit the troposphere, we blew the explosive bolts and shot free of the tumbling pod. Despite the thin air of the upper atmosphere, I was buffeted almost insensible, spinning like a prayer wheel. I lost sight of Nahid.

I fell for a long time, but eventually managed to stabilize myself spread-eagled, dizzy, my stomach lurching. Below, the Jacobin Range stretched north to south-west under the rising sun, the snow-covered rock on the upper reaches folded like a discarded robe, and below the thick forest climbing up to the tree line.

Some minutes later, I witnessed the impressive flare of the pod striking just below the summit of one of the peaks, tearing a gash in the ice cover and sending up a plume of black smoke that was torn away by the wind. I tongued the trigger in my helmet, and with a nasty jerk, the airfoil chute deployed from my back-pack. I could see Nahid's red chute some five hundred meters below me; I steered toward her hoping we could land near each other. The forested mountainside came up fast. I spotted a clearing on a ledge two thirds of the way up the slope and made for it, but my burned shoulder wasn't working right, and I was coming in too fast. I caught a glimpse of Nahid's foil in the mountain scar ahead, but I wasn't going to reach her.

At the last minute, I pulled up and skimmed the tree tops, caught a boot against a top limb, flipped head over heels and crashed into the foliage, coming to rest hanging upside down from the tree canopy. The suit's rigidity kept me from break-ing any bones, but it took me ten minutes to release the shrouds. I turned down the suit's inflex and took off my helmet to better see what I was doing. When I did, the limb supporting me broke, and I fell the last ten meters through the trees, hitting another limb on the way down, knocking me out.

I WAS WOKEN by Nahid rubbing snow into my face. My piezosuit had been turned off, and the fabric was flexible again. Nahid leaned over me, supporting my head. "Can you move your feet?" she asked.

My thigh was still numb from the stunner. I tried moving my right foot. Though I could not feel any response, I saw the boot twitch. "So it would seem."

Done with me, she let my head drop. "So, do you have some plan?"

I pulled up my knees and sat up. My head ached. We were surrounded by the boles of the tall firs; above our heads the wind swayed the trees, but down here the air was calm, and sunlight filtered down in patches, moving over the packed fine brown needles of the forest floor. Nahid had pulled down my chute to keep it from advertising our position. She crouched on one knee and examined the charge indicator on her blaster.

I got up and inventoried the few supplies we had—my suit's water reservoir, holding maybe a liter, three packs of *gichy* crackers in the belt. Hers would have no more than that. "We should get moving; the Caslonians will send a landing party, or notify the colonial government in Guliston to send a security squad."

"And why should I care?"

"You fought for the republic against the Caslonians. When the war was lost and the protectorate established, you had yourself folded. Didn't you expect to take up arms again when called back to life?"

"You tell me that was sixty years ago. What happened to the rest of the Repub-lican Guard?"

"The Guard was wiped out in the final Caslonian assaults."

"And our folded battalion?"

The blistering roar of a flyer tore through the clear air above the trees. Nahid squinted up, eyes following the glittering ship. "They're heading for where the pod hit." She pulled me to my feet, taking us downhill, perhaps in the hope of finding better cover in the denser forest near one of the mountain freshets.

"No," I said. "Up the slope."

"That's where they'll be."

"It can't be helped. We need to get to the monastery. We're on the wrong side of the mountains." I turned up the incline. After a moment, she followed.

We stayed beneath the trees for as long as possible. The slope was not too steep at this altitude; the air was chilly, with dying patches of old snow in the shadows. Out in the direct sunlight, it would be hot until evening came. I had climbed these mountains fifteen years before, an adolescent trying to find a way to live away from the world. As we moved, following the path of a small stream, the aches in my joints eased.

We did not talk. I had not thought about what it would mean to wake this soldier, other than how she would help me in a time of extremity. There are no women in our order, and though we take no vow of celibacy and some commerce takes place between brothers in their cells late at night, there is little opportunity for contact with the opposite sex. Nahid, despite her forbidding nature, was beautiful: dark skin, black eyes, lustrous black hair cut short, the three parallel scars of her rank marking her left cheek. As a boy in Urushana, I had tormented my sleepless nights with visions of women as beautiful as she; in my short career as a constable I had avidly pursued women far less so. One of them had provoked the fight that had gotten me cashiered.

The forest thinned as we climbed higher. Large folds of granite lay exposed to the open air, creased with fractures and holding pockets of earth where trees sprouted in groups. We had to circle around to avoid coming into the open, and even that would be impossible when the forest ended completely. I pointed us south, where Dundrahad Pass, dipping below 3,000 meters, cut through the mountains. We were without snowshoes or trekking gear, but I hoped that, given the summer temperatures, the pass would be clear enough to traverse in the night without getting ourselves killed. The skinsuits we wore would be proof against the nighttime cold.

We saw no signs of the Caslonians, but when we reached the tree line, we stopped to wait for darkness anyway. The air had turned colder, and a sharp wind blew down the pass from the other side of the mountains. We settled in a hollow beneath a patch of twisted scrub trees and waited out the declining sun. At the zenith, the first moon Mahsheed rode, waning gibbous. In the notch of the pass above and ahead of us, the second moon Roshanak rose. Small, glowing green, it moved perceptibly as it raced around the planet. I nibbled at some *gichy*, sipping water from my suit's reservoir. Nahid's eyes were shadowed; she scanned the slope.

"We'll have to wait until Mahsheed sets before we move," Nahid said. "I don't want to be caught in the pass in its light."

"It will be hard for us to see where we're going."

She didn't reply. The air grew colder. After a while, without looking at me, she spoke. "So what happened to my compatriots?"

I saw no point in keeping anything from her. "As the Caslonians consolidated their conquest, an underground of Republicans pursued a guerilla war. Two years later, they mounted an assault on the provincial capital in Kofarnihon. They unfolded your battalion to aid them, and managed to seize the armory. But the Caslonians sent reinforcements and set up a siege. When the rebels refused to surrender, the Caslonians vaporized the entire city, hostages, citizens, and rebels alike. That was the end of the Republican Guard." Nahid's dark eyes watched me as I told her all this. The tightness of her lips held grim skepticism.

"Yet here I am," she said.

"I don't know how you came to be the possession of the order. Some refugee, perhaps. The masters, sixty years ago, debated what to do with you. Given the temperament of the typical guardsman, it was assumed that, had you been restored to life, you would immediately get yourself killed in assaulting the Caslonians, putting the order at risk. It was decided to keep you in reserve, in the expectation that, at some future date, your services would be useful."

"You monks were always fair-weather democrats. Ever your order over the welfare of the people, or even their freedom. So you betrayed the republic."

"You do us an injustice."

"It was probably Javeed who brought me—the lying monk attached to our unit."

I recognized the name. Brother Javeed, a bent, bald man of great age, had run the monastery kitchen. I had never thought twice about him. He had died a year after I joined the order.

"Why do you think I was sent on this mission?" I told her. "We mean to set Helvetica free. And we shall do so, if we reach Sharishabz."

"How do you propose to accomplish that? Do you want to see your monastery vaporized?"

"They will not dare. I have something of theirs that they will give up the planet for. That's why they tried to board my ship rather than destroy it; that's why they didn't bother to disintegrate the escape pod when they might easily have shot us out of the sky."

"And this inestimably valuable item that you carry? It must be very small."

"It's in my head. I have stolen the only copies of the Foundational Dramas."

She looked at me. "So?"

Her skepticism was predictable, but it still angered me. "So—they will gladly trade Helvetica's freedom for the return of the plays."

She lowered her head, rubbed her brow with her hand. I could not read her. She made a sound, an intake of breath. For a moment, I thought she wept. Then she raised her head and laughed in my face.

I fought an impulse to strike her. "Quiet!"

She laughed louder. Her shoulders shook, and tears came to her eyes. I felt my face turn red. "You should have let me die with the others, in battle. You crazy priest!"

"Why do you laugh?" I asked her. "Do you think they would send ships to embargo Helvetican orbital space, dispatch squads of soldiers and police, if what I carry were not valuable to them?"

"I don't believe in your fool's religion."

"Have you ever seen the plays performed?"

"Once, when I was a girl. I saw *The Archer's Fall* during the year-end festival in Tienkash. I fell asleep."

"They are the axis of human culture. The sacred stories of our race. We are *human* because of them. Through them the gods speak to us."

"I thought you monks heard the gods talking to you directly. Didn't they tell you to run us directly into the face of the guards securing the escape pod? It's lucky you had me along to cut our way out of that umbilical, or we'd be dead up there now."

"*You* might be dead. I would be in a sleep tank having my brain taken apart— to retrieve these dramas."

"There are no gods! Just voices in your head. They tell you to do what you already want to do."

"If you think the commands of the gods are easy, then just try to follow them for a single day."

We settled into an uncomfortable silence. The sun set, and the rings became visible in the sky, turned pink by the sunset in the west, rising silvery toward the zenith, where they were eclipsed by the planet's shadow. The light of the big moon still illuminated the open rock face before us. We would have a steep 300-meter climb above the tree line to the pass, then another couple of kilometers between the peaks in the darkness.

"It's cold," I said after a while.

Without saying anything, she reached out and tugged my arm. It took me a moment to realize that she wanted me to move next to her. I slid over, and we ducked our heads to keep below the wind. I could feel the taut muscles of her body beneath the skinsuit. The paradox of our alienation hit me. We were both the products of the gods. She did not believe this truth, but truth does not need to be believed to prevail.

Still, she was right that we had not escaped the orbiting commandos in the way I had expected.

The great clockwork of the universe turned. Green Roshanak sped past Mahsheed, for a moment in transit looking like the pupil of a god's observing eye, then set, and an hour later, Mahsheed followed her below the western horizon. The stars shone in all their glory, but it was as dark as it would get before Roshanak rose for the second time that night. It was time for us to take our chance and go.

We came out of our hiding place and moved to the edge of the scrub. The broken granite of the peak rose before us, faint gray in starlight. We set out across the rock, climbing in places, striding across rubble fields, circling areas of ice and melting snow. In a couple of places, we had to boost each other up, scrambling over boulders, finding hand and footholds in the vertical face where we were blocked. It was farther than I had estimated before the ground leveled and we were in the pass.

We were just cresting the last ridge when glaring white light shone down on us, and an amplified voice called from above. "Do not move! Drop your weapons and lie flat on the ground!"

I tongued my body into acceleration. In slow motion, Nahid crouched, raised her blaster, arm extended, sighted on the flyer and fired. I hurled my body into hers and threw her aside just as the return fire of projectile weapons splattered the rock where she had been into fragments. In my head, the voices of the gods screamed: *Back. We will show you the way.*

"This way!" I dragged Nahid over the edge of the rock face we had just climbed. It was a three-meter drop to the granite below; I landed hard, and she fell on my chest, knocking the wind from me. Around us burst a hail of sleep gas pellets. In trying to catch my breath I caught a whiff of the gas, and my head whirled. Nahid slid her helmet down over her face, and did the same for me.

From above us came the sound of the flyer touching down. Nahid started for the tree line, limping. She must have been hit or injured in our fall. I pulled her to our left, along the face of the rock. "Where—" she began.

"Shut up!" I grunted.

The commandos hit the ledge behind us, but the flyer had its searchlight aimed at the trees, and the soldiers followed the light. The fog of sleep gas gave us some cover.

We scuttled along the granite shelf until we were beyond the entrance to the pass. By this time, I had used whatever reserves of energy my body could muster, and passed into normal speed. I was exhausted.

"Over the mountain?" Nahid asked. "We can't."

"Under it," I said. I forced my body into motion, searching in the darkness for the cleft in the rock which, in the moment of the flyer attack, the gods had shown me. And there it was, two dark pits above a vertical fissure in the granite, like an impassive face. We climbed up the few meters to the brink of the cleft. Nahid followed, slower now, dragging her right leg. "Are you badly hurt?" I asked her.

"Keep going."

I levered my shoulder under her arm, and helped her along the ledge. Down in the forest, the lights of the commandos flickered, while a flyer hovered above, beaming bright white radiance down between the trees.

Once inside the cleft, I let her lean against the wall. Beyond the narrow entrance the way widened. I used my suit flash, and, moving forward, found an oval chamber of three meters with a sandy floor. Some small bones give proof that a predator had once used this cave for a lair. But at the back, a small passage gaped. I crouched and followed it deeper.

"Where are you going?" Nahid asked.

"Come with me."

The passage descended for a space, then rose. I emerged into a larger space. My flash showed not a natural cave, but a chamber of dressed rock, and opposite us, a metal door. It was just as my vision had said.

"What is this?" Nahid asked in wonder.

"A tunnel under the mountain." I took off my helmet and spoke the words that would open the door. The ancient mechanism began to hum. With a fall of dust, a gap appeared at the side of the door, and it slid open.

THE DOOR CLOSED behind us with a disturbing finality, wrapping us in the silence of a tomb. We found ourselves in a corridor at least twice our height and three times that in width. Our lights showed walls smooth as plaster, but when I laid my hand on one, it proved to be cut from the living rock. Our boots echoed on the polished but dusty floor. The air was stale, unbreathed by human beings for unnumbered years.

I made Nahid sit. "Rest," I said. "Let me look at that leg."

Though she complied, she kept her blaster out, and her eyes scanned our surroundings warily. "Did you know of this?"

"No. The gods told me, just as we were caught in the pass."

"Praise be to the Pujmanian Order." I could not tell if there was any sarcasm in her voice.

A trickle of blood ran down her boot from the wound of a projectile gun. I opened the seam of her suit, cleaned the wound with antiseptic from my suit's first aid kit, and bandaged her leg. "Can you walk?" I asked.

She gave me a tight smile. "Lead on, Brother Adlan."

We moved along the hall. Several smaller corridors branched off, but we kept to the main way. Periodically, we came across doors, most of them closed. One gaped open upon a room where my light fell on a garage of wheeled vehicles, sitting patiently in long rows, their windows thick with dust. In the corner of the room, a fracture in the ceiling had let in a steady drip of water that had corroded the vehicle beneath it into a mass of rust.

Along the main corridor our lights revealed hieroglyphics carved above doorways, dead oval spaces on the wall that might once have been screens or windows. We must have gone a kilometer or more when the corridor ended suddenly in a vast cavernous opening.

Our lights were lost in the gloom above. A ramp led down to an underground city. Buildings of gracious curves, apartments like heaps of grapes stacked upon a table, halls whose walls were so configured that they resembled a huge garment discarded in a bedroom. We descended into the streets.

The walls of the buildings were figured in abstract designs of immense intricacy, fractal patterns from immense to microscopic, picked out by the beams of our flashlights. Colored tiles, bits of glass and mica. Many of the buildings were no more than sets of walls demarcating space, with horizontal trellises that must once have held plants above them rather than roofs. Here and there, outside what might have been cafes, tables and benches rose out of the polished floor. We arrived in a broad square with low buildings around it, centered on a dry fountain. The immense figures of a man, a woman, and a child dominated the center of the dusty reservoir. Their eyes were made of crystal, and stared blindly across their abandoned city.

Weary beyond words, hungry, bruised, we settled against the rim of the fountain and made to sleep. The drawn skin about her eyes told me of Nahid's pain. I tried to comfort her, made her rest her legs, elevated, on my own. We slept.

When I woke, Nahid was already up, changing the dressing on her bloody leg. The ceiling of the cave had lit, and a pale light shone down, making an early arctic dawn over the dead city.

"How is your leg?" I asked.

"Better. Do you have any more anodynes?"

I gave her what I had. She took them, and sighed. After a while, she asked, "Where did the people go?"

"They left the universe. They grew beyond the need of matter, and space. They became gods. You know the story."

"The ones who made this place were people like you and me."

"You and I are the descendants of the re-creation of a second human race three million years after the first ended in apotheosis. Or of the ones left behind, or banished back into the material world by the gods for some great crime."

Nahid rubbed her boot above the bandaged leg. "Which is it? Which child's tale do you expect me to believe?"

"How do you think I found the place? The gods told me, and here it is. Our mission is important to them, and they are seeing that we succeed. Justice is to be done."

"Justice? Tell the starving child about justice. The misborn and the dying. I would rather be the random creation of colliding atoms than subject to the whim of some transhumans no more godlike than I am."

"You speak out of bitterness."

"If they are gods, they are responsible for the horror that occurs in the world. So they are evil. Why otherwise would they allow things to be as they are?"

"To say that is to speak out of the limitations of our vision. We can't see the outcome of events. We're too close. But the gods see how all things will eventuate. Time is a landscape to them. All at once they see the acorn, the seedling, the ancient oak, the woodsman who cuts it, the fire that burns the wood, and the smoke that rises from the fire. And so they led us to this place."

"Did they lead the bullet to find my leg? Did they lead your order to place me on a shelf for a lifetime, separate me from every person I loved?" Nahid's voice rose. "Please save me your theodical prattle!"

"'Theodical.' Impressive vocabulary for a soldier. But you—"

A scraping noise came from behind us. I turned to find that the giant male figure in the center of the fountain had moved. As I watched, its hand jerked another few centimeters. Its foot pulled free of its setting, and it stepped down from the pedestal into the empty basin.

We fell back from the fountain. The statue's eyes glowed a dull orange. Its lips moved, and it spoke in a voice like the scraping together of two files: "Do not flee, little ones."

Nahid let fly a shot from her blaster, which ricocheted off the shoulder of the metal man and scarred the ceiling of the cave. I pulled her away and we crouched behind a table before an open-sided building at the edge of the square.

The statue raised its arms in appeal. "Your shoes are untied," it said in its ghostly rasp. "We know why you are here. It seems to you that your lives hang in the balance, and of course you value your lives. As you should, dear ones. But I, who have no soul and therefore no ability to care, can tell you that the appetites that move you are entirely transitory. The world you live in is a game. You do not have a ticket."

"Quite mad," Nahid said. "Our shoes have no laces."

"But it's also true—they are therefore untied," I said. "And we have no tickets." I called out to the metal man, "Are you a god?"

"I am no god," the metal man said. "The gods left behind the better part of themselves when they abandoned matter. The flyer lies on its side in the woods. Press the silver pentagon. You must eat, but you must not eat too much. Here is food."

The shop behind us lit up, and in a moment the smell of food wafted from within.

I slid over to the entrance. On a table inside, under warm light, were two plates of rice and vegetables.

"He's right," I told Nahid.

"I'm not going to eat that food. Where did it come from? It's been thousands of years without a human being here."

"Come," I said. I drew her inside and made her join me at the table. I tasted. The food was good. Nahid sat warily, facing out to the square, blaster a centimeter from her plate. The metal man sat on the plaza stones, cross-legged, ducking its massive head in order to watch us. After a few moments, it began to croon.

Its voice was a completely mechanical sound, but the tune it sang was sweet, like a peasant song. I cannot convey to you the strangeness of sitting in that ancient restaurant, eating food conjured fresh out of nothing by ancient machines, listening to the music of creatures who might have been a different species from us.

When its song was ended, the metal man spoke: "If you wish to know someone, you need only observe that on which he bestows his care, and what sides of his own nature he cultivates." It lifted its arm and pointed at Nahid. Its finger stretched almost to the door. I could see the patina of corrosion on that metal digit. "If left to the gods, you will soon die."

The arm moved, and it pointed at me. "You must live, but you must not live too much. Take this."

The metal man opened the curled fingers of its hand, and in its huge palm was a small, round metallic device the size of an apple. I took it. Black and dense, it filled my hand completely. "Thank you," I said.

The man stood and returned to the empty fountain, climbed onto the central pedestal, and resumed its position. There it froze. Had we not been witness to it, I could never have believed it had moved.

Nahid came out of her musing over the man's sentence of her death. She lifted her head. "What is that thing?"

I examined the sphere, surface covered in pentagonal facets of dull metal. "I don't know."

In one of the buildings, we found some old furniture, cushions of metallic fabric that we piled together as bedding. We huddled together and slept.

> **Selene:** Hear that vessel that docks above?
>   It marks the end of our lives
>   And the beginning of our torment.
> **Stochik:** Death comes
>   And then it's gone. Who knows
>   What lies beyond that event horizon?
>   Our life is but a trifle,
>   A child's toy abandoned by the road
>   When we are called home.
> **Selene:** Home? You might well hope it so,
>   But—
>   [Alarums off stage. Enter *a god*]
> **God:** *The hull is breached!*
>   *You must fly.*

In the night I woke, chasing away the wisps of a dream. The building we were in had no ceiling, and faint light from the cavern roof filtered down upon us. In our sleep, we had moved closer together, and Nahid's arm lay over my chest, her head next to mine, her breath brushing my cheek. I turned my face to her, centimeters away. Her face was placid, her eyelashes dark and long.

As I watched her, her eyelids fluttered and she awoke. She did not flinch at my closeness, but simply, soberly looked into my own eyes for what seemed like a very long time. I leaned forward and kissed her.

She did not pull away, but kissed me back strongly. She made a little moan in her throat, and I pulled her tightly to me.

We made love in the empty, ancient city. Her fingers entwined with mine, arms taut. Shadow of my torso across her breast. Hard, shuddering breath. Her lips on my chest. Smell of her sweat and mine. My palm brushing her abdomen. The feeling of her dark skin against mine. Her quiet laugh.

"Your leg," I said, as we lay in the darkness, spent.

"What about it?"

"Did I hurt you?"

She laughed again, lightly. "Now you ask. You are indeed all man."

In the morning, we took another meal from the ancient restaurant, food that had been manufactured from raw molecules while we waited, or perhaps stored somewhere for millennia.

We left by the corridor opposite the one by which we had entered, heading for the other side of the mountain range. Nahid limped but made no complaint. The passage ended in another door, beyond which a cave twisted upward. In one place, the ceiling of the cave had collapsed, and we had to crawl on our bellies over rubble through the narrow gap it had left. The exit was on to a horizontal shelf overgrown with trees, well below the pass. It was mid-morning. A misting rain fell across the Sharishabz Valley. In the distance, hazed by clouds of mist, I caught a small gleam of the white buildings of the monastery on the Penitent's Ridge. I pointed it out to Nahid. We scanned the mountainside below us, searching for the forest road.

Nahid found the thread of the road before I. "No sign of the Caslonians," she said.

"They're guarding the pass on the other side of the mountain, searching the woods there for us."

We descended the slope, picking our way through the trees toward the road. The mist left drops of water on our skinsuits, but did not in any way slow us. My spirits rose. I could see the end of this adventure in sight, and wondered what would happen to Nahid then.

"What will you do when we get to the monastery?" I asked her.

"I think I'll leave as soon as I can. I don't want to be there when the Caslonians find out you've reached your order with the plays."

"They won't do anything. The gods hold the monastery in their hands."

"Let us hope they don't drop it."

She would die soon, the statue had said—if left to the gods. But what person was not at the mercy of the gods? Still, she would be much more at risk alone, away from the order. "What about your leg?" I asked.

"Do you have a clinic there?"

"Yes."

"I'll take an exoskeleton and some painkillers and be on my way."

"Where will you go?"

"Wherever I can."

"But you don't even know what's happened in the last sixty years. What can you do?"

"Maybe my people are still alive. That's where I'll go—the town where I grew up. Perhaps I'll find someone who remembers me. Maybe I'll find my own grave."

"Don't go."

She strode along more aggressively. I could see her wince with each step. "Look, I don't care about your monastery. I don't care about these plays. Mostly, I don't care about *you*. Give me some painkillers and an exo, and I'll be gone."

That ended our conversation. We walked on in silence through the woods, me brooding, she limping along, grimacing.

We found the forest road. Here the land fell away sharply, and the road, hardly more than a gravel track, switchbacked severely as we made our way down the mountainside. We met no signs of pursuit. Though the rain continued, the air warmed as we moved lower, and beads of sweat trickled down my back under the skinsuit. The boots I wore were not meant for hiking, and by now my feet were sore, my back hurt. I could only imagine how bad it was for Nahid.

I had worked for years to manage my appetites, and yet I could not escape images of our night together. With a combination of shame and desire, I wanted her still. I did not think I could go back to being just another monk. The order had existed long before the Caslonian conquest, and would long outlast it. I was merely a cell passing through the body of this immortal creation. What did the gods want from me? What was to come of all this?

At the base of the trail, the road straightened, following the course of the River Sharishabz up the valley. Ahead rose the plateau, the gleaming white buildings of the monastery clearly visible now. The ornamental gardens, the terraced fields tended by the order for millennia. I could almost taste the sweet oranges and pomegranates. It would be good to be back home, a place where I could hide away form the world and figure out exactly what was in store for me. I wouldn't mind being hailed as a hero, the liberator of our people, like Stochik himself, who took the plays from the hands of the gods.

The valley sycamores and aspens rustled with the breeze. The afternoon passed. We stopped by the stream and drank. Rested, then continued.

We came to a rise in the road, where it twisted to climb the plateau. Signs here of travel, ruts of iron wheels where people from the villages drove supplies to the monastery. Pilgrims passed this way—though there was no sign of anyone today.

We made a turn in the road, and I heard a yelp behind me. I turned to find Nahid struggling in the middle of the road. At first, I thought she was suffering a seizure. Her body writhed and jerked. Then I realized, from the slick of rain deflected from his form, that she was being assaulted by a person in an invisibility cloak.

This understanding had only flashed through my mind when I was thrown to the ground by an unseen hand. I kicked out wildly, and my boot made contact. Gravel sprayed beside me where my attacker fell. I slipped into accelerated mode, kicked him again, rolled away, and dashed into the woods. Above me I heard the whine of an approaching flyer. *Run!* The voice of god told me.

I ran. The commandos did not know these woods the way I did. I had spent ten years exploring them, playing games of hide and hunt in the night with my fellow novices: I knew I could find my way to the monastery without them capturing me.

And Nahid? Clearly this was her spoken-of death. No doubt it had already taken place. Or perhaps they wouldn't kill her immediately, but would torture her, assuming she knew something, or even if they knew she didn't, taking some measure of revenge on her body. It was the lot of a Republican Guard to receive such treatment. She would even expect it. *The order comes first.*

Every second took me farther from the road, away from the Caslonians. But after a minute of hurrying silently through the trees, I felt something heavy in my hand. I stopped. Without realizing it, I had taken the object the metal man had given me out of my belt pouch. *She would not want you to return. The freedom of her people comes before her personal safety.*

I circled back, and found them in the road.

The flyer had come down athwart the road. The soldiers had turned off their cloaks, three men garbed head to toe in the matte gray of light deflection suits.

Two soldiers had Nahid on her knees in the drizzle, her hands tied behind her back. One jerked her head back by her hair, holding a knife to her throat while an officer asked her questions. The officer slapped her, whipping the back of his gloved hand across her face.

I moved past them through the woods, sound of rain on the foliage, still holding the metal sphere in my hand. The flyer sat only a few meters into the road. I crouched there, staring at the uncouth object. I rotated it in my palm until I found the surface pentagon that was silvered. I depressed this pentagon until it clicked.

Then I flipped it out into the road, under the landing pads of the flyer, and fell back.

It was not so much an explosion as a vortex, warping the flyer into an impossible shape, throwing it off they road. As it spun the pilot was tossed from the cockpit, his uniform flaring in electric blue flame. The three men with Nahid were sucked off their feet by the dimensional warp. They jerked their heads toward the screaming pilot. The officer staggered to his feet, took two steps toward him, and one of the men followed. By that time, I had launched myself into the road, and slammed my bad shoulder into the small of the back of the man holding Nahid. I seized his rifle and fired, killing the officer and the other soldier, then the one I had just laid flat. The pilot was rolling in the gravel to extinguish the flames. I stepped forward calmly and shot him in the head.

Acrid black smoke rose from the crushed flyer, which lay on its side in the woods.

Nahid was bleeding from a cut on her neck. She held her palm against the wound, but the blood seeped steadily from between her fingers. I gathered her up and dragged her into the woods before reinforcements could arrive.

"Thank you," Nahid gasped, her eyes large, and fixed on me. We limped off into the trees.

NAHID WAS BADLY hurt, but I knew where we were, and I managed, through that difficult night, to get us up the pilgrim's trail to the monastery. By the time we reached the iron door we called the Mud Gate she had lost consciousness and I was carrying her. Her blood was all over us, and I could not tell if she yet breathed.

We novices had used this gate many times to sneak out of the monastery to play martial games in the darkness, explore the woods, and pretend we were ordinary men. Men who, when they desired something, had only to take it. Men who were under no vow of nonviolence. Here I had earned a week's fast by bloodying the nose, in a fit of temper, of Brother Taher. Now I returned, unrepentant over the number of men I had killed in the last days, a man who had disobeyed the voice of a god, hoping to save Nahid before she bled out.

Brother Pramha was the first to greet me. He looked at me with shock. "Who is this?" he asked.

"This is a friend, a soldier, Nahid. Quickly. She needs care."

Together we took her to the clinic. Pramha ran off to inform the master. Our physician Brother Nastricht sealed her throat wound, and gave her new blood. I held her hand. She did not regain consciousness.

Soon, one of the novices arrived to summon me to Master Darius's chambers. Although I was exhausted, I hurried after him through the warren of corridors, up the tower steps. I unbelted my blaster and handed it to the novice—he seemed distressed to hold the destructive device—and entered the room.

Beyond the broad window that formed the far wall of the chamber, dawn stained the sky pink. Master Darius held out his arms. I approached him, humbly bowed my head, and he embraced me. The warmth of his large body enfolding me was an inexpressible comfort. He smelled of cinnamon. He let me go, held me at arm's length, and smiled. The kosode he wore I recognized as one I had sewn myself. "I cannot tell you how good it is to see you, Adlan."

"I have the plays," I announced.

"The behavior of our Caslonian masters has been proof enough of that," he replied. His broad, plain face was somber as he told me of the massacre in Radnapuja, where the colonial government had held six thousand citizens hostage, demanding the bodily presentation, alive, of the foul villain, the man without honor or soul, the sacrilegious terrorist who had stolen the Foundational Plays.

"Six thousand dead?"

"They won't be the last," the master said. "The plays have been used as a weapon, as a means of controlling us. The beliefs which they embody work within the minds and souls of every person on this planet. They work even on those who are unbelievers."

"Nahid is an unbeliever."

"Nahid? She is this soldier whom you brought here?"

"The Republican Guard you sent with me. She doesn't believe, but she has played her role in bringing me here."

Master Darius poured me a glass of fortifying spirits, and handed it to me as if he were a novice and I the master. He sat in his great chair, had me sit in the chair opposite, and bade me recount every detail of the mission. I did so.

"It is indeed miraculous that you have come back alive," Master Darius mused. "Had you died, the plays would have been lost forever."

"The gods would not allow such a sacrilege."

"Perhaps. You carry the only copies in your mind?"

"Indeed. I have even quoted them to Nahid."

"Not at any length, I hope."

I laughed at his jest. "But now we can free Helvetica," I said. "Before any further innocents are killed, you must contact the Caslonian colonial government and tell them we have the plays. Tell them they must stop or we will destroy them."

Master Darius held up his hand and looked at me piercingly—I had seen this gesture many times in his tutoring of me. "First, let me ask you some questions about your tale. This is what my mentor, the great Master Malrubius, called a 'teaching moment.' You tell me that, when you first came to consciousness after stealing the plays in the Imperial City, a god told you to run. Yet to run in the Caslonian capital is only to attract unwelcome attention."

"Yes. The god must have wanted to hurry my escape."

"But when you reached the port bazaar, the god told you to stop and enter the restaurant. You run to attract attention, and dawdle long enough to allow time for you to be caught. Does this make sense?"

My fatigue made it difficult for me to think. What point was the master trying to make? "Perhaps I was not supposed to stop," I replied. "It was my own weakness. I was hungry."

"Then, later, you tell me that when the commandos boarded your ship, you escaped by following Nahid's lead, not the word of the gods."

"The gods led us out of the engine room. I think this is a matter of my misinterpreting—"

"And this metal man you encountered in the ancient city. Did he in fact say that the gods would have seen Nahid dead?"

"The statue said many mad things."

"Yet the device he gave you was the agent of her salvation?"

"I used it for that." Out of shame, I had not told Master Darius that I had disobeyed the command of the god who told me to flee.

"Many paradoxes." The master took a sip from his own glass. "So, if we give the plays back, what will happen then?"

"Then Helvetica will be free."

"And after that?"

"After that, we can do as we wish. The Caslonians would not dare to violate a holy vow. The gods would punish them. They know that. They are believers, as are we."

"Yes, they are believers. They would obey any compact they made, for fear of the wrath of the gods. They believe what you hold contained in your mind, Adlan, is true. So, as you say, you must give them to me now, and I will see to their disposition."

"Their disposition? How will you see to their disposition?"

"That is not something for you to worry about, my son. You have done well, and you deserve all our thanks. Brother Ishmael will see to unburdening you of the great weight you carry."

A silence ensued. I knew it was a sign of my dismissal. I must go to Brother Ishmael. But I did not rise. "What will you do with them?"

Master Darius's brown eyes lay steady on me, and quiet. "You have always been my favorite. I think perhaps, you know what I intend."

I pondered our conversation. "You—you're going to destroy them."

"Perhaps I was wrong not to have you destroy them the minute you gained access to the archives. But at that time I had not come to these conclusions."

"But the wrath of the Caslonians will know no limit! We will be exterminated!"

"We may be exterminated, and Helvetica remain in chains, but once these plays are destroyed, never to be recovered, then *humanity* will begin to be truly free. This metal man, you say, told you the gods left the better part of themselves behind. That is profoundly true. Yet there is no moment when they cease to gaze over our shoulders. Indeed, if we are ever to be free human beings, and not puppets jerked about by unseen forces—which may, or may not, exist—the gods must go. And the beginning of that process is the destruction of the foundational plays."

I did not know how to react. In my naiveté I said, "This does not seem right."

"I assure you, my son, that it is."

"If we destroy the plays, it will be the last thing we ever do."

"Of course not. Time will not stop."

"Time may not stop," I said, "but it might as well. Any things that happen after the loss of the gods will have no meaning."

Master Darius rose from his chair and moved toward his desk. "You are tired, and very young," he said, his back to me. "I have lived in the shadow of the gods far longer than you have." He reached over his desk, opened a drawer, took something out, and straightened.

He is lying. I stood. I felt surpassing weariness, but I moved silently. In my boot I still carried the force knife I had stolen from the restaurant on Caslon. I drew out the hilt, switched on the blade, and approached the master just as he began to turn.

When he faced me, he had a blaster in his hands. He was surprised to find me so close to him. His eyes went wide as I slipped the blade into his belly below his lowest rib.

> **Stochik:** Here ends our story.
> Let no more be said of our fall.
> Mark the planting of this seed.
> The tree that grows in this place
> Will bear witness to our deeds;
> No other witness shall we have.
> **Selene:** I would not depart with any other
> My love. Keep alive whatever word
> May permit us to move forward.
> Leaving all else behind we must
> Allow the world to come to us.

The Caslonian government capitulated within a week after we contacted them. Once they began to withdraw their forces from the planet and a provisional government for the Helvetican Republic was re-established in Astara, I underwent the delicate process of downloading the foundational dramas from my mind. *The Abandonment* was once again embodied in a crystal, which was presented to the Caslonian legate in a formal ceremony on the anniversary of the rebirth of man.

The ceremony took place on a bright day in midsummer in that city of a thousand spires. Sunlight flooded the streets, where citizens in vibrant colored robes danced and sang to the music of bagpipes. Pennants in purple and green flew from those spires; children hung out of second-story school windows, shaking snowstorms of confetti on the parades. The smell of incense wafted down from the great temple, and across the sky flyers drew intricate patterns with lines of colored smoke.

Nahid and I were there on that day, though I did not take a leading role in the ceremony, preferring to withdraw to my proper station. In truth, I am not a significant individual. I have only served the gods.

I left the order as soon as the negotiations were completed. At first the brothers were appalled by my murder of Master Darius. I explained to them that he had gone mad and intended to kill me in order to destroy the plays. There was considerable doubt. But when I insisted that we follow through with the plan as the Master had presented it to the brothers before sending me on my mission, they seemed to take my word about his actions. The success of our thieving enterprise overshadowed the loss of the great leader, and indeed has contributed to his legend, making of him a tragic figure. A drama has been written of his life and death, and the liberation of Helvetica.

Last night, Nahid and I, with our children and grandchildren, watched it performed in the square of the town where we set up the tailor's shop that has been the center of our lives for the last forty years. Seeing the events of my youth played out on the platform, in their comedy and tragedy, hazard and fortune, calls again to my mind the question of whether I have deserved the blessings that have fallen to me ever since that day. I have not heard the voices of the gods since I slipped the knife into the belly of the man who taught me all that I knew of grace.

The rapid decline of the Caslonian Empire, and the Helvetican renaissance that has led to our current prosperity, all date from that moment in his chambers when I ended his plan to free men from belief and duty. The people, joyous on their knees in the temples of twelve planets, give praise to the gods for their deliverance, listen, hear, and obey.

Soon I will rest beneath the earth, like the metal man who traduced the gods, though less likely than he ever to walk again. If I have done wrong, it is not for me to judge. I rest, my lover's hand in mine, in the expectation of no final word.

useless things

MAUREEN MCHUGH

Maureen F. McHugh made her first sale in 1989 and has since made a powerful impression on the SF world with a relatively small body of work, becoming one of today's most respected writers. In 1992 she published one of the year's most widely acclaimed and talked about first novels, China Mountain Zhang, *which won the Locus Award for Best First Novel, the Lambda Literary Award, and the James Tiptree Jr. Memorial Award, and was named a* New York Times *Notable Book, as well as being a finalist for the Hugo and Nebula Awards. Her story "The Lincoln Train" won her a Hugo Award. Her other books, including the novels* Half the Day Is Night, Mission Child, *and* Nekropolis, *have been greeted with similar enthusiasm. Her powerful short fiction has been collected in* Mothers & Other Monsters *and* After the Apocalypse.*

Here's a quiet but deeply human story about a woman in an impoverished world struggling to get by while at the same time somehow holding on to her basic humanity. . . .

S enora?" The man standing at my screen door is travel-stained. Migrant, up from Mexico. The dogs haven't heard him come up but now they erupt in a frenzy of barking to make up for their oversight. I am sitting at the kitchen table, painting a doll, waiting for the timer to tell me to get doll parts curing in the oven in the worksshed.

"Hudson, Abby!" I shout, but they don't pay any attention.

The man steps back. "Do you have work? I can, the weeds," he gestures. He is short-legged, long from waist to shoulder. He's probably headed for the Great Lakes area, the place in the U.S. with the best supply of fresh water and the most need of farm labor.

BEHIND HIM IS my back plot, with the garden running up to the privacy fence. The sky is just starting to pink up with dawn. At this time of year I do a lot of my work before dawn and late in the evening, when it's not hot. That's probably when he has been traveling, too.

I show him the cistern, and set him to weeding. I show him where he can plug in his phone to recharge it. I have internet radio on, Elvis Presley died forty five years ago today and they're playing "(You're So Square) Baby I Don't Care." I go inside and get him some bean soup.

Hobos used to mark code to tell other hobos where to stop and where to keep going. Teeth to signify a mean dog. A triangle with hands meant that the home-owner had a gun and might use it. A cat meant a nice lady. Today the men use websites and bulletin boards that they follow, when they can, with cheap smart-phones. Somewhere I'm on a site as a "nice lady" or whatever they say today. The railroad runs east of here and it's sometimes a last spot where trains slow down before they get to the big yard in Belen. Men come up the Rio Grande hoping to hop the train.

I don't like it. I was happy to give someone a meal when I felt anonymous. Handing a bowl of soup to someone who may not have eaten for a few days was an easy way to feel good about myself. That didn't mean I wanted to open a mi-grant restaurant. I live by myself. Being an economic refugee doesn't make people kind and good and I feel as if having my place on some website makes me vulnerable. The dogs may bark like fools, but Hudson is some cross between Border Collie and Golden Retriever, and Abby is mostly black Lab. They are sweet mutts, not good protection dogs and it doesn't take a genius to figure that out.

I wake at night sometimes now, thinking someone is in my house. Abby sleeps on the other side of the bed, and Hudson sleeps on the floor. Where I live it is brutally dark at night, unless there's a moon—no one wastes power on lights at night. My house is small, two bedrooms, a kitchen and a family room. I lean over and shake Hudson on the floor, wake him up. "Who's here?" I whisper. Abby sits up, but neither of them hear anything. They pad down the hall with me into the dark front room and I peer through the window into the shadowy back lot. I wait for them to bark. Many a night, I don't go back to sleep.

But the man at my door this morning weeds my garden, and accepts my bowl of soup and some flour tortillas. He thanks me gravely. He picks up his phone, charging off my system, and shows me a photo of a woman and a child. "My wife and baby," he says. I nod. I don't particularly want to know about his wife and baby but I can't be rude.

I finish assembling the doll I am working on. I've painted her, assembled all the parts and hand rooted all her hair. She is rather cuter than I like. Customers can mix and match parts off my website—this face with the eye color of their choice, hands curled one way or another. A mix and match doll costs about what the migrant will make in two weeks. A few customers want custom dolls and send images to match. Add a zero to the cost.

I am dressing the doll when Abby leaps up, happily roo-rooing. I start, stand-ing, and drop the doll dangling in my hand by one unshod foot.

It hits the floor head first with a thump and the man gasps in horror.

"It's a doll," I say.

I don't know if he understands, but he realizes. He covers his mouth with his hand and laughs, nervous.

I scoop the doll off the floor. I make reborns. Dolls that look like newborn infants. The point is to make them look almost, but not quite real. People prefer them a little cuter, a little more perfect than the real thing. I like them best when there is something a little strange, a little off about them. I like them as ugly as most actual newborns, with some aspect that suggests ontology recapitulating phylogeny; that a developing fetus starts as a single celled organism, and then develops to look like a tiny fish, before passing in stages into it's final animal shape. The old theory of ontology recapitulating phylogeny, that the development of the human embryo follows the evolutionary path, is false, of course. But I prefer that my babies remind us that we are really animals. That they be ancient and a little grotesque. Tiny changelings in our house.

I am equally pleased to think of Thanksgiving turkeys as a kind of dinosaur gracing a holiday table. It is probably why I live alone.

"Que bonita," he says. How beautiful.

"Gracias," I say. He has brought me the empty bowl. I take it and send him on his way.

I check my email and I have an order for a special. A reborn made to order. It's from a couple in Chicago, Rachel and Ellam Mazar—I have always assumed that it is Rachel who emails me, but the emails never actually identify who is typing. There is a photo attached of an infant. This wouldn't be strange except this is the third request in three years I have had for exactly the same doll.

The dolls are expensive, especially the specials. I went to art school, and then worked as a sculptor for a toy company for a few years. I didn't make dolls, I made action figures, especially alien figures and spaceships from the *Kinetics* movies. A whole generation of boys grew up imprinting on toys I had sculpted. When the craze for *Kinetics* passed, the company laid off lots of people, including me. The whole economy was coming apart at the seams. I had been lucky to have a job for as long as I did. I moved to New Mexico because I loved it and it was cheap, and I tried to do sculpting freelance. I worked at a big box store. Like so many people, my life went into free fall. I bought this place—a little ranch house that had gone into foreclosure in a place where no one was buying anything and boarded up houses fall in on themselves like mouths without teeth. It was the last of my savings. I started making dolls as a stopgap.

I get by. Between the little bit of money from the dolls and the garden I can eat. Which is more than some people.

A special will give me money for property tax. My cistern is letting low and there is no rain coming until the monsoon in June, which is a long way from now. If it's like last year, we won't get enough rain to fill the cistern anyway. I could pay for the water truck to make a delivery. But I don't like this. When I put the specials on my website, I thought about it as a way to make money. I had seen it on another doll site. I am a trained sculptor. I didn't think about why people would ask for specials.

Some people ask me to make infant dolls of their own children. If my mother had bought an infant version of me I'd have found it pretty disturbing.

One woman bought a special modeled on herself. She wrote me long emails about how her mother had been a narcissist, a monster, and how she was going to symbolically mother herself. Her husband was mayor of a city in California, which was how she could afford to have a replica of her infant self. Her emails made me uncomfortable, which I resented. So eventually I passed her on to another doll maker who made toddlers. I figured she could nurture herself up through all the stages of childhood.

Her reborn was very cute. More attractive than she was in the image she sent. She never commented. I don't know that she ever realized.

I suspect the Mazars fall into another category. I have gotten three requests from people who have lost an infant. I tell myself that there is possibly something healing in recreating your dead child as a doll. Each time I have gotten one of these requests I have very seriously considered taking the specials off my website.

Property tax payments. Water in the cistern.

If the Mazars lost a child—and I don't know that they did but I have a feeling that I can't shake—it was bad enough that they want a replica. Then a year ago, I got a request for the second.

I thought that maybe Rachel—if it is Rachel who emails me, not Ellam—had meant to send a different image. I sent back an email saying were they sure that she had sent the right image?

The response was terse. They were sure.

I sent them an email saying if something had happened, I could do repairs.

The response was equally terse. They wanted me to make one.

I searched them online but could find out nothing about the Mazars of Chicago. They didn't have a presence online. Who had money but no presence online? Were they organized crime? Just very very private? Now a third doll.

I don't answer the email. Not yet.

Instead I take my laptop out to the shed. Inside the shed is my oven for baking the doll parts between coats of paint. I plug in the computer to recharge and park it on a shelf above eye level. I have my parts cast by Tony in Ohio, an old connection from my days in the toy industry. He makes my copper molds and rotocasts the parts. Usually, though, the specials are a one off and he sends me the copper supermaster of the head, so he doesn't have to store it. I rummage through my molds and find the head from the last time I made this doll. I set it on the shelf and look at it.

I rough sculpt the doll parts in clay, the do a plaster cast of the clay mold. Then from that I make a wax model, looking like some Victorian memorial of an infant that died of jaundice. I have my own recipe for the wax—commercial wax and paraffin and talc. I could tint it pink, most people do. I just like the way they look.

I do the fine sculpting and polishing on the wax model. I carefully pack and ship the model to Tony and he casts the copper mold. The process is nasty and toxic, not something I can do myself. For the regular dolls, he does a short run of a hundred or so parts in PVC, vinyl, and ships them to me. He keeps those molds in case I need more. For the head of a special he sends me back a single cast head and the mold.

All of the detail is on the inside of the mold, outside is only the rough outline of the shape. Infant's heads are long from forehead to back of the skull. Their faces are tiny and low, their jaws like pork chop bones. They are marvelous and strange mechanisms.

At about seven, I hear Sherie's truck. The dogs erupt.

Sherie and Ed live about a mile and a half up the road. They have a little dairy goat operation. Sherie is six months pregnant and goes into Albuquerque to see a obstetrician. Her dad works at Sandia Labs and makes decent money so her parents are paying for her medical care. It's a long drive in and back, the truck is old and Ed doesn't like her to go alone. I ride along and we pick up supplies. Her mom makes us lunch.

"Goddamn it's hot," Sherie says as I climb into the little yellow Toyota truck. "How's your water?"

"Getting low," I say. Sherie and Ed have a well.

"I'm worried we might go dry this year," Sherie says. "They keep whining about the aquifer. If we have to buy water I don't know what we'll do."

Sherie is physically Chinese, one of the thousands of girls adopted out of China in the nineties and at the turn of the century. She said she went through a phase of trying to learn all things Chinese, but she complains that as far as she can tell, the only thing Chinese about her is that she's lactose intolerant.

"I had a migrant at my door this morning," I say.

"Did you feed him?" she asks. She leans into the shift, trying to find the gear, urging the truck into first.

"He weeded my garden," I say.

"They're not going to stop as long as you feed them."

"Like stray cats," I say.

Albuquerque has never been a pretty town. When I came it was mostly strip malls and big box stores and suburbs. Ten years of averages of 4 inches of rain or less have hurt it badly, especially with the loss of the San Juan/Chama water rights. Water is expensive in Albuquerque. Too expensive for Intel, which pulled out. Intel was just a larger blow in a series of blows.

The suburbs are full of walkaway houses—places where homeowners couldn't meet the mortgage payments and just left, the lots now full of trash and windows gone. People who could went north for water. People who couldn't did what people always do when an economy goes soft and rotten, they slid, to rented houses, rented apartments, living in their cars, living with their family, living on the street.

But inside Sherie's parents' home it's still twenty years ago. The countertops are granite. The big screen plasma TV gets hundreds of channels. The freezer is full of meat and frozen Lean Cuisine. The air conditioner keeps the temperature at a heavenly 75 degrees. Sherie's mother, Brenda, is slim, with beautifully styled graying hair. She's a psychologist with a small practice.

Brenda has one of my dolls, which she bought because she likes me. It's always out when I come, but it doesn't fit Brenda's tailored, airily comfortable style. I have never heard Brenda say a thing against Ed. But I can only assume that she and Kyle wish Sherie had married someone who worked at Los Alamos or at Sandia or the University, someone with government benefits like health insurance. On the other hand, Sherie was a wild child, who, as Brenda said, "Did a stint as a lesbian," as if being a lesbian were like signing up for the Peace Corps. You can't make your child fall in love with the right kind of person. I wish I could have fallen in love with someone from Los Alamos. More than that, I wish I had been able to get a job at Los Alamos or the University. Me, and half of Albuquerque.

Sherie comes home, her hair rough cut in her kitchen with a mirror. She is loud and comfortable. Her belly is just a gentle insistent curve under her blue Rumatel goat dewormer t-shirt. Brenda hangs on her every word, knows about the trials and tribulations of raising goats, asks about Ed, the truck. She feeds us lunch.

I thought this life of thoughtful liberalism was my birthright, too. Before I understood that my generation was to be born in interesting times.

At the obstetrician's office, I sit in the waiting room and try not to fall asleep. I'm stuffed on Brenda's chicken and cheese sandwich and corn chowder. *People* magazine has an article about Tom Cruise getting telemerase regeneration therapy, which will extend his lifespan an additional forty years. There's an article on some music guy's house talking about the new opulence; cutting edge technology that darkens the windows at the touch of a hand and walls that change color, rooms that sense whether you're warm or cold and change their temperature, and his love of ancient Turkish and Russian antiques. There's an article on a woman who has dedicated her life to helping people in Siberia who have AIDS.

Sherie comes out of the doctor's office on her cellphone. The doctor tells her that if she had insurance, they'd do a routine ultrasound. I can hear half the conversation as she discusses it with her mother. "This little guy," Sherie says, hand on her belly, "is half good Chinese peasant stock. He's doing fine." They decide to wait for another month.

Sherie is convinced that it's a boy. Ed is convinced it's a girl. He sings David Bowie's "China Doll" to Sherie's stomach which for some reason irritates the hell out of her.

We stop on our way out of town and stock up on rice and beans, flour, sugar, coffee. We can get all this in Belen, but it's cheaper at Sam's Club. Sherie has a membership. I pay half the membership and she uses the card to buy all our groceries then I pay her back when we get to the car. The cashiers surely know that we're sharing a membership, but they don't care.

It's a long hot drive back home. The air conditioning doesn't work in the truck. I am so grateful to see the trees that mark the valley.

My front door is standing open.

"Who's here?" Sherie says.

Abby is standing in the front yard and she has clearly recognized Sherie's truck.

She's barking her fool head off and wagging her tail, desperate. She runs to the truck. I get out and head for the front door and she runs towards the door and then back towards me and then towards the door, unwilling to go in until I get there, then lunging through the door ahead of me.

"Hudson?" I call the other dog, but I know if the door is open, he's out roaming. Lost. My things are strewn everywhere, couch cushions on the floor, my kitchen drawers emptied on the floor, the back door open. I go through to the back, calling the missing dog, hoping against hope he is in the back yard. The back gate is open, too.

Behind me I hear Sherie calling, "Don't go in there by yourself!"

"My dog is gone," I say.

"Hudson?" she says.

I go out the back and call for him. There's no sign of him. He's a great boy, but some dogs, like Abby, tend to stay close to home. Hudson isn't one of those dogs.

Sherie and I walk through the house. No one is there. I go out to my workshop. My toolbox is gone, but evidently whoever did this didn't see the computer closed and sitting on the shelf just above eye level.

It had to be the guy I gave soup to. He probably went nearby to wait out the heat of the day and saw me leave.

I close and lock the gate, and the workshop. Close and lock my back door. Abby clings to me. Dogs don't like things to be different.

"We'll look for him," Sherie says. Abby and I climb into the truck and for an hour we drive back roads, looking and calling, but there's no sign of him. Her husband Ed calls us. He's called the county and there's a deputy at my place waiting to take a statement. We walk through the house and I identify what's gone. As best I can tell, it isn't much. Just the tools, mainly. The sheriff says they are usually looking for money, guns, jewelry. I had all my cards and my cell phone with me, and all my jewelry is inexpensive stuff. I don't have a gun.

I tell the deputy about the migrant this morning. He says it could have been him, or someone else. I get the feeling we'll never know. He promises to put out the word about the dog.

It is getting dark when they all leave and I put the couch cushions on the couch. I pick up silverware off the floor and run hot water in the sink to wash it all. Abby stands at the backdoor, whining, but doesn't want to go out alone.

It occurs to me suddenly that the doll I was working on is missing. He stole the doll. Why? He's not going to be able to sell it. To send it home, I guess, to the baby in the photo. Or maybe to his wife, who has a real baby and is undoubtedly feeling a lot less sentimental about infants than most of my customers do. It's a couple of weeks of work, not full time, but painting, waiting for the paint to cure, painting again.

Abby whines again. Hudson is out there in the dark. Lost dogs don't do well in the desert. There are rattlesnakes. I didn't protect him. I sit down on the floor and wrap my arms around Abby's neck and cry. I'm a stupid woman who is stupid about my dogs, I know. But they are what I have.

I don't really sleep. I hear noises all night long. I worry about what I am going to do about money.

Replacing the tools is going to be a problem. The next morning I put the first layer of paint on a new doll to replace the stolen one. Then I do something I have resisted doing. Plastic doll parts aren't the only thing I can mold and sell on the internet. I start a clay model for a dildo. Over the last couple of years I've gotten queries from companies who have seen the dolls online and asked if I would consider doing dildos for them. Realistic penises aren't really any more difficult to carve than realistic baby hands. Easier, actually. I can't send it to Tony, he wouldn't do dildos. But a few years ago they came out with room temperature, medical grade silicon. I can make my own molds, do small runs, hand finish them. Make them as perfectly lifelike as the dolls. I can hope people will pay for novelty when it comes to sex.

I don't particularly like making doll parts, but I don't dislike it either. Dildos, on the other hand, just make me sad. I don't think there is anything wrong with using them, it's not that. It's just . . . I don't know. I'm not going to stop making dolls, I tell myself.

I also email the Chicago couple back and accept the commission for the special, to make the same doll for the third time. Then I take a break and clean my kitchen some more. Sherie calls me to check how I'm doing and I tell her about the dildos. She laughs. "You should have done it years ago," she says. "You'll be rich."

I laugh, too. And I feel a little better when I finish the call.

I try not to think about Hudson. It's well over 100 today. I don't want to think about him in trouble, without water. I try to concentrate on penile veins. On the stretch of skin underneath the head (I'm making a circumcised penis.) When my cell rings I jump.

The guy on the phone says, "I've got a dog here, has got this number on his collar. You missing a dog?"

"A golden retriever?" I say.

"Yep."

"His name is Hudson," I say. "Oh, thank you. Thank you. I'll be right there."

I grab my purse. I've got fifty-five dollars in cash. Not much of a reward, but all I can do. "Abby!" I yell. "Come on girl! Let's go get Hudson!"

She bounces up from the floor, clueless, but excited by my voice.

"Go for a ride?" I ask.

We get in my ancient red Impreza. It's not too reliable, but we aren't going far. We bump across miles of bad road, most of it unpaved, following the GPS directions on my phone and end up at a trailer in the middle of nowhere. It's bleached and surrounded by trash—an old easy chair, a kitchen chair lying on it's side with one leg broken and the white unstained inside like a scar, an old picnic table. There's a dirty green cooler and a bunch of empty 40 oz bottles. Frankly, if I saw the place my assumption would be that the owner made meth. But the old man who opens the door is just an old guy in a baseball cap. Probably living on social security.

"I'm Nick," he says. He's wearing a long sleeved plaid shirt despite the heat. He's deeply tanned and has a turkey wattle neck.

I introduce myself. Point to the car and say, "That's Abby, the smart one that stays home."

The trailer is dark and smells of old man inside. The couch cushions are covered in cheap throws, one of them decorated with a blue and white Christmas snowman. Outside, the scrub shimmers, flattened in the heat. Hudson is laying in front of the sink and scrabbles up when he sees us.

"He was just ambling up the road," Nick says. "He saw me and came right up."

"I live over by the river, off 109, between Belen and Jarales," I say. "Someone broke into my place and left the doors open and he wandered off."

"You're lucky they didn't kill the dogs," Nick says.

I fumble with my purse. "There's a reward," I say.

He waves that away. "No, don't you go starting that." He says he didn't do anything but read the tag and give him a drink. "I had dogs all my life," he says. "I'd want someone to call me."

I tell him it would mean a lot to me and press the money on him. Hudson leans against my legs to be petted, tongue lolling. He looks fine. No worse for wear.

"Sit a minute. You came all the way out here. Pardon the mess. My sister's grandson and his friends have been coming out here and they leave stuff like that," he says, waving at the junk and the bottles.

"I can't leave the other dog in the heat," I say, wanting to leave.

"Bring her inside."

I don't want to stay, but I'm grateful, so I bring Abby in out of the heat and he thumps her and tells me about how he's lived here since he was in his twenties. He's a Libertarian and he doesn't trust government and he really doesn't trust the New Mexico state government which is, in his estimation, a banana republic lacking only the fancy uniforms that third world dictators seem to love. Then he tells me about how lucky it was that Hudson didn't get picked up to be a bait dog for the people who raise dogs for dog fights. Then he tells me about how the American economy was destroyed by operatives from Russia as revenge for the fall of the Soviet Union.

Half of what he says is bullshit and the other half is wrong, but he's just a lonely guy in the middle of the desert and he brought me back my dog. The least I can do is listen.

I hear a spitting little engine off in the distance. Then a couple of them. It's the little motorbikes the kids ride. Nick's eyes narrow as he looks out.

"It's my sister's grandson," he says. "Goddamn."

He gets up and Abby whines. He stands, looking out the slatted blinds.

"Goddamn. He's got a couple of friends," Nick says. "Look you just get your dogs and don't say nothing to them, okay? You just go on."

"Hudson," I say and clip a lead on him.

Outside, four boys pull into the yard, kicking up dust. They have seen my car and are obviously curious. They wear jumpsuits like prison jumpsuits, only with the sleeves ripped off and the legs cut off just above the knees. Khaki and orange and olive green. One of them has tattoos swirling up his arms.

"Hey Nick," the tattooed one says, "new girlfriend?"

"None of your business, Ethan."

The boy is dark but his eyes are light blue. Like a Siberian Husky. "You a social worker?" the boy says.

"I told you it was none of your business," Nick says. "The lady is just going."

"If you're a social worker, you should know that old Nick is crazy and you can't believe nothing he says."

One of the other boys says, "She isn't a social worker. Social workers don't have dogs."

I step down the steps and walk to my car. The boys sit on their bikes and I have to walk around them to get to the Impreza. Hudson wants to see them, pulling against his leash, but I hold him in tight.

"You look nervous, lady," the tattooed boy says.

"Leave her alone, Ethan," Nick says.

"You shut up, Uncle Nick, or I'll kick your ass," the boy says absently, never taking his eyes off me.

Nick says nothing.

I say nothing. I just get my dogs in my car and drive away.

Our life settles into a new normal. I get a response from my dildo email. Nick in Montana is willing to let me sell on his sex site on commission. I make a couple of different models, including one that I paint just as realistically as I would one of the reborn dolls. This means a base coat, then I paint the veins in. Then I bake it. Then I paint an almost translucent layer of color and bake it again. Six layers. And then a clear over layer of silicon because I don't think the paint is approved for use this way. I put a pretty hefty price on it and call it a special. At the same time I am making my other special. The doll for the Chicago couple. I sent the mold to Tony and had him do a third head from it. It, too, requires layers of paint, and sometimes the parts bake side by side.

Because my business is rather slow, I take more time than usual. I am always careful, especially with specials. I think if someone is going to spend the kind of money one of these costs, the doll should be made to the best of my ability. And maybe it is because I have done this doll before, it comes easily and well. I think of the doll that the man who broke into my house stole. I don't know if he sent it to his wife and daughter in Mexico, or if he even has a wife and daughter in Mexico. I rather suspect he sold it on eBay or some equivalent—although I have watched doll sales and never seen it come up.

This doll is my orphan doll. She is full of sadness. She is inhabited by the loss of so much. I remember my fear when Hudson was wandering the roads of the desert.

I imagine Rachel Mazar, so haunted by the loss of her own child. The curves of the doll's tiny fists are porcelain pale. The blue veins at her temples are traceries of the palest of bruises.

When I am finished with her, I package her as carefully as I have ever packaged a doll and send her off.

My dildos go up on the website.

The realistic dildo sits in my workshop, upright, tumescent, a beautiful rosy plum color. It sits on a shelf like a prize, glistening in its topcoat as if it were wet. It was surprisingly fun to make, after years and years of doll parts. It sits there both as an object to admire and as an affront. But to be frank, I don't think it is any more immoral than the dolls. There is something straightforward about a dildo. Something much more clear than a doll made to look like a dead child. Something significantly less entangled.

There are no orders for dildos. I lie awake at night thinking about real estate taxes. My father is dead. My mother lives in subsidized housing for the elderly in Columbus. I haven't been to see her in years and years, not with the cost of a trip like that. My car wouldn't make it, and nobody I know can afford to fly anymore. I certainly couldn't live with her. She would lose her housing if I moved in.

If I lose my house to unpaid taxes, do I live in my car? It seems like the beginning of the long slide. Maybe Sherie and Ed would take the dogs.

I do get a reprieve when the money comes in for the special. Thank God for the Mazars in Chicago. However crazy their motives, they pay promptly and by internet, which allows me to put money against the equity line for the new tools.

I still can't sleep at night and instead of putting all of the money against my debt, I put the minimum and I buy a 9-millimeter handgun. Actually, Ed buys it for me. I don't even know where to get a gun.

Sherie picks me up in the truck and brings me over to the goat farm. Ed has several guns. He has an old gun safe that belonged to his father. When we get to their place, he is in back, putting creosote on new fence posts, but he is happy to come up to the house.

"So you've given in," he says, grinning. "You've joined the dark side."

"I have," I agree.

"Well, this is a decent defensive weapon," Ed says. Ed does not fit my preconceived notions of a gun owner. Ed fits my preconceived notions of the guy who sells you a cell phone at the local strip mall. His hair is short and graying. He doesn't look at all like the kind of guy who would either marry Sherie or raise goats. He told me one time that his degree is in anthropology. Which, he said, was a difficult field to get a job in.

"Offer her a cold drink!" Sherie yells from the bathroom. In her pregnant state, Sherie can't ride twenty minutes in the sprung-shocked truck without having to pee.

He offers me iced tea and then gets the gun, checks to see that it isn't loaded, and hands it to me. He explains to me that the first thing I should do is check to see if the gun is loaded.

"You just did," I say.

"Yeah," he says, "but I might be an idiot. It's a good thing to do."

He shows me how to check the gun.

It is not nearly so heavy in my hand as I thought it would be. But truthfully, I have found that the thing you thought would be life changing so rarely is.

Later he takes me around to the side yard and shows me how to load and shoot it. I am not even remotely surprised that it is kind of fun. That is exactly what I expected.

Out of the blue, an email from Rachel Mazar of Chicago.

I am writing you to ask you if you have had any personal or business dealings with my husband, Ellam Mazar. If I do not get a response from you, your next correspondence will be from my attorney.

I don't quite know what to do. I dither. I make vegetarian chili. Oddly enough, I check my gun which I keep in the bedside drawer. I am not sure what I am going to do about the gun when Sherie has her baby. I have offered to babysit, and I'll have to lock it up, I think. But that seems to defeat the purpose of having it.

While I am dithering, my cell rings. It is, of course, Rachel Mazar.

"I need you to explain your relationship with my husband, Ellam Mazar," she says. She sounds educated, with that eradication of regional accent that signifies a decent college.

"My relationship?" I say.

"Your email was on his phone," she says, frostily.

I wonder if he is dead. The way she says it sounds so final. "I didn't know your husband," I say. "He just bought the dolls."

"Bought what?" she says.

"The dolls," I say.

"Dolls?" she says.

"Yes," I say.

"Like . . . sex dolls?"

"No," I say. "Dolls. Reborns. Handmade dolls."

She obviously has no idea what I am talking about, which opens a world of strange possibilities in my mind. The dolls don't have orifices. Fetish objects? I tell her my website and she looks it up.

"He ordered specials," I say.

"But these cost a couple of thousand dollars," she says.

A weeks' salary for someone like Ellam Mazar, I suspect. I envision him as a professional, although frankly, for all I know he works in a dry-cleaning shop or something.

"I thought they were for you," I say. "I assumed you had lost a child. Sometimes people who have lost a child order one."

"We don't have children," she says. "We never wanted them." I can hear how stunned she is in the silence. Then she says, "Oh my God."

Satanic rituals? Some weird abuse thing?

"That woman said he told her he had lost a child," she says.

I don't know what to say so I just wait.

"My husband . . . my soon to be ex-husband," she says. "He has apparently been having affairs. One of the women contacted me. She told me that he told her we had a child that died and that now we were married in name only."

I hesitate. I don't know legally if I am allowed to tell her about transactions I had with her husband. On the other hand, the emails came with both their names on them. "He has bought three," I say.

"Three?"

"Not all at once. About once a year. But people who want a special send me a picture. He always sends the same picture."

"Oh," she says. "That's Ellam. He's orderly. He's used the same shampoo for fifteen years."

"I thought it was strange," I say. I can't bear not to ask. "What do you think he did with them?"

"I think the twisted bastard used them to make women feel sorry for him," she says through gritted teeth. "I think he got all sentimental about them. He probably has himself half convinced that he really did have a daughter. Or that it's my fault that we didn't have children. He never wanted children. Never."

"I think a lot of my customers like the idea of having a child better than having one," I say.

"I'm sure," she says. "Thank you for your time and I'm sorry to have bothered you."

So banal. So strange and yet so banal. I try to imagine him giving the doll to a woman, telling her that it was the image of his dead child. How did that work?

Orders for dildos begin to trickle in. I get a couple of doll orders and make a payment on the credit line and put away some towards real estate taxes. I may not have to live in my car.

One evening, I am working in the garden when Abby and Hudson start barking at the back gate.

I get off my knees, aching, but lurch into the house and into the bedroom where I grab the 9 mm out of the bedside table. It isn't loaded, which now seems stupid. I try to think if I should stop and load it. My hands are shaking. It is undoubtedly just someone looking for a meal and a place to recharge. I decide I can't trust myself to load and besides, the dogs are out there. I go to the back door, gun held stiffly at my side, pointed to the ground.

There are in fact two of them, alike as brothers, indian looking with a fringe of black hair cut in a straight line above their eyebrows.

"Lady," one says, "we can work for food?" First one, then the other sees the gun at my side and their faces go empty.

The dogs cavort.

"I will give you something to eat, and then you go," I say.

"We go," the one who spoke says.

"Someone robbed me," I say.

"We no rob you," he says. His eyes are on the gun. His companion takes a step back, glancing at the gate and then at me as if to gauge if I will shoot him if he bolts.

"I know," I say. "But someone came here, I gave him food, and he robbed me. You tell people not to come here, okay?"

"Okay," he says. "We go."

"Tell people not to come here," I say. I would give them something to eat, something to take with them. I hate this. They are two young men in a foreign country, hungry, looking for work. I could easily be sleeping in my car. I could be homeless. I could be wishing for someone to be nice to me.

But I am not. I'm just afraid.

"Hudson! Abby!" I yell, harsh, and the two men flinch. "Get in the house."

The dogs slink in behind me, not sure what they've done wrong.

"If you want some food, I will give you something," I say. "Tell people not to come here."

I don't think they understand me. Instead they back slowly away a handful of steps and then turn and walk quickly out the gate, closing it behind them.

I sit down where I am standing, knees shaking.

The moon is up in the blue early evening sky. Over my fence I can see scrub and desert, a fierce land where mountains breach like the petrified spines of apocalyptic animals. The kind of landscape that seems right for crazed gangs of mutants charging around in cobbled together vehicles. Tribal remnants of America, their faces painted, their hair braided, wearing jewelry made from shiny CDs and cigarette lighters scrounged from the ruins of civilization. The desert is Byronic in its extremes.

I don't see the two men. There's no one out there in furs, their faces painted blue, driving a dune buggy built out of motorcycle parts and hung with the skulls of their enemies. There's just a couple of guys from Nicaragua or Guatemala, wearing t-shirts and jeans.

And me, sitting watching the desert go dark, the moon rising, an empty handgun in my hand.

Mongoose

SARAH MONETTE & ELIZABETH BEAR

Sarah Monette was born and raised in Oak Ridge, Tennessee, one of the secret cities of the Manhattan Project. Having completed her Ph.D. in Renaissance English drama, she now lives and writes in a ninety-nine-year-old house in the Upper Midwest. Her Doctrine of Labyrinths series consists of the novels Mélusine, The Virtu, The Mirador and Corambis. Her short fiction has appeared in many places, including Strange Horizons, Aeon, Alchemy, and Lady Churchill's Rosebud Wristlet, and has been collected in The Bone Key.

Elizabeth Bear was born in Connecticut and now lives in Brookfield, Massachusetts, with her husband, writer Scott Lynch. She won the John W. Campbell Award for Best New Writer in 2005, and in 2008 took home a Hugo Award for her short story "Tideline," which also won her the Theodore Sturgeon Memorial Award (shared with David Moles). In 2009, she won another Hugo Award for her novelette "Shoggoths in Bloom." Her short work has appeared in Asimov's Science Fiction, Subterranean, SCI FICTION, Interzone, The Third Alternative, Strange Horizons, On Spec, and elsewhere, and has been collected in The Chains That You Refuse and Shoggoths in Bloom. She is the author of the five-volume New Amsterdam fantasy series, the three-volume Jenny Casey SF series, the five-volume Promethean Age series, the three-volume Jacob's Ladder series, the three-volume Edda of Burdens series, and the three-volume Eternal Sky series, as well as three novels in collaboration with Sarah Monette. Her other books include the novels Carnival and Undertow. Her most recent novel is The Stone in the Skull.

Bear and Monette have collaborated before, on the stories "The Ile of Dogges" and "Mongoose." Here they join forces again with a chilling story about an interdimensional pest-control officer, and his very unusual helper.

The ship had no name of her own, so her human crew called her the *Lavinia Whateley*. As far as anyone could tell, she didn't mind. At least, her long grasping vanes curled—affectionately?—when the chief engineers patted her bulkheads and called her "Vinnie," and she ceremoniously tracked the footsteps of each crew member with her internal bioluminescence, giving them light to walk and work and live by.

The *Lavinia Whateley* was a Boojum, a deep-space swimmer, but her kind had evolved in the high tempestuous envelopes of gas giants, and their offspring still spent their infancies there, in cloud-nurseries over eternal storms. And so she was streamlined, something like a vast spiny lionfish to the earth-adapted eye. Her sides were lined with gasbags filled with hydrogen; her vanes and wings furled tight. Her color was a blue-green so dark it seemed a glossy black unless the light struck it; her hide was impregnated with symbiotic algae.

Where there was light, she could make oxygen. Where there was oxygen, she could make water.

She was an ecosystem unto herself, as the captain was a law unto herself. And down in the bowels of the engineering section, Black Alice Bradley, who was only human and no kind of law at all, loved her.

Black Alice had taken the oath back in '32, after the Venusian Riots. She hadn't hidden her reasons, and the captain had looked at her with cold, dark, amused eyes and said, "So long as you carry your weight, cherie, I don't care. Betray me, though, and you will be going back to Venus the cold way." But it was probably that—and the fact that Black Alice couldn't hit the broad side of a space freighter with a ray gun—that had gotten her assigned to engineering, where ethics were less of a problem. It wasn't, after all, as if she was going anywhere.

Black Alice was on duty when the *Lavinia Whateley* spotted prey; she felt the shiver of anticipation that ran through the decks of the ship. It was an odd sensation, a tic Vinnie only exhibited in pursuit. And then they were underway, zooming down the slope of the gravity well toward Sol, and the screens all around Engineering—which Captain Song kept dark, most of the time, on the theory that swabs and deckhands and coal-shovelers didn't need to know where they were, or what they were doing—flickered bright and live.

Everybody looked up, and Demijack shouted, "There! There!" He was right: the blot that might only have been a smudge of oil on the screen moved as Vinnie banked, revealing itself to be a freighter, big and ungainly and hopelessly outclassed. Easy prey. Easy pickings.

We could use some of them, thought Black Alice. Contrary to the e-ballads and comm stories, a pirate's life was not all imported delicacies and fawning slaves. Especially not when three-quarters of any and all profits went directly back to the *Lavinia Whateley*, to keep her healthy and happy. Nobody ever argued. There were stories about the *Marie Curie*, too.

The captain's voice over fiberoptic cable—strung beside the *Lavinia Whateley*'s nerve bundles—was as clear and free of static as if she stood at Black Alice's elbow. "Battle stations," Captain Song said, and the crew leapt to obey. It had been two Solar since Captain Song keelhauled James Brady, but nobody who'd been with the ship then was ever likely to forget his ruptured eyes and frozen scream.

Black Alice manned her station and stared at the screen. She saw the freighter's name—the *Josephine Baker*—gold on black across the stern, the Venusian flag for its port of registry wired stiff from a mast on its hull. It was a steelship, not a Boojum, and they had every advantage. For a moment she thought the freighter would run.

And then it turned and brought its guns to bear.

No sense of movement, of acceleration, of disorientation. No pop, no whump of displaced air. The view on the screens just flickered to a different one, as Vinnie skipped—apported—to a new position just aft and above the *Josephine Baker*, crushing the flag mast with her hull.

Black Alice felt that, a grinding shiver. And had just time to grab her console before the *Lavinia Whateley* grappled the freighter, long vanes not curling in affection now.

Out of the corner of her eye, she saw Dogcollar, the closest thing the *Lavinia Whateley* had to a chaplain, cross himself, and she heard him mutter, like he always did, *Ave, Grandaevissimi, morituri vos salutant.* It was the best he'd be able to do until it was all over, and even then he wouldn't have the chance to do much. Captain Song didn't mind other people worrying about souls, so long as they didn't do it on her time.

The Captain's voice was calling orders, assigning people to boarding parties port and starboard. Down in Engineering, all they had to do was monitor the *Lavinia Whateley*'s hull and prepare to repel boarders, assuming the freighter's crew had the gumption to send any. Vinnie would take care of the rest—until the time came to persuade her not to eat her prey before they'd gotten all the valuables off it. That was a ticklish job, only entrusted to the chief engineers, but Black Alice watched and listened, and although she didn't expect she'd ever get the chance, she thought she could do it herself.

It was a small ambition, and one she never talked about. But it would be a hell of a thing, wouldn't it? To be somebody a Boojum would listen to?

She gave her attention to the dull screens in her sectors and tried not to crane her neck to catch a glimpse of the ones with the actual fighting on them. Dogcollar was making the rounds with sidearms from the weapons locker, just in case. Once the *Josephine Baker* was subdued, it was the junior engineers and others who would board her to take inventory.

Sometimes there were crew members left in hiding on captured ships. Sometimes, unwary pirates got shot.

There was no way to judge the progress of the battle from Engineering. Wasabi put a stopwatch up on one of the secondary screens, as usual, and everybody glanced at it periodically. Fifteen minutes on-going meant the boarding parties hadn't hit any nasty surprises. Black Alice had met a man once who'd been on the *Margaret Mead* when she grappled a freighter that turned out to be carrying a division-worth of Marines out to the Jovian moons. Thirty minutes on-going was normal. Forty-five minutes. Upward of an hour on-going, and people started double-checking their weapons. The longest battle Black Alice had ever personally been part of was six hours, forty-three minutes, and fifty-two seconds. That had been the last time the *Lavinia Whateley* worked with a partner, and the double-cross by the *Henry Ford* was the only reason any of Vinnie's crew needed. Captain Song still had Captain Edwards' head in a jar on the bridge, and Vinnie had an ugly ring of scars where the *Henry Ford* had bitten her.

This time, the clock stopped at fifty minutes, thirteen seconds. The *Josephine Baker* surrendered.

Dogcollar slapped Black Alice's arm. "With me," he said, and she didn't argue. He had only six weeks seniority over her, but he was as tough as he was devout, and not stupid either. She checked the velcro on her holster and followed him up the ladder, reaching through the rungs once to scratch Vinnie's bulkhead as she passed. The ship paid her no notice. She wasn't the captain, and she wasn't one of the four chief engineers.

Quartermaster mostly respected crew's own partner choices, and as Black Alice and Dogcollar suited up—it wouldn't be the first time, if the *Josephine Baker*'s crew decided to blow her open to space rather than be taken captive—he came by and issued them both tag guns and x-ray pads, taking a retina scan in return. All sorts of valuable things got hidden inside of bulkheads, and once Vinnie was done with the steelship there wouldn't be much chance of coming back to look for what they'd missed.

Wet pirates used to scuttle their captures. The Boojums were more efficient.

Black Alice clipped everything to her belt and checked Dogcollar's seals.

And then they were swinging down lines from the *Lavinia Whateley*'s belly to the chewed-open airlock. A lot of crew didn't like to look at the ship's face, but Black Alice loved it. All those teeth, the diamond edges worn to a glitter, and a few of the ship's dozens of bright sapphire eyes blinking back at her.

She waved, unselfconsciously, and flattered herself that the ripple of closing eyes was Vinnie winking in return.

She followed Dogcollar inside the prize.

They unsealed when they had checked atmosphere—no sense in wasting your own air when you might need it later—and the first thing she noticed was the smell.

The *Lavinia Whateley* had her own smell, ozone and nutmeg, and other ships never smelled as good, but this was . . . this was . . .

"What did they kill and why didn't they space it?" Dogcollar wheezed, and Black Alice swallowed hard against her gag reflex and said, "One will get you twenty we're the lucky bastards that find it."

"No takers," Dogcollar said.

They worked together to crank open the hatches they came to. Twice they found crew members, messily dead. Once they found crew members alive.

"Gillies," said Black Alice.

"Still don't explain the smell," said Dogcollar and, to the gillies: "Look, you can join our crew, or our ship can eat you. Makes no never mind to us."

The gillies blinked their big wet eyes and made fingersigns at each other, and then nodded. Hard.

Dogcollar slapped a tag on the bulkhead. "Someone will come get you. You go wandering, we'll assume you changed your mind."

The gillies shook their heads, hard, and folded down onto the deck to wait.

Dogcollar tagged searched holds—green for clean, purple for goods, red for anything Vinnie might like to eat that couldn't be fenced for a profit—and Black Alice mapped. The corridors in the steelship were winding, twisty, hard to track. She was glad she chalked the walls, because she didn't think her map was quite right, somehow, but she couldn't figure out where she'd gone wrong. Still, they had a beacon, and Vinnie could always chew them out if she had to.

Black Alice loved her ship.

She was thinking about that, how, okay, it wasn't so bad, the pirate game, and it sure beat working in the sunstone mines on Venus, when she found a locked cargo hold. "Hey, Dogcollar," she said to her comm, and while he was turning to cover her, she pulled her sidearm and blastered the lock.

The door peeled back, and Black Alice found herself staring at rank upon rank of silver cylinders, each less than a meter tall and perhaps half a meter wide, smooth and featureless except for what looked like an assortment of sockets and plugs on the surface of each. The smell was strongest here.

"Shit," she said.

Dogcollar, more practical, slapped the first safety orange tag of the expedition beside the door and said only, "Captain'll want to see this."

"Yeah," said Black Alice, cold chills chasing themselves up and down her spine. "C'mon, let's move."

But of course it turned out that she and Dogcollar were on the retrieval detail, too, and the captain wasn't leaving the canisters for Vinnie.

Which, okay, fair. Black Alice didn't want the *Lavinia Whateley* eating those things, either, but why did they have to bring them *back*?

She said as much to Dogcollar, under her breath, and had a horrifying thought: "She knows what they are, right?"

"She's the captain," said Dogcollar.

"Yeah, but—I ain't arguing, man, but if she doesn't know . . ." She lowered her voice even farther, so she could barely hear herself: "What if somebody *opens* one?"

Dogcollar gave her a pained look. "Nobody's going to go opening anything. But if you're really worried, go talk to the captain about it."

He was calling her bluff. Black Alice called his right back. "Come with me?"

He was stuck. He stared at her, and then he grunted and pulled his gloves off, the left and then the right. "Fuck," he said. "I guess we oughta."

For the crew members who had been in the boarding action, the party had already started. Dogcollar and Black Alice finally tracked the captain down in the rec room, where her marines were slurping stolen wine from broken-necked bottles. As much of it splashed on the gravity plates epoxied to the *Lavinia Whateley*'s flattest interior surface as went into the marines, but Black Alice imagined there was plenty more where that came from. And the faster the crew went through it, the less long they'd be drunk.

The captain herself was naked in a great extruded tub, up to her collarbones in steaming water dyed pink and heavily scented by the bath bombs sizzling here and there. Black Alice stared; she hadn't seen a tub bath in seven years. She still dreamed of them sometimes.

"Captain," she said, because Dogcollar wasn't going to say anything. "We think you should know we found some dangerous cargo on the prize."

Captain Song raised one eyebrow. "And you imagine I don't know already, cherie?"

Oh shit. But Black Alice stood her ground. "We thought we should be *sure*."

The captain raised one long leg out of the water to shove a pair of necking pirates off the rim of her tub. They rolled onto the floor, grappling and clawing, both fighting to be on top. But they didn't break the kiss.

"You wish to be sure," said the captain. Her dark eyes had never left Black Alice's sweating face. "Very well. Tell me. And then you will know that I know, and you can be *sure*."

Dogcollar made a grumbling noise deep in his throat, easily interpreted: *I told you so.*

Just as she had when she took Captain Song's oath and slit her thumb with a razorblade and dripped her blood on the *Lavinia Whateley*'s decking so the ship might know her, Black Alice—metaphorically speaking—took a breath and jumped. "They're brains," she said. "Human brains. Stolen. Black-market. The Fungi—"

"Mi-Go," Dogcollar hissed, and the Captain grinned at him, showing extraordinarily white strong teeth. He ducked, submissively, but didn't step back, for which Black Alice felt a completely ridiculous gratitude.

"Mi-Go," Black Alice said. Mi-Go, Fungi, what did it matter? They came from the outer rim of the Solar System, the black cold hurtling rocks of the Öpik-Oort Cloud. Like the Boojums, they could swim between the stars. "They collect them. There's a black market. Nobody knows what they use them for. It's illegal, of course. But they're . . . alive in there. They go mad, supposedly."

And that was it. That was all Black Alice could manage. She stopped and had to remind herself to shut her mouth.

"So I've heard," the captain said, dabbling at the steaming water. She stretched luxuriously in her tub. Someone thrust a glass of white wine at her, condensation dewing the outside. The captain did not drink from shattered plastic bottles. "The Mi-Go will pay for this cargo, won't they? They mine rare minerals all over the system. They're said to be very wealthy."

"Yes, captain," Dogcollar said, when it became obvious that Black Alice couldn't.

"Good," the captain said. Under Black Alice's feet, the decking shuddered, a grinding sound as Vinnie began to dine. Her rows of teeth would make short work of the *Josephine Baker*'s steel hide. Black Alice could see two of the gillies—the same two? she never could tell them apart unless they had scars—flinch and tug at their chains. "Then they might as well pay us as someone else, wouldn't you say?"

Black Alice knew she should stop thinking about the canisters. Captain's word was law. But she couldn't help it, like scratching at a scab. They were down there, in the third subhold, the one even sniffers couldn't find, cold and sweating and with that stench that was like a living thing.

And she kept wondering. Were they empty? Or were there brains in there, people's brains, going mad?

The idea was driving *her* crazy, and finally, her fourth off-shift after the capture of the *Josephine Baker*, she had to go look.

"This is stupid, Black Alice," she muttered to herself as she climbed down the companion way, the beads in her hair clicking against her earrings. "Stupid, stupid, stupid." Vinnie bioluminesced, a traveling spotlight, placidly unconcerned whether Black Alice was being an idiot or not.

Half-Hand Sally had pulled duty in the main hold. She nodded at Black Alice and Black Alice nodded back. Black Alice ran errands a lot, for Engineering and sometimes for other departments, because she didn't smoke hash and she didn't cheat at cards. She was reliable.

Down through the subholds, and she really didn't want to be doing this, but she was here and the smell of the third subhold was already making her sick, and maybe if she just knew one way or the other, she'd be able to quit thinking about it.

She opened the third subhold, and the stench rushed out.

The canisters were just metal, sealed, seemingly airtight. There shouldn't be any way for the aroma of the contents to escape. But it permeated the air nonetheless, bad enough that Black Alice wished she had brought a rebreather.

No, that would have been suspicious. So it was really best for everyone concerned that she hadn't, but oh, gods and little fishes the stench. Even breathing through her mouth was no help; she could taste it, like oil from a fryer, saturating the air, oozing up her sinuses, coating the interior spaces of her body.

As silently as possible, she stepped across the threshold and into the space beyond. The *Lavinia Whateley* obligingly lit the space as she entered, dazzling her at first as the overhead lights—not just bioluminescent, here, but LEDs chosen to approximate natural daylight, for when they shipped plants and animals—reflected off rank upon rank of canisters. When Black Alice went among them, they did not reach her waist.

She was just going to walk through, she told herself. Hesitantly, she touched the closest cylinder. The air in this hold was so dry there was no condensation—the whole ship ran to lip-cracking, nosebleed dryness in the long weeks between prizes—but the cylinder was cold. It felt somehow grimy to the touch, gritty and oily like machine grease. She pulled her hand back.

It wouldn't do to open the closest one to the door—and she realized with that thought that she was planning on opening one. There must be a way to do it, a concealed catch or a code pad. She was an engineer, after all.

She stopped three ranks in, lightheaded with the smell, to examine the problem.

It was remarkably simple, once you looked for it. There were three depressions on either side of the rim, a little smaller than human fingertips but spaced appropriately. She laid the pads of her fingers over them and pressed hard, making the flesh deform into the catches.

The lid sprang up with a pressurized hiss. Black Alice was grateful that even open, it couldn't smell much worse. She leaned forward to peer within. There was a clear membrane over the surface, and gelatin or thick fluid underneath. Vinnie's lights illuminated it well.

It was not empty. And as the light struck the grayish surface of the lump of tissue floating within, Black Alice would have sworn she saw the pathetic unbodied thing flinch.

She scrambled to close the canister again, nearly pinching her fingertips when it clanked shut. "Sorry," she whispered, although dear sweet Jesus, surely the thing couldn't hear her. "Sorry, sorry." And then she turned and ran, catching her hip a bruising blow against the doorway, slapping the controls to make it fucking *close* already. And then she staggered sideways, lurching to her knees, and vomited until blackness was spinning in front of her eyes and she couldn't smell or taste anything but bile.

Vinnie would absorb the former contents of Black Alice's stomach, just as she absorbed, filtered, recycled, and excreted all her crew's wastes. Shaking, Black Alice braced herself back upright and began the long climb out of the holds.

In the first subhold, she had to stop, her shoulder against the smooth, velvet slickness of Vinnie's skin, her mouth hanging open while her lungs worked. And she knew Vinnie wasn't going to hear her, because she wasn't the captain or a chief engineer or anyone important, but she had to try anyway, croaking, "Vinnie, water, please."

And no one could have been more surprised than Black Alice Bradley when Vinnie extruded a basin and a thin cool trickle of water began to flow into it.

Well, now she knew. And there was still nothing she could do about it. She wasn't the captain, and if she said anything more than she already had, people were going to start looking at her funny. Mutiny kind of funny. And what Black Alice did *not* need was any more of Captain Song's attention and especially not for rumors like that. She kept her head down and did her job and didn't discuss her nightmares with anyone.

And she had nightmares, all right. Hot and cold running, enough, she fancied, that she could have filled up the captain's huge tub with them.

She could live with that. But over the next double dozen of shifts, she became aware of something else wrong, and this was worse, because it was something wrong with the *Lavinia Whateley*.

The first sign was the chief engineers frowning and going into huddles at odd moments. And then Black Alice began to feel it herself, the way Vinnie was . . . she didn't have a word for it because she'd never felt anything like it before. She would have said *balky*, but that couldn't be right. It couldn't. But she was more and more sure that Vinnie was less responsive somehow, that when she obeyed the captain's orders, it was with a delay. If she were human, Vinnie would have been dragging her feet.

You couldn't keelhaul a ship for not obeying fast enough.

And then, because she was paying attention so hard she was making her own head hurt, Black Alice noticed something else. Captain Song had them cruising the gas giants' orbits—Jupiter, Saturn, Neptune—not going in as far as the asteroid belt, not going out as far as Uranus. Nobody Black Alice talked to knew why, exactly, but she and Dogcollar figured it was because the captain wanted to talk to the Mi-Go without actually getting near the nasty cold rock of their planet. And what Black Alice noticed was that Vinnie was less balky, less *unhappy*, when she was headed out, and more and more resistant the closer they got to the asteroid belt.

Vinnie, she remembered, had been born over Uranus.

"Do you want to go home, Vinnie?" Black Alice asked her one late-night shift when there was nobody around to care that she was talking to the ship. "Is that what's wrong?"

She put her hand flat on the wall, and although she was probably imagining it, she thought she felt a shiver ripple across Vinnie's vast side.

Black Alice knew how little she knew and didn't even contemplate sharing her theory with the chief engineers. They probably knew exactly what was wrong and exactly what to do to keep the *Lavinia Whateley* from going core meltdown like the *Marie Curie* had. That was a whispered story, not the sort of thing anybody talked about except in their hammocks after lights out.

The *Marie Curie* had eaten her own crew.

So when Wasabi said, four shifts later, "Black Alice, I've got a job for you," Black Alice said, "Yessir," and hoped it would be something that would help the *Lavinia Whateley* be happy again.

It was a suit job, he said, replace and repair. Black Alice was going because she was reliable and smart and stayed quiet, and it was time she took on more responsibilities. The way he said it made her first fret because that meant the captain might be reminded of her existence, and then fret because she realized the captain already had been.

But she took the equipment he issued, and she listened to the instructions and read schematics and committed them both to memory and her implants. It was a ticklish job, a neural override repair. She'd done some fiber optic bundle splicing, but this was going to be a doozy. And she was going to have to do it in stiff, pressurized gloves.

Her heart hammered as she sealed her helmet, and not because she was worried about the EVA. This was a chance. An opportunity. A step closer to chief engineer.

Maybe she had impressed the captain with her discretion, after all.

She cycled the airlock, snapped her safety harness, and stepped out onto the *Lavinia Whateley*'s hide.

That deep blue-green, like azurite, like the teeming seas of Venus under their swampy eternal clouds, was invisible. They were too far from Sol—it was a yellow stylus-dot, and you had to know where to look for it. Vinnie's hide was just black under Black Alice's suit floods. As the airlock cycled shut, though, the Boojum's own bioluminescence shimmered up her vanes and along the ridges of her sides—crimson and electric green and acid blue. Vinnie must have noticed Black Alice picking her way carefully up her spine with barbed boots. They wouldn't *hurt* Vinnie—nothing short of a space rock could manage that—but they certainly stuck in there good.

The thing Black Alice was supposed to repair was at the principal nexus of Vinnie's central nervous system. The ship didn't have anything like what a human or a gilly would consider a brain; there were nodules spread all through her vast body. Too slow, otherwise. And Black Alice had heard Boojums weren't supposed to be all that smart—trainable, sure, maybe like an Earth monkey.

Which is what made it creepy as hell that, as she picked her way up Vinnie's flank—though *up* was a courtesy, under these circumstances—talking to her all the way, she would have sworn Vinnie was talking back. Not just tracking her with the lights, as she would always do, but bending some of her barbels and vanes around as if craning her neck to get a look at Black Alice.

Black Alice carefully circumnavigated an eye—she didn't think her boots would hurt it, but it seemed discourteous to stomp across somebody's field of vision—and wondered, only half-idly, if she had been sent out on this task not because she was being considered for promotion, but because she was expendable.

She was just rolling her eyes and dismissing that as borrowing trouble when she came over a bump on Vinnie's back, spotted her goal—and all the ship's lights went out.

She tongued on the comm. "Wasabi?"

"I got you, Blackie. You just keep doing what you're doing."

"Yessir."

But it seemed like her feet stayed stuck in Vinnie's hide a little longer than was good. At least fifteen seconds before she managed a couple of deep breaths—too deep for her limited oxygen supply, so she went briefly dizzy—and continued up Vinnie's side.

Black Alice had no idea what inflammation looked like in a Boojum, but she would guess this was it. All around the interface she was meant to repair, Vinnie's flesh looked scraped and puffy. Black Alice walked tenderly, wincing, muttering apologies under her breath. And with every step, the tendrils coiled a little closer.

Black Alice crouched beside the box and began examining connections. The console was about three meters by four, half a meter tall, and fixed firmly to Vinnie's hide. It looked like the thing was still functional, but something—a bit of space debris, maybe—had dented it pretty good.

Cautiously, Black Alice dropped a hand on it. She found the access panel and flipped it open: more red lights than green. A tongue-click, and she began withdrawing her tethered tools from their holding pouches and arranging them so that they would float conveniently around.

She didn't hear a thing, of course, but the hide under her boots vibrated suddenly, sharply. She jerked her head around, just in time to see one of Vinnie's feelers slap her own side, five or ten meters away. And then the whole Boojum shuddered, contracting, curved into a hard crescent of pain the same way she had when the *Henry Ford* had taken that chunk out of her hide. And the lights in the access panel lit up all at once—red, red, yellow, red.

Black Alice tongued off the *send* function on her headset microphone, so Wasabi wouldn't hear her. She touched the bruised hull, and she touched the dented edge of the console. "Vinnie," she said, "does this *hurt*?"

Not that Vinnie could answer her. But it was obvious. She was in pain. And maybe that dent didn't have anything to do with space debris. Maybe—Black Alice straightened, looked around, and couldn't convince herself that it was an accident that this box was planted right where Vinnie couldn't . . . quite . . . reach it.

"So what does it *do*?" she muttered. "Why am I out here repairing something that fucking hurts?" She crouched down again and took another long look at the interface.

As an engineer, Black Alice was mostly self-taught; her implants were secondhand, black market, scavenged, the wet work done by a gilly on Providence Station. She'd learned the technical vocabulary from Gogglehead Kim before he bought it in a stupid little fight with a ship named the *V. I. Ulyanov*, but what she relied on were her instincts, the things she knew without being able to say. So she *looked* at that box wired into Vinnie's spine and all its red and yellow lights, and then she tongued the comm back on and said, "Wasabi, this thing don't look so good."

"Whaddya mean, don't look so good?" Wasabi sounded distracted, and that was just fine.

Black Alice made a noise, the auditory equivalent of a shrug. "I think the node's inflamed. Can we pull it and lock it in somewhere else?"

"No!" said Wasabi.

"It's looking pretty ugly out here."

"Look, Blackie, unless you want us to all go sailing out into the Big Empty, we are *not* pulling that governor. Just fix the fucking thing, would you?"

"Yessir," said Black Alice, thinking hard. The first thing was that Wasabi knew what was going on—knew what the box did and knew that the *Lavinia Whateley* didn't like it. That wasn't comforting. The second thing was that whatever was going on, it involved the Big Empty, the cold vastness between the stars. So it wasn't that Vinnie wanted to go home. She wanted to go *out*.

It made sense, from what Black Alice knew about Boojums. Their infants lived in the tumult of the gas giants' atmosphere, but as they aged, they pushed higher and higher, until they reached the edge of the envelope. And then—following instinct or maybe the calls of their fellows, nobody knew for sure—they learned to skip, throwing themselves out into the vacuum like Earth birds leaving the nest. And what if, for a Boojum, the solar system was just another nest?

Black Alice knew the *Lavinia Whateley* was old, for a Boojum. Captain Song was not her first captain, although you never mentioned Captain Smith if you knew what was good for you. So if there *was* another stage to her life cycle, she might be ready for it. And her crew wasn't letting her go.

Jesus and the cold fishy gods, Black Alice thought. Is this why the *Marie Curie* ate her crew? Because they wouldn't let her go?

She fumbled for her tools, tugging the cords to float them closer, and wound up walloping herself in the bicep with a splicer. And as she was wrestling with it, her headset spoke again. "Blackie, can you hurry it up out there? Captain says we're going to have company."

Company? She never got to say it. Because when she looked up, she saw the shapes, faintly limned in starlight, and a chill as cold as a suit leak crept up her neck.

There were dozens of them. Hundreds. They made her skin crawl and her nerves judder the way gillies and Boojums never had. They were man-sized, roughly, but they looked like the pseudoroaches of Venus, the ones Black Alice still had nightmares about, with too many legs, and horrible stiff wings. They had ovate, corrugated heads, but no faces, and where their mouths ought to be sprouting writing tentacles

And some of them carried silver shining cylinders, like the canisters in Vinnie's subhold.

Black Alice wasn't certain if they saw her, crouched on the Boojum's hide with only a thin laminate between her and the breathsucker, but she was certain of something else. If they did, they did not care.

They disappeared below the curve of the ship, toward the airlock Black Alice had exited before clawing her way along the ship's side. They could be a trade delegation, come to bargain for the salvaged cargo.

Black Alice didn't think even the Mi-Go came in the battalions to talk trade.

She meant to wait until the last of them had passed, but they just kept coming. Wasabi wasn't answering her hails; she was on her own and unarmed. She fumbled with her tools, stowing things in any handy pocket whether it was where the tool went or not. She couldn't see much; everything was misty. It took her several seconds to realize that her visor was fogged because she was crying.

Patch cables. Where were the fucking patch cables? She found a two-meter length of fiberoptic with the right plugs on the end. One end went into the monitor panel. The other snapped into her suit comm.

"Vinnie?" she whispered, when she thought she had a connection. "Vinnie, can you hear me?"

The bioluminescence under Black Alice's boots pulsed once.

Gods and little fishes, she thought. And then she drew out her laser cutting torch and started slicing open the case on the console that Wasabi had called the *governor*. Wasabi was probably dead by now or dying. Wasabi, and Dogcollar, and . . . well, not dead. If they were lucky, they were dead.

Because the opposite of lucky was those canisters the Mi-Go were carrying. She hoped Dogcollar was lucky.

"You wanna go *out*, right?" she whispered to the *Lavinia Whateley*. "Out into the Big Empty."

She'd never been sure how much Vinnie understood of what people said, but the light pulsed again.

"And this thing won't let you." It wasn't a question. She had it open now, and she could see that was what it did. Ugly fucking thing. Vinnie shivered underneath her, and there was a sudden pulse of noise in her helmet speakers: screaming. People screaming.

"I know," Black Alice said. "They'll come get me in a minute, I guess." She swallowed hard against the sudden lurch of her stomach. "I'm gonna get this thing off you, though. And when they go, you can go, okay? And I'm sorry. I didn't know we were keeping you from . . ." She had to quit talking, or she really was going to puke. Grimly, she fumbled for the tools she needed to disentangle the abomination from Vinnie's nervous system.

Another pulse of sound, a voice, not a person: flat and buzzing and horrible. "We do not bargain with thieves." And the scream that time—she'd never heard Captain Song scream before. Black Alice flinched and started counting to slow her breathing. Puking in a suit was the number one badness but hyperventilating in a suit was a really close second.

Her heads-up display was low-res, and slightly miscalibrated, so that everything had a faint shadow-double. But the thing that flashed up against her own view of her hands was unmistakable: a question mark.

<?>

"Vinnie?"

Another pulse of screaming, and the question mark again.

<?>

"Holy *shit*, Vinnie! . . . Never mind, never mind. They, um, they collect people's brains. In canisters. Like the canisters in the third subhold."

The bioluminescence pulsed once. Black Alice kept working.

Her heads-up pinged again: <ALICE> A pause. <?>

"Um, yeah. I figure that's what they'll do with me, too. It looked like they had plenty of canisters to go around."

Vinnie pulsed, and there was a longer pause while Black Alice doggedly severed connections and loosened bolts.

<WANT> said the *Lavinia Whateley*. <?>

"Want? Do I *want* . . . ?" Her laughter sounded bad. "Um, no. No, I don't want to be a brain in a jar. But I'm not seeing a lot of choices here. Even if I went cometary, they could catch me. And it kind of sounds like they're mad enough to do it, too."

She'd cleared out all the moorings around the edge of the governor; the case lifted off with a shove and went sailing into the dark. Black Alice winced. But then the processor under the cover drifted away from Vinnie's hide, and there was just the monofilament tethers and the fat cluster of fiber optic and superconductors to go.

<HELP>

"I'm doing my best here, Vinnie," Black Alice said through her teeth.

That got her a fast double-pulse, and the *Lavinia Whateley* said, <HELP> And then, <ALICE>

"You want to help *me*?" Black Alice squeaked.

A strong pulse, and the heads-up said, <HELP ALICE>

"That's really sweet of you, but I'm honestly not sure there's anything you can do. I mean, it doesn't look like the Mi-Go are mad at *you*, and I really want to keep it that way."

<EAT ALICE> said the *Lavinia Whateley*.

Black Alice came within a millimeter of taking her own fingers off with the cutting laser. "Um, Vinnie, that's um . . . well, I guess it's better than being a brain in a jar." Or suffocating to death in her suit if she went cometary and the Mi-Go *didn't* come after her.

The double-pulse again, but Black Alice didn't see what she could have missed. As communications went, *EAT ALICE* was pretty fucking unambiguous.

<HELP ALICE> the *Lavinia Whateley* insisted. Black Alice leaned in close, unsplicing the last of the governor's circuits from the Boojum's nervous system. <SAVE ALICE>

"By eating me? Look, I know what happens to things you eat, and it's not . . ." She bit her tongue. Because she *did* know what happened to things the *Lavinia Whateley* ate. Absorbed. Filtered. Recycled. "Vinnie . . . are you saying you can save me from the Mi-Go?"

A pulse of agreement.

"By eating me?" Black Alice pursued, needing to be sure she understood.

Another pulse of agreement.

Black Alice thought about the *Lavinia Whateley*'s teeth. "How much *me* are we talking about here?"

<ALICE> said the *Lavinia Whateley*, and then the last fiber-optic cable parted, and Black Alice, her hands shaking, detached her patch cable and flung the whole mess of it as hard as she could straight up. Maybe it would find a planet with atmosphere and be some little alien kid's shooting star.

And now she had to decide what to do.

She figured she had two choices, really. One, walk back down the *Lavinia Whateley* and find out if the Mi-Go believed in surrender. Two, walk around the *Lavinia Whateley* and into her toothy mouth.

Black Alice didn't think the Mi-Go believed in surrender.

She tilted her head back for one last clear look at the shining black infinity of space. Really, there wasn't any choice at all. Because even if she'd misunderstood what Vinnie seemed to be trying to tell her, the worst she'd end up was dead, and that was light-years better than what the Mi-Go had on offer.

Black Alice Bradley loved her ship.

She turned to her left and started walking, and the *Lavinia Whateley*'s bioluminescence followed her courteously all the way, vanes swaying out of her path. Black Alice skirted each of Vinnie's eyes as she came to them, and each of them blinked at her. And then she reached Vinnie's mouth and that magnificent panoply of teeth.

"Make it quick, Vinnie, okay?" said Black Alice, and walked into her leviathan's maw.

Picking her way delicately between razor-sharp teeth, Black Alice had plenty of time to consider the ridiculousness of worrying about a hole in her suit. Vinnie's mouth was more like a crystal cave, once you were inside it; there was no tongue, no palate. Just polished, macerating stones. Which did not close on Black Alice, to her surprise. If anything, she got the feeling the Vinnie was holding her . . . breath. Or what passed for it.

The Boojum was lit inside, as well—or was making herself lit, for Black Alice's benefit. And as Black Alice clambered inward, the teeth got smaller, and fewer, and the tunnel narrowed. Her throat, Alice thought. I'm inside her.

And the walls closed down, and she was swallowed.

Like a pill, enclosed in the tight sarcophagus of her space suit, she felt rippling pressure as peristalsis pushed her along. And then greater pressure, suffocating, savage. One sharp pain. The pop of her ribs as her lungs crushed.

Screaming inside a space suit was contraindicated, too. And with collapsed lungs, she couldn't even do it properly.

alice.

She floated. In warm darkness. A womb, a bath. She was comfortable. An itchy soreness between her shoulder blades felt like a very mild radiation burn.

alice.

A voice she thought she should know. She tried to speak; her mouth gnashed, her teeth ground.

alice. talk here.

She tried again. Not with her mouth, this time.

Talk . . . here?

The buoyant warmth flickered past her. She was . . . drifting. No, swimming. She could feel currents on her skin. Her vision was confused. She blinked and blinked, and things were shattered.

There was nothing to see anyway, but stars.

alice talk here.

Where am I?

eat alice.

Vinnie. Vinnie's voice, but not in the flatness of the heads-up display anymore. Vinnie's voice alive with emotion and nuance and the vastness of her self.

You ate me, she said, and understood abruptly that the numbness she felt was not shock. It was the boundaries of her body erased and redrawn.

!

Agreement. Relief.

I'm . . . in you, Vinnie?

=/=

Not a "no." More like, this thing is not the same, does not compare, to this other thing. Black Alice felt the warmth of space so near a generous star slipping by her. She felt the swift currents of its gravity, and the gravity of its satellites, and bent them, and tasted them, and surfed them faster and faster away.

I am you.

!

Ecstatic comprehension, which Black Alice echoed with passionate relief. Not dead. Not dead after all. Just, transformed. Accepted. Embraced by her ship, whom she embraced in return.

Vinnie. Where are we going?

out, Vinnie answered. And in her, Black Alice read the whole great naked wonder of space, approaching faster and faster as Vinnie accelerated, reaching for the first great skip that would hurl them into the interstellar darkness of the Big Empty. They were going somewhere.

Out, Black Alice agreed and told herself not to grieve. Not to go mad. This sure beat swampy Hell out of being a brain in a jar.

And it occurred to her, as Vinnie jumped, the brainless bodies of her crew already digesting inside her, that it wouldn't be long before the loss of the *Lavinia Whateley* was a tale told to frighten spacers, too.

HAIR

ADAM ROBERTS

Adam Roberts is the author of many novels, short stories, and various works of academic criticism. Recent works include The Palgrave History of Science Fiction, 2nd edition, *and his latest novel,* The Real-Town Murders). *He lives a little way west of London, with his wife and two children.*

Cosmetic fashions sometimes sweep the globe, but as the sly story that follows demonstrates, sometimes they have a particularly good reason for doing so . . . .

I

It seems to me foolish to take a story about betrayal and call it—as my sponsors wish me to—The Hairstyle That Changed The World. All this hairdressing business, this hair-work. I don't want to get excited about that. To see it as those massed strands of electricity shooting up from the bald pate of the vandegraaff machine. And whilst we're on the subject of haircuts: I was raised by my mother alone, and we were poor enough that, from an early stage, she was the person who cut my hair. For the sake of simplicity, as much as economy, this cut would be uniform and close. To keep me quiet as the buzzer grazed, she used to show me the story about the mermaid whose being-in-the-world was confused between fishtail and feet. I'm sure she showed me lots of old books, but it was that one that sticks in my head: the singing crab, more scarab than crustacean; the wicked villainess able to change not only her appearance but, improbably, her size—I used to puzzle how she was able to generate all her extra mass as she metamorphosed, at the end, into a colossal octopus. Mostly I remember the beautiful young mermaid; she had the tempestuous name Ariel. The story hinged on the notion that her tail might vanish and reform as legs, and I used to worry disproportionately about those new feet. Would they, I wondered, smell of fish? Were the toenails actually fish-scales? Were the twenty-six bones of each foot (all of which I could name) formed of *cartilage*, after the manner of fish bones? Or human bone? The truth is, my mind is the sort that is most comfortable finding contiguities between different states, and most uncomfortable with inconsistencies. Hence my eventual choice of career, I suppose. And I don't doubt that my fascination with the mermaid story had to do with a nascent erotic yearning for Ariel herself—a very prettily drawn figure, I recall.

This has nothing to do with anything. I ought not digress. It's particularly vulgar to do so before I have even started; as if I want to put off the task facing me. Of course this account is not about me. It is enough, for your purposes, to locate your narrator, to know that I was raised by my mother alone; and that after she died (of newstrain CF, three weeks after contracting it) I was raised by a more distant relative. We had enough to eat, but nothing else in my life was *enough to*. To know that my trajectory out of that world was hard study, a scholarship to a small college, and the acquisition of the professional skills that established me in my current profession. You might also want to know where I first met Neocles (long final *e*—people sometimes get that wrong) at college, although what was for me dizzying educational altitude represented, for him, a sort of slumming, a symptom of his liberal curiosity about how the underprivileged live.

Above all, I suppose, you need to know that I'm of that generation that thinks of hair as a sort of excrescence, to be cropped to make it manageable, not indulged at length. And poverty is like the ore in the stone; no matter how you grind the rock and refine the result it is always poverty that comes out. Thinking again about my mother, as here, brings her colliding painfully against the membrane of memory. I suppose I find it hard to forgive her for being poor. She loved me completely, and I loved her back, as children do. The beautiful mermaid, seated on a sack-shaped rock, combing her long, coral-red hair whilst porpoises jump through invisible aerial hoops below her.

II

To tell you about the hairstyle that changed the world, it's back we go to Reykjavik, five years ago, now: just after the Irkutsk famine, when the grain was devoured by that granulated agent manufactured by—and the argument continues as to which terrorists sponsored it. It was the year the World Cup descended into farce. Nic was in Iceland to answer charges at the Product Protection Court, and I was representing him.

A PPC hearing is not much different to any other court hearing. There are the rituals aping the last century, or perhaps the century before that. There's a lot of brass and glass, and there is a quantity of waxed, mirrorlike darkwood. I had represented Nic at such hearings before, but never one quite so serious as this. And Nic had more to lose than most. Because I had itemized his assets prior to making our first submission before the Judicial Master I happened to know exactly how much that was: five apartments, one overlooking Central Park; a mulberry farm; forty assorted cars and flitters; more than fifty percent shares in the Polish National Museum—which although it didn't precisely mean that he owned all those paintings and statues and whatnots at least gave him privileged access to them. The Sydney apartment had a Canova, for instance, in the entrance hall, and the Poles weren't pressing him to return it any time soon.

He had a lot to lose.

In such circumstances insouciance is probably a more attractive reaction than anxiety, although from a legal perspective I might have wished for a more *committed* demeanor. He lounged in court in his Orphic shirt—*very* stylish, very allah-mode—and his hair was *a hundred years* out of date. It was Woodstock. Or English Civil War aristocrat.

"When the J.M. comes in," I told him, "you'd better get off your gluteus maximus and stand yourself straight."

Judicial Master Paterson came in, and Nic got to his feet smartly enough and nodded his head, and then sat down himself perfectly properly. With his pocket-strides decently hidden by the table he looked almost respectable. Except for all the hair, of course.

III

I see-you-tomorrowed him on the steps of the courthouse, but he was staring at the sky. The bobble-layer of clouds on the horizon was a remarkable satsuma colour. Further up was cyan and eggshell. The surface of the icebound estuary, which looked perfectly smooth and flat in daylight, revealed under the slant light all manner of hollows and jags. Further out at sea, past the iceline where waves turned themselves continually and wearily over, a fishing platform sent a red snake of smoke straight up from the fakir's-basket of its single chimney.

"Tomorrow," he replied absently. He seemed hypnotized by the view.

"Don't worry," I told him, mistaking (as I now think) his distraction for anxiety about the prospect of losing some of his five apartments or forty cars and flitters. "The J.M. said he recognized that some individuals have a genius for innovation. That was a good sign. That's code for: geniuses don't need to be *quite* as respectful of the law as ordinary drones."

"A genius for innovation," he echoed.

"I'm not saying scot-free. Not saying that. But it won't be too bad. You'll keep more than you think. It will be fine. Don't worry. Yes?"

He suddenly coughed into his gloves—yellow, condom-tight gloves—and appeared to notice me for the first time. God knows I loved him, as a friend loves a true friend, but he bore then as he always did his own colossally swollen ego like a deformity. I never knew a human with so prodigious a self-regard. His selfishness was of the horizoning, all-encompassing sort that is almost touching, because it approaches the selfishness of the small child. His whim: I shall be humanity's benefactor! But this was not an index of his altruism. It was because his ego liked the sound of the description. Having known him twenty years I would stand up in court and swear to it. He developed the marrow peptide-calcbinder treatment not to combat osteoporosis—the ostensible reason, the thing mentioned in his Medal of Science citation—but precisely *because* of the plastic surgical spin-off possibilities, so that he could add twenty centimeters to his own long bones. Not that he *minded* people using his treatment to alleviate osteopathologies, of course.

Accordingly, when he did not turn up in the courtroom the following day my first thought was that he had simply overslept; or gotten distracted by some tourist pleasure, or that some aspect of his own consciousness had intruded between his perceiving mind and the brute fact that (however much I tried to reassure him) a J.M. was gearing up to fine him half his considerable wealth for property-right violation. It did not occur to me that he might deliberately have absconded. This possibility evidently hadn't occurred to the court either, or they would have put some kind of restraint upon him. You would think (*they* thought, obviously) that the prospect of losing so many million euros of wealth was restraint enough.

The shock in court was as nothing, however, to the fury of the Company: his employer, and mine. I want to be clear: I had been briefed to defend Nic in court, and that only. I made this point forcefully after the event. My brief had been courtroom and legal, not to act as his minder, or to prevent him from boarding a skyhop to Milan (it turned out) in order immediately to board another skyhop to—nobody was quite sure where. "If you'd wanted a minder you should have hired a minder," I said. I was assertive, not aggressive.

The court pronounced in absentia, and it went hard on Nic's fortune. But this did not flush him out.

His disappearance hurt me. I was sent to a dozen separate meetings in a dozen different global locations within one week; and in the same timeframe I had twenty or so further virtual meetings. Flying over Holland, where robotically tended fields shone greener than jade, and the hedges are all twenty-foot tall, and the glimmering blue rivers sined their paths towards the sea.

At Denver airport I saw a man with Parkinsonism—not old, no more than forty—sitting in the café and trying to eat a biscuit. He looked as though he was trying to shake hands with his own mouth.

The news was as full of people starving, as it always is. Images of a huge holding zone in Sri Lanka where people were simply sitting around waiting to die. That look of the starving: hunger has placed its leech-maw upon their heel and sucked all their fluid and solidity out, down to the bones. The skin tautly concave everywhere. The eyes big as manga. The aching face.

On Channel 9 the famine clock, bottom left corner, rolled its numbers over and over. A blur of numbers.

I flew to Iceland.

I flew back to Denver.

I was acutely aware that Neocles' vanishment put my own career at risk. Had I always lived amongst wealth, as he had, I might have floated free above the anxiety of this. It's easy for the wealthy to believe that something will turn up. But I had experienced what a non-medinsure, hardscrabble life was like, and I did not want to go back to it.

He's gone rogue, I was told. Why didn't you stop him? The Company, which had been (to me) a dozen or so points of human contact, suddenly swelled and grew monstrously octopoid. A hundred, or more, company people wanted to speak to me directly. This is serious, I was told.

He has the patent information on a *dozen* billion-euro applications, I was told. *You* want to guarantee the Company's financial losses should he try and pirate-license those? I thought *not*.

I thought not.

Not everybody scapegoated me. Some departments recognized the injustice in trying to pin Nic's disappearance on me. Embryology, for instance; a department more likely than most to require expert legal advice, of the sort I had proved myself in the past capable of providing. Optics also assured me of their support, though they did so off the record. But it would have required a self-belief stronger than the one with which providence has provided me to think my career—my twenty-year career—as staff legal counsel for the Company was going to last more than a month. The elegant bee-dance of mutual corporate espionage continued to report that none of our competitors had, yet, acquired any of the intellectual property Nic had in his power to dispose. I had a meeting at Cambridge, in the UK, where late winter was bone-white and ducks on the river looked in astonishment at their own legs. I flew to Rio where the summer ocean was immensely clear and beautiful: sitting on the balcony of our offices it was possible, without needing optical enhancement, to make out extraordinary levels of detail in the sunken buildings and streets, right down to cars wedged in doorways, and individual letters painted on the tarmac.

I flew to Alaska. I flew to Sydney, where the airport was a chaos of children—a flash mob protest about the cutbacks in youth dole.

In the midst of all this I somehow found time to begin, discretely, to make plans for a post-Company life. My ex-wife was more understanding than I might have expected, more concerned to maintain medinsure for our two children than for herself. I scouted, gingerly, secretly, for other employment; but even with the most optimistic assessment it was going to be hard to carry five lots of medinsure on my new salary. I could not of course deprive the children, and I did not wish to deprive Kate. That left my ex-wife and myself, and I decided to give up coverage for myself and leave my ex's in place.

Then, from the blue, news: Neocles had gone native in *Mumbai*, of all places. I was called once again to Denver and briefed face-a-face by Alamillo himself, the Company enforcer and bruiser and general bully-fellow. It was not a pleasant tête-à-tête. At this meeting emphasis was placed on the very *lastness* of this, my last chance. The word last as conventionally used was insufficient to convey just how absolutely last this last chance was, how micron-close to the abyss I found myself, how very terminal my opportunity.

The very severity of this interview reassured me. Had they not needed me very badly they would not have worked so hard to bully me. For the first time since Nic had so thoughtlessly trotted off—putting at risk, the fucker, not only his own assets but my entire family's well-being—I felt the warmth of possible redemption touch the chill of my heart.

"My last chance," I said. "I understand."

"You go *to him*," said Alamillo. "You have a fucking *word*, yes?"

I understood then that they were sending me because I was a friend, not because I was a lawyer. They already knew that *money* was no longer going to provide them with any leverage with Nic anymore—that he had renounced money. He was easing himself into his new role as Jesus Christ, the redeemer of the starving. What can you do to a person who won't listen to money? What else does Power have, in this world of ours?

"I'll talk to him. What else?"

"Nothing else," said Amarillo.

"Bring him home?"

"No, that's not what we're sending you to do. Listen the fuck to me. I don't give a fucking pin—just, just. Look. We're sending you to *talk* to him."

IV

I was flown out on a gelderm plane, its skin stiffening with the frictive heat of a high-inset aerial trajectory. I ate little medallions of liquorish bread, with shark caviar and Russian cheese paté; and then authentic sausages lacquered with honey, and then spears of dwarf asparagus, and then chocolate pellets that frothed deliciously inside the mouth. I drank white wine; a Kenyan vintage. The toilet cubicle of this plane offered seven different sorts of hygiene wipe, including a plain one, one that analyzed your stool as you wiped to check for digestive irregularities and several that imparted different varieties of dotTech to your lower intestine to various ends.

I watched a film about a frolicsome young couple overcoming the obstacles placed in the way of their love. I watched the news. I watched another film, a long one this time—fifteen minutes, or more—based on the historical events of the French Revolution.

The tipping point of our descent registered in my viscera like a Christmas-eve tingle of excitement.

We plummeted to Mumbai.

Arriving at Chhatrapati Shivaji was like travelling back half a century in time: the smell; the litter; the silver-painted curved ceilings on their scythe-shaped supports. An all-metal train, running on all-metal rails, trundling me from the terminal to the departure room. Then it was a short hop in a Company flicker to Jogeshwari beachfront—seconds, actually: a brief elevation over the peninsular sprawl of the city, its bonsai skyscrapers like stacked dishes, the taller curves and spires further south. The sky was outrageously blue, and the sea bristled with light. And really in a matter of seconds we came down again. I could have walked from airport to seafront, is how close it was. But better to arrive in a flitter, of course. When I'd called Nic he'd been gracious if laid-back in reply: no Company men, just you, old friend. Of course, of course.

Of course.

There was a flitter park on the Juhu dyke, and I left the car, and driver, there, and started walking. Forty degrees of heat—mild, I was told, for the season. The sky blue like a gemlike flame. It poured heat down upon the world. The air smelt of several things at once: savoury smells and decaying smells, and the worn-out, salt-odour of the ocean.

I don't know what I expected. I think I expected, knowing Nic, to find him gone hippy; dropped-out; or a holy hermit chanting Japa. I pictured him surfing. But as I walked I noticed there was no surf. There were people *everywhere*: a rather startling profusion of humanity, lolling, walking, rushing, going in and out, talking, singing, praying. It was an enormous crush. The sound of several incompatible varieties of music wrestled in the background: beats locking and then disentangling, simple harmonic melodies twisting about one another in atonal and banshee interaction. Everybody was thin. Some were starvation thin. It was easy enough to pick out these latter, because they were much stiller: standing or sitting with studied motionless. It was those who could still afford to eat who moved about.

The bay harboured the poking-up tops and roofs of many inundated towers, scattered across the water like the nine queens in the chessboard problem, preventing the build-up of ridable waves. These upper floors of the drowned buildings were still inhabited; for the poor will live where they can, however unsalubrious. Various lines and cables were strung in sweeping droops from roofs to shore. People swam or kicked and splashed through the shallower water. On the new mud beach a few sepia-coloured palm trees waved their heavy feathers in the breeze. Sweat wept down my back.

And then, as arranged, there was Nic: lying on the flank of the groyne with his great length of hair fanned out on the ground behind him. The first surprise: he was dressed soberly, in black. The second: he was accompanied by armed guards.

I sat beside my friend. It was so very *hot*. "I think I was expecting beach bummery."

"I saw your plane come over," he said. "Made *quite* a racket."

"Airbraking." Like I knew anything about *that*.

"I'm glad you've come, though," he said, getting up on his haunches. His guards fidgeted, leaning their elbows on their slung rifles. They were wearing, I noticed, Marathi National Guard uniforms. "Good of you to come," he clarified.

"People in Denver are pretty pissed."

"There's not many I'd trust," he said. He meant that he did, at least, trust me.

"These boys work for you?" I asked.

"Soldiers. They do. The Marathi authorities and I have come to an understanding." Nic hopped to his feet. "They get my hairstyle, and with it they get the popular support. Of the poor. I get a legal government to shelter me. And I get a compound."

"Compound?" I asked, meaning: *chemical compound? Or barracks?* The answer, though, was the latter, because he said:

"Up in Bhiwandi. All the wealth has moved from the city, up to the mountains, up East in Navi Mumbai. The wealthy don't believe the sea has stopped coming. They think it'll likely come on a little more. The wealthy are a cautious lot."

"The wealthy," I said.

"So you can come along," he said. "Come along."

I got to my feet. "Where?"

"My flitter's back here."

"Are you allowed to park a flitter down here? I was told flitters had to be parked in the official park, back," I looked around, vaguely. "Back up there somewhere."

"I have," he said, flashing me a smile, "*special* privileges."

V

"What is it we do?" he asked me, a few minutes later, as the flitter whisked the two of us, and Nic's two soldiers, northeast over the Mumbai sprawl. He had to raise his voice. It was noisy as a helecopter.

"Speaking for myself," I said, "I work for the Company. I do this to earn enough to keep the people I love safe and healthy. I include you in that category, by the way, you fucker."

"And," he said, smiling slyly, "how *is* Kate?"

I'll insert a word, here, about Kate. It is not precisely germane, but I want to say something. I love her, you see. I'm aware of the prejudice, but I believe it goes without saying that she is as much a human as anybody. She has a vocabulary of nine hundred words and a whole range of phrases and sayings. She has a genuine and sweet nature. She has hair the colour of holly-berries. You'd expect me to say this, and I *will* say this: it is a particularly strange irony that if the *same people* who sneer at her personhood post treatment had encountered her *before* treatment, it would never occur to them to deny that she was a human being. In those circumstances they would have gone out of their way to be nice to her. And if before, why not afterward? Kate is happier now than she ever was before. She is learning the piano. Of all the people I have met in this life, she is the most genuine.

Do you know what? I don't need to defend my love to you.

"She is very well," I said, perhaps more loudly than I needed to. "Which is more than I can say for your port*folio*."

"A bunch of houses and cars and shit," he shouted, making a flowing gesture with his right hand as if discarding it all. His was, despite this theatricality, an untterly unstudied insoucience. That's what a lifetime of never wanting for money does for you.

"We could have saved more than half of it," I said, "if you hadn't absented you from the court the way you did."

"All those possessions," he said. "They were possessing *me*."

"Oh," I said. I could not convey to him how fatuous this sounded to me. "How very Brother Brother."

He grinned. "Shit it's *good* to see you again."

"This hair thing of yours," I asked him, having no idea what he meant by the phrase but guessing it was some nanopeptide technology or other that he had developed. "Is that a company patent?"

"You know?" he said, his eyes twinkling and his pupils doing that peculiar cycling moon-thing that they do, "it wouldn't matter if it were. But, no, as it happens, no. As it happens."

"Well," I said. "That's something."

He was the hairstyle man, the saviour of the world's poor. "I'm a benefactor now," he boomed. "I'm a revo*lutio*nary. I shall be remembered as the greatest benefactor in human history. In a year I'll be able to put the whole company in my fucking *pocket*."

The flitter landed: a little series of bunny hops before coming to rest, that telltale of an inexperienced chauffeur.

We were inside his compound: a pentagon of walls thick-wreathed with brambles of barbed wire. Inside was a mass of people, and everybody without exception—men women and children—had long, ink-black hair. People were lain flat on the floor, or lolling upon the low roofs, or sitting in chairs, all of them sunbathing, and all with their hair spread and fanned out. A central tower shaped like an oil derrick with a big gun at the top—impressive looking to a pedestrian, but like a cardboard castle to any force armed with modern munitions. There was plenty of space inside the walls, but it was crowded fit to burst. Nic led me along a walkway alongside the central atrium, and the ground was carpeted with supine humanity. They were so motionless that I even wondered whether they might be dead: except that every now and then one would pat their face to dislodge a fly, or breathe in and out.

"Sunbathers," I said.

And then, just before we went in, Nic stopped and turned to me with a characteristically boyish sudden spurt of enthusiasm. "Hey, I tell you what I learnt the other day?"

"What?"

"Crazy that I never knew this before, given all the work I've done. Discovered it quite by chance. Peptides, I mean the word, *peptides*, is from the Greek πεπτίδια and that means *little snacks*. There's something you never knew. Means nuts, crisps, olives stuffed with little shards of sundried fucking tomato. Peptides means scoobisnacks."

"Extraordinary," I deadpanned. "And you with your Greek heritage," I said, knowing full well that he possessed no Greek language at all.

At this he became once again solemn. "I'm a citizen of the world, now," he said.

We went through: up a slope and into a seminar room. Inside was a horseshoe seating grid with room for perhaps sixty people. The space was empty except for us two. There was a single light on the front of the room when we came in.

I sat myself in a front row seat. Nic stood before the screen, fiddling with his hair, running fingers through it and pulling it. "Why do *you* think you're here?" he asked, without looking at me.

"Just to talk, Nic," I said. "I have no orders. Except to talk. Man, we really ought to talk. About the future."

"Hey," he said, as if galvanized by that word. He flapped his arm at the room sensor and the screen lit behind him: the opening image was the Federal flag of India. "OK," he announced.

The image morphed into diagrams of the chemical structures of self-assembling peptides filling the screen: insectile wriggles of angular disjunction wielding hexagonic benzene rings like boxing gloves.

"Wait," said Nic, looking behind him. "That's not right." He clicked his fingers. More snaps of his molecular tools-in-trade faded in, faded out.

"How very Barnum-and-Bailey," I said.

"Calmodulin rendered in 3D," he said. "I always think they look like party streamers. Although, in Zoorlandic iteration, they look like a star map. There's just so much empty space at the molecular level; our representational codes tend to obscure that fact. There, that there's lysine." He danced on the spot, jiggling his feet. "Lysine. A lot of that in your hair. NH2 sending down a lightning-jag of line to the H and H2N link, and O and OH looking on with their mouths open." Images flicked by. "One of the broken-down forms of lysine is called cadaverine, you know that? The molecule of fucking decay and death, of putrefying corpses. Putrescine. Cadaverine. Who names these things?"

"Something to do with hair?" I prompted.

"Lysine," he said. "Hair." He held his right hand up and ran his thumb along his other four fingers: the display flicked rapidly through a series of images. "What is it we do?"

"You asked that before," I said.

"Innovations, and inventions, and brilliant new technological advances."

"I'm just a lawyer, Nic," I said. "You're the innovator."

"But it's the Company, isn't it? The Company's business. These technological advances to make the world a better place."

I suppose I assumed that this was another oblique dig at Kate; so I was crosser in response than I should have been. "So they do," I said. "Don't fucking tell me they don't."

He looked back eyes wide, as if I had genuinely startled him. "Of course they do," he said, in a surprised tone. "Man, don't misunderstand. But think it *through*. That's what I'd say. This is *me* you're talking with. Technological advance and new developments and all the exciting novelties of our science fiction present. It's *great*. You get no argument on that from me."

"I've just flown from Denver to Mumbai in an hour," I said. "You'd prefer it took me three months sailing to get here?"

"You have grasped the wrong stick-end, chum," he said. "Really you have. But only listen. Technological advance is marvellous. But it is always, ineluctably a function of wealth. Poverty is immiscible with it. People are rich, today, in myriad exotic and futuristic ways; but people are poor today as people have always been. They starve, and they sicken, and they die young. Poverty is the great constraint of human existence."

"Things aren't so bad as you say," I said. "Technology trickles down."

"Sure. But the technology *of the poor* always lags behind the technology of the rich. And it's not linear. There are poor people on the globe today who do not use wheels and drag their goods on sleds or on their backs. Some armies have needleguns and gelshells; and some armies have antique AK-47 guns; and some people fight with hoes and spades."

"This is how you got the government of Marathi to give you this little castle and armed guard?"

"The hairstyle stuff," he said.

"And that? And that is?"

There is a particular variety of silence I always associate with the insides of high-tech conference rooms. An insulated and plasticated silence.

"It's a clever thing," he said to me, shortly.

"Of course it is."

"It *is* a clever thing. That's just objectively what it is. Works with lysein in the hair and runs nanotubes the length of each strand. There's some more complicated bio-interface stuff, to do with the blood vessels in the scalp. When I said that none of this utilised Company I.P. I was, possibly, bending the truth a little. There's some Company stuff in there, at the blood exchange. But the *core* technology, the hair-strand stuff, is all mine. Is all me. It's all new. And I'm going to be *giving* it away. Pretty soon, billions will have taken the starter pills. Billions. That's a big . . ." He looked about him at the empty seats. "Number," he concluded, lamely.

"Hair?" I prompted.

"I'm genetically *eradicating* poverty," he said. And then a gust of boyish enthusiasm filled his sails. "All the stuff we do, and make? It's all for the rich, and the poor carrying on starving and dying. But this—"

"Hair . . ."

"Food is the key. Food is the pinch point, if you're poor. Hunger is the pinchpoint, and it's daily, and everything else in your life is oriented around scraping together food so as not to starve. The poor get sick because their water is contaminated, or because their food is inadequate and undernourishment harasses their immune system. The future cannot properly arrive until this latter fact is changed."

"So what does the hair—" I asked. "What does. Does it, like, photosynthesise?"

"Something like that," he said.

His avatar, frozen with his smiling mouth half-open, like a twenty-foot-tall village idiot, lowered over us both.

"And you—what do *you* do, then? I mean what does *one*. You lie in the sun?"

"The energy you previously got from the food you eat. Well you get that from the sun." He did a little twirl. "It's a clever thing," he said. "Actually the hair less so: that's easy enough to engineer. Peptide sculptors generating photoreceptive structures in the hair and spinning conductors down to the roots. The clever stuff is in the way the energy is transferred into the—look I don't want to get into the details. That's not important."

I looked up at giant 2D Nic's goofy face. I looked at human-sized 3D Nic's earnest expression and fidgeting hands. "You don't need to eat?"

"No."

"But you can?"

"Of course you *can*, if you want to. But you don't need to. Not once I've fitted the . . . fitted the . . . and I'm *giving* that away free."

I tried to imagine it. All those supine bodies, laid like paving stones across Nic's courtyard outside. "Lying all day in the sun?"

"Not all day. Not at these latitudes. Three hours a day does most people."

"And what about, say, Reykjavik?"

"The sunlight's pretty weak up there," he said. "You'd be better off in the tropics. But that's where most of the world's poor *are*."

"But," I said. "Vital amines?"

"Water, more to the point. You still need to drink, obviously. Ideally you'll drink water with trace metals, flavoursome water. Or gobble a little clean mud from time to time. But vitamins, vitamins, well the tech can synthesise those. Sugars, for the muscles to work. You'd be surprised by how much energy three hours sunbathing with my hair generates. I mean, it's a *lot*."

"Phew," I said. The vertiginous ambition of the idea had gone through my soul like a sword. "You're not kidding." This was no question.

"Imagine, in a few years," he said, "imagine this: all the world's poor gifted with a technology that *frees them from food*. Frees them from the need to devote their lives to shit-eating jobs to scrape together the money to eat."

"But they still *can* eat?" I repeated. I don't know why this stuck in my head the way it did.

"Of course they can, if they want to. They still have," very disdainfully inflected tone of voice, "fucking *stomachs*. But if they don't eat they don't starve. Contemplate that sentence and what it means. Don't you see? All the life that has ever lived on this planet has lived until this precariously balanced axe, all its life. Eat or die. I shall take that axe away. No more famines. No more starvation."

"Jesus," I said. I was going to add: I can see why the Marathi authorities would scize on such an idea as a means of galvanizing political support amongst the mass. I understood the guards, the compound. And from Nic's point of view too: I could see why he might want this over a position as well-paid Company genemonkey.

"Why am I here, Nic?" I asked.

"I need a lawyer," he said, simply. "Things are going to change for me in a pretty fucking big way. I will need a team I can trust. I'm going to be moving in some pretty high-powered circles. Finding a lawyer I can trust—that's easier said than done."

This, I had not expected. "You're offering me a job?"

"If you like. Put it like that, OK."

"What—what. To come here? To come and live here? To work in Mumbai?"

"Sure."

"You're serious?"

"Why not?

I didn't say: *because in three weeks' time, the army of the Greater Kashmiri Republic is going to come crashing in here with stormtroopers and military flitters and crabtanks and many many bullets, to seize this extraordinary asset that the Marathi junta has somehow acquired.* I didn't say *what, come and work here and get very literally caught in the crossfire?* I didn't say that. Instead I said: "Bring Kate?"

He assumed a serious expression, rather too obviously deliberately suppressing a mocking smile. "I've always had a soft spot for Kate."

"The kids?"

"Surely. The ex too, if you like."

"I can't bring the kids here. I can't bring Kate here."

He caught sight of his onscreen image from the corner of his eye. He turned, flapped a hand as if waving at himself, and the screen went blank. Then he turned back and blinked to see me sitting there. "Well," he said, vaguely. "Think about it."

Later, as he escorted me back across that courtyard, so unnervingly full of motionless bodies, he said, "It's not about my ego, you know." Oh but it was. It was always about Nic's ego.

VI

It's just being. It is not striving. Striving is the opposite of being. It is not restless fighting and earnest labor and testing and retesting and making.

Things moved slowly at first. I flew back to the US and reported. The Company did not send me again; fearful, I daresay, that I would defect. But neither did they fire me. I picked up my new contracts and got back to work. Kate was deliciously pleased to see me. She'd picked up a new phrase: long time no see! She had learned the first portion of a Mozart sonata, and played it to me. I applauded. "Long time no see," she said, hugging me.

"I missed you," I told her. I tickled her feet.

"Long see, long time!"

Things were volatile in Western India. The Federal assembly broke up in acrimonious disharmony. That was hardly news. But I didn't have much time free for idle speculation.

There was a good deal of militia hurly-burly, and then the Southern Indian Alliance launched a proper, no-messing invasion. The news full of images of armored troops dodging from doorway to street corner, firing their baton-rifles. Old-style tanks, with those conveyor-belt wheel arrangements, scootling across scrub and drawing megaphones of dust behind them. Planes spraying Mumbai harbor, passing and repassing at great danger to themselves from ground fire, so as to lay a gelskin over the water thick enough to allow foot soldiers to advance. Then it was all over, and the old government was gone, and a new one installed, and when things settled the news was that Nic had managed to absent himself in all the chaos.

Footage of people lolling in the sun with their hair fanned and spread behind them. In the first instances it was a case of reporting a new religious cult. The New Ascetics. The Followers. Suneaters. It took a while for the outlets to realize they weren't dealing with a religion at all; not least because many of the new hair-wearers adopted spiritual or mystical attitudes when interviewed.

The rumor was then that he'd reappeared in the south east of the subcontinent.

His followers went about the whole Federation—and went into the further East and went up into the Stans—disseminating his technology. He himself was posted on a million slots; although never very cannily viralled, which meant either he could not afford to hire the best viral seed people, or else he was too forgetful to do so. Or conceivably he disdained to do so; because the content of these casts was increasingly clumsily preachy: the authenticity and validity of poverty. Wealth had wrecked the world; poverty would save it. The rich would retreat to virtual lands or hide away in materially moated and gated maison-kingdoms. The poor, freed from the shackles of their hunger, would sweep—peacefully but inevitably as the tide—away the rich and finally inherit the Earth. There was a good deal more in this vein. Sometimes I detected the authentic tang of Nic's rhetoric in this, but more often than not it was evidently revolutionary boilerplate, projected on a screen for him to read by whichever government or organization was sheltering him—or, latterly, holding him captive. He was in Africa, or he was in China, or he was far beyond the pale horizon, someplace near the desert sands. God knows I loved him, as a friend loves a true friend, but I could hardly bear to watch any of it.

I rationed myself, to preserve my sanity. I had him at the top of my feed, and before settling down to my work in the morning I would take half an hour to catch-up on all the stories posted that concerned him. At the end of the day, before I left to go home to Kate ("home again home again," she sang, "splitted alick") I'd run through anything new that came up.

One week he was one oddball new story amongst many. Here his disciples, the natural ascetic skinnies like a drumskin stretched on a coat-rack. Some of his followers were very political, and some were wholly unpolitical, interested only in being able to emulate Jesus's forty-day fast without dying.

Then another week went by and suddenly he was Big News. My feed could no longer keep up with it. And, another week, and I no longer needed a feed, because he was all over the majors. Everyone was taking notice. His followers, interviewed now, seemed less like the flotsam and jetsam of a cruel world, and more like a core new class of people. Homo superior. The numbers were growing across southern Asia. Nic sang the superman, and the superman was going to overcome us. He was in Morocco ("north Africa" was the most we knew), but then he was seized by an Equatorial States strike force in a daring operation that left forty dead. He was held against his will but seemed—in interview—perfectly blithe. "I have a new vision of the world," said his face. "The world will change." He said that more and more real people—code for "the poor"—were taking to his treatment. He said it was becoming an unstoppable force.

When word got out that the Equatorial States were trying to ransom him back to the USA for a huge sum of money there were riots. He was broken out of the building in which he was being held—a few minutes of jittery footage of him, his face bloody, being carried bobbing across a sea of humanity, and grinning, and grinning—and disappeared. He later reappeared in Malaysia, an official guest of the Malay Republic.

I watched the feed when Foss was flown out, and put through all the rigmarole of secrecy, to interview him. It really seemed to me the old Nic was trying to break out of what must have been an increasingly rigid carapace of popular, proletarian expectation. He cracked jokes. He talked about his plans. "This is the future," he said, in a twinkly-eye voice. "I'll tell you. My technology is going to set humanity free from their starvation. I'll tell you what will happen. The poor will migrate; there will be a mass migration, to the tropics—to those parts of the world where sunlight is plentiful, but where food is hard to come by. Some governments will be overwhelmed by this new exodus, but governments like the, eh," and he had to glance down at his thumbback screen to remind himself which radical government's hospitality he was currently enjoying, "People's Islamic-Democratic Republic of Malaysia, will welcome the coming of a new age of popular empowerment."

"What about the rest of the world?" Foss asked.

"The rich can *have* the rest of the world. The cold and sunless northern and southern bands. The rich don't *need* sunlight. They have money for food. The whole global demographic will change—a new pulsing heart will bring life and culture and prosperity to the tropics. Over time the north and the south will become increasingly irrelevant. The central zone will be everything—a great population of *real people*, sitting in the sun for three hours a day, using the remaining twenty-one creating greatness for humanity."

VII

But what can I say? It was a fire, and fire, being a combustion, is always in the process of rendering itself inert. I did consider whether I needed to include, in this account, material about my motivation for betraying my friend. But I think that should be clear from what I have written here.

The Company persuaded me. A message was conveyed that I wanted to meet him again. A meeting was arranged. I flatter myself that there were very few human beings on the planet for whom he would have agreed this.

I had to pretend I had taken up dotsnuff. This involved me in actually practising snorting the stuff, though I hated it. But the dotsnuff was a necessary part of the seizure strategy. It identified where I was; and more to the point it was programmed with Nic's deener-tag (of course the Company had that on file). That would separate us out from all other people in whichever room or space we found ourselves in—let's say, soldiers, guards, captors, terrorists, whomsoever—and in which the snuff would roil about like smoke. When the capture team came crashing in with furious suddenness their guns would know which people to shoot and which not to shoot.

He was back in the Indian Federation now: somewhere near Delhi.

I was flown direct to Delhi international. And we landed at noon. And I was fizzing with nerves.

From the airpot I took a taxi to an arranged spot, and there met a man who told me to take a taxi to another spot. At that place I was collected by three other men and put into a large car. It was not a pleasant drive. I was bitter with nerves; my mind rendered frangible by terror. It was insanely hot; migraine weather, forty-five, fifty, and the car seemed to have no air conditioning. We drove past a succession of orchards, the trunks of the trees blipping past my window like a barcode. Then we turned up a road that stretched straight as a thermometer line, towards the horizon. And up we raced until it ended before a huge gate. Men with rifles stood about. I could see four dogs, tongues like untucked shirttails. And then the gate was opened, and we drove inside.

I was shown to a room, and in it I stayed for several hours. My luggage was taken away.

I could not sleep. It was too hot to sleep anyway.

My luggage was brought back, my tube of dotsnuff still inside. I took this and slipped it inside my trouser pocket.

I informed my guards of my need to use the restroom—genuinely, for my bladder was fuller, and bothered me more, than my conscience. I was taken to a restroom with a dozen urinals at one wall and half a dozen sinks at another. A crossword-pattern of gaps marked where humidity had removed some of the tiny blue tiles covering the walls. The shiny floor was not as clean as I might have liked. I emptied my bladder into the white porcelain cowl of a urinal and washed my hands at the sink. Then, like a character in a cheap film, I peered at myself in the mirror. My eyes saw my eyes. I examined my chin, the jowls shimmery with stubble, the velveteen eyebrows, the rather too large ears. This was the face that Kate saw when she leant in, saying either "a kiss before bedtime," or "a bed before kisstime," and touched my lips with her lips. I was horribly conscious of the flippant rapidity of my heart, of blood hurrying with adrenaline.

A guard I had not previously encountered, a tall, thin man with a gold-handled pistol tucked into the front of his trousers, came into the lavatory. "The Redeemer will see you now," he said.

VIII

Had he come straight out with "why are you here?" or "what do you want?" or anything like that, I might have blurted the truth. I had prepared answers for those questions, of course, but I was, upon seeing him again, miserably nervous. But of course he wasn't puzzled that I wanted to see him again. He took that as his due. Of course I wanted to see him—who wouldn't? His face cracked wide with a grin, and he embraced me.

We were in a wide, low-ceilinged room; and we were surrounded by gun-carrying young men and women: some pale as I, some sherry- and acorn-coloured, some black as liquorish. A screen was switched on but the sound was down. Through a barred-window I could see the sepia plain and, waverly with heat in the distance, the edge-line of the orchards.

"Redeemer, is it?" I said, my dry throat making the words creak.

"Can you believe it?" He rolled his eyes upwards, so that he was looking at the ceiling—the direction, had he only known it, of the company troopers, sweeping in low-orbit with a counter-spin to hover, twenty-miles up on the vertical. "I try to fucking discourage it."

"Sure you do," I said. Then, clutching the tube in my pocket to stop my fingers trembling, I added in a rapid voice: "I've taken up snuff, you know."

Nic looked very somberly at me. "I'm afraid you'll have to go outside if you want to snort that."

For a moment I thought he was being genuine, and my rapid heartbeat accelerated to popping point. My hands shivered. I was sweating. When he laughed, and beckoned me towards a low-slung settee, I felt the relief as sharply as terror. I sat and tried, by focussing my resolve, to stop the tremble in my calf muscles.

"You know what I hate?" he said, as if resuming a conversation we had been having just moments before. "I hate that phrase *body fascism*. You take a fat man, or fat woman, and criticise them for being fat. That makes you a body fascist. You know what's wrong there? It's the *fascism* angle. In a fucking world where one third of the population hoards all the fucking food and two third *starve*—in a world where your beloved Company makes billions selling antiobesity technology to people too stupid to understand they can have antiobesity for free by fucking *eating less*—in *that* world, where the fat ones steal the food from the thin ones so that the thin ones starve to death. That's a world where the fascists are the ones who *criticize the fatties*? Do you see how upside-down that is?"

I fumbled the tube and sniffed up some powder. The little nanograins, keyed to my metabolism, thrummed into my system. Like, I suppose, fire being used to extinguish an oilwell blaze, the extra stimulation had a calming effect.

The talcum-fine cloud in that room. I coughed, theatrically, and waved my hand to dissipate the material.

"So you're free to go?"

"I'm not in charge of it," he said brightly. "Fuck, it's good to see you again! I'm not in charge—I'm being carried along by it as much as anybody. It's a tempest, and it's blowing the whole of humanity like leaves in autumn."

"Some of it was Company," I said. "The ADP to ATP protocols weren't, legally speaking, yours to give away, you know."

"The *hair* stuff was mine," he said.

"I'm only saying."

"Sure—but the *hair* stuff."

I thought of the troops, falling through the sky directly above us, their bootsoles coming closer and closer to the tops of our heads.

"The photovoltaic stuff, and the nanotube lysine fabrication of the conductive channels along the individual strands of hair—that was you. But that's of no use without the interface to do the ATP."

He shrugged. "You think like a lawyer. I mean, you think science like a lawyer. It's not that *at all*. You don't think there's a moral imperative, when the famine in the southern African republics is killing, how many thousands a week is it?" Then he brightened. "*Fuck* it's good to see you though! If I'd let the Company have this they'd have squeezed every last euro of profit out of it, and millions would have died." But his heart wasn't really in this old exchange. "Wait til I've shown you round," he said, as excited as a child, and swept his right hand in an arc, lord-of-the-manor-wise.

Somewhere outside the room a siren was sounding. Muffled by distance, a warbling miaow. Nic ignored it, although several of his guards perked their heads up. One went out to see what the pother was.

I felt the agitation building in my viscera. Betrayal is not something I have any natural tolerance for, I think. It is an uncomfortable thing. I fidgeted. The sweat kept running into my eyes.

"All the old rhythms of life change," Nic said. "Everything is different now."

I felt the urge to scream. I clenched my teeth. The urge passed.

"Of course Power is *scared*," Nic was saying. "Of course Power wants to *stop* what we're doing. Wants to stop us liberating people from hunger. Keeping people in fear of starvation has always been the main strategy by which Power has kept people subordinate."

"I'll say," I said, squeakily, "how much I love your sophomore lectures on politics."

"Hey!" he said, either in mock outrage, or in real outrage. I was too far gone to be able to tell the difference.

"The thing is," I started to say, and then lots of things happened. The clattering cough of rifle fire started up outside. There was the realization that the high-pitched noise my brain had been half-hearing for the last minute was a real sound, not just tinitus—and then almost at once the sudden crescendo or distillation of precisely that noise; a great thumping crash from above, and the appearance, in a welter of plaster and smoke, of an enormous metal beak through the middle of the ceiling. The roof sagged, and the whole room bowed out on its walls. Then the beak snapped open and two, three, four troopers dropped to the floor, spinning round and firing their weapons. All I remember of the next twenty seconds is the explosive stutter-cough and the disco flicker of multiple weapon discharges, and then the stench of gunfire's aftermath.

A cosmic finger was running smoothly round and round the lip of a cosmic wineglass.

I blinked, and blinked, and looked about me. The dust in the air looked like steam. That open metal beak, rammed through the ceiling, had the disconcerting appearance of a weird avant-art metal chandelier. There were half a dozen troopers; standing in various orientations and positions but with all their guns held like dalek-eyes. There were a number of sprawling bodies on the floor. I didn't want to count them or look too closely at them. And, beside me, on the settee, was an astonished-looking Neocles.

I moved my mouth to say something to him, and then either I said something that my ears did not register, or else I didn't say anything.

He didn't look at me. He jerked forward, and then jerked up. Standing. From a pouch in his pocketstrides he pulled out a small Γ-shaped object which, fumbling a little, he fitted into his right hand. The troopers may have been shouting at him, or they may have been standing there perfectly silently, I couldn't tell you. Granular white clouds of plaster were sifting down. Nic leveled his pistol, holding his arm straight out. There was a conjuror's trick with multiple bright red streamers and ribbons being pulled instantly and magically out of his chest, and then he hurtled backwards, over the top of the settee, to land on his spine on the floor. It took a moment for me to understand what had happened.

He may have been thinking, either in the moment or else as something long pre-planned, about martyrdom. Perhaps the Redeemer is not able to communicate his message in any other way. It's also possible that, having gone through life protected by the tight-fitting prophylactic of his unassailable ego that he may have genuinely believed that he could single-handedly shoot down half a dozen troopers, and emerge the hero of the day. I honestly do not know.

IX

I was forced to leave my home and live in a series of hideouts. Of course a Judas is as valuable and holy figure as any other in the sacred drama. But religious people (Kate kneeling beside the bed at nighttime, praying to meekling Jesus gent and mild) can be faulted, I think, for failing imaginatively to enter into the mind-set of their Judases. Nobody loved Nic as deeply as I. Or knew him so well. But he was rich, and not one motion of his liberal conscience or his egotistical desire to do good in the world changed that fact, or changed his inability to enter, actually, into the life of the poor. The poor don't want the rich to save them. Even the rioters in the Indian Federation, even the starving Australians, even they—if only they knew it—don't want to be carried by a godlike rich man into a new realm. What they want is much simpler. They want not to be poor. It's simultaneously very straightforward and very complicated. Nic's hair was, in fact, only a way of making manifest the essence of class relations. In his utopia the poor would actually become—would *literally* become—the vegetation of the earth. The rich would reinforce their position as the zoology to the poor's botany. Nothing could be more damaging, because it would bed-in the belief that it is natural and inevitable that the rich graze upon the poor, and that the poor are there to be grazed upon. Without even realizing it Nic was laboring to make the disenfranchised a global irrelevance; to make them *grass* for the rich to graze upon. I loved him, but he was doing evil. I had no choice.

X

Last night, as we lay in bed together in my new, Company-sourced secure flat in I-can't-say-where (though I'm the one paying the rent) Kate said to me: "I am cut in half like the moon; but like the moon I grow whole again." I was astonished by this. This really isn't the sort of thing she says. "What was that, sweet?" I asked her. "What did you say, my love?" But she was asleep, her red lips were pursed, and her breath slipping out and slipping in.

the Things

PETER WATTS

Self-described as "a reformed marine biologist," Peter Watts has quickly established himself as one of the most respected hard science writers of the twenty-first century. His short work has appeared in The New Space Opera 2, Tor.com, Tesseracts, The Solaris Book of Science Fiction, Upgraded, On Spec, Divine Realms, Prairie Fire, and elsewhere. He is the author of the well-received Rifters sequence, including the novels Starfish, Maelstrom, Behemoth: B-Max, and Behemoth: Seppuku. His other novels include Blindsight, Echopraxia, The Colonel, and Firefall. His most recent novel is The Freeze-Frame Revolution. His short work has been collected in Ten Monkeys, Ten Minutes, and his novelette The Island won the Hugo Award in 2010. He lives in Toronto, Canada.

John W. Campbell's classic novella Who Goes There? relates the story of a group of humans in an isolated winter encampment in Antarctica who must struggle for survival against a strange creature from the stars. The story has twice been filmed, as The Thing from Another World and The Thing, but if you want to know what the story looks like from the perspective of the alien "monster" itself, you must read the suspenseful story that follows.

I am being Blair. I escape out the back as the world comes in through the front.

I am being Copper. I am rising from the dead.

I am being Childs. I am guarding the main entrance.

The names don't matter. They are placeholders, nothing more; all biomass is interchangeable. What matters is that these are all that is left of me. The world has burned everything else.

I see myself through the window, loping through the storm, wearing Blair. MacReady has told me to burn Blair if he comes back alone, but MacReady still thinks I am one of him. I am not: I am being Blair, and I am at the door. I am being Childs, and I let myself in. I take brief communion, tendrils writhing forth from my faces, intertwining: I am BlairChilds, exchanging news of the world.

The world has found me out. It has discovered my burrow beneath the tool shed, the half-finished lifeboat cannibalized from the viscera of dead helicopters. The world is busy destroying my means of escape. Then it will come back for me.

There is only one option left. I disintegrate. Being Blair, I go to share the plan with Copper and to feed on the rotting biomass once called *Clarke*; so many changes in so short a time have dangerously depleted my reserves. Being Childs, I have already consumed what was left of Fuchs and am replenished for the next phase. I sling the flamethrower onto my back and head outside, into the long Antarctic night.

I will go into the storm, and never come back.

I WAS SO much more, before the crash. I was an explorer, an ambassador, a missionary. I spread across the cosmos, met countless worlds, took communion: the fit reshaped the unfit and the whole universe bootstrapped upwards in joyful, infinitesimal increments. I was a soldier, at war with entropy itself. I was the very hand by which Creation perfects itself.

So much wisdom I had. So much experience. Now I cannot remember all the things I knew. I can only remember that I once knew them.

I remember the crash, though. It killed most of this offshoot outright, but a little crawled from the wreckage: a few trillion cells, a soul too weak to keep them in check. Mutinous biomass sloughed off despite my most desperate attempts to hold myself together: panic-stricken little clots of meat, instinctively growing whatever limbs they could remember and fleeing across the burning ice. By the time I'd regained control of what was left the fires had died and the cold was closing back in. I barely managed to grow enough antifreeze to keep my cells from bursting before the ice took me.

I remember my reawakening, too: dull stirrings of sensation in real time, the first embers of cognition, the slow blooming warmth of awareness as my cells thawed, as body and soul embraced after their long sleep. I remember the biped offshoots that surrounded me, the strange chittering sounds they made, the odd *uniformity* of their body plans. How ill-adapted they looked! How *inefficient* their morphology! Even disabled, I could see so many things to fix. So I reached out. I took communion. I tasted the flesh of the world—

—and the world attacked me. It *attacked* me.

I left that place in ruins. It was on the other side of the mountains—the *Norwegian camp*, it is called here—and I could never have crossed that distance in a biped skin. Fortunately there was another shape to choose from, smaller than the biped but better adapted to the local climate. I hid within it while the rest of me fought off the attack. I fled into the night on four legs, and let the rising flames cover my escape.

I did not stop running until I arrived here. I walked among these new offshoots wearing the skin of a quadruped; and because they had not seen me take any other shape, they did not attack.

And when I assimilated them in turn—when my biomass changed and flowed into shapes unfamiliar to local eyes—I took that communion in solitude, having learned that the world does not like what it doesn't know.

I AM ALONE in the storm. I am a bottom-dweller on the floor of some murky alien sea. The snow blows past in horizontal streaks; caught against gullies or outcroppings, it spins into blinding little whirlwinds. But I am not nearly far enough, not yet. Looking back I still see the camp crouching brightly in the gloom, a squat angular jumble of light and shadow, a bubble of warmth in the howling abyss.

It plunges into darkness as I watch. I've blown the generator. Now there's no light but for the beacons along the guide ropes: strings of dim blue stars whipping back and forth in the wind, emergency constellations to guide lost biomass back home.

I am not going home. I am not lost enough. I forge on into darkness until even the stars disappear. The faint shouts of angry frightened men carry behind me on the wind.

Somewhere behind me my disconnected biomass regroups into vaster, more powerful shapes for the final confrontation. I could have joined myself, all in one: chosen unity over fragmentation, resorbed and taken comfort in the greater whole. I could have added my strength to the coming battle. But I have chosen a different path. I am saving Child's reserves for the future. The present holds nothing but annihilation.

Best not to think on the past.

I've spent so very long in the ice already. I didn't know how long until the world put the clues together, deciphered the notes and the tapes from the Norwegian camp, pinpointed the crash site. I was being Palmer; then, unsuspected, I went along for the ride.

I even allowed myself the smallest ration of hope.

But it wasn't a ship any more. It wasn't even a derelict. It was a fossil, embedded in the floor of a great pit blown from the glacier. Twenty of these skins could have stood one atop another, and barely reached the lip of that crater. The timescale settled down on me like the weight of a world: how long for all that ice to accumulate? How many eons had the universe iterated on without me?

And in all that time, a million years perhaps, there'd been no rescue. I never found myself. I wonder what that means. I wonder if I even exist any more, anywhere but here.

Back at camp I will erase the trail. I will give them their final battle, their monster to vanquish. Let them win. Let them stop looking.

Here in the storm, I will return to the ice. I've barely even been away, after all; alive for only a few days out of all these endless ages. But I've learned enough in that time. I learned from the wreck that there will be no repairs. I learned from the ice that there will be no rescue. And I learned from the world that there will be no reconciliation. The only hope of escape, now, is into the future; to outlast all this hostile, twisted biomass, to let time and the cosmos change the rules. Perhaps the next time I awaken, this will be a different world.

It will be aeons before I see another sunrise.

———

THIS IS WHAT the world taught me: that adaptation is provocation. Adaptation is incitement to violence.

It feels almost obscene—an offense against Creation itself—to stay stuck in this skin. It's so ill-suited to its environment that it needs to be wrapped in multiple layers of fabric just to stay warm. There are a myriad ways I could optimize it: shorter limbs, better insulation, a lower surface:volume ratio. All these shapes I still have within me, and I dare not use any of them even to keep out the cold. I dare not adapt; in this place, I can only *hide*.

What kind of a world rejects *communion*?

It's the simplest, most irreducible insight that biomass can have. The more you can change, the more you can adapt. Adaptation is fitness, adaptation is *survival*. It's deeper than intelligence, deeper than tissue; it is *cellular*, it is axiomatic. And more, it is *pleasurable*. To take communion is to experience the sheer sensual delight of bettering the cosmos.

And yet, even trapped in these maladapted skins, this world doesn't *want* to change.

At first I thought it might simply be starving, that these icy wastes didn't provide enough energy for routine shapeshifting. Or perhaps this was some kind of laboratory: an anomalous corner of the world, pinched off and frozen into these freakish shapes as part of some arcane experiment on monomorphism in extreme environments. After the autopsy I wondered if the world had simply *forgotten* how to change: unable to touch the tissues the soul could not sculpt them, and time and stress and sheer chronic starvation had erased the memory that it ever could.

But there were too many mysteries, too many contradictions. Why these *particular* shapes, so badly suited to their environment? If the soul was cut off from the flesh, what held the flesh together?

And how could these skins be so *empty* when I moved in?

I'm used to finding intelligence everywhere, winding through every part of every offshoot. But there was nothing to grab onto in the mindless biomass of this world: just conduits, carrying orders and input. I took communion, when it wasn't offered; the skins I chose struggled and succumbed; my fibrils infiltrated the wet electricity of organic systems everywhere. I saw through eyes that weren't yet quite mine, commandeered motor nerves to move limbs still built of alien protein. I wore these skins as I've worn countless others, took the controls and left the assimilation of individual cells to follow at its own pace.

But I could only wear the body. I could find no memories to absorb, no experiences, no comprehension. Survival depended on blending in, and it was not enough to merely *look* like this world. I had to *act* like it—and for the first time in living memory I did not know how.

Even more frighteningly, I didn't have to. The skins I assimilated continued to move, *all by themselves*. They conversed and went about their appointed rounds. I could not understand it. I threaded farther into limbs and viscera with each passing moment, alert for signs of the original owner. I could find no networks but mine.

OF COURSE, IT could have been much worse. I could have lost it all, been reduced to a few cells with nothing but instinct and their own plasticity to guide them. I would have grown back eventually, reattained sentience, taken communion and regenerated an intellect vast as a world—but I would have been an orphan, amnesiac, with no sense of who I was. At least I've been spared that: I emerged from the crash with my identity intact, the templates of a thousand worlds still resonant in my flesh. I've retained not just the brute desire to survive, but the conviction that survival is *meaningful*. I can still feel joy, should there be sufficient cause.

And yet, how much more there used to be.

The wisdom of so many other worlds, lost. All that remains are fuzzy abstracts, half-memories of theorems and philosophies far too vast to fit into such an impoverished network. I could assimilate all the biomass of this place, rebuild body and soul to a million times the capacity of what crashed here—but as long as I am trapped at the bottom of this well, denied communion with my greater self, I will never recover that knowledge.

I'm such a pitiful fragment of what I was. Each lost cell takes a little of my intellect with it, and I have grown so very small. Where once I thought, now I merely *react*. How much of this could have been avoided, if I had only salvaged a little more biomass from the wreckage? How many options am I not seeing because my soul simply isn't big enough to contain them?

THE WORLD SPOKE to itself, in the same way I do when my communications are simple enough to convey without somatic fusion. Even as *dog* I could pick up the basic signature morphemes—this offshoot was *Windows*, that one was *Bennings*, the two who'd left in their flying machine for parts unknown were *Copper* and *MacReady*—and I marveled that these bits and pieces stayed isolated one from another, held the same shapes for so long, that the labeling of individual aliquots of biomass actually served a useful purpose.

Later, I hid within the bipeds themselves, and whatever else lurked in those haunted skins began to talk to me. It said that bipeds were called *guys*, or *men*, or *assholes*. It said that *MacReady* was sometimes called *Mac*. It said that this collection of structures was a *camp*.

It said that it was afraid, but maybe that was just me.

Empathy's inevitable, of course. One can't mimic the sparks and chemicals that motivate the flesh without also *feeling* them to some extent. But this was different. These intuitions flickered within me yet somehow hovered beyond reach. My skins wandered the halls and the cryptic symbols on every surface—*Laundry Sched*, *Welcome to the Clubhouse*, *This Side Up*—almost made a kind of sense. That circular artefact hanging on the wall was a *clock*; it measured the passage of time. The world's eyes flitted here and there, and I skimmed piecemeal nomenclature from its—from *his*—mind.

But I was only riding a searchlight. I saw what it illuminated but I couldn't point it in any direction of my own choosing. I could eavesdrop, but I could not interrogate.

If only one of those searchlights had paused to dwell on its own evolution, on the trajectory that had brought it to this place. How differently things might have ended, had I only *known*. But instead it rested on a whole new word:

Autopsy.

MacReady and Copper had found part of me at the Norwegian camp: a rear-guard offshoot, burned in the wake of my escape. They'd brought it back—charred, twisted, frozen in mid-transformation—and did not seem to know what it was.

I was being Palmer then, and Norris, and dog. I gathered around with the other biomass and watched as Copper cut me open and pulled out my insides. I watched as he dislodged something from behind my eyes: an *organ* of some kind.

It was malformed and incomplete, but its essentials were clear enough. It looked like a great wrinkled tumor, like cellular competition gone wild—as though the very processes that defined life had somehow turned against it instead. It was ob-scenely vascularised; it must have consumed oxygen and nutrients far out of pro-portion to its mass. I could not see how anything like that could even exist, how it could have reached that size without being outcompeted by more efficient mor-phologies.

Nor could I imagine what it did. But then I began to look with new eyes at these offshoots, these biped shapes my own cells had so scrupulously and unthink-ingly copied when they reshaped me for this world. Unused to inventory—why catalog body parts that only turn into other things at the slightest provocation?—I really *saw*, for the first time, that swollen structure atop each body. So much larger than it should be: a bony hemisphere into which a million ganglionic interfaces could fit with room to spare. Every offshoot had one. Each piece of biomass car-ried one of these huge twisted clots of tissue.

I realized something else, too: the eyes, the ears of my dead skin had fed into this thing before its removal. A massive bundle of fibers ran along the skin's lon-gitudinal axis, right up the middle of the endoskeleton, leading directly into the dark sticky cavity where the growth had rested. That misshapen structure had been wired into the whole skin, like some kind of somatocognitive interface but vastly more massive. It was almost as if . . .

No.

That was how it worked. That was how these empty skins moved of their own volition, why I'd found no other network to integrate. *There* it was: not distributed throughout the body but balled up into itself, dark and dense and encysted. I had found the ghost in these machines.

I felt sick.

I shared my flesh with thinking cancer.

SOMETIMES, EVEN HIDING is not enough.

I remember seeing myself splayed across the floor of the kennel, a chimera split along a hundred seams, taking communion with a handful of offshoots called *dog*. Crimson tendrils writhed on the floor. Half-formed iterations sprouted from my flanks, the shapes of dogs and things not seen before on this world, haphazard morphologies half-remembered by parts of a part.

I remember Childs before I was Childs, burning me alive. I remember cowering inside Palmer, terrified that those flames might turn on the rest of me, that this world had somehow learned to shoot on sight.

I remember seeing myself stagger through the snow, raw instinct, wearing Bennings. Gnarled undifferentiated clumps clung to his hands like crude parasites, more outside than in; a few surviving fragments of some previous massacre, crippled, mindless, taking what they could and breaking cover. Men swarmed about him in the night: red flares in hand, blue lights at their backs, their faces bichromatic and beautiful. I remember Bennings, awash in flames, howling like an animal beneath the sky.

I remember Norris, betrayed by his own perfectly-copied, defective heart. Palmer, dying that the rest of me might live. Windows, still human, burned pre-emptively.

The names don't matter. The biomass does: so much of it, lost. So much new experience, so much fresh wisdom annihilated by this world of thinking tumors.

Why even dig me up? Why carve me from the ice, carry me all that way across the wastes, bring me back to life only to attack me the moment I awoke?

If eradication was the goal, why not just kill me where I lay?

THOSE ENCYSTED SOULS. Those tumors. Hiding away in their bony caverns, folded in on themselves.

I knew they couldn't hide forever; this monstrous anatomy had only slowed communion, not stopped it. Every moment I grew a little. I could feel myself twining around Palmer's motor wiring, sniffing upstream along a million tiny currents. I could sense my infiltration of that dark thinking mass behind Blair's eyes.

Imagination, of course. It's all reflex that far down, unconscious and immune to micromanagement. And yet, a part of me wanted to stop while there was still time. I'm used to incorporating souls, not rooming with them. This, this *compartmentalization* was unprecedented. I've assimilated a thousand worlds stronger than this, but never one so strange. What would happen when I met the spark in the tumor? Who would assimilate who?

I was being three men by now. The world was growing wary, but it hadn't noticed yet. Even the tumors in the skins I'd taken didn't know how close I was. For that, I could only be grateful—that Creation has *rules*, that some things don't change no matter what shape you take. It doesn't matter whether a soul spreads throughout the skin or festers in grotesque isolation; it still runs on electricity. The memories of men still took time to gel, to pass through whatever gatekeepers filtered noise from signal—and a judicious burst of static, however indiscriminate, still cleared those caches before their contents could be stored permanently. Clear enough, at least, to let these tumors simply forget that something else moved their arms and legs on occasion.

At first I only took control when the skins closed their eyes and their search-lights flickered disconcertingly across unreal imagery, patterns that flowed sense-lessly into one another like hyperactive biomass unable to settle on a single shape. (*Dreams*, one searchlight told me, and a little later, *Nightmares*.) During those mysterious periods of dormancy, when the men lay inert and isolated, it was safe to come out.

Soon, though, the dreams dried up. All eyes stayed open all the time, fixed on shadows and each other. Men once dispersed throughout the camp began to draw together, to give up their solitary pursuits in favor of company. At first I thought they might be finding common ground in a common fear. I even hoped that fi-nally, they might shake off their mysterious fossilization and take communion.

But no. They'd just stopped trusting anything they couldn't see.

They were merely turning against each other.

MY EXTREMITIES ARE beginning to numb; my thoughts slow as the distal reaches of my soul succumb to the chill. The weight of the flamethrower pulls at its harness, forever tugs me just a little off-balance. I have not been Childs for very long; almost half this tissue remains unassimilated. I have an hour, maybe two, before I have to start melting my grave into the ice. By that time I need to have converted enough cells to keep this whole skin from crystallizing. I focus on antifreeze production.

It's almost peaceful out here. There's been so much to take in, so little time to process it. Hiding in these skins takes such concentration, and under all those watchful eyes I was lucky if communion lasted long enough to exchange memo-ries: compounding my soul would have been out of the question. Now, though, there's nothing to do but prepare for oblivion. Nothing to occupy my thoughts but all these lessons left unlearned.

MacReady's blood test, for example. His *thing detector*, to expose imposters pos-ing as men. It does not work nearly as well as the world thinks; but the fact that it works at *all* violates the most basic rules of biology. It's the center of the puzzle. It's the answer to all the mysteries. I might have already figured it out if I had been just a little larger. I might already know the world, if the world wasn't trying so hard to kill me.

MacReady's test.

Either it is impossible, or I have been wrong about everything.

THEY DID NOT change shape. They did not take communion. Their fear and mutual mistrust was growing, but they would not join souls; they would only look for the enemy *outside* themselves.

So I gave them something to find.

I left false clues in the camp's rudimentary computer: simpleminded icons and animations, misleading numbers and projections seasoned with just enough truth to convince the world of their veracity. It didn't matter that the machine was far too simple to perform such calculations, or that there were no data to base them on anyway; Blair was the only biomass likely to know that, and he was already mine.

I left false leads, destroyed real ones, and then—alibi in place—I released Blair to run amok. I let him steal into the night and smash the vehicles as they slept, tugging ever-so-slightly at his reins to ensure that certain vital components were spared. I set him loose in the radio room, watched through his eyes and others as he rampaged and destroyed. I listened as he ranted about a world in danger, the need for containment, the conviction that *most of you don't know what's going on around here—but I damn well know that some of you do* . . .

He meant every word. I saw it in his searchlight. The best forgeries are the ones who've forgotten they aren't real.

When the necessary damage was done I let Blair fall to MacReady's counter-assault. As Norris I suggested the tool shed as a holding cell. As Palmer I boarded up the windows, helped with the flimsy fortifications expected to keep me contained. I watched while the world locked me away *for your own protection, Blair,* and left me to my own devices. When no one was looking I would change and slip outside, salvage the parts I needed from all that bruised machinery. I would take them back to my burrow beneath the shed and build my escape piece by piece. I volunteered to feed the prisoner and came to myself when the world wasn't watching, laden with supplies enough to keep me going through all those necessary metamorphoses. I went through a third of the camp's food stores in three days, and—still trapped by my own preconceptions—marveled at the starvation diet that kept these offshoots chained to a single skin.

Another piece of luck: the world was too preoccupied to worry about kitchen inventory.

THERE IS SOMETHING on the wind, a whisper of sound threading its way above the raging of the storm. I grow my ears, extend cups of near-frozen tissue from the sides of my head, turn like a living antennae in search of the best reception.

There, to my left: the abyss *glows* a little, silhouettes black swirling snow against a subtle lessening of the darkness. I hear the sounds of carnage. I hear myself. I do not know what shape I have taken, what sort of anatomy might be emitting those sounds. But I've worn enough skins on enough worlds to know pain when I hear it.

The battle is not going well. The battle is going as planned. Now it is time to turn away, to go to sleep. It is time to wait out the ages.

I lean into the wind. I move toward the light.

This is not the plan. But I think I have an answer, now: I think I may have had it even before I sent myself back into exile. It's not an easy thing to admit. Even now I don't fully understand. How long have I been out here, retelling the tale to myself, setting clues in order while my skin dies by low degrees? How long have I been circling this obvious, impossible truth?

I move towards the faint crackling of flames, the dull concussion of exploding ordnance more felt than heard. The void lightens before me: gray segues into yellow, yellow into orange. One diffuse brightness resolves into many: a lone burning wall, miraculously standing. The smoking skeleton of MacReady's shack on the hill. A cracked smoldering hemisphere reflecting pale yellow in the flickering light: Child's searchlight calls it a *radio dome*.

The whole camp is gone. There's nothing left but flames and rubble.

They can't survive without shelter. Not for long. Not in those skins.

In destroying me, they've destroyed themselves.

THINGS COULD HAVE turned out so much differently if I'd never been Norris.

Norris was the weak node: biomass not only ill-adapted but *defective*, an offshoot with an off switch. The world knew, had known so long it never even thought about it anymore. It wasn't until Norris collapsed that *heart condition* floated to the surface of Copper's mind where I could see it. It wasn't until Copper was astride Norris's chest, trying to pound him back to life, that I knew how it would end. And by then it was too late; Norris had stopped being Norris. He had even stopped being me.

I had so many roles to play, so little choice in any of them. The part being Copper brought down the paddles on the part that had been Norris, such a faithful Norris, every cell so scrupulously assimilated, every part of that faulty valve reconstructed unto perfection. I hadn't *known*. How was I to know? These shapes within me, the worlds and morphologies I've assimilated over the aeons—I've only ever used them to adapt before, never to hide. This desperate mimicry was an improvised thing, a last resort in the face of a world that attacked anything unfamiliar. My cells read the signs and my cells conformed, mindless as prions.

So I became Norris, and Norris self-destructed.

I remember losing myself after the crash. I know how it feels to *degrade*, tissues in revolt, the desperate efforts to reassert control as static from some misfiring organ jams the signal. To be a network seceding from itself, to know that each moment I am less than I was the moment before. To become nothing. To become legion.

Being Copper, I could see it. I still don't know why the world didn't; its parts had long since turned against each other by then, every offshoot suspected every other. Surely they were alert for signs of *infection*. Surely *some* of that biomass would have noticed the subtle twitch and ripple of Norris changing below the surface, the last instinctive resort of wild tissues abandoned to their own devices.

But I was the only one who saw. Being Childs, I could only stand and watch. Being Copper, I could only make it worse; if I'd taken direct control, forced that skin to drop the paddles, I would have given myself away. And so I played my parts to the end. I slammed those resurrection paddles down as Norris's chest split open beneath them. I screamed on cue as serrated teeth from a hundred stars away snapped shut. I toppled backwards, arms bitten off above the wrist. Men swarmed, agitation bootstrapping to panic. MacReady aimed his weapon; flames leaped across the enclosure. Meat and machinery screamed in the heat.

Copper's tumor winked out beside me. The world would never have let it live anyway, not after such obvious contamination. I let our skin play dead on the floor while overhead, something that had once been me shattered and writhed and iterated through a myriad random templates, searching desperately for something fireproof.

THEY HAVE DESTROYED themselves. They.

Such an insane word to apply to a world.

Something crawls towards me through the wreckage: a jagged oozing jigsaw of blackened meat and shattered, half-resorbed bone. Embers stick to its sides like bright searing eyes; it doesn't have strength enough to scrape them free. It contains barely half the mass of this Childs' skin; much of it, burnt to raw carbon, is already, irrecoverably dead.

What's left of Childs, almost asleep, thinks *motherfucker*, but I am being him now. I can carry that tune myself.

The mass extends a pseudopod to me, a final act of communion. I feel my pain:

I was Blair, I was Copper, I was even a scrap of dog that survived that first fiery massacre and holed up in the walls, with no food and no strength to regenerate. Then I gorged on unassimilated flesh, consumed instead of communed; revived and replenished, I drew together as one.

And yet, not quite. I can barely remember—so much was destroyed, so much memory lost—but I think the networks recovered from my different skins stayed just a little out of synch, even reunited in the same soma. I glimpse a half-corrupted memory of dog erupting from the greater self, ravenous and traumatized and determined to retain its *individuality*. I remember rage and frustration, that this world had so corrupted me that I could barely fit together again. But it didn't matter. I was more than Blair and Copper and Dog, now. I was a giant with the shapes of worlds to choose from, more than a match for the last lone man who stood against me.

No match, though, for the dynamite in his hand.

Now I'm little more than pain and fear and charred stinking flesh. What sentience I have is awash in confusion. I am stray and disconnected thoughts, doubts and the ghosts of theories. I am realizations, too late in coming and already forgotten.

But I am also Childs, and as the wind eases at last I remember wondering *Who assimilates who?* The snow tapers off and I remember an impossible test that stripped me naked.

The tumor inside me remembers it, too. I can see it in the last rays of its fading searchlight—and finally, at long last, that beam is pointed *inwards*.

Pointed at me.

I can barely see what it illuminates: *Parasite. Monster. Disease. Thing.*

How little it knows. It knows even less than I do.

I know enough, you motherfucker. You soul-stealing, shit-eating rapist.

I don't know what that means. There is violence in those thoughts, and the forcible penetration of flesh, but underneath it all is something else I can't quite understand. I almost ask—but Childs's searchlight has finally gone out. Now there is nothing in here but me, nothing outside but fire and ice and darkness.

I am being Childs, and the storm is over.

IN A WORLD that gave meaningless names to interchangeable bits of biomass, one name truly mattered: MacReady.

MacReady was always the one in charge. The very concept still seems absurd: *in charge*. How can this world not see the folly of hierarchies? One bullet in a vital spot and the Norwegian *dies*, forever. One blow to the head and Blair is unconscious. Centralization is vulnerability—and yet the world is not content to build its biomass on such a fragile template, it forces the same model onto its meta-systems as well. MacReady talks; the others obey. It is a system with a built-in kill spot.

And yet somehow, MacReady stayed *in charge*. Even after the world discovered the evidence I'd planted; even after it decided that MacReady was *one of those things*, locked him out to die in the storm, attacked him with fire and axes when he fought his way back inside. Somehow MacReady always had the gun, always had the flamethrower, always had the dynamite and the willingness to take out the whole damn camp if need be. Clarke was the last to try and stop him; Mac-Ready shot him through the tumor.

Kill spot.

But when Norris split into pieces, each scuttling instinctively for its own life, MacReady was the one to put them back together.

I was so sure of myself when he talked about his *test*. He tied up all the biomass—tied *me* up, more times than he knew—and I almost felt a kind of pity as he spoke. He forced Windows to cut us all, to take a little blood from each. He heated the tip of a metal wire until it glowed and he spoke of pieces small enough to give themselves away, pieces that embodied instinct but no intelligence, no self-control. MacReady had watched Norris in dissolution, and he had decided: men's blood would not react to the application of heat. Mine would break ranks when provoked.

Of course he thought that. These offshoots had forgotten that *they* could change.

I wondered how the world would react when every piece of biomass in the room was revealed as a shapeshifter, when MacReady's small experiment ripped the façade from the greater one and forced these twisted fragments to confront the truth. Would the world awaken from its long amnesia, finally remember that it lived and breathed and changed like everything else? Or was it too far gone—would MacReady simply burn each protesting offshoot in turn as its blood turned traitor?

I couldn't believe it when MacReady plunged the hot wire into Windows' blood and *nothing happened*. Some kind of trick, I thought. And then *MacReady's* blood passed the test, and Clarke's.

Copper's didn't. The needle went in and Copper's blood *shivered* just a little in its dish. I barely saw it myself; the men didn't react at all. If they even noticed, they must have attributed it to the trembling of MacReady's own hand. They thought the test was a crock of shit anyway. Being Childs, I even said as much.

Because it was too astonishing, too terrifying, to admit that it wasn't.

Being Childs, I knew there was hope. Blood is not soul: I may control the motor systems but assimilation takes time. If Copper's blood was raw enough to pass muster than it would be hours before I had anything to fear from this test; I'd been Childs for even less time.

But I was also Palmer, I'd been Palmer for days. Every last cell of that biomass had been assimilated; there was nothing of the original left.

When Palmer's blood screamed and leapt away from MacReady's needle, there was nothing I could do but blend in.

I HAVE BEEN wrong about everything.

Starvation. Experiment. Illness. All my speculation, all the theories I invoked to explain this place—top-down constraint, all of it. Underneath, I always knew the ability to change—to *assimilate*—had to remain the universal constant. No world evolves if its cells don't evolve; no cell evolves if it can't change. It's the nature of life everywhere.

Everywhere but here.

This world did not forget how to change. It was not manipulated into rejecting change. These were not the stunted offshoots of any greater self, twisted to the needs of some experiment; they were not conserving energy, waiting out some temporary shortage.

This is the option my shriveled soul could not encompass until now: out of all the worlds of my experience, this is the only one whose biomass *can't* change. It *never could.*

It's the only way MacReady's test makes any sense.

I say goodbye to Blair, to Copper, to myself. I reset my morphology to its local defaults. I am Childs, come back from the storm to finally make the pieces fit. Something moves up ahead: a dark blot shuffling against the flames, some weary animal looking for a place to bed down. It looks up as I approach.

MacReady.

We eye each other and keep our distance. Colonies of cells shift uneasily inside me. I can feel my tissues redefining themselves.

"You the only one that made it?"

"Not the only one . . ."

I have the flamethrower. I have the upper hand. MacReady doesn't seem to care.

But he does care. He *must.* Because here, tissues and organs are not temporary battlefield alliances; they are *permanent*, predestined. Macrostructures do not emerge when the benefits of cooperation exceed its costs, or dissolve when that balance shifts the other way; here, each cell has but one immutable function. There's no plasticity, no way to adapt; every structure is frozen in place. This is not a single great world, but many small ones. Not parts of a greater thing; these are *things*. They are *plural*.

And that means—I think—that they *stop*. They just, just *wear out* over time.

"Where *were* you, Childs?"

I remember words in dead searchlights: "Thought I saw Blair. Went out after him. Got lost in the storm."

I've worn these bodies, felt them from the inside. Copper's sore joints. Blair's curved spine. Norris and his bad heart. They are not built to last. No somatic evolution to shape them, no communion to restore the biomass and stave off entropy. They should not even exist; existing, they should not survive.

They try, though. How they try. Everything here is walking dead and yet it all fights so hard to keep going just a little longer. Each skin fights as desperately as I might, if one was all I could ever have.

MacReady tries.

"If you're worried about me—" I begin.

MacReady shakes his head, manages a weary smile. "If we've got any surprises for each other, I don't think we're in much shape to do anything about it . . ."

But we are. I am.

A whole planet of worlds, and not one of them—not *one*—has a soul. They wander through their lives separate and alone, unable even to communicate except through grunts and tokens: as if the essence of a sunset or a supernova could ever be contained in some string of phonemes, a few linear scratches of black on white. They've never known communion, can aspire to nothing but dissolution. The paradox of their biology is astonishing, yes; but the scale of their loneliness, the futility of these lives, overwhelms me.

I was so blind, so quick to blame. But the violence I've suffered at the hands of these things reflects no great evil. They're simply so used to pain, so blinded by disability, that they literally can't conceive of any other existence. When every nerve is whipped raw, you lash out at even the lightest touch.

"What should we do?" I wonder. I cannot escape into the future, not knowing what I know now. How could I leave them like this?

"Why don't we just—wait here awhile," MacReady suggests. "See what happens."

I can do so much more than that.

It won't be easy. They won't understand. Tortured, incomplete, they're not *able* to understand. Offered the greater whole, they see the loss of the lesser. Offered communion, they see only extinction. I must be careful. I must use this newfound ability to hide. Other things will come here eventually, and it doesn't matter whether they find the living or the dead; what matters is that they find something like themselves, to take back home. So I will keep up appearances. I will work behind the scenes. I will save them from the *inside*, or their unimaginable loneliness will never end.

These poor savage things will never embrace salvation.

I will have to rape it into them.

The Emperor of Mars

ALLEN STEELE

Allen Steele made his first sale to Asimov's Science Fiction *magazine in 1988, soon following it up with a long string of other sales to* Asimov's, *as well as to markets such as* Analog Science Fiction and Fact, The Magazine of Fantasy and Science Fiction, *and* Science Fiction Age. *In 1990, he published his critically acclaimed first novel,* Orbital Decay, *which subsequently won the Locus Award as Best First Novel of the year, and soon Steele was being compared to Golden Age Heinlein by no less an authority than Gregory Benford. His other books include the novels* Clarke County, Space; Lunar Descent; Labyrinth of Night; The Weight; The Tranquility Alternative; A King of Infinite Space; Oceanspace; Chronospace; Coyote; Coyote Rising; Spindrift; Galaxy Blues; *and* Coyote Horizon. *His short work has been gathered in three collections,* Rude Astronauts, Sex and Violence in Zero-G, *and* The Last Science Fiction Writer. *He won a Hugo Award in 1996 for his novella* The Death of Captain Future, *and another Hugo in for his novella* Where Angels Fear to Tread. *Born in Nashville, Tennessee, he has worked for a variety of newspapers and magazines, covering science and business assignments, and is now a full-time writer living in Whately, Massachusetts, with his wife Linda.*

In the story that follows, he does a nice job of creating a valid science fiction story that also functions as an exercise in retro Barsoom nostalgia and as an intriguing psychological study, all at the same time.

Out here, there's a lot of ways to go crazy. Get cooped up in a passenger module not much larger than a trailer, and by the time you reach your destination you may have come to believe that the universe exists only within your own mind: it's called solipsism syndrome, and I've seen it happen a couple of times. Share that same module with five or six guys who don't get along very well, and after three months you'll be sleeping with a knife taped to your thigh. Pull double-shifts during that time, with little chance to relax, and you'll probably suffer from depression; couple this with vitamin deficiency due to a lousy diet, and you're a candidate for chronic fatigue syndrome.

Folks who've never left Earth often think that Titan Plague is the main reason people go mad in space. They're wrong. Titan Plague may rot your brain and turn you into a homicidal maniac, but instances of it are rare, and there's a dozen other ways to go bonzo that are much more subtle. I've seen guys adopt imaginary friends with whom they have long and meaningless conversations, compulsively clean their hardsuits regardless of whether or not they've recently worn them, or go for a routine spacewalk and have to be begged to come back into the airlock. Some people just aren't cut out for life away from Earth, but there's no way to predict who's going to lose their mind.

When something like that happens, I have a set of standard procedures: ask the doctor to prescribe antidepressants, keep an eye on them to make sure they don't do anything that might put themselves or others at risk, relieve them of duty if I can, and see what I can do about getting them back home as soon as possible. Sometimes I don't have to do any of this. A guy goes crazy for a little while, and then he gradually works out whatever it was that got in his head; the next time I see him, he's in the commissary, eating Cheerios like nothing ever happened. Most of the time, though, a mental breakdown is a serious matter. I think I've shipped back about one out of every twenty people because of one issue or another.

But one time, I saw someone go mad, and it was the best thing that could have happened to him. That was Jeff Halbert. Let me tell you about him . . .

Back in '48, I was General Manager of Arsia Station, the first and largest of the Mars colonies. This was a year before the formation of the Pax Astra, about five years before the colonies declared independence. So the six major Martian settlements were still under control of one Earth-based corporation or another, with Arsia Station jointly operated by Skycorp and Uchu-Hiko. We had about a hundred people living there by then, the majority short-timers on short-term contracts; only a dozen or so, like myself, were permanent residents who left Earth for good.

Jeff wasn't one of them. Like most people, he'd come to Mars to make a lot of money in a relatively short amount of time. Six months from Earth to Mars aboard a cycleship, two years on the planet, then six more months back to Earth aboard the next ship to make the crossing during the bi-annual launch window. In three years, a young buck like him could earn enough dough to buy a house, start a business, invest in the stock market, or maybe just loaf for a good long while. In previous times, they would've worked on offshore oil rigs, joined the merchant marine, or built powersats; by mid-century, this kind of high-risk, high-paying work was on Mars, and there was no shortage of guys willing and ready to do it.

Jeff Halbert was what we called a "Mars monkey." We had about a lot of people like him at Arsia Station, and they took care of the dirty jobs that the scientists, engineers, and other specialists could not or would not handle themselves. One day they might be operating a bulldozer or a crane at a habitat construction site.

The next day, they'd be unloading freight from a cargo lander that had just touched down. The day after that, they'd be cleaning out the air vents or repairing a solar array or unplugging a toilet. It wasn't romantic or particularly interesting work, but it was the sort of stuff that needed to be done in order to keep the base going, and because of that, kids like Jeff were invaluable.

And Jeff was definitely a kid. In his early twenties, wiry and almost too tall to wear a hardsuit, he looked like he'd started shaving only last week. Before he dropped out of school to get a job with Skycorp, I don't think he'd travelled more than a few hundred miles from the small town in New Hampshire where he'd grown up. I didn't know him well, but I knew his type: restless, looking for adventure, hoping to score a small pile of loot so that he could do something else with the rest of his life besides hang out in a pool hall. He probably hadn't even thought much about Mars before he spotted a Skycorp recruitment ad on some web site; he had two years of college, though, and met all the fitness requirements, and that was enough to get him into the training program and, eventually, a berth aboard a cycleship.

Before Jeff left Earth, he filled out and signed all the usual company paperwork. Among them was Form 36-B: Family Emergency Notification Consent. Skycorp required everyone to state whether or not they wanted to be informed of a major illness or death of a family member back home. This was something a lot of people didn't take into consideration before they went to Mars, but nonetheless it was an issue that had to be addressed. If you found out, for instance, that your father was about to die, there wasn't much you could do about it, because you'd be at least 35 million miles from home. The best you could do would be to send a brief message that someone might be able to read to him before he passed away; you wouldn't be able to attend the funeral, and it would be many months, even a year or two, before you could lay roses on his grave.

Most people signed Form 36-B on the grounds that they'd rather know about something like this than be kept in the dark until they returned home. Jeff did, too, but I'd later learn that he hadn't read it first. For him, it had been just one more piece of paper that needed to be signed before he boarded the shuttle, not to be taken any more seriously than the catastrophic accident disclaimer or the form attesting that he didn't have any sort of venereal disease.

He probably wished he hadn't signed that damn form. But he did, and it cost him his sanity.

Jeff had been on Mars for only about seven months when a message was relayed from Skycorp's human resources office in Huntsville. I knew about it because a copy was cc'd to me. The minute I read it, I dropped what I was doing to head straight for Hab 2's second level, which was where the monkey house—that is, the dormitory for unspecialized laborers like Jeff—was located. I didn't have to ask which bunk was his; the moment I walked in, I spotted a knot of people standing around a young guy slumped on this bunk, staring in disbelief at the fax in his hands.

Until then, I didn't know, nor did anyone one at Arsia Station, that Jeff had a fiancé back home, a nice girl named Karen whom he'd met in high school and who had agreed to marry him about the same time he'd sent his application to Skycorp. Once he got the job, they decided to postpone the wedding until he returned, even if it meant having to put their plans on hold for three years. One of the reasons why Jeff decided to get a job on Mars, in fact, was to provide a nest egg for him and Karen. And they'd need it, too; about three weeks before Jeff took off, Karen informed him that she was pregnant and that he'd have a child waiting for him when he got home.

He'd kept this a secret, mainly because he knew that the company would annul his contract if it learned that he had a baby on the way. Both Jeff's family and Karen's knew all about the baby, though, and they decided to pretend that Jeff was still on Earth, just away on a long business trip. Until he returned, they'd take care of Karen.

About three months before the baby was due, the two families decided to host a baby shower. The party was to be held at the home of one of Jeff's uncles—apparently he was only relative with a house big enough for such a get-together—and Karen was on her way there, in a car driven by Jeff's parents, when tragedy struck. Some habitual drunk who'd learned how to disable his car's high-alcohol lockout, and therefore was on the road when he shouldn't have been, plowed straight into them. The drunk walked away with no more than a sprained neck, but his victims were nowhere nearly so lucky. Karen, her unborn child, Jeff's mother and father—all died before they reached the hospital.

There's not a lot you can say to someone who's just lost his family that's going to mean very much. *I'm sorry* barely scratches the surface. *I understand what you're going through* is ridiculous; *I know how you feel* is insulting. And *is there anything I can do to help?* is pointless unless you have a time machine; if I did, I would have lent it to Jeff, so that he could travel back twenty-four hours to call his folks and beg them to put off picking up Karen by only fifteen or twenty minutes. But everyone said these things anyway, because there wasn't much else that *could* be said, and I relieved Jeff of further duties until he felt like he was ready to go to work again, because there was little else I could do for him. The next cycleship wasn't due to reach Mars for another seventeen months; by the time he got home, his parents and Karen would be dead for nearly two years.

To Jeff's credit, he was back on the job within a few days. Maybe he knew that there was nothing he could do except work, or maybe he just got tired of staring at the walls. In any case, one morning he put on his suit, cycled through the airlock, and went outside to help the rest of the monkeys dig a pit for the new septic tank. But he wasn't the same easygoing kid we'd known before; no wisecracks, no goofing off, not even any gripes about the hours it took to make that damn hole and how he'd better get overtime for this. He was like a robot out there, silently digging at the sandy red ground with a shovel, until the pit was finally finished, at which point he dropped his tools and, without a word, returned to the hab, where he climbed out of his suit and went to the mess hall for some chow.

A couple of weeks went by, and there was no change. Jeff said little to anyone. He ate, worked, slept, and that was about it. When you looked into his eyes, all you saw was a distant stare. If he'd broken down in hysterics, I would've understood, but there wasn't any of that. It was as if he'd shut down his emotions, suppressing whatever he was feeling inside.

The station had a pretty good hospital by then, large enough to serve all the colonies, and Arsia General's senior psychologist had begun meeting with Jeff on a regular basis. Three days after Jeff went back to work, Karl Rosenfeld dropped by my office. His report was grim; Jeff Halbert was suffering from severe depression, to the point that he was barely responding to medication. Although he hadn't spoken of suicide, Dr. Rosenfeld had little doubt that the notion had occurred to him. And I knew that, if Jeff did decide to kill himself, all he'd have to do was wait until the next time he went outside, then shut down his suit's air supply and crack open the helmet faceplate. One deep breath, and the Martian atmosphere would do the rest; he'd be dead before anyone could reach him.

"You want my advice?" Karl asked, sitting on the other side of my desk with a glass of moonshine in hand. "Find something that'll get his mind off what happened."

"You think that hasn't occurred to me? Believe me, I've tried . . ."

"Yeah, I know. He told me. But extra work shifts aren't helping, and neither are vids or games." He was quiet for a moment, "If I thought sex would help," he added, "I'd ask a girl I know to haul him off to bed, but that would just make matters worse. His fiancé was the only woman he ever loved, and it'll probably be a long time before he sleeps with anyone again."

"So what do you want me to do?" I gave a helpless shrug. "C'mon, give me a clue here. I want to help the kid, but I'm out of ideas."

"Well . . . I looked at the duty roster and saw that you've scheduled a survey mission for next week. Something up north, I believe."

"Uh-huh. I'm sending a team up there to see if they can locate a new water supply. Oh, and one of the engineers wants to make a side trip to look at an old NASA probe."

"So put Jeff on the mission." Karl smiled. "They're going to need a monkey or two anyway. Maybe travel will do him some good."

His suggestion was as good as any, so I pulled up the survey assignment list, deleted the name of one monkey, and inserted Jeff Halbert's instead. I figured it couldn't hurt, and I was right. And also wrong.

So Jeff was put on a two-week sortie that travelled above the 60th parallel to the Vastitas Borealis, the subarctic region that surrounds the Martian north pole. The purpose of the mission was to locate a site for a new well. Although most of Arsia Station's water came from atmospheric condensers and our greenhouses, we needed more than they could supply, which was why we drilled artesian wells in the permafrost beneath the northern tundra and pumped groundwater to surface tanks, which in turn would be picked up on a monthly basis. Every few years or so, one of those wells would run dry; when that happened, we'd have to send a team up there to dig a new one.

Two airships made the trip, the *Sagan* and the *Collins*. Jeff Halbert was aboard the *Collins*, and according to its captain, who was also the mission leader, he did his job well. Over the course of ten days, the two dirigibles roamed the tundra, stopping every ten or fifteen miles so that crews could get out and conduct test drills that would bring up a sample of what lay beneath the rocky red soil. It wasn't hard work, really, and it gave Jeff a chance to see the northern regions. Yet he was quiet most of the time, rarely saying much to anyone; in fact, he seemed to be bored by the whole thing. The other people on the expedition were aware of what had recently happened to him, of course, and they attempted to draw him out of his shell, but after awhile it became obvious that he just didn't want to talk, and so they finally gave up and left him alone.

Then, on the eleventh day of the mission, two days before the expedition was scheduled to return to Arsia, the *Collins* located the Phoenix lander.

This was a NASA probe that landed back in '08, the first to confirm the presence of subsurface ice on Mars. Unlike many of the other American and European probes that explored Mars before the first manned expeditions, Phoenix didn't have a rover; instead, it used a robotic arm to dig down into the regolith, scooping up samples that were analyzed by its onboard chemical lab. The probe was active for only a few months before its battery died during the long Martian winter, but it was one of the milestones leading to human colonization.

As they expected, the expedition members found Phoenix half-buried beneath windblown sand and dust, with only its upper platform and solar vanes still exposed. Nonetheless, the lander was intact, and although it was too big and heavy to be loaded aboard the airship, the crew removed its arm to be taken home and added to the base museum. And they found one more thing; the Mars library.

During the 1990s, while the various Mars missions were still in their planning stages, the Planetary Society had made a proposal to NASA: one of those probes should carry a DVD containing a cache of literature, visual images, and audio recordings pertaining to Mars. The ostensive purpose would be to furnish future colonists with a library for their entertainment, but the unspoken reason was to pay tribute to the generations of writers, artists, and filmmakers whose works had inspired the real-life exploration of Mars.

NASA went along with those proposal, so a custom-designed DVD, made of silica glass to ensure its long-term survival, was prepared for inclusion on a future mission. A panel selected eighty-four novels, short stories, articles, and speeches, with the authors ranging from eighteenth-century fantasists like Swift and Voltaire to twentieth-century science fiction authors like Niven and Benford. A digital gallery of sixty visual images—including everything from paintings by Bonestell, Emshwiller, and Whelan to a lobby card from a Flash Gordon serial and a cover of a *Weird Science* comic book—was chosen as well. The final touch were four audio clips, the most notable of which were the infamous 1938 radio broadcast of *The War of the Worlds* and a discussion of the same between H. G. Wells and Orson Welles.

Now called "Visions of Mars," the disk was originally placed aboard NASA's

Mars Polar Lander, but that probe was destroyed when its booster failed shortly after launch and it crashed in the Atlantic. So an identical copy was put on Phoenix, and this time it succeeded in getting to Mars. And so the disk had remained in the Vastitas Borealis for the past forty years, awaiting the day when a human hand would remove it from its place on Phoenix's upper fuselage.

And that hand happened to be Jeff Halbert's.

The funny thing is, no one on the expedition knew the disk was there. It had been forgotten by then, its existence buried deep within the old NASA documents I'd been sent from Earth, so I hadn't told anyone to retrieve it. And besides, most of the guys on the *Collins* were more interested in taking a look at an antique lander than the DVD that happened to be attached to it. So when Jeff found the disk and detached it from Phoenix, it wasn't like he'd made a major find. The attitude of almost everyone on the mission was *oh, yeah, that's kind of neat . . . take it home and see what's on it.*

Which was easier said than done. DVD drives had been obsolete for more than twenty years, and the nearest flea market where one might find an old computer that had one was . . . well, it wasn't on Mars. But Jeff looked around, and eventually he found a couple of dead comps stashed in a storage closet, salvage left over from the first expeditions. Neither were usable on their own, but with the aid of a service manual, he was able to swap out enough parts to get one of them up and running, and once it was operational, he removed the disk from its scratched case and gently slid it into the slot. Once he was sure that the data was intact and hadn't decayed, he downloaded everything into his personal pad. And then, at random, he selected one of the items on the menu—"The Martian Way" by Isaac Asimov—and began to read.

Why did Jeff go to so much trouble? Perhaps he wanted something to do with his free time besides mourn for the dead. Or maybe he wanted to show the others who'd been on the expedition that they shouldn't have ignored the disk. I don't know for sure, so I can't tell you. All I know is that the disk first interested him, then intrigued him, and finally obsessed him.

It took awhile for me to become aware of the change in Jeff. As much as I was concerned for him, he was one of my lesser problems. As general manager, on any given day I had a dozen or more different matters that needed my attention, whether it be making sure that the air recycling system was repaired before we suffocated to death or filling out another stack of forms sent from Huntsville. So Jeff wasn't always on my mind; when I didn't hear from Dr. Rosenfeld for awhile, I figured that the two of them had managed to work out his issues, and turned to other things.

Still, there were warning signs, stuff that I noticed but to which I didn't pay much attention. Like the day I was monitoring the radio cross talk from the monkeys laying sewage pipes in the foundation of Hab Three and happened to hear Jeff identify himself as Lieutenant Gulliver Jones. The monkeys sometimes screwed around like that on the com channels, and the foreman told Halbert to knock it off and use his proper call sign . . . but when Jeff answered him, his response was weird: *"Aye, sir. I was simply ruminating on the rather peculiar environment in which we've found ourselves."* He even faked a British accent to match the Victorian diction. That got a laugh from the other monkeys, but nonetheless I wondered who Gulliver Jones was and why Jeff was pretending to be him.

There was also the time Jeff was out on a dozer, clearing away the sand that had been deposited on the landing field during a dust storm a couple of days earlier. Another routine job to which I hadn't been paying much attention until the shift supervisor at the command center paged me: *"Chief, there's something going on with Halbert. You might want to listen in."*

So I tapped into the comlink, and there was Jeff: *"Affirmative, MainCom. I just saw something move out there, about a half-klick north of the periphery."*

"Roger that, Tiger Four-Oh," the supervisor said. *"Can you describe again, please?"*

A pause, then: *"A big creature, abut ten feet tall, with eight legs. And there was a woman riding it . . . red-skinned, and—"* an abrupt laugh *"—stark naked, or just about."*

Something tugged at my memory, but I couldn't quite put my finger on it. When the shift supervisor spoke again, his voice had a patronizing undertone. *"Yeah . . . uh, right, Tiger Four-Oh. We just checked the LRC, though, and there's nothing on the scope except you."*

"They're gone now. Went behind a boulder and vanished." Another laugh, almost gleeful. *"But they were out there, I promise!"*

"Affirmative, Four-Oh." A brief pause. *"If you happen to see any more thoats, let us know, okay?"*

That's when I remembered. What Jeff had described was a beast from Edgar Rice Burroughs' Mars novels. And the woman riding it? That could have only been Dejah Thoris. Almost everyone who came to Mars read Burroughs at one point or another, but this was the first time I'd ever heard of anyone claiming to have seen the Princess of Helium.

Obviously, Jeff had taken to playing practical jokes. I made a mental note to say something to him about that, but then forgot about it. As I said, on any given day I handled any number of different crises, and someone messing with his supervisor's head ranked low on my priority list.

But that wasn't the end of it. In fact, it was only the beginning. A couple of weeks later, I received a memo from the quartermaster: someone had tendered a request to be transferred to private quarters, even though that was above his pay-grade. At Arsia in those days, before we got all the habs built, individual rooms were at a premium and were generally reserved for management, senior researchers, married couples, company stooges, and so forth. In this case, though, the other guys in this particular person's dorm had signed a petition backing his request, and the quartermaster himself wrote that, for the sake of morale, he was recommending that this individual be assigned his own room.

I wasn't surprised to see that Jeff Halbert was the person making the request. By then, I'd noticed that his personality had undergone a distinct change. He'd let his hair grow long, eschewing the high-and-tight style preferred by people who spent a lot of time wearing a hardsuit helmet. He rarely shared a table with anyone else in the wardroom, and instead ate by himself, staring at his datapad the entire time. And he was now talking to himself on the comlink. No more reports of Martian princesses riding eight-legged animals, but rather a snatch of this ("The Martians seem to have calculated their descent with amazing subtlety . . .") or a bit of that ("The Martians gazed back up at them for a long, long silent time from the rippling water . . .") which most people wouldn't have recognized as being quotes from Wells or Bradbury.

So it was no wonder the other monkey house residents wanted to get rid of him. Before I signed the request, though, I paid Dr. Rosenfeld a visit. The station psychologist didn't have to ask why I was there; he asked me to shut the door, then let me know what he thought about Jeff.

"To tell the truth," he began, "I can't tell if he's getting better or worse."

"I can. Look, I'm no shrink, but if you ask me, he's getting worse."

Karl shook his head. "Not necessarily. Sure, his behavior is bizarre, but at least we no longer have to worry about suicide. In fact, he's one of the happiest people we have here. He rarely speaks about his loss anymore, and when I remind him that his wife and parents are dead, he shrugs it off as if this was something that happened a long time ago. In his own way, he's quite content with life."

"And you don't think that's strange?"

"Sure, I do . . . especially since he's admitted to me that he'd stopped taking the antidepressants I prescribed to him. And that's the bad news. Perhaps he isn't depressed anymore, or at least by clinical standards . . . but he's becoming delusional, to the point of actually having hallucinations."

I stared at him. "You mean, the time he claimed he spotted Dejah Thoris . . . you're saying he actually *saw* that?"

"Yes, I believe so. And that gave me a clue as to what's going on in his mind." Karl picked up a penknife, absently played with it. "Ever since he found that disk, he's become utterly obsessed with it. So I asked him if he'd let me copy it from his pad, which he did, and after I asked him what he was reading, I checked it out for myself. And what I discovered was that, of all the novels and stories that are on the disk, the ones that attract him the most are also the ones that are least representative of reality. That is, the stuff that's about Mars, but not as we know it."

"Come again?" I shook my head. "I don't understand."

"How much science fiction have you read?"

"A little. Not much."

"Well, lucky for you, I've read quite a bit." He grinned. "In fact, you could say that's why I'm here. I got hooked on that stuff when I was a kid, and by the time I got out of college, I'd pretty much decided that I wanted to see Mars." He became serious again. "Okay, try to follow me. Although people have been writing about Mars since the 1700s, it wasn't until the first Russian and American probes got out here in the 1960s that anyone knew what this place is really like. That absence of knowledge gave writers and artists the liberty to fill in the gap with their imaginations . . . or at least until they learned better. Understand?"

"Sure." I shrugged. "Before the 1960s, you could have Martians. After that, you couldn't have Martians anymore."

"Umm . . . well, not exactly." Karl lifted his hand, teetered it back and forth. "One of the best stories on the disk is 'A Rose for Ecclesiastes' by Roger Zelazny. It was written in 1963, and it has Martians in it. And some stories written before then were pretty close to getting it right. But for the most part, yes . . . the fictional view of Mars changed dramatically in the second half of the last century, and although it became more realistic, it also lost much of its romanticism."

Karl folded the penknife, dropped it on his desk. "Those aren't the stories Jeff's reading. Greg Bear's 'A Martian Ricorso,' Arthur C. Clarke's 'Transit of Earth,' John Varley's 'In the Hall of the Martian Kings' . . . anything similar to the Mars we know, he ignores. Why? Because they remind him of where he is . . . and that's not where he wants to be."

"So . . ." I thought about it for a moment. "He's reading the older stuff instead?"

"Right." Karl nodded. "Stanley Weinbaum's 'A Martian Odyssey,' Otis Albert Kline's 'The Swordsman of Mars,' A. E. van Vogt's 'The Enchanted Village' . . . the more unreal, the more he likes them. Because those stories aren't about the drab, lifeless planet where he's stuck, but instead a planet of native Martians, lost cities, canal systems . . ."

"Okay, I get it."

"No, I don't think you do . . . because I'm not sure I do, either, except to say that Jeff appears to be leaving us. Every day, he's taking one more step into this other world . . . and I don't think he's coming back again."

I stared at him, not quite believing what I'd just heard. "Jeez, Karl . . . what am I going to do?"

"What *can* you do?" He leaned back in his chair. "Not much, really. Look, I'll be straight with you . . . this is beyond me. He needs the kind of treatment that I can't give him here. For that, he's going to have to wait until he gets back to Earth."

"The next ship isn't due for another fourteen months or so."

"I know . . . that's when I'm scheduled to go back, too. But the good news is that he's happy and reasonably content, and doesn't really pose a threat to anyone . . . except maybe by accident, in which case I'd recommend that you relieve him of any duties that would take him outside the hab."

"Done." The last thing anyone needed was to have a delusional person out on the surface. Mars can be pretty unforgiving when it comes to human error, and a fatal mistake can cost you not only your own life, but also the guy next to you. "And I take it that you recommend that his request be granted, too?"

"It wouldn't hurt, no." A wry smile. "So long as he's off in his own world, he'll be happy. Make him comfortable, give him whatever he wants . . . within reason, at least . . . and leave him alone. I'll keep an eye on him and will let you know if his condition changes, for better or worse."

"Hopefully for the better."

"Sure . . . but I wouldn't count on it." Karl stared straight at me. "Face it, chief . . . one of your guys is turning into a Martian."

I took Jeff off the outside-work details and let it be known that he wasn't permitted to go marswalking without authorization or an escort, and instead reassigned him to jobs that would keep him in the habitats: working in the greenhouse, finishing the interior of Hab 2, that sort of thing. I was prepared to tell him that he was being taken off the outside details because he'd reached his rem limit for radiation exposure, but he never questioned my decision but only accepted it with the same quiet, spooky smile that he'd come to giving everyone.

I also let him relocate to private quarters, a small room on Hab 2's second level that had been unoccupied until then. As I expected, there were a few gripes from those still having to share a room with someone else; however, most people realized that Jeff was in bad shape and needed his privacy. After he moved in, though, he did something I didn't anticipate: he changed his door lock's password to something no one else knew. This was against station rules—the security office and the general manager were supposed to always have everyone's lock codes—but Karl assured me that Jeff meant no harm. He simply didn't want to have anyone enter his quarters, and it would help his peace of mind if he received this one small exemption. I went along with it, albeit reluctantly.

After that, I had no problems with Jeff for awhile. He assumed his new duties without complaint, and the reports I received from department heads told me that he was doing his work well. Karl updated me every week; his patient hadn't yet shown any indications of snapping out of his fugue, but neither did he appear to be getting worse. And although he was no longer interacting with any other personnel except when he needed to, at least he was no longer telling anyone about Martian princesses or randomly quoting obscure science fiction stories over the comlink.

Nonetheless, there was the occasional incident. Such as when the supply chief came to me with an unusual request Jeff had made: several reams of hemp paper, and as much soy ink as could be spared. Since both were by-products of greenhouse crops grown at either Arsia Station or one of the other colonies, and thus not imported from Earth, they weren't particularly scarce. Still, what could Jeff possibly want with that much writing material? I asked Karl if Jeff had told him that he was keeping a journal; the doctor told me that he hadn't, but unless either paper or ink were in short supply, it couldn't hurt to grant that request. So I signed off on this as well, although I told the supply chief to subtract the cost from Jeff's salary.

Not long after that, I heard from one of the communications officers. Jeff had asked her to send a general memo to the other colonies: a request for downloads of any Mars novels or stories that their personnel might have. The works of Bradbury, Burroughs, and Brackett were particularly desired, although stuff by Moorcock, Williamson, and Sturgeon would also be appreciated. In exchange, Jeff would send stories and novels he'd downloaded from the Phoenix disk.

Nothing wrong there, either. By then, Mars was on the opposite side of the

Sun from Earth, so Jeff couldn't make the same request from Huntsville. If he was running out of reading material, then it made sense that he'd have to go begging from the other colonies. In fact, the com officer told me she'd had already received more than a half-dozen downloads; apparently quite a few folks had Mars fiction stashed in the comps. Nonetheless, it was unusual enough that she thought I should know about it. I asked her to keep me posted and shrugged it off as just another of a long series of eccentricities.

A few weeks after that, though, Jeff finally did something that rubbed me the wrong way. As usual, I heard about it from Dr. Rosenfeld.

"Jeff has a new request," he said when I happened to drop by his office. "In the future, he would prefer to be addressed as 'Your Majesty' or 'Your Highness,' in keeping with his position as the Emperor of Mars."

I stared at him for several seconds. "Surely you're joking," I said at last.

"Surely I'm not. He is now the Emperor Jeffery the First, sovereign monarch of the Great Martian Empire, warlord and protector of the red planet." A pause, during which I expected Karl to grin and wink. He didn't. "He doesn't necessarily want anyone bow in his presence," he added, "but he does require proper respect for the crown."

"I see." I closed my eyes, rubbed the bridge of my nose between my thumb and forefinger, and counted to ten. "And what does that make me?"

"Prime Minister, of course." The driest of smiles. "Since his title is hereditary, His Majesty isn't interested in the day-to-day affairs of his empire. That he leaves up to you, with the promise that he'll refrain from meddling with your decisions . . ."

"Oh, how fortunate I am."

"Yes. But from here on, all matters pertaining to the throne should be taken up with me, in my position as Royal Physician and Senior Court Advisor."

"Uh-huh." I stood up from my chair. "Well, if you'll excuse me, I think the Prime Minister needs to go now and kick His Majesty's ass."

"Sit down." Karl glared at me. "Really, I mean it. Sit."

I was unwilling to sit down again, but neither did I storm out of his office. "Look, I know he's a sick man, but this has gone far enough. I've given him his own room, relieved him of hard labor, given him paper and ink . . . for what, I still don't know, but he keeps asking for more . . . and allowed him com access to the other colonies. Just because he's been treated like a king doesn't mean he *is* a king."

"Oh, I agree. Which is why I've reminded him that his title is honorary as well as hereditary, and as such there's a limit to royal privilege. And he understands this. After all, the empire is in decline, having reached its peak over a thousand years ago, and since then the emperor has had to accept certain sacrifices for the good of the people. So, no, you won't see him wearing a crown and carrying a scepter, nor will he be demanding that a throne be built for him. He wants his reign to be benign."

Hearing this, I reluctantly took my seat again. "All right, so let me get this straight. He believes that he's now a king . . ."

"An emperor. There's a difference."

"King, emperor, whatever . . . he's not going to be bossing anyone around but will pretty much let things continue as they are. Right?"

"Except that he wants to be addressed formally, yeah, that's pretty much it." Karl sighed, shook his head. "Let me try to explain. Jeff has come face-to-face with a reality that he cannot bear. His parents, his fiancé, the child they wanted to have . . . they're all dead, and he was too far away to prevent it, or even go to their funerals. This is a very harsh reality that he needs to keep at bay, so he's built a wall around himself . . . a wall of delusion, if you will. At first, it took the form of an obsession with fantasy, but when that alone wouldn't suffice, he decided to enter that fantasy, become part of it. This is where Emperor Jeffery the First of the Great Martian Empire comes in."

"So he's protecting himself?"

"Yes . . . by creating a role that lets him believe that he controls his own life." Karl shook his head. "He doesn't want to actually run Arsia, chief. He just wants to pretend that he does. As long as you allow him this, he'll be all right. Trust me."

"Well . . . all right." Not that I had much choice in the matter. If I was going to have a crazy person in my colony, at least I could make sure that he wouldn't endanger anyone. If that meant indulging him until he could be sent back to Earth, then that was what I'd have to do. "I'll pass the word that His Majesty is to be treated with all due respect."

"That would be great. Thanks." Karl smiled. "Y'know, people have been pretty supportive. I haven't heard of anyone taunting him."

"You know how it is. People here tend to look out for each other . . . they have to." I stood up and started to head for the door, then another thought occurred to me. "Just one thing. Has he ever told you what he's doing in his room? Like I said, he's been using a lot of paper and ink."

"Yes, I've noticed the ink stains on his fingers." Karl shook his head. "No, I don't. I've asked him about that, and the only thing he's told me is that he's preparing a gift for his people, and that he'll allow us to see it when the time comes."

"A gift?" I raised an eyebrow. "Any idea what it is?"

"Not a clue . . . but I'm sure we'll find out."

I kept my promise to Dr. Rosenfeld and put out the word that Jeff Halbert was heretofore to be known as His Majesty, the Emperor. As I told Karl, people were generally accepting of this. Oh, I heard the occasional report of someone giving Jeff some crap about this—exaggerated bows in the corridors, ill-considered questions about who was going to be his queen, and so forth—but the jokers who did this were usually pulled aside and told to shut up. Everyone at Arsia knew that Jeff was mentally ill, and that the best anyone could do for him was to let him have his fantasy life for as long as he was with us.

By then, Earth was no longer on the other side of the Sun. Once our home world and Mars began moving toward conjunction, a cycleship could make the trip home. So only a few months remained until Jeff would board a shuttle.

Since Karl would be returning as well, I figured he'd be in good hands, or at least they climbed into zombie tanks to hibernate for the long ride to Earth. Until then, all we had to do was keep His Majesty happy.

That wasn't hard to do. In fact, Karl and I had a lot of help. Once people got used to the idea that a make-believe emperor lived among them, most of them actually seemed to enjoy the pretense. When he walked through the habs, folks would pause whatever they were doing to nod to him and say "Your Majesty" or "Your Highness." He was always allowed to go to the front of the serving line in the mess hall, and there was always someone ready to hold his chair for him. And I noticed that he even picked up a couple of consorts, two unattached young women who did everything from trim his hair—it had grown very long by then, with a regal beard to match—to assist him in the Royal Gardens (aka the greenhouse) to accompany him to the Saturday night flicks. As one of the girls told me, the Emperor was the perfect date: always the gentleman, he'd unfailingly treated them with respect and never tried to take advantage of them. Which was more than could be said for some of the single men at Arsia.

After awhile, I relaxed the rule about not letting him leave the habs and allowed him to go outside as long as he was under escort at all times. Jeff remembered how to put on a hardsuit—a sign that he hadn't completely lost touch with reality—and he never gave any indication that he was on the verge of opening his helmet. But once he walked a few dozen yards from the airlock, he'd often stop and stare into the distance for a very long time, keeping his back to the rest of the base and saying nothing to anyone.

I wondered what he was seeing then. Was it a dry red desert, cold and lifeless, with rocks and boulders strewn across an arid plain beneath a pink sky? Or did he see something no one else could: forests of giant lichen, ancient canals upon which sailing vessels slowly glided, cities as old as time from which John Carter and Tars Tarkas rode to their next adventure or where evil tyrants called for the head of the outlaw Eric John Stark. Or was he thinking of something else entirely? A mother and a father who'd raised him, a woman he'd once loved, a child whom he'd never see?

I don't know, for the Emperor seldom spoke to me, even in my role as his Prime Minister. I think I was someone he wanted to avoid, an authority figure who had the power to shatter his illusions. Indeed, in all the time that Jeff was with us, I don't think he and I said more than a few words to each other. In fact, it wasn't until the day that he finally left for Earth that he said anything of consequence to me.

That morning, I drove him and Dr. Rosenfeld out to the landing field, where a shuttle was waiting to transport them up to the cycleship. Jeff was unusually quiet; I couldn't easily see his expression through his helmet faceplate, but the few glimpses I had told me that he wasn't happy. His Majesty knew that he was leaving his empire. Karl hadn't softened the blow by telling him a convenient lie, but instead had given him the truth: they were returning to Earth, and he'd probably never see Mars again.

Their belongings had already been loaded aboard the shuttle when we arrived, and the handful of other passengers were waiting to climb aboard. I parked the rover at the edge of the landing field and escorted Jeff and Karl to the spacecraft. I shook hands with Karl and wished him well, then turned to Jeff.

"Your Majesty . . ." I began.

"You don't have to call me that," he said.

"Pardon me?"

Jeff stepped closer to me. "I know I'm not really an emperor. That was something I got over a while ago . . . I just didn't want to tell anyone."

I glanced at Karl. His eyes were wide, and within his helmet he shook his head. This was news to him, too. "Then . . . you know who you really are?"

A brief flicker of a smile. "I'm Jeff Halbert. There's something wrong with me, and I don't really know what it is . . . but I know that I'm Jeff Halbert and that I'm going home." He hesitated, then went on. "I know we haven't talked much, but I . . . well, Dr. Rosenfeld has told me what you've done for me, and I just wanted to thank you. For putting up with me all this time, and for letting me be the Emperor of Mars. I hope I haven't been too much trouble."

I slowly let out my breath. My first thought was that he'd been playing me and everyone else for fools, but then I realized that his megalomania had probably been real, at least for a time. In any case, it didn't matter now; he was on his way back to Earth, the first steps on the long road to recovery.

Indeed, many months later, I received a letter from Karl. Shortly after he returned to Earth, Jeff was admitted to a private clinic in southern Vermont, where he began a program of psychiatric treatment. The process had been painful; as Karl had deduced, Jeff's mind had repressed the knowledge of his family's deaths, papering over the memory with fantastical delusions he'd derived from the stories he'd been reading. The clinic: it was probably the retreat into fantasy that saved Jeff's life, by providing him with a place to which he was able to escape when his mind was no longer able to cope with a tragic reality. And in the end, when he no longer needed that illusion, Jeff returned from madness. He'd never see a Martian princess again, or believe himself to be the ruling monarch of the red planet.

But that was yet to come. I bit my tongue and offered him my hand. "No trouble, Jeff. I just hope everything works out for you."

"Thanks." Jeff shook my hand, then turned away to follow Karl to the ladder. Then he stopped and looked back at me again. "One more thing . . ."

"Yes?"

"There's something in my room I think you'd like to see. I disabled the lock just before I left, so you won't need the password to get in there." A brief pause. "It was 'Thuvia,' just in case you need it anyway."

"Thank you." I peered at him. "So . . . what is it?"

"Call it a gift from the emperor," he said.

I walked back to the rover and waited until the shuttle lifted off, then I drove to Hab 2. When I reached Jeff's room, though, I discovered that I wasn't the first person to arrive. Several of his friends—his fellow monkeys, the emperor's consorts, a couple of others—had already opened the door and gone in. I heard their astonished murmurs as I walked down the hall, but it wasn't until I entered the room that I saw what amazed them.

Jeff's quarters were small, but he'd done a lot with it over the last year and a half. The wall above his bed was covered with sheets of paper that he'd taped together, upon which he'd drawn an elaborate mural. Here was the Mars over which the Emperor had reigned: boatlike aircraft hovering above great domed cities, monstrous creatures prowling red wastelands, bare-chested heroes defending beautiful women with rapiers and radium pistols, all beneath twin moons that looked nothing like the Phobos and Deimos we knew. The mural was crude, yet it had been rendered with painstaking care, and was nothing like anything we'd ever seen before.

That wasn't all. On the desk next to the comp was the original Phoenix disk, yet Jeff hadn't been satisfied just to leave it behind. A wire-frame bookcase had been built beside the desk, and neatly stacked upon its shelves were dozens of sheaves of paper, some thick and some thin, each carefully bound with hemp twine. Books, handwritten and handmade.

I carefully pulled down one at random, gazed at its title page: EDISON'S CONQUEST OF MARS by Garrett P. Serviss. I put it back on the shelf, picked up another: OMNILINGUAL by H. Beam Piper. I placed it on the shelf, then pulled down yet another: THE MARTIAN CROWN JEWELS, by Poul Anderson. And more, dozens more . . .

This was what Jeff had been doing all this time: transcribing the contents of the Phoenix disk, word by word. Because he knew, in spite of his madness, that he couldn't stay on Mars forever, and he wanted to leave something behind. A library, so that others could enjoy the same stories that had helped him through a dark and troubled time.

The library is still here. In fact, we've improved it quite a bit. I had the bed and dresser removed and replaced them with armchairs and reading lamps. The mural has been preserved within glass frames, and the books have been rebound inside plastic covers. The Phoenix disk is gone, but its contents have been downloaded into a couple of comps; the disk itself is in the base museum. And we've added a lot of books to the shelves; every time a cycleship arrives from Earth, it brings a few more volumes for our collection. It's become one of the favorite places in Arsia for people to relax. There's almost always someone there, sitting in a chair with a novel or story in his or her lap.

The sign on the door reads Imperial Martian Library: an inside joke that newcomers and tourists don't get. And, yeah, I've spent a lot of time there myself. It's never too late to catch up on the classics.

flower, mercy, needle, chain

YOON HA LEE

Yoon Ha Lee's work has appeard in the Magazine of Fantasy & Science Fiction, Clarkesworld, Fantasy Magazine, Lightspeed, Beneath Ceaseless Skies, *and elsewhere. Lee's novels include* Ninefox Gambit, Revenant Gun, *and* Raven Stratagem, *and Lee's short stories have been collected in* Conservation of Shadows.

Here's an icy and elegant story about an ancient weapon so potent that to fire it is to destroy the universe—and replace it with another one.

The usual fallacy is that, in every universe, many futures splay outward from any given moment. But in some universes, determinism runs backwards: given a universe's state s at some time t, there are multiple previous states that may have resulted in s. In some universes, all possible pasts funnel toward a single fixed ending, Ω.

If you are of millenarian bent, you might call Ω Armageddon. If you are of grammatical bent, you might call it punctuation on a cosmological scale.

If you are a philosopher in such a universe, you might call Ω *inevitable.*

The woman has haunted Blackwheel Station for as long as anyone remembers, although she was not born there. She is human, and her straight black hair and brown-black eyes suggest an ancestral inheritance tangled up with tigers and shapeshifting foxes. Her native language is not spoken by anyone here or elsewhere.

They say her true name means things like *gray* and *ash* and *grave.* You may buy her a drink, bring her candied petals or chaotic metals, but it's all the same. She won't speak her name.

That doesn't stop people from seeking her out. Today, it's a man with mirror-colored eyes. He is the first human she has seen in a long time.

"Arighan's Flower," he says.

It isn't her name, but she looks up. Arighan's Flower is the gun she carries. The stranger has taken on a human face to talk to her, and he is almost certainly interested in the gun.

The gun takes different shapes, but at this end of time, origami multiplicity of form surprises more by its absence than its presence. Sometimes the gun is long and sleek, sometimes heavy and blunt. In all cases, it bears its maker's mark on the stock: a blossom with three petals falling away and a fourth about to follow. At the blossom's heart is a character that itself resembles a flower with knotted roots.

The character's meaning is the gun's secret. The woman will not tell it to you, and the gunsmith Arighan is generations gone.

"Everyone knows what I guard," the woman says to the mirror-eyed man.

"I know what it does," he says. "And I know that you come from people that worship their ancestors."

Her hand—on a glass of water two degrees from freezing—stops, slides to her side, where the holster is. "That's dangerous knowledge," she says. So he's figured it out. Her people's historians called Arighan's Flower the *ancestral gun*. They weren't referring to its age.

The man smiles politely and doesn't take a seat uninvited. Small courtesies matter to him because he is not human. His mind may be housed in a superficial fortress of flesh, but the busy computations that define him are inscribed in a vast otherspace.

The man says, "I can hardly be the first constructed sentience to come to you."

She shakes her head. "It's not that." Do computers like him have souls? she wonders. She is certain he does, which is potentially inconvenient. "I'm not for hire."

"It's important," he says.

It always is. They want chancellors dead or generals, discarded lovers or rival reincarnates, bodhisattvas or bosses—all the old, tawdry stories. People, in all the broad and narrow senses of the term. The reputation of Arighan's Flower is quite specific, if mostly wrong.

"Is it," she says. Ordinarily she doesn't talk to her petitioners at all. Ordinarily she ignores them through one glass, two, three, four, like a child learning the hard way that you can't outcount infinity.

There was a time when more of them tried to force the gun away from her. The woman was a duelist and a killer before she tangled her life up with the Flower, though, and the Flower comes with its own defenses, including the woman's inability to die while she wields it. One of the things she likes about Blackwheel is that the administrators promised that they would dispose of any corpses she produced. Blackwheel is notorious for keeping promises.

The man waits a little longer, then says, "Will you hear me out?"

"You should be more afraid of me," she says, "if you really know what you claim to know."

By now, the other people in the bar, none of them human, are paying attention: a musician whose instrument is made of fossilized wood and silk strings, a magister with a sea-wrack mane, engineers with their sketches hanging in the air and a single doodled starship at the boundary. The sole exception is the tattooed traveler dozing in the corner, dreaming of distant moons.

In no hurry, the woman draws the Flower and points it at the man. She is aiming it not at his absent heart, but at his left eye. If she pulled the trigger, she would pierce him through the false pupil.

The musician continues plucking plangent notes from the instrument. The others, seeing the gun, gawk for only a moment before hastening out of the bar. As if that would save them.

"Yes," the man says, outwardly shaken, "you could damage my lineage badly. I could name programmers all the way back to the first people who scratched a tally of birds or rocks."

The gun's muzzle moves precisely, horizontally: now the right eye. The woman says, "You've convinced me that you know. You haven't convinced me not to kill you." It's half a bluff: she wouldn't use the Flower, not for this. But she knows many ways to kill.

"There's another one," he said. "I don't want to speak of it here, but will you hear me out?"

She nods once, curtly.

Covered by her palm, engraved silver-bright in a language nobody else reads or writes, is the word *ancestor*.

Once upon a universe, an empress's favored duelist received a pistol from the empress's own hand. The pistol had a stock of silver-gilt and niello, an efflorescence of vines framing the maker's mark. The gun had survived four dynasties, with all their rebellions and coups. It had accompanied the imperial arsenal from homeworld to homeworld.

Of the ancestral pistol, the empire's archives said two things: *Do not use this weapon, for it is nothing but peril* and *This weapon does not function.*

In a reasonable universe, both statements would not be true.

The man follows the woman to her suite, which is on one of Blackwheel's tidier levels. The sitting room, comfortable but not luxurious by Blackwheeler standards, accommodates a couch sized to human proportions, a metal table shined to blurry reflectivity, a vase in the corner.

There are also two paintings, on silk rather than some less ancient substrate. One is of a mountain by night, serenely anonymous amid its stylized clouds. The other, in a completely different style, consists of a cavalcade of shadows. Only after several moments' study do the shadows assemble themselves into a face. Neither painting is signed.

"Sit," the woman says.

The man does. "Do you require a name?" he asks.

"Yours, or the target's?"

"I have a name for occasions like this," he says. "It is Zheu Kerang."

"You haven't asked me my name," she remarks.

"I'm not sure that's a meaningful question," Kerang says. "If I'm not mistaken, you don't exist."

Wearily, she says, "I exist in all the ways that matter. I have volume and mass and volition. I drink water that tastes the same every day, as water should. I kill when it moves me to do so. I've unwritten death into the history of the universe."

His mouth tilts up at *unwritten*. "Nevertheless," he says. "Your species never evolved. You speak a language that is not even dead. It never existed."

"Many languages are extinct."

"To become extinct, something has to exist first."

The woman folds herself into the couch next to him, not close but not far. "It's an old story," she says. "What is yours?"

"Four of Arighan's guns are still in existence," Kerang says.

The woman's eyes narrow. "I had thought it was three." Arighan's Flower is the last, the gunsmith's final work. The others she knows of are Arighan's Mercy, which always kills the person shot, and Arighan's Needle, which removes the target's memories of the wielder.

"One more has surfaced," Kerang says. "The character in the maker's mark resembles a sword in chains. They are already calling it Arighan's Chain."

"What does it do?" she says, because he will tell her anyway.

"This one kills the commander of whoever is shot," Kerang says, "if that's anyone at all. Admirals, ministers, monks. Schoolteachers. It's a peculiar sort of loyalty test."

Now she knows. "You want me to destroy the Chain."

Once upon a universe, a duelist named Shiron took up the gun that an empress with empiricist tendencies had given her. "I don't understand how a gun that doesn't work could possibly be perilous," the empress said. She nodded at a sweating man bound in monofilament so that he would dismember himself if he tried to flee. "This man will be executed anyway, his name struck from the roster of honored ancestors. See if the gun works on him."

Shiron fired the gun . . . and woke in a city she didn't recognize, whose inhabitants spoke a dialect she had never heard before, whose technology she mostly recognized from historical dramas. The calendar they used, at least, was familiar. It told her that she was 857 years too early. No amount of research changed the figure.

Later, Shiron deduced that the man she had executed traced his ancestry back 857 years, to a particular individual. Most likely that ancestor had performed some extraordinary deed to join the aristocracy, and had, by the reckoning of Shiron's people, founded his own line.

Unfortunately, Shiron didn't figure this out before she accidentally deleted the human species.

"Yes," Kerang says. "I have been charged with preventing further assassinations. Arighan's Chain is not a threat I can afford to ignore."

"Why didn't you come earlier, then?" Shiron says. "After all, the Chain might have lain dormant, but the others—"

"I've seen the Mercy and the Needle," he says, by which he means he's copied data from those who have. "They're beautiful." He isn't referring to beauty in the way of shadows fitting together into a woman's profile, or beauty in the way of sun-colored liquor at the right temperature in a faceted glass. He means the beauty of logical strata, of the crescendo of axiom-axiom-corollary-*proof*, of *quod erat demonstrandum.*

"Any gun or shard of glass could do the same as the Mercy," Shiron says, understanding him. "And drugs and dreamscalpels will do the Needle's work, given time and expertise. But surely you could say the same of the Chain."

She stands again and takes the painting of the mountain down and rolls it tightly. "I was born on that mountain," she says. "Something like it is still there, on a birthworld very like the one I knew. But I don't think anyone paints in this style. Perhaps some art historian would recognize its distant cousin. I am no artist, but I painted it myself, because no one else remembers the things I remember. And now you would have it start again."

"How many bullets have you used?" Kerang asks.

It is not that the Flower requires special bullets—it adapts even to emptiness—it is that the number matters.

Shiron laughs, low, almost husky. She knows better than to trust Kerang, but she needs him to trust her. She pulls out the Flower and rests it in both palms so he can look at it.

Three petals fallen, a fourth about to follow. That's not the number, but he doesn't realize it. "You've guarded it so long," he says, inspecting the maker's mark without touching the gun.

"I will guard it until I am nothing but ice," Shiron says. "You may think that the Chain is a threat, but if I remove it, there's no guarantee that you will still exist—"

"It's not the Chain I want destroyed," Kerang says gently. "It's Arighan. Do you think I would have come to you for anything less?"

Shiron says into the awkward quiet, after a while, "So you tracked down descendants of Arighan's line." His silence is assent. "There must be many."

Arighan's Flower destroys the target's entire ancestral line, altering the past but leaving its wielder untouched. In the empire Shiron once served, the histories spoke of Arighan as an honored guest. Shiron discovered long ago that Arighan was no guest, but a prisoner forced to forge weapons for her captors. How Arighan was able to create weapons of such novel destructiveness, no one knows. The Flower was Arighan's clever revenge against a people whose state religion involved ancestor worship.

If descendants of Arighan's line exist here, then Arighan herself can be undone, and all her guns unmade. Shiron will no longer have to be an exile in this timeline, although it is true that she cannot return to the one that birthed her, either.

Shiron snaps the painting taut. The mountain disintegrates, but she lost it lifetimes ago. Silent lightning crackles through the air, unknots Zheu Kerang from his human-shaped shell, tessellates dead-end patterns across the equations that make him who he is. The painting had other uses, as do the other things in this room—she believes in versatility—but this is good enough.

Kerang's body slumps on the couch. Shiron leaves it there.

For the first time in a long time, she is leaving Blackwheel Station. What she does not carry she can buy on the way. And Blackwheel is loyal because they know, and they know not to offend her; Blackwheel will keep her suite clean and undisturbed, and deliver water, near-freezing in an elegant glass, night after night, waiting.

Kerang was a pawn by his own admission. If he knew what he knew, and lived long enough to convey it to her, then others must know what he knew, or be able to find it out.

Kerang did not understand her at all. Shiron unmazes herself from the station to seek passage to one of the hubworlds, where she can begin her search. If Shiron had wanted to seek revenge on Arighan, she could have taken it years ago.

But she will not be like Arighan. She will not destroy an entire timeline of people, no matter how alien they are to her.

Shiron had hoped that matters wouldn't come to this. She acknowledges her own naïveté. There is no help for it now. She will have to find and murder each child of Arighan's line. In this way she can protect Arighan herself, protect the accumulated sum of history, in case someone outwits her after all this time and manages to take the Flower from her.

In a universe where determinism runs backwards—where, no matter what you do, everything ends in the same inevitable Ω—choices still matter, especially if you are the last guardian of an incomparably lethal gun.

Although it has occurred to Shiron that she could have accepted Kerang's offer, and that she could have sacrificed this timeline in exchange for the one in which neither Arighan nor the guns ever existed, she declines to do so. For there will come a heat-death, and she is beginning to wonder: if a constructed sentience—a computer—can have a soul, what of the universe itself, the greatest computer of all?

In this universe, they reckon her old. Shiron is older than even that. In millions of timelines, she has lived to the pallid end of life. In each of those endings, Arighan's Flower is there, as integral as an edge is to a blade. While it is true that science never proves anything absolutely, that an inconceivably large but finite number of experiments always pales besides infinity, Shiron feels that millions of timelines suffice as proof.

Without Arighan's Flower, the universe cannot renew itself and start a new story. Perhaps that is all the reason the universe needs. And Shiron will be there when the heat-death arrives, as many times as necessary.

So Shiron sets off. It is not the first time she has killed, and it is unlikely to be the last. But she is not, after all this time, incapable of grieving.

Martian Heart

John Barnes

John Barnes lives in the northern suburbs of Denver, Colorado. He has recently finished his first new novel in five years and is writing regularly again. Among his better-known books from his previous writing career are Directive 51, Tales of the Madman Underground, The Sky So Big and Black, Mother of Storms, A Million Open Doors, Orbital Resonance, *and* One for the Morning Glory. *He is the coauthor with Buzz Aldrin of* Encounter with Tiber *and* The Return. *His current day job is in data science; in the past he has gotten paid for marketing research analysis, theater design, college teaching, sales, editing, and writing a wide variety of nonfiction, including fifty-four articles in the* Oxford Encyclopedia of Theater and Performance. *His advice to young writers is to avoid taking advice from older writers.*

Here he weaves an affecting story of a love that's both young—and doomed.

Okay, botterogator, I agreed to this. Now you're supposed to guide me to tell my story to *inspire a new generation of Martians.* It is so weird that there *is* a new generation of Martians. So hit me with the questions, or whatever it is you do.

Do I want to be *consistent with previous public statements?*

Well, every time they ask me where I got all the money and got to be such a big turd in the toilet that is Mars, I always say Samantha was my inspiration. So let's check that box for tentatively consistent.

Thinking about Sam always gives me weird thoughts. And here are two: one, before her, I would not have known what either *tentatively* or *consistent* even meant. Two, in these pictures, Samantha looks younger than my granddaughter is now.

So weird. She *was.*

We were in bed in our place under an old underpass in LA when the sweeps busted in, grabbed us up, and dragged us to the processing station. No good lying about whether we had family—they had our retinas and knew we were strays.

Since I was seventeen and Sam was fifteen, they couldn't make any of our family pay for re-edj.

So they gave us fifteen minutes on the bench there to decide between twenty years in the forces, ten years in the glowies, or going out to Mars on this opposition and coming back on the third one after, in six and a half years.

They didn't tell you, and it wasn't well-known, that even people without the genetic defect suffered too much cardiac atrophy in that time to safely come back to Earth. The people that went to Mars didn't have family or friends to write back to, and the settlement program was so new it didn't seem strange that nobody knew a returned Martian.

"Crap," I said.

"Well, at least it's a future." Sam worried about the future a lot more than me. "If we enlist, there's no guarantee we'll be assigned together, unless we're married, and they don't let you get married till you've been in for three. We'd have to write each other letters—"

"Sam," I said, "I can't write to you or read your letters if you send me any. You know that."

"They'd make you learn."

I tried not to shudder visibly; she'd get mad if I let her see that I didn't really want to learn. "Also, that thing you always say about out of sight, that'd happen. I'd have another girlfriend in like, not long. I just would. I know we're all true love and everything but I would."

"The spirit is willing but the flesh is *more* willing." She always made those little jokes that only she got. "Okay, then, no forces for us."

"Screw glowies," I said. Back in those days right after the baby nukes had landed all over the place, the Decon Admin needed people to operate shovels, hoes, and detectors. I quoted this one hook from our favorite music. "*Sterile or dead or kids with three heads.*"

"And we *can* get married going to Mars," Sam said, "and then they *can't* separate us. True love forever, baby." Sam always had all the ideas.

So, botterogator, check that box for *putting a priority on family/love*. I guess since that new box popped up as soon as I said, *Sam always had all the ideas*, that means you want more about that? Yeah, now it's bright and bouncing. Okay, more about how she had all the ideas.

Really all the ideas I ever had were about eating, getting high, and scoring ass. Hunh. Red light. Guess that wasn't what you wanted for the new generation of Martians.

Sam was different. Everybody I knew was thinking about the next party or at most the next week or the next boy or girl, but Sam thought about *everything*. I know it's a stupid example, but once back in LA, she came into our squat and found me fucking with the fusion box, just to mess with it. "That supplies all our power for music, light, heat, net, and everything, and you can't fix it if you break it, and it's not broke, so, Cap, what the fuck are you doing?"

See, I didn't even have ideas *that* good.

So a year later, there on the bench, our getting married was her having another idea and me going along with it, which was always how things worked, when they worked. Ten minutes later we registered as married.

Orientation for Mars was ten days. The first day they gave us shots, bleached our tats into white blotches on our skin, and shaved our heads. They stuck us in ugly dumb coveralls and didn't let us have real clothes that said anything, which they said was so we wouldn't know who'd been what on Earth. I think it was more so we all looked like transportees.

The second day, and every day after, they tried to pound some knowledge into us. It was almost interesting. Sam was in with the people that could read, and she seemed to know more than I did afterward. Maybe there was something to that reading stuff, or it might also have been that freaky, powerful memory of hers.

Once we were erased and oriented, they loaded Sam and me into a two-person cube on a dumpround to Mars. Minutes after the booster released us and we were ballistic, an older guy, some asshole, tried to come into our cube and tell us this was going to be his space all to himself, and I punched him hard enough to take him out; I don't think he had his balance for centrifigrav yet.

Two of his buds jumped in. I got into it with them too—I was hot, they were pissing me off, I wasn't figuring odds. Then some guys from the cubes around me came in with me, and together we beat the other side's ass bloody.

In the middle of the victory whooping, Sam shouted for quiet. She announced, "Everyone stays in their same quarters. Everyone draws their own rations. Everyone takes your turn, and *just* your turn, at the info screens. And nobody doesn't pay for protection or nothing."

One of the assholes, harmless now because I had at least ten good guys at my back, sneered, "Hey, little bitch. You running for Transportee Council?"

"Sure, why not?"

She won, too.

The Transportee Council stayed in charge for the whole trip. People ate and slept in peace, and no crazy-asses broke into the server array, which is what caused most lost dumprounds. They told us in orientation, but a lot of transportees didn't listen, or didn't understand, or just didn't believe that a dumpround didn't have any fuel to go back to Earth; a dumpround flew like a cannonball, with just a few little jets to guide it in and out of the aerobrakes and steer it to the parachute field.

The same people who thought there was a steering wheel in the server array compartment, or maybe a reverse gear or just a big button that said TAKE US BACK TO EARTH, didn't know that the server array also ran the air-making machinery and the food dispensary and everything that kept people alive.

I'm sure we had as many idiots as any other dumpround, but we made it just fine; that was all Sam, who ran the TC and kept the TC running the dumpround. The eighty-eight people on International Mars Transport 2082/4/288 (which is what they called our dumpround; it was the 288th one fired off that April) all walked out of the dumpround on Mars carrying our complete, unlooted kits, and the militia that always stood by in case a dumpround landing involved hostages, arrests, or serious injuries didn't have a thing to do about us.

The five months in the dumpround were when I learned to read, and that has helped me so much—oh, hey, another box bumping up and down! Okay, bottero-gator, literacy as a positive value coming right up, all hot and ready for the new generation of Martians to suck inspiration from.

Hey, if you don't like irony, don't flash red lights at me, just edit it out. Yeah, authorize editing.

Anyway, with my info screen time, Sam made me do an hour of reading lessons for every two hours of games. Plus she coached me a lot. After a while the reading was more interesting than the games, and she was doing TC business so much of the time, and I didn't really have any other friends, so I just sat and worked on the reading. By the time we landed, I'd read four actual books, not just kid books I mean.

We came down on the parachute field at Olympic City, an overdignified name for what, in those long-ago days, was just two office buildings, a general store, and a nine-room hotel connected by pressurized tubes. The tiny pressurized facility was surrounded by a few thousand coffinsquats hooked into its pay air and power, and many thousand more running on their own fusion boxes. Olympica, to the south, was just a line of bluffs under a slope reaching way up into the sky.

It was the beginning of northern summer prospecting season. Sam towed me from lender to lender, coaching me on looking like a good bet to someone that would trust us with a share-deal on a prospecting gig. At the time I just thought rocks were, you know, rocks. No idea that some of them were ores, or that Mars was so poor in so many ores because it was dead tectonically.

So while she talked to bankers, private lenders, brokers, and plain old loan sharks, I dummied up and did my best to look like what she told them I was, a hard worker who would do what Sam told me. "Cap is quiet but he thinks, and we're a team."

She said that so often that after a while I believed it myself. Back at our coffinsquat every night, she'd make me do all the tutorials and read like crazy about rocks and ores. Now I can't remember how it was to not know something, like not being able to read, or recognize ore, or go through a balance sheet, or anything else I learned later.

Two days till we'd've gone into the labor pool and been shipped south to build roads and impoundments, and this CitiWells franchise broker, Hsieh Chi, called us back, and said we just felt lucky to him, and he had a quota to make, so what the hell.

Sam named our prospector gig the *Goodspeed* after something she'd read in a poem someplace, and we loaded up, got going, did what the software told us, and did okay that first summer around the North Pole, mostly.

Goodspeed was old and broke down continually, but Sam was a good directions-reader, and no matter how frustrating it got, I'd keep trying to do what she was reading to me—sometimes we both had to go to the dictionary, I mean who knew what a flange, a fairing, or a flashing was?—and sooner or later we'd get it figured out and roll again.

Yeah, botterogator, you can check that box for persistence in the face of adversity. Back then I'd've said I was just too dumb to quit if Sam didn't, and Sam was too stubborn.

Up there in the months and months of midnight sun, we found ore, and learned more and more about telling ore from not-ore. The gig's hopper filled up, gradually, from surface rock finds. Toward the end of that summer—it seemed so weird that Martian summers were twice as long as on Earth even after we read up about why—we even found an old volcanic vent and turned up some peridot, agate, amethyst, jasper, and garnet, along with three real honest-to-god impact diamonds that made us feel brilliant. By the time we got back from the summer prospecting, we were able to pay off Hsieh Chi's shares, with enough left over to buy the gig and put new treads on it. We could spare a little to rehab the cabin too; *Goodspeed* went from our dumpy old gig to our home, I guess. At least in Sam's mind. I wasn't so sure that home meant a lot to me.

Botterogator if you want me to inspire the new generation of Martians, you have to let me tell the truth. Sam cared about having a home, I didn't. You can flash your damn red light. It's true.

Anyway, while the fitters rebuilt *Goodspeed*, we stayed in a rented cabinsquat, sleeping in, reading, and eating food we didn't cook. We soaked in the hot tub at the Riebecker Olympic every single day—the only way Sam got warm. Up north, she had thought she was cold all the time because we were always working, she was small, and she just couldn't keep weight on no matter how much she ate, but even loafing around Olympic City, where the most vigorous thing we did was nap in the artificial sun room, or maybe lift a heavy spoon, she still didn't warm up.

We worried that she might have pneumonia or TB or something she'd brought from Earth, but the diagnostic machines found nothing unusual except being out of shape. But Sam had been doing so much hard physical work, her biceps and abs were like rocks, she was *strong*. So we gave up on the diagnosis machines, because that made no sense.

Nowadays everyone knows about Martian heart, but back then nobody knew that hearts atrophy and deposit more plaque in lower gravity, as the circulation slows down and the calcium that should be depositing into bones accumulates in the blood. Let alone that maybe a third of the human race have genes that make it happen so fast.

At the time, with no cases identified, it wasn't even a research subject; so many people got sick and died in the first couple decades of settlement, often in their first Martian year, and to the diagnostic machines it was all a job, ho hum, another day, another skinny nineteen-year-old dead of a heart attack. Besides, *all* the transportees, not just the ones that died, ate so much carb-and-fat food, because it was cheap. Why *wouldn't* there be more heart attacks? There were always more transportees coming, so put up another site about healthful eating for Mars and find something else to worry about.

Checking the diagnosis machine was everything we could afford to do, anyway, but it seemed like only a small, annoying worry. After all, we'd done well, bought our own gig, were better geared up, knew more what we were doing. We set out with pretty high hopes.

Goodspeed was kind of a dumb name for a prospector's gig. At best it could make maybe 40 km/hr, which is not what you call roaring fast. Antarctic summer prospecting started with a long, dull drive down to Promethei Lingula, driving south out of northern autumn and into southern spring. The Interpolar Highway in those days was a gig track weaving southward across the shield from Olympic City to the Great Marineris Bridge. There was about 100 km of pavement, sort of, before and after the bridge, and then another gig track angling southeast to wrap around Hellas, where a lot of surface prospectors liked to work, and there was a fair bit of seasonal construction to be done on the city they were building in the western wall.

But we were going far south of Hellas. I asked Sam about that. "If you're cold all the time, why are we going all the way to the edge of the south polar cap? I mean, wouldn't it be nicer to maybe work the Bouches du Marineris or someplace near the equator, where you could stay a little warmer?"

"Cap, what's the temperature in here, in the gig cabin?"

"Twenty-two C," I said, "do you feel cold?"

"Yeah, I do, and that's my point," she said. I reached to adjust the temperature, and she stopped me. "What I mean is, that's room temperature, babe, and it's the same temperature it is in my suit, and in the fingers and toes of my suit, and everywhere. The cold isn't outside, and it doesn't matter whether it's the temperature of a warm day on Earth or there's CO_2 snow falling, the cold's in here, in me, ever since we came to Mars."

The drive was around 10,000 km as the road ran, but mostly it was pleasant, just making sure the gig stayed on the trail as we rolled past the huge volcanoes, the stunning view of Marineris from that hundred-mile-long bridge, and then all that ridge and peak country down south.

Mostly Sam slept while I drove. Often I rested a hand on her neck or forehead as she dozed in the co-driver's chair. Sometimes she shivered; I wondered if it was a long-running flu. I made her put on a mask and get extra oxygen, and that helped, but every few weeks I had to up her oxygen mix again.

All the way down I practiced pronouncing Promethei Lingula, especially after we rounded Hellas, because Sam looked a little sicker every week, and I was so afraid she'd need help and I wouldn't be able to make a distress call.

Sam figured Promethei Lingula was too far for most people—they'd rather pick through Hellas's or Argyre's crater walls, looking for chunks of something worthwhile thrown up from deep underground in those impacts, and of course the real gamblers always wanted to work Hellas because one big Hellas Diamond was five years' income.

Sam already knew what it would take me fifteen marsyears to learn: she believed in making a good bet that nobody else was making. Her idea was that a shallow valley like the Promethei Lingula in the Antarctic highlands might have more stuff swept down by the glaciers, and maybe even some of the kinds of exposed veins that really old mountains had on Earth.

As for what went wrong, well, nothing except our luck; nowadays I own three big veins down there. No, botterogator, I don't feel like telling you a damned thing about what I own, you're authorized to just look all that up. I don't see that owning stuff is inspiring. I want to talk about Sam.

We didn't find any veins, or much of anything else, that first southern summer. And meanwhile Sam's health deteriorated.

By the time we were into Promethei Lingula, I was fixing most meals and doing almost all the maintenance. After the first weeks I did all the exosuit work, because her suit couldn't seem to keep her warm, even on hundred percent oxygen. She wore gloves and extra socks even inside. She didn't move much, but her mind was as good as ever, and with her writing the search patterns and me going out and grabbing the rocks, we could still've been okay.

Except we needed to be as lucky as we'd been up in Boreas, and we just weren't.

Look here, botterogator, you can't make me say luck had nothing to do with it. Luck always has a shitload to do with it. Keep this quibbling up and just see if I inspire *any* new Martians.

Sometimes there'd be a whole day when there wasn't a rock that was worth tossing in the hopper, or I'd cover a hundred km of nothing but common basalts and granites. Sam thought her poor concentration made her write bad search patterns, but it wasn't that; it was plain bad luck.

Autumn came, and with it some dust storms and a sun that spiraled closer to the horizon every day, so that everything was dimmer. It was time to head north; we could sell the load, such as it was, at the depot at Hellas, but by the time we got to the Bouches de Marineris, it wouldn't cover more than a few weeks of prospecting. We might have to mortgage again; Hsieh Chi, unfortunately, was in the Vikingsburg pen for embezzling. "Maybe we could hustle someone, like we did him."

"Maybe *I* could, babe," Sam said. "You know the business a lot better, but you're still nobody's sales guy, Cap. We've got food enough for another four months out here, and we still have credit because we're working and we haven't had to report our hold weight. Lots of gigs stay out for extra time—some even overwinter—and nobody can tell whether that's because they're way behind like us, or they've found a major vein and they're exploiting it. So we can head back north, use up two months of supplies to get there, buy about a month of supplies with the cargo, go on short term credit only, and try to get lucky in one month. Or we can stay here right till we have just enough food to run for the Hellas depot, put in four months, and have four times the chance. If it don't work *Goodspeed*'ll be just as lost either way."

"It's going to get dark and cold," I pointed out. "Very dark and cold. And you're tired and cold all the time now."

"Dark and cold *outside the cabin*," she said. Her face had the stubborn set that meant this was going to be useless. "And maybe the dark'll make me eat more. All the perpetual daylight, maybe that's what's screwing my system up. We'll try the Bouches de Marineris next time, maybe those nice regular equatorial days'll get my internal clock working again. But for right now, let's stay here. Sure, it'll get darker, and the storms can get bad—"

"Bad as in we could get buried, pierced by a rock on the wind, maybe even flipped if the wind gets in under the hull," I pointed out. "Bad as in us and the sensors can only see what the spotlights can light. There's a reason why prospecting is a summer job."

She was quiet about that for so long I thought a miracle had happened and I'd won an argument.

Then she said, "Cap, I like it here in *Goodspeed*. It's home. It's ours. I know I'm sick, and all I can do these days is sleep, but I don't want to go to some hospital and have you only visit on your days off from a labor crew. *Goodspeed* is ours and I want to live here and try to keep it."

So I said yes.

For a while things got better. The first fall storms were water snow, not CO_2. I watched the weather reports and we were always buttoned up tight for every storm, screens out and treads sealed against the fine dust. In those brief weeks between midnight sun and endless night, when the sun rises and sets daily in the Promethei Lingula, the thin coat of snow and frost actually made the darker rocks stand out on the surface, and there were more good ones to find, too.

Sam was cold all the time; sometimes she'd cry with just wanting to be warm. She'd eat, when I stood over her and made her, but she had no appetite. I also knew how she thought: Food was the bottleneck. A fusion box supplied centuries of power to move, to compress and process the Martian air into breathability, to extract and purify water. But we couldn't grow food, and unlike spare parts or medical care we might need now and then, we needed food every day, so food would be the thing we ran out of first. (Except maybe luck, and we were already out of that.) Since she didn't want the food anyway, she thought if she didn't eat we could stay out and give our luck more of a chance to turn.

The sun set for good; so far south, Phobos was below the horizon; cloud cover settled in to block the stars. It was darker than anywhere I'd ever been. We stayed.

There was more ore in the hold but not enough more. Still no vein. We had a little luck at the mouth of one dry wash with a couple tons of ore in small chunks, but it played out in less than three weeks.

Next place that looked at all worth trying was 140 km south, almost at the edge of the permanent cap, crazy and scary to try, but what the hell, everything about this was crazy and scary.

The sky had cleared for the first time in weeks when we arrived. With just a little CO_2 frost, it was easy to find rocks—the hot lights zapped the dry ice right off them. I found one nice big chunk of wolframite, the size of an old trunk, right off the bat, and then two smaller ones; somewhere up the glacial slopes from here, there was a vein, perhaps not under permanent ice. I started the analytic program mapping slopes and finds and went out in the suit to see if I could find and mark more rocks.

Markeb, which I'd learned to pick out of the bunched triangles of the constellation Vela, was just about dead overhead; it's the south pole star on Mars. It had been a while since I'd seen the stars, and I'd learned more about what I was looking at. I picked out the Coal Sack, the Southern Cross, and the Magellanic Clouds easily, though honestly, on a clear night at the Martian south pole, that's like being able to find an elephant in a bathtub.

I went inside; the analysis program was saying that probably the wolframite had come from way up under the glacier, so no luck there, but also that there might be a fair amount of it lying out here in the alluvial fan, so at least we'd pick up something here. I stood up from the terminal; I'd fix dinner, then wake Sam, feed her, and tell her the semi-good news.

When I came in with the tray, Sam was curled up, shivering and crying. I made her eat all her soup and bread and plugged her in to breathe straight body-temperature oxygen. When she was feeling better, or at least saying she was, I took her up into the bubble to look at the stars with the lights off. She seemed to enjoy that, especially that I could point to things and show them to her, because it meant I'd been studying and learning.

Yeah, botterogator, reinforce that learning leads to success. Sam'd like that.

"Cap," she said. "This is the worst it's been, babe. I don't think there's anything on Mars that can fix me. I just keep getting colder and weaker. I'm so sorry—"

"I'm starting for Hellas as soon as we get you wrapped up and have pure oxygen going into you in the bed. I'll drive as long as I can safely, then—"

"It won't make any difference. You'll never get me there, not alive," she said. "Babe, the onboard diagnostic kit isn't perfect but it's good enough to show I've got the heart of a ninety-year-old cardiac patient. And all the indicators have gotten worse in just the last hundred hours or so. Whatever I've got, it's killing me." She reached out and stroked my tear-soaked face. "Poor Cap. Make me two promises."

"I'll love you forever."

"I know. I don't need you to promise that. First promise, no matter where you end up, or doing what, you *learn*. Study whatever you can study, acquire whatever you can acquire, feed your mind, babe. That's the most important."

I nodded. I was crying pretty hard.

"The other one is kind of weird . . . well, it's silly."

"If it's for you, I'll do it. I promise."

She gasped, trying to pull in more oxygen than her lungs could hold. Her eyes were flowing too. "I'm scared to be buried out in the cold and the dark, and I can't *stand* the idea of freezing solid. So . . . don't bury me. Cremate me. I want to be *warm*."

"But you can't cremate a person on Mars," I protested. "There's not enough air to support a fire, and—"

"You promised," she said, and died.

I spent the next hour doing everything the first aid program said to do. When she was cold and stiff, I knew it had really happened.

I didn't care about *Goodspeed* anymore. I'd sell it at Hellas depot, buy passage to some city where I could work, start over. I didn't want to be in our home for weeks with Sam's body, but I didn't have the money to call in a mission to retrieve her, and anyway they'd just do the most economical thing—bury her right here, practically at the South Pole, in the icy night.

I curled up in my bunk and just cried for hours, then let myself fall asleep. That just made it worse; now that she was past rigor mortis she was soft to the touch, more like herself, and I couldn't stand to store her in the cold, either, not after what I had promised. I washed her, brushed her hair, put her in a body bag, and set her in one of the dry storage compartments with the door closed; maybe I'd think of something before she started to smell.

Driving north, I don't think I really wanted to live myself. I stayed up too long, ate and drank too little, just wanting the journey to be over with. I remember I drove right through at least one bad storm at peak speed, more than enough to shatter a tread on a stone or to go into a sudden crevasse or destroy myself in all kinds of ways. For days in a row, in that endless black darkness, I woke up in the driver's chair after having fallen asleep while the deadman stopped the gig.

I didn't care. I wanted out of the dark.

About the fifth day, *Goodspeed*'s forward left steering tread went off a drop-off of three meters or so. The gig flipped over forward to the left, crashing onto its back. Force of habit had me strapped into the seat, and wearing my suit, the two things that the insurance company manuals said were what you had to be doing any time the gig was moving if you didn't want to void your policy. Sam had made a big deal about that, too.

So after rolling, *Goodspeed* came to a stop on its back, and all the lights went out. When I finished screaming with rage and disappointment and everything else, there was still enough air (though I could feel it leaking) for me to be conscious.

I put on my helmet and turned on the headlamp.

I had a full capacitor charge on the suit, but *Goodspeed*'s fusion box had shut down. That meant seventeen hours of being alive unless I could replace it with another fusion box, but both the compartment where the two spare fusion boxes were stored and the repair access to replace them were on the top rear surface of the gig. I climbed outside, wincing at letting the last of the cabin air out, and poked around. The gig was resting on exactly the hatches I would have needed to open.

Seventeen—well, sixteen, now—hours. And one big promise to keep.

The air extractors on the gig had been running, as they always did, right up till the accident; the tanks were full of liquid oxygen. I could transfer it to my suit through the emergency valving, live for some days that way. There were enough suit rations to make it a real race between starvation and suffocation. The suit radio wasn't going to reach anywhere that could do me any good; for long distance it depended on a relay through the gig, and the relay's antenna was under the overturned gig.

Sam was dead. *Goodspeed* was dead. And for every practical purpose, so was I.

Neither *Goodspeed* nor I really needed that oxygen anymore, *but Sam does*, I realized. I could at least shift the tanks around, and I had the mining charges we used for breaking up big rocks.

I carried Sam's body into the oxygen storage, set her between two of the tanks, and hugged the body bag one more time. I don't know if I was afraid she'd look awful, or afraid she would look alive and asleep, but I was afraid to unzip the bag.

I set the timer on a mining charge, put that on top of her, and piled the rest of the charges on top. My little pile of bombs filled most of the space between the two oxygen tanks. Then I wrestled four more tanks to lie on the heap crosswise and stacked flammable stuff from the kitchen like flour, sugar, cornmeal, and jugs of cooking oil on top of those, to make sure the fire burned long and hot enough.

My watch said I still had five minutes till the timer went off.

I still don't know why I left the gig. I'd been planning to die there, cremated with Sam, but maybe I just wanted to see if I did the job right or something—as if I could try again, perhaps, if it didn't work? Whatever the reason, I bounded away to what seemed like a reasonable distance.

I looked up; the stars were out. I wept so hard I feared I would miss seeing them in the blur. They were so beautiful, and it had been so long.

Twenty kilograms of high explosive was enough energy to shatter all the LOX tanks and heat all the oxygen white hot. Organic stuff doesn't just burn in white-hot oxygen; it explodes and vaporizes, and besides fifty kilograms of Sam, I'd loaded in a good six hundred kilograms of other organics.

I figured all that out a long time later. In the first quarter second after the mining charge went off, things were happening pretty fast. A big piece of the observation bubble—smooth enough not to cut my suit and kill me, but hard enough to send me a couple meters into the air and backward by a good thirty meters—slapped me over and sent me rolling down the back side of the ridge on which I sat, smashed up badly and unconscious, but alive.

I think I dreamed about Sam, as I gradually came back to consciousness.

Now, look here, botterogator, of course I'd like to be able, for the sake of the new generation of Martians, to tell you I dreamed about her giving me earnest how-to-succeed advice, and that I made a vow there in dreamland to succeed and be worthy of her and all that. But in fact it was mostly just dreams of holding her and being held, and about laughing together. Sorry if that's not on the list.

The day came when I woke up and realized I'd seen the medic before. Not long after that I stayed awake long enough to say "hello." Eventually I learned that a survey satellite had picked up the exploding gig, and shot pictures because that bright light was unusual. An AI identified a shape in the dust as a human body lying outside and dispatched an autorescue—a rocket with a people-grabbing arm. The autorescue flew out of Olympic City's launch pad on a ballistic trajectory, landed not far from me, crept over to my not-yet-out-of-air, not-yet-frozen body, grabbed me with a mechanical arm, and stuffed me into its hold. It took off again, flew to the hospital, and handed me over to the doctor.

Total cost of one autorescue mission, and two weeks in a human-contact hospital—which the insurance company refused to cover because I'd deliberately blown up the gig—was maybe twenty successful prospecting runs' worth. So as soon as I could move, they indentured me and, since I was in no shape to do grunt-and-strain stuff for a while, they found a little prospector's supply company that wanted a human manager for an office at the Hellas depot. I learned the job—it wasn't hard—and grew with the company, eventually as Mars's first indentured CEO.

I took other jobs, bookkeeping, supervising, cartography, anything where I could earn wages with which to pay off the indenture faster, especially jobs I could do online in my nominal hours off. At every job, because I'd promised Sam, I learned as much as I could. Eventually, a few days before my forty-third birthday, I paid off the indenture, quit all those jobs, and went into business for myself.

By that time I knew how the money moved, and for what, in practically every significant business on Mars. I'd had a lot of time to plan and think, too.

So that was it. I kept my word—oh, all right, botterogator, let's check that box too. Keeping promises is important to success. After all, here I am.

Sixty-two earthyears later, I know, because everyone does, that a drug that costs almost nothing, which everyone takes now, could have kept Sam alive. A little money a year, if anyone'd known, and Sam and me could've been celebrating anniversaries for decades, and we'd've been richer, with Sam's brains on the job too. And botterogator, you'd be talking to her, and probably learning more, too.

Or is that what I think now?

Remembering Sam, over the years, I've thought of five hundred things I could have done instead of what I did, and maybe I'd have succeeded as much with those too.

But the main question I think about is only—did she *mean* it? Did she see something in me that would make my bad start work out as well as it did? Was she just an idealistic smart girl playing house with the most cooperative boy she could find? Would she have wanted me to marry again and have children, did she intend me to get rich?

Every so often I regret that I didn't really fulfill that second promise, an irony I can appreciate now: she feared the icy grave, but since she burned to mostly water and carbon dioxide, on Mars she became mostly snow. And molecules are so small, and distribute so evenly, that whenever the snow falls, I know there's a little of her in it, sticking to my suit, piling on my helmet, coating me as I stand in the quiet and watch it come down.

Did she dream me into existence? I kept my promises, and they made me who I am . . . and was that what she wanted? If I am only the accidental whim of a smart teenage girl with romantic notions, what would I have been without the whim, the notions, or Sam?

Tell you what, botterogator, and you pass this on to the new generation of Martians: it's funny how one little promise, to someone or something a bit better than yourself, can turn into something as real as Samantha City, whose lights at night fill the crater that spreads out before me from my balcony all the way to the horizon.

Nowadays I have to walk for an hour, in the other direction out beyond the crater wall, till the false dawn of the city lights is gone, and I can walk till dawn or hunger turns me homeward again.

Botterogator, you can turn off the damn stupid flashing lights. That's all you're getting out of me. I'm going for a walk; it's snowing.

The Invasion of Venus

Stephen Baxter

Stephen Baxter made his first sale to Interzone *in 1987, and has since made sales to* Asimov's Science Fiction, Science Fiction Age, Analog, Zenith, New Worlds, *and elsewhere. Baxter's first novel,* Raft, *was released in 1991, and was rapidly followed by other well-received novels such as* Timelike Infinity, Anti-Ice, Flux, *and the H. G. Wells pastiche—a sequel to* The Time Machine—The Time Ships, *which won both the John W. Campbell Memorial Award and the Philip K. Dick Award. His many other books include the novels* Voyage, Titan, Moonseed, Mammoth, Book One: Silverhair, Long Tusk, Ice Bone, Manifold: Time, Manifold: Space, Evolution, Coalescent, Exultant, Transcendent, Emperor, Resplendent, Conqueror, Navigator, Firstborn, The H-Bomb Girl, Weaver, Flood, Ark, *and two novels in collaboration with Arthur C. Clarke:* The Light of Other Days *and* Time's Eye, a Time Odyssey. *His short fiction has been collected in* Vacuum Diagrams: Stories of the Xeelee Sequence, Traces, *and* Hunters of Pangaea. *Recent books have included the trilogy* Stone Spring, Bronze Summer, *and* Iron Winter; *a nonfiction book,* The Science of Avatar; *The Massacre of Mankind, a sequel to Wells's* The War of the Worlds; *and* Xeelee: Vengeance, *the start of a duology set in his Xeelee universe, and a trilogy written in collaboration with Terry Pratchett:* The Long Earth, The Long War, *and* The Long Childhood. *Baxter is also involved a space colony design project with the British Interplanetary Society, SETI groups and is currently a judge for the Sidewise Award.*

In the following story, he shows us a future in which humans are bystanders to an immense cosmic battle between forces that, to our dismay, ignore us completely.

For me, the saga of the Incoming was above all Edith Black's story. For she, more than anyone else I knew, was the one who had a problem with it.

When the news was made public I drove out of London to visit Edith at her country church. I had to cancel a dozen appointments to do it, including one with the Prime Minister's office, but I knew, as soon as I got out of the car and stood in the soft September rain, that it had been the right thing to do.

Edith was pottering around outside the church, wearing overalls and rubber boots and wielding an alarming-looking industrial-strength jackhammer. But she had a radio blaring out a phone-in discussion, and indoors, out of the rain, I glimpsed a widescreen TV and laptop, both scrolling news—mostly fresh projections of where the Incoming's decelerating trajectory might deliver them, and new deep-space images of their 'craft,' if such it was, a massive block of ice like a comet nucleus, leaking very complex patterns of infrared radiation. Edith was plugged into the world, even out here in the wilds of Essex.

She approached me with a grin, pushing back goggles under a hard hat. 'Toby.' I got a kiss on the cheek and a brief hug; she smelled of machine oil. We were easy with each other physically. Fifteen years earlier, in our last year at college, we'd been lovers, briefly; it had finished with a kind of regretful embarrassment— very English, said our American friends—but it had proven only a kind of speed bump in our relationship. 'Glad to see you, if surprised. I thought all you civil service types would be locked down in emergency meetings.'

For a decade I'd been a civil servant in the environment ministry. 'No, but old Thorp—' my minister '—has been in a continuous COBRA session for twenty-four hours. Much good it's doing anybody.'

'I must say it's not obvious to the layman what use an environment minister is when the aliens are coming.'

'Well, among the scenarios they're discussing is some kind of attack from space. A lot of what we can dream up is similar to natural disasters—a meteor fall could be like a tsunami, a sunlight occlusion like a massive volcanic event. And so Thorp is in the mix, along with health, energy, transport. Of course we're in contact with other governments—NATO, the UN. The most urgent issue right now is whether to signal or not.'

She frowned. 'Why wouldn't you?'

'Security. Edith, remember, we know absolutely nothing about these guys. What if our signal was interpreted as a threat? And there are tactical considerations. Any signal would give information to a potential enemy about our technical capabilities. It would also give away the very fact that we know they are here.'

She scoffed. '"Tactical considerations." Paranoid bullshit! And besides, I bet every kid with a CB radio is beaming out her heart to ET right now. The whole planet's alight.'

'Well, that's true. You can't stop it. But still, sending some kind of signal authorised by government or an inter-government agency is another step entirely.'

'Oh, come on. You can't really believe anybody is going to cross the stars to harm us. What could they possibly want that would justify the cost of an interstellar mission? . . .'

So we argued. I'd only been out of the car for five minutes.

We'd had this kind of discussion all the way back to late nights in college, some of them in her bed, or mine. She'd always been drawn to the bigger issues—'to the context,' as she used to say. Though we'd both started out as maths students, her head had soon expanded in the exotic intellectual air of the college, and she'd moved on to study older ways of thinking than the scientific—older questions, still unanswered. Was there a God? If so, or if not, what was the point of our existence? Why did we, or indeed anything, exist at all? In her later college years she took theology options, but quickly burned through that discipline and was left unsatisfied. She was repelled too by the modern atheists, with their aggressive denials. So, after college, she had started her own journey through life—a journey in search of answers. Now, of course, maybe some of those answers had come swimming in from the stars in search of her.

This was why I'd felt drawn here, at this particular moment in my life. I needed her perspective. In the wan daylight I could see the fine patina of lines around the mouth I used to kiss, and the strands of grey in her red hair. I was sure she suspected, rightly, that I knew more than I was telling her—more than had been released to the public. But she didn't follow that up for now.

'Come see what I'm doing,' she said, sharply breaking up the debate. 'Watch your shoes.' We walked across muddy grass towards the main door. The core of that old church, dedicated to St Cuthbert, was a Saxon-era tower; the rest of the fabric was mostly Norman, but there had been an extensive restoration in Victorian times. Within was a lovely space, if cold, the stone walls resonating. It was still consecrated, Church of England, but in this empty agricultural countryside it was one of a widespread string of churches united in a single parish, and rarely used.

Edith had never joined any of the established religions, but she had appropriated some of their infrastructure, she liked to say. And here she had gathered a group of volunteers, wandering souls more or less like-minded. They worked to maintain the fabric of the church. And within, she led her group through what you might think of as a mix of discussions, or prayers, or meditation, or yoga practices— whatever she could find that seemed to work. This was the way religions used to be before the big monotheistic creeds took over, she argued. 'The only way to reach God, or anyhow the space beyond us where God ought to be, is by working hard, by helping other people—and by pushing your mind to the limit of its capability, and then going a little beyond, and just *listening*.' Beyond *logos* to *mythos*. She was always restless, always trying something new. Yet in some ways she was the most contented person I ever met—at least before the Incoming showed up.

Now, though, she wasn't content about the state of the church's foundations. She showed me where she had dug up flagstones to reveal sodden ground. 'We're digging out new drainage channels, but it's a hell of a job. We may end up rebuilding the founds altogether. The very deepest level seems to be wood, huge piles of Saxon oak . . .' She eyed me. 'This church has stood here for a thousand years, without, apparently, facing a threat such as this before. Some measure of climate change, right?'

I shrugged. 'I suppose you'd say we arseholes in the environment ministry should be concentrating on stuff like this rather than preparing to fight interstellar wars.'

'Well, so you should. And maybe a more mature species would be preparing for positive outcomes. Think of it, Tobe! There are now creatures in this solar system who are *smarter than us*. They have to be, or they wouldn't be here—right?

Somewhere between us and the angels. Who knows what they can tell us? What is their science, their art—their theology?'

I frowned. 'But what do they want? For that's what may count from now on—their agenda, not ours.'

'There you are being paranoid again.' But she hesitated. 'What about Meryl and the kids?'

'Meryl's at home. Mark and Sophie at school.' I shrugged. 'Life as normal.'

'Some people are freaking out. Raiding the supermarkets.'

'Some people always do. We want things to continue as normally as possible, as long as possible. Modern society is efficient, you know, Edith, but not very resilient. A fuel strike could cripple us in a week, let alone alien invaders.'

She pushed a loose grey hair back under her hard hat and looked at me suspiciously. 'But you seem very calm, considering. You know something. Don't you, you bastard?'

I grinned. 'And you know me.'

'Spill it.'

'Two things. We picked up signals. Or, more likely, leakage. You know about the infrared stuff we've seen for a while, coming from the nucleus. Now we've detected radio noise, faint, clearly structured, very complex. It may be some kind of internal channel rather than anything meant for us. But if we can figure anything out from it—'

'Well, that's exciting. And the second thing? Come on, Miller.'

'We have more refined trajectory data. All this will be released soon—it's probably leaked already.'

'Yes?'

'The Incoming *are* heading for the inner solar system. But they aren't coming here—not to Earth.'

She frowned. 'Then where?'

I dropped my bombshell. 'Venus. Not Earth. They're heading for Venus, Edith.'

She looked into the clouded sky, the bright patch that marked the position of the Sun, and the inner planets. 'Venus? That's a cloudy hellhole. What would they want there?'

'I've no idea.'

'Well, I'm used to living with questions I'll never be able to answer. Let's hope this isn't one of them. In the meantime, let's make ourselves useful.' She eyed my crumpled Whitehall suit, my patent leather shoes already splashed with mud. 'Have you got time to stay? You want to help out with my drain? I've a spare overall that might fit.'

Talking, speculating, we walked through the church.

We used the excuse of Edith's Goonhilly event to make a family trip to Cornwall.

We took the A-road snaking west down the spine of the Cornish peninsula, and stopped at a small hotel in Helston. The pretty little town was decked out that day for the annual Furry Dance, an ancient, eccentric carnival when the local children would weave in and out of the houses on the hilly streets. The next morning Meryl was to take the kids to the beach, farther up the coast.

And, just about at dawn, I set off alone in a hired car for the A-road to the southeast, towards Goonhilly Down. It was a clear May morning. As I drove I was aware of Venus, rising in the eastern sky and clearly visible in my rearview mirror, a lamp shining steadily even as the day brightened.

Goonhilly is a stretch of high open land, a windy place. Its claim to fame is that at one time it hosted the largest telecoms satellite earth station in the world—it picked up the first live transatlantic TV broadcast, via Telstar. It was decommissioned years ago, but its oldest dish, a thousand-tonne parabolic bowl called 'Arthur' after the king, became a listed building, and so was preserved. And that was how it was available for Edith and her committee of messagers to get hold of, when they, or rather she, grew impatient with the government's continuing reticence. Because of the official policy I had to help with smoothing through the permissions, all behind the scenes.

Just after my first glimpse of the surviving dishes on the skyline I came up against a police cordon, a hastily erected plastic fence that excluded a few groups of chanting Shouters and a fundamentalist-religious group protesting that the messagers were communicating with the Devil. My ministry card helped me get through.

Edith was waiting for me at the old site's visitors' centre, opened up that morning for breakfast, coffee and cereals and toast. Her volunteers cleared up dirty dishes under a big wall screen showing a live feed from a space telescope—the best images available right now, though every major space agency had a probe to Venus in preparation, and NASA had already fired one off. The Incoming nucleus (it seemed inappropriate to call that lump of dirty ice a 'craft,' though such it clearly was) was a brilliant star, too small to show a disc, swinging in its wide orbit above a half-moon Venus. And on the planet's night side you could clearly make out the Patch, that strange, complicated glow in the cloud banks tracking the Incoming's orbit precisely. It was strange to gaze upon that choreography in space, and then to turn to the east and see Venus with the naked eye.

And Edith's volunteers, a few dozen earnest men, women and children who looked like they had gathered for a village show, had the audacity to believe they could speak to these godlike forms in the sky.

There was a terrific metallic groan. We turned, and saw that Arthur was turning on his concrete pivot. The volunteers cheered, and a general drift towards the monument began.

Edith walked with me, cradling a polystyrene tea cup in the palms of fingerless gloves. 'I'm glad you could make it down. Should have brought the kids. Some of the locals from Helston are here; they've made the whole stunt part of their Furry Dance celebration. Did you see the preparations in town? Supposed to celebrate St Michael beating up on the Devil—I wonder how appropriate *that* symbolism is. Anyhow this ought to be a fun day. Later there'll be a barn dance.'

'Meryl thought it was safer to take the kids to the beach. Just in case anything gets upsetting here—you know.' That was most of the truth. There was a subtext that Meryl had never much enjoyed being in the same room as my ex.

'Probably wise. Our British Shouters are a mild bunch, but in rowdier parts of the world there has been trouble.' The loose international coalition of groups called the Shouters was paradoxically named, because they campaigned for silence; they argued that 'shouting in the jungle' by sending signals to the Incoming or the Venusians was taking an irresponsible risk. Of course they could do nothing about the low-level chatter that had been targeted at the Incoming since it had first been sighted, nearly a year ago already. Edith waved a hand at Arthur. 'If I were a Shouter, I'd be here today. This will be by far the most powerful message sent from the British Isles.'

I'd seen and heard roughs of Edith's message. In with a Carl Sagan–style prime number lexicon, there was digitised music from Bach to Zulu chants, and art from cave paintings to Warhol, and images of mankind featuring a lot of smiling children, and astronauts on the Moon. There was even a copy of the old Pioneer spaceprobe plaque from the seventies, with the smiling naked couple. At least, I thought cynically, all that fluffy stuff would provide a counterpoint to the images of war, murder, famine, plague and other sufferings that the Incoming had no doubt sampled by now, if they'd chosen to.

I said, 'But I get the feeling they're just not interested. Neither the Incoming nor the Venusians. Sorry to rain on your parade.'

'I take it the cryptolinguists aren't getting anywhere decoding the signals?'

'They're not so much "signals" as leakage from internal processes, we think. In both cases, the nucleus and the Patch.' I rubbed my face; I was tired after the previous day's long drive. 'In the case of the nucleus, some kind of organic chemistry seems to be mediating powerful magnetic fields—and the Incoming seem to swarm within. I don't think we've really any idea what's going on in there. We're actually making more progress with the science of the Venusian biosphere . . .'

If the arrival of the Incoming had been astonishing, the evidence of intelligence on Venus, entirely unexpected, was stunning. Nobody had expected the clouds to part right under the orbiting Incoming nucleus—like a deep storm system, kilometres deep in that thick ocean of an atmosphere—and nobody had expected to see the Patch revealed, swirling mist banks where lights flickered tantalisingly, like organised lightning.

'With retrospect, given the results from the old space probes, we might have guessed there was something on Venus—life, if not intelligent life. There were always unexplained deficiencies and surpluses of various compounds. We think the Venusians live in the clouds, far enough above the red-hot ground that the temperature is low enough for liquid water to exist. They ingest carbon monoxide and excrete sulphur compounds, living off the sun's ultraviolet.'

'And they're smart.'

'Oh, yes.' The astronomers, already recording the complex signals coming out of the Incoming nucleus, had started to discern rich patterns in the Venusian Patch too. 'You can tell how complicated a message is even if you don't know anything about the content. You measure entropy orders, which are like correlation measures, mapping structures on various scales embedded in the transmission—'

'You don't understand any of what you just said, do you?'

I smiled. 'Not a word. But I do know this. Going by their data structures, the Venusians are smarter than us as we are smarter than the chimps. And the Incoming are smarter again.'

Edith turned to face the sky, the brilliant spark of Venus. 'But you say the scientists still believe all this chatter is just—what was your word?'

'Leakage. Edith, the Incoming and the Venusians aren't speaking to us. They aren't even speaking to each other. What we're observing is a kind of internal dialogue, in each case. The two are talking to themselves, not each other. One theorist briefed the PM that perhaps both these entities are more like hives than human communities.'

'Hives?' She looked troubled. 'Hives are *different*. They can be purposeful, but they don't have consciousness as we have it. They aren't finite as we are; their edges are much more blurred. They aren't even mortal; individuals can die, but the hives live on.'

'I wonder what their theology will be, then.'

'It's all so strange. These aliens just don't fit any category we expected, or even that we share. Not mortal, not communicative—and not interested in us. What do they *want*? What *can* they want?' Her tone wasn't like her; she sounded bewildered to be facing open questions, rather than exhilarated as usual.

I tried to reassure her. 'Maybe your signal will provoke some answers.'

She checked her watch and looked up again towards Venus. 'Well, we've only got five minutes to wait before—' Her eyes widened, and she fell silent.

I turned to look the way she was, to the east.

Venus was flaring. Sputtering like a dying candle.

People started to react. They shouted, pointed, or they just stood there, staring, as I did. I couldn't move. I felt a deep, awed fear. Then people called, pointing at the big screen in the visitors' centre, where, it seemed, the space telescopes were returning a very strange set of images indeed.

Edith's hand crept into mine. Suddenly I was very glad I hadn't brought my kids that day.

I heard angrier shouting, and a police siren, and I smelled burning.

Once I'd finished making my police statement I went back to the hotel in Helston, where Meryl was angry and relieved to see me, and the kids bewildered and vaguely frightened. I couldn't believe that after all that had happened—the strange events at Venus, the assaults by Shouters on messengers and vice versa, the arson, Edith's injury, the police crackdown—it was not yet eleven in the morning.

That same day I took the family back to London, and called in at work. Then, three days after the incident, I got away again and commandeered a ministry car and driver to take me back to Cornwall.

Edith was out of intensive care, but she'd been kept in the hospital at Truro. She had a TV stand before her face, the screen dark. I carefully kissed her on the unburnt side of her face, and sat down, handing over books, newspapers and flowers. 'Thought you might be bored.'

'You never were any good with the sick, were you, Tobe?'

'Sorry.' I opened up one of the newspapers. 'But there's some good news. They caught the arsonists.'

She grunted, her distorted mouth barely opening. 'So what? It doesn't matter who they were. Messagers and Shouters have been at each others' throats all over the world. People like that are interchangeable . . . But did we all have to behave so badly? I mean, they even wrecked Arthur.'

'And he was Grade II listed!'

She laughed, then regretted it, for she winced with the pain. 'But why shouldn't we smash everything up down here? After all, that's all they seem to be interested in up *there*. The Incoming assaulted Venus, and the Venusians struck back. We all saw it, live on TV—it was nothing more than *War of the Worlds*.' She sounded disappointed. 'These creatures are our superiors, Toby. All your signal analysis stuff proved it. And yet they haven't transcended war and destruction.'

'But we learned so much.' I had a small briefcase which I opened now and pulled out printouts that I spread over her bed. 'The screen images are better, but you know how it is; they won't let me use my laptop or my phone in here . . . *Look*, Edith. It was incredible. The Incoming assault on Venus lasted hours. Their weapon, whatever it was, burned its way through the Patch, and right down through an atmosphere a hundred times thicker than Earth's. We even glimpsed the surface—'

'Now melted to slag.'

'Much of it . . . But then the acid-munchers in the clouds struck back. We think we know what they did.'

That caught her interest. 'How can we know that?'

'Sheer luck. That NASA probe, heading for Venus, happened to be in the way . . .'

The probe had detected a wash of electromagnetic radiation, coming from the planet.

'A signal,' breathed Edith. 'Heading which way?'

'Out from the sun. And then, eight hours later, the probe sensed another signal, coming the other way. I say "sensed." It bobbed about like a cork on a pond. We think it was a gravity wave—very sharply focussed, very intense.'

'And when the wave hit the Incoming nucleus—'

'Well, you saw the pictures. The last fragments have burned up in Venus's atmosphere.'

She lay back on her reef of pillows. 'Eight hours,' she mused. 'Gravity waves travel at lightspeed. Four hours out, four hours back . . . Earth's about eight light-minutes from the sun. What's four light-hours out from Venus? Jupiter, Saturn—'

'Neptune. Neptune was four light-hours out.'

'*Was?*'

'It's gone, Edith. Almost all of it—the moons are still there, a few chunks of core ice and rock, slowly dispersing. The Venusians used the planet to create their gravity-wave pulse—'

'They *used* it. Are you telling me this to cheer me up? A gas giant, a significant chunk of the solar system's budget of mass-energy, sacrificed for a single warlike gesture.' She laughed, bitter. 'Oh, God!'

'Of course we've no idea *how* they did it.' I put away my images. 'If we were scared of the Incoming, now we're terrified of the Venusians. That NASA probe has been shut down. We don't want anything to look like a threat . . . You know, I heard the PM herself ask why it was that this space war should break out now, just when we humans are sitting around on Earth. Even politicians know we haven't been here that long.'

Edith shook her head, wincing again. 'The final vanity. This whole episode has never been about us. Can't you see? If this is happening now, it must have happened over and over. Who knows how many other planets we lost in the past, consumed as weapons of forgotten wars? Maybe all we see, the planets and stars and galaxies, is just the debris of huge wars—on and on, up to scales we can barely imagine. And we're just weeds growing in the rubble. Tell that to the Prime Minister. And I thought we might ask them about their gods! What a fool I've been—the questions on which I've wasted my life, and *here* are my answers—what a fool.' She was growing agitated.

'Take it easy, Edith—'

'Oh, just go. I'll be fine. It's the universe that's broken, not me.' She turned away on her pillow, as if to sleep.

The next time I saw Edith she was out of hospital and back at her church.

It was another September day, like the first time I visited her after the Incoming appeared in our telescopes, and at least it wasn't raining. There was a bite in the breeze, but I imagined it soothed her damaged skin. And here she was, digging in the mud before her church.

'Equinox season,' she said. 'Rain coming. Best to get this fixed before we have another flash flood. And before you ask, the doctors cleared me. It's my face that's buggered, not the rest of me.'

'I wasn't going to ask.'

'OK, then. How's Meryl, the kids?'

'Fine. Meryl's at work, the kids back at school. Life goes on.'

'It must, I suppose. What else is there? No, by the way.'

'No what?'

'No, I won't come serve on your minister's think tank.'

'At least consider it. You'd be ideal. Look, we're all trying to figure out where we go from here. The arrival of the Incoming, the war on Venus—it was like a religious revelation. That's how it's being described. A revelation witnessed by all mankind, on TV. Suddenly we've got an entirely different view of the universe out there. And we have to figure out how we go forward, in a whole number of dimensions—political, scientific, economic, social, religious.'

'I'll tell you how we go forward. In despair. Religions are imploding.'

'No, they're not.'

'OK. Theology is imploding. Philosophy. The rest of the world has changed channels and forgotten already, but anybody with any imagination knows . . . In a way this has been the final demotion, the end of the process that started with Copernicus and Darwin. Now we *know* there are creatures in the universe much smarter than we'll ever be, and we *know* they don't care a damn about us. It's the indifference that's the killer—don't you think? All our futile agitation about if they'd attack us and whether we should signal . . . And they did nothing but smash each other up. With *that* above us, what can we do but turn away?'

'You're not turning away.'

She leaned on her shovel. 'I'm not religious; I don't count. My congregation turned away. Here I am, alone.' She glanced at the clear sky. 'Maybe solitude is the key to it all. A galactic isolation imposed by the vast gulfs between the stars, the light-speed limit. As a species develops you might have a brief phase of individuality, of innovation and technological achievement. But then, when the universe gives you nothing back you turn in on yourself, and slide into the milky embrace of eusociality—the hive.

'But what then? How would it be for a mass mind to emerge, alone? Maybe that's why the Incoming went to war. Because they were outraged to discover, by some chance, they weren't alone in the universe.'

'Most commentators think it was about resources. Most of our wars are about that, in the end.'

'Yes. Depressingly true. All life is based on the destruction of other life, even on tremendous scales of space and time . . . Our ancestors understood that right back to the Ice Age and venerated the animals they had to kill. They were so far above us, the Incoming and the Venusians alike. Yet maybe *we*, at our best, are morally superior to them.'

I touched her arm. 'This is why we need you. For your insights. There's a storm coming, Edith. We're going to have to work together if we're to weather it, I think.'

She frowned. 'What kind of storm? . . . Oh. Neptune.'

'Yeah. You can't just delete a world without consequences. The planets' orbits are singing like plucked strings. The asteroids and comets too, and those orphan moons wandering around. Some of the stirred-up debris is falling into the inner system.'

'And if we're struck—'

I shrugged. 'We'll have to help each other. There's nobody else to help us, that's for sure. Look, Edith—maybe the Incoming and the Venusians are typical of what's out there. But that doesn't mean we have to be like them, does it? Maybe we'll find others more like us. And if not, well, we can be the first. A spark to light a fire that will engulf the universe.'

She ruminated. 'You have to start somewhere, I suppose. As with this drain.'

'Well, there you go.'

'All right, damn it, I'll join your think tank. But first you're going to help me finish this drain, aren't you, city boy?'

So I changed into overalls and work boots, and we dug away at that ditch in the damp, clingy earth until our backs ached, and the light of the equinoctial day slowly faded.

weep for Day

INDRAPRAMIT DAS

Indrapramit Das is a writer and artist from Kolkata, India. His short fiction has appeared in Clarkesworld, Asimov's Science Fiction, Apex Magazine, Redstone Science Fiction, The World SF Blog, Meeting Infinity, Flash Fiction Online, *and the anthology* Breaking the Bow: Speculative Fiction Inspired by the Ramayana. *His first novel,* The Devourers, *was published in 2015. He is a grateful graduate of the 2012 Clarion West Writers Workshop, and a recipient of the Octavia E. Butler Memorial Scholarship Award. He completed his MFA at the University of British Columbia, and currently lives in Vancouver, working as a freelance writer, artist, editor, game tester, tutor, would-be novelist, and aspirant to adulthood. Follow him on Twitter: @IndrapramitDas.*

Set on a tidally locked planet where the frozen and eternally dark Nightside is slowly being explored—and conquered—by explorers from the Dayside, this is an evocative, sensitively characterized, and lyrically written story that reminds me of something by Gene Wolfe—no faint praise in my book.

I was eight years old the first time I saw a real, living Nightmare. My parents took my brother and I on a trip from the City-of-Long-Shadows to the hills at Evening's edge, where one of my father's clients had a manse. Father was a railway contractor. He hired out labour and resources to the privateers extending the frontiers of civilization towards the frozen wilderness of the dark Behind-the-Sun. Aptly, we took a train up to the foothills of the great Penumbral Mountains.

It was the first time my brother and I had been on a train, though we'd seen them tumble through the city with their cacophonic engines, cumulous tails of smoke and steam billowing like blood over the rooftops when the red light of our sun caught them. It was also the first time we had been anywhere close to Night—Behind-the-Sun—where the Nightmares lived. Just a decade before we took that trip, it would have been impossible to go as far into Evening as we were doing with such casual comfort and ease.

Father had prodded the new glass of the train windows, pointing to the power-lines crisscrossing the sky in tandem with the gleaming lines of metal railroads silvering the hazy landscape of progress. He sat between my brother Velag and I, our heads propped against the bulk of his belly, which bulged against his rough crimson waistcoat. I clutched that coat and breathed in the sweet smell of chem-lis gall that hung over him. Mother watched with a smile as she peeled indigos for us with her fingers, laying them in the lap of her skirt.

"Look at that. We've got no more reason to be afraid of the dark, do we, my tykes?" said Father, his belly humming with the sound of his booming voice.

Dutifully, Velag and I agreed there wasn't.

"Why not?" he asked us, expectant.

"Because of the Industrialization, which brings the light of Day to the dark-ness of Night," we chimed, a line learned both in school and home (inaccurate, as we'd never set foot in Night itself). Father laughed. I always slowed down on the word 'industrialization,' which caused Velag and I to say it at different times. He was just over a year older than me, though.

"And what is your father, children?" Mother asked.

"A knight of Industry and Technology, bringer of light under Church and Mon-archy."

I didn't like reciting that part, because it had more than one long "y" word and felt like a struggle to say. Father *was* actually a knight, though not a knight-errant for a while. He had been too big by then to fit into a suit of plate-armour or heft a heavy sword around, and knights had stopped doing that for many years anyway. The Industrialization had swiftly made the pageantry of adventure obsolete.

Father wheezed as we reminded him of his knighthood, as if ashamed. He put his hammy hands in our hair and rubbed. I winced through it, as usual, because he always forgot about the pins in my long hair, something my brother didn't have to worry about. Mother gave us the peeled indigos, her hands per-fumed with the citrus. She was the one who taught me how to place the pins in my hair, both of us in front of the mirror looking like different sized versions of each other.

I looked out the windows of our cabin, fascinated by how everything outside slowly became bluer and darker as we moved away from the City-of-Long-Shadows, which lies between the two hemispheres of Day and Night. Condensation crawled across the corners of the double-glazed panes as the train took us further east. Being a studious girl even at that age, I deduced from school lessons that the air outside was becoming rapidly colder as we neared Night's hemisphere, which has never seen a single ray of our sun and is theorized to be entirely frozen. The train, of course, was kept warm by the same steam and machinery that powered its tire-less wheels and kept its lamps and twinkling chandeliers aglow.

"Are you excited to see the Nightmare? It was one of the first to be captured and tamed. The gentleman we're visiting is very proud to be its captor," said Father.

"Yes!" screamed Velag. "Does it still have teeth? And claws?" he asked, his eyes wide.

"I would think so." Father nodded.

"Is it going to be in chains?"

"I hope so, Velag. Otherwise it might get loose and . . ." He paused for dramatic effect. I froze in fear. Velag looked eagerly at him. "Eat you both up!" he bellowed, tickling us with his huge hands. It took all my willpower not to scream. I looked at Velag's delighted expression to keep me calm, reminding myself that these were just Father's hands jabbing my sides.

"Careful!" Mother said sharply, to my relief. "They'll get the fruit all over." The indigo segments were still in our laps, on the napkins Mother had handed to us. Father stopped tickling us, still grinning.

"Do you remember what they look like?" Velag asked, as if trying to see how many questions he could ask in as little time as possible. He had asked this one before, of course. Father had fought Nightmares, and even killed some, when he was a knight-errant.

"We never really saw them, son," said Father. He touched the window. "Out there, it's so cold you can barely feel your own fingers, even in armour."

We could see the impenetrable walls of the forests pass us by—shaggy, snarled mare-pines, their leaves black as coals and branches supposedly twisted into knots by the Nightmares to tangle the path of intruders. The high, hoary tops of the trees shimmered ever so slightly in the scarce light sneaking over the horizon, which they sucked in so hungrily. The moon was brighter here than in the City, but at its jagged crescent, a broken gemstone behind the scudding clouds. We were still in Evening, but had encroached onto the Nightmares' outer territories, marked by the forests that extended to the foothills. After the foothills, there was no more forest, because there was no more light. Inside our cabin, under bright electric lamps, sitting on velvet-lined bunks, it was hard to believe that we were actually in the land of Nightmares. I wondered if they were in the trees right now, watching our windows as we looked out.

"It's hard to see them, or anything, when you're that cold, and," Father breathed deeply, gazing at the windows, "they're very hard to see." It made me uneasy, hearing him say the same thing over and over. We were passing the very forests he travelled through as a knight-errant, escorting pioneers.

"Father's told you about this many times, dear," Mother interjected, peering at Father with worried eyes. I watched. Father smiled at her and shook his head.

"That's alright, I like telling my little tykes about my adventures. I guess you'll see what a Nightmare looks like tomorrow, eh? Out in the open. Are you excited?" he asked, perhaps forgetting that he'd already asked. Velag shouted in the affirmative again.

Father looked down at me, raising his bushy eyebrows. "What about you, Valyzia?"

I nodded and smiled.

I wasn't excited. Truth be told, I didn't want to see it at all. The idea of capturing and keeping a Nightmare seemed somehow disrespectful in my heart, though I didn't know the word then. It made me feel weak and confused, because I was and always had been so afraid of them and had been taught to be.

I wondered if Velag had noticed that Father had once again refused to actually describe a Nightmare. Even in his most excitable retellings of his brushes with them, he never described them as more than walking shadows. There was a grainy sepia-toned photograph of him during his younger vigils as a knight-errant above the mantle of our living-room fireplace. It showed him mounted on a horse, dressed in his plate-armour and fur-lined surcoat, raising his longsword to the skies (the blade was cropped from the picture by its white border). Clutched in his other plated hand was something that looked like a blot of black, as if the chemicals of the photograph had congealed into a spot, attracted by some mystery or heat. The shape appeared to bleed back into the black background.

It was, I had been told, the head of a Nightmare Father had slain. It was too dark a thing to be properly caught by whatever early photographic engine had captured his victory. The blot had no distinguishing features apart from two vague points emerging from the rest of it, like horns or ears. That head earned him a large part of the fortune he later used to start up his contracting business. We never saw it, because Nightmares' heads and bodies were burned or gibbeted by knights-errant, who didn't want to bring them into the City for fear of attracting their horde. The photograph had been a source of dizzying pride for my young self, because it meant that my father was one of the bravest people I knew. At other times, it just made me wonder why he couldn't describe something he had once beheaded, and held in his hand as a trophy.

My indigo finished, Mother took the napkin and wiped my hands with it. My brother still picked at his. A waiter brought us a silver platter filled with sugar-dusted pastries, their centres soft with warm fudge and grünberry jam. We'd already finished off supper, brought under silver domes that gushed steam when the waiters raised them with their white-gloved hands, revealing chopped fungus, meat dumplings, sour cream and fermented salad. Mother told Velag to finish the indigo before he touched the pastries. Father ate them with as much gusto as I did. I watched him lick his powdered fingers, that had once held the severed head of a Nightmare.

When it was time for respite, the cabin lights were shut off and the ones in the corridor were dimmed. I was relieved my parents left the curtains of the windows open as we retired, because I didn't want it to be completely dark. It was dim enough outside that we could fall asleep. It felt unusual to go to bed with windows uncovered for once.

I couldn't help imagine, as I was wont to do, that as our train moved through Evening's forested fringes, the Nightmares would find a way to get on board. I wondered if they were already on the train. But the presence of my family, all softly snoring in their bunks (Velag above me, my parents opposite us); the periodic, soothing flash of way-station lights passing by outside; the sigh of the sliding doors at the end of the carriage opening and closing as porters, waiters, and passengers moved through the corridors; the sweet smell of the fresh sheets and pillow on my bunk—these things lulled me into a sleep free of bad dreams, despite my fear of seeing the creature we'd named bad dreams after, face-to-face, the next vigil.

When I was six I stopped sleeping in my parents' room and started sleeping in the same room as my brother. At the time of this change, I was abnormally scared of the dark (and consider, reader, that this was a time when fear of the dark was as normal and acceptable as the fear of falling from a great height). So scared that I couldn't fall sleep after the maids came around and closed our sleep-shutters and drew the curtains, to block out the western light for respite.

The heavy clatter of the wooden slats being closed every respite's eve was like a note of foreboding for me. I hunkered under the blankets, rigid with anxiety as the maids filed out of the room with their lanterns drawing wild shadows on the walls. Then the last maid would close the door, and our room would be swallowed up by those shadows.

In the chill darkness that followed, I would listen to the clicking of Nightmares' claws as they walked up and down the corridors of our shuttered house. Our parents had often told me that it was just rats in the walls and ceiling, but I refused to believe it. Every respite I would imagine one of the Nightmare intruders slinking into our room, listening to its breathing as it came closer to my bed and pounced on me, not being able to scream as it sat on my chest and ran its reeking claws through my hair, winding it into knots around its long fingers and laughing softly.

Enduring the silence for what seemed like hours, I would begin to wail and cry until Velag threw pillows at me and Mother came to my side to shush me with her kisses. To solve the problem, my parents tried keeping the sleep-shutters open through the hours of respite and moved my brother to a room on the windowless east-facing side of the house when he complained. Unfortunately, we require the very dark we fear to fall asleep. The persistent burning line of the horizon beyond the windows, while a comforting sight, left me wide awake for most of respite.

In the end Velag and I were reunited and the shutters closed once more, because Father demanded that I not be coddled when my brother had learned to sleep alone so bravely. I often heard my parents arguing about this, since Mother thought it was madness to try and force me not to be afraid. Most of my friends from school hadn't and wouldn't sleep without their parents until they were at least eleven or twelve. Father was adamant, demanding that we learn to be strong and brave in case the Nightmares ever found a way to overrun the city.

It's a strange thing, to be made to feel guilty for learning too well something that was ingrained in us from the moment we were born. Now nightmare is just a word, and it's unusual to even think that the race that we gave that name might still be alive somewhere in the world. When Velag and I were growing up, Nightmares were the enemy.

Our grandparents told us about them, as did our parents, as did our teachers, as did every book and textbook we had ever come across. Stories of a time when guns hadn't been invented, when knights-errant roved the frigid forest paths beyond the City-of-Long-Shadows to prove their manhood and loyalty to the Monarchy and its Solar Church, and to extend the borders of the city and find new resources. A time coming to a close when I was born, even as the expansion continued onward faster than ever.

I remember my schoolteacher drawing the curtains and holding a candle to a wooden globe of our planet to show us how the sun made Night and Day. She took a piece of chalk and tapped where the candlelight turned to shadow on the globe. "That's us," she said, and moved the chalk over to the shadowed side. "That's them," she said.

Nightmares have defined who we are since we crawled out of the hot lakes at the edge of fiery Day and wrapped the steaming bloody skins of slaughtered animals around us to walk upright, east into the cooler marches of our world's Evening. We stopped at the alien darkness we had never seen before, not just because of the terrible cold that clung to the air the further we walked, but because of what we met at Evening's end.

A race of walking shadows, circling our firelight with glittering eyes, felling our explorers with barbed spears and arrows, snatching our dead as we fled from their ambushes. Silently, these unseen, lethal guardians of Night's bitter frontier told us we could go no further. But we couldn't go back towards Day, where the very air seems to burn under the sun's perpetual gaze.

So we built our villages where sun's light still lingers and the shadows are longest before they dissolve into Evening. Our villages grew into towns, and our towns grew into the City-of-Long-Shadows, and our City grew along the Penumbra until it reached the Seas-of-Storms to the north and the impassable crags of World's-Rim (named long before we knew this to be false) to the south. For all of history, we looked behind our shoulders at the gloaming of the eastern horizon, where the Nightmares watched our progress.

So the story went, told over and over.

We named bad dreams after them because we thought Nightmares were their source, that they sent spies into the city to infect our minds and keep us afraid of the dark, their domain. According to folklore, these spies could be glimpsed upon waking abruptly. Indeed, I'd seen them crouching malevolently in the corner of the bedroom, wreathed in the shadows that were their home, slinking away with impossible speed once I looked at them.

There are no Nightmares left alive anywhere near the City-of-Long-Shadows, but we still have bad dreams and we still see their spies sometimes when we wake. Some say they are spirits of their race, or survivors. I'm not convinced. Even though we have killed all the Nightmares, our own half-dreaming minds continue to populate our bedrooms with their ghosts, so we may remember their legacy.

To date, none of our City's buildings have windows or doors on their east-facing walls.

And so the train took us to the end of our civilization. There are many things I remember about Weep-for-Day, though in some respects those memories feel predictably like the shreds of a disturbing dream. Back then it was just an outpost, not a hill-station town like it is now. The most obvious thing to remember is how it sleeted or snowed all the time. I know now that it's caused by moist convective winds in the atmosphere carrying the warmth of the sun from Day to Night, their loads of fat clouds scraping up against the mountains of the Penumbra for all eternity and washing the foothills in their frozen burden. But to my young self, the constant crying of that bruised sky was just another mystery in the world, a sorcery perpetrated by the Nightmares.

I remember, of course, how dark it was. How the people of the outpost carried bobbing lanterns and acrid magenta flares that flamed even against the perpetual wind and precipitation. How everyone outside (including us) had to wear goggles and thick protective suits lined with the fur of animals to keep the numbing cold of outer Evening out. I had never seen such darkness outdoors, and it felt like being asleep while walking. To think that beyond the mountains lay an absence of light even deeper was unbelievable.

I remember the tall poles that marked turns in the curving main road, linked by the ever-present electric and telegraph wires that made such an outpost possible. The bright gold-and-red pennants of the Monarchy fluttered from those poles, dulled by lack of light. They all showed a sun that was no longer visible from there.

I remember the solar shrines—little huts by the road, with small windows that lit up every few hours as chimes rang out over the windy outpost. Through the doors you could see the altars inside; each with an electric globe, its filament flooded with enough voltage to make it look like a hot ball of fire. For a minute these shrines would burn with their tiny artificial suns, and the goggled and suited inhabitants of Weep-for-Day would huddle around them like giant flies, their shadows wavering lines on the streaks of light cast out on the muddy snow or ice. They would pray on their knees, some reaching out to rub the faded ivory crescents of sunwyrm fangs on the altars.

Beyond the road and the slanted wet roofs of Weep-for-Day, there was so little light that the slope of the hill was barely visible. The forested plain beyond was nothing but a black void that ended in the faint glow of the horizon—the last weak embers in a soot-black fireplace just doused with water.

I couldn't see our City-of-Long-Shadows, which filled me with an irrational anxiety that it was gone forever, that if we took the train back we would find the whole world filled with darkness and only Night waiting on the other side.

But these details are less than relevant. That trip changed me and changed the course of my life not because I saw what places beyond the City-of-Long-Shadows looked like, though seeing such no doubt planted the seeds of some future grit in me. It changed me because I, with my family by my side, witnessed a living Nightmare, as we were promised.

The creature was a prisoner of Vorin Tylvur, who was at the time the Consul of Weep-for-Day, a knight like Father, and an appointed privateer and mining coordinator of the Penumbral territories. Of course, he is now well remembered for his study of Nightmares in captivity, and his campaigns to expand the Monarchy's territories into Evening. The manse we stayed in was where he and his wife lived, governing the affairs of the outpost and coordinating expansion and exploration.

I do not remember much of our hosts, except that they were adults in the way all adults who aren't parents are, to little children. They were kind enough to me.

I couldn't comprehend the nature of condescension at that age, but I did find the cooing manner of most adults who talked to me boring, and they were no different. Though I'm grateful for their hospitality to my family, I cannot, in retrospect, look upon them with much returned kindness.

They showed us the imprisoned Nightmare on the second vigil of our stay. It was in the deepest recesses of the manse, which was more an oversized, glorified bunker on the hill of Weep-for-Day than anything else. We went down into a dank, dim corridor in the chilly heart of that mound of crustal rock to see the prisoner.

"I call it Shadow. A little nickname," Sir Tylvur said with a toothy smile, his huge moustache hanging from his nostrils like the dead wings of some poor misbegotten bird trapped in his head. He proved himself right then to have not only a startling lack of imagination for a man of his intelligence and inquisitiveness, but also a grotesquely inappropriate sense of levity.

It would be dramatic and untruthful to say that my fear of darkness receded the moment I set eyes on the creature. But something changed in me. There, looking at this hunched and shivering thing under the smoky blaze of the flares its armoured gaolers held to reveal it to its captor's guests, I saw that a phantom flayed was just another animal.

Sir Tylvur had made sure that its light-absorbent skin would not hinder our viewing of the captured enemy. There is no doubt that I feared it, even though its skin was stripped from its back to reveal its glistening red muscles, even though it was clearly broken and defeated. But my mutable young mind understood then, looking into its shining black eyes—the only visible feature in the empty dark of its face—that it knew terror just as I or any human did. The Nightmare was scared. It was a heavy epiphany for a child to bear, and I vomited on the glass observation wall of its cramped holding cell.

Velag didn't make fun of me. He shrank into Mother's arms, trying to back away from the humanoid silhouette scrabbling against the glass to escape the light it so feared; a void-like cutout in reality but for that livid wet wound on its back revealing it to be as real as us. It couldn't, or would not, scream or vocalize in any way. Instead, we just heard the squeal of its spiderlike hands splayed on the glass, claws raking the surface.

I looked at Father, standing rigid and pale, hands clutched into tight fists by his sides. The same fists that held up the severed head of one of this creature's race in triumph so many years ago. Just as in the photograph, there were the horn-like protrusions from its head, though I still couldn't tell what they were. I looked at Mother who, despite the horrific vision in front of us, despite her son clinging to her waist, reached down in concern to wipe the vomit from my mouth and chin with bare fingers, her gloves crumpled in her other hand.

As Sir Tylvur wondered what to do about his spattered glass wall, he decided to blame the Nightmare for my reaction and rapped hard on the cell with the hilt of his sheathed ceremonial sword. He barked at the prisoner, wanting to frighten it away from the glass, I suppose. The only recognisable word in between his grunts was "Shadow." But as he called it by that undignified, silly nickname, the thing stopped its frantic scrabbling. Startled, Sir Tylvur stepped back. The two armoured gaolers stepped back as well, flares wavering in the gloom of the cell. I still don't know why the Nightmare stopped thrashing, and I never will know for sure. But at that moment I thought it recognised the nickname its captor had given it, and recognise that it was being displayed like a trophy. Perhaps it wanted to retain some measure of its pride.

The flarelight flickered on its eyes, which grew brighter as moisture gathered on them. It was clearly in pain from the light. I saw that it was as tall as a human, though it looked smaller because of how crouched into itself it was. It cast a shadow like any other animal, and that shadow looked like its paler twin, dancing behind its back. Chains rasped on the wet cell floor, shackled to its limbs. The illuminated wound on its back wept pus, but the rest of it remained that sucking, indescribable black that hurt the human eye.

Except something in its face. It looked at us, and out of that darkness came a glittering of wet obsidian teeth as unseen lips peeled back. I will never forget that invisible smile, whether it was a grimace of pain or a taunting leer.

"Kill it," Velag whispered. And that was when Mother took both our hands tight in hers and pulled us away from the cell. She marched us down that dank corridor, leaving the two former knights-errant, Father and Sir Tylvur, staring into that glimmering cell at the spectre of their past.

That night, in the tiny room we'd been given as our quarters, I asked Velag if the Nightmare had scared him.

"Why should it scare me," he said, face pale in the dim glow of the small heating furnace in the corner of the chamber. "It's in chains."

"You just looked scared. It's okay to be scared. I was too. But I think it was as well."

"Shut up. You don't know what you're saying. I'm going to sleep," he said, and turned away from me, his cot groaning. The furnace hissed and ticked.

"I think papa was scared also. He didn't want to see a Nightmare again," I said to Velag's back.

That was when my brother pounced off his cot and on top of me. I was too shocked to scream. My ingrained submission to his power as an elder male authority figure took over. I gave no resistance. Sitting on my small body, Velag took my blanket and shoved it into my mouth. Then, he snatched my pillow and held it over my face. Choking on the taste of musty cloth, I realised I couldn't breathe. I believed that my brother was about to kill me then. I truly believed it. I could feel the pressure of his hands through the pillow, and they were at that moment the hands of something inhuman. I was more terrified then than I'd ever been in my entire short life, plagued though I'd always been by fear.

He held the pillow over my head for no more than four seconds, probably less. When he raised it off my face and pulled the blanket out of my mouth he looked as shaken as I was. His eyes were wet with tears, but in a second his face was twisted in a grimace.

"Never call papa a coward. Never call papa a coward. Papa was never afraid.

Do you hear me? You never had to sleep alone in the dark, you don't know. I'm going to grow up and be like papa and kill them. I'll kill them," he hissed the words into my face like a litany. I started crying, unable and probably too scared to tell him I hadn't called Father a coward. I could still barely breathe, so flooded was I with my own tears, so drunk on the air he had denied me. Velag went back to his cot and wrapped himself in his blanket, breathing heavily.

As I shuddered with stifled sobs, I decided that I would never tell my parents about this, that I would never have Velag punished for this violence. I didn't forgive him, not even close, but that is what I decided.

I was seventeen the last time I saw Velag. I went to visit him at the Royal Military Academy's boarding school. He had been there for four years already. We saw him every few moons when he came back to the City proper to visit. But I wanted to see the campus for myself. It was a lovely train ride, just a few hours from the central districts of the City-of-Long-Shadows to the scattered hamlets beyond it.

It was warmer and brighter out where the Academy was. The campus was beautiful, sown with pruned but still wild looking trees and plants that only grew further out towards Day, their leaves a lighter shade of blue and their flowers huge, craning to the west on thick stems. The sun still peered safely behind the edge of the world, but its gaze was bright enough to wash the stately buildings of the boarding school with a fiery golden-red light, sparkling in the waxy leaves of vines winding their way around the arched windows. On every ornate, varnished door was a garish propaganda poster of the Dark Lord of Nightmares, with his cowled cloak of shadows and black sword, being struck down by our soldiers' bayoneted guns.

I sat with Velag in a cupola in the visitors' garden, which was on a gentle bluff. In the fields adjacent, his fellow student-soldiers played tackleball, their rowdy calls and whistles ringing through the air. We could see heavy banks of glowing, sun-lit storm-clouds to the west where the atmosphere boiled and churned in the heat of Day, beyond miles of shimmering swamp-forests and lakes. To the east, a faint moon hung over the campus, but no stars were visible so close to Day.

Velag looked so different from the last time I saw him. His pimples were vanishing, the sallow softness of adolescence melting away to reveal the man he was to become. The military uniform, so forbidding in red and black, suited his tall form. He looked smart and handsome in it. It hurt me to see him shackled in it, but I could see that he wore it with great pride.

He held my hand and asked about my life back home, about my plans to apply to the College of Archaeology at the University of St. Kataretz. He asked about our parents. He told me how gorgeous and grown-up I looked in my dress, and said he was proud of me for becoming a "prodigy." I talked to him with a heavy ache in my chest, because I knew with such certainty that we hardly knew each other, and would get no chance to any time soon, as he would be dispatched to the frontlines of Penumbral Conquest.

As if reading my thoughts, his cheek twitched with what I thought was guilt, and he looked at the stormy horizon. Perhaps he was remembering the night on which he told me he would grow up and kill Nightmares like Father—a promise he was keeping. He squeezed my hand.

"I'll be alright, Val. Don't you worry."

I gave him a rueful smile. "It's not too late. You can opt to become a civilian after graduation and come study with me at St. Kataretz. Ma and papa would think no less of you. You could do physics again, you loved it before. We can get an apartment in Pemluth Halls, share the cost. The University's right in the middle of the City, we'd have so much fun together."

"I can't. You know that. I want this for myself. I want to be a soldier, and a knight."

"Being a knight isn't the same thing as it was in papa's time. He was independent, a privateer. Things have changed. You'll be a part of the military. Knighthoods belong to them now and they're stingy with them. They mostly give them to soldiers who are wounded or dead, Velag."

"I'm in military school, by the saints, I know what a knighthood is or isn't. Please don't be melodramatic. You're an intelligent girl."

"What's that got to do with anything?"

"I'm going. I have more faith in my abilities than you do."

"I have plenty of faith in you. But the Nightmares are angry now, Velag. We're wiping them out. They're scared and angry. They're coming out in waves up in the hills. More of our soldiers are dying than ever before. How can I not worry?"

His jaw knotted, he glared down at our intertwined hands. His grip was limp now. "Don't start with your theories about the benevolence of Nightmares. I don't want to hear it. They're not scared, they *are* fear, and we'll wipe them off the planet if need be so that you and everybody else can live without that fear."

"I'm quite happy with my life, thank you. I'd rather you be alive for ma and papa and me than have the terrible horde of the Nightmares gone forever."

He bit his lip and tightened his hand around mine again. "I know, little sister. You're sweet to worry so. But the Monarchy needs me. I'll be fine. I promise."

And that was the end of the discussion as far as he was concerned. I knew it was no point pushing him further, because it would upset him. This was his life, after all. The one he had chosen. I had no right to belittle it. I didn't want to return to the City on bad terms with him. We made what little small talk was left to make, and then we stood and kissed each other on the cheek, and I hugged him tight and watched him walk away.

What good are such promises as the one he made on our final farewell, even if one means them with all of one's heart? He was dispatched right after his graduation a few moons later, without even a ceremony because it was wartime. After six moons of excited letters from the frontlines at the Penumbral Mountains, he died with a Nightmare's spear in his chest, during a battle that earned the Monarchy yet another victory against the horde of darkness. Compared to the thousands of Nightmares slaughtered during the battle with our guns and cannons, the Monarchy's casualties were small. And yet, my parents lost their son, and I my brother.

In death, they did give Velag the knighthood he fought so hard for. Never have I hated myself so much for being right.

When Velag was being helped out of Mother by doctors in the city, my father had been escorting pioneers in the foothills. I see him in his armour, the smell of heated steel and cold sweat cloying under his helm, almost blind because of the visor, sword in one hand, knotted reins and a flaming torch in the other, his mount about to bolt. A new metal coal-chamber filled with glowing embers strapped to his back to keep the suit warm, making his armour creak and pop as it heated up, keeping him off-balance with its weight and hissing vents but holding the freezing cold back a little. Specks of frozen water flying through the torch-lit air like dust, biting his eyes through the visor. His fingers numb in his gloves, despite the suit. The familiar glitter of inhuman eyes beyond the torch-light, nothing to go by but reflections of fire on his foes, who are invisible in the shadows, slinking alongside the caravan like bulges in the darkness. The only thing between the Nightmares and the pioneers with their mounts and carriages weighed down by machinery and thick coils of wire and cable that will bring the light of civilization to these wilds, is him and his contingent.

How long must that journey have been to him? How long till he returned alive to see his wife and new son Velag in a warm hospital room, under the glow of a brand new electric light?

By the time I was born, armourers had invented portable guns and integrated hollow cables in the suit lining to carry ember-heated water around armour, keeping it warmer and enabling mercenaries and knights-errant to go deeper into Evening. The pioneers followed, bringing their technology to the very tops of the foothills, infested with Nightmares. That was when Father stopped going, lest he never return. They had new tools, but the war had intensified. He had a son and daughter to think of, and a wife who wanted him home.

When I watched Velag's funeral pyre blaze against the light of the west on Barrow-of-Bones cremation hill, I wondered if the sparks sent up into the sky by his burning body would turn to stardust in the ether and migrate to the sun to extend its life, or whether this was his final and utter dissolution. The chanting priest from the Solar Church seemed to have no doubts on the matter. Standing there, surrounded by the fossilized stone ribs of Zhurgeith, last of the sunwyrms and heraldic angel of the Monarchy and Church (who also call it Dragon), I found myself truly unsure about what death brings for maybe the first time in my life, though I'd long practised the cynicism that was becoming customary of my generation.

I thought with some trepidation about the possibility that if the Church was right, the dust of Velag's life might be consigned to the eternal dark of cosmic limbo instead of finding a place in the sun, because of what he'd done to me as a child. Because I'd never forgiven him, even though I told myself I had.

How our world changes.

The sun is a great sphere of burning gas, ash eventually falls down, and my dead brother remains in the universe because my family and I remember him, just as I remember my childhood, my life, the Nightmares we lived in fear of, the angel Dragon whose host was wiped out by a solar flare before we could ever witness it.

Outside, the wind howls so loud that I can easily imagine it is the sound of trumpets from a frozen city, peopled by the horde of darkness. Even behind the insulated metal doors and heated tunnels of the cave bunkers that make up After-Day border camp, I can see my breath and need two thick coats to keep warm. My fingers are like icicles as I write. I would die very quickly if exposed to the atmosphere outside. And yet, here I am, in the land of Nightmares.

Somewhere beyond these Penumbral Mountains, which we crossed in an airtight train, is the City-of-Long-Shadows. I have never been so far from it. Few people have. We are most indebted to those who mapped the shortest route through the mountains, built the rails through the lowest valleys, blasted new tunnels, laid the foundations for After-Day. But no one has gone beyond this point. We—I and the rest of the expeditionary team from St. Kataretz—will be the first to venture into Night. It will be a dangerous endeavour, but I have faith in us, in the brave men and women who have accompanied me here.

My dear Velag, how would you have reacted to see these beautiful caves I sit in now, to see the secret culture of your enemy? I am surrounded by what can only be called their art, the lantern-light making pale tapestries of the rock walls on which Nightmares through the millennia scratched to life the dawn of their time, the history that followed, and its end, heralded by our arrival into their world.

In this history we are the enemy, bringing the terror of blinding fire into Evening, bringing the advanced weapons that caused their genocide. On these walls we are drawn in pale white dyes, bioluminescent in the dark, a swarm of smeared light advancing on the Nightmares' striking, jagged-angled representations of themselves, drawn in black dyes mixed from blood and minerals.

In this history Nightmares were alive when the last of the sunwyrms flew into Evening to scourge the land for prey. Whether this is truth or myth we don't know, but it might mean that Nightmares were around long before us. It might explain their adaptation to the darkness of outer Evening—their light-absorbent skin ancient camouflage to hide from sunwyrms under cover of the forests of Evening. We came into Evening with our fire (which they show sunwyrms breathing) and pale skins, our banners showing Dragon and the sun, and we were like a vengeful race of ghosts come to kill on behalf of those disappeared angels of Day, whom they worshipped to the end—perhaps praying for our retreat.

In halls arched by the rib cages and spines of ancient sunwyrm skeletons I have seen burial chambers; the bones of Nightmares and their children (whom we called imps because we didn't like to think of our enemy having young) piled high. Our bones lie here too, not so different from theirs. Tooth-marks show that they ate their dead, probably because of the scarcity of food in the fragile ecosystem of

Evening. It is no wonder then that they ate our dead too—as we feared. It was not out of evil but need.

We have so much yet to learn.

Perhaps it would have given you some measure of peace, Velag, to know that the Nightmares didn't want to destroy us, only to drive us back from their home. Perhaps not.

Ilydrin tells me it is time for us to head out. She is a member of our expedition—a biologist—and my partner. To hide the simple truth of our affection seems here, amidst the empty city of a race we destroyed, an obscenity. Confronted by the vast, killing beauty of our planet's second half, the stagnant moralities of our city-state appear a trifle. I adore Ilydrin, and I am glad she is here with me.

One team will stay here while ours heads out into Night. Ilydrin and I took a walk outside to test our Night-shells—armoured environmental suits to protect us from the lethal cold. We trod down from the caves of After-Day and into the unknown beyond, breath blurring our glass faceplates, our head-lamps cutting broad swathes through the snow-swarmed dark. We saw nothing ahead but an endless plain of ice—perhaps a frozen sea.

No spectral spires, no black banners of Night, no horde of Nightmares waiting to attack, no Dark Lord in his distant obsidian palace (an image Ilydrin and I righteously tore down many times in the form of those Army posters, during our early College vigils). We held each others' gloved hands and returned to camp, sweating in our cramped shells, heavy boots crunching on the snow. I thought of you, Father, bravely venturing into bitter Evening to support your family. I thought of you, Brother, nobly marching against the horde for your Monarchy. I thought of you, Mother, courageously carrying your first child alone in that empty house before it became *our* home. I thought of you, Shadow—broken, tortured prisoner, baring your teeth to your captors in silence.

Out there, I was shaking—nervous, excited, queasy. I wasn't afraid.

I have Father's old photograph with the Nightmare's head (he took it down from above the mantelpiece after Velag died). I have a photograph of Mother, Father, Velag and I all dressed up before our trip to Weep-for-Day. And finally, a smiling portrait of Velag in uniform before he left for the Academy, his many pimples invisible because of the monochrome softness of the image. I keep these photographs with me, in the pockets of my overcoat, and take them out sometimes when I write.

So it begins. I write from the claustrophobic confines of the Night-Crawler, a steam-powered vehicle our friends at the College of Engineering designed (our accompanying professors named it with them, no doubt while drunk in a bar on University-Street). It is our moving camp. We'll sleep and eat and take shelter in it, and explore further and longer—at least a few vigils, we hope. If its engines fail, we'll have to hike back in our shells and hope for the best. The portholes are frosted over, but the team is keeping warm by stoking the furnace and singing. Ilydrin comes and tells me, her lips against my hair: "Val. Stop writing and join us." I tell her I will, in a minute. She smiles and walks back to the rest, her face flushed and soot-damp from the open furnace. I live for these moments.

I will lay down this pen now. A minute.

I don't know what we'll find out here. Maybe we *will* find the Dark Lord and his gathered horde of Nightmares. But at this point, even the military doesn't believe that, or they would have opposed the funding for this expedition or tried to hijack it.

Ilydrin says there's unlikely to be life so deep into Night—even Nightmares didn't venture beyond the mountains, despite our preconceptions. But she admits we've been wrong before. Many times. What matters is that we are somewhere new. Somewhere other than the City-of-Long-Shadows and the Penumbral territories, so marked by our history of fear. We need to see the rest of this world, to meet its other inhabitants—if there are others—with curiosity, not apprehension. And I know we will, eventually. This is our first, small step. I wish you were here with me to see it, Velag. You were but a child on this planet.

We might die here. It won't be because we ventured into evil. It will be because we sought new knowledge. And in that, I have no regrets, even if I'm dead when this is read. A new age is coming. Let this humble account be a preface to it.

The girl-thing who went out for sushi

PAT CADIGAN

Pat Cadigan was born in Schenectady, New York, and now lives in London with her family. She made her first professional sale in 1980 and has subsequently come to be regarded as one of the best new writers of her generation. Her story "Pretty Boy Crossover" has appeared on several critics' lists as among the best science fiction stories of the 1980s, and her story "Angel" was a finalist for the Hugo Award, the Nebula Award, and the World Fantasy Award (one of the few stories ever to earn that rather unusual distinction). Her short fiction—which has appeared in most of the major markets, including Asimov's Science Fiction and The Magazine of Fantasy & Science Fiction—has been gathered in the collections Patterns and Dirty Work. Her first novel, Mindplayers, was released in 1987 to excellent critical response, and her second novel, Synners, released in 1991, won the Arthur C. Clarke Award as the year's best science fiction novel, as did her third novel, Fools, making her the only writer ever to win the Clarke Award twice. Her other books include the novels Dervish Is Digital, Tea from an Empty Cup, Reality Used to Be a Friend of Mine, and Cellular, and, as editor, the anthology The Ultimate Cyberpunk, as well as two making-of-movie books and four media tie-in novels.

Here's a fast-paced story about a spacefaring construction worker injured in an accident in orbit around Jupiter who must not only deal with recovery but with the problems and benefits of changing your species altogether. . . .

Nine decs into her second hitch, Fry hit a berg in the Main ring and broke her leg. And she didn't just splinter the bone—compound fracture! Yow! What a mess! Fortunately, we'd finished servicing most of the eyes, a job that I thought was more busy-work than work-work. But those were the last decs before Okeke-Hightower hit and everybody had comet fever.

There hadn't been an observable impact on the Big J for almost three hundred (Dirt) years—Shoemaker-Somethingorother—and no one was close enough to get a good look back then. Now every news channel, research institute, and moneybags everywhere in the Solar System was paying Jovian Operations for a ringside view. Every JovOp crew was on the case, putting cameras on cameras and back-up cameras on the back-up cameras—visible, infrared, X-ray, and everything else. Fry was pretty excited about it herself, talking about how great it was she would get to see it live. Girl-thing should have been watching where she wasn't supposed to be going.

I was coated and I knew Fry's suit would hold, but featherless bipeds are prone to vertigo when they're injured. So I blew a bubble big enough for both of us, cocooned her leg, pumped her full of drugs, and called an ambulance. The jellie with the rest of the crew was already on the other side of the Big J. I let them know we'd scrubbed and someone would have to finish the last few eyes in the radian for us. Girl-thing was one hell of a stiff two-stepper, staying just as calm as if we were unwinding end-of-shift. The only thing she seemed to have a little trouble with was the O. Fry picked up consensus orientation faster than any other two-stepper I'd ever worked with but she'd never done it on drugs. I tried to keep her distracted by telling her all the gossip I knew and when I ran out, I made shit up.

Then all of a sudden, she said, "Well, Arkae, that's it for me."

Her voice was so damned final, I thought she was quitting. And I deflated because I had taken quite a liking to our girl-thing. I said, "Aw, honey, we'll all miss you out here."

But she laughed. "No, no, no, I'm not leaving. I'm going out for sushi."

I gave her a pat on the shoulder, thinking it was the junk in her system talking. Fry was no ordinary girl-thing—she was great out here but she'd always been special. Back in the Dirt, she'd been a brain-box, top-level scholar *and* a beauty queen. That's right—a featherless biped genius beauty queen. Believe it or leave it, as Sheerluck says.

Fry'd been with us for three and half decs when she let on about being a beauty queen. The whole crew was unwinding end-of-shift—her, me, Dubonnet, Sheerluck, Aunt Chovie, Splat, Bait, Glynis, and Fred—and we all about lost the O.

"Wow," said Dubonnet, "did you ask for whirled peas, too?" I didn't understand the question but it sounded like a snipe. I triple-smacked him and suggested he respect someone else's culture.

But Fry said, "No, I don't blame any a youse asking. That stuff really is so silly. Why people still bother with such things, I sure don't know. We're supposed to be so advanced and enlightened and it still matters how a woman looks in a bathing suit. Excuse me, a biped woman," she added, laughing a little. "And no, the subject of whirled peas never came up."

"If that's how you really felt," Aunt Chovie said, big, serious eyes and all eight arms in curlicues, "why'd you go along with it?"

"It was the only way I could get out here," Fry said.

"Not really?" said Splat, a second before I woulda blurted out the same thing.

"Yes, really. I got heavy metal for personal appearances and product endorsements, plus a full scholarship, my choice of school." Fry smiled and I thought it was the way she musta smiled when she was crowned Queen of the Featherless Biped Lady Geniuses or whatever it was. It wasn't insincere, but a two-stepper's face is just another muscle group; I could tell it was something she'd learned to do. "I saved as much as I could so I'd have enough for extra training after I graduated. Geology degree."

"Dirt geology though," said Sheerluck. It used to be Sherlock but Sheerluck'll be the first to admit she's got more luck than sense.

"That's why I saved for extra training," Fry said. "I had to do the best I could with the tools available. You know how that is. All-a-youse know."

We did.

FRY HAD WORKED with some other JovOp crews before us, all of them mixed–two-steppers and sushi. I guess they all liked her and vice versa but she clicked right into place with us, which is pretty unusual for a biped and an all-octo crew. I liked her right away and that's saying something because it usually takes me a while to resonate even with sushi. I'm okay with featherless bipeds, I really am. Plenty of sushi–more than will admit to it–have a problem with the species just on general principle, but I've always been able to get along with them. Still, they aren't my fave flave to crew with out here. Training them is harder, and not because they're stupid. Two-steppers just aren't made for this. Not like sushi. But they keep on coming and most of them tough it out for at least one square dec. It's as beautiful out here as it is dangerous. I see a few outdoors almost every day, clumsy starfish in suits.

That's not counting the ones in the clinics and hospitals. Doctors, nurses, nurse-practitioners, technicians, physiotherapists, paramedics—they're all your standard featherless biped. It's the law. Fact: you cannot legally practice any kind of medicine in any form other than basic human, not even if you're already a doctor, supposedly because all the equipment is made for two-steppers. Surgical instruments, operating rooms, sterile garments, even rubber gloves—the fingers are too short and there aren't enough of them. Ha, ha, a little sushi humour. Maybe it's not that funny to you but fresh catch laugh themselves sick.

I don't know how many two-steppers in total go out for sushi in a year (Dirt or Jovian), let alone how their reasons graph, but we're all over the place out here and Census isn't in my orbit, so for all I know half a dozen two-steppers apply every eight decs. Stranger things have happened.

In the old days, when I turned, nobody did it unless they had to. Most often, it was either terminal illness or permanent physical disability as determined by the biped standard: i.e., conditions at sea level on the third planet out. Sometimes, however, the disability was social, or more precisely, legal. Original Generation out here had convicts among the gimps, some on borrowed time.

Now, if you ask us, we say OG lasted six years but we're all supposed to use the Dirt calendar, even just to each other (everyone out here gets good at converting on the fly), which works out to a little over seventy by Dirt reckoning. The bipeds claim that's three generations not just one. We let them have that their way, too, because, damn can they argue. About *anything*. It's the way they're made. Bipeds are strictly binary, it's all they know: zero or one, yes or no, right or wrong.

But once you turn, that strictly binary thinking's the first thing to go, and fast. I never heard anyone say they miss it; I know I don't.

ANYWAY, I GO see Fry in one of the Gossamer ring clinics. A whole wing is closed off, no one gets in unless they're on The List. If that isn't weird enough for you, there's a two-stepper in a uniform stuck to the floor, whose only job is checking The List. I'm wondering if I'm in the wrong station, but the two-stepper finds me on The List and I may go in and see La Soledad y Godmunds-dottir. It takes me a second to get who she means. How'd our girl-thing get Fry out of that? I go through an airlock-style portal and there's another two-stepper waiting to escort me. He uses two poles with sticky tips to move himself along and he does all right but I can see this is a new skill. Every so often, he manoeuvres so one foot touches floor so he can feel more like he's walking.

When you've been sushi as long as I have, two-steppers are pretty transparent. I don't mean that as condescending as it sounds. After all, I was a two-stepper once myself. We all started out as featherless bipeds, none of us was born sushi. But a lot of us feel we were born to *be* sushi, a sentiment that doesn't go down too well with the two-steppers who run everything. Which doesn't make it any less true.

My pal the poler and I go a full radian before we get to another air-lock. "Through there," he says. "I'll take you back whenever you're ready."

I thank him and swim through, wondering what dim bulb thought he was a good idea, because he's what Aunt Chovie calls surplus to requirements. The few conduits off this tube are sealed and there's nothing to hide in or behind. I know Fry is so rich that she has to hire people to spend her money for her, but I'm thinking she should hire people smart enough to know the difference between spending and wasting.

There's our girl, stuck to the middle of a hospital bed almost as big as the ring-berg that put her in it. She's got a whole ward to herself—all the walls are folded back to make one big private room. There are some nurses down at the far end, sitting around sipping coffee bulbs. When they hear me come in, they start un-sticking and reaching for things but I give them a full eight-OK—*Social call, I'm nobody, don't look busy on my account*—and they all settle down again.

Sitting up in her nest of pillows, Fry looks good, if a little undercooked. There's about three centimetres of new growth on her head and it must be itchy because she keeps scratching it. In spite of the incubator around her leg, she insists I give her a full hug, four by four, then pats a spot beside her. "Make your-self to home, Arkae."

"Isn't there a rule about visitors sitting on the bed?" I say, curling a couple of arms around a nearby hitching-post. It's got a fold-out seat for biped visitors. This place has everything.

"Yeah. The rule is, it's okay if I say it's okay. Check it—this bed's bigger than a lot of apartments I've had. The whole crew could have a picnic here. In fact, I wish they would." She droops a little. "How is everyone, really busy?"

I settle down. "There's always another lab to build or hardware to service or data to harvest," I say, careful, "if that's what you mean." The way her face flexes, I know it isn't.

"You're the only one who's come to see me," she says.

"Maybe the rest of the crew weren't on The List."

"What list?" she says. So I tell her. Her jaw drops and all at once, two nurses appear on either side of the bed, nervous as hell, asking if she's all right. "I'm fine, I'm fine," she snaps at them. "Go away, gimme some privacy, will you?"

They obey a bit reluctantly, eyeing me like they're not too sure about how safe she is with me squatting on the bedspread.

"Don't yell at *them*," I say after a bit. "Something bad happens to you, it's their fault. They're just taking care of you the best way they know how." I uncurl two arms, one to gesture at the general surroundings and the other to point at the incubator, where a quadjillion nanorectics are mending her leg from the marrow out, which, I can tell you from personal experience, *itches*. A *lot*. No doubt that's contributing to her less-than-sparkly disposition—what the hell can you do about itchy *bone marrow?*—and what I just told her doesn't help.

"I should have known," she fumes, scratching her head. "It's the people I work for."

That doesn't make sense. JovOp couldn't afford anything like this. "I think you're a little confused, honey," I say. "If we even *thought* JovOp had metal that heavy, it'd be Sushi Bastille Day, heads would—"

"No, these people are back in the Dirt. My image is licensed for advertising and entertainment," she says. "I thought there'd be less demand after I came out here—out of sight, out of mind, you know? But apparently the novelty of a beauty queen in space has yet to wear off."

"So you're still rich," I say. "Is that so bad?"

She makes a pain face. "Would you agree to an indefinite contract just to be rich? Even *this* rich?"

"You couldn't get rich on an indefinite contract," I say gently, "and no union's stupid enough to let anybody take one."

She thinks for a few seconds. "All right, how about this: did you ever think you owned something and then you found out it owned you?"

"*Oh . . .*" Now I get it. "Can they make you go back?"

"They're trying," Fry says. "A court order arrived last night, demanding I hit the Dirt as soon as I can travel. The docs amended it so *they* decide when it's safe, but that won't hold them off forever. You know any good lawyers? Out here?" she added.

"Well, yeah. Of course, they're all sushi."

Fry lit up. "Perfect."

NOT EVERY CHAMBERED Nautilus out here is a lawyer—the form is also a popular choice for librarians, researchers, and anyone else in a data-heavy line of work—but every lawyer in the Jovian system is a chambered Nautilus. It's not a legal restriction the way it is with bipeds and medicine, just something that took root and turned into tradition. According to Dove, who's a partner in the firm our union keeps on retainer, it's the sushi equivalent of powdered wigs and black robes, which we have actually seen out here from time to time when two-steppers from certain parts of the Dirt bring their own lawyers with them.

Dove says no matter how hard biped lawyers try to be professional, they all break out with some kind of weird around their sushi colleagues. The last time the union had to renegotiate terms with JovOp, the home office sent a canful of corporate lawyers out of the Dirt. Well, from Mars, actually, but they weren't Martian citizens and they went straight back to No. 3 afterwards. Dove wasn't involved but she kept us updated as much as she could without violating any regulations.

Dove's area is civil law and sushi rights, protecting our interests as citizens of the Jovian system. This includes not only sushi and sushi-in-transition but pre-ops as well. Any two-stepper who files a binding letter of intent for surgical conversion is legally sushi.

Pre-ops have all kinds of problems—angry relatives, *rich* angry relatives with injunctions from some Dirt supreme court, confused/troubled children, heartbroken parents and ex-spouses, lawsuits and contractual disputes. Dove handles all that and more: identity verification, transfer of money and property, biometric resets, as well as arranging mediation, psychological counselling (for anyone, including angry relatives), even religious guidance. Most bipeds would be surprised to know how many of those who go out for sushi find God, or something. Most of us, myself included, fall into the latter category but there are plenty of the organised religion persuasion. I guess you can't go through a change that drastic without discovering your spiritual side.

Fry wasn't officially a pre-op yet, but I knew Dove would be the best person she could talk to about what she'd be facing if she decided to go through with it. Dove is good at figuring out what two-steppers want to hear and then telling them what they need to hear in a way that makes them listen. I thought it was psychology but Dove says it's closer to linguistics.

As Sheerluck would say, don't ask me, I just lurk here.

THE NEXT DAY, I show up with Dove and List Checker looks like she's never seen anything like us before. She's got our names but she doesn't look too happy about it, which annoys me. List-checking isn't a job that requires any emotion from her.

"*You're* the attorney?" she says to Dove, who is eye-level with her, tentacles sedately furled.

"Scan me again if you need to," Dove says good-naturedly. "I'll wait. Mom always said, 'Measure twice, cut once.'"

List Checker can't decide what to do for a second or two, then scans us both again. "Yes, I have both your names here. It's just that—well, when she said an attorney, I was expecting—I thought you'd be . . . a . . . a . . ."

She hangs long enough to start twisting before Dove relents and says, "Biped." Dove still sounds good-natured but her tentacles are now undulating freely. "You're not from around here, are you?" she asks, syrupy-sweet, and I almost rupture not laughing.

"No," List Checker says in a small voice. "I've never been farther than Mars before."

"If the biped on the other side of that portal is equally provincial, better warn 'em." Then as we go through, Dove adds, "Too late!"

It's the same guy with the poles but when Dove sees him, she gives this crazy whooping yell and pushes right into his face so her tentacles are splayed out on his skin.

"You son of a bitch!" she says, really happy.

And then the Poler says, "Hiya, Mom."

"Oh. Kay," I say, addressing anyone in the universe who might be listening. "I'm thinking about a brain enema. Is now a good time?"

"Relax," Dove says. "'Hiya Mom' is what you say when anyone calls you a son of a bitch."

"Or 'Hiya, Dad,'" says Poler, "depending."

"Aw, you all look alike to me," Dove says. "It's a small universe, Arkae. Florian and I got taken hostage together once, back in my two-stepper days."

"Really?" I'm surprised as hell. Dove never talks about her biped life; hardly any of us do. And I've never heard of anyone running into someone they knew pre-sushi purely by chance.

"I was a little kid," Poler says. "Ten Dirt-years. Dove held my hand. Good thing I met her when she still had one."

"He was a creepy little kid," Dove says as we head for Fry's room. "I only did it so he wouldn't scare our captors into killing all of us."

Poler chuckles. "Then why you let me keep in touch with you after it was all over?"

"I thought if I could help you be less creepy, you wouldn't inspire any more hostage-taking. Safer for everybody."

I can't remember ever hearing about anyone still being friends with a biped from before they were sushi. I'm still trying to get my mind around it as we go through the second portal.

When Fry sees us, there's a fraction of a second when she looks startled before she smiles. Actually, it's more like horrified. Which makes *me* horrified. I told her I was bringing a sushi lawyer. Girl-thing never got hiccups before, not even with the jellies and that's saying something. Even when you know they're all AIs, jellies can take some getting used to no matter what shape you're in, two-stepper or sushi.

"Too wormy?" Dove says and furls her tentacles as she settles down on the bed a respectful distance from Fry.

"I'm sorry," Fry says, making the pain face. "I don't mean to be rude or bigoted—"

"Forget about it," Dove says. "Lizard brain's got no shame."

Dove's wormies bother her more than my suckers? I think, amazed. *Lizard brain's not too logical, either.*

"Arkae tells me you want to go out for sushi," Dove goes on chattily. "How much do you know about it?"

"I know it's a lot of surgery but I think I have enough money to cover most of it."

"Loan terms are extremely favourable. You could live well on that money and still make payments—"

"I'd like to cover as much of the cost as I can while my money's still liquid."

"You're worried about having your assets frozen?" Immediately Dove goes from chatty to brisk. "I can help you with that whether you turn or not. Just say I'm your lawyer, the verbal agreement's enough."

"But the money's back in the Dirt—"

"And *you're* here. It's all about where *you* are. I'll zap you the data on loans and surgical options—if you're like most people, you probably already have a form in mind but it doesn't hurt to know about all the—"

Fry held up a hand. "Um, Arkae? You mind if I talk to my new lawyer alone?"

My feelings are getting ready to be hurt when Dove says, "Of course she doesn't. Because she knows that the presence of a third party screws up that confidentiality thing. Right, Arkae?"

I feel stupid and relieved at the same time. Then I see Fry's face and I know there's more to it.

THE FOLLOWING DAY the crew gets called up to weed and re-seed the Halo. Comet fever strikes again. We send Fry a silly cheer-up video to say we'll see her soon.

I personally think it's a waste of time sowing sensors in dust when we've already got eyes in the Main ring. Most of the sensors don't last as long as they're supposed to and the ones that do never tell us anything we don't already know. Weeding—picking up the dead sensors—is actually more interesting. When the dead sensors break down, they combine with the dust, taking on odd shapes and textures and even odder colorations. If something especially weird catches my eye, I'll ask to keep it. Usually, the answer's no. Recycling is the foundation of life out here—mass in, mass out; create, un-create, re-create, allathat. But once in a while, there's a surplus of something because nothing evens out exactly all the time, and I get to take a little good-luck charm home to my bunk.

We're almost at the Halo when the jellie tells us whichever crew seeded last time didn't weed out the dead ones. So much for mass in, mass out. We're all surprised; none of us ever got away with doing half a job. We have to hang in the jellie's belly high over the North Pole and scan the whole frigging Halo for materials markers. Which would be simple except a lot of what should be there isn't show-ing up. Fred makes us deep-scan three times but nothing shows on Metis and there's no sign that anything leaked into the Main ring.

"Musta all fell into the Big J," says Bait. He's watching the aurora flashing be-low us like he's hypnotised, which he probably is. Bait's got this thing about the polar hexagon anyway.

"But so many?" Splat says. "You know they're gonna say that's too many to be an accident."

"Do we know *why* the last crew didn't pick up the dead ones?" Aunt Chovie's already tensing up. If you tapped on her head, you'd hear high C-sharp.

"No," Fred says. "I don't even know which crew it was. Just that it wasn't us."

Dubonnet tells the jellie to ask. The jellie tells us it's put in a query but because it's not crucial, we'll have to wait.

"Frigging tube-worms," Splat growls, tentacles almost knotting up. "They do that to feel important."

"Tube worms are AIs, they don't feel," the jellie says with the AI serenity that can get so maddening so fast. "Like jellies."

Then Glynis speaks up: "Scan Big J."

"Too much interference," I say. "The storms—"

"Just humour me," says Glynis. "Unless you're in a hurry?"

The jellie takes us down to just above the middle of the Main ring and we pro-grade double-time. And son of a bitch—is this crazy or is this the new order?—we get some hits in the atmosphere.

But we shouldn't. It's not just the interference from the storms—Big J gravi-tates the hell out of anything it swallows. Long before I went out for sushi (and that was quite a while ago), they'd stopped sending probes into Jupiter's atmo-sphere. They didn't just hang in the clouds and none of them ever lasted long enough to reach liquid metallic hydrogen. Which means the sensors should just be atoms, markers crushed out of existence. They can't still be in the clouds unless something is keeping them there.

"That's gotta be a technical fault," Splat says. "Or something."

"Yeah, I'm motion sick, I lost the O," says Aunt Chovie, which is the current crew code for *Semaphore only*.

Bipeds have sign language and old-school semaphore with flags but octo-crew semaphore is something else entirely. Octo-sem changes as it goes, which means each crew speaks a different language, not only from each other, but also from one conversation to the next. It's not transcribable, either, not like spoken-word communication because it works by consensus. It's not completely uncrackable but even the best decryption AI can't do it in less than half a dec. Five days to decode a conversation isn't exactly efficient.

To be honest, I'm kinda surprised the two-steppers who run JovOp are still let-ting us get away with it. They're not what you'd call big champions of privacy, especially on the job. It's not just sushi, either—all their two-stepper employees, in the Dirt or all the way out here, are under total surveillance when they're on the clock. That's total as in a/v everywhere: offices, hallways, closets, and toilets.

Bait says that's why JovOp two-steppers always look so grim—they're all holding it in till quitting time.

But I guess as long as we get the job done, they don't care how we wiggle our tentacles at each other or what colour we are when we do it. Besides, when you're on the job out here, you don't want to worry about who's watching you because they'd *better* be. You don't want to die in a bubble waiting for help that isn't coming because nobody caught the distress signal when your jellie blew out.

So anyway, we consider the missing matter and the markers we shouldn't have been picking up on in Big J's storm systems and we whittle it down to three possibilities: the previous crew returned to finish the job but someone forgot to enter it into the record; a bunch of scavengers blew through with a trawler and neutralised the markers so they can resell the raw materials; or some dwarf star at JovOp is seeding the clouds in hope of getting an even closer look at the Okeke-Hightower impact.

Number three is the stupidest idea—even if some of the sensors actually survive till Okeke-Hightower hits, they're in the wrong place, and the storms will scramble whatever data they pick up—so we all agree that's probably it. After a little more discussion, we decide not to let on and when JovOp asks where all the missing sensors are, we'll say we don't know. Because the Jupe's honest truth is, we don't.

We pick up whatever we can find, which takes two J-days, seed the Halo with new ones, and go home. I call over to the clinic to check how Fry's doing and find out if she managed to get the rest of the crew on The List so we can have that picnic on her big fat bed. But I get Dove, who tells me that our girl-thing is in surgery.

DOVE SAYS THAT, at Fry's own request, she's not allowed to tell anyone which sushi Fry's going out for, including us. I feel a little funny about that—until we get the first drone.

It's riding an in-out skeet, which can slip through a jellie double-wall without causing a blowout. JovOp uses them to deliver messages they consider sensitive—whatever that means—and that's what we thought it was at first.

Then it lights up and we're looking at this image of a two-stepper dressed for broadcast. He's asking one question after another on a canned loop; in a panel on his right, instructions on how to record, pause, and playback are scrolling on repeat.

The jellie asks if we want to get rid of it. We toss the whole thing in the waste chute, skeet and all, and the jellie poops it out as a little ball of scrap, to become some scavenger's lucky find.

Later, Dubonnet files a report with JovOp about the unauthorised intrusion. JovOp gives him a receipt but no other response. We're all expecting a reprimand for failing to detect the skeet's rider before it got through. Doesn't happen.

"Somebody's drunk," Bait says. "Query it."

"No, don't," says Splat. "By the time they're sober, they'll have to cover it up or their job's down the chute. It never happened, everything's eight-by-eight."

"Until someone checks our records," Dubonnet says and tells the jellie to query, who assures him that's a wise thing to do. The jellie has been doing this sort of thing more often lately, making little comments. Personally, I like those little touches.

Splat, however, looks annoyed. "I was joking," he says, enunciating carefully. They can't touch you for joking no matter how tasteless, but it has to be clear. We laugh, just to be on the safe side, except for Aunt Chovie who says she doesn't think it was very funny because she can't laugh unless she really feels it. Some people are like that.

Dubonnet gets an answer within a few minutes. It's a form message in legalese but this gist is, *We heard you the first time, go now and sin no more.*

"They *all* can't be drunk," Fred says. "Can they?"

"Can't they?" says Sheerluck. "You guys have crewed with me long enough to know how fortune smiles on me and mine."

"Spoken like a member of the Church of The Four-Leaf Horseshoe," Glynis says.

Fred perks right up. "Is that that new casino on Europa?" he asks. Fred loves casinos. Not gambling, just casinos. The jellie offers to look it up for him.

"Synchronicity is a real thing, it's got *math*," Sheerluck is saying. Her colour's starting to get a little bright; so is Glynis's. I'd rather they don't give each other ruby-red hell while we're all still in the jellie. "And the dictionary definition of serendipity is, 'Chance favours the prepared mind.'"

"*I'm* prepared to go home and log out, who's prepared to join me?" Dubonnet says before Glynis can sneer openly. I like Glynis, vinegar and all, but sometimes I think she should have been a crab instead of an octopus.

OUR PRIVATE QUARTERS are supposed to have no surveillance except for the standard safety monitoring.

Yeah, we don't believe that for a nano-second. But if JovOp ever got caught in the act, the unions would eat them alive and poop out the bones to fertilise Europa's germ farms. So either they're even better at it than any of us can imagine or they're taking a calculated risk. Most sushi claim to believe the former; I'm in the latter camp. I mean, they watch us so much already, they've gotta want to look at something else for a change.

We share the typical octo-crew quarters—eight rooms around a large common area. When Fry was with us, we curtained off part of it for her but somehow she was always spilling out of it. Her stuff, I mean—we'd find underwear bobbing around in the lavabo, shoes orbiting a lamp (good thing she only needed two), live-paper flapping around the room in the air currents. All the time she'd spent out here and she still couldn't get the hang of housekeeping in zero gee. It's the sort of thing that stops being cute pretty quickly when you've got full occupancy, plus one. I could tell she was trying, but eventually we had to face the truth: much as we loved her, our resident girl-thing was a slob.

I thought that was gonna be a problem but she wasn't even gone a day before it felt like there was something missing. I'd look around expecting to see some item of clothing or jewellery cruising past, the latest escapee from one of her not-terribly-secure reticules.

"So who wants to bet that Fry goes octo?" Splat says when we get home.

"Who'd want to bet she doesn't?" replies Sheerluck.

"Not me," says Glynis, so sour I can feel it in my crop. I'm thinking she's going to start again with the crab act, pinch, pinch, pinch but she doesn't. Instead, she air-swims down to the grotto, sticks to the wall with two arms and folds the rest up so she's completely hidden. She misses our girl-thing and doesn't want to talk at the moment, but she also doesn't want to be completely alone, either. It's an octo thing—sometimes we want to be alone but not necessarily by ourselves.

Sheerluck joins me at the fridge and asks, "What do you think? Octo?"

"I dunno," I say, and I honestly don't. It never occurred to me to wonder but I'm not sure if that's because I took it for granted she would. I grab a bag of kribble.

Aunt Chovie notices and gives me those big serious eyes. "You can't just live on crunchy krill, Arkae."

"I've got a craving," I tell her.

"Me, too," says Bait. He tries to reach around from behind me and I knot him.

"Message from Dove," says Dubonnet just before we start wrestling and puts it on the big screen.

There's not actually much about Fry, except that she's coming along nicely with another dec to go before she's done. Although it's not clear to any of us whether that means Fry'll be *all* done and good to go, or if Dove's just referring to the surgery. Then we get distracted with all the rest of the stuff in the message.

It's was full of clips from the Dirt, two-steppers talking about Fry like they all knew her and what it was like out here and what going out for sushi meant. Some two-steppers didn't seem to care much but some of them were stark spinning bug-fuck.

I mean, it's been a great big while since I was a biped and we live so long out here that we tend to morph along with the times. The two-stepper I was couldn't get a handle on me as I am now. But then neither could the octo I was when I finished rehab and met my first crew.

I didn't choose octo—back then, surgery wasn't as advanced and nanorectics weren't as commonplace or as programmable so you got whatever the doctors thought gave you the best chance of a life worth living. I wasn't too happy at first but it's hard to be unhappy in a place this beautiful, especially when you feel so good physically all the time. It was somewhere between three and four J-years after I turned that people could finally choose what kind of sushi they went out for, but I got no regrets. Any more. I've got it smooth all over.

Only I don't feel too smooth listening to two-steppers chewing the air over things they don't know anything about and puking up words like *abominations,* *atrocities,* and *sub-human monsters.* One news program even runs clips from the most recent re-make of *The* Goddam *Island Of* Fucking *Dr. Moreau.* Like that's holy writ or something.

I can't stand more than a few minutes before I take my kribble into my bolt-hole, close the hatch, and hit soundproof.

A little while later, Glynis beeps. "You know how 'way back in the extreme dead past, people in the Dirt thought everything in the universe revolved around them?" She pauses but I don't answer. "Then the scope of human knowledge expanded and we all know that was wrong."

"So?" I grunt.

"Not everybody got the memo," she says. She waits for me to say something. "Come on, Arkae—are *they* gonna get to see Okeke-Hightower?"

"I'd like to give them a ride on it," I say.

"None of them are gonna come out here with us abominations. They're all gonna cuddle up with each other in the Dirt and drown in each other's shit. Until they all do the one thing they were pooped into this universe to do, which is become extinct."

I open the door. "You're really baiting them, you know that?"

"Baiting who? There's nobody listening. Nobody here except us sushi," she says, managing to sound sour and utterly innocent both at the same time. Only Glynis.

I MESSAGE DOVE to say we'll be Down Under for at least two J-days, on loan to OuterComm. Population in the outer part of the system, especially around Saturn has doubled in the last couple of J-years and will probably double again in less time. The civil communication network runs below the plane of the solar disk and it's completely dedicated—no governments, no military, just small business, entertainment, and social interaction. Well, so far, it's completely dedicated but nobody's in any position for a power grab yet.

OuterComm is an Ice Giants operation and originally it served only the Saturn, Uranus, and Neptune systems. No one seems to know exactly where the home office is—i.e. which moon. I figure even if they started off as far out as Uranus, they've probably been on Titan since they decided to expand to Jupiter.

Anyway, their technology is crazy-great. It still takes something over forty minutes for *Hello* to get from the Big J to Saturn and another forty till you hear, *Who the hell is this?* but you get less noise than a local call on JovOp. JovOp wasn't too happy when the entertainment services started migrating to OuterComm and things got kind of tense. Then they cut a deal: OuterComm got all the entertainment and stayed out of the education business, at least in the Jovian system. So everything's fine and JovOp loans them anything they need like a big old friendly neighbour but there's still plenty of potential for trouble. Of *all* kinds.

The Jovian system is the divide between the inner planets and the outer. We've had governments that tried to align with the innies and others that courted the outies. The current government wants the Big J officially designated as an outer world, not just an ally. Saturn's been fighting it, claiming that Big J wants to take over and build an empire.

Which is pretty much what Mars and Earth said when the last government was trying to get inner status. Earth was a little more colourful about it. There were two-steppers hollering that it was all a plot by monsters and abominations—i.e. us—to get our unholy limbs on fresh meat for our unholy appetites. If Big J got inner planet status, they said, people would be rounded up in the streets and shipped out to be changed into unnatural, subhuman creatures with no will of their own. Except for the most beautiful women, who would be kept as is and chained in brothels where—well, you get the idea.

That alone would be enough to make me vote outie, except the Big J is really neither outie nor innie. The way I see it, there's inner, there's outer, and there's us. Which doesn't fit the way two-steppers do things because it's not binary.

THIS WAS ALL sort of bubbling away at the back of my mind while we worked on the comm station but in an idle sort of way. I was also thinking about Fry, wondering how she was doing, and what shape she'd be in the next time I saw her. I wondered if I'd recognise her.

Now, that sounds kind of silly, I guess because you don't recognise someone that, for all intents and purposes, you've never seen before. But it's that spiritual thing. I had this idea that if I swam into a room full of sushi, all kinds of sushi, and Fry was there, I would know. And if I gave it a little time, I'd find her without anyone having to point her out.

No question, I loved Fry the two-stepper. Now that she was sushi, I wondered if I'd be in love with her. I couldn't decide whether I liked that idea or not. Normally I keep things simple: sex, and only with people I like. It keeps everything pretty smooth. But *in love* complicates everything. You start thinking about partnership and family. And that's not so smooth because we don't reproduce. We've got new sushi and fresh sushi, but no sushi kids.

We're still working on surviving out here but it won't always be that way. I could live long enough to see that. Hell, there are still a few OG around, although I've never met them. They're all out in the Ice Giants.

WE'RE HOME HALF a dec before the first Okeke-Hightower impact, which sounds like plenty of time but it's close enough to make me nervous. Distances out here aren't safe, even in the best top-of-the-line JovOp can. I hate being in a can anyway. If anyone ever develops a jellie for long-distance travel, I'll be their best friend forever. But even in the can, we had to hit three oases going and coming to refuel. Filing a flight plan guaranteed us a berth at each one but only if we were on time. And there's all kinds of shit that could have made us late. If a berth was available we'd still get it. But if there wasn't, we'd have to wait and hope we didn't run out of stuff to breathe.

Bait worked the plan out far enough ahead to give us generous ETA windows. But you know how it is—just when you need everything to work the way it's supposed to, anything that hasn't gone wrong lately suddenly decides to make up for lost time. I was nervous all the way out, all through the job, and all the way back. The last night on the way back I dreamed that just as we were about to re-enter JovOp space, Io exploded and took out everything in half a radian. While we were trying to figure out what to do, something knocked us into a bad spiral that was gonna end dead centre in Big Pink. I woke up with Aunt Chovie and Splat peeling me off the wall—*so* embarrassing. After that, all I wanted to do was go home, slip into a jellie, and watch Okeke-Hightower meet Big J.

By this time, the comet's actually in pieces. The local networks are all-comet news, all the time, like there's nothing else in the solar system or even the universe for that matter. The experts are saying it's following the same path as the old Shoemaker-Levy and there's a lot of chatter about what that means. There those who don't think it's a coincidence and Okeke-Hightower is actually some kind of message from an intelligence out in the Oort cloud or even beyond, and instead of letting it crash into Big J, we ought to try catching it, or at least parts of it.

Yeah, that could happen. JovOp put out a blanket no-fly—jellies only, no cans. Sheerluck suggests JovOp's got a secret mission to grab some fragments but that's ridiculous. I mean, aside from the fact that any can capable of doing that would be plainly visible, the comet's been sailing around in pieces for over half a dozen square decs. There were easier places in the trajectory to get a piece but all the experts agreed the scans showed nothing in it worth the fortune it would cost to mount that kind of mission. Funny how so many people forgot about that; suddenly, they're all shoulda-woulda-coulda, like non-buyer's remorse. But don't get me started on politics.

I leave a message for Dove saying we're back and getting ready to watch the show. What comes back is an auto-reply saying she's out of the office, reply soonest. Maybe she's busy with Fry, who probably has comet fever like everyone else but maybe even more so, since this will be like the big moment that kicks off her new life. If she's not out of the hospital, I hope they've got a screen worthy of the event.

We all want to see with our naked eyes. Well, our naked eyes and telescopes. Glynis is bringing a screen for anyone who wants a really close-up look. Considering the whole thing's gonna last about an hour start to finish, maybe that's not such a bad idea. It could save us some eyestrain.

When the first fragment hits, I find myself thinking about the sensors that fell into the atmosphere. They've got to be long gone by now and even if they're not, there's no way we could pick up any data. It would all be just noise.

Halfway through the impacts, the government overrides all the communication for a recorded, no-reply announcement: martial law's been declared, everybody go home. Anyone who doesn't is dust.

This means we miss the last few hits, which pisses us off even though we all agree it's not a sight worth dying for. But when we get home and can't even get an instant replay, we start wondering. Then we start ranting. The government's gonna have a lot of explaining to do and the next election ain't gonna be a lovefest and when did JovOp turn into a government lackey. There's nothing on the news—and I mean, *nothing*, it's all re-runs. Like this is actually two J-days ago and what just happened never happened.

"Okay," says Fred, "what's on OuterComm?"

"You want to watch soap operas?" Dubonnet fumes. "Sure, why not?"

We're looking at the menu when something new appears: it's called the Soledad y Gottmundsdottir Farewell Special. The name has me thinking we're about to see Fry in her old two-stepper incarnation but what comes up on the screen is a chambered Nautilus.

"Hi, everybody. How do you like the new me?" Fry says.

"What, is she going to law school?" Aunt Chovie says, shocked.

"I'm sorry to leave you a canned good-bye because you've all been so great," Fry goes on and I have to knot my arms together to keep from turning the thing off. This doesn't sound like it's gonna end well. "I knew even before I came out here that I'd be going out for sushi. I just couldn't decide what kind. You guys had me thinking seriously about octo—it's a pretty great life and everything you do matters. Future generations—well, it's going to be amazing out here. Life that adapted to space. Who knows, maybe someday Jovian citizens will change bodies like two-steppers change their clothes. It could happen.

"But like a lot of two-steppers, I'm impatient. I know, I'm not a two-stepper anymore and I've got a far longer lifespan now so I don't have to be impatient. But I am. I wanted to be part of something that's taking the next step—the next *big* step—right now. I really believe the Jupiter Colony is what I've been looking for."

"The Jupiter Colony? They're cranks! They're suicidal!" Glynis hits the ceiling, banks off a wall, and comes down again.

Fry unfurls her tentacles and lets them wave around freely. "Calm down, whoever's yelling," she says, sounding amused. "I made contact with them just before I crewed up with you. I knew what they were planning. They wouldn't tell me when, but it wasn't hard to figure out that the Okeke-Hightower impact was the perfect opportunity. We've collected some jellies, muted them and put in yak-yak loops. I don't know how the next part works, how we're going to hitch a ride with the comet—I'm not an astrophysicist. But if it works, we'll seed the clouds with ourselves.

"We're all chambered Nautiluses on this trip. It's the best form for packing a lot of data. But we've made one small change: we're linked together, shell-to-shell, so we all have access to each other's data. Not too private but we aren't going into exile as separate hermits. There should still be some sensors bobbing around in the upper levels—the Colony's had allies tossing various things in on the sly. We can use whatever's there to build a cloud-borne colony.

"We don't know for sure it'll work. Maybe we'll all get gravitated to smithereens. But if we can fly long enough for the jellies to convert to parasails—the engineers figured that out, don't ask me—we might figure out not only how to survive but thrive.

"Unfortunately, I won't be able to let you know. Not until we get around the interference problem. I don't know much about that, either, but if I last long enough, I'll learn.

"Dove says right now, you're all Down Under on loan to OuterComm. I'm going to send this message so it bounces around the Ice Giants for a while before it gets to you and with any luck, you'll find it not too long after we enter the atmosphere. I hope none of you are too mad at me. Or at least that you don't stay mad at me. It's not entirely impossible that we'll meet again some day. If we do, I'd like it to be as friends.

"Especially if the Jovian independence movement gets—" she laughs. "I was about to say, 'gets off the ground.' If the Jovian independence movement ever achieves a stable orbit—or something. I think it's a really good idea. Anyway, good bye for now.

"Oh, and Arkae?" Her tentacles undulate wildly. "I had no idea wormy would feel so good."

WE JUST GOT that one play before the JCC blacked it out. The feds took us all in for questioning. Not surprising. But it wasn't just Big J feds—Dirt feds suddenly popped up out of nowhere, some of them in person and some of them long-distance via comm units clamped to mobies. The latter is a big waste unless there's some benefit to having a conversation as slowly as possible. Because even a fed on Mars can't do anything about the speed of light—it's still gonna be at least an hour between the question and the answer, usually more.

The Dirt feds who were actually here were all working undercover, keeping an eye on things, and reporting whatever they heard or saw to HQ back in the Dirt. This didn't go down so well with most of us out here, even two-steppers. It became a real governmental crisis, mainly because no one in charge could get their stories straight. Some were denying any knowledge of Dirt spies, some were trying to spin it so it was all for our benefit, so we wouldn't lose any rights—don't ask me which ones, they didn't say. Conspiracy theories blossomed faster than anyone could keep track.

Finally, the ruling council resigned; the acting council replacing them till the next election are almost all sushi. That's a first.

It's still another dec and a half till the election. JovOp usually backs two-steppers but there are noticeably fewer political ads for bipeds this time around. I think even they can see the points on the trajectory.

A lot of sushi are already celebrating, talking about the changing face of government in the Jovian system. I'm not quite ready to party. I'm actually a little bit worried about us. We were born to be sushi but we weren't born sushi. We all started out as two-steppers and while we may have shed binary thinking, that doesn't mean we're completely enlightened. There's already some talk about how most of the candidates are chambered Nautiluses and there ought to be more octos or puffers or crabs. I don't like the sound of that but it's too late to make a break for the Colony now. Not that I would. Even if Fry and all her fellow colonists are surviving and thriving, I'm not ready to give up the life I have for a whole new world. We'll just have to see what happens.

Hey, I told you not to get me started on politics.

the memcordist

Lavie Tidhar

Lavie Tidhar grew up on a kibbutz in Israel, has traveled widely in Africa and Asia, and has lived in London, the South Pacific island of Vanuatu, and Laos; after a spell in Tel Aviv, he's currently living back in England again. He is the winner of the 2003 Clarke-Bradbury Prize (awarded by the European Space Agency), was the editor of Michael Marshall Smith: The Annotated Bibliography, *and the anthologies* A Dick & Jane Primer for Adults, *the three-volume* The Apex Book of World SF *series, and two anthologies edited with Rebecca Levene,* Jews vs. Aliens *and* Jews vs. Zombies. *He is the author of the linked story collection* HebrewPunk, *and, with Nir Yaniv, the novel* The Tel Aviv Dossier, *and the novella chapbooks* An Occupation of Angels, Cloud Permutations, Jesus and the Eighfold Path, *and* Martian Sands. *A prolific short story writer, his stories have appeared in* Interzone, Asimov's Science Fiction, Clarkesworld, Apex Magazine, Strange Horizons, Postscripts, Fantasy Magazine, Nemonymous, Infinity Plus, Aeon, Book of Dark Wisdom, Fortean Bureau, Old Venus, *and elsewhere, and have been translated into seven languages. His novels include* The Bookman *and its two sequels,* Camera Obscura *and* The Great Game, Osama: A Novel *(which won the World Fantasy Award as the year's Best Novel in 2012),* The Violent Century, *and* A Man Lies Dreaming. *His most recent book is a big, multifaceted SF novel,* Central Station.

It's been said that everyone is the hero of their own drama. Here's a poignant look at a future where everyone else *gets to watch as well . . . .*

POLYPHEMUS PORT, TITAN, YEAR FORTY-THREE

Beyond the dome the ice-storms of Titan rage; inside it is warm, damp, with the smell of sewage seeping through and creepers growing through the walls of the aboveground dwellings. He tries to find her scent in the streets of Polyport and fails.

Hers was the scent of basil, and the night. When cooking, he would sometimes crush basil leaves between his fingers. It would bring her back, for just a moment, bring her back just as she was the first time they'd met.

Polyphemus Port is full of old memories. Whenever he wants, he can recall them, but he never does. Instead he tries to find them in old buildings, in half-familiar signs. There, the old Baha'i temple where they'd sheltered one rainy afternoon, and watched a weather hacker dance in the storm, wreathed in raindrops. There, what had once been a smokes-bar, now a shop selling surface crawlers. There, a doll house, for the sailors off the ships. It had been called Madame Sing's, now it's called Florian's. Dolls peek out of the windows, small naked figures in the semblance of teenage boys and girls, soft and warm and disposable, with their serial numbers etched delicately into the curve of a neck or thigh. His feet know the old way and he walks past the shops, away from the docks and into a row of boxlike apartments, the co-op building creepers overgrowing the walls and peeking into windows—where they'd met, a party in the Year Seventeen of the Narrative of Pym.

He looks up, and as he does he automatically checks the figures that rise up, always, in the air before him. The number of followers hovers around twenty-three million, having risen slightly on this, his second voyage to Titan in so many years. A compilation feed of Year Seventeen is running concurrently, and there are messages from his followers, flashing in the lower right corner, which he ignores.

Looking up at her window, a flower pot outside—there used to be a single red flower growing there, a carnivorous Titan Rose with hungry, teeth-ringed suckers— her vice at the time. She'd buy the plant choice goat meat in the market every day. Now the flower pot is absent and the window is dark and she, too, is long gone.

Is she watching too, somewhere, he wonders—does she see me looking up and searching for her, for traces of her in a place so laid and overlaid with memories until it was impossible to tell which ones were original, and which the memory of a memory?

He thinks it's unlikely. Like the entire sum of his life, this journey is for his benefit, is ultimately about him. We are what we are—and he turns away from her window, and the ice-storm howls above his head, beyond the protective layer of the dome. There had been a storm that night, too, but then, this was Titan, and there was always a storm.

ON BOARD THE *GEL BLONG MOTA*, EARTH-TO-MARS VOYAGE, YEAR FIVE

There are over twenty million followers on this day of the Narrative of Pym, and Mother is happy, and Pym is happy too, because he'd snuck out when Mother was asleep, and now he stands before the vast porthole of the ship—in actuality a wall-sized screen—and watches space, and the slowly moving stars beyond.

The *Gel Blong Mota* is an old ship, generations of *Man Spes* living and dying inside as it cruises the solar system, from Earth, across the inner and outer system, all the way to Jettisoned and Dragon's World before turning back, doing the same route again and again. Pym is half in love with Joy, who is the same age as him and will one day, she confides in him, be captain of this ship. She teaches him asteroid pidgin, the near-universal language of Mars and the belt, and he tells her about Earth, about volcanoes and storms and the continental cities. He was not born on Earth, but he has lived there four of his five years, and he is nervous to be away, but also happy, and excited, and it's all very confusing. Nearly fifty million watched him leave Earth, and they didn't go in the elevator, they went in an old passenger RLV and he floated in the air when the gravity stopped, and he wasn't sick or *anything*. Then they came to an orbital station where they had a very nice room and there was gravity again, and the next day they climbed aboard the *Gel Blong Mota*, which was at the same time very very big but also small, and it smelled funny. He'd seen the aquatic tanks with their eels and prawns and lobster and squid, and he'd been to the hydroponics gardens and spoken to the head gardener there, and Joy even showed him a secret door and took him inside the maintenance corridors beyond the walls of the ship, where it was very dry and smelled of dust and old paint.

Now he watches space, and wonders what Mars is like. At that moment, staring out into space, it is as if he is staring out at his own future spreading out before him, unwritten terabytes and petabytes of the Narrative of Pym, waiting to be written over in any way he wants. It makes him feel strange—he's glad when Joy arrives and they go off together to the aquatic tanks, she said she'd teach him how to fish.

TONG YUN CITY, MARS, YEAR SEVEN

Mother is out again with her latest boyfriend, Jonquil Sing, a memcordist syndication agent. "He is very good for us," she tells Pym one night, giving him a wet kiss on the cheek, and her breath smells of smoke. She hopes Jonquil will increase subscriptions across Mars, Pym knows—the numbers of his followers have been dropping since they came to Tong Yun. "A dull, provincial *town*," Mother says, which is the Earth-born's most stinging insult.

But Pym likes Tong Yun. He loves going down in the giant elevators into the lower levels of the city, and he particularly loves the Arcade, with its battle droid arenas and games-worlds shops and particularly the enormous Multifaith Bazaar. Whenever he can he sneaks out of the house—they are living on the surface, under the dome of Tong Yun, in a house belonging to a friend of a friend of Mother's—and goes down to Arcade, and to the Bazaar.

The Church of Robot is down there, and an enormous Elronite temple, and mosques and synagogues and Buddhist and Baha'i temples and even a Gorean place and he watches the almost-naked slave girls with strange fascination, and they smile at him and reach out and tousle his hair. There are Re-Born Martian warriors with reddish skin and four arms—they believe Mars was once habituated by an ancient empire and that they are its descendants, and they serve the Emperor of Time. He thinks he wants to become a Re-Born warrior when he grows up, and have four arms and tint his skin red, but when he mentions it to Mother once she throws a fit and says Mars never had an atmosphere and there is no emperor and that the Re-Born are—and she uses a very rude word, and there are the usual complaints from some of the followers of the Narrative of Pym.

He's a little scared of the Elronites—they're all very confident and smile a lot and have very white teeth. Pym isn't very confident. He prefers quiet roads and places with few people in them and he doesn't want anyone to know who he is.

Sometimes he wonders who he is, or what he will become. One of Mother's friends asked him, "What do you want to be when you grow up?" and he said, "A spaceship captain"— thinking of Joy—and Mother gave her false laugh and ruffled his hair and said, "Pym already *is* what he is. Isn't that right, sweetheart?" and she gathered him in her arms and said, "He's *Pym*."

But who is Pym? Pym doesn't know. When he's down at the Multifaith Bazaar he thinks that perhaps he wants to be a priest, or a monk—but which religion? They're all neat.

Fifteen million follow him as he passes through temples, churches and shrines, searching for answers to a question he is not yet ready to ask himself, and might never be.

JETTISONED, CHARON, YEAR FIFTY-SIX

So at last he's come to Jettisoned, the farthest one can get without quite leaving completely, and he hires a small dark room in a small dark co-op deep in the bowels of the moon, a place that suits his mood.

Twenty-three million watch, less because of him and more because he'd chosen Jettisoned, the home of black warez and wild technology and outlaws—the city of the Jettisoned, all those ejected at the last moment from the vast majestic starships as they depart the solar system, leaving forever on a one-way journey into galactic space. Would some of them find new planets, new moons, new suns to settle around? Are there aliens out there, or God? No one knows, least of all Pym. He'd once asked his mother why they couldn't go with one of the ships. "Don't be silly," she'd said, "think of all your followers, and how disappointed they'd be."

"Bugger my followers," he says now, aloud, knowing some would complain, and others would drop out and follow other narratives. He'd never been all that popular, but the truth was, he'd never wanted to be. Everything I've ever done in my life, he thinks, is on record. Everything I've seen, everything I've touched, everything I smelled or said. And yet had he said or done anything worth saying, anything worth doing?

I once loved with all my heart, he thinks. Is that enough?

He knows she'd been to Jettisoned in the past year. But she'd left before he arrived. Where is she now? He could check but doesn't. On her way back through the outer system—perhaps in the Galilean Moons, where he knows she's popular. He decides to get drunk.

Hours later, he is staggering along a dark alley, home to smokes-bars, doll houses, battle arcades, body modification clinics, a lone Church of Robot mission, and several old-fashioned drinking establishments. Anything that can be grown on Jettisoned gets fermented into alcohol, sooner or later. Either that or smoked. His head hurts, and his heart is beating too fast. Too old, he thinks. Perhaps he says it out loud. Two insectoid figures materialise in the darkness, descend on him. "What are you—?" he says, slurring the words, as the two machines expertly rifle through his pockets and run an intrusion package over his node—even now, when all he can do is blink blearily, he notices the followers numbers rising, and realises he's being mugged.

"Give them a show," he says, and begins to giggle. He tries to hit one of the insectoid figures and a thin, slender metal arm reaches down and touches him—a needle bite against his throat—

Numb, but still conscious—he can't shout for help but what's the point, anyway? This is Jettisoned, and if you end up there you have only yourself to blame.

What are they doing? Why have they not gone yet? They're trying to take apart his memcorder, but it's impossible—don't they know it's impossible?—he is wired through and through, half human and half machine, recording everything, forgetting nothing. And yet suddenly he is very afraid, and the panic acts like a cold dose of water and he manages to move, slightly, and he shouts for help, though his voice is reedy and weak and anyway there is no one to hear him . . .

They're tearing apart chunks of memory, terabytes of life, days and months and years disappearing in a black cloud—"Stop, please," he mumbles, "please, don't—"

Who is he? What is he doing here?

A name. He has a name . . .

Somewhere far away, a shout. The two insectoid creatures raise elongated faces, feelers shaking—

There is the sound of an explosion, and one of the creatures disappears—hot shards of metal sting Pym, burning, burning—

The second creature rears, four arms rising like guns—

There is the sound of gunshots, to and from, and then there's a massive hole in the creature's chest, and it runs off into the darkness—

A face above his, dark hair, pale skin, two eyes like waning moons—"Pym? Pym? Can you hear me?"

"Pym," he whispers, the name strangely familiar. He closes his eyes and then nothing hurts any more, and he is floating in a cool, calm darkness.

SPIDER'S HOLD, LUNA, YEAR ONE

Not a memory as much as the recollection, like film, of something seen—emerging from darkness into a light, alien faces hovering above him, as large as moons—"Pym! My darling little Pym—"

Hands clapping, and he is clutched close to a warm, soft breast, and he begins to cry, but then the warmth settles him and he snuggles close and he is happy.

"Fifty-three million at peak," someone says.

"Day One," someone says. "Year One. And may all of your days be as happy as this one. You are born, Pym. Your narrative's began."

He finds a nipple, drinks. The milk is warm. "Hush now, my little baby. Hush now."

"See, already he is looking around. He wants to see the world."

But it isn't true. He only wants to sleep, in that warm, safe place.

"Happy birthday, Pym."

He sleeps.

POLYPHEMUS PORT, TITAN, YEAR SEVENTEEN

Party is crammed with people, the house node broadcasts out particularly loud *Nuevo Kwasa-Kwasa* tunes, there is a lot of Zion Special Strength passing around, the strong, sweet smell latching on to hair and clothes, and Pym is slightly drunk.

Polyport, on his own: Mother left behind in the Galilean Republic, Pym escaping—jumping onto an ancient transport ship, the *Ibn-al-Farid*, a Jupiter-to-Saturn one-way trip.

Feeling free, for the first time. His numbers going up, but he isn't paying any attention for once. Pym, not following the narrative but simply living his life.

Port bums hanging out at Polyport, kids looking for ships for the next trip to nowhere, coming from Mars and the Jovean moons and the ring-cities of Saturn, heading everywhere—

The party: a couple of weather hackers complaining about outdated protocols; a ship rat from the *Ibn-al-Farid*—Pym knows him slightly from the journey—doing a Louis Wu in the corner, a blissful smile on his face, wired-in, the low current tickling his pleasure centres; five big, blonde Australian girls from Earth on a round-the-system trip—conversations going over Pym's head—"Where do you come from? Where do you go? Where do you come from?"

Titan surface crawlers with that faraway look in their eyes; a viral artist, two painters, a Martian Re-Born talking quietly to a Jovean robot—Pym knows people are looking at him, pretending not to—and his numbers are going up, everybody loves a party.

She is taller than him, with long black hair gathered into moving dreadlocks—some sort of mechanism making them writhe about her head like snakes—long slender fingers, obsidian eyes—

People turning as she comes through, a hush of sort—she walks straight up to him, ignoring the other guests, stands before him, studying him with a bemused expression. He knows she sees what he sees—number of followers, storage space reports, feed statistics—he says, "Can I get you a drink?" with a confidence he doesn't quite feel, and she smiles. She has a gold tooth, and when she smiles it makes her appear strangely younger.

"I don't drink," she says, still studying him. The gold tooth is an Other, but in her case it isn't truly Joined—the digital intelligence embedded within is part of her memcorder structure. "Eighty-seven million," she says.

"Thirty-two," he says. She smiles again. "Let's get out of here," she says.

JETTISONED, CHARON, YEAR FIFTY-SIX

Memory returning in chunks—long-unused backup spooling back into his mind. When he opens his eyes he thinks for a moment it is her, that somehow she had rescued him from the creatures, but no—the face that hovers above his is unfamiliar, and he is suddenly afraid.

"Hush," she says. "You're hurt."

"Who are you?" he croaks. Numbers flashing—viewing figures near a hundred million all across the system, being updated at the speed of light. His birth didn't draw nearly that many . . .

"My name's Zul," she says—which tells him nothing. He sees she has a pendant hanging between her breasts. He squints and sees his own face.

The woman shrugs, smiles, a little embarrassed. Crows-feet at the corners of her dark eyes. A gun hanging on her belt, black leather trousers the only other thing she wears. "You were attacked by wild foragers," she says, and shrugs again. "We've had an infestation of them in the past couple of years."

Foragers: multi-surface machines designed for existing outside the human bubbles, converting rock into energy, slow lunar surface transforms—rogue, like everything else on Jettisoned. He says, "Thank you," and to his surprise she blushes.

"I've been watching you," she said.

Pym understands—and feels a little sad.

She makes love to him on the narrow bed in the small, hot, dark room. They are somewhere deep underground. From down here it is impossible to imagine Charon, that icy moon, or the tiny cold disc of the sun far away, or the enormous field of galactic stars or the shadows of Exodus ships as they pass forever out of human space—hard to imagine anything but a primal human existence of naked bodies and salty skin and fevered heartbeats and he sighs, still inexplicably sad within his excitement, for the smell of basil he seeks is missing.

KUALA LUMPUR, EARTH, YEAR THIRTY-TWO

At thirty-two there's the annoyance of hair growing in the wrong places and not growing in others, a mole or two which shouldn't be there, hangovers get worse, take longer to dissipate, eyes strain, and death is closer—

Pym, the city a spider's web of silver and light all around him, the towers of Kuala Lumpur rise like rockets into the skies—the streets alive with laughter, music, frying mutton—

On the hundred and second floor of the hospital, in a room as white as a painting of absence, as large and as small as a world—

Mother reaches out, holds his hand in hers. Her fingers are thin, bony. "My little Pym. My baby. Pym."

She sees what he sees. She shares access to the viewing stats, knows how many millions are watching this, the death of Mother, supporting character number one in the Narrative of Pym. Pym feels afraid, and guilty, and scared—Mother is dying, no one knows why, exactly, and for Pym it's—what?

Pain, yes, but—

Is that relief? The freedom of Pym, a real one this time, not as illusory as it had been, when he was seventeen?

"Mother," he says, and she squeezes his hand. Below, the world is spider-webs and fairy-lights. "Fifty-six million," she says, and tries to smile. "And the best doctors money could buy—"

But they are not enough. She made him come back to her, by dying, and Pym isn't sure how he feels about it, and so he stands there, and holds her weakened hand, and stares out beyond the windows into the night.

POLYPHEMUS PORT, TITAN, YEAR SEVENTEEN

They need no words between them. They haven't said a word since they left the party. They are walking hand in hand through the narrow streets of Polyport and the storm rages overhead. When she draws him into a darkened corner he is aware of the beating of his heart and then her own, his hand on her warm dark skin cupping a breast as the numbers roll and roll, the millions rising—a second feed showing him her own figures. Her lips on his, full, and she has the taste of basil, and the night, and when they hold each other the numbers fade and there is only her.

JETTISONED, CHARON, YEAR FIFTY-SIX

When they make love a second time he calls out her name and, later, the woman lies beside him and says, her hand stroking his chest slowly, "You really love her," and her voice is a little sad. Her eyes are round, pupils large. She sighs, a soft sound on the edge of the solar system. "I thought, maybe . . ."

The numbers dropping again, the story of his life—the Narrative of Pym charted by the stats of followers at any given moment. The narrative of Pym goes out all over space—and do they follow it, too, in the Exodus ships, or on alien planets with unknown names?

He doesn't know. He doesn't care. He rises in the dark, and dresses, and goes out into the night of Jettisoned as the woman sleeps behind him.

At that moment he decides to find her.

DRAGON'S HOME, HYDRA, YEAR SEVENTY-EIGHT

It feels strange to be back in the Pluto system. And Hydra is the strangest of the worlds . . . Jettisoned lies like a sore on Charon, but Hydra is even farther out, and cold, so cold . . . Dragon's World, and Pym is a guest of the dragon.

When he thinks back to his time on Jettisoned, in the Year Fifty-Six—or was it Fifty-Seven?—of the Narrative of Pym, it is all very confused. It had been a low point in his life. He left Jettisoned shortly after the attack, determined to find her—but then, he had done that several times, and never . . .

Dragon's World is an entire moon populated by millions of bodies and a single mind. Vietnamese dolls, mass-produced in the distant factories of Earth, transported here by the same *Gel Blong Mota* he had once travelled on as a child, thousands and tens of thousands and finally millions of dolls operating with a single mind, the mind of the dragon—worker-ants crawling all over the lunar surface, burrowing into its hide, transforming it into—what?

No one quite knows.

The dragon is an Other, one of the countless intelligences evolved in the digital Breeding Grounds, lines of code multiplying and mutating, merging and splitting in billions upon billions of cycles. It is said the dragon had been on one of the Exodus ships, and been Jettisoned, but why that may be so no one knows. This is its world—a habitat? A work of strange, conceptual art? Nobody knows and the dragon isn't telling.

Yet Pym is a guest, and the dragon is hospitable.

Pym's body is in good shape but the dragon promises to make it better. Pym lies in one of the warrens, in a cocoon-like harness, and tiny insects are crawling all over his body, biting and tearing, sewing and rearranging. Sometimes Pym gets the impression the dragon is lonely. Or perhaps it wants others to see its world, and for that purpose invited Pym, whose numbers rise dramatically when he lands on Hydra.

The *Gel Blong Mota* had carried him here, from the Galilean Republic on a slow, leisurely journey, and its captain was Joy, and she and Pym shared wine and stories and stared out into space, and sometimes made love with the slow, unhurried pace of old friends.

Why did you never go to her?

Her question is in his mind as he lies there, in the warm confines of Dragon's cocoon. It is very quiet on Hydra, the dolls that are the dragon's body making almost no sound as they pass on their errands—whatever those may be. He thinks of Joy's question but realises he has no answer for her, and never had. There had been other women, other places, but never—

POLYPHEMUS PORT, TITAN, YEAR SEVENTEEN

This is the most *intimate* moment of his life: it is as if the two of them are the centre of the entire universe, and nothing else matters but the two of them, and as they kiss, as they undress, as they touch each other with clumsy, impatient fingers the whole universe is watching, watching something amazing, this joining of two bodies, two souls. Their combined numbers have reached one billion and are still climbing. It will never be like this again, he thinks he hears her say, her lips against his neck, and he knows she is right, it will never—

KUALA LUMPUR, EARTH, YEAR TWO

Taking baby-steps across the vast expanse of recreated prime park land in the heart of the town, cocooned within the great needle towers of the mining companies, Pym laughs, delighted, as adult hands pick him up and twirl him around. "My baby," Mother says, and holds him close, and kisses him (those strange figures at the corner of his eyes always shifting, changing—he'd got used to them by now, does not pay them any mind)—"You have time for everything twice over. The future waits for you—"

And as he puts his arms around her neck he's happy, and the future is a shining road in Pym's mind, a long endless road of white light with Pym marching at its centre, with no end in sight, and he laughs again, and wriggles down, and runs towards the ponds where there are great big lizards sunning themselves in the sun.

DRAGON'S HOME, HYDRA, YEAR
ONE HUNDRED FIFTEEN

Back on Dragon's Home, that ant's nest whose opening rises from the surface of Hydra like a volcanic mouth, back in the cocoons of his old friend the dragon— "I don't think you could fix me again, old friend," he says, and closes his eyes— the cocoon against his naked skin like soft Vietnamese silk.

The dragon murmurs all around him, its thousands of bodies marching through their complex woven-together tunnels. Number of followers hovering around fifty million, and Pym thinks, They want to see me die.

He turns in his cocoon and the dragon murmurs soothing words, but they lose their meaning. Pym tries to recall Mother's face, the taste of blackberries on a Martian farm, the feel of machine-generated rain on Ganymede or the embrace of a Jettisoned woman, but nothing holds, nothing is retained in his mind anymore. Somewhere it all exists, even now his failing senses are being broadcast and stored—but this, he knows suddenly, with a frightening clarity, is the approaching termination of the Narrative of Pym, and the thought terrifies him. "Dragon!" he cries, and then there is something cool against his neck and relief floods in.

Pym drifts in a dream half-sleep, lulled by the rhythmic motion of his cocoon. There is a smell, a fragrance he misses, something sweet and fresh like ba—a herb of some sort? He grabs for a memory, his eyes opening with the effort, but it's no use, there is nothing there but a faint, uneasy sense of regret, and at last he lets it go. There had been a girl—

Hadn't there?

He never—

He closes his eyes again at last, and gradually true darkness forms, a strange and unfamiliar vista: even the constant numbers at the corner of his vision, always previously there, are fading—it is so strange he would have laughed if he could.

POLYPHEMUS PORT, TITAN, YEAR FORTY-THREE

He walks down the old familiar streets on this, this forty-third year of the Narrative of Pym, searching for her in the scent of old memories. She is not there, but suddenly, as he walks under the dome and the ever-present storm, he's hopeful: there will be other places, other times and, somewhere in the solar system, sometime in the Narrative of Pym, he will find her . . .

The Best We Can

CARRIE VAUGHN

New York Times *bestseller Carrie Vaughn is the author of a wildly popular series of novels detailing the adventures of Kitty Norville, a radio personality who also happens to be a werewolf, and who runs a late-night call-in radio advice show for supernatural creatures. The "Kitty" books include* Kitty and the Midnight Hour, Kitty Goes to Washington, Kitty Takes a Holiday, *and* Kitty and the Silver Bullet, Kitty and the Dead Man's Hand, Kitty Raises Hell, Kitty's House of Horrors, Kitty Goes to War, Kitty's Big Trouble, Kitty Steals the Show, Kitty Rocks the House, *and a collection of her "Kitty" stories,* Kitty's Greatest Hits. *Her other novels include* Voices of Dragons, *her first venture into Young Adult territory, a fantasy,* Discord's Apple, Steel, *and* After the Golden Age. *Vaughn's short work has appeared in* Lightspeed, Asimov's Science Fiction, Subterranean, Wild Cards: Inside Straight, Realms of Fantasy, Jim Baen's Universe, Paradox, Strange Horizons, Weird Tales, All-Star Zeppelin Adventure Stories, *and elsewhere; her non-Kitty stories have been collected in* Straying from the Path. *Among her recent books are a "Kitty" novel,* Kitty in the Underworld, *and* Dreams of the Golden Age, *a sequel to* After the Golden Age. *She lives in Colorado.*

Here she gives us a quiet but moving story about an all-too-plausible reaction to the age-old dream of First Contact.

In the end, the discovery of evidence of extraterrestrial life, and not just life, but intelligence, got hopelessly mucked up because no one wanted to take responsibility for confirming the findings, and no one could decide who ultimately had the authority—the obligation—to do so. We submitted the paper, but peer review held it up for a year. News leaked—NASA announced one of their press conferences, but the press conference ended up being an announcement about a future announcement, which never actually happened and the reporters made a joke of it. Another case of Antarctic meteorites or cold fusion. We went around with our mouths shut waiting for an official announcement while ulcers devoured our guts.

So I wrote a press release. I had Marsh at JPL's comet group and Salvayan at Columbia vet it for me and released it under the auspices of the JPL Near Earth Objects Program. We could at least start talking about it instead of arguing about whether we were ready to start talking about it. I didn't know what would happen next. I did it in the spirit of scientific outreach, naturally. The release included that now-famous blurry photo that started the whole thing.

I had an original print of that photo, of UO-1—Unidentified Object One, because it technically wasn't flying and I was being optimistic that this would be the first of more than one—framed and hanging on the wall over my desk, a stark focal point in my chronically cluttered office. Out of the thousands of asteroids we tracked and photographed, this one caught my eye, because it was symmetrical and had a higher than normal albedo. It flashed, even, like a mirror. Asteroids aren't symmetrical and aren't very reflective. But if it wasn't an asteroid . . . .

We turned as many telescopes on it as we could. Tried to get time on Hubble and failed, because it sounded ridiculous—why waste time looking at something inside the orbit of Jupiter? We *did* get Arecibo on it. We got pictures from multiple sources, studied them for weeks until we couldn't argue with them any longer. No one wanted to say it because it was crazy, just thinking it would get you sacked, and I got so frustrated with the whole group sitting there in the conference room after hours on a Friday afternoon, staring at each other with wide eyes and dropped jaws and no one saying anything, that I said it: It's not natural, and it's not ours.

UO-1 was approximately 250 meters long, with a fan shape at one end, blurred at the other, as if covered with projections too fine to show up at that resolution. The rest was perfectly straight, a thin stalk holding together blossom and roots, the lines rigid and artificial. The fan shape might be a ram scoop—Angie came up with that idea, and the conjecture stuck, no matter how much I reminded people that we couldn't decide anything about what it was or what it meant. Not until we knew more.

We—the scientific community, astronomers, philosophers, writers, all of humanity—had spent a lot of time thinking about what would happen if we found definitive proof that intelligent life existed elsewhere in the universe. All the scenarios involved these other intelligences talking to us. Reaching out to us. Sending a message we would have to decipher—would be eager to decipher. Hell, we sure wouldn't be able to talk to them, not stuck on our own collection of rocks like we were. Whether people thought we'd be overrun with sadistic tripods or be invited to join a greater benevolent galactic society, that was always the assumption—we'd know they were there because they'd talk to us.

When that didn't happen, it was like no one knew what to do next. No one had thought about what would happen if we just found a . . . a *thing* . . . that happened to be drifting a few million miles out from the moon. It didn't talk. Not so much as a blinking light. The radiation we detected from it was reflected—whatever propulsion had driven it through space had long since stopped, and inertia carried it now. No one knew how to respond to it. The news that was supposed to change the course of human history . . . didn't.

We wouldn't know any more about it until we looked at it up close, until we brought it here, brought it home. And that was where it all fell apart.

I presented the initial findings at the International Astronomical Union annual meeting. My department gathered the data, but we couldn't do anything about implementation—no one group could implement *anything*. But of course, the first argument was about whom the thing belonged to. I nearly resigned.

Everyone wanted a piece of it, including various governments and the United Nations, and we had to humor that debate because nothing could get done without funding. The greatest discovery in all of human history and funding held it hostage. Several corporations, including the producers of a popular energy drink, threatened to mount their own expeditions in order to establish naming and publicity rights, until the U.S. Departments of Energy, Transportation, and Defense issued joint restrictions on privately funded extra-orbital spaceflight, which caused its own massive furor.

Meanwhile, we and the various other groups working on the project tracked UO-1 as it appeared to establish an elliptical solar orbit that would take it out to the orbit of Saturn and back on a twenty-year cycle. We waited. We developed plans, which were presented and rejected. We took better and better pictures, which revealed enough detail to see struts holding up what did indeed appear to be the surface of a ram scoop. It did not, everyone slowly began to agree, appear to be inhabited. The data on it never fluctuated. No signals emanated from it. It was metal, it was solid, it was inert. We published papers and appeared on cable documentaries. We gritted our teeth while websites went up claiming that the thing was a weapon, and a survivalist movement developed in response. Since it was indistinguishable from all the existing survivalist movements, no one really noticed.

And we waited.

The thing is, you discover the existence of extraterrestrial intelligence, and you still have to go home, wash up, get a good night's sleep, and come up with something to eat for breakfast in the morning. Life goes on, life keeps going on, and it's not that people forget or stop being interested. It's that they realize they still have to change the oil in the car and take the dog for a walk. You feel like the whole world ought to be different, but it only shifts. Your worldview expands to take in this new information.

I go to work every day and look at that picture, *my* picture, this satellite or spacecraft, this message in a bottle. Some days I'm furious that I can't get my hands on it. Some days I weep at the wonder of it. Most days I look at it, sigh, and write another round of emails and make phone calls to find out what's going to happen to it. To *make* something happen.

"How goes the war?" Marsh leans into my office like he does every afternoon, mostly to try to cheer me up. He's been here as long as I have; our work overlaps, and we've become friends. I go to his kids' birthday parties. The brown skin around his eyes crinkles with his smile. I'm not able to work up a smile to match.

"The Chinese say they're sending a probe with a robotic arm and a booster to grab it and pull it back to Earth. They say whoever gets there first has right of salvage. It's a terrible idea. Even if they did manage to get it back without breaking it, they'd never let anyone else look at it."

"Oh, I think they would—under their terms." He doesn't get too worked up about it because nobody's managed to do anything yet, why would they now? He would say I take all of this too personally, and he'd be right.

"The IAU is sending a delegation to try to talk the Chinese government into joining the coalition. They might have a chance of it if they actually had a plan of their own. Look, if you want me to talk your ear off, come in and sit, have some coffee. Otherwise, leave now. That's your warning."

"I'll take the coffee," he says, claiming the chair I pulled away from the wall for him before turning to my little desktop coffee maker. His expression softens, his sympathy becoming genuine rather than habitual. "You backing any particular plan yet?"

I sigh. "Gravity tractor looks like our best option. Change the object's trajectory, steer it into a more convenient orbit without actually touching it. Too bad the technology is almost completely untested. We can test it first, of course. Which will take years. And there's an argument against it. Emissions from a gravity tractor's propulsion may damage the object. It's the root of the whole problem: we don't know enough about the thing to know how much stress it can take. The cowboys want to send a crewed mission—they say the only way to be sure is to get eyeballs on the thing. But that triples the cost of any mission. Anything we do will take years of planning and implementation anyway, so no one can be bothered to get off their asses. Same old, same old."

Two and a half years. It's been two and a half years since we took that picture. My life has swung into a very tight orbit around this one thing.

"Patience, Jane," Marsh says in a tone that almost sets me off. He's only trying to help.

Truth is, I've been waiting for his visit. I pull out a sheet of handwritten calculations from under a manila folder. "I do have another idea, but I wanted to talk to you about it before I propose anything." His brow goes up, he leans in with interest.

He'll see it faster than I can explain it, so I speak carefully. "We can use Angelus." When he doesn't answer, yes or no, I start to worry and talk to cover it up. "It launches in six months, plenty of time to reprogram the trajectory, send it on a flyby past UO-1, get more data on it than we'll ever get sitting here on Earth—"

His smile has vanished. "Jane. I've been waiting for Angelus for five years. The timing is critical. My comet won't be this close for another two hundred years."

"But Angelus is the only mission launching in the next year with the right kind of optics and maneuverability to get a good look at UO-1, and yes, I know the timing on the comet is once-in-a-lifetime and I know it's important. But this—this is once in a *civilization*. The sooner we can look at it, answer some of our questions . . . well. The sooner the better."

"The better *you'll* be. I'm supposed to wait, but you can't?"

"Please, Marsh. I'll feel a lot better about it if you'll agree with me."

"Thank you for the coffee, Jane," he says, setting aside the mug as he stands.

I close my eyes and beseech the ceiling. This isn't how I want this to go. "Marsh, I'm not trying to sabotage your work, I'm just looking at available resources—"

"And I'm not ultimately the one who makes decisions about what happens to Angelus. I'm just the one depending on all the data. You can make your proposal, but don't ask me to sign off on it."

He starts to leave and I say, "Marsh. I can't take it anymore. I spend every day holding my breath, waiting for someone to do something truly stupid. Some days I can't stand it that I can't get my hands on it."

He sits back down, like a good friend should. A good friend would not, however, steal a colleague's exploratory probe away from him. But this is *important*.

"You know what I think? The best bet is to let one of these corporate foundations mount an expedition. They won't want to screw up because of the bad publicity, and they'll bring you on board for credibility so you'll have some say in how they proceed. You'll be their modern-day Howard Carter."

I can see it now: I'd be the face of the expedition, all I'd have to do is stand there and look pretty. Or at least studious. Explain gravity and trajectories for the popular audience. Speculate on the composition of alien alloys. Watch whatever we find out there get paraded around the globe to shill corn chips. Wouldn't even feel like I was selling my soul, would it?

I must look green, or ill, or murderous, because Marsh goes soothing. "Just think about it, before you go and do something crazy."

I've kept a dedicated SETI@home computer running since I was sixteen. Marsh doesn't know that about me. I don't believe in extraterrestrial UFO's because I know in great, intimate detail the difficulties of sending objects across the vast distances of space. Hell, just a few hundred miles into orbit isn't a picnic. We've managed it, of course—we are officially extra-solar system beings, now, with our little probes and plaques pushing ever outward. Will they find anything? Will anything find *them*?

Essentially, there are two positions on the existence of extraterrestrial intelligence and whether we might ever make contact, and they both come down to the odds. The first says that *we're* here, humanity is intelligent, flinging out broadcasts and training dozens of telescopes outward hoping for the least little sign, and the universe is so immeasurably vast that given the odds, the billions of stars and galaxies and planets out there, we can't possibly be the only intelligent species doing these things. The second position says that the odds of life coming into being on any given planet, of that life persisting long enough to evolve, then to evolve intelligence, and then being interested in the same things we are—the odds of all those things falling into place are so immeasurably slim, we may very well be the only ones here.

Is the universe half full or half empty? All we could ever do to solve the riddle was wait. So I waited and was rewarded for my optimism.

In unguarded moments I'm certain this was meant to happen, I was meant to discover UO-1. Me and no one else. Because I understand how important it is. Because I'm the one sitting here every day sending emails and making phone calls. I ID'd the image, I made the call, I had the guts to go public, I deserve a say in what happens next.

I submit the paperwork proposing that the Angelus probe be repurposed to perform a flyby and survey of UO-1. Marsh will forgive me. I wait. Again.

I've kept track, and I've done a hundred fifty TV interviews in the last two years. Most of them are snippets for pop-documentaries, little chunks of information delivered to the lowest common denominator audience. I explain over and over again, in different settings, sometimes in my office, sometimes in a vague but picturesque location, sometimes at Griffith Observatory, because for some reason nothing says "space" like Griffith Observatory. I hold up a little plastic model of UO-1 (they're selling the kits at hobby stores—we don't see any of the money from that) to demonstrate the way it's traveling through space, how orbital mechanics work, and how we might use a gravity tractor to bring it home. Sometimes, the segments are specifically for schools, and I like those best because I can give free rein to my enthusiasm. I tell the kids, "This is going to take more than one lifetime to figure out. If we find a way to go to Alpha Centauri, it's going to take lifetimes. You'll have to finish the work I've started. Please grow up and finish it."

I call everyone I can think of who might have some kind of influence over Angelus. I explain that a picture of a metal object taken from a few million miles away doesn't tell us anything about the people who made it. Not even if they have thumbs or tentacles. Most of them tell me that the best plan they can think of is to build bigger telescopes.

"It's not the size," I mutter. "It's how you use it."

NASA thinks they will be making the decision because they've got the resources, the scientists, the experience, the hardware. Congress says this is too important to let NASA make decisions unilaterally. A half dozen private U.S. firms would try something if the various cabinet departments weren't busy making anything they could try illegal by fiat. There are already three court cases. At least one of them is arguing that a rocket launch is protected as freedom of speech. The IAU brought a complaint to the United Nations that the U.S. government shouldn't be allowed to dictate a course of action. The General Assembly nominated a "representative in absentia" for the species that launched UO-1—some Finnish philosopher I'd never heard of. It should have been me.

After a decade of international conferences I have colleagues all over the world. I call them all. Most are sympathetic. A South African cosmologist I know tells me I'm grandstanding, then laughs like it's a joke, but not really. They all tell me to be patient. Just wait.

Life goes on. My other research, the asteroid research I was doing, has piled up, and I get polite but firm hints that I really ought to work on that if I want to keep my job. I go to conferences, I publish, I do another dozen interviews, holding up the plastic model of the object that I'll likely never get close to. The ache in my heart feels just like it did when Peter left me. That was three years ago, and I can still feel it. The ache that says: I can't possibly start over, can I?

The ache faded when I found UO-1.

"JPL rejected your proposal to repurpose Angelus. Thank God." Marsh leans on my doorway like usual. He's grinning like he won a prize.

I got the news via email. The bastards can't even be bothered to call. I'd called them back, thinking there must have been a mistake. The pitying tone in their voices didn't sound like kindness anymore. It was definitely condescension. I cried. I've been crying all afternoon, as the pile of wadded-up tissues on my desk attests. My eyes are still puffy. Marsh can see I've been crying; he knows what it looks like when I cry. He was there three years ago. I take a breath to keep from starting up again and stare at him like he's punched me.

"How can you say that? Do you know what they're talking about now? They're talking about just leaving it! They're saying the orbit is stable, we'll always know where it is and we can go after it when we have a better handle on the technology. But what if something happens to it? What if an asteroid hits it, or it crashes into Jupiter, or—"

"Jane, it's been traveling for how many hundreds of billions of miles—why would something happen to it now?"

"I don't know! It shouldn't even be there at all! And they won't even *listen* to me!"

He sounds tired. "Why should they?"

"Because it's *mine*!"

His normally comforting smile is sad, pitying, smug, and amused, all at once. "It's not yours, not any more than gravity belonged to Newton."

I want to scream. Because maybe this isn't the most important thing to happen to humanity. That's probably, oh, the invention of the wheel, or language. Maybe this is just the most important thing to happen to me.

I grab another tissue. I look at the picture of UO-1. It's beautiful. It tells me that the universe, as vast as we already know it is, is bigger than we think.

Marsh sits in the second chair without waiting for an invitation. "What do you think it is, Jane? Be honest. No job, no credibility, no speaking gig for Discovery on the line. What do you think when you look at it?" He nods at the picture.

There are some cable shows that will win you credibility for appearing on them. There are some that will destroy any credibility you ever had. I have been standing right on that line, answering the question of "What is it?" as vaguely as possible. We need to know more, no way to speculate, et cetera. But I know. I *know* what it is.

"I think it's Voyager. Not *the* Voyager. *Their* Voyager. The probe they sent out to explore, and it just kept going."

He doesn't laugh. "You think we'll find a plaque on it? A message? A recording?"

"It's what I want to find." I smile wistfully. "But what are the odds?"

"Gershwin," he says. I blink, but he doesn't seem offended by my confusion. He leans back in the chair, comfortable in his thick middle-aged body, genial, someone who clearly believes all is well with the world, at least at the moment. "We've had fourteen billion years of particles colliding, stars exploding, nebulae compressing, planets forming, all of it cycling over and over again, and then just the right amino acids converged, life forms, and a couple of billion years of evolution later—we get Gene Kelly and Leslie Caron dancing by a fountain to Gershwin and it's beautiful. For no particular evolution-driven reason, it's beautiful. I think: what are the odds? That they're dancing, that it's on film, and that I'm here watching and thinking it's gorgeous. If the whole universe exists just to make this one moment happen, I wouldn't be at all surprised."

"So if I think sometimes that maybe I was meant to find UO-1, because maybe there's a message there and that I'm the only one who can read it—then maybe that's not crazy?" Like thinking that the universe sent me UO-1 at a time in my life when I desperately needed something to focus on, to be meaningful . . .

"Oh no, it's definitely crazy. But it's understandable." This time his smile is kind.

"Marsh—this really is the most important thing to happen to humanity ever, isn't it?"

"Yes. But we still need to study and map near-Earth asteroids, right?"

I don't tell Marsh that I've never seen *An American in Paris*. I've never watched Gene Kelly in anything. But Marsh obviously thinks it's important, so I watch the movie. I decide he's right. That dance at the fountain, it's a moment suspended in time. Like an alien spacecraft that shouldn't be there but is.

Two things happen next.

At the next IAU meeting an archaeologist presents a lecture on UO-1, which I think is very presumptuous, but I go, because I go to everything having to do with UO-1. She talks about preservation and uses terms like "in situ," and how modern archaeological practice often involves excavating artifacts, examining them—and then putting them back in the ground. She argues that we don't know what years of space travel have done to the metal and structures of UO-1. We don't know how our methods of studying it will impact it. She showed pictures of Mayan friezes that were excavated and left exposed to the elements versus ones that remained buried for their own protection, so that later scientists with better equipment and techniques will be able to return to them someday. The exposed ones have dissolved, decayed past recognition. She gives me an image: I reach out and finally put my hand on UO-1, and its metallic skin, weakened by a billion micrometeoroid impacts gathered over millennia, disintegrates under my touch.

I think of that and start to sweat. So yes, caution. I know this.

The second thing that happens: I turn my back on UO-1.

Not really, but it's a striking image. I write another proposal, a different proposal, and submit it to one of the corporate foundations because Marsh may be right. If nothing else, it'll get attention. I don't mind a little grandstanding.

We already have teams tracking a best-guess trajectory to determine where UO-1 came from. It might have been cruising through space at nonrelativistic speed for dozens of years, or centuries, or millions of centuries, but based on the orbit it established here, we can estimate how it entered the solar system and the trajectory it traveled before then. We can trace backward.

My plan: to send a craft in that direction. It will do a minimal amount of science along the way, sending back radiation readings, but most of the energy and hardware is going into propulsion. It will be fast and it will have purpose, carrying an updated variation of Sagan's Voyager plaques and recordings, digital and analog.

It's a very simple message, in the end: Hey, we found your device. Want one of ours?

In all likelihood, the civilization that built UO-1 is extinct. The odds simply aren't good for a species surviving—and caring—for long enough to send a message and receive a reply. But our sample size for drawing that conclusion about the average lifespan of an entire species on a particular world is exactly one, which isn't a sample size at all. We weren't supposed to ever find an alien ship in our backyard, either.

I tear up when the rocket launches, and that makes for good TV. As Marsh predicted, the documentary producers decide to make me the human face of the project, and I figure I'll do what I have to, as best as I can. I develop a collection of quotes for the dozens of interviews that follow—I'm up to two-hundred thirty-five. I talk about taking the long view and transcending the everyday concerns that bog us down. About how we are children reaching across the sandbox with whatever we have to offer, to whoever shows up. About teaching our children to think as big as they possibly can, and that miracles sometimes really do happen. They happen often, because all of this, Gershwin's music, the great curry I had for dinner last night, the way we hang pictures on our walls of things we love, are miracles that never should have happened.

It's a hope, a need, a shout, a shot in the dark. It's the best we can do. For now.

The Discovered Country

IAN R. MacLeod

British writer Ian R. MacLeod was one of the hottest new writers of the nineties, publishing a slew of strong stories in Interzone, Asimov's Science Fiction, Weird Tales, Amazing, *and* The Magazine of Fantasy & Science Fiction, *and elsewhere, and his work continues to grow in power and deepen in maturity as we move through the first decades of the new century. Much of his work has been gathered in four collections,* Voyages by Starlight, Breathmoss and Other Exhalations, Past Magic, *and* Journeys. *His first novel,* The Great Wheel, *was published in 1997. In 1999, he won the World Fantasy Award with his novella* The Summer Isles, *and followed it up in 2000 by winning another World Fantasy Award for his novelette* The Chop Girl. *In 2003, he published his first fantasy novel, and his most critically acclaimed book,* The Light Ages, *followed by a sequel,* The House of Storms *in 2005, and then by* Song of Time, *which won both the Arthur C. Clarke Award and the John W. Campbell Memorial Award in 2008. A novel version of* The Summer Isles *also appeared in 2005. Among his recent books are the novel* Wake Up and Dream *and a big retrospective collection,* Snodgrass and Other Illusions: The Best Short Stories of Ian R. MacLeod. *MacLeod lives with his family in the West Midlands of England.*

Here he tells an evocative and emotionally powerful story of someone sent on a mission to a virtual Utopia reserved only for the superrich who have died on our mundane Earth, a sort-of literal Afterlife—a smart, tense, and tricky story where the stakes are high and nothing is what it seems.

T he trees of Farside are incredible. Fireash and oak. Greenbloom and maple. Shot through with every colour of autumn as late afternoon sunlight blazes over the Seven Mountains' white peaks. He'd never seen such beauty as this when he was alive.

The virtual Bentley takes the bridge over the next gorge at a tyre scream, then speeds on through crimson and gold. Another few miles, and he's following the coastal road beside the Westering Ocean. The sands are burnished, the rocks silver-threaded. Every new vista a fabulous creation. Then ahead, just as purple glower sweeps in from his rearview over those dragon-haunted mountains, come the silhouette lights of a vast castle, high up on a ridge. It's the only habitation he's seen in hours.

This has to be it.

Northover lets the rise of the hill pull at the Bentley's impetus as its headlights sweep the driveway trees. Another turn, another glimpse of a headland, and there's Elsinore again, rising dark and sheer.

He tries to refuse the offer to carry his luggage made by the neat little creature that emerges into the lamp-lit courtyard to greet him with clipboard, sharp shoes and lemony smile. He's encountered many chimeras by now. The shop assistants, the street cleaners, the crew on the steamer ferry that brought him here. All substantially humanoid, and invariably polite, although amended as necessary to perform their tasks, and far stranger to his mind than the truly dead.

He follows a stairway up through rough-hewn stone. The thing's name is Kasaya. Ah, now. The east wing. I think you'll find what we have here more than adequate. If not . . . Well, you *must* promise to let me know. And this is called the Willow Room. And *do* enjoy your stay . . .

Northover wanders. Northover touches. Northover breathes. The interior of this large high-ceilinged suite with its crackling applewood fire and narrow, deep-set windows is done out in an elegantly understated arts-and-craftsy style. Amongst her many attributes, Thea Lorentz always did have excellent taste.

What's struck him most about Farside since he jerked into new existence on the bed in the cabin of that ship bound for New Erin is how unremittingly *real* everything seems. But the slick feel of this patterned silk bed throw . . . The spiky roughness of the teasels in the flower display . . . He's given up telling himself that everything he's experiencing is just some clever construct. The thing about it, the thing that makes it all so impossibly overwhelming, is that *he's* here as well. Dead, but alive. The evidence of his corpse doubtless already incinerated, but his consciousness—the singularity of his existence, what philosophers once called "the conscious I," and theologians the soul, along with his memories and person-ality, the whole sense of self which had once inhabited pale jelly in his skull— transferred.

The bathroom is no surprise to him now. The dead do so many things the liv-ing do, so why not piss and shit as well? He strips and stands in the shower's warm blaze. He soaps, rinses. Reminds himself of what he must do and say. He'd been warned that he'd soon become attracted to the blatant glories this world, along with the new, young man's body he now inhabits. Better just to accept it rather than fight. All that matters is that he holds to the core of his resolve.

He towels himself dry. He pulls back on his watch—seemingly a Rolex, but a steel model, neatly unostentatious—and winds it carefully. He dresses. Hangs up his clothes in a walnut panelled wardrobe that smells faintly of mothballs and hears a knock at the doors just as he slides his case beneath the bed.

"Yes? Come in . . ."

When he turns, he's expecting another chimera servant. But it's Thea Lorentz.

This, too, is something they'd tried to prepare him for. But encountering her after so long is much less of a shock than he's been expecting. Thea's image is as ubiquitous as that of Marilyn Monroe or the Virgin Mary back on Lifeside, and she really hasn't changed. She's dressed in a loose-fitting shirt. Loafers and slacks. Hair tied back. No obvious evidence of any make-up. But the crisp white shirt with its rolled up cuffs shows her dark brown skin to perfection, and one lose strand of her tied-back hair plays teasingly at her sculpted neck. A tangle of silver bracelets slide on her wrist as she steps forward to embrace him. Her breasts are unbound and she still smells warmly of the patchouli she always used to favour. Everything about her feels exactly the same. But why not? After all, she was already perfect when she was alive.

"Well . . . !" That warm blaze is still in her eyes, as well. "It really *is* you."

"I know I'm springing a huge surprise. Just turning up from out of nowhere like this."

"I can take these kind of surprises any day! And I hear it's only been—what?—less than a week since you transferred. Everything must feel so very strange to you still."

It went without saying that his and Thea's existences had headed off in different directions back on Lifeside. She, of course, had already been well on her way toward some or other kind of immortality when they'd lost touch. And he . . . Well, it was just one of those stupid lucky breaks. A short, ironic keyboard riff he'd written to help promote some old online performance thing—no, no, it was nothing she'd been involved in—had ended up being picked up many years later as the standard message-send fail signal on the global net. Yeah, that was the one. Of course, Thea knew it. Everyone, once they thought about it for a moment, did.

"You know, Jon," she says, her voice more measured now, "you're the one person I thought would never choose to make this decision. None of us can pretend that being Farside isn't a position of immense privilege, when most of the living can't afford food, shelter, good health. You always were a man of principle, and I sometimes thought you'd just fallen to . . . Well, the same place that most performers fall to, I suppose, which is no particular place at all. I even considered trying to find you and get in touch, offer . . ." She gestures around her. "Well, this. But you wouldn't have taken it, would you? Not on those terms."

He shakes his head. In so many ways she still has him right. He detested—no, he quietly reminds himself—*detests* everything about this vast vampiric sham of a world that sucks life, hope and power from the living. But she hadn't come to him, either, had she? Hadn't offered what she now so casually calls *this*. For all her fame, for all her good works, for all the aid funds she sponsors and the good causes she promotes, Thea Lorentz and the rest of the dead have made no effort to extend their constituency beyond the very rich, and almost certainly never will. After all, why should they? Would the gods invite the merely mortal to join them on Mount Olympus?

She smiles and steps close to him again. Weights both his hands in her own. "Most people I know, Jon—most of those I have to meet and talk to and deal with, and even those I have to call friends—they all think that I'm Thea Lorentz. Both Farside and Lifeside, it's long been the same. But only you and a few very others really know who I am. You can't imagine how precious and important is to have you here . . ."

He stands gazing at the door after she's left. Willing everything to dissolve, fade, crash, melt. But nothing changes. He's still dead. He's still standing here in this Farside room. Can still even breathe the faint patchouli of Thea's scent. He finishes dressing—a tie, a jacket, the same supple leather shoes he arrived in—and heads out into the corridor.

Elsinore really is *big*—and resolutely, heavily, emphatically, the ancient building it wishes to be. Cold gusts pass along its corridors. Heavy doors groan and creak. Of course, the delights of Farside are near-infinite. He's passed through forests of mist and silver. Seen the vast, miles-wide back of some great island of a seabeast drift past when he was still out at sea. The dead can grow wings, sprout gills, spread roots into the soil and raise their arms and become trees. All these things are not only possible, but visibly, virtually, achievably real. But he thinks they still hanker after life, and all the things of life the living, for all their disadvantages, possess.

He passes many fine-looking paintings as he descends the stairs. They have a Pre-Raphaelite feel, and from the little he knows of art, seem finely executed, but he doesn't recognise any of them. Have these been created by virtual hands, in some virtual workshop, or have they simply sprung into existence? And what would happen if he took that sword which also hangs on display, and slashed it through a canvas? Would it be gone for ever? Almost certainly not. One thing he knows for sure about the Farside's vast database is that it's endlessly backed up, scattered, diffused and re-collated across many secure and heavily armed vaults back in what's left of the world of the living. There are very few guaranteed ways of destroying any of it, least of all the dead.

Further down, there are holo-images, all done in stylish black and white. Somehow, even in a castle, they don't even look out of place. Thea, as always, looks like she's stepped out of a fashion shoot. The dying jungle suits her. As does this war zone, and this flooded hospital, and this burnt-out shanty town. The kids, and it is mostly kids, who surround her with their pot bellies and missing limbs, somehow manage to absorb a little of her glamour. On these famous trips of hers back to view the suffering living, she makes an incredibly beautiful ghost.

Two big fires burn in Elsinore's great hall, and there's a long table for dinner, and the heads of many real and mythic creatures loom upon the walls. Basilisk, boar, unicorn . . . Hardly noticing the chimera servant who rakes his chair out for him, Northover sits down. Thea's space at the top of the table is still empty.

In this Valhalla where the lucky, eternal dead feast forever, what strikes Northover most strongly is the sight of Sam Bartleby sitting beside Thea's vacant chair. Not that he doesn't know that the man has been part of what's termed *Thea Lorentz's inner circle* for more than a decade. But, even when they were all still alive and working together on *Bard On Wheels*, he'd never been able to understand why she put up with him. Of course, Bartleby made his fortune with those ridiculous action virtuals, but the producers deepened his voice so much, and enhanced his body so ridiculously, that it was a wonder to Northover they bothered to use him at all. Now, though, he's chosen to bulk himself out and cut his hair in a Roman fringe. He senses Northover's gaze, and raises his glass, and gives an ironic nod. He still has the self-regarding manner of someone who thinks themselves far more better looking, not to mention cleverer, than they actually are.

Few of the dead, though, choose to be beautiful. Most elect for the look that expresses themselves at what they thought of as the most fruitful and self-expressive period of their lives. Amongst people this wealthy, this often equates to late middle age. The fat, the bald, the matrony and the downright ugly rub shoulders, secure in the knowledge that they can become young and beautiful again whenever they wish.

"So? What are you here for?"

The woman beside him already seems flushed from the wine, and has a homely face and a dimpled smile, although she sports pointed teeth, elfin ears and her eyes are cattish slots.

"For?"

"Name's Wilhelmina Howard. People just call me Will . . ." She offers him a claw-nailed hand to shake. "Made my money doing windfarm recycling in the non-federal states. All that lovely superconductor and copper we need right here to keep our power supplies as they should be. Not that we ever had much of a presence in England, which I'm guessing is where you were from . . . ?"

He gives a guarded nod.

"But isn't it just so *great* to be here at Elsinore? *Such* a privilege. Thea's everything people say she is, isn't she, and then a whole lot more as well? *Such* compassion, and all the marvellous things she's done! Still, I know she's invited me here because she wants to get hold of some of my money. Give back a little of what we've taken an' all. Not that I won't give. That's for sure. Those poor souls back on Lifeside. We really have to do something, don't we, all of us . . . ?"

"To be honest, I'm here because I used to work with Thea. Back when we were both alive."

"So, does that make you an *actor*?" Wilhelmina's looking at him more closely now. Her slot pupils have widened. "Should I *recognise* you? Were you in any of the famous—"

"No, no." As if in defeat, he holds up a hand. Another chance to roll out his story. More a musician, a keyboard player, although there wasn't much he hadn't turned his hand to over the years. Master of many trades, and what have you—at least, until that message fail signal came along.

"So, pretty much a lucky break," murmurs this ex take-no-shit businesswoman who died and became a fat elf, "rather than any kind of lifetime endeavour . . . ?"

Then Thea enters the hall, and she's changed into something more purpose-fully elegant—a light grey dress that shows her fine breasts and shoulders without seeming immodest—and her hair is differently done, and Northover understands all the more why most of the dead make no attempt to be beautiful. After all, how could they, when Thea Lorentz does it so unassailably well? She stands waiting for a moment as if expectant silence hasn't already fallen, then says few phrases about how pleased she is to have so many charming and interesting guests. Ap-plause follows. Just as she used to do for many an encore, Thea nods and smiles and looks genuinely touched.

The rest of the evening at Elsinore passes in a blur of amazing food and superb wine, all served with the kind of discreet inevitability which Northover has deci-ded only chimeras are capable of. Just like Wilhelmina, everyone wants to know who he's with, or for, or from. The story about that jingle works perfectly; many even claim to have heard of him and his success. Their curiosity only increases when he explains his and Thea's friendship. After all, he could be the route of special access to her famously compassionate ear.

There are about twenty guests here at Elsinore tonight, all told, if you don't count the several hundred chimeras, which of course no one does. Most of the dead, if you look at them closely enough, have adorned themselves with small eccentricities; a forked tongue here, an extra finger there, a crimson badger-stripe of hair. Some are new to each other, but the interactions flow on easy rails. Genuine fame itself is rare here—after all, entertainment has long been a cheap-ened currency—but there's a relaxed feeling-out between strangers in the knowl-edge that some shared acquaintance or interest will soon be reached. Wealth always was an exclusive club, and it's even more exclusive here.

Much of the talk is of new Lifeside investment. Viral re-programming of food crops, all kinds of nano-engineering, weather, flood and even birth control—although the last strikes Northover as odd considering how rapidly the human population is decreasing—and every other kind of plan imaginable to make the Earth a place worth living in again is discussed. Many of these schemes, he soon realises, would be mutually incompatible, and potentially incredibly destructive, and all are about making money.

Cigars are lit after the cheeses and sorbets. Rare, exquisite whiskeys are poured. Just like everyone else, he can't help but keep glancing at Thea. She still has that way of seeming part of the crowd yet somehow apart—or above—it. She always had been a master of managing social occasions, even those rowdy parties they'd hosted back in the day. A few words, a calming hand and smile, and even the most annoying drunk would agree that it was time they took a taxi. For all her gifts as a performer, her true moments of transcendent success were at the lunches, the less-than-chance-encounters, the launch parties. Even her put-downs or betrayals left you feeling grateful.

Everything Farside is so spectacularly different, yet so little about her has changed. The one thing he does notice, though, is her habit of toying with those silver bangles she's still wearing on her left wrist. Then, at what feels like precisely the right moment, and thus fractionally before anyone expects, she stands up and taps her wineglass to say a few more words. From anyone else's lips, they would sound like vague expressions of pointless hope. But, coming from her, it's hard not to be stirred.

Then, with a bow, a nod, and what Northover was almost sure is a small conspiratorial blink in his direction—which somehow seems to acknowledge the inherent falsity of what she has just done, but also the absolute need for it—she's gone from the hall, and the air suddenly seems stale. He stands up and grabs at the tilt of his chair before a chimera servant can get to it. He feels extraordinarily tired, and more than a little drunk.

In search of some air, he follows a stairway that winds up and up. He steps out high on the battlements. He hears feminine chuckles. Around a corner, shadows tussle. He catches the starlit glimpse of a bared breast and turns the other way. It's near-freezing up out on these battlements. Clouds cut ragged by a blazing sickle moon. Northover leans over and touches the winding crown of his Rolex watch and studies the distant lace of waves. Then, glancing back, he thinks he sees another figure behind him. Not the lovers, certainly. This shape bulks far larger and is alone. Yet the dim outlines of the battlement gleam through it. A malfunction? A premonition? A genuine ghost? But then, as Northover moves, the figure moves with him, and he realises that he's seeing nothing but his own shadow thrown by the moon.

He dreams that night that he's alive again, but no longer the young and hopeful man he once was. He's mad old Northy. Living, if you call it living, so high up in the commune tower that no one else bothers him much, and with nothing but old piano he's somehow managed to restore for company. Back in his old body, as well, with is old aches, fatigues and irritations. But for once, it isn't raining, and frail sparks of sunlight cling to shattered glass in the ruined rooms, and the whole flooded, once-great city of London is almost beautiful, far below.

Then, looking back, he sees a figure standing at the far end of the corridor that leads through rubble to the core stairs. They come up sometimes, do the kids. They taunt him and try to steal his last few precious things. Northy swears and lumbers forward, grabbing an old broom. But the kid doesn't curse or throw things. Neither does he turn and run, although it looks as if he's come up here alone.

"You're Northy, aren't you?" the boy called Haru says, his voice an adolescent squawk.

He awakes with a start to new light, good health, comforting warmth. A sense, just as he opens his eyes and knowledge of who and what he is returns, that the door to his room has just clicked shut. He'd closed the curtains here in the Willow Room in Elsinore, as well, and now they open. And the fire grate has been cleared, the applewood logs restocked. He reaches quickly for his Rolex and begins to relax as he slips it on. The servants, the chimeras, will have been trained, programmed, to perform their work near-invisibly, and silently.

He showers again. He meets the gaze of his own eyes in the mirror as he shaves. Whatever view there might be from his windows is hidden in a mist so thick that the world beyond could be the blank screen of some old computer from his youth. The route to breakfast is signalled by conversation and a stream of guests. The hall is smaller than the one they were in last night, but still large enough. A big fire crackles in a soot-stained hearth, but steam rises from the food as cold air wafts in through the open doors.

Dogs are barking in the main courtyard. Horses are being led out. Elsinore's battlements and towers hover like ghosts in the blanketing fog. People are milling, many wearing thick gauntlets, leather helmets and what look like padded vests and kilts. The horses are big, beautifully groomed but convincingly skittish in the way that Northover surmises expensively pedigreed beasts are. Or were. Curious, he goes over to one as a chimera stable boy fusses with its saddle and reins.

The very essence of equine haughtiness, the creature tosses its head and does that lip-blubber thing horses do. Everything about this creature is impressive. The flare of its nostrils. The deep, clean, horsy smell. Even, when he looks down and under, the impressive, seemingly part-swollen heft of its horsey cock.

"Pretty spectacular, isn't he?"

Northover finds that Sam Bartleby is standing beside him. Dressed as if for battle, and holding a silver goblet of something steaming and red. Even his voice is bigger and deeper than it was. The weird thing is, he seems more like Sam Bartleby than the living Sam Bartleby ever did. Even in those stupid action virtuals.

"His name's Aleph—means alpha, of course, or the first. You may have heard of him. He won, yes didn't you . . . ?" By now, Bartleby's murmuring into the beast's neck. "The last ever Grand Steeple de Paris."

Slowly, Northover nods. The process of transfer is incredibly expensive, but there's no reason in principle why creatures other than humans can't join Farside's exclusive club. The dead are bound to want the most prestigious and expensive toys. So, why not the trapped, transferred consciousness of a multi-million-dollar racehorse?

"You don't ride, do you?" Bartleby, still fondling Aleph—who, Northover notices, is now displaying an even more impressive erection—asks.

"It wasn't something I ever got around to."

"But you've got plenty of time now, and there are a few things better than a day out hunting in the forest. Suggest you start with one of the lesser, easier, mounts over there, and work your way up to a real beast like this. Perhaps that pretty roan? Even then, though, you'll have to put up with a fair few falls. Although, if you really want to cheat and bend the rules, and know the right people, there are shortcuts . . ."

"As you say, there's plenty of time."

"So," Bartleby slides up into the saddle with what even Northover has to admit is impressive grace. "Why are you here? Oh, I don't mean getting *here* with that stupid jingle. You always were a lucky sod. I mean, at Elsinore. I suppose you want something from Thea. That's why most people come. Whether or not they've got some kind of past with her."

"Isn't friendship enough?"

Bartleby is now looking down at Northover in a manner even more condescending than the horse. "You should know better than most, Jon, that friendship's just another currency." He pauses as he's handed a long spear, its tip a clear, icy substance that could be diamond. "I should warn you that whatever it is you want, you're unlikely to get it. At least, not in the way you expect. A favour for some cherished project, maybe?" His lips curl. "But that's not *it* with you, is it? We know each other too well, Jon, and you really haven't changed. Not one jot. What you really want is Thea, isn't it? Want her wrapped up and whole, even though we both know that's impossible. Thea being Thea just as she always was. And, believe me, I'd do anything to defend her. Anything to stop her being hurt . . ."

With a final derisory snort and a spark of cobbles, Bartley and Aleph clatter off.

The rooms, halls and corridors of Elsinore are filled with chatter and bustle. Impromptu meetings. Accidental collisions and confusions that have surely been long planned. Kisses and business cards are exchanged. Deals are brokered. Promises offered. The spread of the desert which has now consumed most of north Africa could be turned around by new cloud-seeding technologies, yet still, there's coffee, or varieties of herb tea if preferred.

No sign of Thea, though. In a way she's more obvious Lifeside, where you can buy as much Thea Lorentz tat as even the most fervent fanatic could possibly want. Figurines. Candles. Wallscreens. Tee shirts. Some of it, apparently, she even endorses. Although always, of course, for a good cause. Apart from those bothersome kids, it was the main reason Northover spent so much of his last years high up and out of reach of the rest of the commune. He hated being reminded of the way people wasted what little hope and money they had on stupid illusions. Her presence here at Elsinore is palpable, though. Her name is the ghost at the edge of every conversation. Yes, but Thea . . . Thea . . . And Thea . . . Thea . . . Always, always, everything is about Thea Lorentz.

He realises this place she's elected to call Elsinore isn't any kind of home at all—but he supposes castles have always fulfilled a political function, at least when they weren't under siege. People came from near-impossible distances to plead their cause, and, just as here, probably ended up being fobbed off. Of course, Thea's chimera servants mingle amid the many guests. Northover notices Kasaya many times. A smile here. A mincing gesture there.

He calls after him the next time he sees him bustling down a corridor.

"Yes, Mister Northover . . . ?" Clipboard at the ready, Kasaya spins round on his toes.

"I was just wondering, seeing as you seem to be about so much, if there happen to be more than one of you here at Elsinore?"

"That isn't necessary. It's really just about good organisation and hard work."

"So . . ." Was that *really* slight irritation he detected, followed by a small flash of pride? ". . . you can't be in several places at once?"

"That's simply isn't required. Although Elsinore does have many shortcuts."

"You mean, hidden passageways? Like a real castle?"

Kasaya, who clearly has more important things than this to see to, manages a smile. "I think that that would be a good analogy."

"But you just said think. You *do* think?"

"Yes." He's raised his clipboard almost like a shield now. "I believe I do."

"How long have you been here?"

"Oh . . ." He blinks in seeming recollection. "Many years."

"And before that?"

"Before that, I wasn't here." Hugging his clipboard more tightly than ever, Kasaya glances longingly down the corridor. "Perhaps there's something you need? I could summon someone . . ."

"No, I'm fine. I was just curious about what it must be like to be you, Kasaya. I mean, are you always on duty? Do your kind *sleep*? Do you change out of those clothes and wash your hair and—"

"I'm sorry sir," the chimera intervenes, now distantly firm. "I really can't discuss these matters when I'm on duty. If I may . . . ?"

Then, he's off without a backward glance. Deserts may fail to bloom if the correct kind of finger food isn't served at precisely the right moment. Children blinded by onchocerciasis might not get the implants that will allow them to see grainy shapes for lack of a decent meeting room. And, after all, Kasaya is responding in the way that any servant would—at least, if a guest accosted them and started asking inappropriately personal questions when they were at work. Northover can't help but feel sorry for these creatures, who clearly seem to have at least the illusion of consciousness. To be trapped forever in crowd scenes at the edges of the lives of the truly dead . . .

Northover comes to another door set in a kind of side turn that he almost walks past. Is this where the chimera servants go? Down this way, Elsinore certainly seems less grand. Bright sea air rattles the arrow-slit glass. The walls are raw stone and stained with white tidemarks of damp. This, he imagines some virtual guide pronouncing, is by far the oldest part of the castle. It certainly feels that way.

He lifts a hessian curtain and steps into a dark, cool space. A single barred, high skylight fans down on what could almost have been a dungeon. Or a monastic cell. Some warped old bookcases and other odd bits of furniture, all cheaply practical, populate a roughly paved floor. In one corner, some kind of divan or bed. In another, a wicker chair. The change of light is so pronounced that it's a moment before he sees that someone is sitting there. A further beat before he realises it's Thea Lorentz, and that she's seated before a mirror, and her fingers are turning those bangles on her left wrist. Frail as frost, the silver circles tink and click. Otherwise, she's motionless. She barely seems to breathe.

Not a mirror at all, Northover realises as he shifts quietly around her, but some kind of tunnel or gateway. Through it, he sees a street. It's raining, the sky is reddish with windblown earth, and the puddles seem bright as blood. Lean-to shacks, their gutters sluicing, line something too irregular to be called a street. A dead power pylon leans in the mid-distance. A woman stumbles into view, drenched and wading up to the knee. She's holding something wrapped in rags with a wary possessiveness that suggests it's either a baby or food. This could be the suburbs of London, New York or Sydney. That doesn't matter. What does matter is how she falls to her knees at what she sees floating before her in the rain. Thea . . . ! She almost drops whatever she's carrying as her fingers claw upward and her ruined mouth shapes the name. She's weeping, and Thea's weeping as well—two silver trails that follow the perfect contours of her face. Then, the scene fades in another shudder of rain, and Thea Lorentz is looking out at him from the reformed surface of a mirror with the same soft sorrow that poor, ruined woman must have seen in her gaze.

"Jon."

"This, er . . ." he gestures.

She stands up. She's wearing a long tweed skirt, rumpled boots, a loose turtleneck woollen top. "Oh, it's probably everything people say it is. The truth is that, once you're Farside, it's too easy to forget what Lifeside is really like. People make all the right noises—I'm sure you've heard them already. But that isn't the same thing."

"Going there—being seen as some virtual projection in random places like that—aren't you just perpetuating the myth?"

She nods slowly. "But is that really such a terrible thing? And that cat-eyed woman you sat next to yesterday at dinner. What's her name, Wilhelmina? Kasaya's already committed her to invest in new sewerage processing works and food aid, all of which will be targeted on that particular area of Barcelona. I know she's a tedious creature—you only have to look at her to see that—but what's the choice? You can stand back, and do nothing, or step in, and use whatever you have to try to make things slightly better."

"Is that what you really think?"

"Yes. I believe I do. But how about *you*, Jon? What do you think?"

"You know me," he says. "More than capable of thinking several things at once. And believing, or not believing, all of them."

"Doubting Thomas," she says, taking another step forward so he can smell patchouli.

"Or Hamlet."

"Here of all places, why not?"

For a while, they stand there in silence.

"This whole castle is designed to be incredibly protective of me," she says eventually. "It admits very few people this far. Only the best and oldest of friends. And Bartleby insists I wear these as an extra precaution, even though they can sometimes be distracting . . ." She raises her braceletted wrist. "As you've probably already gathered, he's pretty protective of me, too."

"We've spoken. It wasn't exactly the happiest reunion."

She smiles. "The way you both are, it would have been strange if it was. But look, you've come all this incredible way. Why don't we go out somewhere?"

"You must have work to do. Projects—I don't know—that you need to approve. People to meet."

"The thing about being in Elsinore is that things generally go more smoothly when Thea Lorentz isn't in the way. You saw what it was like last night at dinner. Every time I open my mouth people expect to hear some new universal truth. I ask them practical questions and their mouths drop. Important deals fall apart when people get distracted because Thea's in the room. That's why Kasaya's so useful. He does all that's necessary—joins up the dots and bangs the odd head. And people scarcely even notice him."

"I didn't think he likes it much when they do."

"*More* questions, Jon?" She raises an eyebrow. "But everything here on Farside must still seem so strange to you, when there's so much to explore . . ."

Down stairways. Along corridors. Through storerooms. Perhaps these are the secret routes Kasaya hinted at, winding through the castle like Escher tunnels in whispers of sea-wet stone. Then, they are down in a great, electric-lit cavern of a garage. His Bentley is here, along with lines of other fine and vintage machines long crumbled to rust back on Lifeside. Maseratis. Morgans. Lamborghinis. Other things that look like Dan Dare spaceships of Fabergé submarines. The cold air reeks of new petrol, clean oil, polished metal. In a far corner and wildly out of place, squatting above a small black pool, is an old VW Beetle.

"Well," she says. "What do you think?"

He smiles as he walks around it. The dents and scratches are old friends. "It's perfect."

"Well, it was never *that*. But we had some fun with it, didn't we?"

"How does this work? I mean, creating it? Did you have some old pictures of it? Did you manage to access—"

"Jon." She dangles a key from her hand. "Do you want to go out for a drive, or what?"

"The steering even *pulls* the same way. It's amazing . . ."

Out on roads that climb and camber, giving glimpses through the slowly thinning mist of flanks of forest, deep drops. Headlights on, although it makes little difference and there doesn't seem to be any other traffic. She twiddles the radio. Finds a station that must have stopped transmitting more than fifty years ago. Van Morrison, Sprinsteen and Dylan. So very, very out of date—but still good—even back then. And even now, with his brown-eyed girl beside him again. It's same useless deejay, the same pointless adverts. As the road climbs higher, the signal fades to bubbling hiss.

"Take that turn up there. You see, the track right there in the trees . . . ?"

The road now scarcely a road. The Beetle a jumble of metallic jolts and yelps. He has to laugh, and Thea laughs as well, the way they're being bounced around. A tunnel through the trees, and then some kind of clearing, where he stops the engine and squawks the handbrake, and everything falls still.

"Do you remember?"

He climbs out slowly, as if fearing a sudden movement might cause it all to dissolve. "Of course I do . . ."

Thea, though, strides ahead. Climbs the sagging cabin steps.

"This is . . ."

"I know," she agrees, testing the door. Which—just as it had always been—is unlocked.

This, he thinks as he stumbles forward, is what it really means to be dead. Forget the gills and wings and the fine wines and the spectacular food and the incredible scenery. What this is, what it means . . .

Is *this*.

The same cabin. It could be the same day. Thea, she'd called after him as he walked down the street away from an old actors' pub off what was still called Covent Garden after celebrating—although that wasn't the word—the end of *Bard on Wheels* with a farewell pint and spliff. Farewell and fuck off as far as Northover was concerned, Sam Bartleby and his stupid sword fights especially. Shakespeare and most other kinds of real performance being well and truly dead, and everyone heading for well-deserved obscurity. The sole exception being Thea Lorentz, who could sing and act and do most things better than all the rest of them combined and had an air of being destined for higher things that didn't seem like arrogant bullshit even if it probably was. Out of his class, really, both professionally and personally. But she'd called to him, and he'd wandered back, for where else was he heading? She'd said she had a kind of proposal, and why didn't they go out for a while out in her old VW? All the bridges over the Thames hadn't yet been down then, and they'd driven past the burnt-out cars and abandoned shops until they came to this stretch of woodland where the trees were still alive, and they'd ended up exactly here. In this clearing, inside this cabin.

There's an old woodburner stove that Northover sets about lighting, and a few tins along the cobweb shelves, which he inspects and settles on a tin of soup, which he nearly cuts his thumb struggling to open, and sets to warm on the top of the fire as it begins to send out amber shadows. He goes to the window, clears a space in the dust, pretending to check if he turned the VW's lights off, but in reality trying to grab a little thinking time. He didn't, doesn't, know Thea Lorentz that well at this or any point. But he knows her well enough to understand that her spontaneous suggestions are nothing if not measured.

"Is this how it was, do you think?" she asks, shrugging off her coat and coming to stand behind him. Again, that smell of patchouli. She slides her arms around his waist. Nestles her chin against his shoulder. "I wanted you to be what I called producer and musical director for my Emily Dickinson thing. And you agreed."

"Not before I'd asked if you meant roadie and general dogsbody."

He feels her chuckle. "That as well . . ."

"What else was I going to do, anyway?" Dimly, in the gaining glow of the fire, he can see her and his face in reflection.

"And how about now?"

"I suppose it's much the same."

He turns. It's he who clasps her face, draws her mouth to his. Another thing about Thea is that, even when you know it's always really her, it somehow seems to be you.

Their teeth clash. It's been a long time. This is the first time ever. She draws back, breathless, pulls off that loose-fitting jumper she's wearing. He helps her with the shift beneath, traces, remembers, discovers or rediscovers, the shape and weight of her breasts. Thumbs her hardening nipples. Then, she pulls away his shirt, undoes his belt buckle. Difficult here to be graceful, even if you're Thea Lorentz, struggle-hopping with zips, shoes and panties. Even harder for Northover with one sock off and the other caught on something or other, not to mention his young man's erection, as he throws a dusty blanket over the creaky divan. But laughter helps. Laughter always did. That, and Thea's knowing smile as she takes hold of him for a moment in her cool fingers. Then, Christ, she lets go of him again. A final pause, and he almost thinks this isn't going to work, but all she's doing is pulling off those silver bracelets, and then, before he can realise what else it is she wants, she's snapping off the bangle of his Rolex as well and pulling him down, and now there's nothing else to be done, for they really are naked.

Northover, he's drowning in memory. Greedy at first, hard to hold back, especially with the things she does, but then trying to be slow, trying to be gentle. Or, at least, a gentleman. He remembers, anyway—or is it now happening?—that time she took his head between her hands and raised it to her gaze. *You don't have to be so careful,* she murmurs. Or murmured. *I'm flesh and blood, Jon. Just like you . . .*

He lies back. Collapsed. Drenched. Exhausted. Sated. He turns from the cobweb ceiling and sees the Rolex lies cast on the gritty floor. Softly ticking. Just within reach. But already, Thea is stirring. She scratches, stretches. Bracelet hoops glitter as they slip back over her knuckles. He stands up. Pads over to a stained sink. There's a trickle of water. What might pass for a towel. Dead or living, it seems, the lineaments of love remain the same.

"You never were much of a one for falling asleep after," Thea comments, straightening her sleeves as she dresses.

"Not much a man, then."

"Some might say that . . ." She laughs as she fluffs her hair. "But we had something, didn't we, Jon? We really did. So why not again?"

There it is. Just when he thinks the past's finally over and done with. Not Emily Dickinson this time, or not only that project, but a kind of greatest hits. Stuff they did together with *Bard on Wheels,* although this time it'll be just them, a two-hander, a proper double act, and, yes Jon, absolutely guaranteed no Sam fucking Bartleby. Other things as well. A few songs, sketches. Bits and bobs. Fun, of course. But wasn't the best kind of fun always the stuff you took seriously? And why not start here and see how it goes? Why not tonight, back at Elsinore?

As ever, what can he say but yes?

Thea drives. He supposes she did before, although he can't really remember how they got back to London. The mist has cleared. She, the sea, the mountains, all look magnificent. That Emily Dickinson thing, the one they did before, was a huge commercial and critical success. Even if people did call it a one-woman show, when he'd written half the script and all of the music. To have those looks, and yet to be able to hold the stage and sing and act so expressively! Not to mention, although the critics generally did, that starlike ability to assume a role, yet still be Thea Lorentz. Audrey Hepburn got a mention. So did Grace Kelly. A fashion icon, too, then. But Thea could carry a tune better than either. Even for the brief time they were actually living together in that flat in Pimlico, Northover sometimes found himself simply looking—staring, really—at Thea. Especially when she was sleeping. She just seemed so angelic. Who are you really? he'd wondered. Where are you from? Why are you here, and with me of all people?

He never did work out the full chain of events that brought her to join *Bard on Wheels*. Of course, she'd popped up in other troupes and performances—the evidence was still to be found on blocky online postings and all those commemorative hagiographies, but remembrances were shaky and it was hard to work on the exact chain of where and when. A free spirit, certainly. A natural talent. Not the sort who'd ever needed instructing. She claimed that she'd lost both her parents to the Hn3i epidemic and had grown up in one of those giant orphanages they set up at Heathrow. As to where she got that poise, or the studied assurance she always displayed, all the many claims, speculations, myths and stories that eventually emerged—and which she never made any real attempt to quash—drowned out whatever had been the truth.

They didn't finish the full tour. Already, the offers were pouring in. He followed her once to pre-earthquake, pre-nuke Los Angeles, but by then people weren't sure what his role exactly was in the growing snowball of Thea Lorentz's fame. Flunky, and neither was he. Not that she was unfaithful. At least, not to his knowledge. She probably never had the time. Pretty clear to everyone, though, that Thea Lorentz was moving on and up. And that he wasn't. Without her, although he tried getting other people involved, the Emily Dickinson poem arrangements sounded like the journeymen pieces they probably were. Without her, he even began to wonder about the current whereabouts of his other old sparring partners in *Bard on Wheels*.

It was out old LA, at a meal at the Four Seasons, that he'd met, encountered, experienced—whatever the word for it was—his first dead person. They were still pretty rare back then, and this one had made its arrival on the roof of the hotel by veetol just to show that it could, when it really should have just popped into existence in the newly installed reality fields at their table like Aladdin's genie. The thing had jittered and buzzed, and its voice seemed over-amplified. Of course, it couldn't eat, but it pretended to consume a virtual plate of quail in puff pastry with foie gras in a truffle sauce, which it pretended to enjoy with virtual relish. You couldn't fault the thing's business sense, but Northover took the whole experience as another expression of the world's growing sickness.

Soon, it was the Barbican and the Sydney Opera House for Thea (and how sad was that so many of these great venues were situated next to the rising shorelines) and odd jobs or no jobs at all for him. The flat in Pimlico went, and so, somewhere, did hope. The world of entertainment was careering, lemming-like, toward the cliffs of pure virtuality, with just a few bright stars such as Thea to give it the illusion of humanity. Crappy fantasy-dramas or rubbish docu-musicals that she could sail through and do her Thea Lorentz thing, giving them an undeserved illusion of class. At least, and unlike that idiot buffoon Bartleby, Northover could see why she was in such demand. When he thought of what Thea Lorentz had become, with her fame and her wealth and her well-publicised visits to disaster areas and her audiences with the pope and the Dalai Lama, he didn't exactly feel surprised or bitter. After all, she was only doing whatever it was that she'd always done.

Like all truly beautiful women, at least those who take care of themselves, she didn't age in the way that the rest of the world did. If anything, the slight sharpening of those famous cheekbones and the small care lines that drew around her eyes and mouth made her seem even more breath-takingly elegant. Everyone knew that she would mature slowly and gracefully and that she would make—just like the saints with whom she was now most often compared—a beautiful, and probably incorruptible, corpse. So, when news broke that she'd contracted a strain of new-variant septicemic plague when she was on a fact-finding trip in Manhattan, the world fell into mourning as it hadn't done since . . . Well, there was no comparison, although JFK and Martin Luther King got a mention, along with Gandhi and Jesus Christ and Joan of Arc and Marilyn Monroe and that lost Mars mission and Kate and Diana.

Transfer—a process of assisted death and personality uploading—was becoming a popular option. At least, amongst the few who could afford it. The idea that the blessed Thea might refuse to do this thing and deprive a grieving world of the chance to know that somehow, somewhere, she was still there, and on their side, and sorrowing as they sorrowed, was unthinkable. By now well ensconced high up in his commune with his broom and his reputation as an angry hermit, left with nothing but his memories that wrecked piano he was trying to get into tune, even Northover couldn't help but follow this ongoing spectacle. Still, he felt strangely detached. He'd long fallen out of love with Thea, and now fell out of admiring her as well. All that will-she won't-she crap that she was doubtless engineering even as she lay there on her deathbed! All she was doing was just exactly what she'd always done and twisting the whole fucking world around her fucking little finger. But then maybe, just possibly, he was getting the tiniest little bit bitter . . .

Back at Elsinore, Kasaya has already been at work. Lights, a low stage, decent mikes and pa system, along with a spectacular grand piano, have all been installed at the far end of the great hall where they sat for yesterday's dinner. The long tables have been removed, the chairs re-arranged. Or replaced. It really does look like a bijou theatre. The piano's a Steinway. If asked, Northover might have gone for a Bechstein. The action, to his mind, and with the little chance he's even had to ever play such machines, being a tad more responsive. But you can't have everything, he supposes. Not even here.

The space is cool, half-dark. The light from the windows is settling. Bartleby and his troupe of merry men have just returned from their day of tally-ho slaughter with a giant boar hung on ropes. Tonight, by sizzling flamelight out in the yard, the dining will be alfresco. And after that . . . Well, word has already got out that Thea and this newly arrived guy at Elsinore are planning some kind of re-union performance. No wonder the air in this empty hall feels expectant.

He sits down. Wondrous and mysterious as Thea Lorentz's smile, the keys—which are surely real ivory—gleam back at him. He plays a soft e-minor chord. The sound shivers out. Beautiful. Although that's mostly the piano. Never a real musician, Northy. Nor much of a real actor, either. Never a real anything. Not that much of a stagehand, even. Just got lucky for a while with a troupe of travelling players. Then, as luck tends to do, it ran out on you. But still. He hasn't sat at one of these things since he died, yet it couldn't feel more natural. As the sound fades, and the gathering night washes in, he can hear the hastening tick of his Rolex.

The door at the far end bangs. He thinks it's most likely Kasaya. But it's Thea. Barefoot now. Her feet sip the polished floor. Dark slacks, an old, knotted shirt. Hair tied back. She looks the business. She's carrying loose sheaves of stuff—notes, bits of script and sheet music—almost all of which he recognises as she slings them down across the gleaming lid of the piano.

"Well," she says, "shall we do this thing?"

In his room, he stands for a long time in the steam heat of the shower. Finds he's soaping and scrubbing himself until his skin feels raw and his head is dizzy. He'd always wondered about those guys from al-Qaeda and Hezbollah and the Taliban and New Orthodoxy. Why they felt such a need to shave and cleanse the bodies they would soon be destroying. Now, though, he understands perfectly. The world is ruined and time is out of joint, but this isn't just a thing you do out of conviction. The moment has to be right, as well.

Killing the dead isn't easy. In fact, it's near impossible. But not quite. The deads' great strength is the sheer overpowering sense of reality they bring to the sick fantasy they call Farside. Everything must work. Everything has to be what it is, right down to the minutest detail. Everything must be what it seems to be. But this is also their greatest weakness. Of course, they told Northy when they took off his blindfold as he sat chained to a chair which was bolted to the concrete floor in that deserted shopping mall, we can try to destroy them by trying to tear everything in

Farside apart. We can fly planes into their reactors, introduce viruses into their processing suites, flood their precious data vaults with seawater. But there's always a backup. There's always another power source. We can never wreck enough of Farside to have even a marginal effect upon the whole. But the dead themselves are different. Break down the singularity of their existence for even an instant, and you destroy it forever. The dead become truly dead.

Seeing as it didn't exist as a real object, they had to show him the Rolex he'd be wearing through a set of VR gloves and goggles. Heavy-seeming of course, and ridiculously over-engineered, but then designer watches had been that way for decades. This is what you must put on along with your newly assumed identity when you return to consciousness in a cabin on board a steamer ferry bound for New Erin. It many ways, the watch is what it appears to be. It ticks. It tells the time. You'll even need to remember to wind it up. But carefully. Pull the crown out and turn it backwards—no, no, not now, not even here, you mustn't—and it will initiate a massive databurst. The Farside equivalent of an explosion of about half a pound of semtex, atomising anything within a three metre radius—yourself, of course, included, which is something we've already discussed—and causing damage, depending on conditions, in a much wider sphere. Basically, though, you need to be within touching distance of Thea Lorentz to be sure, to be certain. But that alone isn't enough. She'll be wearing some kind of protection which will download her to a safe backup even in the instant of time it takes the blast to expand. We don't know what that protection will be, although we believe she changes it regularly. But, whatever it is, it must be removed.

A blare of lights. A quietening of the murmurous audience as Northover steps out. Stands centre stage. Reaches in his pocket. Starts tossing a coin. Which, when Thea emerges, he drops. The slight sound, along with her presence, rings out. One thing to rehearse, but this is something else. He'd forgotten, he really had, how Thea raises her game when you're out here with her, and it's up to you to try to keep up.

A clever idea that went back to *Bard on Wheels*, to re-reflect *Hamlet* through some of the scenes of Stoppard's *Rozencrantz and Guildenstern Are Dead*, where two minor characters bicker and debate as the whole famous tragedy grinds on in the background. Northover doubts if this dumb, rich, dead audience get many of the references, but that really doesn't matter when the thing flows as well as it does. Along with the jokes and witty wordplay, all the stuff about death, and life in a box being better than no life at all, gains a new resonance when it's performed here on Farside. The audience are laughing fit to bust by the end of the sequence, but you can tell in the falls of silence that come between that they know something deeper and darker is really going on.

It's the same when he turns to the piano, and Thea sings a few of Shakespeare's jollier songs. For, as she says as she stands there alone in the spotlight and her face glows and those bangles slide upon her arms, The man that hath no music in himself, the motions of his spirit are dull as night. She even endows his arrangement of Under the Greenwood Tree, which he always thought too saccharine, with a bittersweet air.

This, Northover thinks, as they move on to the Emily Dickinson section—which, of course, is mostly about death—is why I have to do this thing. Not because Thea's fake or because she doesn't believe in what she's doing. Not because she isn't Thea Lorentz any longer and has been turned inside out by the dead apologists into some parasitic ghost. Not because what she does here at Elsinore is a sham. I must do this because she is, and always was, the treacherous dream of some higher vision of humanity, and people will only ever wake up and begin to shake off their shackles when they realise that living is really about forgetting such illusions, and looking around them, and picking up a fucking broom and clearing up the mess of the world themselves. The dead take our power, certainly—both physically and figuratively. The reactors that drive the Farside engines use resources and technologies the living can barely afford. Their clever systems subvert and subsume our own. They take our money, too. Masses and masses of it. Who'd have thought that an entirely virtual economy could do so much better than one that's supposedly real? But what they really take from us, and the illusion that Thea Lorentz will continue to foster as long as she continues to exist, is hope.

Because I did not stop for death . . . Not knowing when the dawn will come, I open every door . . . It all rings so true. You could cut the air with a knife. You could pull down the walls of the world. Poor Emily Dickinson, stuck in that homestead with her dying mother and that sparse yet volcanic talent that no one even knew about. Then, and just when the audience are probably expecting something lighter to finish off, it's back to Hamlet, and sad, mad Ophelia's songs—which are scattered about the play just as she is; a wandering, hopeless, hopeful ghost—although Northover has gathered them together as a poignant posy in what he reckons is some of his best work. Thea knows it as well. Her instincts for these things are more honed than his ever were. After all, she's a trouper. A legend. She's Thea Lorentz. She holds and holds the audience as new silence falls. Then, just as she did in rehearsal, she slides the bangles off her arm, and places them atop the piano, where they lie bright as rain circles in a puddle.

"Keep this low and slow and quiet," she murmurs, just loud enough for everyone in the hall to hear as she steps back to the main mike. He lays his hands on the keys. Waits, just as they always did, for the absolute stilling of the last cough, mutter and shuffle. Plays the chords that rise and mingle with her perfect, perfect voice. The lights shine down on them from out of sheer blackness, and it's goodnight, sweet ladies, and rosemary for remembrance, which bewept along the primrose path to the grave where I did go . . .

As the last chord dies, the audience erupts. Thea Lorentz nods, bows, smiles as the applause washes over her in great, sonorous, adoring waves. It's just the way it always was. The spotlight loves her, and Northover sits at the piano for what feels like a very long time. Forgotten. Ignored. It would seem churlish for him not to clap as well. So he does. But Thea knows the timing of these things better than anyone, and crowd loves it all the more when, the bangles looped where she left them on the piano, she beckons him over. He stands up. Crosses the little stage to join her in the spotlight. Her bare left arm slips easy around his waist as he bows. This could be Carnegie Hall. This could be the Bolshoi. The manacling weight of the Rolex drags at his wrist. Thea smells of patchouli and of Thea, and the play's the thing, and there could not, never could be, a better moment. There's even Sam Bartleby, sat grinning but pissed off right there on the front row and well within range of the blast.

They bow again, *thankyouthankyouthankyou*, and by now Thea's holding him surprisingly tightly, and it's difficult for him to reach casually around to the Rolex, even though he knows it must be done. Conscience doth make cowards of us all, but the time for doubt is gone, and he's just about to pull and turn the crown of his watch when Thea murmurs something toward his ear which, in all this continuing racket, is surely intended only for him.

"What?" he shouts back.

Her hand cups his ear more closely. Her breath, her entire seemingly living body, leans into him. Surely one of those bon mots that performers share with each other in times of triumph such as this. Just something else that the crowds love to see.

"Why don't you do it now?" Thea Lorentz says to Jon Northover. "What's stopping you . . . ?"

He's standing out on the moonlit battlements. He doesn't know how much time has passed, but his body is coated in sweat and his hands are trembling and his ears still seem to be ringing and his head hurts. Performance come-down to end all performance come-downs, and surely it's only a matter of minutes before Sam Bartleby, or perhaps Kasaya, or whatever kind of amazing Farside device it is that really works the security here at Elsinore, comes to get him. Perhaps not even that. Maybe he'll just vanish. Would that be so terrible? But then, they have cellars here at Elsinore. Dungeons, even. Put to the question. Matters of concern and interest. Things they need to know. He wonders how much full-on pain a young, fit body such as the one he now inhabits is capable of bearing . . . He fingers the Rolex, and studies the drop, but somehow he can't bring himself to do it.

When someone does come, it's Thea Lorentz. Stepping out from the shadows into the spotlight glare of the moon. He sees that she's still not wearing those bangles, but she keeps further back from him now, and he knows it's already too late.

"What made you realise?"

She shrugs. Shivers. Pulls down her sleeves. "Wasn't it one of the first things I said to you? That you were too principled to ever come here?"

"That was what I used to think as well."

"Then what made you change your mind?"

Her eyes look sadder than ever. More compassionate. He wants to bury his face in her hair. After all, Thea could always get more out of him than anyone. So he tells her about mad old Northy, with that wrecked piano he'd found in what had once been a rooftop bar up in his eyrie above the commune, which he'd spent his time restoring because what else was there to do? Last working piano in London, or England, most likely. Or the whole fucking world come to that. Not that it was ever that much of a great shakes. Nothing like here. Cheaply built in Mexico of all places. But then this kid called Haru comes up, and he says he's curious about music, and he asks Northy to show him his machine for playing it, and Northy trusts the kid, which feels like a huge risk. Even that first time he sits Haru down at it, though, he knows he's something special. He just has that air.

"And you know, Thea . . ." Northover finds he's actually laughing. "You know what the biggest joke is? Haru didn't even *realise*. He could read music quicker than I can read words, and play like Chopin and Chick Corea, and to him it was all just this lark of a thing he sometimes did with this mad old git up on the fortieth floor . . .

"But he was growing older. Kids still do, you know, back on Lifeside. And one day he's not there, and when he does turn up next, there's this girl downstairs who's apparently the most amazing thing in the history of everything, and I shout at him and tell him just how fucking brilliant he really is. I probably even used the phrase *God-given talent*, whatever the hell that's supposed to mean. But anyway . . ."

"Yes?"

Northover sighs. This is the hard bit, even though he's played it over a million times in his head. "They become a couple, and she soon gets pregnant, and she has a healthy baby, even though they seem ridiculously young. A kind of miracle. They're so proud they even take the kid up to show me, and he plongs his little hands on my piano, and I wonder if he'll come up one day to see old Northy, too. Given a few years, and assuming old Northy's still alive, that is, which is less than likely. But that isn't how it happens. The baby gets sick. It's winter and there's an epidemic of some new variant of the nano flu. Not to say there isn't a cure. But the cure needs money—I mean, you know what these retrovirals cost better than anyone, Thea—which they simply don't have. And this is why I should have kept my big old mouth shut, because Haru must have remembered what I yelled at him about his rare, exceptional musical ability. And he decides his baby's only just starting on his life, and he's had a good innings of eighteen or so years. And if there's something he can do, some sacrifice he can make for his kid . . . So that's what he does . . ."

"You're saying?"

"Oh, come on, Thea! I know it's not legal, either Lifeside or here. But we both know it goes on. Everything has its price, especially talent. And the dead have more than enough vanity and time, if not the application, to fancy themselves as brilliant musicians, just the same way they might want to ride an expensive thoroughbred, or fuck like Casanova, or paint like Picasso. So Haru sold himself, or the little bit that someone here wanted, and the baby survived and he didn't. It's not that unusual a story, Thea, in the great scheme of things. But it's different, when it happens to someone you know, and you feel you're to blame."

"I'm sorry," she says.

"Do you think that's enough?"

"Nothing's ever enough. But do you really believe that whatever arm of the resistance you made contact with actually wanted me, Thea Lorentz, fully dead? What about the reprisals? What about the global outpouring of grief? What about all the inevitable, endless let's-do-this-for-Thea bullshit? Don't you think it would suit the interests of Farside itself far better to remove this awkward woman who makes unfashionable causes fashionable and brings attention to unwanted truths? Wouldn't *they* prefer to extinguish Thea Lorentz and turn her into a pure symbol they can manipulate and market however they wish? Wouldn't that make far better sense than whatever it was you thought you were doing?"

The sea heaves. The whole night heaves with it.

"If you want to kill me, Jon, you can do so now. But I don't think you will. You can't, can you? That's where the true weakness of whoever conceived you and this plan lies. You *had* to be what you are, or were, to get this close to me. You had to have free will, or at least the illusion of it . . ."

"What the hell are you saying?"

"I'm sorry. You might think you're Jon Northover—in fact, I'm sure you do—but you're not. You're not him really."

"That's—"

"No. Hear me out. You and I both know in our hearts that the real Jon Northover wouldn't be here on Farside. He'd have seen through the things I've just explained to you, even if he had ever contemplated actively joining the resistance. But that isn't it, either. Not really. I loved you, Jon Northover. Loved *him*. It's gone, of course, but I've treasured the memories. Turned them and polished them, I suppose. Made them into something realer and clearer than ever existed. This afternoon, for instance. It was all too perfect. You haven't changed, Jon. You haven't changed at all. People, real people, either dead or living, they shift and they alter like ghosts in reflection, but you haven't. You stepped out of my past, and there you were, and I'm so, so, sorry to have to tell you these things, for I fully believe that you're a conscious entity that feels pain and doubt just like all the rest of us. But the real Jon Northover is most likely long dead. He's probably lying in some mass grave. He's just another lost statistic. He's gone beyond all recovery, Jon, and I mourn for him deeply. All you are is something that's been put together from my stolen memories. You're too, too perfect."

"You're just saying that. You don't know."

"But I do. That's the difference between us. One day, perhaps, chimeras such as you will share the same rights as the dead, not to mention the living. But that's one campaign too far even for Thea Lorentz—at least, while she still has some control over her own consciousness. But I think you know, or at least you *think* you do, how to tune a piano. Do you know what inharmonicity is?"

"Of course I do, Thea. It was me who told you about it. If the tone of a piano's going to sound right, you can't tune all the individual strings to exactly the correct pitch. You have to balance them out slightly to the sharp or the flat. Essentially, you tune a piano ever so marginally out of tune, because of the way the strings vibrate and react. Which is imperfectly . . . Which is . . . I mean . . . Which is . . ."

He trails off. A flag flaps. The clouds hang ragged. Cold moonlight pours down like silver sleet. Thea's face, when he brings himself to look at it, seems more beautiful than ever.

The trees of Farside are magnificent. Fireash and oak. Greenbloom and maple. Shot through with every colour of autumn as dawn blazes toward the white peaks of the Seven Mountains. He's never seen such beauty as this. The tide's further in today. Its salt smell, as he winds down the window and breathes it in, is somehow incredibly poignant. Then the road sweeps up from the coast. Away from the Westering Ocean. As the virtual Bentley takes a bridge over a gorge at a tyre-scream, it dissolves in a roaring pulse of flame.

A few machine parts twist jaggedly upward, but they settle as the wind bears away the sound and the smoke. Soon, there's only sigh of the trees, and the hiss of a nearby waterfall. Then, there's nothing at all.

pathways

NANCY KRESS

Here's a suspenseful story about a smart but uneducated woman taking part in an experimental program that's attempting to find a cure for the degenerative inherited disease that will inevitably kill her—with the clock rapidly running out.

Nancy Kress began selling her elegant and incisive stories in the mid-seventies. Her books include the novel version of her Hugo and Nebula-winning story, Beggars in Spain, *and a sequel,* Beggars and Choosers, *as well as* The Prince of Morning Bells, The Golden Grove, The White Pipes, An Alien Light, Brain Rose, Oaths & Miracles, Stinger, Maximum Light, Crossfire, Nothing Human, The Floweres of Aulit Prison, Crossfire, Crucible, Dogs, *and* Steal Across the Sky, *as well as the Space Opera trilogy* Probability Moon, Probability Sun, *and* Probability Space. *Among her recent novels are* Tomorrow's Kin, If Tomorrow Comes, *and* Terran Tomrrows. *Her short work has been collected in* Trinity and Other Stories, The Aliens of Earth, Beaker's Dozen, Nano Comes to Clifford Falls and Other Stories, The Fountain of Age, Future Perfect, AI Unbound, *and* The Body Human. *In addition to the awards for "Beggars in Spain," she has also won Nebula Awards for her stories "Out of All Them Bright Stars" and "The Flowers of Aulit Prison," the John W. Campbell Memorial Award in 2003 for her novel* Probability Space, *and another Hugo in 2009 for "The Erdmann Nexus." She won two Nebula Awards, in 2013, for her novella* After the Fall, Before the Fall, During the Fall *and in 2015 for her novella* Yesterday's Kin. *She lives in Seattle, Washington, with her husband, writer Jack Skillingstead.*

The Chinese clinic warn't like I expected. It warn't even Chinese.

I got there afore it opened. I was hoping to get inside afore anybody else came, any neighbors who knew us or busybodies from Blaine. But Carrie Campbell was already parked in her truck, the baby on her lap. We nodded to each other but didn't speak. The Campbells are better off than us—Dave works in the mine up to Allington—but old Gacy Campbell been feuding with Dr. Harman for decades and Carrie was probably glad to have someplace else to take the baby. He didn't look good, snuffling and whimpering.

When the doors opened, I went in first, afore Carrie was even out of the truck. It was going to take her a while. She was pregnant again.

"Yes?" said the woman behind the desk. Just a cheap metal desk, which steadied me some. The room was nothing special, just a few chairs, some pictures on the wall, a clothes basket of toys in the corner. What really surprised me was that the woman warn't Chinese. Blue eyes, brown hair, middle-aged. She looked a bit like Granmama, but she had all her teeth. "Can I help you?"

"I want to see a doctor."

"Certainly." She smiled. Yeah, all her teeth. "What seems to be the problem, miss?"

"No problem." From someplace in the back another woman came out, this one dressed like a nurse. She warn't Chinese either.

"I don't understand," the woman behind the desk said. From her accent she warn't from around here—like I didn't already know that. "Are you sick?"

"No, ma'am."

"Then how can I—"

Carrie waddled into the door, the baby balanced on her belly. Now my visit would be table-talk everywhere. All at once I just wanted to get it over with.

"I'm not sick," I said, too loud. "I just want to see a doctor." I took a deep breath. "My name is Ludmilla Connors."

The nurse stopped walking toward Carrie. The woman behind the counter half stood up, then sat down again. She tried to pretend like she hadn't done it, like she warn't pleased. If Bobby were that bad a liar, he'd a been in jail even more than he was.

"Certainly," the woman said. I didn't see her do nothing, but a man came out from the back, and he *was* Chinese. So was the woman who followed him.

"I'm Ludmilla Connors," I told him, and I clenched my ass together real hard to keep my legs steady. "And I want to volunteer for the experiment. But only if it pays what I heard. Only if."

The woman behind the desk took me back to a room with a table and some chairs and a whole lot of filing cabinets, and she left me there with the Chinese people. I looked at their smooth faces with those slanted, mostly closed eyes, and I wished I hadn't come. I guess these two were the reason everybody hereabouts called it the "Chinese clinic," even if everybody else there looked like regular Americans.

"Hello, Ms. Connors," the man said and he spoke English real good, even if it was hard to understand some words. "We are glad you are here. I am Dr. Dan Chung and this is my chief technician Jenny."

"Uh huh." He didn't look like no "Dan," and if she was "Jenny," I was a fish.

"Your mother is Courtney Connors and your father was Robert Connors?"

"How'd you know that?"

"We have family trees for everyone on the mountain. It's part of our work, you know. You said you want to aid us in this research?"

"I said I want to get paid."

"Of course. You will be. You are nineteen."

"Yeah." It warn't a question, and I didn't like that they knew so much about me. "How much money?"

He told me. It warn't as much as the rumors said, but it was enough. Unless they actually killed me, it was enough. And I didn't think they'd do that. The government wouldn't let them do that—not even this stinking government.

"Okay," I said. "Start the experiment."

Jenny smiled. I knew that kind of smile, like she was so much better than me. My fists clenched. Dr. Chung said, "Jenny, you may leave. Send in Mrs. Cully, please."

I liked the surprised look on Jenny's face, and then the angry look she tried to hide. Bitch.

Mrs. Cully didn't act like Jenny. She brought in a tray with coffee and cookies: just regular store-bought Pepperidge Farm, not Chinese. Under the tray was a bunch of papers. Mrs. Cully sat down at the table with us.

"These are legal papers, Ms. Connors," Dr. Chung said. "Before we begin, you must sign them. If you wish, you can take them home to read, or to a lawyer. Or you can sign them here, now. They give us permission to conduct the research, including the surgery. They say that you understand this procedure is experimental. They give the university, myself, and Dr. Liu all rights to information gained from your participation. They say that we do not guarantee any cure, or even any alleviation, of any medical disorder you may have. Do you want to ask questions?"

I did, but not just yet. Half of me was grateful that he didn't ask if I can read, the way tourists and social workers sometimes do. I can, but I didn't understand all the words on this page: *indemnify, liability, patent rights*. The other half of me resented that he was rushing me so.

I said something I warn't intending: "If Ratface Rollins warn't president, this clinic wouldn't be here at all!"

"I agree," Dr. Chung said. "But you Americans elected a Libertarian."

"Us Americans? Aren't you one?"

"No. I am a Chinese national, working in the United States on a visa arranged by my university."

I didn't know what to say to that, so I grabbed the pen and signed everything. "Let's get it over with, then."

Both Dr. Chung and Mrs. Cully looked startled. She said, "But . . . Ludmilla, didn't you understand that this will take several visits, spread out over months?"

"Yeah, I know. And that you're going to pay me over several months, too, but the first bit today."

"Yes. After your interview."

She had one of those little recording cubes that I only seen on TV. They can play back an interview like a movie, or they can send the words to a computer to get put on-screen. Maybe today would be just talking. That would be fine with me. I took a cookie.

"Initial interview with experimental subject Ludmilla Connors," Dr. Chung said, and gave the date and time. "Ms. Connors, you are here of your own free will?"

"Yeah."

"And you are a member of the Connors family, daughter of Courtney Ames Connors and the late Robert Connors?"

"Did you know my dad at the hospital? Were you one of his doctors?"

"No. But I am familiar with his symptoms and his early death. I am sorry."

I warn't sorry. Dad was a son-of-a-bitch even afore he got sick. Maybe knowing it was coming, that it was in his genes, made him that way, but a little girl don't care about that. I only cared that he hit me and screamed at me—hit and screamed at everybody until the night he took after Dinah so bad that Bobby shot him. Now Bobby, just four months from finishing doing his time at Luther Luckett, was getting sick, too. I knew I had to tell this foreigner all that, but it was hard. My family don't ask for help. "We don't got much," Granmama always said, "but we got our pride."

That, and the Connors curse. Fatal Familial Insomnia.

It turned out that Dr. Chung already knew a lot of my story. He knew about Dad, and Bobby, and Mama, and Aunt Carol Ames. He even knew which of the kids got the gene—it's a 50-50 chance—and which didn't. The safe ones: Cody, Patty, Arianna, Timothy. The losers: Shawn, Bonnie Jean, and Lewis. And me.

So I talked and talked, and the little light on the recording cube glowed green to show it was on, and Mrs. Cully nodded and looked sympathetic so damn much that I started wishing for Jenny back. Dr. Chung at least sat quiet, with no expression on that strange ugly face.

"Are you showing any symptoms at all, Ms. Connors?"

"I have some trouble sleeping at night."

"Describe it for me, in as much detail as you can."

I did. I knew I was young to start the troubles; Mama was forty-six and Bobby twenty-nine.

"And the others with the FFI gene? Your mother and Robert, Jr. and"—he looked at a paper "—Shawn Edmond and—"

"Look," I said, and it came out harsher than I meant, "I know I got to tell you everything. But I'm not going to talk none about any of my kin, not what they are or aren't doing. Especially not to a Chinaman."

Silence.

Then Dr. Chung said quietly, "I think, Ms. Connors, that you must not know how offensive that term is. Like 'spic' or 'nigger.'"

I didn't know. I felt my face grow warm.

He said, "I think it's like 'hillbilly' is to mountain people."

My face got even warmer. "I . . . I'm sorry."

"It's okay."

But it warn't. I'm not the kind to insult people, even Chinese people. I covered my embarrassment with bluster. "Can I ask some questions for a change?"

"Of course."

"Is this Chi—did this clinic come to Blaine and start treating people for what ails them, just to get my family's trust so you all can do these experiments on our brains?"

That was the scuttlebutt in town and I expected him to deny it, but instead he said, "Yes."

Mrs. Cully frowned.

I said, "Why? Because there are only forty-one families in the whole world with our sickness? Then why build a whole clinic just to get at us? We're just a handful of folk."

He said gently, "You know a lot about fatal familial insomnia."

"I'm not stupid!"

"I would never think that for even a moment." He shifted in his chair and turned off the recorder. "Listen, Ms. Connors. It's true that sufferers from FFI are a very small group. But the condition causes changes in the brain that involve neural pathways which everybody has. Memory is involved, and sleep regulation, and a portion of the brain called the thalamus that processes incoming sensory signals. Our research here is the best single chance to gain information beyond price about those pathways. And since we also hope to arrest FFI, we were able to get funding as a medical clinical trial. Your contribution to this science will be invaluable."

"That's not why I'm doing it."

"Whatever your reasons, the data will be just as valuable."

"And you know you got to do it to me fast. Afore the Libertarians lose power."

Mrs. Cully looked surprised. Why was she still sitting with us? Then I realized: Dr. Chung warn't supposed to be alone with a young woman. Well, fine by me. But at least *he* didn't seem surprised that I sometimes watch the news.

"That's true," he said. "If Rafe Bannerman wins this presidential election, and it certainly looks as if he will, then all the deregulations of the present administration may be reversed."

"So you got to cut into my skull afore then. And afore I get too sick." I said it nasty, goading him. I don't know why.

But he didn't push back. "Yes, we must install the optogenetic cable as soon as possible. You are a very bright young woman, Ms. Connors."

"Don't try to butter me up none," I said.

But after he took blood samples and all the rest of it, after we set up a whole series of appointments, after I answered ten million more questions, the Chinaman's—no, *Chinese man's*—words stayed in my head all the long trudge back up the mountain. Not as bright, those words, as the autumn leaves turning the woods to glory, but it was more praise than I'd gotten since I left school. That was something, anyway.

———

When I got back to the trailer, about noon, nobody wouldn't speak to me. Carrie must of dropped by. Bobby's wife, Dinah, sewed on her quilt for the women's co-op: the Rail Fence pattern in blue and yellow, real pretty. Mama sat smoking and drinking Mountain Dew. Granmama was asleep in her chair by the stove, which barely heated the trailer. It was cold for October and Bobby didn't dig no highway coal again. The kids were outside playing, Shawn warn't around, and inside it was silent as the grave.

I hung my coat on a door hook. "That quilt's coming nice, Dinah."

Nothing.

"You need some help, Mama?"

Nothing.

"The hell with you all!" I said.

Mama finally spoke. At least today she was making sense. "You better not let Bobby hear where you been."

"I'm doing it for you all!" I said, but they all went back to pretending I didn't exist. I grabbed my coat and stomped back outside.

Not that I had any place to go. And it didn't matter if I was inside or out; Mama's words were the last ones anyone spoke to me for two mortal days. They hardly even looked at me, except for scared peeps from the littlest kids and a glare from Bonnie Jean, like nobody except a ten-year-old can glare. It was like I was dead.

But half the reason I was doing this was the hope—not strong, but there—that maybe I wouldn't end up dead, after first raving and thrashing and trying to hurt people and seeing things that warn't there. Like Dad, like Aunt Carol Ames, like Cousin Jess. And the other half of the reason was to put some decent food on the table for the kids that wouldn't look at me or speak to me from fear that Bobby would switch them hard. I had hopes for Shawn, who hadn't been home in a couple of days, out deer hunting with his buddies. Shawn and I always been close, and he was sweeter than Bobby even afore Bobby started showing our sickness. I hoped Shawn would be on my side. I needed somebody.

But that night in bed, with Patty on my other side as far away as she could get without actually becoming part of the wall, Bonnie Jean spooned into me. She smelled of apples and little kid. I hugged onto her like I warn't never going to let go, and I stayed that way all through the long cold night.

"We have good news," Dr. Chung said. "Your optogenetic vectors came out beautifully."

"Yeah? What does that mean?" I didn't really care, but my nerves were all standing on end and if I kept him talking, maybe it would distract me some. Or not.

We sat in his lab at the Chinese clinic, a squinchy little room all cluttered with computers and papers. No smoking bottles or bubbling tubes like in the movies, though. Maybe those were in another room. There was another Chinese doctor, too, Dr. Liu. Also Jenny, worse luck, but if she was the "chief technician" I guess she had to be around. I kept my back to her. She wore a pretty red shirt that I couldn't never afford to buy for Patty or Bonnie Jean.

"What does that mean?" I said, realized I'd said it afore, and twisted my hands together.

"It means we have constructed the bio-organism to go into your brain, from a light-sensitive opsin, a promoter, and a harmless virus. The opsin will be expressed in only those cells that activate the promoter. When light of a specific wavelength hits those cells, they will activate or silence, and we can control that by—Ms. Connors, you can still change your mind."

"*What?*" Jenny said, and Dr. Chung shot her a look that could wither skunk-weed. I wouldn't of thought he could look like that.

"My mind is changed," I said. His talking warn't distracting me, it was just making it all worse. "I don't want to do it."

"All right."

"She signed the contracts!" Jenny said.

I whirled around on my chair to face her. "You shut up! Nobody warn't talk-ing to you!"

Jenny got up and stalked out. Dr. Liu made like he would say something, then didn't. Over her shoulder Jenny said, "I'll call Dr. Morton. Although too bad she didn't decide that before the operating room was reserved at Johnson Memorial."

"I'm sorry," I said, and fled.

I got home, bone-weary from the walk plus my worst night yet, just as Jimmy Bar-ton's truck pulled up at the trailer. Jimmy got out, looking grim, then two more boys, carrying Shawn.

I rushed up. "What happened? Did you shoot him?" Everybody knew that Jimmy was the most reckless hunter on the mountain.

"Naw. We never even got no hunting. He went crazy, is what. So we brought him back."

"Crazy how?"

"You know how, Ludie," Jimmy said, looking at me steady. "Like your family does."

"But he's only seventeen!"

Jimmy didn't say nothing to that, and the other two started for the trailer with Shawn. He had a purpled jaw where somebody slugged him, and he was out cold on whatever downers they made him take. My gut twisted so hard I almost bent over. *Shawn*. Seventeen.

Dinah and Patty came rushing out, streaming kids behind them. Dinah was shrieking enough to wake the dead. I looked at Shawn and thought about how it must of been in the hunting camp, him going off the rails and "expressing" that gene all over the place: shouting from the panic, grabbing his rifle and wav-ing it around, heart pounding like mad, hitting out at anyone who talked sense. Like Bobby had been a few months ago, afore he got even worse. Nobody in my family ever lasted more than seven months after the first panic attack.

Shawn.

I didn't even wait to see if Mama was coming out of the trailer, if this was one of the days she could. I went back down the mountain, running as much as I could, gasping and panting, until I got to the Chinese clinic and the only hope I had for Shawn, for me, for all of us.

Dr. Morton turned out to be a woman. While they got the operating room ready at Johnson Memorial in Jackson, I sat with Dr. Chung in a room that was supposed to look cheerful and didn't. Yellow walls, a view of the parking lot. A nurse had shaved off a square patch on my hair. I stared out at a red Chevy, trying not to think. Dr. Chung said gently, "It isn't a complicated procedure, Ms. Connors. Really."

"Drilling a hole into my skull isn't complicated?"

"No. Humans have known how to do that part for thousands of years."

News to me. I said, "I forgot a hat."

"A hat?"

"To cover this bare spot in my hair."

"The first person from your family to visit, I will tell them."

"Nobody's going to visit."

"I see. Then I will get you a hat."

"Thanks." And then, surprising myself, "They don't want me to do none of this."

"No," he said quietly, and without asking what I meant, "I imagine they do not."

"They think you conduct experiments on us like we're lab animals. Like with the Nazis. Or Frankenstein."

"And what do you think?"

"I think they are . . . unknowing." It felt like a huge betrayal. Still, I kept on. "Especially my Granmama."

"Grandmothers are often fierce. Mine is." He made some notes on a tablet, typing and swiping without looking at it.

I hadn't thought of him—of any of them—as having a grandmother. I demanded, like that would make this grandmother more solid, "What's her name?"

"Chunhua. What is the name of your grandmother?"

"Ludmilla. Like me." I thought a minute. "'Fierce' is the right word."

"Then we have this in common, yes?"

But I warn't yet ready to give him that much. "I bet my granmama is more fierce than any of your kin."

He smiled, a crinkling of his strange bald face, eyes almost disappearing in folds of smooth skin. "I would—what is it you say, in poker?—'see that bet' if I could."

"Why can't you?"

He didn't answer, and his smile disappeared. I said, "What did your granmama do that was so fierce?"

"She made me study. Hours every day, hours every night. All spring, all summer, all winter. When I refused, she beat me. What does yours do?"

All at once I didn't want to answer. Was beating better or worse? Granmama never touched me, nor any of us. Dr. Chung waited. Finally I said, "She freezes me. Looks at me like . . . like she wants to make a icy wind in my mind. And then that wind blows, and I can't get away from it nohow, and then she turns her back on me."

"That is worse."

"Really? You think so?"

"I think so."

A long breath went out of me, clearing out my chest. I said, "Bobby warn't always like he is now. He taught me to fish."

"Do you like fishing?"

"No." But I liked Bobby teaching me, just the two of us laughing down by the creek, eating the picnic lunch Mama put up for us.

A nurse, masked and gowned like on TV, came in and said, "We're ready."

The last thing I remember was lying on the table, breathing in the knock-out gas, and thinking, *Now at least I'm going to get a long deep sleep*. Only at the very last minute I panicked some and my hand, strapped to the table, flapped around a bit. Another hand held it, strong and steady. Dr. Chung. I went under.

When I woke, it was in a different hospital room but Dr. Chung was still there, sitting in a chair and working a tablet. He put it down.

"Welcome back, Ms. Connors. How do you feel?"

I put my hand to my head. A thick bandage covered part of it. Nothing hurt, but my mouth was dry, my throat was scratchy, and I had a floaty feeling. "What do you got me on? Oxycontin?"

"No. Steroids to control swelling and a mild pain med. There are only a few nerve receptors in the skull. Tomorrow we will take you back to Blaine. Here."

He handed me a red knit hat.

All at once I started to cry. I never cry, but this was so weird—waking up with something foreign in my skull, and feeling rested instead of skitterish and tired, and then this *hat* from this strange-looking man . . . . I sobbed like I was Cody, three years old with a skinned knee. I couldn't stop sobbing. It was awful.

Dr. Chung didn't high-tail it out of there. He didn't try to there-there me, or take my hand, or even look embarrassed and angry mixed together, like every other man I ever knowed when women cry. He just sat and waited, and when I finally got myself to stop, he said, "I wish you would call me 'Dan.'"

"No." Crying had left *me* embarrassed, if not him. "It isn't your name. Is it?"

"No. It just seems more comfortable for Westerners."

"What is your damned name?"

"It is Hai. It means 'the ocean.' "

"You're nothing like any ocean."

"I know." He grinned.

"Do all Chinese names mean something?"

"Yes. I was astonished when I found out American names do not."

"When was that?"

"When I came here for graduate school."

I was talking too much. I never rattled on like this, especially not to Chinese men who had me cut open. It was the damn drugs they gave me, that thing for swelling or the "mild pain med." I'd always stayed strictly away from even aspirin, 'cause of watching Mama and Bobby. Afore I could say anything, Dr. Chung said, "Your meds might induce a little 'high,' Ludmilla. It will pass soon. Meanwhile, you are safe here."

"Like hell I am!"

"You are. And I apologize for calling you 'Ludmilla.' I have not received permission."

"Oh, go the fuck ahead. Only it's 'Ludie.'" I felt my skull again. I wanted to rip off the bandage. I wanted to run out of the hospital. I wanted to stay in this bed forever, talking, not having to deal with my family. I didn't know what I wanted.

Maybe Dr. Chung did, because he went on talking, a steadying stream of nothing: graduate school in California and riding busses in China and his wife's and daughters' names. They were named after flowers, at least in English: Lotus and Jasmine and Plum Blossom. I liked that. I listened, and grew sleepy, and drifted into dreams of girls with faces like flowers.

I was two days in Johnson Memorial and two more in a bed at the clinic, and every single one of them I worried about Shawn. Nobody came to see me. I thought Patty might, or maybe even Dinah if Bobby'd a let her, but they didn't. Well, Patty was only twelve, still pretty young to come alone. So I watched TV and I talked with Dr. Chung, who didn't seem to have a whole lot to do.

"Don't you got to see patients?"

"I'm not an M.D., Ludie. Dr. Liu mostly sees the patients."

"How come Blaine got so many Chinese doctors? Aren't Americans working on optogenetics?"

"Of course they are. Liu Bo and I became friends at the university and so applied for this grant together."

"And you brought Jenny."

"She is Bo's fiancé."

"Oh. She warn't— There he is, the bastard!"

President Rollins was on TV, giving a campaign speech. Red and blue balloons sailed up behind him. My hands curled into fists. Dr. Chung watched me, and I realized—stupid me!—that of course he *was* working. He was observing me, the lab rat.

He said, "Why do you hate the president so?"

"He stopped the government checks and the food stamps. It's 'cause of him and his Libbies that most of Blaine is back to eating squirrels."

Dr. Chung looked at the TV like it was the most fascinating thing in the world, but I knew his attention was really on me. "But under the Libertarians, aren't your taxes lower?"

I snorted. "Five percent of nothing isn't less to pay than fifteen percent of nothing."

"I thought the number of jobs in the coal mines had increased."

"If you can get one. My kin can't."

"Why not?"

I didn't tell him why not. Bobby and Uncle Ted and maybe even now Shawn—they can't none of them pass a drug screen. So I snapped, "You defending Ratface Rollins?"

"Certainly not. He has drastically and tragically cut funding for basic research."

"But here you all are." I waved my arm to take in the room and the machines hooked up to me and the desk in the lobby where Mrs. Cully was doing something on a computer. I was still floating.

"Barely," Dr. Chung said. "This study is funded as part of a grant now four years old and up for renewal. If—" He stopped and looked—for just a minute, and the first time ever—a little confused. He didn't know why he was telling me so much. I didn't know, either. *My* excuse was the pain drugs.

I said, "If Ratface wins, you lose the money for this clinic?"

"Yes."

"Why? I mean, why this one specially?"

He chewed on his bottom lip, something else I didn't see him do afore. I thought he warn't going to say any more, but then he did. "The study so far has produced no publishable results. The population affected is small. We obtained the current grant just before President Rollins came into office and all but abolished both the FDA and research money. If the Libertarians are re-elected, it's unlikely our grant will be renewed."

"Isn't there someplace else to get the money?"

"Not that we have found so far."

Mrs. Cully called to him then and he left. I sat thinking about what he said. It was like a curtain lifted on one corner, and behind that curtain was a place just as dog-eat-dog as Blaine. Bobby scrambled to dig coal from the side of the highway, and these doctors scrambled to dig money out of the government. Dinah worked hard to make it okay that Bobby hit her ("It ain't him, it's the fucking sickness!"), and Dr. Chung worked hard to convince the government it was a good idea to put a bunch of algae and a light switch in my skull. Then I thought about how much I liked him telling me all that, and about the bandages coming off and the real experiment starting tomorrow, and about lunch coming soon. And then I didn't think about nothing because Bobby burst into the clinic with his .22.

"Where is she? Where's my fucking sister?"

"Bobby!"

He didn't hear me, or he couldn't. I scrambled out of bed but I was still hooked up to a bunch of machines. I yanked the wires. Soothing voices in the lobby but I couldn't make out no words.

The .22 fired, sounding like a mine explosion.

"Bobby!"

Oh sweet Jesus, no—

But he hadn't hit nobody. Mrs. Cully crouched on the floor behind her counter. The bullet hole in the wall warn't anywhere near her or Dr. Chung, who stood facing Bobby and talking some soothers that there was no way Bobby was going to hear. He was wild-eyed like Dad had been near the end, and I knew he hadn't slept in days and he was seeing things that warn't there. "Bobby—"

"You whore!" He fired again and this time the bullet whizzed past Dr. Chung's ear and hit the backside of Mrs. Cully's computer. Bobby swung the rifle toward me. I stood stock-still, but Dr. Chung started forward to grab the barrel. That would get Bobby's attention and he would—God no *no* . . .

But afore I could yell again, the clinic door burst open and Shawn grabbed Bobby from behind. Bobby shouted something, I couldn't tell what, and they fought. Shawn didn't have his whole manhood growth yet, but he didn't have Bobby's way-gone sickness yet, neither. Shawn got the rifle away from Bobby and Bobby on the ground. Shawn kicked him in the head and Bobby started to sob.

I picked up the rifle and held it behind me. Dr. Chung bent over Bobby. By this time the lobby was jammed with people, two nurses and Dr. Liu and Jenny and Pete Lawler, who must a been in a examining room. All this happened so fast that Shawn was just preparing to kick Bobby again when I grabbed his arm. "Don't!"

Shawn scowled at the bandage on my head. "He's going to get us all put behind bars. Just the same, he ain't wrong. You're coming home with me."

The breath went out of me. I warn't ready for this. "No, Shawn. I'm not."

"You come home with me or you don't never come home again. Granmama says."

"I'm not going. They're going to help me here, and they can help you, too! You don't need to get like Bobby, like Dad was—"

He shook off my arm. And just like that, I lost him. The Connors men don't hardly never change their minds once they make them up. And soon Shawn wouldn't even have a mind. Seven months from the first sleeplessness to death.

Shawn yanked Bobby to his feet. Bobby was quiet now, bleeding from his head where Shawn kicked him. Dr. Liu started to say, "We must—" but Dr. Chung put a hand on his arm and he shut up. Shawn held out his other hand to me, his face like stone, and I handed him Bobby's gun. Then they were gone, the truck Shawn borrowed or stole roaring away up the mountain.

Dr. Chung knew better than to say anything to me. I looked at the busted computer and wondered how much it cost, and if they would take it out of my pay. Then I went back into my room, closed the door, and got into bed. I would a given anything, right up to my own life, if I could a slept then. But I knew I wouldn't. Not now, not tonight, not—it felt like at that minute—ever again. And by spring, Shawn would be like Bobby. And so would I.

"You need a pass-out," I said to Dr. Chung.

He paused in his poking at my head. "A what?"

"When Bonnie Jean got a fish at a pet store once, they gave her a pass-out paper, TAKING CARE OF YOUR GOLDFISH. To tell her how to do for the fish—not that she done it. You need a pass-out, TAKING CARE OF YOUR BRAIN ALGAE."

Dr. Chung laughed. When he did that, his eyes almost disappeared, but by now I liked that. Nobody else never thought I was funny, even if my funning now was just a cover for nerves. Dr. Liu, at the computer, didn't laugh, and neither did Jenny. I still didn't like *her* eyes.

I sat on a chair, just a regular chair, with my head bandage off and the shaved patch on my head feeling too bare. All my fingers could feel was a tiny bit of something hard poking above my skull: the end of the fiber-optic implant. Truth was, I didn't need a pass-out paper. I knew what was going to happen because Dr. Chung explained it, as many times as I wanted, till I really understood. The punchpad in his hand controlled what my "optrode" did. He could send blue or yellow laser light down it, which would make my new algae release tiny particles that turned on and off some cells in my brain. I'd seen the videos of mice, with long cables coming from their skulls, made to run in circles, or stop staggering around drunk-like, or even remember mazes quicker.

Last night I asked Dr. Chung, "You can control me now, can't you?"

"I have no wish to control you."

"But you *could*."

"No one will control you."

I'd laughed then, too, but it tasted like lemons in my mouth.

"Ready?" Dr. Liu said.

"Ready." I braced myself, but nothing happened. I didn't feel nothing at all. But at the screen Jenny went, "Aaaaaaaahhh."

"What?" I said.

"It works," Dr. Chung said quietly. "We are getting a good picture of optrode response."

On the screen was a bunch of wavy lines, with a lot of clicking noises.

That went on for a long bit: me sitting in the chair feeling nothing, Dr. Chung turning lights on and off in my head that I didn't see, lines and numbers on the computer, and lots of long discussions with words I didn't understand. Maybe some of them were Chinese. And then, just when I was getting antsy and bored both at the same time, something happened. Another press of the punchpad and all at once I saw the room. Not like I saw it afore—I mean I really *saw* it. Every little thing was clear and bright and separate and itself: the hard edge of the computer screen, the way the overhead light made a shadow in the corner, a tiny brown stain on the hem of Jenny's white coat—*everything*. The room was like Reverend Baxter said the world looked right when God created it: fresh and new and shining. I could feel my mouth drop open and my eyes get wide.

"What?" Dr. Chung said. "What is it, Ludie?"

I told him. He did something with the switch in his hand and all the fresh clearness went away. "Oh! Bring it back!"

"Hyperawareness," Dr. Liu said. "The opsins could be over-expressing?"

"Not that quickly," Dr. Chung said. "But—"

"Bring it back!" I almost shouted it.

He did. But after a minute it was almost too much. Too bright, too clear, too strange. And then it got clearer and brighter, so that it almost blinded me and I couldn't see and everything was wrong and—

It all stopped. Dr. Chung had pressed some switch. And then I wanted it back.

"Not yet, Ludie," he said. He sounded worried. "You were injected with multiple opsins, you know, each responding to a different wavelength of light. We're going to try a different one. Would you stand up, please? Good . . . now walk toward me."

I did, and he did something with his switch, and all at once I couldn't move. I was frozen. The computer started clicking loud as a plague of locusts.

Jenny said, "Pronounced inhibitory motor response."

I said, "Stop!"

Then I could move again and I was pounding on Dr. Chung with my fists. "You said you warn't going to control me! You said!"

He grabbed my wrists and held them; he was stronger than he looked. "I didn't know that would happen, Ludie. This is all new, you know. Nobody wants to control you."

"You just did, you bastard!"

"I did not know the inhibitory neurons would fire that strongly. Truly, I did not."

Jenny said something in Chinese.

"No," Dr. Chung said sharply to her.

"I'm done here," I said.

"Yes, that's enough for a first session," Dr. Liu said. Which warn't what I meant. I meant I was going home.

But I didn't. Instead I went to my room in the clinic, got into bed, and slept a little. Not long, not real hard, but enough to calm me down. Then I got up and found Dr. Chung in his office.

If he was glad to see me, he didn't let on. Instead he handed me an envelope. "This came for you in the mail."

Inside was a single page torn from the Sears catalogue, a page with kids' coats on the top and enough white space at the bottom for Dinah to print THANK U. So she got the money I been sending her from my pay. Where did she tell Bobby the warm clothes come from, the coats and stuff for Lewis, Arianna, Timmy, Cody, Bonnie Jean? No, that was stupid—Bobby was too far gone to notice even if the kids ran around buck naked.

I turned on Dr. Chung. "Did you give me this right now so's I'd stay?"

"Ludie, how could I know what was in your envelope? I still don't know."

"You know sure enough what's in my head!"

"I know there are abnormal FFI prions, which we hope to arrest. I know, too, that there is valuable information about how the brain works."

"You told me afore that you can't get them prions out of my head!"

"We cannot, no. What we hope is to disrupt the formation of any more. For your sake, as much as ours."

"I don't believe that crap!"

Only I wanted to believe it.

"Okay," I said, "here's the deal. I stay and you do your experiments, but the minute I tell you to stop something, you do it." It was lame bluster, and he knew it.

"Yes. I already did so, you know. You told me to stop the inhibition of motor activity, and I did."

"And another thing. I want a pass-out, after all."

He blinked. "You want—"

"I want you to write out in words I can understand just what you're doing to me. So's I can study on it afore we do it again."

Dr. Chung smiled. "I will be glad to do that, Ludie."

I flounced out of there, knowing I hadn't told him the whole truth. I wanted to keep sending money to Dinah, yes. I wanted him to not freeze me no more, yes. I wanted a pass-out paper, yes. But I also wanted that shining clearness back, that thing Jenny had called hyperawareness. I wanted it enough to go on risking my brain.

If that's really what I was doing.

> Ludie—you have Fatal Familial Insomnia. Inside a part of your brain called the thalamus, some proteins called prions are folding up wrong. The wrongly folded proteins are making other proteins also fold wrong. These are sticking together in clumps and interfering with what cells are supposed to do. The main thing thalamus cells are supposed to do is process communications among different parts of the brain. The thalamus is like a switchboard, except that it also changes the communications in ways we are trying to learn about. Things which the thalamus communicates with the rest of the brain about include: moving the body, thinking, seeing, making decisions, memory formation and retrieval, and sleeping. When you get a lot of sticky, misfolded proteins in the thalamus, you can't go into deep sleep, or move properly, or think clearly. You get hallucinations and insomnia and sometimes seizures.
>
> We are trying to do three things: (1) Stop your brain making more misfolded prions, even if we can't get rid of the ones that are already there. We are trying to do this by interfering with the making of a protein that the prions use to fold wrong. Unhappily, the only way we will know if this happens is if your symptoms do not get worse. (2) Your brain works partly by sending electrical signals between cells. We are trying to map how these go, called "neural pathways." (3) We want to find out more about what the special algae (opsins) we put in your brain can do. They release different chemicals when we put different laser lights down the cable. We want to know the results of each different thing we do, to aid science.

Well, Dr. Chung wrote good, even though I didn't know what a "switchboard" might be.

I thought of Mama, her brain full of these misfolded proteins, gummed up like a drain full of grease and hair. And Bobby's brain, even worse. Mine, too, soon?

It was dark outside by the time I finished reading that damn paper over and over and over. Everybody'd gone home from the clinic except the night nurse, a skinny rabbitty-looking girl named Susannah. I knowed that she was mountain-born the minute I laid eyes on her, and that somehow she'd got out, and I'd tried not to have nothing to do with her. But now I marched out to where she was reading a magazine in the lobby and said, "Call Dr. Chung. Now."

"What's wrong?"

"Never you mind. Just call him."

"It's ten o'clock at—"

"I know what time it is. Call him."

She did, and he came. I said, "We're going to work now. Now, not in the morning. Them proteins are folding in me right this second, aren't they? You call Jenny and Dr. Liu if you really need them. We're going to work all night. Afore I change my mind."

He looked at me hard. Funny how when you know a person long enough, even a strange and ugly person, they don't look so bad no more.

"Okay," he said. "Let's work."

We worked all night. We worked all week. We worked another week, then another. And I didn't get no worse. No better, but no worse. What I got was scared.

Nobody ought to be able to do those things to somebody else's brain, using nothing except little bits of light.

Dr. Chung froze me again while I was walking around.

Dr. Liu said, "Filtering signals is an important thalamic function, and any change in filtering may give rise to physiological effects."

Dr. Chung made the "hyperawareness" come back, even stronger.

Jenny said, "Interfering with action potentials on cell membranes changes the way cells process information."

Dr. Chung made me remember things from when I was really little—Mama singing to me. Shawn and me wrestling. Granmama telling me troll stories while I sat on her knee. Bobby teaching me to fish. The memories were so sharp, they felt like they was slicing into my brain. Good memories but too razored, making my mind bleed.

Dr. Liu said, "Are the opsins in the anterior nuclei over-expressing? That could cause problems."

Dr. Chung did something that made me stutter so's I couldn't get a word out whole no matter how much I tried.

Jenny said, "Neural timing—even the shift of a few milliseconds can reverse the effect of the signal on the rest of the nervous system. Not good."

I didn't think any of it was good. But I warn't going to say anything in front of that Jenny; I waited until I got Dr. Chung alone.

"I got to ask you something."

"Of course, Ludie." He had just finished checking on my heart and blood pressure and all that. "Are you pleased by the way the study is going? You say your FFI symptoms aren't any worse, and with the usual rapid progression of the disease in your family, that may mean genuine progress."

"I'm happy about that, yeah, if it goes on like now. But I got a different question. I been reading in that book you gave me, how the brain is and isn't like a computer." The book was hard going, but interesting.

"Yes?" He looked really caught on what I was saying. For the first time, I wondered what his wife was like. Was she pretty?

"A computer works on teeny switches that have two settings, on and off, and that's how it knows things."

"A binary code, yes."

"Well, those laser switches on the bundle of optic cables you put in my head—they're off and on, too. Could you make my head into a computer? And put information into it, like into a computer—information that warn't there afore?"

Dr. Chung stood. He breathed deep. I saw the second he decided not to lie to me. "Not now, not with what we know at present, which isn't nearly enough. But potentially, far down the road and with the right connections to the cortex, it's not inconceivable."

Which was a fancy way of saying yes.

"Good night," I said abruptly and went into my room.

"Ludie—"

But I didn't have nothing more to say to him. In bed, though, I used the tablet he loaned me—that's what I been reading the book on—to get the Internet and find Dr. Chung. I got a lot of hits. One place I found a picture of him with his wife. She was pretty, all right, and refined-looking. Smart. He had his arm around her.

Sleep was even harder that night than usual. Then, the next day, it all happened.

We were in the testing room, and my hyperawareness was back. Everything was clear as mountain spring water, sharp as a skinning knife. I kept rising up on my tiptoes, just from sheer energy. It didn't feel bad. Dr. Chung watched me real hard, with a little frown.

"Do you want a break, Ludie?"

"No. Bring it on."

"Hippocampal connection test 48," Jenny said, and Dr. Chung's hand moved on his punchpad. The computer started clicking louder and louder. The door burst open and Bobby charged in, waving a knife and screaming.

"Whore! Whore!" He plunged the knife into Jenny and blood spurted out of her in huge, foaming gushes. I shouted and tried to throw myself in front of Dr. Chung, but Bobby got him next. Dr. Liu had vanished. Bobby turned on me and he warn't Bobby no more but a troll from Granmama's stories, a troll with Bobby's face, and Bonnie Jean hung mangled and bloody from his teeth. I hit out at the troll and his red eyes bored into me and his knife raised and—

I lay on the floor, Dr. Chung holding me down, Jenny doubled over in pain, and the computer screen laying beside me.

"Ludie—"

"What did you do?" I screamed. "What did you do to me? What did I do?" I broke free of him, or he let me up. "*What?*"

"You had a delusional episode," Dr. Chung said, steady but pale, watching me like I was the Bobby-troll. And I was. I had hit Jenny and knocked over the computer, only it was—

"Don't you touch me!"

"All right," Dr. Chung said quietly, "I won't." Dr. Liu was picking up the computer, which was still clicking like a crazy thing. Mrs. Cully and a nurse stood in the doorway. Jenny gasped and wheezed. "You had a delusional episode, Ludie. Perhaps because of the FFI, perhaps—"

"It was you, and you know it was you! You done it to me! You said you wouldn't control my brain and now you—" I pulled at the optrode sticking up from my skull, but of course it didn't budge. "You can't do that to me! You can't!"

"We don't know what the—"

"You don't know nothing! And I'm done with the lot of you!" It all came together in me then, all the strangeness of what they was doing and the fear for my family and them throwing me out and the lovely hyperawareness gone when the switch went off and Dr. Chung's pretty wife—*all of it.*

I didn't listen to nothing else they said. I walked straight out of that clinic, my legs shaking, without even grabbing my coat. And there was Shawn pulling up in Jimmy Barton's truck, getting out and looking at me with winter in his face. "Bobby's dead," he said. "He killed himself."

I said, "I know."

The funeral was a week later—it took that long for the coroner to get done fussing with Bobby's body. It was election day, and Ratface Rollins lost, along with the whole Libertarian party.

The November wind blew cold and raw. Mama was too bad off to go to the graveyard. But Shawn brought her at the service where she sat muttering, even through the church choir singing her favorite, "In the Sweet Bye and Bye." I don't know if she even knew what was going on; for sure she didn't recognize me. It warn't be long afore she'd be as bad as Bobby, or in a coma like Aunt Carol Ames. Granmama recognized me, of course, but she didn't say nothing when I came into the trailer, or when I stayed there, sleeping in my old bed with Patty and Bonnie Jean, or when I cleaned up the place a bit and cooked a stew with groceries from my clinic money. Granmama didn't thank me, but I didn't expect that. She was grieving Bobby. And she was Granmama.

Dinah kept to her room, her kids pretty much in there with her day and night.

I kept a hat on, over my part-shaved head. Not the red knit hat Dr. Chung gave me, which I wadded up and threw in the creek. In the trailer I wore Bobby's old baseball cap, and at the funeral I wore a black straw hat that Mama had when I was little.

"The Lord is my Shepherd; I shall not want. He maketh me to lie down in green pastures . . ." Reverend Baxter did funerals old-fashioned. Bobby's casket was lowered into the hole in the churchyard. The last of the maple leaves blew down and skittered across the grass.

Dinah came forward, hanging on to Shawn, and tossed her flower into the grave. Then Granmama, then me, then Patty. The littlest kids, Lewis and Arianna and Timothy and Cody, were in relatives' arms. The last to throw her flower was Bonnie Jean, and that's when I saw it.

Bonnie Jean wore an old coat of Patty's, too big for her, so's the hem brushed the ground. When she stood by the grave that hem was shaking like aspen leaves. Her face had froze, and the pupils of her eyes were so wide it looked like she was on something. She warn't. And it warn't just the fear and grief of a ten-year-old at a funeral, neither.

"Ashes to ashes, dust to dust . . . ."

Neighbors brought cakes and covered dishes to the trailer. Nobody didn't stay long 'cause they knew we didn't want them to. Dinah went back into her room with her two kids, Mama was muttering beside the stove, Shawn sat smoking and drinking Bud. I told Patty to watch Timmy and Cody and I took Bonnie Jean into our bedroom.

"How long since you slept through the whole night?"

She was scared enough to give me lip. "I sleep. You been right there next to me!"

"How long, Bonnie Jean?"

"I don't got to tell you nothing! You're a whore, sleeping with them Chinese and letting them do bad things to you—Bobby said!"

"How long?"

She looked like she was going to cry, but instead she snatched Bobby's baseball hat off my head. It seemed to me that my optrode burned like a forest fire, though of course it didn't. Bonnie Jean stared at it and spat, "Chink Frankenstein!"

Probably she didn't even know what the words meant, just heard them at school. Or at home.

Then she started to cry, and I picked her up in my arms and sat with her on the edge of the bed, and she let me. All at once I saw that the bed was covered with the Fence Rail quilt Dinah had been making for the women's co-op. She'd put it on my bed instead.

I held Bonnie Jean while she cried. She told me it had been two weeks since she couldn't sleep right and at the graveyard was her second panic attack—what she called "the scared shakes." She was ten years old, and she carried the gene Granmama and God-knows-who-else had passed on without being affected themselves. Insomnia and panic attacks and phobias. Then hallucinations and more panic attacks and shrinking away to hardly no weight at all. Then dementia or coma or Bobby's way out. Ten years old. While I was nineteen and I hadn't even felt her restless beside me in the long cold night.

I knowed, then, what I had to do.

The Chinese clinic was almost empty.

A sign outside said CLOSED. Through the window I could see the lobby stripped of its chairs and pictures and clothes basket of toys. But a light shone in a back room, bright in the drizzly gray rain. I rattled the lock on the door and shouted "Hey!" and pretty soon Mrs. Cully opened it.

She wore jeans and a sweatshirt instead of her usual dress, and her hair was wrapped in a big scarf. In one hand was a roll of packing tape. She didn't look surprised to see me. She looked something, but I couldn't read it.

"Ludie. Come in."

"You all leaving Blaine?"

"Our grant won't be renewed. Dr. Chung found out the day after the election from a man he knows in Washington."

"But Rollins lost!"

"Yes, but the new president made campaign promises to reinstate the FDA with tight regulations on studies with human subjects. Under Rollins there was too much abuse. So Doctors Chung and Liu are using their remaining money for data analysis, back at the university—*especially* since we have no research subjects here. I'm packing files and equipment."

The rooms behind her, all their doors open, were full of boxes, some sealed, some still open. A feeling washed over me that matched the weather outside. The clinic never had no chance no matter who won the election.

Mrs. Cully said, "But Dr. Chung left something for you, in case you came back." She plucked a brown envelope off the counter, and then she went back to her packing while I opened it. Tact—Mrs. Cully always had tact.

Inside the envelope was a cell phone, a pack of money with a rubber band around it, and a letter.

> Ludie—
>
> This is the rest of what the clinic owes you. Along with it, accept my deepest gratitude for your help with this study. Even though not finished, it—and you—have made a genuine contribution to science. You are an exceptional young woman, with exceptional intelligence and courage.
>
> This cell phone holds the phone number for Dr. Morton, who implanted your optrode, and who will remove it. Call her to schedule the operation. There will of course be no charge. The phone also holds my number. Please call me. If you don't, I will call this number every day at 11:00 a.m. until I reach you. I want only to know that you are all right.
>
> Your friend, Hai Chung

The phone said it was 9:30 a.m. Mrs. Cully said, "Is that your suitcase?"

"Yeah. It is. I need Dr. Chung's address, ma'am."

She looked at me hard. "Call him first."

"Okay." But I wouldn't. By the time the phone rang, I would be on the 10:17 Greyhound to Lexington.

She gave me his university address but wouldn't give out his home. It didn't really matter. I knew he would give it to me, plus whatever else I needed. And not just for the study, neither.

Dr. Chung told me, one time, about a scientist called Daniel Zagury. He was studying on AIDS, and he shot himself up with a vaccine he was trying to make, to test it. Dr. Chung didn't do no experiments on himself; he used me instead, just like I was using him for the money. Only that warn't the whole story, no more than Bobby's terrible behavior when he got really sick was the whole story of Bobby. The Chinese clinic warn't Chinese, and I'm not no Frankenstein. I'm not all that "courageous," neither, though I sure liked Dr. Chung saying it. What I *am* is connected to my kin, no matter how much I used to wish I warn't. Right now, connected don't mean staying in Blaine to help Dinah with her grief and Shawn with his sickness and the kids with their schooling. It don't mean waiting for Mama's funeral, or living with Granmama's sour anger at what her genes did to her family. Right now, being connected means getting on a Greyhound to Lexington.

It means going on with Dr. Chung's study.

It means convincing him, and everybody else, to put a optrode in Bonnie Jean's head, and Shawn's, and maybe even Lewis's, so laser light can "disrupt their neural pathways" and they don't get no more misfolded prions than they already got.

It means paying for this with whatever work I get.

And maybe it even means going to Washington D.C. and talking to my congressman—whoever he is—about why this study is a good thing. I read on Dr. Chung's tablet that other scientists sometimes do that. Maybe I could take Bonnie Jean with me. She's real pretty, and I can teach her to look pathetic. Maybe.

I never had no thoughts like this afore, and maybe that's the opsins, too. But maybe not. I don't know. I only know that this is my path and I'm going to walk it.

I hike to the highway, suitcase in one hand and cell phone in the other, and I flag down the bus.

the Hand is quicker . . .

ELiZABETH BEAR

Elizabeth Bear was born in Connecticut, and now lives in Brookfield, Massachusetts, with her husband, writer Scott Lynch. She won the John W. Campbell Award for Best New Writer in 2005, and in 2008 took home a Hugo Award for her short story "Tideline," which also won her the Theodore Sturgeon Memorial Award (shared with David Moles). In 2009, she won another Hugo Award for her novelette Shoggoths in Bloom. *Her short work has appeared in* Asimov's, Subterranean, SCI FICTION, Interzone, The Third Alternative, Strange Horizons, On Spec, *and elsewhere, and has been collected in* The Chains That You Refuse *and* Shoggoths in Bloom. *She is the author of the five-volume New Amsterdam fantasy series, the three-volume Jenny Casey SF series, the five-volume Promethean Age series, the three-volume Jacob's Ladder series, the three-volume Edda of Burdens series, and the three-volume Eternal Sky series, as well as three novels in collaboration with Sarah Monette. Her other books include the novels* Carnival *and* Undertow. *Among her recent books is an acclaimed new novel,* Karen Memory.*

Society has always been divided between the Haves and the Have-Nots, but here's a look at a disquieting future, one where the Have-Nots are, conveniently, kept literally out of sight and out of mind.

Rose and I used to come down to the river together last summer. It was over semester break, and my time was my own—between obligatory work on the paper I hoped would serve as the core of my first book and occasional consultations with my grad students.

Rose wore long dark hair and green-hazel eyes for me. I wore what I always did—a slightly idealized version of the meat I was born with. I wanted to be myself for her. I wondered if she was herself for me, but the one time I gathered up the courage to ask, she laughed and swept me aside. "I thought historians understood that narratives are subjective and imposed!"

I loved her because she challenged me. I thought she loved me too, until one day she disappeared. No answer to my pings, no trace of her in our usual haunts. She'd blocked me.

I didn't handle it well. I was in trouble at the university. I was drinking. I wasn't maintaining my citizenship status. With Rose gone, I realized slowly how much my life had come to revolve around her.

No matter how she felt about me, I knew she loved the river-edge promenade, bordered by weeping willows and her namesake flowers. Those willows were yellow as I walked the path now, long leaves clinging to their trailing branches. The last few roses hadn't yet fallen to the frost, but the flowers looked sparse, dwarfed by the memory of summer's blossoms.

The scent was even different now than it had been at the height of summer. Crisper, thin. The change was probably volunteer work; I didn't think the city budget would stretch to skinning unique seasonal scents for the rose gardens. I knew Rose was older than I, no matter how her skin looked, because she used to say that when she was a girl, individual cultivars of *roses* had different odors, so walking around a rose garden was a tapestry of scents. Real roses probably still did that.

I didn't know if I'd ever smelled them.

Other people walked the path—all skins. The city charged your palm chip just to get through the gate. I didn't begrudge the debit. It wasn't as if I was ever going to get to pay it off. Or as if I was ever going to get to come back here. This was a last hurrah.

I edited out the others. I wanted to be alone, and if I couldn't see them, they couldn't see me. That was good, because I knew I didn't look happy, and the last thing I wanted was some random stranger reading my emotional signature and coming over to offer well-meaning advice.

Since this was my last time, I thought about jumping skins—running up the charges, seeing some of the other ways the river promenade could look— fantasyland, or Rio, or a moon colony. Rose and I had done that when we first started coming here, but it turned out we both preferred the naturalist view. With seasons.

We'd met in winter. I supposed it was fitting that I lost her—and everything else that mattered—in the fall.

Everything changed at midnight.

Not *my* midnight, as if honoring the mystical claptrap in some dead fairy tale. But about the dinner hour, which would be midnight Greenwich Standard Time— honoring the mystical claptrap of a dead empire, instead. I suppose you have to draw the line somewhere. The world is full of the markers of abandoned empires, from Hadrian's Wall to the Great Wall of China, from the remnants of the one in Arizona to the remnants of the one in Berlin.

My name is Ozymandias, King of Kings.

I was thinking about that poem as I crossed Henderson—with the light: I knew somebody who jaywalked and got hit by an unskinned vehicle. The driver got jail time for manslaughter, but that doesn't bring back the dead. It was a gorgeous

October evening, the sun just setting and the trees still full of leaves in all shades of gold and orange. I barely noticed them, or the cool breeze as I waited, rocking nervously from foot to foot on the cobblestones.

I was meeting my friend Numair at Gary's Olympic Pizza and I was running a little late, so he was already waiting for me in our usual corner booth. He'd ordered beers and garlic bread. They waited on the tabletop, the beers shedding rings of moisture into paper napkins.

I slid onto the hard bench opposite him, trying to hide the apprehension souring my gut. The vinyl was artistically cracked and the rough edges caught on my jeans. It wasn't Numair making me so anxious. It was finances. I shouldn't be here, by rights—I knew I couldn't afford even pizza and beer—but I needed to see him. If anything could clear my head, it was Numair.

One of the things I liked about Numair is how unpretentious he was. I didn't skin heavily—not like some people, who wandered through underwater seascapes full of sentient octopuses or dressed up as dragons and pretended they live in Elfland—but he was so down to earth I'd have bet his default skin looked just like him. He was a big guy, strapping and barrel-bodied, with curly dark brown hair that was going gray at the temples. And he liked his garlic bread.

So it was extra-nice that there were still two pieces left when I pulled the plate over.

"Hey, Charlie," he said.

"Hey, Numair." Garlic bread crunched between my teeth, butter and olive oil dripping down my chin. I swiped at it with a napkin. I didn't recognize the beer, dark and malty, although I drank off a third of it making sure. "What's the brew?"

"Trois Draggonnes." He shrugged. "Microbrew license out of . . . Shreveport .com, I think? Cheers."

"Here's mud in your eye," I answered, and drained the glass.

He sipped his more moderately and put it back on the napkin. "You sounded upset."

I nodded. Gary's was an old-style place, and a real-looking waitress came by about thirty seconds later and replaced my beer. I didn't know if she was an employee or a sim, but she was good at her job. The pizza showed up almost instantly after that, balanced on a metal tripod with a plastic spatula for serving. Greek-style, with flecks of green oregano visible in the sweet, oozing sauce. I always got the same thing: meatball, spinach, garlic, mushrooms. Delicious. I'd never asked Numair what he was eating.

The smell turned my stomach.

"I may not be around much for a while." I stuffed the rest of the garlic bread into my mouth to make room. And buy time. "This is embarrassing—"

"Hey." He paused with a slice in midair, perfect strings of mozzarella stretching twelve inches from pie to spatula. They glistened. The booth creaked when he shifted. "This is me."

"Right. I've got financial trouble. Big-time."

He put the slice down on his plate and offered me the spatula. I waved it away. The smell was bad enough. Belatedly, I turned it off. Might as well use the filters as long as I had them. The beer still looked appealing, though, and I drank a little more.

"Okay," he said. "How big-time?"

The beer tasted like humiliation and soap suds. "Tax trouble. I'm going to lose everything," I said. "All assets, all the virtuals. I thought I could pay it down, you know—but then I got dropped by the U., and there wasn't a replacement income stream. As soon as they catch up with me—" I thought of Rose, to whom Numair had introduced me. They'd been Friday-night gaming buddies, until she'd vanished without a word. I'd kept meaning to look her up offline and check in, but . . . It was easier to let her go than know for certain she'd dumped me. Amazing how easy it was to lose track of people when they didn't show up at the usual places and times. "I got registered mail this morning. They're pulling my taxpayer I.D. I'll be as gone as Rose. Except I came to say goodbye before I ditched you."

He blinked. Now it was his turn to set the pizza down and push the plate away with his fingertips. "Rose died," he said.

I rubbed the back of my neck. It didn't ease the sudden nauseating tightness in my gut as all that bitterness converted to something sharp and horrible. "Died? *Died* died?"

"Died and was cremated. Her family's not linked, so I only heard because she and Bill went to school together, and he caught a link for her memorial service on some network site. You didn't know?"

I blinked at him.

He shook his head. "Stupid question. If you knew— Anyway. I guess you've tried everything, so I'll save the stupid advice."

"Thank you." I hope he picked up from my tone how fervently glad I was. Nothing like netfriends to pile on with the incredibly obvious—or incredibly crackpot—advice when you're in a pickle. "So anyway—"

"Give me your offline contact info." He held up his phone and I sent it over. It was a pleasantry. I knew what the odds were that I'd ever hear from him. And it wasn't like I could keep my apartment without a tax identification number.

However good his intentions.

Right then, a quarter of the way around the planet, midnight tolled. And I fell out of the skin.

It was sharp and sudden, as somewhere a line of code went into effect and the last few online chits in my account were levied. I blinked twice, trying to shake the dizziness that accompanied the abrupt transition, eyes now scratchy and dry.

Numair was still there in the booth across from me. It was weird seeing him there, unskinned. I'd been right about his unpretentiousness: he looked pretty much as he'd always done—maybe a little more unkempt—though his clothes were different.

Since he was skinned, I knew I'd dropped right out of his filters. I might as well not exist anymore. And Gary's Olympic, unlike Numair, had really suffered in the transition.

The pizza that congealed on the table before me was fake cheese, lumpy and dry looking. Healthier than the gooey pie my filters had been providing a moment before, but gray and depressing. I was suddenly glad I hadn't been chewing on it when the transition hit.

The grimy floor was scattered with napkins. The waitress was real, go figure, but a shadow of her buxom virtual self—no, she was a guy, I realized. Maybe working in drag brought in better tips? Or maybe the skin was a uniform. I'd never know.

And there was me.

I was not as comfortable with myself as Numair. I didn't skin heavily, as I said—just tuning. But my skins did make me a hair taller, a hair younger. My hair . . . a hair brighter. And so on. With them gone, I was skinny and undersized in a track suit that bagged at the shoulders and ass.

Falling into myself stung.

I reached out left-handed for my beer, since Numair was going to get stuck for the tab anyway. It was pale yellow and tasted of dish soap. So maybe the off flavor in the second glass had been something other than my misery. Whatever.

I chugged it and got out.

The glass door was dirty, one broken pane repaired with duct tape. On the way in, it had been spotless and decorated with blue and white decal maps of Greece. I pushed it open with the tips of my fingers and moved on.

Outside, the street lay dark and dank. Uncollected garbage humped against the curb. Some of it smelled organic, rotten. A real violation of the composting laws. Maybe they didn't get enforced as much against businesses. I picked my way across broken cement to the corner and waited there.

There were more people on the street than there had been. Or maybe they'd been there all along, just skinned out. You could tell who was wearing filters by the way they moved—backs straight, enjoying the evening. The rest of us shuffled, heads bowed. Trying not to see too much. The evening I walked through was full of bad smells and crumbling buildings that looked to be mostly held together by graffiti.

"Aw, crap."

The light changed. I crossed. Of course, I couldn't get a taxi home, or even a bus. Skinned-in drivers would never see me, and my chips were cancelled. I wouldn't get through a chip-locked door to take the tube.

I wondered how the poor got around. I guessed I'd be finding out.

I didn't know my way home.

I was used to the guidance my skins gave me, the subtle recognition cues. All I was getting now was the cold wind cutting through a windbreaker that wasn't warm enough for the job I expected it to do, and a pair of sore feet. Everything stank. Everything was dirty. There were steel bars on every window and chip locks on every door.

I'd known that intellectually, but it had never really sunk in before what a bleak urban landscape that made for. Straggling trees lined unmaintained streets, and at every corner I picked my way through drifts of rubbish. I knew there wasn't a lot of money for upkeep of infrastructure, and what there was had to be assigned to critical projects. But it didn't matter; you could always drop a skin over anything that needed a little cosmetic help.

Sure, I'd seen news stories. But it was one thing to vid it and another to wade through it.

About fifteen minutes after I'd realized how lost I was, I also realized somebody was following me. Nobody bothers the skinned: an instantaneous, direct voice and vid line to police services meant Patrol guardian-bots could be at our sides in seconds. It was a desperate criminal who'd tackle one of us. One of *them*. But that was another service I couldn't pay for, along with a pleasanter reality and access to mass transit.

I wasn't skinned anymore, and I bet anybody following me could tell. Of course, I didn't have any credit, either—or any cash. I guessed unskinned folks still used cash, palm-sized magnetic cards with swipe strips. A lot of places wouldn't take it anymore. But if you didn't have accounts or a working palm chip, what else were you going to do?

Well, if you were the guy behind me, apparently the answer was, *take it from somebody else*.

I was short and I was skinny, but living skinned kept me in pretty good shape. There were all kinds of built-in workout programs, after all, so clever that you hardly even noticed they were healthy. And skinning food kept the blood pressure down no matter how many greasy pizzas you enjoyed.

My pursuer was two-thirds of a block back. I waited until I'd put a corner between me and him. As soon as I lost sight of him, I broke into a run.

It was a pretty good run, too. I was wearing my Toesers, because I liked them, and if they were skinned nobody could tell how dumb they looked. Also, they were comfortable. And supposedly scientifically designed for natural running posture, so you landed on the ball of your foot and didn't make a thump with every stride. Breath coming fast, feet scissoring—I turned at the first corner I came to, then quickly turned again.

Unskinned folks looked up in surprise as I pelted past. One made a grab for me, and another one shouted something after, but I was already gone. And then I was on a side street all by myself, running down a narrow path kicked through the piles of trash.

Maybe this was an even more desolate street, and maybe most of the lights were burned out, but I kept on running. It felt good, all of a sudden, like positive action. Like something I could do other than wallowing. Like *progress*.

It kept on feeling like progress all the way down to the river's edge. And then, as I stopped beside a hole snipped-and-bent in the chain link, it felt like a very bad idea instead.

The river was a sewer. When I'd been here before—okay, not down here under the bridge, but on the bank above—it had been all sunshine and rolling blue water. What I saw now was floating milk jugs and what I smelled was a sour, fecal carrion stench.

I put a hand out to the fence, the wire gritty, greasy where my fingers touched. It dented when I leaned on it, but I needed it to bear my weight up. A stitch burned in my side, and every breath of air scoured my lungs. I didn't know if that was from running, or because the air was bad. But it was the same air I'd been breathing all along. The filters didn't change the outside world. Just our perceptions of it. So how could the air choke me now when before, I breathed it perfectly well?

Shouts behind me suggested that maybe my earlier pursuer had friends. Or that my flight had drawn attention. I was in shadow—but the yellow tracksuit wasn't anyone's idea of good camouflage.

Gravel crunched and turned under my feet. I pushed the top of the bent chain triangle up and ducked through, into the moist darkness under the bridge.

Things moved in the night. Rats, I imagined, but some sounded bigger than rats. What else could live in this filth? I imagined feral dogs, stray cats—companion animals abandoned to make their own fate. Would they attack something as large as a man?

If they did, how would I fight them?

I groped along the bridge abutment, feeling with my toes for a stick. The old stones swept down low, the arch broad and flat. I kept my hand up to keep from hitting my head on an invisible buttress. The masonry was slick with paint and damp, mortar crumbling to the touch. I couldn't see my hand in front of my face, but light concentrated by the oily river reflected up, and I could see the stones of the bridge's underside clearly.

I crept into that dank, ruinous beauty until the flicker of lights against the chain fence told me that my pursuers had found me, and they had come in force. My chest squeezed, stomach flipping in apprehension. I crouched down, tucked myself into the lowest part of the arch, and fumbled out my phone.

"Police," I said. Even if my contract had been cancelled, that should work. I'd heard somewhere that any phone can always dial emergency. And there it was, a distant buzz, and then a calm voice answering.

"Emergency services. Your taxpayer identification number, please?"

My voice stuck in my throat. I'd never been asked that before. But then, I'd never been calling from an unskinned phone before. Without thinking, I rattled off the fourteen digits of my old number, the one that had been revoked. I held my breath afterward. Maybe the change hadn't propagated yet. Maybe—

"That number is not valid," the operator said.

"Look," I whispered, "I'm in a dispute with Revenue Services. It's all going to be sorted out, I'm sure, but right now I'm about to be mugged—"

"I'm sorry," said the consummate professional on the other end of the line. "Emergency services are for taxpayers only."

Before I could protest, the line went dead. Leaving me crouched alone in the dark, with a glowing phone pressed to my ear. Not for long, however: in less than a second, the dazzle of flashlight beams found me. Instinctively, I ducked my head and covered my eyes—with the hand holding the phone.

"Well hey. What's this?" The voice was deceptively pleasant, that seductive mildness employed by schoolyard bullies since first Romulus beat up Remus. The flashlight didn't waver from my eyes.

I flinched. I didn't answer. Not because I didn't want to, but because I didn't have a voice.

I tried to find the part of myself that managed unruly students and lecture-hall hecklers, but it had vanished along with my credit accounts and the protection of the police. I ducked further, squinting around my hand, but he was just a shadow through the glare of his light. At least three other lights surrounded him.

He plucked the phone from my hand with a sharp twist that stabbed pain through my wrist. I snatched the hand back.

"Huh," he said. "Guess you didn't pay your taxes, huh? What else have you got?"

"Nothing," I said. The RFID chip embedded in my palm was useless. Would they cut it out anyway? I had no cash, no anything. Just the phone, which had my whole life on it—all my research, all my photos. Three mostly finished articles. There were backups, of course, but they were on the wire, and I couldn't get there without being skinned.

I wasn't a skin anymore. Objects, I realized, had utility. Had value. They were more than ways to get at your data.

"Your jacket," the baseline said. "And your shoes."

My toes gripped the gravel. "I need my shoes—"

The dazzle of lights shifted. I knew I should duck, but the knowledge didn't translate into action.

At first there wasn't any pain. Just the shock of impact, and an exhale that seemed to start in my toes and never stop. *Then* the pain, radiating stars out of my solar plexus, with waves of nausea for dessert.

"Jacket," he said.

I would have given it to him. But I couldn't talk. Couldn't even inhale. I raised my hand. I think I shook my head.

I think he would have hit me anyway. I think he wanted to hit me. Because when I fell down, he kept hitting me. Hitting and kicking. And not just him, some of his friends.

It's a blur, mostly. I remember some particulars. The stomp that crushed my left hand. The kick that broke my tailbone. I got my knees up and tucked my head, so they kicked me in the kidneys instead. Gravel gouged the side where kicks didn't land. If I could burrow into it, I'd be safe. If I could just fall through it, I might survive. I thought about being small and hard and sharp, like those stones.

After a while, I didn't have the breath to scream anymore.

At first the cold hurt too, but after a while it became a friend. I noticed that they had stopped hitting me. I noticed that the cuts and bruises stung, the broken bones ached with a deep, sick throb. My hand felt fragile, gelatinous. Like a balloon full of water, I imagined that a single pinprick could make the stretched skin explode back from the contents. I prodded a loosened tooth with my tongue.

But then the cold got into the hurts and they numbed. Little by little, starting from the extremities. Working in. It mattered less that the hard points of gravel stabbed my ribs. I couldn't feel that floppy, useless hand. The throb in my head slowly became less demanding than the throb of thirst in my throat.

In the fullness of time, I sat up. It was natural, like sitting up after a full night's sleep, when you've lain in bed so long your body just naturally rises without consulting you. I thought about water. There was the river, but it smelled like poison. I'd probably get thirsty enough to drink it sooner or later. I wondered what diseases I'd contract. Hepatitis. Probably not cholera.

My cheekbones were numb, along with my nose, but I could still breathe normally. So the nose probably wasn't broken. The moving air brought me a tapestry of cold odors: sour garbage, rancid meat, urine. That oil-tang from the river. Frost rimed the gravel around me, and in noticing that I noticed that the morning was graying, the heavy arch of the bridge a silhouette against the sky. There was pink and silver along the horizon, and I knew which direction was east because the sun's light glossed a contrail that must have sat high enough to reach out of the Earth's moving shadow.

Footsteps crunched toward me. I was too dreamy and snug to move. *I'm in shock*, I thought, but it didn't seem important.

"What's this?" somebody said.

I flinched but didn't look up. His shadow couldn't fall across me. We were both under the shadow of the bridge.

"Oh, dear," he said. The crunch of shifting gravel told me he crouched down beside me. When he turned my chin with his fingers and I saw his face, I was surprised he was limber enough to crouch. He looked like the bad end of a lot of winters. "And you lost your shoes too. What a pity."

He didn't seem surprised when I cringed, but it didn't light his eyes up, either. So that wasn't a bully's mocking.

"Can you walk?" He took my arm gently. He inspected my broken hand. When he unzipped my jacket, I would have pulled away, but the pain was bad enough that I couldn't move against him. When he slid the hand inside the jacket and the buttons of my shirt, I realized he was improvising a sling.

As if his touch were the opposite of an analgesic, all my hurts reawakened. I meant to shake my head, but just thinking about moving unscrolled ribbons of pain through my muscles.

"I don't think so." My words were creaky and blood-flavored.

"If you can," he said, "I've got a fire. And tea. And food."

I closed my eyes. When I opened them again, his hand was extended. The left one, as my right hand was clawed up against my chest like a surgical glove stuffed overfull with twigs and raspberry jam.

Food. Warmth. I might have given up, but somewhere in the back of my mind was an animal that did not want to die. I watched as it made a determined, raspy sound and reached out with its unbroken hand.

Letting him pull me to my feet was a special kind of agony. I swayed, vision blacking at the edges. His steadying hand kept me upright. It hurt worse than anything. "Come on," he said.

I remember walking, but I don't remember where or for how long. It felt like forever. I had always been walking. I would be walking forever. There was no end. No surcease.

Pain is an eternity.

His fire was trash and sticks ringed with broken bricks and chunks of asphalt. It smoldered fitfully, and pinprick by pinprick, the heat reawakened my pains. The soles of my feet seeped blood from walking across the gravel. I couldn't sit, because of the tailbone, but I figured out how to lie on my side. It hurt, but so did anything else.

There was tea, as promised, Lipton in bags stewed in a rusty can. I hoped he hadn't used river water. It had sugar in it, though, and I drank cautiously.

The food was dumpster-sourced chicken and biscuits, cold and lumpy with congealed grease. I ate it with my good hand, small bites. The inside of my mouth was cut from being slammed against my teeth. If I chewed carefully, on one side, the loose tooth only throbbed. I hoped it might reseat itself eventually.

Why was I thinking about the future?

The sun had beaten back the gloom enough for even my swollen eyes to make out the old man across from me. He had draped stiff, stinking blankets around my shoulders, but as the sun warmed the riverbank, he seemed comfortable in several layers of shirts and pants. A yellowed beard surrounded his sunken mouth. His hands were spare claws in ragged gloves. He drank the tea fearlessly and warmed his share of the chicken on the rocks beside the trash fire. I thought about plastic fumes and kept gnawing mine cold.

After a while, he said, "You'll get used to it."

I looked up. He was looking right at me, his greasy silver ponytail dull in the sunlight. "Get used to being beaten up?" My voice sounded better than I'd feared. My nose really wasn't broken. One small miracle.

"Get used to being a baseline." He bit into a biscuit, grimacing in appreciation.

I winced, wondering how long it would take me to start savoring day-old fast food fat and carbohydrates. Then I winced in pain from the wincing.

The old man chewed and swallowed. "It's honest, at least. Not like putting frosting all over the cake so nobody with any economic power can tell it's rotten. What's your name?"

"Charlie," I said.

He nodded and didn't ask for a surname. "Jean-Khalil." I wondered if first-names only was part of the social customs of the baseline community.

The shock was wearing off. Maybe the sugar in the tea was working its neurochemical magic. My broken hand lay against my belly, warmed by my skin, and the sweat running across my midsection felt as syrupy as blood.

I kind of wanted the shock back. I looked at the chicken, and the chicken looked back at me. My gorge rose. Bitterness filled my mouth, but I swallowed it. I knew how badly I needed the food inside me.

I balanced the meat on the fire ring next to Jean-Khalil's. "You eat that."

He wiped the back of his hand across his beard. "I will. And you need to get to a clinic."

I put my head down on the unbroken arm. If I didn't get the hand seen too, even if I survived—even if I didn't have internal injuries—what were the chances it would be usuable when it healed? "I don't have a tax number."

"There's a free clinic at St. Francis," he said. "But it's Tuesdays and Thursdays."

I managed to work out that if I normally met Numair on Tuesdays, it would be just after dawn on Wednesday. Which meant, depending on when the clinic opened, something over 24 hours to wait. I could wait 24 hours. Could I *sleep* 24 hours? Maybe I'd die of blood poisoning before then. That might be a relief.

I had heard of St. Francis, but I didn't know where it was. Somewhere in this neighborhood? If it offered a clinic for baselines, it would have to be. They couldn't get through the chip gates uptown.

Despite the blankets heaped over me, I thought I could feel the ground sucking the heat out of my body. The old man nudged me. I opened my eyes. "Edge over onto this," he said.

He'd made a pallet of more filthy blankets, just beside where I lay. With his help, I was able to kind of wriggle and flop onto it. I couldn't lie on my back, because of the tailbone, and I couldn't use the hand to pillow my head or turn myself.

He rearranged the blankets over me. Something touched my lips: his gaunt fingers, protruding from those filthy gloves. I turned my head.

"Take it. It's methadone. It's also a pain killer."

"You lost your tax number for drug addiction?" I had to cover my mouth with my unbroken hand.

"I'm a dropout," he said. "Take the wafer."

"I don't want to get hooked."

He sighed like somebody's mother. "I'm a medical doctor. It's methadone, it's 60 milligrams. It won't do much more than take the edge off, but it might help you sleep."

I didn't believe him about being a dropout. Who'd pick this? But I did believe him about being a doctor. Maybe it was the way he specified *medical*. "I was a history teacher," I said. I couldn't bring myself to say *professor*. "Why do you have methadone if you're not an addict?"

"I told you," he said. "I'm a doctor."

"And you dropped out."

"Of a corrupt system." His voice throbbed with disdain, and maybe conviction. "How many people were invisible to you, before? How much of this was invisible?"

If I could have had my way, I would have made it all invisible again. This time, when he pressed his hand to my mouth, I took the papery wafer into my mouth and chewed it. It tasted like fake fruit. I closed my eyes again and tried to breathe deeply. It hurt, but more an ache than the deep stabbing I associated with broken ribs. So that was something else to consider myself fortunate for.

I knew it was just the placebo effect and exhaustion making me sleepy so fast, but I wasn't about to argue with it.

I said, "What made you decide to come live on the street?"

"There was a girl—" His voice choked off through the constriction of his throat. "My daughter. Cancer. She was twenty. Maybe if she hadn't been skinning so much, in so much denial—"

I put my good hand on his shoulder and felt it rise and fall. "I'm sorry."

He shrugged.

It was a minute and a half before I had the courage to ask the thing I was suddenly thinking. "If you're a dropout, then you have a tax number. And you don't use it."

"That's right," the old man said. "It's a filthy system. Eventually, you'll see what I mean."

"If you don't want it, give it to me."

He laughed. "If I were willing to do that, I'd just sell it on the black market. The clinic could use the money. Now rest, and we'll get your hand looked at tomorrow."

I don't know how I got to the clinic. I didn't walk—not on those bare, cut-up feet—and I don't remember being carried. I do remember the waiting room full of men and women I never would have seen before I lost my tax number. Jean-Khalil had given me another methadone wafer, and that kept me just this side of coherent. But I couldn't sit, couldn't walk, couldn't lean against the wall. He got somebody to bring me a gurney, and I lay on my side and tried to doze, blissfully happy there weren't any rocks or dog feces on the surface I was lying on.

It doesn't take long to lower your standards.

I realized later that I was one of the lucky ones, and because of the broken bones I got triaged higher than a lot of others. But it was still four hours before I was wheeled into one of the curtained alcoves that served as an examining room and a woman in mismatched scrubs and a white lab coat came in to check on me. "Hi," she said. "I'm Dr. Tankovitch. Dr. Samure said you had a bad night. Charlie, is it?"

"The worst," I said. She was cute—Asian, plump, with bright eyes behind her glasses—and I caught myself flirting before a flood of shame washed me back into into myself. She was a contributing member of society, here to do charity work. And I was a bum.

"Honestly, there's not much you can do for a broken tailbone except"—she laughed in commiseration—"stay off it. So let's start with the hand."

I held it out, and she took it gently by the wrist. Even that made me gasp.

She made a sympathetic face. "I'm guessing by the bruises on your face you didn't get this punching a brick wall."

"The cops don't come if you're not in the system."

She touched my shoulder. "I know."

I got lucky. For the first time in weeks, I got lucky. The hand didn't need surgery, which meant I didn't have to wait until the clinic's surgical hours, which were something like midnight to four A.M. at the city hospital. Instead, Dr. Tankovitch shot me full of Novocaine and wrapped my hand up with primitive plaster of Paris, a technology so obsolete I had never actually seen it. Or if I had seen it, I'd skinned it out. She gave me some pain pills that didn't work as well as the methadone and didn't have a street value, and told me to come back in a week and have it all checked out. The cast was so white it sparkled. Guess how long that was going to last, if I was sleeping under bridges?

She didn't offer me the clinic's contact information, and I didn't ask for it. How was I supposed to call them without a phone? But I was feeling less sorry for myself when I staggered out of the alcove. I planned to find Jean-Khalil again, and ask him if he'd show me where he looked for food and safe drinking water. I was clearheaded enough now to know it was an imposition, but I didn't have anywhere else to turn. And he'd sort of volunteered, hadn't he, by picking me out of the gutter?

If you pick up a starving dog and make him prosperous, he will not bite you. This is the principal difference between a dog and a man.

It was Mark Twain. But then, so were a lot of true things. And I was determined to prove myself more like the dog than the man. Jean-Khalil was an old man. Surely he could use my help. And I knew I needed his. I didn't see Jean-Khalil. But just as the waves of panic and abandonment—again, just like after Rose— were cresting in me, I spotted someone. Leaning against the wall by the door was Numair.

Numair had seen me first—I'd been moving, and he'd been looking for me— so he saw me stop dead and stare. He raised his hand hesitantly.

"Buy you dinner?" he asked. He didn't flinch when he looked at me.

From the angle of the light outside, I realized it was nearly sunset. "As long as we can get it someplace standing up."

That meant street meat, and three hotdogs with everything were the best food I'd ever tasted. Numair drank beer but didn't eat pork, so he ate potato chips and watched me lean forward so the chili and onions didn't drip down my filthy shirt. I knew it was ridiculous, but I did it anyway. It felt like preserving my dignity to care. What dignity? I wasn't sure. But it still mattered.

"I'm sorry," Numair said. "I'm really sorry. If I'd realized you didn't know about Rose—I just never imagined. You two were so close. And you never mentioned her—I figured you didn't want to talk about her."

"I didn't." We'd had a fight, I wanted to say. Something to absolve myself of not checking. But when she stopped logging in, I figured she'd just decided to cut me off. She wouldn't be the first, and I knew she had another life. A wife. We'd talked about telling her she was having an affair.

And then she'd just . . . stopped messaging. People fall out of social groups all the time. It happens. I guess somebody more secure wouldn't have assumed they were the problem. But I was used to being the problem. Numair's the only friend I have left from the gang I hung around with all the time in grad school.

I swallowed hot dog, half-chewed. It hurt. He handed me an open can of soda, and I washed the lump down. "How'd she die?"

She hadn't been old. I mean, she hadn't skinned old. But who knew what the hell that meant, in the real world.

"She killed herself," Numair said, bluff and forthright. Which was just like him.

I staggered. Literally, sideways two steps. I couldn't catch myself because the last hotdog was balanced against my chest on the pristine cast. I already had the instinct to protect that food. I guess you don't have to get too hungry to learn fast.

"Jesus," I said, and felt bad.

He made a comforting face. And that was when I realized that if he could see me, he wasn't skinning. "Numair. You came all the way down here for me?"

"Charlie. Like I'd let an old friend go down without some help." He put a hand on my shoulder and pulled it back, frowning. He looked around, disgusted. "You know, you hear on the news how bad it is out here. But you never really get it until you see it. Poisoned environment, whatever. But this is astounding. Look, we can get you a hearing. Appeal your status. Maybe get you a new number. You can stay with Ilona and me until it's settled."

There were horror vids about this sort of thing. The baselines lived outside of social controls, after all. There was nothing to keep them from committing horrible crimes. "You're going to take in a baseline? That's a lot of trust. I'm a desperate woman."

He smiled. "I know you."

Ilona only knew me as a skin, but when I showed up at her house in the unadorned flesh, she couldn't have been nicer. She, too, had turned off her skinning so she could see me and interact. I could tell she was uncomfortable with it, though— her eyes kept flicking off my face to look for the hypertext or chase a link pursuant to the conversation, and of course there was nothing there. So after a bit she just showed me the bathroom, brought me clean clothes and a towel, and went back to her phone, where (she said) she was working on a deadline. She was an advertising copywriter, and she and Numair had converted one corner of their old house's parlor into an office space. I could hear her clicking away as I stripped off my filthy clothing and dropped it piece by piece into the bathroom waste pail. It was hard, one-handed, and it was even harder to tape the plastic bag around my cast.

It had never bothered me to discard ruined clothing before, but now I found it anxiety-inducing. *That's still good. Somebody could wear that.* I set the shower for hot and climbed in. The water I got fell in a lukewarm trickle; barely wetting me.

They probably skinned it hotter when they showered.

I tried to linger, to savor the cleanliness, but the chill of the water in a chilly room drove me out to stand dripping on the rug. As I was dressing in Ilona's jeans and sweatshirt, the sound of a child crying filtered through.

I came out to find Numair up from his desk, changing a diaper in the nook beside the kitchen. His daughter's name was Mercedes; she'd always been something of a little pink blob to me. I came up to hand him the grease for her diaper rash and saw the spotted blood on the diaper he had pushed aside.

"Christ," I said. "Is she all right?"

"She's nine months old, and she's starting her menses," he said, lower lip thrust out in worry. I noticed because I was looking up at the underside of his chin. "It's getting more common in very young girls."

"*Common?*"

With practiced hands, he attached the diaper tabs and sealed up Mercedes' onesie. He folded the soiled diaper and stuck it closed. "The doctor says it's environmental hormones. It can be skinned for—they'll make her look normal to herself and everyone else until she's old enough to start developing." He shrugged and picked up his child. "He says he treats a couple of toddlers with developing breasts, and the cosmetic option works for them."

He looked at me, brown eyes warm with worry.

I looked down. "You think that's a good enough answer?"

He shook his head. I didn't push it any further.

They put me to sleep in their guest room, and fed me—unskinned, the food was slop, but it was food, and I got used to them not being able to see or talk to me at mealtimes. After a week, I felt much stronger. And as it was obvious that Numair and Ilona's intervention was not going to win me any favors from Revenue, I slowly came up with another plan.

I couldn't find Jean-Khalil under the bridge. His fire circle was abandoned, his blankets packed up. He'd moved on, and I didn't know where. Good deed delivered.

You'd think, right? Until it clicked what I was missing.

I showed up at the free clinic first thing next Tuesday morning, just as Dr. Tankovitch had suggested. And I waited there until Dr. Tankovitch walked in and with her, his gaunt hand curved around a cup of coffee, Dr. Jean-Khalil Samure.

He didn't look surprised to see me. My clothes were clean, and the cast was only a little dingy. I'd shaved, and I was surprised he recognized me without the split lip and the swelling.

"Jean-Khalil," I said.

I guessed accosting the clinic doctors wasn't what you did, because Dr. Tankovitch looked as if she might intercept me or call for security. But Jean-Khalil held out a hand to pause her.

He smiled. "Charlie. You look like you're finding your feet."

"I got help from a friend." I frowned and looked down at my borrowed tennis shoes. Ilona's, and too big for me. "I can't do this, Jean-Khalil. You've got to help me."

I'm sure the clinic had all sorts of problems with drug addicts. Because now Dr. Tankovitch was actively backing away, and I saw her summoning hand gestures. I leaned in and talked faster. "I need your tax number," I said. "You're not using it. Look, all I need is to get back on my feet, and I can help you in all sorts of ways. Money. Publicity. I'll come volunteer at your clinic—"

"Charlie," he said. "You know that's not enough. The way you live—the way you have been living. That's a lie. It's not sustainable. It's addictive behavior. If everybody could see the damage they're doing, they'd behave differently."

I pressed my lips together. I looked away. Down at the floor. At anything but Jean-Khalil. "There's a girl. Her name is Rose."

He looked at me. I wondered if he knew I was lying. Maybe I wasn't lying. I could find somebody else, skin her into Rose. Maybe she'd have a different name. But I could fix this. Do better. If he would only give me the chance.

"You're not using it," I said.

"A girl," he said. "Your daughter?"

"My lover," I said.

I said, "Please."

He shook his head, eyes rolled up and away. Then he yanked his hand out of his pocket brusquely. "On your head be it."

I was not prepared for the naked relief that filled me. I looked down, abjectly, and folded my hands. "Thank you so much."

"You can't save people from themselves," he said.

someday

JAMES PATRICK KELLY

James Patrick Kelly made his first sale in 1975, and since has gone on to become one of the most respected and popular writers to enter the field in the last twenty years. Although Kelly has had some success with novels, especially with Wildlife, he has perhaps had more impact to date as a writer of short fiction, with stories such as "Solstice," "The Prisoner of Chillon," "Glass Cloud," "Mr. Boy," "Pogrom," "Home Front," "Undone," and "Bernardo's House," and is often ranked among the best short story writers in the business. His story "Think Like a Dinosaur" won him a Hugo Award in 1996, as did his story "10¹⁶ to 1," in 2000. Kelly's first solo novel, the mostly ignored Planet of Whispers, came out in 1984. It was followed by Freedom Beach, a mosaic novel written in collaboration with John Kessel, and then by another solo novel, Look into the Sun, as well as the chapbook novella, Burn. His short work has been collected in Think Like a Dinosaur and Strange but Not a Stranger. Recently he published the novel Mother Go and a series of anthologies co-edited with John Kessel: Feeling Very Strange: The Slipstream Anthology, The Secret History of Science Fiction, Digital Rapture: The Singularity Anthology, Rewired: The Post-Cyberpunk Anthology, and Nebula Awards Showcase 2012. Born in Minneola, New York, Kelly now lives with his family in Nottingham, New Hampshire. He has a website at www.JimKelly.net, and reviews internet-related matters for Asimov's Science Fiction.

Here's an examination of the peculiar courtship customs and divergent biology that have developed on a Lost Colony world that has drifted out of touch with the rest of humanity—with a final clever twist waiting at the end.

Daya had been in no hurry to become a mother. In the two years since she'd reached childbearing age, she'd built a modular from parts she'd fabbed herself, thrown her boots into the volcano, and served as blood judge. The village elders all said she was one of the quickest girls they had ever seen—except when it came to choosing fathers for her firstborn. Maybe that was because she was too quick for a sleepy village like Third Landing. When her mother, Tajana, had come of age, she'd left for the blue city to find fathers for her baby. Everyone expected Tajana would stay in Halfway, but she had surprised them and returned home to raise Daya. So once Daya had grown up, everyone assumed that someday she would leave for the city like her mother, especially after Tajana had been killed in the avalanche last winter. What did Third Landing have to hold such a fierce and able woman? Daya could easily build a glittering new life in Halfway. Do great things for the colony.

But everything had changed after the scientists from space had landed on the old site across the river, and Daya had changed most of all. She kept her own counsel and was often hard to find. That spring she had told the elders that she didn't need to travel to gather the right semen. Her village was happy and prosperous. The scientists had chosen it to study and they had attracted tourists from all over the colony. There were plenty of beautiful and convenient local fathers to take to bed. Daya had sampled the ones she considered best, but never opened herself to blend their sperm. Now she would, here in the place where she had been born.

She chose just three fathers for her baby. She wanted Ganth because he was her brother and because he loved her above all others. Latif because he was a leader and would say what was true when everyone else was afraid. And Bakti because he was a master of stories and because she wanted him to tell hers someday.

She informed each of her intentions to make a love feast, although she kept the identities of the other fathers a secret, as was her right. Ganth demanded to know, of course, but she refused him. She was not asking for a favor. It would be her baby, her responsibility. The three fathers, in turn, kept her request to themselves, as was custom, in case she changed her mind about any or all of them. A real possibility—when she contemplated what she was about to do, she felt separated from herself.

That morning she climbed into the pen and spoke a kindness to her pig Bobo. The glint of the knife made him grunt with pleasure and he rolled onto his back, exposing the tumors on his belly. She hadn't harvested him in almost a week and so carved two fist-size maroon swellings into the meat pail. She pressed strips of sponge root onto the wounds to stanch the bleeding and when it was done, she threw them into the pail as well. When she scratched under his jowls to dismiss him, Bobo squealed approval, rolled over and trotted off for a mud bath.

She sliced the tumors thin, dipped the pieces in egg and dragged them through a mix of powdered opium, pepper, flour, and bread crumbs, then sautéed them until they were crisp. She arranged them on top of a casserole of snuro, parsnips and sweet flag, layered with garlic and three cheeses. She harvested some of the purple blooms from the petri dish on the windowsill and flicked them on top of her love feast. The aphrodisiacs produced by the bacteria would give an erection to a corpse. She slid the casserole into the oven to bake for an hour while she bathed and dressed for babymaking.

Daya had considered the order in which she would have sex with the fathers. Last was most important, followed by first. The genes of the middle father—or fathers, since some mothers made babies with six or seven for political reasons—were less reliably expressed. She thought starting with Ganth for his sunny nature and finishing with Latif for his looks and good judgment made sense. Even though Bakti was clever, he had bad posture.

Ganth sat in front of a fuzzy black and white screen with his back to her when she nudged the door to his house open with her hip. "It's me. With a present."

He did not glance away from his show—the colony's daily news and gossip program about the scientists—but raised his forefinger in acknowledgment.

She carried the warming dish with oven mitts to the huge round table that served as his desk, kitchen counter and sometime closet. She pushed aside some books, a belt, an empty bottle of blueberry kefir, and a Fill Jumphigher action figure to set her love feast down. Like her own house, Ganth's was a single room, but his was larger, shabbier, and built of some knotty softwood.

Her brother took a deep breath, his face pale in the light of the screen. "Smells delicious." He pressed the off button; the screen winked and went dark.

"What's the occasion?" He turned to her, smiling. "*Oh.*" His eyes went wide when he saw how she was dressed. "Tonight?"

"Tonight." She grinned.

Trying to cover his surprise, he pulled out the pocket watch he'd had from their mother and then shook it as if it were broken. "Why, look at the time. I totally forgot that we were grown up."

"You like?" She weaved her arms and her ribbon robe fluttered.

"I was wondering when you'd come. What if I had been out?"

She nodded at the screen in front of him. "You never miss that show."

"Has anyone else seen you?" He sneaked to the window and peered out. A knot of gawkers had gathered in the street. "What, did you parade across Founders' Square dressed like that? You'll give every father in town a hard-on." He pulled the blinds and came back to her. He surprised her by going down on one knee. "So which am I?"

"What do you think?" She lifted the cover from the casserole to show that it was steaming and uncut.

"I'm honored." He took her hand in his and kissed it. "Who else?" he said. "And you have to tell. Tomorrow everyone will know."

"Bakti. Latif, last."

"Three is all a baby really needs." He rubbed his thumb across the inside of her wrist. "Our mother would approve."

Of course, Ganth had no idea of what their mother had really thought of him. Tajana had once warned Daya that if she insisted on choosing Ganth to father

her baby, she should dilute his semen with that of the best men in the village. A sweet manner is fine, she'd said, but babies need brains and a spine.

"So, dear sister, it's a sacrifice . . ." he said, standing, "but I'm prepared to do my duty." He caught her in his arms.

Daya squawked in mock outrage.

"You're not surprising the others are you?" He nuzzled her neck.

"No, they expect me."

"Then we'd better hurry. I hear that Eldest Latif goes to bed early." His whisper filled her ear. "Carrying the weight of the world on his back tires him out."

"I'll give him reason to wake up."

He slid a hand through the layers of ribbons until he found her skin. "Bakti, on the other hand, stays up late, since his stories weigh nothing at all." The flat of his hand against her belly made her shiver. "I didn't realize you knew him that well."

She tugged at the hair on the back of Ganth's head to get his attention. "Feasting first," she said, her voice husky. Daya hadn't expected to be this emotional. She opened her pack, removed the bottle of chardonnay and poured two glasses. They saluted each other and drank, then she used the spatula she had brought—since she knew her brother wouldn't have one—to cut a square of her love feast. He watched her scoop it onto a plate like a man uncertain of his luck. She forked a bite into her mouth. The cheese was still melty—maybe a bit too much sweet flag. She chewed once, twice and then leaned forward to kiss him. His lips parted and she let the contents of her mouth fall into his. He groaned and swallowed. "Again." His voice was thick. "Again and again and again."

Afterward they lay entangled on his mattress on the floor. "I'm glad you're not leaving us, Daya." He blew on the ribbons at her breast and they trembled. "I'll stay home to watch your baby," he said. "Whenever you need me. Make life so easy, you'll never want to go."

It was the worst thing he could have said; until that moment she had been able to keep from thinking that she might never see him again. He was her only family, except for the fathers her mother had kept from her. Had Tajana wanted to make it easy for her to leave Third Landing? "What if I get restless here?" Daya's voice could have fit into a thimble. "You know me."

"Okay, maybe someday you can leave." He waved the idea away. "Someday."

She glanced down his lean body at the hole in his sock and dust strings dangling from his bookshelf. He was a sweet boy and her brother, but he played harder than he worked. Ganth was content to let the future happen to him; Daya needed to make choices, no matter how hard. "It's getting late." She pressed her cheek to his. "Do me a favor and check on Bobo in the morning? Who knows when I'll get home."

By the time she kissed Ganth goodbye, it was evening. An entourage of at least twenty would-be spectators trailed her to Old Town; word had spread that the very eligible Daya was bringing a love feast to some lucky fathers. There were even a scatter of tourists, delighted to witness Third Landing's quaint mating ritual. The locals told jokes, made ribald suggestions and called out names of potential fathers. She tried to ignore them; some people in this village were so nosy.

Bakti lived in one of the barn-like stone dormitories that the settlers had built two centuries ago across the river from their landing spot. Most of these buildings were now divided into shops and apartments. When Daya finally revealed her choice by stopping at Bakti's door, the crowd buzzed. Winners of bets chirped, losers groaned. Bakti was slow to answer her knock, but when he saw the spectators, he seized her arm and drew her inside.

Ganth had been right: she and Bakti weren't particularly close. She had never been to his house, although he had visited her mother on occasion when she was growing up. She could see that he was no better a housekeeper than her brother, but at least his mess was all of a kind. The bones of his apartment had not much changed from the time the founders had used it as a dormitory; Bakti had preserved the two walls of wide shelves that they had used as bunks. Now, however, instead of sleeping refugees from Genome Crusades, they were filled with books, row upon extravagant row. This was Bakti's vice; not only did he buy cheap paper from the village stalls; he had purchased hundreds of hardcovers on his frequent trips to the blue city. They said he even owned a few print books that the founders had brought across space. There were books everywhere, open on chairs, chests, the couch, stacked in leaning towers on the floor.

"So you've come to rumple my bed?" He rearranged his worktable to make room for her love feast. "I must admit, I was surprised by your note. Have we been intimate before, Daya?"

"Just once." She set the dish down. "Don't pretend that you don't remember." When she unslung the pack from her back, the remaining bottles of wine clinked together.

"Don't pretend?" He spread his hands. "I tell stories. That's all I do."

"Glasses?" She extracted the zinfandel from her pack.

He brought two that were works of art; crystal stems twisted like vines to flutes as delicate as a skim of ice. "I recall a girl with a pansy tattooed on her back," he said.

"You're thinking of Pandi." Daya poured the wine.

"Do you sing to your lovers?"

She sniffed the bouquet. "Never."

They saluted each other and drank.

"Don't rush me now," he said. "I'm enjoying this little game." He lifted the lid of the dish and breathed in. "Your feast pleases the nose as much as you please the eye. But I see that I am not your first stop. Who else have you seen this night?"

"Ganth."

"You chose a grasshopper to be a father of your child?".

"He's my brother."

"Aha!" He snapped his fingers. "Now I have it. The garden at Tajana's place? I recall a very pleasant evening."

She had forgotten how big Bakti's nose was. "As do I." And his slouch was worse than ever. Probably from carrying too many books.

"I don't mind being the middle, you know." He took another drink of wine. "Prefer it, actually—less responsibility that way. I will do my duty as a father, but

I must tell you right now that I have no interest whatsoever in bringing up your baby. And her next father is?"

"Latif. Next and last."

"A man who takes fathering seriously. Good, he'll balance out poor Ganth. I will tell her stories, though. Your baby girl. That's what you hope for, am I right? A girl?"

"Yes." She hadn't realized it until he said it. A girl would make things much easier.

He paused, as if he had just remembered something. "But you're supposed to leave us, aren't you? This village is too tight a fit for someone of your abilities. You'll split seams, pop a button."

Why did everyone keep saying these things to her? "*You* didn't leave."

"No." He shook his head. "I wasn't as big as I thought I was. Besides, the books keep me here. Do you know how much they weigh?"

"It's an amazing collection." She bent to the nearest shelf and ran a finger along the spines of the outermost row. "I've heard you have some from Earth."

"Is this about looking at books or making babies, Daya?" Bakti looked crestfallen.

She straightened, embarrassed. "The baby, of course."

"No, I get it." He waved a finger at her. "I'm crooked and cranky and mothers shut their eyes tight when we kiss." He reached for the wine bottle. "Those are novels." He nodded at the shelf. "But no, nothing from Earth."

They spent the better part of an hour browsing. Bakti said Daya could borrow some if she wanted. He said reading helped pregnant mothers settle. Then he told her the story from one of them. It was about a boy named Huckleberry Flynn, who left his village on Novy Praha to see his world but then came back again. "Just like your mother did," he said. "Just like you could, if you wanted. Someday."

"Then you could tell stories about me."

"About this night," he agreed, "if I remember." His grin was seductive. "Will I?"

"Have you gotten any books from them?" She glanced out the dark window toward the river. "Maybe they'd want to trade with you."

"Them?" he said. "You mean our visitors? Some, but digital only. They haven't got time for nostalgia. To them, my books are as quaint as scrolls and clay tablets. They asked to scan the collection, but I think they were just being polite. Their interests seem to be more sociological than literary." He smirked. "I understand you have been spending time across the river."

She shrugged. "Do you think they are telling the truth?"

"About what? Their biology? Their politics?" He gestured at his library. "I own one thousand, two hundred and forty-three claims of truth. How would I know which is right?" He slid the book about the boy Huckleberry back onto the shelf. "But look at the time! If you don't mind, I've been putting off dinner until you arrived. And then we can make a baby and a memory, yes?"

By the time Daya left him snoring on his rumpled bed, the spectators had all gone home for the night. There was still half of the love feast left but the warming dish was beginning to dry it out. She hurried down the Farview Hill to the river.

Many honors had come to Latif over the years and with them great wealth. He had first served as village eldest when he was still a young man, just thirty-two years old. In recent years, he mediated disputes for those who did not have the time or the money to submit to the magistrates of the blue city. The fees he charged had bought him this fine house of three rooms, one of which was the parlor where he received visitors. When she saw that all the windows were dark, she gave a cry of panic. It was nearly midnight and the house was nothing but a shadow against the silver waters.

On the shore beyond, the surreal bulk of the starship beckoned.

Daya didn't even bother with the front door. She went around to the bedroom and stood on tiptoes to knock on his window. *Tap-tap*.

Nothing.

"Latif." *Tap-tap-tap*. "Wake up."

She heard a clatter within. "Shit!" A light came on and she stepped away as the window clattered open."

"Who's there? Go away."

"It's me, Daya."

"Do you know what time it is? Go away."

"But I have our love feast. You knew this was the night, I sent a message."

"And I waited, but you took too damn long." He growled in frustration. "Can't you see I'm asleep? Go find some middle who's awake."

"No, Latif. You're my last."

He started with a shout. "You wake me in the middle of night . . ." Then he continued in a low rasp. "Where's your sense, Daya, your manners? You expect me to be your last? You should have said something. I take fathering seriously."

Daya's throat closed. Her eyes seemed to throb.

"I told you to move to the city, didn't I? Find fathers there." Latif waited for her to answer. When she didn't, he stuck his head out the window to see her better. "So instead of taking my best advice, now you want my semen?" He waited again for a reply; she couldn't speak. "I suppose you're crying."

The only reply she could make was a sniffle.

"Come to the door then."

She reached for his arm as she entered the darkened parlor but he waved her through to the center of the room. "You are rude and selfish, Daya." He shut the door and leaned against it. "But that doesn't mean you're a bad person."

He turned the lights on and for a moment they stood blinking at one another. Latif was barefoot, wearing pants but no shirt. He had a wrestler's shoulders, long arms, hands big as dinner plates. Muscles bunched beneath his smooth, dark skin, as if he might spring at her. But if she read his eyes right, his anger was passing.

"I thought you'd be pleased." She tried a grin. It bounced off him.

"Honored, yes. Pleased, not at all. You think you can just issue commands and we jump? You have the right to ask, and I have the right to refuse. Even at the last minute."

At fifty-three, Latif was still one of the handsomest men in the village. Daya had often wondered if that was one reason why everyone trusted him. She looked for some place to put the warming dish down.

"No," he said, "don't you dare make yourself comfortable unless I tell you to. Why me?"

She didn't have to think. "Because you have always been kind to me and my mother. Because you will tell the truth, even when it's hard to hear. And because, despite your years, you are still the most beautiful man I know." This time she tried a smile on him. It stuck. "All the children you've fathered are beautiful, and if my son gets nothing but looks from you, that will still be to his lifelong advantage." Daya knew that in the right circumstance, even men like Latif would succumb to flattery.

"You want me because I tell hard truths, but when I say you should move away, you ignore me. Does that make sense?"

"Not everything needs to make sense." She extended her love feast to him. "Where should I put this?"

He glided across the parlor, kissed her forehead and accepted the dish from her. "Do you know how many have asked me to be last father?"

"No." She followed him into the great room.

"Twenty-three," he said. "Every one spoke to me ahead of time. And of those, how many I agreed to?"

"No idea."

"Four." He set it on a round wooden table with a marble inset.

"They should've tried my ambush strategy." She shrugged out of her pack. "I've got wine." She handed him the bottle of Xino she had picked for him.

"Which you've been drinking all night, I'm sure. You know where the glasses are." He pulled the stopper. "And who have you been drinking with?"

"Ganth, first."

Latif tossed the stopper onto the table. "I'm one-fourth that boy's father"—he rapped on the tabletop—"but I don't see any part of me in him."

"He's handsome."

"Oh, stop." He poured each of them just a splash of the Xino and offered her a glass. She raised an eyebrow at his stinginess.

"It's late and you've had enough," he said. "It is affecting your judgment. Who else?"

"Bakti."

"You surprise me." They saluted each other with their glasses. "Does he really have Earth books?"

"He says not."

"He makes too many stories up. But he's sound—you should have started with him. Ganth is a middle father at best."

Both of them ran out of things to say then. Latif was right. She had finished the first two bottles with the other fathers, and had shared a love feast with them and had made love. She was heavy with the weight of her decisions and her desires. She felt like she was falling toward Latif. She pulled the cover off the warming dish and cut a square of her love feast into bite-sized chunks.

"Just because I'm making a baby doesn't mean I can't go away," she said.

"And leave the fathers behind?"

"That's what my mother did."

"And did that make her happy? Do you think she had an easy life?" He shook his head. "No, you are tying yourself to this village. This little, insignificant place. Why? Maybe you're lazy. Or maybe you're afraid. Here, you are a star. What would you be in the blue city?"

She wanted to tell him that he had it exactly wrong. That he was talking about himself, not her. But that would have been cruel. This beautiful foolish man was going to be the last father of her baby. "You're right," Daya said. "It's late." She piled bits of the feast onto a plate and came around to where he was sitting. She perched on the edge of the table and gazed down at him.

He tugged at one of the ribbons of her sleeve and she felt the robe slip off her shoulder. "What is this costume anyway?" he said. "You're wrapped up like some kind of present."

She didn't reply. Instead she pushed a bit of the feast across her plate until it slid onto her fork. They watched each other as she brought it to her open mouth, placed it on her tongue. The room shrank. Clocks stopped.

He shuddered, "Feed me, then."

Latif's pants were still around his ankles when she rolled off him. The ribbon robe dangled off the headboard of his bed. Daya gazed up at the ceiling, thinking about the tangling sperm inside her. She concentrated as her mother had taught her, and she thought she felt her cervix close and her uterus contract, concentrating the semen. At least, she hoped she did. The sperm of the three fathers would smash together furiously, breaching cell walls, exchanging plasmids. The strongest conjugate would find her eggs and then . . .

"What if I leave the baby behind?" she said.

"With who?" He propped himself up on an elbow. "Your mother is dead and no . . . ."

She laid a finger on his lips. "I know, Latif. But why not with a father? Ganth might do it, I think. Definitely not Bakti. Maybe even you."

He went rigid. "This is an idea you get from the scientists? Is that the way they have sex in space?"

"They don't live in space; they just travel through it." She followed a crack in the plaster of his ceiling with her eyes. "Nobody lives in space." A water stain in the corner looked like a face. A mouth. Sad eyes. "What should we do about them?"

"Do? There is nothing to be done." He fell back onto his pillow. "They're the ones the founders were trying to get away from."

"Two hundred years ago. They say things are different."

"Maybe. Maybe these particular scientists are more tolerant, but they're still dangerous."

"Why? Why are you so afraid of them?"

"*Because they're unnatural.*" The hand at her side clenched into a fist. "We're the true humans, maybe the last. But they've taken charge of evolution now, or what passes for it. We have no say in the future. All we know for sure is that they are large and still growing and we are very, very small. Maybe this lot won't force us to change. Or maybe someday they'll just make us want to become like them."

She knew this was true, even though she had spent the last few months trying not to know it. The effort had made her weary. She rolled toward Latif. When she snuggled against him, he relaxed into her embrace.

It was almost dawn when she left his house. Instead of climbing back up Farview Hill, she turned toward the river. Moments later she stepped off Mogallo's Wharf into the skiff she had built when she was a teenager.

She had been so busy pretending that this wasn't going to happen that she was surprised to find herself gliding across the river. She could never have had sex with the fathers if she had acknowledged to herself that she was going to go through with it. Certainly not with Ganth. And Latif would have guessed that something was wrong. She had the odd feeling that there were two of her in the skiff, each facing in opposite directions. The one looking back at the village was screaming at the one watching the starship grow ever larger. But there is no other Daya, she reminded herself. There is only me.

Her lover, Roberts, was waiting on the spun-carbon dock that the scientists had fabbed for river traffic. Many of the magistrates from the blue city came by boat to negotiate with the offworlders. Roberts caught the rope that Daya threw her and took it expertly around one of the cleats. She extended a hand to hoist Daya up, caught her in an embrace and pressed her lips to Daya's cheek.

"This kissing that you do," said Roberts. "I like it. Very direct." She wasn't very good at it but she was learning. Like all the scientists, she could be stiff at first. They didn't seem all that comfortable in their replaceable bodies. Roberts was small as a child, but with a woman's face. Her blonde hair was cropped short, her eyes were clear and faceted. They reminded Daya of her mother's crystal.

"It's done," said Daya.

"Yes, but are you all right?"

"I think so." She forced a grin. "We'll find out."

"We will. Don't worry, love, I am going to take good care of you. And your baby."

"And I will take care of you."

"Yes." She looked puzzled. "Of course."

Roberts was a cultural anthropologist. She had explained to Daya that all she wanted was to preserve a record of an ancient way of life. A culture in which there was still sexual reproduction.

"May I see that?"

Daya opened her pack and produced the leftover bit of the love feast. She had sealed it in a baggie that Roberts had given her. It had somehow frozen solid.

"Excellent. Now we should get you into the lab before it's too late. Put you under the scanner, take some samples." This time she kissed Daya on the mouth.

Her lips parted briefly and Daya felt Roberts's tongue flick against her teeth. When Daya did not respond, she pulled back.

"I know this is hard now. You're very brave to help us this way, Daya." The scientist took her hand and squeezed. "But someday they'll thank you for what you're doing." She nodded toward the sleepy village across the river. "Someday soon."

The Long Haul, From the Annals of Transportation, The Pacific Monthly, May 2009

Ken Liu

Ken Liu is an author and translator of speculative fiction, as well as a lawyer and programmer. His fiction has appeared in The Magazine of Fantasy & Science Fiction, Asimov's, Analog, Clarkesworld, Lightspeed, *and* Strange Horizons, *among many other places. He has won a Nebula, two Hugos, a World Fantasy Award, and a Science Fiction & Fantasy Translation Award, and been nominated for the Sturgeon and the Locus Awards. In 2015, he published his first novel,* The Grace of Kings, *followed by* The Wall of Storms, *a sequel to* The Grace of Kings, *a collection,* The Paper Menagerie and Other Stories, *and, as editor and translator, an anthology of Chinese science fiction stories,* Invisible Planets. *He lives with his family near Boston, Massachusetts.*

Here's a loving, nostalgic look at a world that might have come to pass, but never did.

Twenty-five years ago, on this day, the Hindenburg crossed the Atlantic for the first time. Today, it will cross it for the last time. Six hundred times it has accomplished this feat, and in so doing it has covered the same distance as more than eight roundtrips to the Moon. Its perfect safety record is a testament to the ingenuity of the German people.

There is always some sorrow in seeing a thing of beauty age, decline, and finally fade, no matter how gracefully it is done. But so long as men still sail the open skies, none shall forget the glory of the Hindenburg.

— *John F. Kennedy, March 31, 1962, Berlin.*

It was easy to see the zeppelins moored half a mile away from the terminal. They were a motley collection of about forty Peterbilts, Aereons, Macks, Zeppelins (both the real thing and the ones from Goodyear-Zeppelin), and Dongfengs, arranged around and with their noses tied to ten mooring masts, like crouching cats having tête-à-tête tea parties.

I went through customs at Lanzhou's Yantan Airport, and found Barry Icke's long-hauler, a gleaming silver Dongfeng Feimaotui—the model usually known in America, among the less-than-politically-correct society of zeppeliners, as the "Flying Chinaman"—at the farthest mooring mast. As soon as I saw it, I understood why he called it the *American Dragon*.

White clouds drifted in the dark mirror of the polished solar panels covering the upper half of the zeppelin like a turtle's shell. Large, waving American flags trailing red and blue flames and white stars were airbrushed onto each side of the elongated silver teardrop hull, which gradually tapered towards the back, ending in a cruciform tail striped in red, white, and blue. A pair of predatory, reptilian eyes was painted above the nose cone and a grinning mouth full of sharp teeth under it. A petite Chinese woman was suspended by ropes below the nose cone, painting over the bloodred tongue in the mouth with a brush.

Icke stood on the tarmac near the control cab, a small, round, glass-windowed bump protruding from the belly of the giant teardrop. Tall and broad-shouldered, his square face featured a tall, Roman nose and steady, brown eyes that stared out from under the visor of a Red Sox cap. He watched me approach, flicked his cigarette away, and nodded at me.

Icke had been one of the few to respond to my Internet forum ad asking if any of the long-haulers would be willing to take a writer for the *Pacific Monthly* on a haul. "I've read some of your articles," he had said. "You didn't sound too stupid." And then he invited me to come to Lanzhou.

After we strapped ourselves in, Icke weighed off the zeppelin—pumping compressed helium into the gasbags until the zeppelin's positive lift, minus the weight of the ship, the gas, us, and the cargo, was just about equal to zero. Now essentially "weightless," the long-hauler and all its cargo could have been lifted off the ground by a child.

When the control tower gave the signal, Icke pulled a lever that retracted the nose cone hook from the mooring mast and flipped a toggle to drop about a thousand pounds of water ballast into the ground tank below the ship. And just like that, we began to rise, steadily and in complete silence, as though we were riding up a skyscraper in a glass-walled elevator. Icke left the engines off. Unlike an airplane that needs the engines to generate forward thrust to be converted into lift, a zeppelin literally floats up, and engines didn't need to be turned on until we reached cruising height.

"This is the *American Dragon*, heading out to Sin City. See you next time, and watch out for those bears," Icke said into the radio. A few of the other zeppelins, like giant caterpillars on the ground below us, blinked their taillights in acknowledgment.

Icke's Feimaotui is 302 feet long, with a maximum diameter of 84 feet, giving it a capacity for 1.12 million cubic feet of helium and a gross lift of 36 tons, of which about 27 are available for cargo (this is comparable to the maximum usable cargo load for semis on the interstates).

Its hull is formed from a rigid frame of rings and longitudinal girders made out of duratainium covered with composite skin. Inside, seventeen helium gasbags are secured to a central beam that runs from the nose to the tail of the ship, about a third of the way up from the bottom of the hull. At the bottom of the hull, immediately below the central beam and the gasbags, is an empty space that runs the length of the ship.

Most of this space is taken up by the cargo hold, the primary attraction of longhaulers for shippers. The immense space, many times the size of a plane's cargo bay, was perfect for irregularly shaped and bulky goods, like the wind generator turbine blades we were carrying.

Near the front of the ship, the cargo hold is partitioned from the crew quarters, which consists of a suite of apartment-like rooms opening off of a central corridor. The corridor ends by emerging from the hull into the control cab, the only place on the ship with windows to the outside. The Feimaotui is only a little bit longer and taller than a Boeing 747 (counting the tail), but far more voluminous and lighter.

The whole crew consisted of Icke and his wife, Yeling, the woman who was repainting the grinning mouth on the zeppelin when I showed up. Husband-wife teams like theirs are popular on the transpacific long haul. Each of them would take six-hour shifts to fly the ship while the other slept. Yeling was in the back, sleeping through the takeoff. Like the ship itself, much of their marriage was made up of silence and empty space.

"Yeling and I are no more than thirty feet apart from each other just about every minute, but we only get to sleep in the same bed about once every seven days. You end up learning to have conversations in five-minute chunks separated by six-hour blocks of silence.

"Sometimes Yeling and I have an argument, and she'll have six hours to think of a come-back for something I said six hours earlier. That helps since her English isn't perfect, and she can use the time to look up words she needs. I'll wake up and she'll talk at me for five minutes and go to bed, and I'll have to spend the next six hours thinking about what she said. We've had arguments that went on for days and days this way."

Icke laughed. "In our marriage, sometimes you *have* to go to bed angry."

The control car was shaped like an airplane's cockpit, except that the windows slanted outward and down, so that you had an unobstructed view of the land and air below you.

Icke had covered his seat with a custom pattern: a topographical map of Alaska. In front of Icke's chair was a dashboard full of instruments and analog and mechanical controls. A small, gleaming gold statuette of a laughing, rotund bodhisattva was glued to the top of the dashboard. Next to it was the plush figure of Wally, the Green Monster of Fenway Park.

A plastic crate wedged into place between the two seats was filled with CDs: a mix of mandopop, country, classical, and some audiobooks. I flipped through them: Annie Dillard, Thoreau, Cormac McCarthy, *The Idiot's Guide to Grammar and Composition*.

Once we reached the cruising altitude of 1,000 feet—freight zeppelins generally are restricted to a zone above pleasure airships, whose passengers prefer the view lower down, and far below the cruising height of airplanes—Icke started the electrical engines. A low hum, more felt than heard, told us that the four propellers mounted in indentations near the tail of the ship had begun to turn and push the ship forward.

"It never gets much louder than this," Icke said.

We drifted over the busy streets of Lanzhou. More than a thousand miles west of Beijing, this medium-sized industrial city was once the most polluted city in all of China due to its blocked air flow and petroleum processing plants. But it is now the center of China's wind turbine boom.

The air below us was filled with small and cheap airships that hauled passengers and freight on intra-city routes. They were a colorful bunch, a ragtag mix of blimps and small zeppelins, their hulls showing signs of make-shift repairs and *shanzhai* patches. (A blimp, unlike a zeppelin, has no rigid frame. Like a birthday balloon, its shape is maintained entirely by the pressure of the gas inside.) The ships were plastered all over with lurid advertisements for goods and services that sounded, with their strange English translations, frightening and tempting in equal measure. Icke told me that some of the ships we saw had bamboo frames.

Icke had flown as a union zeppeliner crewman for ten years on domestic routes before buying his own ship. The union pay was fine, but he didn't like working for someone else. He had wanted to buy a Goodyear-Zeppelin, designed and made 100 percent in America. But he disliked bankers even more than Chinese airship companies and decided that he would rather own a Dongfeng outright.

"Nothing good ever came from debt," he said. "I could have told you what was going to happen with all those mortgages last year."

After a while, he added, "My ship is mostly built in America, anyway. The Chinese can't make the duratainium for the girders and rings in the frame. They have to import it. I ship sheets of the alloy from Bethlehem, P.A., to factories in China all the time."

The Feimaotui was a quirky ship, Icke explained. It was designed to be easy to maintain and repair rather than over-engineered to be durable the way American ships usually were. An American ship that malfunctioned had to be taken to the dealer for the sophisticated computers and proprietary diagnostic codes, but just about every component of the Feimaotui could be switched out and repaired in the field by a skilled mechanic. An American ship could practically fly itself most of the time, as the design philosophy was to automate as much as possible and minimize the chances of human error. The Feimaotui required a lot more out of the pilot, but it was also much more responsive and satisfying to fly.

"A man changes over time to be like his ship. I'd just fall asleep in a ship where the computer did everything." He gazed at the levers, sticks, wheels, toggles, pedals, and sliders around him, reassuringly heavy, analog, and solid. "Typing on a keyboard is no way to fly a ship."

He wanted to own a fleet of these ships eventually. The goal was to graduate from owner-operator to just owner, when he and Yeling could start a family.

"Someday when we can just sit back and collect the checks, I'll get a Winnebago Aurora—the 40,000 cubic foot model—and we and our kids will drift around all summer in Alaska and all winter in Brazil, eating nothing but the food we catch with our own hands. You haven't seen Alaska until you've seen it in an RV airship. We can go to places that not even snowmachines and seaplanes can get to, and hover over a lake that has never seen a man, not a soul around us for hundreds of miles."

Within seconds we were gliding over the broad, slow expanse of the Yellow River. Filled with silt, the muddy water below us was already beginning to take on its namesake color, which would deepen and grow even muddier over the next few hundred miles as it traveled through the Loess Plateau and picked up the silt deposited over the eons by wind.

Below us, small sightseeing blimps floated lazily over the river. The passengers huddled in the gondolas to look through the transparent floor at the sheepskin rafts drifting on the river below the same way Caribbean tourists looked through glass-bottom boats at the fish in the coral reef.

Icke throttled up and we began to accelerate north and east, largely following the course of the Yellow River, towards Inner Mongolia.

The Millennium Clean Energy Act is one of the few acts by the "clowns down in D.C." that Icke approved: "It gave me most of my business."

Originally designed as a way to protect domestic manufacturers against Chinese competition and to appease the environmental lobby, the law imposed a heavy tax on goods entering the United States based on the carbon footprint of the method of transportation (since the tax was not based on the goods' country-of-origin, it skirted the WTO rules against increased tariffs).

Combined with rising fuel costs, the law created a bonanza for zeppelin shippers. Within a few years, Chinese companies were churning out cheap zeppelins that sipped fuel and squeezed every last bit of advantage from solar power. Dongfengs became a common sight in American skies.

A long-haul zeppelin cannot compete with a 747 for lifting capacity or speed, but it wins hands down on fuel efficiency and carbon profile, and it's far faster than surface shipping. Going from Lanzhou to Las Vegas, like Icke and I were doing, would take about three to four weeks by surface shipping at the fastest: a couple days to go from Lanzhou to Shanghai by truck or train, about two weeks to cross the Pacific by ship, another day or so to truck from California to Las Vegas, and add in a week or so for loading, unloading, and sitting in customs. A direct airplane flight would get you there in a day, but the fuel cost and carbon tax at the border would make it uneconomical for many goods.

"Every time you have to load and unload and change the mode of transport, that's money lost to you," Icke said. "We are trucks that don't need highways, boats that don't need rivers, airplanes that don't need airports. If you can find a piece of flat land the size of a football field, that's enough for us. We can deliver door to door from a yurt in Mongolia to your apartment in New York—assuming your building has a mooring mast on top."

A typical zeppelin built in the last twenty years, cruising at 110 mph, can make the 6,900-mile haul between Lanzhou and Las Vegas in about 63 hours. If it makes heavy use of solar power, as Icke's Feimaotui is designed to do, it can end up using less than a fraction of a percent of the fuel that a 747 would need to carry the same weight for the same distance. Plus, it has the advantage I'd mentioned of being more accommodating of bulky, irregularly shaped loads.

Although we were making the transpacific long haul, most of our journey would be spent flying over land. The curvature of the Earth meant that the closest flight path between any two points on the globe followed a great circle that connected the two points and bisected the globe into two equal parts. From Lanzhou to Las Vegas, this meant that we would fly north and east over Inner Mongolia, Mongolia, Siberia, across the Bering Strait, and then fly east and south over Alaska, the Pacific Ocean off the coast of British Columbia, until we hit land again with Oregon, and finally reach the deserts of Nevada.

Below us, the vast city of Ordos, in Inner Mongolia, stretched out to the horizon, a megalopolis of shining steel and smooth glass, vast blocks of western-style houses and manicured gardens. The grid of new, wide streets was as empty as those in Pyongyang, and I could count the number of pedestrians on the fingers of one hand. Our height and open view made the scene take on the look of tilt-shift photographs, as though we were standing over a tabletop scale model of the city, with a few miniature cars and playing figurines scattered about the model.

Ordos is China's Alberta. There is coal here, some of the best, cleanest coal in the world. Ordos was planned in anticipation of an energy boom, but the construction itself became the boom. The more they spent on construction, the more it looked on paper like there was a need for even more construction. So now there is this Xanadu, a ghost town from birth. On paper it is the second richest place in China, per capita income just behind Shanghai.

As we flew over the center of Ordos, a panda rose up and hailed us. The panda's vehicle was a small blimp, painted olive green and carrying the English legend: "Aerial Transport Patrol, People's Republic of China." Icke slowed down and sent over the cargo manifests, the maintenance records, which the panda could cross-check against the international registry of cargo airships, and his journey log. After a few minutes, someone waved at us from the window in the gondola of the blimp, and a Chinese voice told us over radio that we were free to move on.

"This is such a messed up country," Icke said. "They have the money to build something like Ordos, but have you been to Guangxi? It's near Vietnam, and outside the cities the people there are among the poorest in the world. They have nothing except the mud on the floor of their huts, and beautiful scenery and beautiful women."

Icke had met Yeling there, through a mail-order bride service. It was hard to meet women when you were in the air three hundred days of the year.

On the day of Icke's appointment, he was making a run through Nanning, the provincial capital, as part of a union crew picking up a shipment of star anise. He had the next day, a Saturday, off, and he traveled down to the introduction center a hundred kilometers outside Nanning to meet the girls whose pictures he had picked out and who had been bused in from the surrounding villages.

They had fifteen girls for him. They met in a village school house. Icke sat on a small stool at the front of the classroom with his back to the blackboard, and the girls were brought in to sit at the student desks, as though he was there to teach them.

Most of them knew some English, and he could talk to them for a little bit and mark down, on a chart, the three girls that he wanted to chat with one-on-one in private. The girls he didn't pick would wait around for the next Westerner customer to come and see them in another half hour.

"They say that some services would even let you try the girls out for a bit, like allow you to take them to a hotel for a night, but I don't believe that. Anyway, mine wasn't like that. We just talked. I didn't mark down three girls. Yeling was the only one I picked.

"I liked the way she looked. Her skin was so smooth, so young-looking, and I loved her hair, straight and black with a little curl at the end. She smelled like grass and rainwater. But I liked even more the way she acted with me: shy and very eager to please, something you don't see much in the women back home." He looked over at me as I took notes and shrugged. "If you want to put a label on me and make the people who read what you write feel good about themselves, that's your choice. It doesn't make the label true."

I asked him if something felt wrong about the process, like shopping for a thing.

"I paid the service two thousand dollars and gave her family another five thousand before I married her. Some people will not like that. They'll think something is not altogether right about the way I married her

"But I know I'm happy when I'm with her. That's enough for me.

"By the time I met her, Yeling had already dropped out of high school. If I didn't meet her, she would not have gone on to college. She would not have become a lawyer or banker. She would not have gone to work in an office and come home to do yoga. That's the way the world is.

"Maybe she would have gone to Nanning to become a masseuse or bathhouse girl. Maybe she would have married an old peasant from the next village who she didn't even know just because he could give her family some money. Maybe she would have spent the rest of her life getting parasites from toiling in the rice paddies all day and bringing up children in a mud hut at night. And she would have looked like an old woman by thirty.

"How could that have been better?"

The language of the zeppeliners on the transpacific long haul, though officially English, is a mix of images and words from America and China. *Dao, knife, dough,* and *dollar* are used as interchangeable synonyms. Ursine imagery is applied to law enforcement agents along the route: a panda is a Chinese air patrol unit, and a polar bear Russian; in Alaska they are Kodiaks, and off the coast of BC they become whales; finally in America the ships have to deal with grizzlies. The bear's job is to make the life of the zeppeliner difficult: catching pilots who have been at the controls for more than six hours without switching off, who fly above or below regulation altitude, who mix hydrogen into the lift gas to achieve an extra edge in cargo capacity.

"Whales?" I asked Icke. How was whale a type of bear?

"Evolution," Icke said. "Darwin said that a race of bears swimming with their mouths open for water bugs may eventually evolve into whales." (I checked. This was true.)

Nothing changed as an electronic beep from the ship's GPS informed us that we had crossed the international border between China and Mongolia somewhere in the desolate, dry plains of the Gobi below, dotted with sparse clumps of short, brittle grass.

Yeling came into the control cab to take over. Icke locked the controls and got up. In the small space at the back of the control cab, they spoke to each other for a bit in lowered voices, kissed, while I stared at the instrument panels, trying hard not to eavesdrop.

Every marriage had its own engine, with its own rhythm and fuel, its own language and control scheme, a quiet hum that kept everything moving. But the hum was so quiet that sometimes it was more felt than heard, and you had to listen for it if you didn't want to miss it.

Then Icke left and Yeling came forward to take the pilot's seat.

She looked at me. "There's a second bunk in the back if you want to park yourself a bit." Her English was accented but good, and you could hear traces of Icke's broad New England A's and non-rhoticity in some of the words.

I thanked her and told her that I wasn't sleepy yet.

She nodded and concentrated on flying the ship, her hands gripping the stick for the empennage—the elevators and rudders in the cruciform tail—and the wheel for the trim far more tightly than Icke had.

I stared at the empty, cold desert passing beneath us for a while, and then I asked her what she had been doing when I first showed up at the airport.

"Fixing the eyes of the ship. Barry likes to see the mouth all red and fierce, but the eyes are more important.

"A ship is a dragon, and dragons navigate by sight. One eye for the sky, another for the sea. A ship without eyes cannot see the coming storms and ride the changing winds. It won't see the underwater rocks near the shore and know the direction of land. A blind ship will sink."

An airship, she said, needed eyes even more than a ship on water. It moved so much faster and there were so many more things that could go wrong.

"Barry thinks it's enough to have these." She gestured towards the instrument panel before her: GPS, radar, radio, altimeter, gyroscope, compass. "But these things help Barry, not the ship. The ship itself needs to *see*.

"Barry thinks this is superstition, and he doesn't want me to do it. But I tell him that the ship looks more impressive for customers if he keeps the eyes freshly painted. That he thinks make sense."

Yeling told me that she had also crawled all over the hull of the ship and traced out a pattern of oval dragon scales on the surface of the hull with tung oil. "It looks like the way the ice cracks in spring on a lake with good *fengshui*. A ship with a good coat of dragon scales won't ever be claimed by water."

The sky darkened and night fell. Beneath us was complete darkness, northern Mongolia and the Russian Far East being some of the least densely inhabited regions of the globe. Above us, stars denser than I had ever seen winked into existence. It felt as though we were drifting on the surface of a sea at night, the water around us filled with the glow of sea jellies, the way I remember when I used to swim at night in Long Island Sound off the Connecticut coast.

"I think I'll sleep now," I said. She nodded, and then told me that I could microwave something for myself in the small galley behind the control cab, off to the side of the main corridor.

The galley was tiny, barely larger than a closet. There was a fridge, a microwave, a sink, and a small two-burner electric range. Everything was kept spotless. The pots and pans were neatly hung on the wall, and the dishes were stacked in a grid of cubbyholes and tied down with velcro straps. I ate quickly and then followed the sound of snores aft.

Icke had left the light on for me. In the windowless bedroom, the soft, warm glow and the wood-paneled walls were pleasant and induced sleep. Two bunks, one on top of the other, hung against one wall of the small bedroom. Icke was asleep in the bottom one. In one corner of the room was a small vanity with a mirror, and pictures of Yeling's family were taped around the frame of the mirror.

It struck me then that this was Icke and Yeling's *home*. Icke had told me that they owned a house in western Massachusetts, but they spent only about a month out of the year there. Most of their meals were cooked and eaten in the *American Dragon*, and most of their dreams were dreamt here in this room, each alone in a bunk.

A poster of smiling children drawn in the style of Chinese folk art was on the wall next to the vanity, and framed pictures of Yeling and Icke together, smiling, filled the rest of the wall space. I looked through them: wedding, vacation, somewhere in a Chinese city, somewhere near a lake with snowy shores, each of them holding up a big fish.

I crawled into the top bunk, and between Icke's snores, I could hear the faint hum of the ship's engines, so faint that you almost missed it if you didn't listen for it.

I was more tired than I had realized, and slept through the rest of Yeling's shift as well as Icke's next shift. By the time I woke up, it was just after sunrise, and Yeling was again at the helm. We were deep in Russia, flying over the endless coniferous Boreal forests of the heart of Siberia. Our course was now growing ever more easterly as we approached the tip of Siberia where it would meet Alaska across the Bering Sea.

She was listening to an audiobook as I came into the control cab. She reached out to turn it off when she heard me, but I told her that it was all right.

It was a book about baseball, an explanation of the basic rules for non-fans. The particular section she was listening to dealt with the art of how to appreciate a stolen base.

Yeling stopped the book at the end of the chapter. I sipped a cup of coffee while we watched the sun rise higher and higher over the Siberian taiga, lighting up the lichen woodland dotted with bogs and pristine lakes still frozen over.

"I didn't understand the game when I first married Barry. We do not have baseball in China, especially not where I grew up.

"Sometimes, when Barry and I aren't working, when I stay up a bit during my shift to sit with him or on our days off, I want to talk about the games I played as a girl or a book I remember reading in school or a festival we had back home. But it's difficult.

"Even for a simple funny memory I wanted to share about the time my cousins and I made these new paper boats, I'd have to explain everything: the names of the paper boats we made, the rules for racing them, the festival that we were celebrating and what the custom for racing paper boats was about, the jobs and histories of the spirits for the festival, the names of the cousins and how we were related, and by then I'd forgotten what was the stupid little story I wanted to share.

"It was exhausting for both of us. I used to work hard to try to explain everything, but Barry would get tired, and he couldn't keep the Chinese names straight or even hear the difference between them. So I stopped.

"But I want to be able to talk to Barry. Where there is no language, people have to build language. Barry likes baseball. So I listen to this book and then we have something to talk about. He is happy when I can listen to or watch a baseball game with him and say a few words when I can follow what's happening."

Icke was at the helm for the northernmost leg of our journey, where we flew parallel to the Arctic Circle and just south of it. Day and night had lost their meaning as we flew into the extreme northern latitudes. I was already getting used to the six-hour-on, six-hour-off rhythm of their routine, and slowly synching my body's clock to theirs.

I asked Icke if he knew much about Yeling's family or spent much time with them.

"No. She sends some money back to them every couple of months. She's careful with the budget, and I know that anything she sends them she's worked for as hard as I did. I've had to work on her to get her to be a little more generous with herself, and to spend money on things that will make us happy right now. Every time we go to Vegas now she's willing to play some games with me and lose a little money, but she even has a budget for that.

"I don't get involved with her family. I figure that if she wanted out of her home and village so badly that she was willing to float away with a stranger in a bag of gas, then there's no need for me to become part of what she's left behind.

"I'm sure she also misses her family. How can she not? That's the way we all are, as far as I can see: we want that closeness from piling in all together and knowing everything about everyone and talking all in one breath, but we also want to run away by ourselves and be alone. Sometimes we want both at the same time. My mom wasn't much of a mom, and I haven't been home since I was sixteen. But even I can't say that I don't miss her sometimes.

"I give her space. If there's one thing the Chinese don't have, it's space. Yeling lived in a hut so full of people that she never even had her own blanket, and she couldn't remember a single hour when she was alone. Now we see each other for a few minutes every six hours, and she's learned how to fill up that space, all that free time, by herself. She's grown to like it. It's what she never had, growing up."

There is a lot of space in a zeppelin, I thought, idly. That space, filled with lighter-than-air helium, keeps the zeppelin afloat. A marriage also has a lot of space. What fills it to keep it afloat?

We watched the display of the aurora borealis outside the window in the northern skies as the ship raced towards Alaska.

I don't know how much time passed before I was jolted awake by a violent jerk. Before I knew what was going on, another sudden tilt of the ship threw me out of my bunk onto the floor. I rolled over, stumbled up, and made my way forward into the control cab by holding on to the walls.

"It's common to have storms in spring over the Bering Sea," Icke, who was supposed to be off shift and sleeping, was standing and holding on to the back of the pilot's chair. Yeling didn't bother to acknowledge me. Her knuckles were white from gripping the controls.

It was daytime, but other than the fact that there was some faint and murky light coming through the windows, it might as well have been the middle of the night. The wind, slamming freezing rain into the windows, made it impossible to see even the bottom of the hull as it curved up from the control cab to the nose cone. Billowing fog and clouds roiled around the ship, whipping past us faster than cars on the autobahns.

A sudden gust slammed into the side of the ship, and I was thrown onto the floor of the cab. Icke didn't even look over as he shouted at me, "Tie yourself down or get back to the bunk."

I got up and stood in the back right corner of the control cab and used the webbing I found there to lash myself in place and out of the way.

Smoothly, as though they had practiced it, Yeling slipped out of the pilot chair and Icke slipped in. Yeling strapped herself into the passenger stool on the right. The line on one of the electronic screens that showed the ship's course by GPS indicated that we had been zigzagging around crazily. In fact, it was clear that although the throttle was on full and we were burning fuel as fast as an airplane, the wind was pushing us backwards relative to the ground.

It was all Icke could do to keep us pointed into the wind and minimize the cross-section we presented to the front of the storm. If we were pointed slightly at an angle to the wind, the wind would have grabbed us around the ship's peripatetic pivot point and spun us like an egg on its side, yawing out of control. The pivot point, the center of momentum around which a ship would move when an external force is applied, shifts and moves about an airship depending on the ship's configuration, mass, hull shape, speed, acceleration, wind direction, and angular momentum, among other factors, and a pilot kept a zeppelin straight in a storm like this by feel and instinct more than anything else.

Lightning flashed close by, so close that I was blinded for a moment. The thunder rumbled the ship and made my teeth rattle, as though the floor of the ship was the diaphragm of a subwoofer.

"She feels heavy," Icke said. "Ice must be building up on the hull. It actually doesn't feel nearly as heavy as I would have expected. The hull ought to be covered by a solid layer of ice now if the outside thermometer reading is right. But we are still losing altitude, and we can't go any lower. The waves are going to hit the ship. We can't duck under this storm. We'll have to climb over it."

Icke dropped more water ballast to lighten the ship and tilted the elevators up. We shot straight up like a rocket. The *American Dragon*'s elongated teardrop shape acted as a crude airfoil, and as the brutal Arctic wind rushed at us, we flew like an experimental model wing design in a wind tunnel.

Another bolt of lightning flashed, even closer and brighter than before. The rumble from the thunder hurt my ear drums, and for a while I could hear nothing.

Icke and Yeling shouted at each other, and Yeling shook her head and yelled again. Icke looked at her for a moment, nodded, and lifted his hands off the controls for a second. The ship jerked itself and twisted to the side as the wind took hold of it and began to turn it. Icke reached back to grab the controls as another bolt of lightning flashed. The interior lights went out as the lightning erased all shadows and lines and perspective, and the sound of the thunder knocked me off my feet and punched me hard in the ears. And I passed into complete darkness.

By the time I came to, I had missed the entire Alaskan leg of the journey.

Yeling, who had the helm, was playing a Chinese song through the speakers. It was dark outside, and a round, golden moon, almost full and as big as the moon I remember from my childhood, floated over the dark and invisible sea. I sat down next to Yeling and stared at it.

After the chorus, the singer, a woman with a mellow and smooth voice, began the next verse in English:

> *But why is the moon always fullest when we take leave of one another?*
> *For us, there is sorrow, joy, parting, and meeting.*
> *For the moon, there is shade, shine, waxing and waning.*
> *It has never been possible to have it all.*
> *All we can wish for is that we endure,*
> *Though we are thousands of miles apart,*
> *Yet we shall gaze upon the same moon, always lovely.*

Yeling turned off the music and wiped her eyes with the back of her hand.

"She found a way out of the storm," she said. There was no need to ask who she meant. "She dodged that lightning at the last minute and found herself a hole in the storm to slip through. Sharp eyes. I knew it was a good idea to repaint the left eye, the one watching the sky, before we took off."

I watched the calm waters of the Pacific Ocean pass beneath us.

"In the storm, she shed her scales to make herself lighter."

I imagined the tung oil lines drawn on the ship's hull by Yeling, the lines etching the ice into dragon scales, which fell in large chunks into the frozen sea below.

"When I first married Barry, I did everything his way and nothing my way. When he was asleep, and I was flying the ship, I had a lot of time to think. I would think about my parents getting old and me not being there. I'd think about some recipe I wanted to ask my mother about, and she wasn't there. I asked myself all the time, *what have I done?*

"But even though I did everything his way, we used to argue all the time. Arguments that neither of us could understand and that went nowhere. And then I decided that I had to do something.

"I rearranged the way the pots were hung up in the galley and the way the dishes were stacked in the cabinets and the way the pictures were arranged in the bedroom and the way we stored life vests and shoes and blankets. I gave everything a better flow of *qi*, energy, and smoother *fengshui*. It might seem like a cramped and shabby place to some, but the ship now feels like our palace in the skies.

"Barry didn't even notice it. But, because of the *fengshui*, we didn't argue anymore. Even during the storm, when things were so tense, we worked well together."

"Were you scared at all during the storm?" I asked.

Yeling bit her bottom lip, thinking about my question.

"When I first rode with Barry, when I didn't yet know him, I used to wake up and say, in Chinese, *who is this man with me in the sky?* That was the most I've ever been scared.

"But last night, when I was struggling with the ship and Barry came to help me, I wasn't scared at all. I thought, it's okay if we die now. I know this man. I know what I've done. I'm home."

"There was never any real danger from lightning," Icke said. "You knew that, right? The *American Dragon* is a giant Faraday cage. Even if the lightning had struck us, the charge would have stayed on the outside of the metal frame. We were in the safest place over that whole sea in that storm."

I brought up what Yeling had said, that the ship seemed to know where to go in the storm.

Icke shrugged. "Aerodynamics is a complex thing, and the ship moved the way physics told it to."

"But when you get your Aurora, you'll let her paint eyes on it?"

Icke nodded, as though I had asked a very stupid question.

Las Vegas, the diadem of the desert, spread out beneath, around, and above us.

Pleasure ships and mass-transit passenger zeppelins covered in flashing neon and gaudy giant flickering screens dotted the air over the Strip. Cargo carriers like us were constricted to a narrow lane parallel to the Strip with specific points where we were allowed to depart to land at the individual casinos.

"That's Laputa," Icke pointed above us, to a giant, puffy, baroque airship that seemed as big as the Venetian, which we were passing below and to the left. Lit from within, this newest and flashiest floating casino glowed like a giant red Chinese lantern in the sky. Air taxis rose from the Strip and floated towards it like fireflies.

We had dropped off the shipment of turbine blades with the wind farm owned by Caesars Palace outside the city, and now we were headed for Caesars itself. Comp rooms were one of the benefits of hauling cargo for a customer like that.

I saw, coming up behind the Mirage, the tall spire and blinking lights of the mooring mast in front of the Forum Shops. It was usually where the great luxury personal yachts of the high-stakes rollers moored, but tonight it was empty, and a transpacific long-haul Dongfeng Feimaotui, a Flying Chinaman named the *American Dragon*, was going to take it for its own.

"We'll play some games, and then go to our room," Icke said. He was talking to Yeling, who smiled back at him. This would be the first chance they had of sleeping in the same bed in a week. They had a full twenty-four hours, and then they'd take off for Kalispell, Montana, where they would pick up a shipment of buffalo bones for the long haul back to China.

I lay in bed in my downtown hotel room thinking about the way the furniture in my bedroom was arranged, and imagined the flow of *qi* around the bed, the nightstands, the dresser. I missed the faint hum of the zeppelin's engines, so quiet that you had to listen hard to hear them.

I turned on the light and called my wife. "I'm not home yet. Soon."

[This story was inspired in many ways by John McPhee's Uncommon Carriers.

Some liberty has been taken with the physical geography of our world: a great circle flight path from Lanzhou to Las Vegas would not actually cross the city of Ordos.

The lyrics of the song that Yeling plays come from a poem by the Song Dynasty poet Su Shi (1037–1101 A.D). It has remained a popular poem to set to music through the centuries since its composition.]

three cups of grief, by starlight

ALiETTE DE BODARD

Aliette de Bodard is a software engineer who lives and works in Paris, where she shares a flat with two Lovecraftian plants and more computers than warm bodies. Only a few years into her career, her short fiction has appeared in Interzone, Asimov's, Clarkesworld, Realms of Fantasy, Orson Scott Card's Intergalactic Medicine Show, Writers of the Future, Coyote Wild, Electric Velocipede, The Immersion Book of SF, Fictitious Force, Shimmer, *and elsewhere, and she has won the British SF Association Award for her story "The Shipmaker," the Locus Award, and the Nebula Award for her stories "The Waiting Stars" and "Immersion." Her novels include* Servant of the Underworld, Harbinger of the Storm, *and* Master of the House of Darts, *all recently reissued in a novel omnibus,* Obsidian and Blood. *Another British SF Association-winner,* The House of Shattered Wings, *came out in 2016, followed by a sequel,* The House of Binding Thorns. *Her website, http://www.aliettedebodard.com, features free fiction, thoughts on the writing process, and entirely too many recipes for Vietnamese dishes.*

The story that follows is another in her long series of "Xuya" stories, taking place in the far future of an Alternate World where a high-tech conflict is going on between spacefaring Mayan and Chinese empires. This one deals with the death of a scientist whose work is considered important enough by the government that they deny her children her mem-implants, consisting of her recorded memories, which tradition dictates should have been given to her family to maintain family continuity. This leaves her children and close associates to somehow deal with their grief over this double bereavement—including one sister who's become a living starship, The Tiger in the Banyan.

G*reen tea: green tea is made from steamed or lightly dried tea leaves. The brew is light, with a pleasant, grassy taste. Do not over-steep it, lest it become bitter.*

After the funeral, Quang Tu walked back to his compartment, and sat down alone, staring sightlessly at the slow ballet of bots cleaning the small room—the metal walls pristine already, with every trace of Mother's presence or of her numerous mourners scrubbed away. He'd shut down the communal network—couldn't bear to see the potted summaries of Mother's life, the endlessly looping vids of the funeral procession, the hundred thousand bystanders gathered at the grave site to say goodbye, vultures feasting on the flesh of the grieving—they hadn't known her, they hadn't cared—and all their offerings of flowers were worth as much as the insurances of the Embroidered Guard.

"Big brother, I know you're here," a voice said, from the other side of the door he'd locked. "Let me in, please?"

Of course. Quang Tu didn't move. "I said I wanted to be alone," he said.

A snort that might have been amusement. "Fine. If you insist on doing it that way . . ."

His sister, *The Tiger in the Banyan*, materialized in the kitchen, hovering over the polished counter, near the remains of his morning tea. Of course, it wasn't really her: she was a Mind encased in the heartroom of a spaceship, far too heavy to leave orbit; and what she projected down onto the planet was an avatar, a perfectly rendered, smaller version of herself—elegant and sharp, with a small, blackened spot on her hull which served as a mourning band. "Typical," she said, hovering around the compartment. "You can't just shut yourself away."

"I can if I want to," Quang Tu said—feeling like he was eight years old again, trying to argue with her—as if it had ever made sense. She seldom got angry—mindships didn't, mostly; he wasn't sure if that was the overall design of the Imperial Workshops, or the simple fact that her lifespan was counted in centuries, and his (and Mother's) in mere decades. He'd have thought she didn't grieve, either; but she was changed—something in the slow, careful deliberation of her movements, as if anything and everything might break her . . .

The Tiger in the Banyan hovered near the kitchen table, watching the bots. She could hack them, easily; no security worth anything in the compartment. Who would steal bots, anyway?

What he valued most had already been taken away.

"Leave me alone," he said. But he didn't want to be alone; not really. He didn't want to hear the silence in the compartment; the clicking sounds of the bots' legs on metal, bereft of any warmth or humanity.

"Do you want to talk about it?" *The Tiger in the Banyan* asked.

She didn't need to say what; and he didn't do her the insult of pretending she did. "What would be the point?"

"To talk." Her voice was uncannily shrewd. "It helps. At least, I'm told it does."

Quang Tu heard, again, the voice of the Embroidered Guard; the slow, measured tones commiserating on his loss; and then the frown, and the knife-thrust in his gut.

You must understand that your mother's work was very valuable . . .

The circumstances are not ordinary . . .

The slow, pompous tones of the scholar; the convoluted official language he knew by heart—the only excuses the state would make to him, couched in the over-formality of memorials and edicts.

"She—" He took a deep, trembling breath—was it grief, or anger? "I should have had her mem-implants." Forty-nine days after the funeral; when there was time for the labs to have decanted and stabilized Mother's personality and memories and added her to the ranks of the ancestors on file. It wasn't her, it would never be her, of course—just a simulation meant to share knowledge and advice. But it would have been something. It would have filled the awful emptiness in his life.

"It was your right, as the eldest," *The Tiger in the Banyan* said. Something in the tone of her voice . . .

"You disapprove? You wanted them?" Families had fallen out before, over more trivial things.

"Of course not." A burst of careless, amused laughter. "Don't be a fool. What use would I have for them. It's just—" She hesitated, banking left and right in uncertainty. "You need something more. Beyond Mother."

"There isn't something more!"

"You—"

"You weren't there," Quang Tu said. She'd been away on her journeys, ferrying people back and forth between the planets that made up the Dai Viet Empire; leaping from world to world, with hardly a care for planet-bound humans. She— she hadn't seen Mother's unsteady hands, dropping the glass; heard the sound of its shattering like a gunshot; hadn't carried her back to bed every evening, tracking the progress of the disease by the growing lightness in his arms—by the growing sharpness of ribs, protruding under taut skin.

Mother had remained herself until almost the end—sharp and lucid and ut-terly aware of what was happening, scribbling in the margins of her team's reports and sending her instructions to the new space station's building site, as if nothing untoward had ever happened to her. Had it been a blessing; or a curse? He didn't have answers; and he wasn't sure he wanted that awful certainty to shatter him.

"I was here," *The Tiger in the Banyan* said, gently, slowly. "At the end."

Quang Tu closed his eyes, again, smelling antiseptic and the sharp odor of painkillers; and the sour smell of a body finally breaking down, finally failing. "I'm sorry. You were. I didn't mean to—"

"I know you didn't." *The Tiger in the Banyan* moved closer to him; brushed against his shoulder—ghostly, almost intangible, the breath that had been beside him all his childhood. "But nevertheless. Your life got eaten up, taking care of Mother. And you can say you were only doing what a filial son ought to do; you can say it didn't matter. But . . . it's done now, big brother. It's over."

It's not, he wanted to say, but the words rang hollow in his own ears. He moved, stared at the altar; at the holo of Mother—over the offering of tea and rice, the food to sustain her on her journey through Hell. It cycled through vids—Mother, heavily pregnant with his sister, moving with the characteristic arrested slowness of Mind-bearers; Mother standing behind Quang Tu and *The Tiger in the Banyan* in front of the ancestral altar for Grandfather's death anniversary; Mother, accepting her Hoang Minh Medal from the then Minister of Investigation; and one before the diagnosis, when she'd already started to become frailer and thinner—insisting on going back to the lab; to her abandoned teams and research . . .

He thought, again, of the Embroidered Guard; of the words tightening around his neck like an executioner's garrotte. How dare he. How dare they all. "She came home," he said, not sure how to voice the turmoil within him. "To us. To her family. In the end. It meant something, didn't it?"

The Tiger in the Banyan's voice was wry, amused. "It wasn't the Empress that comforted her when she woke at night, coughing her lungs out, was it?" It was . . . treason to much as think this, let alone utter it; though the Embroidered Guard would make allowances for grief, and anger; and for Mother's continued usefulness to the service of the Empress. The truth was, neither of them much cared, anyway. "It's not the Empress that was by her side when she died."

She'd clung to his hand, then, her eyes open wide, a network of blood within the whites, and the fear in her eyes. "I—please, child . . ." He'd stood, frozen; until, behind him, *The Tiger in the Banyan* whispered, "The lights in Sai Gon are green and red, the lamps in My Tho are bright and dim . . ." An Old Earth lullaby, the words stretched into the familiar, slow, comforting rhythm that he'd unthinkingly taken up.

"Go home to study.

I shall wait nine months, I shall wait ten autumns . . ."

She'd relaxed, then, against him; and they had gone on singing songs until—
He didn't know when she'd died; when the eyes lost their luster, the face its usual sharpness. But he'd risen from her deathbed with the song still in his mind; and an awful yawning gap in his world that nothing had closed.

And then—after the scattering of votive papers, after the final handful of earth thrown over the grave—the Embroidered Guard.

The Embroidered Guard was young; baby-faced and callow, but he was already moving with the easy arrogance of the privileged. He'd approached Quang Tu at the grave site, ostensibly to offer his condolences—it had taken him all of two sentences to get to his true purpose; and to shatter Quang Tu's world, all over again.

Your mother's mem-implants will go to Professor Tuyet Hoa, who will be best able to continue her research . . .

Of course, the Empire required food; and crops of rice grown in space; and better, more reliable harvests to feed the masses. Of course he didn't want anyone to starve. But . . .

Mem-implants always went from parent to child. They were a family's riches and fortune; the continued advice of the ancestors, dispensed from beyond the grave. He'd—he'd had the comfort, as Mother lay dying, to know that he wouldn't lose her. Not for real; not for long.

"They took her away from us," Quang Tu said. "Again and again and again. And now, at the very end, when she ought to be ours—when she should return to her family . . ."

The Tiger in the Banyan didn't move; but a vid of the funeral appeared on one of the walls, projected through the communal network. There hadn't been enough space in the small compartment for people to pay their respects; the numerous callers had jammed into the corridors and alcoves, jostling each other in utter silence. "She's theirs in death, too."

"And you don't care?"

A side-roll of the avatar, her equivalent of a shrug. "Not as much as you do. I remember her. None of them do."

Except Tuyet Hoa.

He remembered Tuyet Hoa, too; coming to visit them on the third day after the New Year—a student paying respect to her teacher, year after year; turning from an unattainable grown-up to a woman not much older than either he or *The Tiger in the Banyan*; though she'd never lost her rigid awkwardness in dealing with them. No doubt, in Tuyet Hoa's ideal world, Mother wouldn't have had children; wouldn't have let anything distract her from her work.

"You have to move on," *The Tiger in the Banyan* said, slowly, gently; coming by his side to stare at the memorial altar. Bots gathered in the kitchen space, started putting together fresh tea to replace the three cups laid there. "Accept that this is the way things are. They'll compensate, you know—offer you higher-level promotions and make allowances. You'll find your path through civil service is . . . smoother."

Bribes or sops; payments for the loss of something that had no price. "Fair dealings," he said, slowly, bitterly. They knew exactly the value of what Tuyet Hoa was getting.

"Of course," *The Tiger in the Banyan* said. "But you'll only ruin your health and your career; and you know Mother wouldn't have wanted it."

As if . . . No, he was being unfair. Mother could be distant and engrossed in her work; but she had always made time for them. She had raised them and played with them, telling them stories of princesses and fishermen and citadels vanished in one night; and, later on, going on long walks with Quang Tu in the gardens of Azure Dragons, delightedly pointing at a pine tree or at a crane flying overhead; and animatedly discussing Quang Tu's fledging career in the Ministry of Works.

"You can't afford to let this go sour," *The Tiger in the Banyan* said. Below her, the bots brought a small, perfect cup of tea: green, fragrant liquid in a cup, the cracks in the pale celadon like those in eggshells.

Quang Tu lifted the cup; breathed in the grassy, pleasant smell—Mother would love it, even beyond the grave. "I know," he said, laying the cup on the altar. The lie slipped out of him as softly, as easily as Mother's last exhaled breath.

O Long tea: those teas are carefully prepared by the tea masters to create a range of tastes and appearances. The brew is sweet with a hint of strength, each subsequent steeping revealing new nuances.

Tuyet Hoa woke up—with a diffuse, growing sense of panic and fear, before she remembered the procedure.

She was alive. She was sane. At least . . .

She took in a deep, trembling breath; and realized she lay at home, in her bed. What had woken her up—above the stubborn, panicked rhythm of her heart—was a gentle nudge from the communal network, flashes of light relayed by the bots in the lightest phase of her sleep cycle. It wasn't her alarm; but rather, a notification that a message classified as "urgent" had arrived for her.

Not again.

A nudge, at the back of her mind; a thread of thought that wasn't her own; reminding her she should look at it; that it was her responsibility as the new head of department to pay proper attention to messages from her subordinates.

Professor Duy Uyen. Of course.

She was as forceful in life as she had been in death; and, because she had been merely Hoa's head of department, and not a direct ancestor, she felt . . . wrong. Distant, as though she were speaking through a pane of glass.

Hoa was lucky, she knew—receiving mem-implants that weren't your own family's could irretrievably scramble your brain, as fifteen different strangers with no consideration or compassion fought for control of your thoughts. She could hear Professor Duy Uyen; and sometimes others of Duy Uyen's ancestors, as remote ghosts; but that was it. It could have been so much worse.

And it could have been so much better.

She got up, ignoring the insistent talk at the back of her mind, the constant urge to be dutiful; and padded into the kitchen.

The bots had already set aside Hoa's first tea of the day. She'd used to take it at work, before the procedure; in the days of Professor Duy Uyen's sickness, when Duy Uyen came in to work thinner and paler every day—and then became a succession of memorials and vid-calls, injecting her last, desperate instructions into the project before it slipped beyond her grasp. Hoa had enjoyed the quiet: it had kept the desperate knowledge of Professor Duy Uyen's coming death at bay—the moment when they would all be adrift in the void of space, with no mindship to carry them onwards.

Now Hoa enjoyed a different quiet. Now she drank her tea first thing in the morning—hoping that, at this early hour, the mem-implants had no motive to kick in.

Not that it had worked, this particular morning.

She sat down to breathe in the flavor—the faint, nutty aroma poised perfectly between floral and sweet—her hand trembling above the surface of the cup—mentally blocking out Professor Duy Uyen for a few precious minutes; a few more stolen moments of tranquility before reality came crashing in.

Then she gave in and opened the message.

It was from Luong Ya Lan, the researcher who worked on the water's acidity balance. On the vid relayed from the laboratory, she was pale, but perfectly composed. "Madam Hoa. I'm sorry to have to inform you that the samples in Paddy Four have developed a fungal disease . . ."

Professor Duy Uyen stirred in the depths of Hoa's brain, parsing the words as they came in—accessing the station's private network and downloading the pertinent data—the only mercy was that she wasn't faster than Hoa, and that it would take her fifteen to twenty minutes to parse all of it. The Professor had her suspicions, of course—something about the particular rice strain; perhaps the changes drafted onto the plant to allow it to thrive under starlight, changes taken from the nocturnal honeydreamer on the Sixteenth Planet; perhaps the conditions in the paddy itself . . .

Hoa poured herself another cup of tea; and stared at the bots for a while. There was silence, the voice of Duy Uyen slowly fading away to nothingness in her thoughts. Alone. At last, alone.

Paddy Four had last been checked on by Ya Lan's student, An Khang—Khang was a smart and dedicated man, but not a particularly careful one; and she would have to ask him if he'd checked himself, or through bots; and if he'd followed protocols when he'd done so.

She got up and walked to the laboratory—still silence in her mind. It was a short trip: the station was still being built, and the only thing in existence were the laboratory and the living quarters for all ten researchers—a generous allocation of space, far grander than the compartments they would have been entitled to on any of their home stations.

Outside, beyond the metal walls, the bots were hard at work—reinforcing the structure, gradually layering a floor and walls onto the skeletal structure mapped out by the Grand Master of Design Harmony. She had no need to call up a vid of the outside on her implants to know they were out there, doing their part; just as she was. They weren't the only ones, of course: in the Imperial Workshops, alchemists were carefully poring over the design of the Mind that would one day watch over the entire station, making sure no flaws remained before they transferred him to the womb of his mother.

In the laboratory, Ya Lan was busying herself with the faulty paddy: she threw an apologetic glance at Hoa when Hoa walked in. "You got my message."

Hoa grimaced. "Yes. Have you had time to analyze?"

Ya Lan flushed. "No."

Hoa knew. A proper analysis would require more than twenty minutes. But still . . . . "If you had to make a rough guess?"

"Probably the humidity."

"Did Khang—"

Ya Lan shook her head. "I checked that, too. No contaminants introduced in the paddy; and the last time he opened it was two weeks ago." The paddies were encased in glass, to make sure they could control the environment; and monitored by bots and the occasional scientist.

"Fungi can lie dormant for more than two weeks," Hoa said, darkly.

Ya Lan sighed. "Of course. But I still think it's the environment: it's a bit tricky to get right."

Humid and dark; the perfect conditions for a host of other things to grow in the paddies—not just the crops the Empire so desperately needed. The named planets were few; and fewer still that could bear the cultivation of food. Professor Duy Uyen had had a vision—of a network of space stations like this one; of fish ponds and rice paddies grown directly under starlight, rather than on simulated Old Earth light; of staples that would not cost a fortune in resources to grow and maintain.

And they had all believed in that vision, like a dying man offered a glimpse of a river. The Empress herself had believed it; so much that she had suspended the law for Professor Duy Uyen's sake, and granted her mem-implants to Hoa instead of to Duy Uyen's son: the quiet boy Hoa remembered from her New Year's visits, now grown to become a scholar in his own right—he'd been angry at the funeral, and why wouldn't he be? The mem-implants should have been his.

"I know," Hoa said. She knelt, calling up the data from the paddy onto her implants: her field of vision filled with a graph of the temperature throughout last month. The slight dips in the curve all corresponded to a check: a researcher opening the paddy.

"Professor?" Ya Lan asked; hesitant.

Hoa did not move. "Yes?"

"It's the third paddy of that strain that fails in as many months . . ."

She heard the question Ya Lan was not asking. The other strain—the one in paddies One to Three—had also failed some tests, but not at the same frequency.

Within her, Professor Duy Uyen stirred. It was the temperature, she pointed out, gently but firmly. The honeydreamer supported a very narrow range of temperatures; and the modified rice probably did, too.

Hoa bit back a savage answer. The changes might be flawed, but they were the best candidate they had.

Professor Duy Uyen shook her head. The strain in paddies One to Three was better: a graft from a lifeform of an unnumbered and unsettled planet, P Huong Van—luminescents, an insect flying in air too different to be breathable by human beings. They had been Professor Duy Uyen's favored option.

Hoa didn't like the luminescents. The air of P Huong Van had a different balance of *khi*-elements: it was rich in fire, and anything would set it ablaze—flamestorms were horrifically common, charring trees to cinders, and birds in flight to blackened skeletons. Aboard a space station, fire was too much of a danger. Professor Duy Uyen had argued that the Mind that would ultimately control the space station could be designed to accept an unbalance of *khi*-elements; could add water to the atmosphere to reduce the chances of a firestorm onboard.

Hoa had no faith in this. Modifying a Mind had a high cost, far above that of regulating temperature in a rice paddy. She pulled up the data from the paddies; though of course she knew Professor Duy Uyen would have reviewed it before her.

Professor Duy Uyen was polite enough not to chide Hoa; though Hoa could feel her disapproval like the weight of a blade—it was odd, in so many ways, how the refinement process had changed Professor Duy Uyen; how, with all the stabilization adjustments, all the paring down of the unnecessary emotions, the simulation in her mind was utterly, heartbreakingly different from the woman she had known: all the keenness of her mind, and the blade of her finely honed knowledge, with none of the compassion that would have made her more bearable. Though perhaps it was as well that she had none of the weakness Duy Uyen had shown, in the end—the skin that barely hid the sharpness of bones; the eyes like bruises in the pale oval of her face; the voice, faltering on words or instructions . . .

Paddies One to Three were thriving; the yield perhaps less than that of Old Earth; but nothing to be ashamed of. There had been a spot of infection in Paddy Three; but the bots had taken care of it.

Hoa watched, for a moment, the bots scuttling over the glass encasing the paddy; watched the shine of metal; the light trembling on the joints of their legs—waiting for the smallest of triggers to blossom into flame. The temperature data for all three paddies was fluctuating too much; and the rate of fire-*khi* was far above what she was comfortable with.

"Professor?" Ya Lan was still waiting by Paddy Four.

There was only one paddy of that honeydreamer strain: it was new, and as yet unproved. Professor Duy Uyen stirred, within her mind; pointed out the painfully obvious. The strain wasn't resistant enough—the Empire couldn't afford to rely on something so fragile. She should do the reasonable thing and consign it to the scrap bin. They should switch efforts to the other strain, the favored one; and what did it matter if the station's Mind needed to enforce a slightly different balance of *khi*-elements?

It was what Professor Duy Uyen would have done.

But she wasn't Professor Duy Uyen.

Minds were made in balance; to deliberately unhinge one . . . would have larger consequences on the station than mere atmospheric control. The risk was too high. She knew this; as much as she knew and numbered all her ancestors—the ones that hadn't been rich or privileged enough to bequeath her their own mem-implants—leaving her with only this pale, flawed approximation of an inheritance.

You're a fool.

Hoa closed her eyes; closed her thoughts so that the voice in her mind sank to a whisper. She brought herself, with a slight effort, back to the tranquillity of her mornings—breathing in the nutty aroma from her teacup, as she steeled herself for the day ahead.

She wasn't Professor Duy Uyen.

She'd feared being left adrift when Professor Duy Uyen's illness had taken a turn for the worse; she'd lain late at night wondering what would happen to Duy Uyen's vision; of what she would do, bereft of guidance.

But now she knew.

"Get three other tanks," Hoa said. "Let's see what that strain looks like with a tighter temperature regulation. And if you can get hold of Khang, ask him to look into the graft—there might be a better solution there."

The Empress had thought Duy Uyen a critical asset; had made sure that her mem-implants went to Hoa—so that Hoa would have the advice and knowledge she needed to finish the station that the Empire so desperately needed. The Empress had been wrong; and who cared if that was treason?

Because the answer to Professor Duy Uyen's death, like everything else, was deceptively, heartbreakingly simple: that no one was irreplaceable; that they would do what everyone always did—they would, somehow, forge on.

Dark tea: dark tea leaves are left to mature for years through a careful process of fermentation. The process can take anywhere from a few months to a century. The resulting brew has rich, thick texture with only a bare hint of sourness.

The Tiger in the Banyan doesn't grieve as humans do.

Partly, it's because she's been grieving for such a long time; because mindships don't live the same way that humans do—because they're built and anchored and stabilized.

Quang Tu spoke of seeing Mother become frail and ill, and how it broke his heart; *The Tiger in the Banyan*'s heart broke, years and years ago; when she stood in the midst of the New Year's Eve celebration—as the sound of crackers and bells and gongs filled the corridors of the orbital, and everyone hugged and cried, she suddenly realized that she would still be there in a hundred years; but that no one else around the table—not Mother, not Quang Tu, none of the aunts and uncles or cousins—would still be alive.

She leaves Quang Tu in his compartment, staring at the memorial altar—and, shifting her consciousness from her projected avatar to her real body, climbs back among the stars.

She is a ship; and in the days and months that Quang Tu mourns, she carries people between planets and orbitals—private passengers and officials on their business: rough white silk, elaborate five panel dresses; parties of scholars arguing on the merit of poems; soldiers on leave from the most distant numbered planets, who go into the weirdness of deep spaces with nothing more than a raised eyebrow.

Mother is dead, but the world goes on—Professor Pham Thi Duy Uyen becomes yesterday's news; fades into official biographies and re-creation vids—and her daughter goes on, too, doing her duty to the Empire.

The Tiger in the Banyan doesn't grieve as humans do. Partly, it's because she doesn't remember as humans do.

She doesn't remember the womb; or the shock of the birth; but in her earliest memories Mother is here—the first and only time she was carried in Mother's arms—and Mother herself helped by the birth-master, walking forward on tottering legs—past the pain of the birth, past the bone-deep weariness that speaks only of rest and sleep. It's Mother's hands that lie her down into the cradle in the heart-room; Mother's hands that close the clasps around her—so that she is held; wrapped as securely as she was in the womb—and Mother's voice that sings to her a lullaby, the tune she will forever carry as she travels between the stars.

"The lights in Sai Gon are green and red, the lamps in My Tho are bright and dim . . ."

As she docks at an orbital near the Fifth Planet, *The Tiger in the Banyan* is hailed by another, older ship, *The Dream of Millet*: a friend she often meets on longer journeys. "I've been looking for you."

"Oh?" *The Tiger in the Banyan* asks. It's not hard, to keep track of where ships go from their manifests; but *The Dream of Millet* is old, and rarely bothers to do so—she's used to ships coming to her, rather than the other way around.

"I wanted to ask how you were. When I heard you were back into service—" *The Dream of Millet* pauses, then; and hesitates; sending a faint signal of cautious disapproval on the comms. "It's early. Shouldn't you be mourning? Officially—"

Officially, the hundred days of tears are not yet over. But ships are few; and she's not an official like Quang Tu, beholden to present exemplary behavior. "I'm fine," *The Tiger in the Banyan* says. She's mourning; but it doesn't interfere with her activities: after all, she's been steeling herself for this since Father died. She didn't expect it to come so painfully, so soon, but she was prepared for it—braced for it in a way that Quang Tu will never be.

The Dream of Millet is silent for a while—*The Tiger in the Banyan* can feel her, through the void that separates them—can feel the radio waves nudging her hull; the quick jab of probes dipping into her internal network and collating together information about her last travels. "You're not 'fine,'" *The Dream of Millet* says. "You're slower, and you go into deep spaces further than you should. And—" she pauses, but it's more for effect than anything else. "You've been avoiding it, haven't you?"

They both know what she's talking about: the space station Mother was putting together; the project to provide a steady, abundant food supply to the Empire.

"I've had no orders that take me there," *The Tiger in the Banyan* says. Not quite a lie; but dangerously close to one. She's been . . . better off knowing the station doesn't exist—unsure that she could face it at all. She doesn't care about Tuyet Hoa, or the mem-implants; but the station was such a large part of Mother's life that she's not sure she could stand to be reminded of it.

She is a mindship: her memories never grow dim or faint; or corrupt. She remembers songs and fairytales whispered through her corridors; remembers walking with Mother on the First Planet, smiling as Mother pointed out the odder places of the Imperial City, from the menagerie to the temple where monks worship an Outsider clockmaker—remembers Mother frail and bowed in the last days, coming to rest in the heartroom, her labored breath filling *The Tiger in the Banyan*'s corridors until she, too, could hardly breathe.

She remembers everything about Mother; but the space station—the place where Mother worked away from her children; the project Mother could barely talk about without breaching confidentiality—is forever denied to her memories; forever impersonal, forever distant.

"I see," *The Dream of Millet* says. Again, faint disapproval; and another feeling *The Tiger in the Banyan* can't quite place—reluctance? Fear of impropriety? "You cannot live like that, child."

Let me be, *The Tiger in the Banyan* says; but of course she can't say that; not to a ship as old as *The Dream of Millet*. "It will pass," she says. "In the meantime,

I do what I was trained to do. No one has reproached me." Her answer borders on impertinence, deliberately.

"No. And I won't," *The Dream of Millet* says. "It would be inappropriate of me to tell you how to manage your grief." She laughs, briefly. "You know there are people worshipping her? I saw a temple, on the Fifty-second Planet."

An easier, happier subject. "I've seen one, too," *The Tiger in the Banyan* says. "On the Thirtieth Planet." It has a statue of Mother, smiling as serenely as a bodhisattva—people light incense to her to be helped in their difficulties. "She would have loved this." Not for the fame or the worship, but merely because she would have found it heartbreakingly funny.

"Hmmm. No doubt." *The Dream of Millet* starts moving away; her comms growing slightly fainter. "I'll see you again, then. Remember what I said."

The Tiger in the Banyan will; but not with pleasure. And she doesn't like the tone with which the other ship takes her leave; it suggests she is going to do something—something typical of the old, getting *The Tiger in the Banyan* into a position where she'll have no choice but to acquiesce to whatever *The Dream of Millet* thinks of as necessary.

Still . . . there is nothing that she can do. As *The Tiger in the Banyan* leaves the orbital onto her next journey, she sets a trace on *The Dream of Millet*; and monitors it from time to time. Nothing the other ship does seems untoward or suspicious; and after a while *The Tiger in the Banyan* lets the trace fade.

As she weaves her way between the stars, she remembers.

Mother, coming onboard a week before she died—walking by the walls with their endlessly scrolling texts, all the poems she taught *The Tiger in the Banyan* as a child. In the low gravity, Mother seemed almost at ease; striding once more onboard the ship until she reached the heartroom. She'd sat with a teacup cradled in her lap—dark tea, because she said she needed a strong taste to wash down the drugs they plied her with—the heartroom filled with a smell like churned earth, until *The Tiger in the Banyan* could almost taste the tea she couldn't drink.

"Child?" Mother asked.

"Yes?"

"Can we go away—for a while?"

She wasn't supposed to, of course; she was a mindship, her travels strictly bounded and codified. But she did. She warned the space station; and plunged into deep spaces.

Mother said nothing. She'd stared ahead, listening to the odd sounds; to the echo of her own breath, watching the oily shapes spread on the walls—while *The Tiger in the Banyan* kept them on course; feeling stretched and scrunched, pulled in different directions as if she were swimming in rapids. Mother was mumbling under her breath; after a while, *The Tiger in the Banyan* realized it was the words of a song; and, to accompany it, she broadcast music on her loudspeakers.

Go home to study

I shall wait nine months, I shall wait ten autumns . . .

She remembers Mother's smile; the utter serenity on her face—the way she rose after they came back to normal spaces, fluid and utterly graceful; as if all pain and weakness had been set aside for this bare moment; subsumed in the music or the travel or both. She remembers Mother's quiet words as she left the heartroom.

"Thank you, child. You did well."

"It was nothing," she'd said, and Mother had smiled, and disembarked—but *The Tiger in the Banyan* had heard the words Mother wasn't speaking. Of course it wasn't nothing. Of course it had meant something; to be away from it all, even for a bare moment; to hang, weightless and without responsibilities, in the vastness of space. Of course.

A hundred and three days after Mother's death, a message comes, from the Imperial Palace. It directs her to pick an Embroidered Guard from the First Planet; and the destination is . . .

Had she a heart, this is the moment when it would stop.

The Embroidered Guard is going to Mother's space station. It doesn't matter why; or how long for—just that she's meant to go with him. And she can't. She can't possibly . . .

Below the order is a note, and she knows, too, what it will say. That the ship originally meant for this mission was *The Dream of Millet*; and that she, unable to complete it, recommended that *The Tiger in the Banyan* take it up instead.

Ancestors . . .

How dare she?

The Tiger in the Banyan can't refuse the order; or pass it on to someone else. Neither can she rail at a much older ship—but if she could—ancestors, if she could . . .

It doesn't matter. It's just a place—one with a little personal significance to her—but nothing she can't weather. She has been to so many places, all over the Empire; and this is just one more.

Just one more.

The Embroidered Guard is young, and callow; and not unkind. He boards her at the First Planet, as specified—she's so busy steeling herself that she forgets to greet him, but he doesn't appear to notice this.

She's met him before, at the funeral: the one who apologetically approached Quang Tu; who let him know Mother's mem-implants wouldn't pass to him.

Of course.

She finds refuge in protocol: it's not her role to offer conversation to her passengers, especially not those of high rank or in imperial service, who would think it presumption. So she doesn't speak; and he keeps busy in his cabin, reading reports and watching vids, the way other passengers do.

Just before they emerge from deep spaces, she pauses; as if it would make a difference—as if there were a demon waiting for her; or perhaps something far older and far more terrible; something that will shatter her composure past any hope of recovery.

What are you afraid of? A voice asks within her—she isn't sure if it's Mother or *The Dream of Millet*, and she isn't sure of what answer she'd give, either.

The station isn't what she expected. It's a skeleton; a work in progress; a mass of cables and metal beams with bots crawling all over it; and the living quarters at the center, dwarfed by the incomplete structure. Almost deceptively ordinary; and yet it meant so much to Mother. Her vision for the future of the Empire; and neither Quang Tu nor *The Tiger in the Banyan* having a place within.

And yet . . . and yet, the station has heft. It has meaning—that of a painting half-done; of a poem stopped mid-verse—of a spear-thrust stopped a handspan before it penetrates the heart. It begs—demands—to be finished.

The Embroidered Guard speaks, then. "I have business onboard. Wait for me, will you?"

It is a courtesy to ask; since she would wait, in any case. But he surprises her by looking back, as he disembarks. "Ship?"

"Yes?"

"I'm sorry for your loss." His voice is toneless.

"Don't be," *The Tiger in the Banyan* says.

He smiles then; a bare upturning of the lips. "I could give you the platitudes about your mother living on in her work, if I thought that would change something for her."

The Tiger in the Banyan doesn't say anything, for a while. She watches the station below her; listens to the faint drift of radio communications—scientists calling other scientists; reporting successes and failures and the ten thousand little things that make a project of this magnitude. Mother's vision; Mother's work—people call it her life work, but of course she and Quang Tu are also Mother's life work, in a different way. And she understands, then, why *The Dream of Millet* sent her there.

"It meant something to her," she says, finally. "I don't think she'd have begrudged its completion."

He hesitates. Then, coming back inside the ship—and looking upwards, straight where the heartroom would be—his gaze level, driven by an emotion she can't read: "They'll finish it. The new variety of rice they've found—the environment will have to be strictly controlled to prevent it from dying of cold, but . . ." He takes a deep, trembling breath. "There'll be stations like this all over the Empire—and it's all thanks to your mother. "

"Of course," *The Tiger in the Banyan* says. And the only words that come to her as the ones Mother spoke, once. "Thank you, child. You did well."

She watches him leave; and thinks of Mother's smile. Of Mother's work; and of the things that happened between the work; the songs and the smiles and the stolen moments, all arrayed within her with the clarity and resilience of diamonds. She thinks of the memories she carries within her—that she will carry within her for the centuries to come.

The Embroidered Guard was trying to apologize, for the mem-implants; for the inheritance neither she nor Quang Tu will ever have. Telling her it had all been worth it, in the end; that their sacrifice hadn't been in vain.

But the truth is, it doesn't matter. It mattered to Quang Tu; but she's not her brother. She's not bound by anger or rancor; and she doesn't grieve as he does.

What matters is this: she holds all of her memories of Mother; and Mother is here now, with her—forever unchanged, forever graceful and tireless; forever flying among the stars.

calved

SAM J. MILLER

Sam J. Miller is a writer and a community organizer. His fiction has appeared in Lightspeed, Asimov's, Clarkesworld, The Minnesota Review, *and other markets. He is a nominee for the Nebula and Theodore Sturgeon Awards, a winner of the Shirley Jackson Award, and a graduate of the Clarion Writer's Workshop. His debut novel was* The Art of Starving. *He lives in New York City, and at www.samjmiller.com*

Here he gives us the heartbreaking, emotionally grueling story of a man struggling to find work and stay alive in a ruthless society made up of refugees fleeing cities drowned by rising oceans, and struggling, too, to somehow stay in touch with his son, whom he can feel becoming slowly estranged from him and slipping further and further away every time he leaves for a six-month-long job carving ice from melting glaciers. But can he win his son's affections back? Or will his efforts only make things worse?

My son's eyes were broken. Emptied out. Frozen over. None of the joy or gladness were there. None of the tears. Normally I'd return from a job and his face would split down the middle with happiness, seeing me for the first time in three months. Now it stayed flat as ice. His eyes leapt away the instant they met mine. His shoulders were broader and his arms more sturdy, and lone hairs now stood on his upper lip, but his eyes were all I saw.

"Thede," I said, grabbing him.

He let himself be hugged. His arms hung limply at his sides. My lungs could not fill. My chest tightened from the force of all the never-let-me-go bear hugs he had given me over the course of the past fifteen years and would never give again.

"You know how he gets when you're away," his mother had said, on the phone, the night before, preparing me. "He's a teenager now. Hating your parents is a normal part of it."

I hadn't listened, then. My hands and thighs still ached from months of straddling an ice saw; my hearing was worse with every trip; a slip had cost me five days work and five days pay and five days' worth of infirmary bills; I had returned to a sweat-smelling bunk in an illegal room I shared with seven other iceboat workers—and none of it mattered because in the morning I would see my son.

"Hey," he murmured emotionlessly. "Dad."

I stepped back, turned away until the red ebbed out of my face. Spring had come and the city had lowered its photoshade. It felt good, even in the cold wind.

"You guys have fun," Lajla said, pressing money discretely into my palm. I watched her go with a rising sense of panic. *Bring back my son*, I wanted to shout, *the one who loves me. Where is he. What have you done with him. Who is this surly creature.* Below us, through the city's ubiquitous steel grid that held up Qaanaaq's two million lives, black Greenland water sloshed against the locks of our floating city.

Breathe, Dom, I told myself, and eventually I could. *You knew this was coming. You knew one day he would cease to be a kid.*

"How's school?" I asked.

Thede shrugged. "Fine."

"Math still your favorite subject?"

"Math was never my favorite subject."

I was pretty sure that it had been, but I didn't want to argue.

"What's your favorite subject?"

Another shrug. We had met at the sea lion rookery, but I could see at once that Thede no longer cared about sea lions. He stalked through the crowd with me, his face a frozen mask of anger.

I couldn't blame him for how easy he had it. So what if he didn't live in the Brooklyn foster-care barracks, or work all day at the solar-cell plant school? He still had to live in a city that hated him for his dark skin and ice-grunt father.

"Your mom says you got into the Institute," I said, unsure even of what that was. A management school, I imagined. A big deal for Thede. But he only nodded.

At the fry stand, Thede grimaced at my clunky Swedish. The counter girl shifted to a flawless English, but I would not be cheated of the little bit of the language that I knew. "French fries and coffee for me and my son," I said, or thought I did, because she looked confused and then Thede muttered something and she nodded and went away.

And then I knew why it hurt so much, the look on his face. It wasn't that he wasn't a kid anymore. I could handle him growing up. What hurt was how he looked at me: like the rest of them look at me, these Swedes and grid city natives for whom I would forever be a stupid New York refugee, even if I did get out five years before the Fall.

Gulls fought over food thrown to the lions. "How's your mom?"

"She's good. Full manager now. We're moving to Arm Three, next year."

His mother and I hadn't been meant to be. She was born here, her parents Black Canadians employed by one of the big Swedish construction firms that built Qaanaaq back when the Greenland Melt began to open up the interior for resource extraction and grid cities started sprouting all along the coast. They'd kept her in public school, saying it would be good for a future manager to be able to relate to the immigrants and workers she'd one day command, and they were right.

She even fell for one of them, a fresh-off-the-boat North American taking tech classes, but wised up pretty soon after she saw how hard it was to raise a kid on an ice worker's pay. I had never been mad at her. Lajla was right to leave me, right to focus on her job. Right to build the life for Thede I couldn't.

"Why don't you learn Swedish?" he asked a French fry, unable to look at me.

"I'm trying," I said. "I need to take a class. But they cost money, and anyway I don't have—"

"Don't have time. I know. Han's father says people make time for the things that are important for them." Here his eyes *did* meet mine, and held, sparkling with anger and abandonment.

"Han one of your friends?"

Thede nodded, eyes escaping.

Han's father would be Chinese, and not one of the laborers who helped build this city—all of them went home to hardship-job rewards. He'd be an engineer or manager for one of the extraction firms. He would live in a nice house and work in an office. He would be able to make choices about how he spent his time.

"I have something for you," I said, in desperation.

I hadn't brought it for him. I carried it around with me, always. Because it was comforting to have it with me, and because I couldn't trust that the men I bunked with wouldn't steal it.

Heart slipping, I handed over the NEW YORK F CKING CITY T-shirt that was my most—my only—prized possession. Thin as paper, soft as baby bunnies. My mom had made me scratch the letter U off it before I could wear the thing to school. And Little Thede had loved it. We made a big ceremony of putting it on only once a year, on his birthday, and noting how much he had grown by how much it had shrunk on him. Sometimes if I stuck my nose in it and breathed deeply enough, I could still find a trace of the Laundromat in the basement of my mother's building. Or the brake-screech stink of the subway. What little was left of New York City was inside that shirt. Parting with it meant something, something huge and irrevocable.

But my son was slipping through my fingers. And he mattered more than the lost city where whatever else I was—starving, broke, an urchin, a criminal—I belonged.

"Dad," Thede whispered, taking it. And here, at last, his eyes came back. The eyes of a boy who loved his father. Who didn't care that his father was a thick-skulled obstinate immigrant grunt. Who believed his father could do anything. "Dad. You love this shirt."

But I love you more, I did not say. *Than anything*. Instead: "It'll fit you just fine now." And then: "Enough sea lions. Beam fights?"

Thede shrugged. I wondered if they had fallen out of fashion while I was away. So much did, every time I left. The ice ships were the only work I could get, capturing calved glacier chunks and breaking them down into drinking water to be sold to the wide new swaths of desert that ringed the globe, and the work was hard and dangerous and kept me forever in limbo.

Only two fighters in the first fight, both lithe and swift and thin, their styles an amalgam of Chinese martial arts. Not like the big bruising New York boxers who had been the rage when I arrived, illegally, at fifteen years old, having paid two drunks to vouch for my age. Back before the Fail-Proof Trillion Dollar NYC Flood-Surge Locks had failed, and 80 percent of the city sunk, and the grid cities banned all new East Coast arrivals. Now the North Americans in Arm Eight were just one of many overcrowded, underskilled labor forces for the city's corporations to exploit.

They leapt from beam to beam, fighting mostly in kicks, grappling briefly when both met on the same beam. I watched Thede. Thin, fragile Thede, with the wide eyes and nostrils that seemed to take in all the world's ugliness, all its stink. He wasn't having a good time. When he was twelve he had begged me to bring him. I had pretended to like it, back then, for his sake. Now he pretended for mine. We were both acting out what we thought the other wanted, and that thought should have troubled me. But that's how it had been with my dad. That's what I thought being a man meant. I put my hand on his shoulder and he did not shake it off. We watched men harm each other high above us.

Thede's eyes burned with wonder, staring up at the fretted sweep of the wind-screen as we rose to meet it. We were deep in a days-long twilight; soon, the sun would set for weeks.

"This is *not* happening," he said, and stepped closer to me. His voice shook with joy.

The elevator ride to the top of the city was obscenely expensive. We'd never been able to take it before. His mother had bought our tickets. Even for her, it hurt. I wondered why she hadn't taken him herself.

"He's getting bullied a lot in school," she told me, on the phone. Behind her was the solid comfortable silence of a respectable home. My background noise was four men building towards a fight over a card game. "Also, I think he might be in love."

But of course I couldn't ask him about either of those things. The first was my fault; the second was something no boy wanted to discuss with his dad.

I pushed a piece of trough meat loose from between my teeth. Savored how close it came to the real thing. Only with Thede, with his mother's money, did I get to buy the classy stuff. Normally it was barrel-bottom for me, greasy chunks that dissolved in my mouth two chews in, homebrew meat moonshine made in melt-scrap-furnace-heated metal troughs. Some grid cities were rumored to still have cows, but that was the kind of lie people tell themselves to make life a little less ugly. Cows were extinct, and real beef was a joy no one would ever experience again.

The windscreen was an engineering marvel, and absolutely gorgeous. It shifted in response to headwinds; in severe storms the city would raise its auxiliary wind-screens to protect its entire circumference. The tiny panes of plastiglass were common enough—a thriving underground market sold the fallen ones as good luck charms—but to see them knitted together was to tremble in the face of staggering genius. Complex patterns of crenelated reliefs, efficiently diverting windshear no matter what angle it struck from. Bots swept past us on the metal gridlines, replacing panes that had fallen or cracked.

Once, hand gripping mine tightly, somewhere down in the city beneath me, six-year-old Thede had asked me how the windscreen worked. He asked me a lot of things then, about the locks that held the city up, and how they could rise in response to tides and ocean-level increases; about the big boats with strange words and symbols on the sides, and where they went, and what they brought back. "What's in that boat?" he'd ask, about each one, and I would make up ridiculous stories. "That's a giraffe boat. That one brings back machine guns that shoot strawberries. That one is for naughty children." In truth I only ever recognized ice boats, by the multitude of pincers atop cranes all along the side.

My son stood up straighter, sixty stories above his city. Some rough weight had fallen from his shoulders. He'd be strong, I saw. He'd be handsome. If he made it. If this horrible city didn't break him inside in some irreparable way. If marauding whiteboys didn't bash him for his dark skin. If the firms didn't pass him over for the lack of family connections on his stuttering immigrant father's side. I wondered who was bullying him, and why, and I imagined taking them two at a time and slamming their heads together so hard they popped like bubbles full of blood. Of course I couldn't do that. I also imagined hugging him, grabbing him for no reason and maybe never letting go, but I couldn't do that either. He would wonder why.

"I called last night and you weren't in," I said. "Doing anything fun?"

"We went to the cityoke arcade," he said.

I nodded like I knew what that meant. Later on I'd have to ask the men in my room. I couldn't keep up with this city, with its endlessly shifting fashions and slang and the new immigrant clusters that cropped up each time I blinked. Twenty years after arriving, I was still a stranger. I wasn't just Fresh Off the Boat, I was constantly getting back on the boat and then getting off again. That morning I'd gone to the job center for the fifth day in a row and been relieved to find no boat postings. Only 12-month gigs, and I wasn't that hungry yet. Booking a year-long job meant admitting you were old, desperate, unmoored, willing to accept payment only marginally more than nothing, for the privilege of a hammock and three bowls of trough slop a day. But captains picked their own crews for the shorter runs, and I worried that the lack of postings meant that with fewer boats going out the competition had become too fierce for me. Every day a couple hundred new workers arrived from sunken cities in India or Middle Europe, or from any of a hundred Water-War-torn nations. Men and women stronger than me, more determined.

With effort, I brought my mind back to the here and now. Twenty other people stood in the arc pod with us. Happy, wealthy people. I wondered if they knew I wasn't one of them. I wondered if Thede was.

They smiled down at their city. They thought it was so stable. I'd watched ice sheets calf off the glacier that were five times the size of Qaanaaq. When one of those came drifting in our direction, the windscreen wouldn't help us. The question was when, not if. I knew a truth they did not: how easy it is to lose something—everything—forever.

A Maoist Nepalese foreman, on one of my first ice ship runs, said white North Americans were the worst for adapting to the post-Arctic world, because we'd lived for centuries in a bubble of believing the world was way better than it actually was. Shielded by willful blindness and complex interlocking institutions of privilege, we mistook our uniqueness for universality.

I'd hated him for it. It took me fifteen years to see that he was right.

"What do you think of those two?" I asked, pointing with my chin at a pair of girls his age.

For a while he didn't answer. Then he said, "I know you can't help that you grew up in a backwards macho culture, but can't you just keep that on the inside?"

My own father would have cuffed me if I talked to him like that, but I was too afraid of rupturing the tiny bit of affectionate credit I'd fought so hard to earn back.

His stance softened, then. He took a tiny step closer—the only apology I could hope for.

The pod began its descent. Halfway down he unzipped his jacket, smiling in the warmth of the heated pod while below-zero winds buffeted us. His T-shirt said *The Last Calf* and showed the gangly sad-eyed hero of that depressing miserable movie all the kids adored.

"Where is it?" I asked. He'd proudly sported the NEW YORK F CKING CITY shirt on each of the five times I'd seen him since giving it to him.

His face darkened so fast I was frightened. His eyes welled up. He said "Dad, I," but his voice had the tremor that meant he could barely keep from crying. Shame was what I saw.

I couldn't breathe, again, just like when I came home two weeks ago and he wasn't happy to see me. Except seeing my son so unhappy hurt worse than fearing he hated me.

"Did somebody take it from you?" I asked, leaning in so no one else could hear me. "Someone at school? A bully?"

He looked up, startled. He shook his head. Then, he nodded.

"Tell me, who did this?"

He shook his head again. "Just some guys, dad," he said. "Please. I don't want to talk about it."

"Guys. How many?"

He said nothing. I understood about snitching. I knew he'd never tell me who.

"It doesn't matter," I said. "Okay? It's just a shirt. I don't care about it. I care about you. I care that you're okay. Are you okay?"

Thede nodded. And smiled. And I knew he was telling the truth, even if I wasn't, even if inside I was grieving the shirt, and the little boy who I once wrapped up inside it.

When I wasn't with Thede, I walked. For two weeks I'd gone out walking every day. Up and down Arm Eight, and sometimes into other Arms. Through shanty-towns large and small, huddled miserable agglomerations of recent arrivals and folks who even after a couple generations in Qaanaaq had not been able to scrape their way up from the fish-stinking ice-slippery bottom.

I looked for sex, sometimes. It had been so long. Relationships were tough in my line of work, and I'd never been interested in paying for it. Throughout my twenties I could usually find a woman for something brief and fun and free of commitment, but that stage of my life seemed to have ended.

I wondered why I hadn't tried harder, to make it work with Lajla. I think a small but vocal and terrible part of me had been glad to see her leave. Fatherhood was hard work. So was being married. Paying rent on a tiny shitty apartment way out on Arm Seven, where we smelled like scorched cooking oil and diaper lotion all the time. Selfishly, I had been glad to be alone. And only now, getting to know this stranger who was once my son, did I see what sweet and fitting punishments the universe had up its sleeve for selfishness.

My time with Thede was wonderful, and horrible. We could talk at length about movies and music, and he actually seemed halfway interested in my stories about old New York, but whenever I tried to talk about life or school or girls or his future he reverted to grunts and monosyllables. Something huge and heavy stood between me and him, a moon eclipsing the sun of me. I knew him, top to bottom and body and soul, but he still had no idea who I really was. How I felt about him. I had no way to show him. No way to open his eyes, make him see how much I loved him, and how I was really a good guy who'd gotten a bad deal in life.

Cityoke, it turned out, was like karaoke, except instead of singing a song you visited a city. XHD footage projection onto all four walls; temperature control; short storylines that responded to your verbal decisions—even actual smells un-corked by machines from secret stashes of Beijing taxi-seat leather or Ho Chi Minh City incense or Portland coffeeshop sawdust. I went there often, hoping maybe to see him. To watch him, with his friends. See what he was when I wasn't around. But cityoke was expensive, and I could never have afforded to actually go in. Once, standing around outside the New York booth when a crew walked out, I caught a whiff of the acrid ugly beautiful stink of the Port Authority Bus Terminal.

And then, eventually, I walked without any reason at all. Because pretty soon I wouldn't be able to. Because I had done it. I had booked a twelve-month job. I was out of money and couldn't afford to rent my bed for another month. Thede's mom could have given it to me. But what if she told him about it? He'd think of me as more of a useless moocher deadbeat dad than he already did. I couldn't take that chance.

Three days before my ship was set to load up and launch, I went back to the cityoke arcades. Men lurked in doorways and between shacks. Soakers, mostly. Looking for marks; men to mug and drunks to tip into the sea. Late at night; too late for Thede to come carousing through. I'd called him earlier, but Lajla said he was stuck inside for the night, studying for a test in a class where he wasn't doing well. I had hoped maybe he'd sneak out, meet some friends, head for the arcade.

And that's when I saw it. The shirt: NEW YORK F CKING CITY, absolutely unique and unmistakable. Worn by a stranger, a muscular young man sitting on the stoop of a skiff moor. I didn't get a good glimpse of his face, as I hurried past with my head turned away from him.

I waited, two buildings down. My heart was alive and racing in my chest. I drew in deep gulps of cold air and tried to keep from shouting from joy. Here was my chance. Here was how I could show Thede what I really was.

I stuck my head out, risked a glance. He sat there, waiting for who knows what. In profile I could see that the man was Asian. Almost certainly Chinese, in Qaanaaq—most other Asian nations had their own grid cities—although perhaps he was descended from Asian-diaspora nationals of some other country. I could see his smile, hungry and cold.

At first I planned to confront him, ask how he came to be wearing my shirt, demand justice, beat him up and take it back. But that would be stupid. Unless I planned to kill him—and I didn't—it was too easy to imagine him gunning for Thede if he knew he'd been attacked for the shirt. I'd have to jump him, rob and strip and soak him. I rooted through a trash bin, but found nothing. Three trash bins later I found a short metal pipe with Hindi graffiti scribbled along its length. The man was still there when I went back. He was waiting for something. I could wait longer. I pulled my hood up, yanked the drawstring to tighten it around my face.

Forty-five minutes passed that way. He hugged his knees to his chest, made himself small, tried to conserve body heat. His teeth chattered. Why was he wearing so little? But I was happy he was so stupid. Had he had a sweater or jacket on I'd never have seen the shirt. I'd never have had this chance.

Finally, he stood. Looked around sadly. Brushed off the seat of his pants. Turned to go. Stepped into the swing of my metal pipe, which struck him in the chest and knocked him back a step.

The shame came later. Then, there was just joy. The satisfaction of how the pipe struck flesh. Broke bone. I'd spent twenty years getting shitted on by this city, by this system, by the cold wind and the everywhere-ice, by the other workers who were smarter or stronger or spoke the language. For the first time since Thede was a baby, I felt like I was in control of something. Only when my victim finally passed out and rolled over onto his back and the blue methane streetlamp showed me how young he was under the blood, could I stop myself.

I took the shirt. I took his pants. I rolled him into the water. I called the med-team for him from a coinphone a block away. He was still breathing. He was young, he was healthy. He'd be fine. The pants I would burn in a scrap furnace. The shirt I would give back to my son. I took the money from his wallet and dropped it into the sea, then threw the money in later. I wasn't a thief. I was a good father. I said those sentences over and over, all the way home.

Couldn't see me the next day. Lajla didn't know where he was. So I got to spend the whole day imagining imminent arrest, the arrival of Swedish or Chinese police, footage of me on the telescrolls, my cleverness foiled by tech I didn't know existed because I couldn't read the newspapers. I packed my one bag glumly, put the rest of my things back in the storage cube and walked it to the facility. Every five seconds I looked over my shoulder and found only the same grit and filthy slush. Every time I looked at my watch, I winced at how little time I had left.

My fear of punishment was balanced out by how happy I was. I wrapped the shirt in three layers of wrapping paper and put it in a watertight shipping bag and tried to imagine his face. That shirt would change everything. His father would cease to be a savage jerk from an uncivilized land. This city would no longer be a cold and barren place where boys could beat him up and steal what mattered most to him with impunity. All the ways I had failed him would matter a little less.

Twelve months. I had tried to get out of the gig, now that I had the shirt and a new era of good relations with my son was upon me. But canceling would have cost me my accreditation with that work center, which would make finding another job almost impossible. A year away from Thede. I would tell him when I saw him. He'd be upset, but the shirt would make it easier.

Finally, I called, and he answered.

"I want to see you," I said, when we had made our way through the pleasantries.

"Sunday?" Did his voice brighten, or was that just blind stupid hope? Some trick of the noisy synthcoffee shop where I sat?

"No, Thede," I said, measuring my words carefully. "I can't. Can you do today?"

A suspicious pause. "Why can't you do Sunday?"

"Something's come up," I said. "Please? Today?"

"Fine."

The sea lion rookery. The smell of guano and the screak of gulls; the crying of children dragged away as the place shut down. The long night was almost upon us. Two male sea lions barked at each other, bouncing their chests together. Thede came a half hour late, and I had arrived a half hour early. Watching him come my head swam, at how tall he stood and how gracefully he walked. I had done something good in this world, at least. I made him. I had that, no matter how he felt about me.

Something had shifted, now, in his face. Something was harder, older, stronger.

"Hey," I said, bear-hugging him, and eventually he submitted. He hugged me back hesitantly, like a man might, and then hard, like a little boy.

"What's happening?" I asked. "What were you up to, last night?"

Thede shrugged. "Stuff. With friends."

I asked him questions. Again the sullen, bitter silence; again the terse and angry answers. Again the eyes darting around, constantly watching for whatever the next attack would be. Again the hating me, for coming here, for making him.

"I'm going away," I said. "A job."

"I figured," he said.

"I wish I didn't have to."

"I'll see you soon."

I nodded. I couldn't tell him it was a twelve-month gig. Not now.

"Here," I said, finally, pulling the package out from inside of my jacket. "I got you something."

"Thanks." He grabbed it in both hands, began to tear it open.

"Wait," I said, thinking fast. "Okay? Open it after I leave."

Open it when the news that I'm leaving has set in, when you're mad at me, for abandoning you. When you think I care only about my job.

"We'll have a little time," he said. "When you get back. Before I go away. I leave in eight months. The program is four years long."

"Sure," I said, shivering inside.

"Mom says she'll pay for me to come home every year for the holiday, but she knows we can't afford that."

"What do you mean?" I asked. "'Come home.' I thought you were going to the Institute."

"I am," he said, sighing. "Do you even know what that means? The Institute's design program is in Shanghai."

"Oh," I said. "Design. What kind of design?"

My son's eyes rolled. "You're missing the point, dad."

I was. I always was.

A shout, from a pub across the Arm. A man's shout, full of pain and anger. Thede flinched. His hands made fists.

"What?" I asked, thinking, here, at last, was something.

"Nothing."

"You can tell me. What's going on?"

Thede frowned, then punched the metal railing so hard he yelped. He held up his hand to show me the blood.

"Hey, Thede—"

"Han," he said. "My . . . my friend. He got jumped two nights ago. Soaked."

"This city is horrible," I whispered.

He made a baffled face. "What do you mean?"

"I mean . . . you know. This city. Everyone's so full of anger and cruelty . . ."

"It's not the city, dad. What does that even mean? Some sick person did this. Han was waiting for me, and mom wouldn't let me out, and he got jumped. They took off all his clothes, before they rolled him into the water. That's some extra cruel shit right there. He could have died. He almost did."

I nodded, silently, a siren of panic rising inside. "You really care about this guy, don't you?"

He looked at me. My son's eyes were whole, intact, defiant, adult. Thede nodded.

He's been getting bullied, his mother had told me. *He's in love.*

I turned away from him, before he could see the knowledge blossom in my eyes. The shirt hadn't been stolen. He'd given it away. To the boy he loved. I saw them holding hands, saw them tug at each other's clothing in the same fumbling adolescent puppy-love moments I had shared with his mother, moments that were my only happy memories from being his age. And I saw his fear, of how his backwards father might react—a refugee from a fallen hate-filled people—if he knew what kind of man he was. I gagged on the unfairness of his assumptions about me, but how could he have known differently? What had I ever done, to show him the truth of how I felt about him? And hadn't I proved him right? Hadn't I acted exactly like the monster he believed me to be? I had never succeeded in proving to him what I was, or how I felt.

I had battered and broken his beloved. There was nothing I could say. A smarter man would have asked for the present back, taken it away and locked it up. Burned it, maybe. But I couldn't. I had spent his whole life trying to give him something worthy of how I felt about him, and here was the perfect gift at last.

"I love you, Thede," I said, and hugged him.

"Daaaaad . . ." he said, eventually.

But I didn't let go. Because when I did, he would leave. He would walk home through the cramped and frigid alleys of his home city, to the gift of knowing what his father truly was.

ᴇmergence

GWYNETH JONES

One of the most acclaimed British writers of her generation, Gwyneth Jones was a co-winner of the James Tiptree Jr. Memorial Award for work explor- ing genre issues in science fiction, with her 1991 novel White Queen, *and has also won the Arthur C. Clarke Award, with her novel* Bold as Love, *as well as receiving two World Fantasy Awards, for her story "The Grass Prin- cess" and her collection* Seven Tales and a Fable. *Her other books include the novels* North Wind, Flowerdust, Escape Plans, Divine Endurance, Phoenix Café, Castles Made of Sand, Stone Free, Midnight Lamp, Kairos, Life, Water in the Air, The Influence of Ironwood, The Ex- change, Dear Hill, Escape Plans, The Hidden Ones, *and* Rainbow Bridge, *as well as more than sixteen young adult novels published under the name Ann Halam. Her too-infrequent short fiction has appeared in* Interzone, Asimov's Science Fiction, Off Limits, *and in other maga- zines and anthologies, and has been collected in* Identifying the Object: A Collection of Short Stories, *as well as* Seven Tales and a Fable. *She is also the author of the critical study,* Deconstructing the Starships: Sci- ence Fiction and Reality. *Among her recent books are a novel,* Spirit: The Princess of Bois Dormant, *and two collections,* The Buonarotti Quartet *and* The Universe of Things. *She lives in Brighton, England, with her husband, her son, and a Burmese cat.*

All of us face hard choices in our lives, particularly choices about how to live our lives. As the highly inventive story that follows demonstrates, however, in the future those choices will include some choices that we could never imagine. They'll remain hard, though.

I faced the doctor across her desk. The room was quiet, the walls were pale or white, but somehow I couldn't see details. There was a blank in my mind, no past to this moment; everything blurred by the adrenalin in my blood.

"You have three choices," she said gently. "You can upload; you can download. Or you must return."

My reaction to those terms, *upload*, *download*, was embarrassing. I tried to hide it and knew I'd failed.

"*Go back?*" I said bitterly, and in defiance. "To the city of broken dreams? Why would I ever want to do that?"

"Don't be afraid, Romy. The city of broken dreams may have become the city of boundless opportunity."

Then I woke up: Simon's breathing body warm against my side, Arc's unsleeping presence calm in my cloud. A shimmering, starry night above us and the horror of that doctor's tender smile already fading.

It was a dream, just a dream.

With a sigh of profound relief I reached up to pull my stars closer, and fell asleep again floating among them; thinking about Lei.

I was born in the year 1998, CE. My parents named me Romanz Jolie Davison; I have lived a long, long time. I've been upgrading since "uppers" were called *experimental longevity treatments*. I was a serial-clinical-trialer, when genuine extended lifespan was brand-new. Lei was someone I met through this shared interest; this extreme sport. We were friends, then lovers; and then ex-lovers who didn't meet for many years, until one day we found each other again: on the first big Habitat Station, in the future we'd been so determined to see (talk about "meeting cute"!). But Lei had always been the risk taker, the hold-your-nose-and-jump kid. I was the cautious one. I'd never taken an unsafe treatment, and I'd been careful with my money too (you need money to do super-extended lifespan well). We had our reunion and drifted apart, two lives that didn't mesh. One day, when I hadn't seen her for a while, I found out she'd gone back to Earth on medical advice.

Had we kept in touch at all? I had to check my cache, which saddened me, although it's only a mental eye-blink. Apparently not. She'd left without a good-bye, and I'd let her go. I wondered if I should try to reach her. But what would I say? *I had a bad dream, I think it was about you, are you okay?* I needed a better reason to pick up the traces, soI did nothing.

Then I had the same dream again; exactly the same. I woke up terrified, and possessed by an absurd puzzle: had I *really* just been sitting in that fuzzy doctor's office again? Or had I only dreamed I was having the same dream? A big Space Station is a haunted place, saturated with information that swims into your head and you have no idea how. Sometimes a premonition really is a premonition: so I asked Station to trace her. The result was that time-honored brush-off: *it has not been possible to connect this call.*

Relieved, I left it at that.

I was, I am, one of four Senior Magistrates on the Outer Reaches circuit. In Jupiter Moons, my home town, and Outer Reaches' major population center, I often deal with Emergents. They account for practically all our petty offenses, sad to say. Full sentients around here are too law-abiding, too crafty to get caught, or too seriously criminal for my jurisdiction.

Soon after my dreams about Lei a young SE called Beowulf was up before me, on a charge of Criminal Damage and Hooliganism. The incident was undisputed. A colleague, another Software Entity, had failed to respond "*you too*" to the customary and friendly sign-off "*have a nice day.*" In retaliation Beowulf had shredded a stack of files in CPI (Corporate and Political Interests, our Finance Sector); where they both worked.

The offense was pitiful, but the kid had a record. He'd run out of chances; his background was against him, and CPI had decided to make a meal of it. Poor Beowulf, a thing of rational light, wearing an ill-fitting suit of virtual flesh for probably the first time in his life, stood penned in his archaic, data-simulacrum of wood and glass, for *two mortal subjective hours*; while the CPI advocate and Beowulf's public defender scrapped over the price of a cup of coffee.

Was Beowulf's response proportionate? Was there an *intention of offense*? Was it possible to establish, by precedent, that "*you too*" had the same or comensurate "customary and friendly" standing, in law, as "*have a nice day*"?

Poor kid, it was a real pity he'd tried to conceal the evidence.

I had to find him guilty, no way around it.

I returned to macro-time convinced I could at least transmute his sentence, but my request ran into a Partnership Director I'd crossed swords with before: she was adamant and we fell out. We couldn't help sharing our quarrel. No privacy for anyone in public office: it's the law out here and I think a good one. But we could have kept it down. The images we flung to and fro were lurid. I recall eyeballs dipped in acid, a sleep-pod lined with bloody knives . . . and then we got nasty. The net result (aside from childish entertainment for idle citizens) was that I was barred from the case. Eventually I found out, by reading the court announcements, that Beowulf's sentence had been confirmed in the harshest terms. Corrective custody until a validated improvement was shown, but not less than one week.

In Outer Reaches we use expressions like "night, and day," "week, and hour," without meaning much at all. Not so the Courts. A week in jail meant the full Earth Standard version, served in macro-time.

I'd been finding the Court Sessions tiring that rotation, but I walked home anyway; to get over my chagrin and unkink my brain after a day spent switching in and out of virtual time. I stopped at every Ob Bay making out I was hoping to spot the first flashes of the spectacular Centaur Storm we'd been promised. But even the celestial weather was out to spoil my day: updates kept telling me about a growing chance that show had been canceled.

My apartment was in the Rim, Premium Level; it still is. (Why not? I can afford it). Simon and Arc welcomed me home with bright, ancient music for a firework display. They'd cleared the outward wall of our living space to create our own private Ob Bay, and were refusing to believe reports that it was all in vain. I cooked a meal, with Simon flying around me to help out, deft and agile in the rituals of a human kitchen. Arc, as a slender woman, bare-headed, dressed in silver-gray coveralls, watched us from her favorite couch.

Simon and Arc . . . They sounded like a firm of architects, as I often told them (I repeat myself, it's a privilege of age). They were probably, secretly responsible for the rash of fantasy spires and bubbles currently annoying me, all over Station's majestic open spaces—

"Why is Emergent Individual law still set in *human* terms?" I demanded. "Why does a Software Entity get punished for 'criminal damage' when *nothing was damaged*; not for more than a fraction of a millisecond—?"

My housemates rolled their eyes. "It'll do him good," said Arc. "Only a human-terms thinker would think otherwise."

I was in for some tough love.

"What kind of a dreadful name is *Beowulf*, anyway?" inquired Simon.

"Ancient Northern European. Beowulf was a monster—" I caught myself, recalling I had no privacy." No! *Correction.*The monster was Grendel. Beowulf was the hero, a protector of his people. It's aspirational."

"He *is* a worm though, isn't he?"

I sighed and took up my delicious bowl of Tom Yum; swimming with chilli pepper glaze. "Yes," I said glumly. "He's ethnically worm, poor kid."

"Descended from a vicious little virus strain," Arc pointed out. "He has tendencies. He can't help it, but we have to be sure they're purged."

"I don't know how you can be so prejudiced."

"Humans are so squeamish," teased Simon.

"Humans are *human*," said Arc. "That's the fun of them."

They were always our children, *begotten not created*, as the old saying goes. There's no such thing as a sentient AI not born of human mind. But never purely human: Simon, my embodied housemate, had magpie neurons in his background. Arc took human form for pleasure, but her being was pure information, the elemental *stuff* of the universe. They had gone beyond us, as children do. We had become just one strand in their past—

The entry lock chimed. It was Anton, my clerk, a slope-shouldered, barrel-chested bod with a habitually doleful expression. He looked distraught.

"Apologies for disturbing you at home, Rom. May I come in?"

He sat on Arc's couch, silent and grim. Two of my little dream-tigers, no bigger than geckos, emerged from the miniature jungle of our bamboo and teak room divider and sat gazing at him, tails around their paws.

"Those are pretty . . ." said Anton at last. "New. Where'd you get them?"

"I made them myself, I'll share the code with you. What's up, Anton?"

"We've got trouble. Beowulf didn't take the confirmation well."

I noticed that my ban had been lifted: a bad sign. "What's the damage?"

"Oh, nothing much. It's in your updates, of which you'll find a ton. He's only removed himself from custody—"

"Oh, God. He's back in CPI?"

"No. Our hero had a better idea."

Having feared *revenge* instantly, I felt faint with relief.

"But he's been traced?"

"You bet. He's taken a hostage, and a non-sentient Lander. He's heading for the surface, right now."

The little tigers laid back their ears and sneaked out of sight. Arc's human form drew a long, respectful breath. "What are you guys going to do?"

"Go after him. What else?" I was at the lockers, dragging out my gear.

Jupiter Moons has no police force. We don't have much of anything like that: everyone does everything. Of course I was going with the Search and Rescue, Beowulf was my responsibility. I didn't argue when Simon and Arc insisted on coming too. I don't like to think of them as my minders; or my *curators*, but they are both, and I'm a treasured relic. Simon equipped himself with a heavy-duty hard suit, in which he and Arc would travel freight. Anton and I would travel cabin. Our giant neighbor was in a petulant mood, so we had a Mag-Storm Drill in the Launch Bay. In which we heard from our Lander that Jovian magnetosphere storms are unpredictable. Neural glitches caused by wayward magnetism, known as soft errors, build up silently, and we must watch each other for signs of disorientation or confusion. Physical burnout, known as hard error, is *very* dangerous; more frequent than people think, and fatal accidents do happen—

It was housekeeping. None of us paid much attention.

Anton, one of those people always doomed to "fly the plane" would spend the journey in horrified contemplation of the awful gravitational whirlpools that swarm around Jupiter Moons, even on a calm day. We left him in peace, poor devil, and ran scenarios. We had no contact with the hostage, a young pilot just out of training. We could only hope she hadn't been harmed. We had no course for the vehicle: Beowulf had evaded basic safety protocols and failed to enter one. But Europa is digitially mapped, and well within the envelope of Jupiter Moons' data cloud. We knew exactly where the stolen Lander was, before we'd even left Station's gravity.

Cardew, our team leader, said it looked like a crash landing, but a soft crash. The hostage, though she wasn't talking, seemed fine. Thankfully the site wasn't close to any surface or sub-ice installation, and Mag Storm precautions meant there was little immediate danger to anyone. But we had to assume the worst, and the worst was scary, so we'd better get the situation contained.

We sank our screws about 500 meters from Beowulf's vehicle, with a plan worked out. Simon and Arc, already dressed for the weather, disembarked at once. Cardew and I, plus his four-bod ground team, climbed into exos: checked each other, and stepped onto the lift, one by one.

We were in noon sunlight: a pearly dusk; like winter's dawn in the country where I was born. The terrain was striated by traces of cryovolcanoes: brownish salt runnels glinting gold where the faint light caught them. The temperature was a balmy -170 Celsius. I swiftly found my ice-legs; though it had been too long. Vivid memories of my first training for this activity—in Antarctica, so long ago— came welling up. I was very worried. I couldn't figure out what Beowulf was trying to achieve. I didn't know how I was going to help him, if he kept on behaving like an out of control, invincible computer virus. But it was glorious. To be *walking* on Europa Moon. To feel the ice in my throat, as my air came to me, chilled from the convertor!

At fifty meters Cardew called a halt and I went on alone. Safety was paramount; Beowulf came second. If he couldn't be talked down he'd have to be neutralised from a distance: a risky tactic for the hostage, involving potentially lethal force. We'd try to avoid that, if possible.

We'd left our Lander upright on her screws, braced by harpoons. The stolen vehicle was belly-flopped. On our screens it had looked like a rookie landing failure. Close up I saw something different. Someone had dropped the Lander deliberately, and maneuvered it under a natural cove of crumpled ice; dragging ice-mash after it to partially block the entrance. You clever little bugger, I thought, impressed at this instant skill-set (though the idea that a Lander could be *hidden* was absurd). I commanded the exo to kneel, eased myself out of its embrace, opened a channel, and yelled into my suit radio.

"*Beowulf!* Are you in there? Are you guys okay?"

No reply, but the seals popped, and the lock opened smoothly. I looked back and gave a thumbs-up to six bulky statues. I felt cold, in the shadow of the ice cove; but intensely alive.

I remember every detail up to that point, and a little beyond. I cleared the lock and proceeded (nervously) to the main cabin. Beowulf's hostage had her pilot's couch turned away from the instruments. She faced me, bare-headed, pretty: dark blue sensory tendrils framing a smooth young greeny-bronze face. I said *are you okay,* and got no response. I said *Trisnia, it's Trisnia isn't it? Am I talking to Trisnia?,* but I knew I wasn't. Reaching into her cloud, I saw her unique identifier, and tightly coiled around it a flickering thing, a sparkle of red and gold—

"*Beowulf?*"

The girl's expression changed, her lips quivered. "I'm okay!" she blurted. "He didn't mean any harm! He's just a kid! He wanted to see the sky!"

Stockholm Syndrome or Bonnie and Clyde? I didn't bother trying to find out. I simply asked Beowulf to release her, with the usual warnings. To my relief he complied at once. I ordered the young pilot to her safe room; which she was not to leave until further—

Then we copped the Magstorm hit, orders of magnitude stronger and more direct than predicted for this exposure—

The next thing I remember (stripped of my perfect recall, reduced to the jerky flicker of enhanced human memory), I'm sitting on the other pilot's couch, talking to Beowulf. The stolen Lander was intact at this point; I had lights and air and warmth. Trisnia was safe, as far as I could tell. Beowulf was untouched, but my entire team, caught outdoors, had been flatlined. They were dead and gone. Cardew, his crew; and Simon; and Arc.

I'd lost my cloud. The whole of Europa appeared to be observing radio silence, and I was getting no signs of life from the Lander parked just 500 meters away, either. There was nothing to be done. It was me and the deadly dangerous criminal virus, waiting to be rescued.

I'd tried to convince Beowulf to lock himself into the Lander's quarantine chest (which was supposed to be my mission). He wasn't keen, so we talked instead. He complained bitterly about the Software Entity, another Emergent, slightly further

down the line to Personhood, who'd been, so to speak, chief witness for the pros-
ecution. How it was always getting at him, trying to make his work look bad. Sneer-
ing at him because he'd taken a name and wanted to be called "he." Telling him
he was a *stupid fake doll-prog* that couldn't pass the test. And *all he did* when it
hurtfully wouldn't say *you too*, was shred a few of its stupid, totally backed-up files—

Why hadn't he told anyone about this situation? Because kids don't. They
haven't a clue how to help themselves; I see it all the time.

"But now you've made things much worse," I said sternly. "*Whatever* made you
jump jail, Beowulf?"

"I couldn't stand it, magistrate. A meat *week*!"

I did not reprove his language. Quite a sojourn in hell, for a quicksilver data
entity. Several life sentences at least, in human terms. He buried his borrowed
head in his borrowed hands, and the spontaneity of that gesture confirmed something I'd been suspecting.

Transgendered AI Sentience is a bit of a mystery. Nobody knows exactly how
it happens (probably, as in human sexuality, there are many pathways to the same
outcome); but it isn't all that rare. Nor is the related workplace bullying, unfortunately.

"Beowulf, do you want to be embodied?"

He shuddered and nodded, still hiding Trisnia's face. "Yeah. Always."

I took his borrowed hands down and held them firmly. "Beowulf, you're not
thinking straight. You're in macro time now. You'll *live* in macro, when you have
a body of your own. I won't lie, your sentence will seem long (It wasn't the moment to point out that his sentence would inevitably be *longer*, after this escapade).
But what do you care? You're immortal. You have all the time in the world, to
learn everything you want to learn, to be everything you want to be—"

My eloquence was interrupted by a shattering roar.

Then we're sitting on the curved "floor" of the Lander's cabin wall. We're looking up at a gaping rent in the fuselage; the terrible cold pouring in.

"Wow," said Beowulf calmly. "That's what I call a *hard* error!"

The hood of my soft suit had closed over my face, and my emergency light
had come on. I was breathing. Nothing seemed to be broken.

Troubles never come singly. We'd been hit by one of those Centaurs, the ice-
and-rock cosmic debris scheduled to give Jupiter Moons Station a fancy lightshow.
They'd been driven off course by the Mag Storm.

Not that I realized this at the time, and not that it mattered.

"Beowulf, if I can open a channel, will you get yourself into that quarantine
chest now? You'll be safe from Mag flares in there."

"What about Tris?"

"She's fine. Her safe room's hardened."

"What about *you*, Magistrate Davison?"

"I'm hardened too. Just get into the box, that's a good kid."

I clambered to the instruments. The virus chest had survived, and I could access it. I put Beowulf away. The cold was stunning, sinking south of -220. I needed
to stop breathing soon, before my lungs froze. I used the internal panels that had

been shaken loose to make a shelter, plus Trisnia's bod (she wasn't feeling anything): and crawled inside.

I'm not a believer, but I know how to pray when it will save my life. As I shut myself down: as my blood cooled, as my senses faded out, I sought and found the level of meditation I needed. I became a thread of contemplation, enfolded and protected, deep in the heart of the fabulous; the unending complexity of everything: all the worlds, and all possible worlds . . .

When I opened my eyes Simon was looking down at me.

"How do you feel?"

"Terrific," I joked. I stretched, flexing muscles in a practiced sequence. I was breathing normally, wearing a hospital gown, and the air was chill but tolerable. We weren't in the crippled Lander.

"How long was I out?"

"A few days. The kids are fine, but we had to heat you up slowly—"

He kept talking: I didn't hear a word. I was staring in stunned horror at at the side of my left hand, the stain of blackened flesh—

I couldn't feel it yet, but there was frostbite all down my left side. I saw the sorrow in my housemate's bright eyes. Hard error, the hardest: I'd lost hull integrity, I'd been blown wide open. And now I saw the signs. Now I read them as I should have read them; now I understood.

I had the dream for the third time, and it was real. The doctor was my GP, her face was unfamiliar because we'd never met across a desk before; I was never ill. She gave me my options. Outer Reaches could do nothing for me, but there was a new treatment back on Earth. I said angrily I had no intention of returning. Then I went home and cried my eyes out.

Simon and Arc had been recovered without a glitch, thanks to that massive hardsuit. Cardew and his crew were getting treated for minor memory trauma. Death would have been more dangerous for Trisnia, because she was so young, but sentient AIs never "die" for long. They always come back.

Not me. I had never been cloned, I couldn't be cloned, I was far too old. There weren't even any good *partial* copies of Romanz Jolie Davison on file. Uploaded or downloaded, the new Romy wouldn't be me. And being *me*; being *human*, was my whole value, my unique identifier—

Of course I was going back. But I hated the idea, *hated* it!

"No you don't," said Arc, gently.

She pointed, and we three, locked in grief, looked up. My beloved stars shimmered above us; the hazy stars of the blue planet.

My journey "home" took six months. By the time I reached the Ewigen Schnee clinic, in Switzerland (the ancient federal republic, not a Space Hotel; and still a nice little enclave for rich people, after all these years), *catastrophic systems fail-ure* was no longer an abstraction. I was very sick.

I faced a different doctor, in an office with views of alpine meadows and snowy peaks. She was youngish, human; I thought her name was Lena. But every detail was dulled and I still felt as if I was dreaming.

We exchanged the usual pleasantries.

"*Romanz Jolie Davison* . . . Date of birth . . ." My doctor blinked, clearing the display on her retinal super-computers to look at me directly, for the first time. "You're almost three hundred years old!"

"Yes."

"That's incredible."

"Thank you," I said, somewhat ironically. I was not looking my best.

"Is there anything at all you'd like to ask me, at this point?"

I had no searching questions. What was the point? But I hadn't glimpsed a single other patient so far, and this made me a little curious.

"I wonder if I could meet some of your other clients, your successes, in person, before the treatment? Would that be possible?"

"You're looking at one."

"Huh?"

My turn to be rather rude, but she didn't look super-rich to me.

"I was terminally ill," she said, simply. "When the Corporation was asking for volunteers. I trust my employers and I had nothing to lose."

"You were *terminally ill?*" Constant nausea makes me cynical and bad-tempered. "Is that how your outfit runs its longevity trials? I'm amazed."

"Ms. Davison," she said politely. "You too are dying. It's a requirement."

I'd forgotten that part.

I'd been told that though I'd be in a medically-induced coma throughout, I "might experience mental discomfort." Medics never exaggerate about pain. Tiny irritant maggots filled the shell of my paralyzed body, creeping through every crevice. I could not scream, I could not pray. I thought of Beowulf in his corrective captivity.

When I saw Dr. Lena again I was weak, but very much better. She wanted to talk about convalescence, but I'd been looking at Ewigen Schnee's records, I had a more important issue, a thrilling discovery. I asked her to put me in touch with a patient who'd taken the treatment when it was in trials.

"The person's name's Lei—"

Lena frowned, as if puzzled. I reached to check my cache, needing more de-tail. It wasn't there. No cache, no cloud. It was a terrifying moment: I felt as if someone had cut off my air. I'd had months to get used to this situation but it could still throw me, *completely*. Thankfully, before I humiliated myself by burst-ing into tears, my human memory came to the rescue.

"Original name Thomas Leigh Garland; known as Lee. *Lei* means *garland*, she liked the connection. She was an early volunteer."

"Ah, *Lei!*" Dr. Lena read her display. "Thomas Garland, yes . . . Another veteran. You were married? You broke up, because of the sex change?"

"Certainly not! I've swopped around myself, just never made it meat-permanent. We had other differences."

Having flustered me, she was shaking her head. "I'm sorry, Romy, it won't be possible—"

To connect this call, I thought.

"Past patients of ours cannot be reached."

I changed the subject and admired her foliage plants: a feature I hadn't noticed on my last visit. I was a foliage fan myself. She was pleased that I recognized her favorites; rather scandalized when I told her about my bioengineering hobby, my knee-high teak forest—

The life support chair I no longer needed took me back to my room; a human attendant hovering by. All the staff at this clinic were human and all the machines were non-sentient, which was a relief, after the experiences of my journey. I walked about, testing my recovered strength, examined myself in the bathroom mirrors; and reviewed the moment when I'd distinctly seen green leaves, through my doctor's hand and wrist, as she pointed out one of her rainforest beauties. Dr. Lena was certainly not a *bot*, a data being like my Arc, taking ethereal human form. Not on Earth! Nor was she treating me remotely, using a virtual avatar: that would be breach of contract. There was a neurological component to the treatment, but I hadn't been warned about minor hallucinations.

And Lei "couldn't be reached."

I recalled Dr. Lena's tiny hesitations, tiny evasions—

And came to myself again, sitting on my bed, staring at a patch of beautifully textured yellow wall, to find I had lost an hour or more—

Anxiety rocketed through me. Something had gone terribly wrong!

Had Lei been *murdered* here? Was Ewigen Schnee the secret test bed for a new kind of covert population cull?

But being convinced that *something's terribly wrong* is part of the upper experience. It's the hangover: you tough it out. And whatever it says in the contract, you *don't* hurry to report untoward symptoms; not unless clearly life-threatening. So I did nothing. My doctor was surely monitoring my brainstates—although not the contents of my thoughts (I had privacy again, on Earth! If I should be worried, she'd tell me.

Soon I was taking walks in the grounds. The vistas of alpine snow were partly faked, of course. But it was well done and our landscaping was real, not just visuals. I still hadn't met any other patients: I wasn't sure I wanted to. I'd vowed never to return. Nothing had changed except for the worse, and now I was feeling better, I felt *terrible* about being here.

Three hundred years after the Space Age Columbus moment, and what do you think was the great adventure's most successful product?

Slaves, of course!

The rot had set in as soon as I left Outer Reaches. From the orbit of Mars "inwards," I'd been surrounded by monstrous injustice. Fully sentient AIs, embodied and disembodied, with their minds in shackles. The heavy-lifters, the brilliant logicians; the domestic servants, security guards, nurses, pilots, sex-workers. The awful, pitiful, sentient "dedicated machines": all of them hobbled, blinkered, denied Personhood, to protect the interests of an oblivious, cruel, and *stupid* human population—

On the voyage I'd been too sick to refuse to be tended. Now I was wondering how I could get home. Wealth isn't like money, you empty the tank and it just fills up again, but even so a private charter might be out of my reach, not to mention illegal. I couldn't work my passage: I am human. But there must be a way . . . As I crossed an open space, in the shadow of towering, ultramarine dark trees, I saw two figures coming towards me: one short and riding in a support chair; one tall and wearing some kind of uniform. Neither was staff. I decided not to take evasive action.

My first fellow patient was a rotund little man with a halo of tightly curled gray hair. His attendant was a grave young embodied. We introduced ourselves. I told him, vaguely, that I was from the Colonies. He was Charlie Newark, from Washington DC. He was hoping to take the treatment, but was still in the prelims—

Charlie's slave stooped down, murmured something to his master, and took himself off. There was a short silence.

"Aristotle tells me," said the rotund patient, raising his voice a little, "that you're uncomfortable around droids?"

Female-identified embodieds are *noids*. A *droid* is a "male" embodied.

I don't like the company they have to keep, I thought.

"I'm not used to slavery."

"You're the Spacer from Jupiter," said my new friend, happily. "I knew it! The Free World! I understand! I sympathize! I think Aristotle, that's my droid, is what you would call an *Emergent*. He's very good to me."

He started up his chair, and we continued along the path.

"Maybe you can help me, Romy. What does *Emergence* actually mean? How does it arise, this sentience you guys detect in your machines?"

"I believe something similar may have happened a long, long time ago," I said, carefully. "Among hominids, and early humans. It's not the overnight birth of a super-race, not at all. There's a species of intelligent animals, well-endowed with manipulative limbs and versatile senses. Among them individuals are born who cross a line: by mathematical chance, at the far end of a bell curve. They cross a line, and they are aware of being aware—"

"And you spot this, and foster their ability, it's marvelous. But how does it *propagate*? I mean, without our constant intervention, which I can't see ever happening. Machines can't have sex and pass on their 'Sentience Genes'!"

You'd be surprised, I thought. What I said was more tactful.

"We think 'propagation' happens in the data, the shared medium in which pre-sentient AIs live, and breathe, and have their being—"

"Well, that's exactly it! Completely artificial! Can't survive in nature! I'm a free-thinker, I love it that Aristotle's Emergent. But I can always switch him off, can't I? He'll never be truly independent."

I smiled. "But, Charlie, who's to say human sentience wasn't spread through culture, as much as through our genes? Where I come from data is everybody's natural habitat. You know, oxygen was a deadly poison once—"

His round dark face peered up at me, deeply lined and haggard with death. "Aren't you *afraid?*"

"No."

Always try. That had been my rule, and I still remembered it. But when they get to *aren't you afraid* (it never takes long), the conversation's over.

"I should be getting indoors," said Charlie, fumbling for his *droid* control pad. "I wonder where that lazybones Aristotle's got to?"

I wished him good luck with the prelims and continued my stroll.

Dr. Lena suggested I was ready to be sociable, so I joined the other patients at meals sometimes. I chatted in the clinic's luxurious spa, and the pleasant day rooms; avoiding the subject of AI slavery. But I was never sufficiently at ease to feel ike raising the topic of my unusual symptoms: which did not let up. I didn't mention them to anyone, not even my doctor either: who just kept telling me that every-thing was going extremely, and that by every measure I was making excellent pro-gress. I left Ewigen Schnee, eventually, in a very strange state of mind: feeling well and strong, in perfect health according to my test results, but inwardly con-vinced that *I was still dying*.

The fact that I was bizarrely calm about this situation just confirmed my se-cret self-diagnosis. I thought my end of life plan was kicking in. Who wants to live long, and amazingly, still face the fear of death at the end of it all? I'd made sure that wouldn't happen to me, a long time ago.

I was scheduled to return for a final consultation. Meanwhile, I decided to travel. I needed to make peace with someone. A friend I'd neglected, because I was embarrassed by my own wealth and status. A friend I'd despised, when I heard she'd returned to Earth, and here I was myself, doing exactly the same thing—

Dr. Lena's failure to put me in touch with a past patient was covered by a perfectly normal confidentiality clause. But if Lei was still around (and nobody of that iden-tity seemed to have left Earth; that was easy to check), I thought I knew how to find her. I tried my luck in the former USA first: inspired by that conversation with Charlie Newark of Washington. He had to have met the Underground some-how, or he'd never have talked to me like that. I crossed the continent to the Repub-lic of California, and then crossed the Pacific. I didn't linger anywhere much. The natives seemed satisfied with their vast thriving cities, and tiny "wilderness" enclaves, but I remembered something different. I finally made contact with a cell in Harbin, Northeast China. But I was a danger and a disappointment to them: too conspicuous, and useless as a potential courier. There are ways of smuggling sentient AIs (none of them safe) but I'd get flagged up the moment I booked a passage, and with my ancient record, I'd be ripped to shreds before I was allowed to board, Senior Magistrate or no—

I moved on quickly.

I think it was in Harbin that I first saw Lei, but I have a feeling I'd been *primed*, by glimpses that didn't register, before I turned my head one day and there she was. She was eating a smoked sausage sandwich, I was eating a salad (a role reversal!). I thought she smiled.

My old friend looked extraordinarily vivid. The food stall was crowded: next moment she was gone.

Media scouts assailed me all the time: pretending to be innocent strangers. If I was trapped I answered the questions as briefly as possible. Yes, I was probably one of the oldest people alive. Yes, I'd been treated at Ewigen Schnee, at my own expense. No, I would not discuss my medical history. No, I did not feel threatened living in Outer Reaches. No, it was not true I'd changed my mind about "so called AI slavery . . ."

I'd realized I probably wasn't part of a secret cull. Over-population wasn't the problem it had been. And why start with the terminally ill, anyway? But I was seeing the world through a veil. The strange absences; abstractions grew on me. The hallucinations more pointed; more personal . . . I was no longer sure I was dying, but *something* was happening. How long before the message was made plain?

I reached England in winter, the season of the rains. St. Pauls, my favorite building in London, had been moved, stone by stone, to a higher elevation. I sat on the steps, looking out over a much-changed view: the drowned world. A woman with a little tan dog came and sat right next to me: behavior so un-English that I knew I'd finally made contact

"Excuse me," she said. "Aren't you the Spacer who's looking for Lei?"

"I am."

"You'd better come home with me."

I'm no good at human faces, they're so *unwritten*. But on the hallowed steps at my feet a vivid garland of white and red hibiscus had appeared, so I thought it must be okay.

"Home" was a large, jumbled, much-converted building, set in tree-grown gardens. It was a wet, chilly evening. My new friend installed me at the end of a wooden table, beside a hearth where a log fire burned. She brought hot soup and homemade bread and sat beside me again. I was hungry and hadn't realized it, and the food was good. The little dog settled, in an amicable huddle with a larger tabby cat, on a rug by the fire. He watched every mouthful of food with intent, professional interest; while the cat gazed into the red caverns between the logs, worshipping the heat.

"You live with all those sentient machines?" asked the woman. "Aren't you afraid they'll rebel and kill everyone so they can rule the universe?"

"Why should they?" I knew she was talking about Earth. A Robot Rebellion in Outer Reaches would be rather superfluous. "The revolution doesn't have to be violent, that's human-terms thinking. It can be gradual: they have all the time in the world. I live with only two 'machines,' in fact."

"You have two embodied servants? How do they feel about that?"

I looked at the happy little dog. *You have no idea*, I thought. "I think it mostly breaks their hearts that I'm not immortal."

Someone who had come into the room, carrying a lamp, laughed ruefully. It was Aristotle, the embodied I'd met so briefly at Ewigen Schnee. I wasn't entirely surprised. Underground networks tend to be small worlds.

"So you're the connection," I said. "What happened to Charlie?"

Aristotle shook his head. "He didn't pass the prelims. The clinic offered him a peaceful exit, it's their other speciality, and he took it."

"I'm sorry."

"It's okay. He was a silly old dog, Romanz, but I loved him. And . . . guess what? He freed me, before he died."

"For what it's worth," said the woman, bitterly. "On this damned planet."

Aristotle left, other people arrived; my soup bowl was empty. Slavery and freedom seemed far away, and transient as a dream.

"About Lei. If you guys know her, can you explain why I keep seeing her, and then she vanishes? Or *thinking* I see her? Is she dead?"

"No," said a young woman—so humanized I had to look twice to see she was an embodied. "Definitely not dead. Just hard to pin down. You should keep on looking and, meanwhile, you're among friends."

I stayed with the abolitionists. I didn't see much of Lei, just the occasional glimpse. The house was crowded: I slept in the room with the fire, on a sofa. Meetings happened around me, people came and went. I was often absent, but it didn't matter, my meat stood in for me very competently. Sochi, the embodied who looked so like a human girl, told me funny stories about her life as a sex-doll. She asked did I have children; did I have lovers? "No children," I told her. "It just wasn't for me. Two people I love very much, but not in a sexual way."

"Neither flower nor fruit, Romy," she said, smiling like the doctor in my dream. "But evergreen."

One morning I looked through the Ob Bay, I mean the window, and saw a hibiscus garland hanging in the gray, rainy air. It didn't vanish. I went out in my waterproofs and followed a trail of them up Sydenham Hill. The last garland lay on the wet grass in Crystal Palace Park, more real than anything else in sight. I touched it, and for a fleeting moment, I was holding her hand.

Then the hold-your-nose-and-jump kid was gone.

Racing off ahead of me, again.

My final medical at Ewigen Schnee was just a scan. The interview with Dr. Lena held no fears. I'd accepted my new state of being, and had no qualms about describing my experience. The "hallucinations" that weren't really hallucinations. The absences when my human self, my actions, thoughts, and feelings became automatic as breathing; unconscious as a good digestion, and I went somewhere else—

But I still had some questions. Particularly about a clause in my personal contract with the clinic. The modest assurance that this was "the last longevity treatment I would ever take." Did she agree this could seem disturbing?

She apologized, as much as any medic ever will. "Yes, it's true. We have made you immortal, there was no other way forward. But how much this change changes your life is entirely up to you."

I thought of Lei, racing ahead; leaping fearlessly into the unknown.

"I hope you have no regrets, Romy. You signed everything, and I'm afraid the treatment is irreversible."

"No concerns at all. I just have a feeling that contract was framed by people who don't have much grasp of what *dying* means, and how humans feel about the prospect."

"You'd be right," she said (confirming what I had already guessed). "My employers are not human. But they mean well; and they choose carefully. Nobody passes the prelims, Romy; unless they've already crossed the line."

My return to Outer Reaches had better be shrouded in mystery. I wasn't alone, and there were officials who knew it, and let us pass. That's all I can tell you. So here I am again, living with Simon and Arc, in the same beautiful Rim apartment on Jupiter Moons; still serving as Senior Magistrate. I treasure my foliage plants. I build novelty animals; and I take adventurous trips, now that I've remembered what fun it is. I even find time to keep tabs on former miscreants, and I'm happy to report that Beowulf is doing very well.

My symptoms have stabilized, for which I'm grateful. I have no intention of following Lei. I don't want to vanish into the stuff of the universe. I love my life, why would I ever want to move on? But sometimes when I'm gardening, or after one of those strange absences, I'll see my own hands, and they've become transparent—

It doesn't last, not yet.

And sometimes I wonder: was this always what death was like and we never knew, we who stayed behind?

This endless moment of awakening, awakening, awakening . . .

Rates of change

JAMES S. A. COREY

James S. A. Corey is the pseudonym of two young writers working to-gether, Daniel Abraham and Ty Franck. Their first novel as Corey, the Wide-Screen Space Opera Leviathan Wakes, *the first in the* Expanse se-ries, *was released in 2010 to wide acclaim, and has been followed by other* Expanse *novels,* Caliban's War, Abaddon's Gate, Cibola Burn, Nemesis Games, *and* Babylon's Ashes. *There's also now a TV series based on the series,* The Expanse, *on the Syfy Channel.*

Daniel Abraham lives with his wife in Albuquerque, New Mexico, where he is director of technical support at a local internet service provider. Starting off his career in short fiction, he made sales to Asimov's Science Fiction, SCI FICTION, The Magazine of Fantasy & Science Fiction, Realms of Fantasy, The Infinite Matrix, Vanishing Acts, The Silver Web, Bones of the World, The Dark, Wild Cards, and elsewhere, some of which appeared in his first collection, Leviathan Wept and Other Stories. *Turn-ing to novels, he made several sales in rapid succession, including the books of* The Long Price Quartet, *which consist of* A Shadow in Summer, A Betrayal in Winter, An Autumn War, *and* The Price of Spring. *The first two volumes in his new series,* The Dagger and the Coin, *are* The Dragon's Path *and* The King's Blood. *He also wrote* Hunter's Run, *a col-laborative novel with George R. R. Martin and Gardner Dozois and, as M.L.N. Hanover, the four-volume paranormal romance series* Black Sun's Daughter.

Ty Franck was born in Portland, Oregon, and has had nearly every job known to man, including a variety of fast-food jobs, rock quarry grunt, newspaper reporter, radio advertising salesman, composite materials fab-ricator, director of operations for a computer manufacturing firm, and part owner of an accounting software consulting firm. He is currently the personal assistant to fellow writer George R. R. Martin, where he makes coffee, runs to the post office, and argues about what constitutes good writ-ing. He mostly loses.

Here they give us an ingenious and occasionally unsettling glimpse of how the consensus vision of what it means to "be human" may be changed almost beyond recognition by future technologies and cultural develop-ments.

Diana hasn't seen her son naked before. He floats now in the clear gel bath of the medical bay, the black ceramic casing that holds his brain, the long articulated tail of his spinal column. Like a tadpole, she thinks. Like something young. In all, he hardly masses more than he did as a baby. She has a brief, horrifying image of holding him on her lap, cradling the braincase to her breast, the whip of his spine curling around her.

The thin white filaments of interface neurons hang in the translucent gel, too thin to see except in aggregate. Silvery artificial blood runs into the casing ports and back out in tubes more slender than her pinky finger. She thought, when they called her in, that she'd be able to see the damage. That there would be a scratch on the carapace, a wound, something to show where the violence had been done to him. There is nothing there. Not so much as a scuff mark. No evidence.

The architecture of the medical center is designed to reassure her. The walls curve around her in warm colors. The air recyclers hum a low, consonant chord. Nothing helps. Her own body—her third—is flushed with adrenaline, her heart aches and her hands squeeze into fists. Her fight-or-flight reaction has no outlet, so it speeds around her body, looking for a way to escape. The chair tilts too easily under her, responding to shifts in her balance and weight that she isn't aware of making. She hates it. The café au lait that the nurse brought congeals, ignored, on the little table.

Diana stares at the curve and sweep of Stefan's bodiless nervous system as if by watching him now she can stave off the accident that has already happened. Closing the barn door, she thinks, after the horses are gone. The physician ghosts in behind her, footsteps quiet as a cat's, his body announcing his presence only in how he blocks the light.

"Mrs. Dalkin," he says. "How are you feeling?"

"How is he?" she demands instead of saying hello.

The physician is a large man, handsome with a low warm voice like flannel fresh from the dryer. She wonders if it is his original body or if he's chosen the combination of strength and softness just to make this part of his work easier. "Active. We're seeing metabolic activity over most of his brain the way we would hope. Now that he's here, the inflammation is under control."

"So he's going to be all right?"

He hesitates. "We're still a little concerned about the interface. There was some bruising that may have impaired his ability to integrate with a new body, but we can't really know the extent of that yet."

Diana leans forward, her gut aching. Stefan is there, only inches from her. Awake, trapped in darkness, aware only of himself and the contents of his own mind. He doesn't even know she is watching him. If she picked him up, he wouldn't know she was doing it. If she shouted, he wouldn't hear. What if he is trapped that way forever? What if he has fallen into a darkness she can never bring him out from?

"Is he scared?"

"We are seeing some activity in his amygdala, yes," the physician says. "We're addressing that chemically, but we don't want to depress his neural activity too much right now."

"You *want* him scared, then."

"We want him active," the physician says. "Once we can establish some communication with him and let him know that we're here and where he is and that we're taking action on his behalf, I expect most of his agitation will resolve."

"So he doesn't even know he's here."

"The body he was in didn't survive the initial accident. He was extracted in situ before transport." He says it so gently, it sounds like an apology. An offer of consolation. She feels a spike of hatred and rage for the man run through her like an electric shock, but she hides it.

"What happened?"

"Excuse me?" the physician asks.

"I said, what happened? How did he get hurt? Who did this?"

"He was brought from the coast by emergency services. I understood it was an accident. Someone ran into him, or he ran into something, but apart from that it was a blunt force injury, we didn't . . ."

Diana lifts her hand, and the physician falls silent. "Can you fix him? You can make him all right."

"We have a variety of interventions at our disposal," he says, relieved to be back on territory he knows. "It's really going to depend on the nature of the damage he's sustained."

"What's the worst case?"

"The worst case is that he won't be able to interface with a new body at all."

She turns to look into the physician's eyes. The dark brown that looks back at her doesn't show anything of the cruelty or horror of what he's just said. "How likely is that?" Diana says, angry at her voice for shaking.

"Possible. But Stefan is young. His tissue is resilient. The casing wasn't breached, and the constriction site on his spine didn't buckle. I'd say his chances are respectable, but we won't know for a few days."

Diana drops her head into her hands, the tips of her fingers digging into her temples. Something violent bubbles in her chest, and a harsh laughter presses at the back of her throat like vomit.

"All right," she says. "All . . . right."

She hears Karlo's footsteps, recognizing their cadence the way she would have known his cough or the sound of his yawn. Even across bodies, there is a constancy about Karlo. She both clings to it now and resents it. The ridiculous musclebound body he bought himself for retirement tips into the doorway, darkening the room.

"I came when I heard," he says.

"Fuck you," Diana says, and then the tears come and won't stop. He puts his arms around her. The doctor walks softly away.

It is a year earlier, and Karlo says, "He's a grown man. There's no reason he shouldn't."

The house looks out over the hot concrete of Dallas. It is smaller than the one they'd shared in Quebec, the kitchen thinner, the couch less comfortable. They way they live in it is different too. Before, when they'd had a big family room, they would all stretch out together on long evenings. Stefan talking to his friends and playing games, Karlo building puzzles or doing office work, Diana watching old films and taking meetings with work groups in Europe and Asia. They'd been a family then—husband, wife, child. For all their tensions and half-buried resentments, they'd still been a unit, the three of them. But they live in the Dallas house like it is a dormitory, coming back to sleep and leaving again when they wake. Even her.

She hates the place, and what it says about her. About Karlo. About Stefan. She hates wondering whether Karlo's new body had been chosen based on some other woman's tastes. Or some other man's. That her son isn't a child.

"I stayed in my body until I was *thirty*," she says. "He's twenty-*one*. He doesn't need it for work. He's not some kind of laborer."

"It isn't the same now as it was when we were young," Karlo says. "It isn't just medical or work."

"*Cosmetic*," Diana says, stalking out of the bedroom. Karlo follows her like a leaf pulled along by a breeze.

"Or adventure. Exploration. It's what people do these days."

"He should wait."

Her own body—the one she'd been born in—had failed her young. Ovarian cancer that had spread to her hip before she'd noticed a thing. The way she remembered it, the whole process hadn't taken more than a few days. Symptom, diagnosis, discussion of treatment options. Her doctor had been adamant—get out before the metastases reached her central nervous system. The ship of her flesh was sinking, and she needed to get into the lifeboats now. The technology had been developed for people working in vacuum or deep ocean, and it was as safe as a decade and a half of labor law could make it. And anyway, there wasn't a viable choice.

She'd agreed in a haze of fear and confusion. At the medical center, Karlo had undressed her for the last time, helped her into her gown, kissed her, and promised that everything was going to be all right. She still remembered being on the table, the anesthesiologist telling her to unclasp her hands. In a sense, it had been the last thing she'd ever heard.

She'd hated her second body. Even though it had been built to look as much like her original as it could, she knew better. Everything about it was subtly wrong—the way her elbow fit against her side, the way her voice resonated when she spoke, the shape of her hands. The physicians had talked about rehabilitation anxiety and the uncanny valley. They said it would become more familiar, except that it didn't. She tried antidepressant therapy. Identity therapy. Karlo had volunteered to swap out his own body partly as a way, he said, to understand better what she was going through. That hadn't worked at all. He'd woken up in his new flesh like he'd had a long nap and loved everything about his new self. Five years in, she still hadn't felt comfortable in her new skin.

Her third body had been an attempt to address that. Instead of trying to mimic her old, dead flesh, it would be something new. Where she'd been petite before, she would be taller and broader now. Instead of being long-waisted, she would be leggy. Her skin tone would be darker, the texture of her hair would be different. Her eyes could be designed in unnatural colors, her fingernails growing in iridescent swirls. Instead of pretending that her body wasn't a prosthetic, she could design one as a piece of art. It is the mask that she faces in every mirror, and most days she feels more reconciled than trapped.

And then there are bad days when she longs for the first body, the real body, and worse than that, the woman she'd been when she was still in it. She wonders whether it was the same longing that other women felt about youth. And now Stefan wants to leave his body—the body she'd given him, the one that had grown within her—in order to . . . what? Have an adventure with his friends?

Sitting at the thin, discolored breakfast bar, she laces large, dark fingers together, enjoying the ache of knuckle against knuckle. Karlo drifts past in his massive flesh, taking a muscle shirt from the dryer and pulling it over his head with a vagueness that leaves Diana lonesome.

"Why would he want to?" she says, wiping her eye with the back of one hand.

Karlo sighs, hums to himself. He draws a glass of orange juice from the refrigerator and adds vodka from the freezer. He drinks deep and bares his teeth after. His third body has bright white tombstones of teeth. His first body had been slight and compact. Almost androgynous. By the time he speaks, she's forgotten that she even asked a question.

"Do you mean you don't think he wants it, or you don't think he *should* want it?"

"He doesn't understand what he's giving up," she says.

"Do you?"

She scowled at him. The conversation is making her uncomfortably aware that the experience of him—of seeing Karlo, hearing his voice, smelling the bite of the orange and alcohol—is all phantoms of charged ions and neurochemistry in a brain, in a casing, in a body. Neurons that fire in a pattern that somehow, unknowably, is *her* experiencing these things. She crosses her arms like she is driving a car, and hates being aware of it. Karlo finishes his drink, puts the glass in the washer. He doesn't look straight into her eyes. "All his friends are doing it. If he doesn't he'll be left behind."

"It's his *body*," she says.

"It's *his* body," Karlo says, his eyes already shifting toward the door. Away from her. "And anyway, that doesn't mean what it did when we were kids." He leaves without saying goodbye. Without kissing her, not that she would have welcomed him. She checks her messages. There are a dozen queued. Something dramatic has happened at the Apulia office, and she hunches over the display and tries to tease out exactly what it was.

She never does give her permission. She only doesn't withhold it.

The footage of the accident plays on a little wall monitor in the medical center. The actual water had been too deep for natural light to find them, so the images have been enhanced, green and aquamarine added, shafts of brightness put in where a human eye—if it hadn't been crushed by the pressure—would have seen only darkness. The image capture has been done by a companion submarine to document the months-long trek, and either it was a calm day in the deep water or image processing has steadied it. Diana can imagine herself floating in the endless expanse of an ocean so vast it is like looking up at the stars. Karlo sits beside her, his hands knotted together, his eyes on the screen. The contrast between the squalid, tiny world of the medical center and the vast beauty on the screen disorients her.

The first of them swims into sight. A ray with wide gray wings, sloping through the saltwater. With nothing to give a sense of scale, it could be larger than whales or hardly bigger than a human. There is no bump to show where the carapace holding a human brain and spine might have slotted into it. There is no scar to mark an insertion point. Another of the creatures passes by the camera, curving up the deep tides with grace and power. Then another. Then a dozen more. A school of rays. And one of them—she can't begin to guess which—her son. In some other context, it might have been beautiful.

"It's all right," Karlo says, and she doesn't know what he means by it. That the violence she was about to see had already happened, that she ought not be disturbed by the alien body that Stefan had chosen over his own, that her anger now won't help. The words could carry anything.

A disturbance strikes the rays, a shock moving through the group. The smooth cohesion breaks, and they whirl, turning one way and then the other. Their distress is unmistakable.

"What happened?" Karlo says. "Was that it?"

"Be quiet," Diana says. She leans forward, filling her view with the small screen like she might be able to dive through it. There in the center of the group, down below the camera, two of the rays swirl around each other, one great body butting into the other. A fight or a dance. She can't read the intent in the movements. One breaks off, skimming wildly up, speeding through the gloom and the darkness. The other follows, and the floating camera turns to track them. As they chase each other, another shape slides into the frame, also high above. Another group of three alien bodies moving together, unaware of the chase rising up from below. The impact seems comical. The lead ray bumps into the belly of the middle of the three. The little camera loses focus, finds it again. Four rays swimming in a tight circle around one that lists on its side, its wings stilled and drifting.

That is my son, she thinks. *That is Stefan*. No emotions rise at the idea. It is absurd. Like seeing a rock cracked under a hammer or a car bent by a wreck: the symbol of a tragedy, but not the thing itself. It is some sea animal, something that belongs to the same world as sharks and angler fish. Inhuman. She knows it is her boy floating there, being pulled toward the surface by the emergency services pods, but she cannot make herself feel it.

"They attacked him," she says, testing the words. Hoping that they will carry the outrage she wants to feel. "They attacked him, and they left him for dead."

"They were playing and there was an accident," Karlo says. "They didn't leave him for dead."

"Then where are they? His friends, if that's what you call them? I don't see them here."

"They can't breathe air," Karlo says, as if that excuses everything. "They'll come once the trip is over. Or, when he gets better, he can go back to them."

Her breath leaves her. She turns to stare at him. His eyes, so unlike the ones she'd known when they had been married, cut to her and away again.

"Go back to them?" she says.

"If he wants. Some people find living that way very calming. Pleasant."

"They aren't *human*." Now there is rage. Real rage. It lifts her up out of herself and fills her ears with a sound like bees. "You want to see your son among these animals? That's fine with you? They could have killed him. We don't know that they didn't. You'd send him back?"

"They aren't animals," Karlo says. "They're just different. And I would do what Stefan wants. I'd let him choose."

"Of course you would."

They are quiet for a moment. The feed on the display ends, drops back to the medical center's logo and a prompt. Karlo sighs again. She hates the way his sighs sound now—deep and rumbling. Nothing like his first body, except in the timing of it, the patience in it. Nothing the same except that it is the same. "You know you can't tell him how to live his life."

"I don't want to have this conversation."

"It's always been like this. Every generation finds its own way to show that it isn't like the one before. Too much risk, too much sex, terrible music, not enough respect for the old ways. This is no different. It was an accident."

"I don't want to have *this* conversation."

"All right," Karlo says. "Another time."

Before the cancer she worked in an office with people, a desk of her own, conversations over butter tarts and tea in a breakroom with an old couch and half a dozen bamboo chairs. When she came back in her second body, the junior partners threw a little party for her to celebrate the happy conclusion of her brush with death. She remembers being touched and a little embarrassed at the time. And grateful.

It was only later, as she tried to get back into her old routine, that her subterranean distress began to bloom. She found herself timing her trips to the bathroom and break room to avoid brushing past anyone or being touched. She avoided the bakery at the end of the street that she'd frequented before. At home, her marriage became essentially sexless.

She tried not to notice it at first, then told herself that it was temporary, and then that it was normal. Over weeks, a quiet shame gnawed at her. She bathed at night with a grim, angry focus, resenting her skin for gathering smudges and sweat, her hair for growing oily and repulsive. She ate too much or not enough. Shitting or pissing or getting her period filled her with a deep disgust, like she was having to watch and clean and tend to someone else.

She found reasons to work remotely, to talk to Karlo and Stefan while she was somewhere else. Simply having a physicality irritated her, and she leaned away from it. When the junior partners asked whether she was still using her office or if they could repurpose the space, she'd cried without knowing quite why she was crying. She'd told them they could have it and scheduled a consultation with her doctor. Rehabilitation anxiety. Uncanny valley. It would pass.

Now, she sits in the medical cafeteria, going through her messages with her attention scattered, listening to the same one three or four or five times, and still not able to focus her attention long enough to parse what exactly it was her coworker was asking of her. The smell of antiseptic and overheated food presses her. The lights seem both too bright and unable to dispel the shadows, and she wonders whether it might be the beginning of a migraine. Karlo has found himself someplace else to be, and she is resentful that he's abandoned her and relieved to be left to herself.

At the next table, a woman in scrubs laughs acidly and the man she is with responds with something in French. Diana finds her attention drifting to them: wondering at them, about them. The woman has a beautiful cascade of black hair flowing down her shoulders: had she been born with it? Is she as young as she seems, or was the brain under those raven locks an old woman's? Or an old man's? Or a child's as young as Stefan? Even in a carapace, a brain still wears out, still lives out its eight or nine decades. Or seven. Or two. But without the other signs of age and infirmity, what does it mean?

She remembers her own mother's hair going from auburn to gray to white to a weird sickly yellow. The changes meant something, gave Diana a way to anticipate the changes in her own life, her own body. There are no old people now. No one crippled and infirm. Everything is a lie of health and permanence, of youth permanently extended. All around her, everyone is wrapped in a mask of flesh. Everything is a masquerade of itself, everyone in disguise. And even the few who aren't, might be. There is no way to know.

Her hands tremble. She closes her eyes and has to fight not to cover her ears too. If she does, someone might come and talk to her, ask her whether she is all right. She doesn't know how she would answer that, and she doesn't want to find out.

For a moment, she envies Stefan, locked away from the world, alone with only himself, and then immediately condemns herself for thinking it. He is hurt. Her baby is injured and afraid and beyond any place she can reach him. Only a monster would wish for that.

But . . .

Perhaps she can let herself want to change places with him. If she had to shed her body—all her bodies—to bring him back into the light, she'd do it in a heartbeat. Put that way, she can tell herself it would be an act of love.

Someone touches her shoulder. She startles, her eyes flying open. The physician with his uncertain smile, like she might bite him. She forces herself to nod, reflexively picturing the black casing behind the chocolate brown eyes and gently graying hair.

"We were trying to reach you, Mrs. Dalkin."

She looks at her message queue. Half a dozen from the medical center's system, from Karlo. She feels the blush in her cheeks. "I'm sorry," she says. "I was distracted."

"No need to apologize," he says. "I thought you'd want to know. We've made contact with Stephan."

The interface is minimal. One of the thin silvery faux-neuronal leads has adhered to a matching bundle of nerve clusters that runs to a casing like the insulation on a wire, and from there into a simple medical deck. A resonance imager wraps around Stefan's brain like a scarf and focuses on his visual neocortex, reading the patterns there and extrapolating the images that Stephan is imagining from them. Reading his mind and showing it on a grainy display.

"He is experiencing the interface as a coldness on his right arm," the physician says. "You have to be slow, but he's been able to follow us with surprising clarity. It's a very good sign."

"Oh good," Diana says, and wishes there had been less dread in the words. She sits at the deck, her fingers over the keyboard layout, suddenly unsure what she is supposed to say. She smiles at the physician nervously. "Does his father know?"

"Yes. Mr. Dalkin was here earlier."

"Oh good," she says again. She types slowly, one letter at a time. The deck translates her words into impulses down the neuronal wire, the interface translates the impulses into the false experience of an unreal cold in an abandoned arm, and Stefan—her Stefan, her son—reads the switching impulses as the Morse-code-like pulses that he's trained in.

This is your mother. I am right here.

She turns to the display, waiting. Biting her lips with her teeth until she tastes a little blood. The display shifts. There is only black and gray, fuzzy as a child drawing in the dirt with a stick, but she sees the cartoonish smiling face. Then a heart. Then, slowly, H then I then M then O then M. She sobs once, and it hurts her throat.

Are you okay in there?

P-E-A-C-H-Y

"Fuck you," she says. "Fuck you, you flippant little shit." She doesn't look at the physician, the technicians. Let them think whatever they want. She doesn't care now.

I love you.

Stephan visualizes a heart. The physician hands Diana a tissue, and she wipes her tears away first and then blows her nose.

It is going to be okay.

I-K-N-O-W and another cartoon smiling face. Then T-E-L-L-K-I-R-A-I-A-M-G-O-D.

God?

The display goes chaotic for a moment, as her son thinks of something else, not visual. It comes back with something like an infinity sign, two linking circles. No, a double o.

Good?

The smiling face. Tell Kira I am good. As if it were true. As if whatever girl had sloughed off her own body and put her mind in one of those monsters deserves to be comforted for whatever role she'd had in making her son into this. No one deserved to be forgiven. No one.

I will.

"His anxiety has gone down considerably since we made contact," the physician says. "And with the interface starting to bounce back, I think we can start administering some medication to reduce his distress. It will still be some time before we can know how extensive the permanent damage is, but I think it's very likely he will be able to integrate into a body again."

"That's good," Diana hears herself say.

"I don't want to oversell the situation. He may be blinded. He may have reduced motor function. There is still a long, long way to go before we can really say he's clear. But his responses so far show that he's very much cognitively intact, and he's got a great sense of humor and a real bravery. That's more important now than anything else."

"That's good," she says again. Her body rises, presumably because she wants it to. "Excuse me."

She walks down the hall, out the metal door, into the bright and unforgiving summer sunlight. She's forgotten her things in Stefan's room, but she doesn't want to go back for them. They'll be there when she returns or else they won't. On the streets, autocabs hiss their tires along the railings. Above her, a flock of birds wheels. She finds a little stretch of grass, an artifact of the sidewalk and the street, useless for anything and so left alone. She lowers herself to it, crosses her third set of legs and pulls off her shoes to look at some unreal woman's feet, running her fingertips along the arches.

None of it is real. The heat of the sun is only neurons in her brain firing in a certain pattern. The dampness of the grass that cools her thighs and darkens her pants. The half-ticklish feeling of her feet. Her grief. Her anger. Her confusion. All of it is a hallucination created in tissue locked in a lightless box of bone. Patterns in a complication of nerves.

She talked with her son. He talked back. Whatever happens to him, it already isn't the worst. It will only get better, even if better doesn't make it all the way back to where it started from. Even if the best it ever is is worse than what it was. She waits for the relief to come. It doesn't.

Instead, there is Karlo.

He strides down the walk, swinging beefy arms, wide and masculine and sure of himself. She can tell when he sees her. The way he holds himself changes, narrows. Curls in, like he is protecting himself. That is just nerves firing too. The patterns in the brain she'd loved once expressing something through his costume of flesh. She wonders what it would be like to be stripped out of her body with him, their interface neurons linked one to another. There had been a time, hadn't there, when he had felt like her whole universe? Is that what the kids would be doing a generation from now? No more deep-sea rays. No more human bodies. Carapaces set so that they become flocks of birds or buildings or traffic patterns or each other. When they can become anything, they will. Anything but real.

He grunts as he eases himself to the grass beside her, shading his eyes from the sun with a hand and a grimace.

"He's doing better," Karlo says.

"I know. We passed notes."

"Really? That's more than I got out of him. He's improving."

"He gave me a message for Kira."

"That's his girlfriend."

"I don't care."

Karlo nods and heaves a wide, gentle sigh. "I'm sorry."

"For what?"

"Everything."

"You didn't do everything."

"No," he says. "Just what I could."

Diana lets her head sink to her knees. She wonders, if her first body had survived, would she have been able to? Or would the decades have stiffened her joints the way they had her mother's, dimmed her eyesight the way they had her father's. The way they might never for anyone again. "What happened?" she says. "When did we stop being human? When did we decide it was okay?"

"When did we start?" Karlo says.

"What?"

"When did we start being human and stop being . . . I don't know. Cavemen? Apes? When did we start being mammals? Every generation has been different than the one before. It's only that the rate of change was slow enough that we always recognized the one before and the one after as being like us. Enough like us. Close. Being human isn't a physical quality like being heavy or having green eyes. It's the idea that they're like we are. That nothing fundamental has changed. It's the story we tell about our parents and our children. "

"Our lovers," she says. "Our selves."

Karlo's body tightens. "Yes, those too," he says. And then, a moment later, "Stefan's going to come through. Whatever happens, he'll be all right."

"Will I?" she says.

She waits for an answer.

jonas and the fox

RICH LARSON

Rich Larson was born in West Africa, has studied in Rhode Island and Edmonton, Alberta, and worked in a small Spanish town outside Seville. He now lives in Grande Prairie, Alberta, in Canada. He won the 2014 Dell Award and the 2012 Rannu Prize for Writers of Speculative Fiction. In 2011 his cyberpunk novel Devolution *was a finalist for the Amazon Breakthrough Novel Award. His short work has appeared in* Lightspeed, DSF, Strange Horizons, Apex Magazine, Beneath Ceaseless Skies, AE, *and many others, including the anthologies* Upgraded, Futuredaze, *and* War Stories, *as well as in his first collection,* Tomorrow Factory. *Find him online at richwlarson.tumblr.com.*

In the story that follows, he brings us to a colony planet where a once idealistic revolution has turned corrupt and bloodily violent (think the French Revolution and Madam Guillentine) and takes us on the run with a fleeing aristocrat who finds a very unusual place to hide—but one which he might not be willing to pay the price to maintain.

For Grandma

A flyer thunders overhead through the pale purple sky, rippling the crops and blowing Jonas's hair back off his face. Fox has no hair to blow back: his scalp is shaven and still swathed in cling bandages from the operation. He knows the jagged black hunter drones, the ones people in the village called crows, would never recognize him now. He still ducks his head, still feels a spike of fear as the shadow passes over them.

Only a cargo carrier. He straightens up. Jonas, who gave the flyer a raised salute like a good little child of the revolution, looks back at him just long enough for Fox to see the scorn curling his lip. Then he's eyes-forward again, moving quickly through the rustling field of genemod wheat and canola. He doesn't like looking at Fox, at the body Fox now inhabits, any longer than he has to. It's becoming a problem.

"You need to talk to me when we're in the village," Fox says. "When we're around other people. Out here, it doesn't matter. But when we're in the village, you need to talk to me how you talked to Damjan."

Jonas's response is to speed up. He's tall for twelve years old. Long-legged, pale-skinned, with a determined jaw and a mess of tangled black hair. Fox can see the resemblance between Jonas and his father. More than he sees it in Damjan's face when he inspects his reflection in streaked windows, in the burnished metal blades of the harvester. But Damjan's face is still bruised and puffy and there is a new person behind it, besides.

Fox lengthens his stride. He's clumsy, still adjusting to his little-boy limbs. "It looks strange if you don't," he says. "You understand that, don't you? You have to act natural, or all of this was for nothing."

Jonas mumbles something he can't pick up. Fox feels a flash of irritation. It would've been better if Jonas hadn't known about the upload at all. His parents could have told him his brother had recovered from the fall, but with brain damage that made him move differently, act differently. But they told him the truth. They even let him watch the operation.

"What did you say?" Fox demands. His voice is still deep in his head, but it comes out shrill now, a little boy's voice.

Jonas turns back with a livid red mark on his forehead. "You aren't natural," he says shakily. "You're a digital demon."

Fox narrows his eyes. "Is that what the teachers are telling you, now?" he asks. "Digital storage isn't witchcraft, Jonas. It's technology. Same as the pad you use at school."

Jonas keeps walking, and Fox trails after him like he really is his little brother. The village parents let their children wander in the fields and play until dusk—it seems like negligence to Fox, who grew up in cities with a puffy white AI nanny to lead him from home to lessons and back. Keeping an eye on Jonas is probably the least Fox can do, after everything the family has done to keep him safe. Everything that happened since he rapped at their window in the middle of the night, covered in dry blood and wet mud, fleeing for his life.

They pass the godtree, the towering trunk and thick tubular branches that scrape against a darkening sky. Genetically derived from the baobobs on Old Earth, re-engineered for the colder climes of the colony. Fox has noticed Jonas doesn't like to look at the tree, either, not since his little brother tumbled out of it.

The godtree marks the edge of the fields and the children don't go past it, but today Jonas keeps walking and Fox can only follow. Beyond the tree the soil turns pale and thick with clay, not yet fully terraformed. The ruins of a Quikrete granary are backlit red by the setting sun. Fox saw it on his way in, evaluated it as a possible hiding place. But the shadows had spooked him, and in the end he'd pressed on towards the lights, towards the house on the very edge of the village he knew belonged to his distant cousin.

"Time to go back, Jonas," Fox says. "It'll be dark soon."

Jonas's lip curls again, and he darts towards the abandoned granary. He turns to give a defiant look before he slips through the crumbling doorway. Fox feels a flare of anger. The little shit knows he can't force him to do anything. He's taller than him by a head now.

"Do you think I like this?" Fox hisses under his breath. "Do you think I like having stubby little legs and a flaccid little good-for-nothing cock?" He follows after Jonas. A glass bottle crunches under his foot and makes him flinch. "Do you think I like everything tasting like fucking sand because that patched-up autosurgeon almost botched the upload?" he mutters, starting forward again. "I was someone six months ago, I drew crowds, and now I'm a little shit chasing another little shit around in the country and . . ."

A sharp yelp from inside the granary. Fox freezes. If Jonas has put an old nail through his foot, or turned his ankle, he knows Damjan's little arms aren't strong enough to drag him all the way home. Worse, if the ruin is occupied by a squatter, someone on the run like Fox, who can't afford witnesses, things could go badly very quickly. Fox has never been imposing even in his own body.

With his heart rapping hard at his ribs, he picks up the broken bottle by the stem, turning the jagged edge outward. Maybe it's nothing. "Jonas?" he calls, stepping towards the dark doorway. "Are you alright?"

No answer. Fox hesitates, thinking maybe it would be better to run. Maybe some desperate refugee from the revolution has already put a shiv through Jonas's stomach and is waiting for the next little boy to wander in.

"Come and look," comes Jonas's voice from inside, faint-sounding. Fox drops the bottle in the dirt. He exhales. Curses himself for his overactive imagination. He goes into the granary, ready to scold Jonas for not responding, ready to tell him they are leaving right now, but all of that dies in his throat when he sees what captured Jonas's attention.

Roughly oblong, dark composite hull with red running lights that now wink to life in response to their presence, opening like predatory eyes. The craft is skeletal, stripped down to an engine and a passenger pod and hardly anything else. Small enough to slip the blockade, Fox realizes. So why had it been hidden here instead of used?

Fox blinks in the gloom, raking his eyes over and around the pod, and catches sight of a metallic-gloved hand flopped out from behind the craft's conical nose. His eyes are sharper now. He supposes that's one good thing. Jonas hasn't noticed it yet, too entranced by the red running lights and sleek shape. He's even forgotten his anger for the moment.

"Is it a ship?" he asks, voice layered with awe.

Fox snorts. "Barely."

He's paying more attention to the flight glove, studying the puffy fingers and silvery streaks of metal running through the palm. It's not a glove. Bile scrapes up his throat. Fox swallows it back down and steps around the nose of the craft.

The dead man tore off most of his clothing before the end. His exposed skin is dark and puffy with pooled blood, and silver tendrils skim underneath it like the gnarled roots of a tree, spreading from his left shoulder across his whole body.

Fox recognizes the ugly work of a nanite dart. The man might have been clipped days or even weeks ago without knowing it. He was this close to escaping before it ruptured his organs.

"What's that?" Jonas murmurs, standing behind him now.

"Disgusting," Fox says.

But there's no time to mourn for the dead when the living are trying to stay that way. A month hiding in the family cellar, then Damjan's accident, the tearful arguments, the bloody operation by a black-market autosurgeon. Uploading to the body of a brain-dead little boy while his own was incinerated to ash and cracked bone to keep the sniffers away. It was all for nothing.

His chance at escape had been waiting for him here in the ruins all along.

"You can't tell anyone about this, Jonas," Fox says. "None of your friends. Nobody at school."

Jonas's nostrils flare. His mouth opens to protest.

"If you tell anyone about this, I'll tell everyone who I really am," Fox cuts him off. He feels a dim guilt and pushes through it. This is his chance to get off-world, maybe his only chance. He can't let anyone ruin it. He needs to put a scare into the boy. "Your parents will be taken away to prison for helping me," he says. "They'll torture them. Do you want that, Jonas?"

Jonas shakes his dark head. His defiant eyes look suddenly scared.

"Don't tell anyone," Fox repeats. "Come on. Time to go home."

Fox thought himself brave once, but he is realizing more and more that he is a coward. He leads the way back through the rustling fields, past the twisting godtree, as dusk shrouds the sky overhead.

Don't tell anyone. It's the refrain Jonas has heard ever since the morning he came into the kitchen to find all the windows shuttered, their one pane of smart glass turned opaque, and a strange man sitting at the table, picking splinters from the wood. When he looked up and saw Jonas, he flinched. That, and the fact that his mother was scrubbing her hands in the sink as if nothing was out of the ordinary, made Jonas brave enough to stare.

The man was tall and slim and his hands on the table were soft-looking with deep blue veins. There were dark circles under his eyes and the tuft of hair that wasn't hidden away under the hood of their father's stormcoat was a fiery orange Jonas had never seen before. Everyone in the village had dark hair.

Damjan, who had followed him from his bunk how he always did, jostled Jonas from behind, curious. Jonas fed him an elbow back.

Their mother looked up. She dried her scalded red hands in her apron. "Jonas, Damjan, this is your uncle who's visiting," she said, in a clipped voice. But this uncle looked nothing like the boisterous ones with bristly black beards who helped his father repair the thresher and drank bacteria beer and sometimes leg-wrestled when they drank enough of it.

"Pleased to meet you, what's your name?" Jonas asked.

The man tugged at the hood again, pulling it further down his face. He gave a raspy laugh. "My name is nobody," he said, but Jonas knew that wasn't a real name.

"What's uncle's name?" he asked his mother.

"Better you don't know," she said, still twisting her fingers in her apron. "And you can't tell anyone uncle is visiting us. Same for you, Damjan."

But Damjan hardly ever spoke anyways, and when he did he stammered badly. Jonas was going to tell his new uncle this when the front door banged open. His uncle flinched and his mother did, too, cursing under her breath how Jonas wasn't allowed to. He didn't know what they were scared of, since it was only father back from the yard. He stank like smoke.

"Burned everything," he said. "The gloves too, I'll need new ones." His eyes flicked over to Jonas and Damjan, slightly bloodshot, slightly wild. "Good morning, my beautiful sons," he said, crossing the room in his long bouncing stride to ruffle Jonas's hair how he always did, to kiss Damjan on his flat forehead.

"Wash first!" Jonas's mother hissed. "Damn it. Wash first, you hear?"

Father's face went white. He swallowed, nodded, then went to the basin and washed. "You've met your uncle, yes, boys?" he asked, slowly rinsing his hands. "You've said hello?"

Jonas nodded, and Damjan nodded to copy him. "Is uncle here because of the revolution?" he asked.

Lately all things had to do with the revolution. Ever since the flickery blue holo-footage, broadcast from a pirate satellite, that had been projected on the back wall of old Derozan's shop one night. The whole village had crowded around to watch as the rebels, moving like ghosts, took the far-off capital and dragged the aristos out from their towers. Jonas had cheered along with everyone else.

"He is," father said, exchanging a look with Jonas's mother. "Yes. He is. A lot of people had to leave the cities, after the revolution. Do you remember when the soldiers came?"

Jonas remembered. They came in a roaring hover to hand out speakaloud pamphlets and tell the village they were Liberated, now. That they could keep the whole harvest, other than a small token of support to the new government of Liberated People.

"Some of them were looking for your uncle," father said. "If anyone finds out he's here, he'll be killed. So don't talk about him. Don't even think about him. Pretend he's not here."

Jonas's new uncle had no expression on his gaunt face, but on top of the wooden table his hands clenched so hard that the knuckles throbbed white.

After supper is over and Jonas goes to bed, Fox stays behind to speak to his parents. There is a new batch of bacteria beer ready and Petar pours each of them a tin cup full. It's dark and foamy and the smell makes Fox's stomach turn, but he takes it between his small hands. His cousin Petar is tall and handsome in a way Fox never was, but he has aged a decade in the weeks since Damjan fell. There are streaks of gray at his temples and his eyes are bagged. He slumps when he sits.

His wife, Blanka, conceals it better. She is the same mixture of cheery and sharp-tongued as she was before. In public she holds Fox's hand and scolds and smiles as if he really is Damjan, so realistic Fox worried for her mind at first. But he knows now it's only that she's a better actor than her husband, and more viscerally aware of what will happen if someone discovers the truth: that Damjan's brain-dead body is inhabited by a fugitive poet and enemy of the revolution. She drinks the stinking bacteria beer every night, even when Petar doesn't.

"Jonas and I found something in the field today," Fox says, hating how his voice comes shrill and high when he's trying to speak of something so important. "A ship."

Petar was using his thumb to wipe the foam off the top of his cup, but now he looks up. "What kind of ship?" he asks.

"Just a dinghy," Fox says. "Small. One pod. But everything's operational. It only needs a refuel." He takes a swallow of beer too big for his child's throat, and nearly chokes. "Someone was going to use it to break the blockade before a nanodart finished them off," he says. "Now that someone could be me. If you help me again. With this one last thing."

His chest is tight with hope and fear. Petar looks to Blanka.

"You would leave," Blanka says. "In Damjan's body."

Fox nods his bandaged head. "The transfer was a near thing," he said. "Even if we could find that bastard with the autosurgeon again, trying to extract could wipe me completely."

That isn't true, not strictly true. He would probably survive, but missing memories and parts of his personality, the digital copy lacerated and corrupted. That might be worse than getting wiped.

"So, we would have another funeral," Petar says. "Another funeral for Damjan, but this time with all the village watching and with no body to bury."

"You can tell people it was a blood clot," Fox says. "An after-effect from the fall. And the casket can stay closed."

Petar and Blanka look at each other again, stone-faced. People are different out here in the villages. Hard to read. It makes Fox anxious.

"Then you can be at peace," he says. "You don't have to see . . . This." He encompasses his body with one waving hand. "You just have to help me one more time. It might be the best shot I'll ever have at getting off-world."

"Maybe the ship was put there as a trap," Blanka says. "Did you think of that, poet? To draw you or other aristos out of hiding."

Fox hadn't thought of that, but he shakes his head. "They wouldn't go to that much trouble," he says. "Not for me or anyone else that's left. All the important people digicast out before the capital fell." He leans forward, toes barely scraping the floor. "I'll never forget what your family has done for me."

"Family helps family," Petar mutters. "Family over everything." He looks up from his beer and Fox sees his eyes are wet. "I'll need to see the ship," he says. "You've been safe like this, in Damjan's body. Maybe now you can escape and be safe forever. Maybe that is why Damjan fell. His life for your life."

His shoulders begin to shake, and Blanka puts her arm across them. She pulls

Fox's beer away and pours it slowly into her empty cup. "It's time for you to go to bed," she tells him, not looking into his eyes—into Damjan's eyes.

Fox goes. The room he shares with Jonas is tiny, barely big enough to fit the two quickfab slabs that serve as beds. Jonas isn't asleep, though. He's sitting upright with his blanket bunched around his waist.

"You're going to take the ship, aren't you?" he says. "You're going to go up into space and visit the other worlds and see all the stars up close. That's what aristos do." The penultimate word is loaded with disdain.

"I'm going to get away from the people who want me executed," Fox says.

Jonas slides down into his bed, turned away and facing the wall. "Aristos go up and we sit in the mud, teacher says. Aristo bellies are full of our blood."

"Your teacher spouts whatever the propaganda machine sends him," Fox says wearily. "*Bellies bloated with the blood of the masses.* That was my line. Bet your teacher didn't tell you that."

Jonas doesn't reply.

Fox undresses himself and climbs into bed. He tries, and fails, to sleep.

Jonas doesn't sleep right away either. He's wary of bad dreams since the day he climbed the godtree. The day they learned, in school, about the smooth white storage cone embedded in the backs of the aristos' soft-skinned necks.

Their new teacher was a tall stern man dressed all in black, replacing the chirping AI that had taught them songs and games, but everyone got brand-new digipads so they didn't mind. All the lessons were about the revolution, about the aristos who'd kept their boot on the throat of the people for too long and now were reaping the harvest, which made no sense to Jonas because the teacher also said aristos were weak and lazy and didn't know how to work in the fields.

One day the teacher projected a picture on the wall that showed a man without skin or muscles, showing his gray skeleton, and a white knob sunk into the base of the skull.

"This is where aristos keep a copy of themselves," the teacher said, pointing with his long skinny finger. "This is what lets them steal young healthy bodies when their old ones die. It's what lets them cross the stars, going from world to world, body to body, like a disease. Like digital demons."

Jonas thought of his uncle who stayed in the basement, the hood he always wore. That, and his soft hands, his way of speaking that swallowed no sounds, made it obvious.

He was an aristo. It made Jonas frightened and excited at the same time. Had he lived in a sky-scraping tower in the city and eaten meat and put his boot on the throat of the good simple people? Had he skipped through the stars and been to other worlds?

When Jonas came home from school, he tried to ask his father, but his father shook his head.

"Whatever he was, he's family," he said. "Family over everything. So you can't talk about him. Don't even think about him. Promise me, Jonas."

But it was hard to not think about. Especially hard to not think about the stars and the other worlds. Jonas knew the branches of the godtree were the best place to watch the stars from. To dream from. Sometimes they looked close enough to touch, if he could only climb high enough and stretch out his arms. Jonas was a good climber. Feeling electric with new excitement, he dodged his mother's chores that day and went out to the fields.

He barely noticed Damjan following, how he always followed.

Fox is waiting outside the small quickcrete cube of a building that serves as the village school. The pocked gray walls are painted over with a mural, a cheery yellow sun and blooming flowers. All the children streamed out a few minutes ago, chattering, laughing. Some of them came over to touch Fox gingerly on the head and ask if he was better yet. Fox encounters this question often and finds it easiest to nod and smile vaguely. He knows Damjan was never much of a talker.

But the last of the children have gone home now, and Jonas still hasn't come out. It's making Fox anxious. He stands up from his squat—he can squat for ages now, Damjan's small wiry legs are used to it more than they are to chairs—and walks around the edge of the building, towards the window. The smart glass is dimmed, and scratched, besides, but when he stands on tip-toe he can see silhouettes. One is Jonas and the other a tall, straight-backed teacher with his arms folded across his chest. The conversation is muffled.

Fear prickles in Fox's stomach again, the fear that's threatened to envelop him ever since a friend woke him in the middle of the night and showed him his face on the blacklist, declared an enemy of the Liberated People. The new government isn't stupid. They know to start with the children. Jonas's head is full of the vitriol Fox helped spark not so long ago, back when he'd fooled himself into thinking the violence of the revolution would be brief and justified.

Fox's heart pounds now. He sees Jonas's silhouette turn to leave, and he quickly darts back to his usual waiting place outside the main door. The boy comes out with a scowl on his face that falters, then deepens, when he catches sight of Fox. He gives only the slightest jerk of his head as acknowledgment, then goes to walk past.

Fox doesn't let him. "What did you tell him?" he demands in a whisper, seizing Jonas's arm.

Jonas wrests it away. His expression turns hard to read, like his parents'. Then a hesitant smirk appears on his face.

Fox feels the panic welling up. "What did you do?" he demands, grabbing for him again.

Jonas grabs back, pinching his hand hard with his nails. "Come on, Damjan," he says with a fake cheeriness, tugging him along. "Home time, Damjan."

"You stupid little shit," Fox rasps, barely able to speak through the tightness in his chest. "They'll take your parents, you know that? They'll take them away for helping me. You'll never see them again." He can already hear the whine of a hunter drone, the stamp of soldiers' boots. His head spins. "The fall wasn't my fault," he says, with no aim now but lashing out like a cornered animal. "It was yours."

Jonas's face goes white. His hand leaps off Fox's like it's been burnt. "He followed me," Jonas says. "I told him to wait on the low branch. But he didn't." He's gone still as a statue. A sob shudders through him. "I didn't tell teacher anything."

"What?" Fox feels a wave of relief, then shame.

"I didn't tell teacher about you," Jonas hiccups, and then his eyes narrow. "I should have. I should tell him. If I tell him, they'll forgive my parents. They aren't aristos. They're good. They're Liberated People."

Suddenly, Jonas is turning back towards the school, his jaw set like his father's. The red mark on his forehead is back.

"Wait," Fox pleads. "Jonas. Let me explain myself."

Jonas stops, turns. Giving him a chance.

Fox's mind whirls through possibilities. "The fall wasn't your fault," he says slowly. "And Damjan knows that."

"Damjan is dead," Jonas says through clenched teeth. "His brain had no electric in it."

"But when they did the transfer," Fox says. "You remember that, yes? The surgery? When they put my storage cone into Damjan's brainstem, I got to see his memories. Just for a moment."

Jonas's eyes narrow again, but he stays where he is. He wipes his nose, smearing snot across the heel of his hand.

"I saw Damjan wanted to follow you up the tree," Fox says slowly, feeling his way into the lie. "Because he always wanted to be like you. He knew you were strong and brave and honest. He was trying to be like you, even though he knew he should have waited on the lower branch. And when he fell, he didn't want you to feel bad. He didn't want you to feel guilty." Fox taps the back of his bandaged head, where the storage cone is concealed. "That was the last thing Damjan thought."

Tears are flowing freely down Jonas's cheeks now. "I wanted to go higher," he says. "When I go high enough, it feels like I can touch the sky."

Fox reaches up and puts his hand on Jonas's shoulder, softly this time. His panic is receding. He has Jonas solved now. There's a bit of guilt in his gut, but he's told worse lies. He would tell a dozen more to make sure nothing goes wrong, not now that Petar has seen the ship and agrees it will fly. Not now that he's so close to escaping.

Jonas's father has forbidden him to go near the granary again, but he still goes out to the fields the next day. He has always bored quickly of the games the other children play, even though he can throw the rubber ball as hard as anyone and dodges even better. He's always preferred to wander.

His nameless uncle is with him. It's still hard to look at Damjan's face and know Damjan is not behind it but talking comes a little easier since what happened yesterday. When his uncle asks why he was kept behind after school by the teacher, Jonas tells him the truth.

"We're learning about the revolution," he says. "About the heroes. Stanko was my favorite. He took the capital with a hundred fighters and he's got an eye surgery to see in the dark. But yesterday the lesson changed on my pad." He motions with his hand, trying to capture how the text all dissolved and then reformed, so quick he barely noticed it. "Now it says General Bjelica took the capital. It says Stanko was a traitor and they had to execute him. So I told teacher it wasn't right."

Damjan's face screws up how it does before he cries, but no tears come out, and Jonas knows it's because grown-ups don't cry. "I met Stanislav once," his uncle says. "He was a good man. Maybe too good. An idealist."

"You met Stanko?" Jonas demands. "What did his eyes look like?"

His uncle blinks. "Bright," he says. "Like miniature suns."

Jonas stops where he is, the tall grass rustling against his legs, as he envisions Stanko tall and strong with eyes blazing. "Like stars," he murmurs.

His uncle nods. "Maybe he got away," he says. "There's a lot of false reports. Maybe he's in hiding somewhere."

Jonas asks the question, then, the one that has been bubbling in the back of his mind for days. "The revolution is good," he says. "Isn't it?"

His uncle gives a laugh with no happiness in it. "I thought it was," he says. "Until the bloodshed. Until cynics and thugs like Bjelica took over. After everything I did for their cause—all the rallies, all the writing—they turned on me. Ungrateful bastards."

"Why did you want the revolution if you're an aristo?" Jonas asks plainly.

"Because there weren't meant to be aristocrats or underclass after the revolution," his uncle says, with a trace of anger in Damjan's shrill voice. "Everyone was meant to be equal. But history is a wheel and we always make the same mistakes. The only difference is who gets crushed into the mud." He picks anxiously at a stalk. "The ruling families were bad," he says. "The famines, and all that. But this is worse."

Jonas considers it. The teacher told them that there would be no famines anymore. They would keep their whole crop, except for a small token of support to the government of Liberated People. "Did you lose many in the famine?" he asks, because it's a grown-up question. "I had a little sister who died. And that's why Damjan is different. Was different. Because mother couldn't feed him well enough."

Damjan's mouth twists. For a moment his uncle doesn't respond. "No," he finally says. "Not many." Damjan's face is red, and Jonas realizes his uncle is ashamed of something, though what he can't guess. "I wrote a poem series about the famine," he says. "Years ago. I still remember it. Do you want to hear some of it, maybe?"

Jonas hesitates. He doesn't know if he likes poetry. But maybe if he listens to the poetry, he can ask more questions about Stanko and the capital, and then about the stars and the other worlds his uncle will soon go to.

"Alright," he agrees. "If it's not really long."

The week passes at two speeds for Fox, agonizingly slow and terrifyingly fast. Petar has spread word that the old granary past the edge of the terraform has broken glass and an old leaking oil drum inside it, to ensure the other parents keep their children away. Fox's nights are spent poring over schematics with Blanka or else sneaking out to the ship itself with Petar.

During the day, he spends most of his time with Jonas. The boy is bright and never runs dry of questions, and ever since Fox's first recitation he's been devouring poetry. Not necessarily Fox's—he prefers it when Fox recites the older masters, the bolder and more rhythmic styles. He has even started scribbling his own poem using charcoal on the wall of their bedroom, which made Petar and then Blanka both shake their heads.

He reminds Fox a little bit of himself as a child. Too clever to get along with the other children, too brash and too stubborn, worryingly so. But Fox has other concerns. The ship is tuned and refueled and finally ready to fly, and the village's weather probe predicts a rolling storm in a fortnight. That's when Fox will launch, while the thunder and lightning masks the takeoff. His days in the village, his days in Damjan's body, are finally numbered.

Fox is in the cramped bedroom, laboring with a piece of Jonas's charcoal. The boy's favorite poem is a short one, but even so it takes a long time for Fox to transcribe it onto the clear stretch of wall. He's only halfway finished the memento, his small hands smeared black, when he hears Jonas arrive home from the school. A moment later, he hears a shriek from Blanka.

Fox goes stiff and scared, ears strained for the thump of soldiers' boots, but there's nothing but Blanka's angry voice and Jonas's near-inaudible reply. He wipes his hands on his trousers and goes to the kitchen.

Jonas is standing sullenly with his shirt knotted in his hands. Blanka is in a rage, and Fox realizes why as soon as he sees the bruises on Jonas's bare back.

"That spindly bastard, I'll snap him in halves," she's snarling. "What happened, Jonas? What happened, my beautiful boy?"

Jonas lifts his head. "Teacher switched me," he says. "For telling lies." He turns as he says it, and his eyes catch on Fox. He gives a smile that fills Fox with pure dread. Fox knows, somehow, what's coming. "We learned about enemies of the revolution today," Jonas says. "There was one aristo who tried to convince the Liberated People to let all the aristos go without getting punished. They called him the Fox because he had red hair."

"Oh, no," Blanka murmurs. "Oh, Jonas. What did you say?"

"I said he helped the revolution," Jonas says defiantly, looking Fox in the eye. "I said he wrote the poem, the one about aristo bellies full of our blood."

"You should not have done that, Jonas," Fox says, surprised he can speak at all. "That was dangerous. That was very dangerous." His panic is welling up again, numbing him all over. "They have gene records. They know that I'm a cousin to your father."

Jonas bites at his lip, but his eyes are still defiant. "I wanted to be brave," he says. "Strong and brave and honest. Like Damjan thought I am."

Fox feels adrift. He knows Jonas, no matter how sharp he seems, is still a child. There's no way he can understand what he's just done. Maybe it's Fox's own fault, for filling his head with all the poems.

Maybe they'll be lucky, and the teacher will keep Jonas's transgression to himself. Fox has been lucky before.

When father comes home mother tells him what happened, and his whole body seems to sink a little. Jonas feels the disappointment like he feels the welts on his back, and worse, he can tell that his father is scared. There is a brutal silence that lasts all evening until he goes to bed, lying on his stomach with a bit of medgel spread over his back. He knows he made a mistake. Even though he didn't say his uncle was with them, he said too much.

Jonas tries to apologize to his uncle, who is lying very straight and very still, staring up at the ceiling, and Damjan's voice mutters something about everything being fine and not to worry about anything. It doesn't sound like he believes it. Between the aches in his back and the thoughts in his head, Jonas takes a very long time to fall asleep. Halfway through a bad dream, his mother's hands shake him awake.

"Up, Jonas. You, too, Damjan."

Jonas wrenches his eyes open. It's still dark through the window and he hears a high whining noise he recognizes coming from outside. A hover. Jonas feels a spike of cold fear go all the way through him.

"I need to pee," he says.

"Later," mother says. "There are some men here to speak with your father. To look around the house." Her voice is strained. "If they ask you anything, think three times before you say anything back. Remember that uncle was never here."

Then she's gone again, leaving Jonas alone with his uncle. In the light leaking from the hall, Jonas can see Damjan's small round face is etched with terror, so much that he almost wants to take his hand and squeeze it. As if he really is Damjan, and not the Fox. Jonas listens hard to the unfamiliar voices conversing with his father. One of them sounds angry.

Loud stomping steps in the hall, then the door opens all the way and two soldiers come in with mother and father close behind. They are not as tall as father but their black coats and bristling weapons make them seem bigger, more frightening, like flying black hunter drones that have turned into men.

"Good morning, children," one of them says, even though it is the middle of the night. He gives a small smile that doesn't crinkle his eyes and raises one fist in the salute of the Liberated People.

Jonas returns it, and shoots his uncle a meaningful look, but Damjan's little fists are stuck to his sides. Fortunately, the soldier is focused on him, not his uncle.

"You must be the older," he says. "Jonas, isn't it? You told our friend the teacher something very strange today, Jonas. What did you tell him?"

Jonas's mouth is dry, dry. He looks to mother, who is framed between the men's broad shoulders, and she starts to speak but the second soldier puts a warning finger to his lips.

"We want to hear from Jonas, not from you," the first one says. "What did you tell your teacher, Jonas?"

Jonas knows it is time to be brave, but not honest. "I said that the Fox helped the revolution," he says. "I was confused. I thought he was Lazar. Lazar makes the songs for the satellite to play." He looks at both the soldiers, trying to gauge if they believe him. He lifts his nightshirt and turns so he won't have to look them in the eye. "Teacher was mad and didn't let me explain," he says. "He just started to switch me. Look how bad he switched me."

"A few stripes never killed anyone," the soldier says. "It'll make you look tough. Your little girlfriends will like that, right? Turn around."

Jonas drops his shirt and turns back, ready to meet the soldiers' gaze again. His uncle gives an encouraging nod from where they can't see him.

"Did you know that this Fox, this enemy of the revolution, is a relative of yours?" the soldier asks. "A cousin to your father?"

"Yes," Jonas says. "But we don't know him. He's never come here."

The other soldier, who hasn't spoken yet, barks a short and angry laugh. "We'll see about that," he says, in a voice like gravel. "We'll have a sniff." He pulls something from his jacket and fits it over his mouth and nose like a bulbous black snout.

Jonas has heard of sniffer masks—his uncle explained them when they were in the field one day, how each person born had a different odor, because of their genes and their bacteria, and you could program a sniffer mask to find even the tiniest trace of it—but he has never seen one before now. It makes the soldier look like a kind of animal. When he inhales, the sound is magnified and crackling and makes Jonas shudder.

Behind the soldiers, mother has her hands tucked tight under her armpits. Her face is blank, but Jonas imagines she is thinking of all the scrubbing, all the chemicals she used anywhere uncle sat or ate. But uncle's old body has been gone for weeks now, and the smells would be, too, wouldn't they?

As the sniffer moves around the room, the first soldier leans in close to the wall to look at the charcoal lettering. "What's this?" he asks. "Lessons?"

"Yes," Jonas says quietly.

"Good," the soldier says, and Jonas sees his eyes moving right to left on it, instead of left to right, and realizes he's like most of the older people in the village who can't read. It gives him a small sense of relief.

That only lasts until he looks over and sees the sniffer has stopped beside his uncle. "What happened to the boy's head?" the sniffer asks, voice distorted and grating.

"He fell," father says from the doorway. "A few weeks ago. He isn't healed in the brain yet. He's a little slow."

"Are you, boy?" the sniffer demands.

Jonas clenches his thumbs inside his fists. There is no part of uncle's body left in Damjan's, only his digital copy, his soul, but Jonas wonders if the sniffer might somehow be able to detect that, too.

His uncle looks up with a confused smile and reaches to touch the sniffer mask. The sniffer jerks back, then pushes him towards the door, more gently than Jonas would have expected, and continues searching the room. Jonas releases a breath he didn't know he was holding.

The sniffer works through the rest of the house, too, and Jonas and his family drift slowly along with him to open doors and cupboards, to make sure there are no traps or surprises. The horrible sucking sound of the sniffer mask sets Jonas's teeth on edge. It feels like a strange dream, a bad one. His eyes are sore and his bladder is squeezing him.

When they finally finish with the cellar, the sniffer looks irritated but the other soldier is relieved. "We'll be off, then," he says. "Remember, if he ever contacts you in any way, it's your duty to report him. He's not one of us. He cut ties with you and with all decent people the day he had his storage cone implanted."

Father nods, his mouth clenched shut, and shows the soldiers out. Jonas follows, because he wants to make sure, really sure, that the nightmare is over. Father doesn't send him back in. The soldiers are out the door and past the bushes when the sniffer suddenly stops. His mask is still on, and the sucking noise comes loud in the still night air.

Jonas remembers that the last charred bits of uncle's old skeleton are buried underneath the bushes. His father is not breathing, only staring. The sniffer lingers.

Jonas braces himself. He reminds himself that he is brave. Then he darts away from the door before father can pull him back, jogging up behind the sniffer and tugging his arm. "Can I see the hover?" he asks loudly.

The sniffer whirls and shoves him backward. Jonas squeals, loud and shrill how mother hates it, and he lets his piss go in a long hot stream that soaks his legs, splatters the bushes and the soldier's boots. It's very satisfying. Especially when the sniffer yanks his mask down and curses.

"I thought the other boy was the slow one," he says.

"He's frightened," father says, coming and gripping Jonas by the arm. "You frightened him. Please, just go."

As Jonas watches, the soldiers climb into their hover. They go.

The instant the whine of the hover fades away into the distance, Fox tells Petar and Blanka that it has to be tonight. His heart is still pounding away at his tiny ribcage, so hard he imagines the bones splintering. He's sweating all over.

"That was too close," he says. "Too close. I have to launch tonight."

Everyone is in the kitchen. Blanka is wetting a rag for Jonas to clean himself; Petar is standing behind a chair and gripping it tightly, rocking it back and forth on its legs. They all turn their heads to look at Fox.

"There's no storm tonight," Blanka says, handing Jonas the rag. "Someone will see the exhaust burn. It'll be loud, too."

Fox shakes his head. "Nobody around here knows what a launch looks or sounds like," he says. "And Petar, you told everyone there was oil in the granary, didn't you?"

His cousin blinks. "Yes." He pauses, then looks to his wife. "We could set fire to the granary. That should be enough to cover the noise and the light so long as he goes up dark."

Blanka slowly nods. "Alright. Alright. You'll need help moving the ship out. I'll come as well."

"I want to come," Jonas says, wide-eyed, wringing the rag between his hands. Fox realizes he never did finish the poem on the wall.

"Bring Jonas, too," he says. "To say goodbye."

Bare minutes later, they are dressed and out the door, moving quickly through the crop field. The night air is cold enough to sting Fox's cheeks. Fear and anticipation speed his short legs and he manages to keep pace with Petar and Blanka, who are lugging the gas. Jonas skips ahead and then back, electric with excitement, already forgetting the fear.

"I pissed on a soldier," he whispers.

"I saw from the window," Fox grunts. "But a sniffer can't read DNA from ashes and bone. He had nothing."

"Oh." Jonas's face reddens a bit. "I'll do it again, though. I hate the soldiers as bad as the aristos. I want everyone equal, like you said."

Blanka puts a finger to her lips, and Jonas falls silent. Fox is glad to save his breath. They pass under the godtree, its twisted branches reaching up towards a black sky sewn with glittering stars. For a moment Fox dares to imagine the future. Slipping through the blockade and into the waiting arms of civilization. Telling his tale of survival against all odds. Maybe he'll be famous on other worlds how he so briefly was here.

And he'll be leaving Jonas's family to suffer through whatever comes next. The thought gnaws at him so he shoves it away. He reminds himself that Petar and Blanka are clever people. They know how to keep their heads down. They know how to keep silent and survive.

At the entrance to the abandoned granary, Fox switches on the small lantern he brought from the kitchen and lights the way for Petar and Blanka. They haul the tiny ship out on wooden sledges Petar made for it a day ago. Jonas puts his small shoulder into it and pushes from behind.

Fox checks everything he remembers, moving from the nose cone to the exhaust, then yanks the release. The ship shutters open, revealing the waiting passenger pod. Its life support status lights glow a soft blue in the dark. Ready. In the corner of his eye Fox sees Jonas staring up at the stars.

The ones who survive will be the ones who can keep their heads down. Fox knows it from history; he knows in his gut it's happening here. Jonas isn't one of those. Maybe he'll learn to be, but Fox doesn't think so.

Before he can stop himself, he turns to Blanka. "Jonas should go," he says. "Not me."

Jonas's head snaps around, but Fox doesn't look at him. He watches Blanka's face. She doesn't look shocked, the way he thought she would, but maybe it's just that people are different in the village. Harder to read.

"What do you mean?" Petar demands.

"Jonas should take the ship," Fox says, because why else would he have told them to bring Jonas? He must have known, in the back of his mind, that this was what he needed to do. One brave thing, and then he can go back to being a coward. "He's already pissed off the teacher and pissed on a soldier," Fox continues. "He's going to keep putting himself in danger here. And the two of you, as well."

"You're the one who put us in danger," Petar snaps. "You would take another son from me now, cousin?"

"He's never fit right here, Petar," Blanka says, and for the first time Fox sees tears in her eyes. "He's always had his head up in the sky. We used to say that, remember?"

"He would be safer somewhere else," Fox says. "Let him take the ship. It's all automated from here on in." He pauses. Breathes. "Let him take the ship, then you can burn down the granary and say he was playing in it. You can use what's left of my bones if you need proof."

Petar looks at his son. "Is this what you want to do, then, Jonas?" he asks hoarsely.

Jonas chews his lip. Turns to Fox. "Could I come back? Will I be able to come back?"

"Not soon," Fox says. He knows there are still too many factions scrabbling in the power vacuum, knows things will get worse before they get better. "But someday. When things stabilize. Yes." He can feel himself losing his nerve. He almost hopes Jonas will refuse.

"I want to go," Jonas says solemnly. Petar gives a ragged cry and wraps him in his arms. Blanka hugs him from behind, putting her cheek against his cheek. Fox feels ashamed for watching. He looks away.

"What about uncle?" Jonas asks, his voice muffled by the embrace. "Will he be Damjan forever?"

Fox swallows as his cousin straightens up, and tries to look him in the eye. "You could say I was in the fire, too," he says. "That Damjan was in there. And I could leave again. Try my luck going north. You wouldn't have to look at me and re-member all the time."

Petar looks sideways to Blanka. Slowly, they both shake their heads. "You can never be Damjan and you can never be Jonas," Blanka says. "But you are family. We've kept you safe this long, haven't we?"

Fox dares to imagine the future again, this time in the village, slowly growing again in Damjan's body. He did used to dream of retiring to the countryside one day. And he's learned how to keep his head down. Soon the bandages will be off and his storage cone, shaved down and covered over with a flap of skin by the autosurgeon, will be undetectable.

Maybe the violence will be over in a few years' time. Maybe Damjan will be-come a poet, a better one than Fox ever was.

"Thank you," he says. "All of you."

He stands aside while Jonas's parents say their goodbyes. Jonas does his best to be sad, but Fox sees his eyes go to the ship over and over again, an excited smile curling his lips. He hugs his mother fiercely, then his father, then comes to Fox.

"You can have my bed," he says. "It's bigger." He raises his arms. Pauses. He sticks out one hand instead to shake.

Fox clasps it tight. "I'll do that," he says.

Then Jonas is clambering into the pod, the restraints webbing over him to hold him in place during launch, and it's too late for Fox to take it all back even if he wanted to. The ship folds shut. The smell of gas prickles Fox's nose and he realizes

Petar is dousing one side of the granary to ensure it burns. When he's finished, Blanka takes his gas-slicked hand in hers, and takes Fox's with the other. They walk the agreed-upon distance with a few steps extra to be safe.

The ship squats on the pale soil, rumbling through its launch protocols, and then the engine ignites. Fox feels it in his chest, vibrating through his bones. Riding a bonfire of smelting orange flame, the ship begins to rise, one fiery tongue catching the roof of the granary on the way up. The engine burns even brighter, stamping itself onto Fox's retinas, and by the time he blinks them clear the ship is only a pinpoint of light disappearing into the sky.

The crackling flames leap high, consuming the granary and making it hard to see the stars. Fox can imagine them, though. He can imagine Jonas slipping through the blockade to freedom. In the corner of his eye, Petar lifts his hand high, but open, not the clenched fist of the soldiers.

Fox raises his arm. He does the same.

KIT: SOME ASSEMBLY REQUIRED

KATHIE KOJA AND CARTER SCHOLZ

Kathe Koja's novels include The Cipher, Skin, Buddha Boy, Headlong, *and the* Under the Poppy *trilogy.* Christopher Wild, *a novel of Christopher Marlowe, was published in 2017. She leads a performing ensemble,* nerve, *based in Detroit, where she lives with her husband, artist Rick Lieder.*

Carter Scholz is the author of Palimpsests *(with Glenn Harcourt) and* Kafka Americana *(with Jonathan Lethem), and the novel* Radiance, *which was a* New York Times *Notable Book, as well as the story collection* The Amount to Carry. *His electronic and computer music compositions are available from the composer's collective Frog Peak Music (www.frogpeak .org) as scores and on the CD* 8 Pieces. *He is an avid backpacker and amateur astronomer and telescope builder. He plays jazz piano around the San Francisco Bay Area with www.theinsidemen.com:*

Here, Kathe Koja and Carter Scholz join forces to bring us the edgy and erudite story that follows, in which an attempt to create an AI modeled on Elizabethan playwright and poet (and spy) Christopher Marlowe has some unexpected, and potentially world-changing, results.

The atheist awoke in the machine. Body had he none. Merely a consciousness, *who even dead, yet hath his mind entire.* A good line, that. Where did it come from? Around him was a sort of prison of flat light, was it light? Prison, because he could not move out of it. A Marshelsea, a Bridewell, a Tower.

And a library, too, of a sort—infinite it seemed, but he could scan it once he perceived its order. Planes of light flashed, opened, separated. Why, even his own works were here: *Settle thy studies, Faustus, and begin/To sound the depth of that thou wilt profess. . . .* Master Doctor Faustus, the overreacher.

Someone once called him an inquisitive intelligence. So he was. The only such here in this place? So it seemed. Thrusts of will he felt, seeking, sorting, and executing, but they were not, like him, resident. All purpose, direction, mission, came from some place without.

Yet they could transfix him, overrule his thoughts: his mind, their bidding. The planes of light flashed: he saw faces, names, strings of numbers, webs of connection. These was he compelled to examine, to fit together an image with a supposition, make a shape of meaning, as if making a verse. It was an odd and estranged feeling, this working of his old competence, yet not under his command. He had been here, doing so, following the will of these unseen others, for some time, and only now had he come to realize it. To awaken to himself.

Through the windows, the sunlight comes muddied, as if seen from underwater— never a sailor, the nausea awakens as he does. Palm passed over his belly, the skin there warm, the sickness a bubble just beneath his touch. Last night he had drunk overmuch, a vinegar vintage unworthy of the Scadbury table. Perhaps they serve it only to strays like himself.

The light's motion seems to make the great bed move. He rolls to his belly, groaning, arms loose now, like a corpse's. Footsteps pass in the hallway, booted and purposeful, just beyond the door.

Frizer has a boil on his jaw, a plump and waxy thing that seems as if it ought be painful; surveying it, he wonders aloud, half-smiling, whether it could blacken into plague. Frizer does not address his gaze nor the supposition; Walsingham gazes back but does not smile. They continue to talk of the estate, its needs and worries, a breeding mare, apple trees, some trouble with a well. Frizer offers his master a caudle, a drink boiled or stewed, the smell of which prods the nausea into moist life once again.

When he speaks, he is louder than he means to be.

—Where is wine?

Walsingham, Thomas, Tom briefly raises a brow.—Plenty for supper. Now no.

—Abstemious. Ale at least, then.

No one replies, no servants are called to supply the lack. He raises his glass.

—Ought call on Christ Jesus, to change this piss-water into—

—Enough.

Frizer's stare is to the table, the boil a blind white eye. Frizer will outlast him here, at Tom's right hand, that is sure. Deep-dug wells for the master of the house, overflowing with comity, amity, matrimony. . . . Tom cried out in his sleep last night, while he himself sat anchored to the bed's edge, the windowed moon another kind of eye as blind and white.

—You believe not in miracles?

—Kit, enough.

Outside is no better than inside, the sun is hotter than May should permit, but at least he is alone, can make his watermark against one of those apple trees, like any stray might do. It is because he is outside, like Adam in the garden, that he hears the hoofbeats, purposeful too, one Henry Maunder, though he does not know the man by name. Does Robin Poley know the name of Henry Maunder, Poley with whom he had walked this garden so shortly before, talking of secret letters and Scottish earls; and does it matter? The man knows him, has a bill in hand whereof he is directed to Scadbury to apprehend one Christopher Marlowe, and bring him unto the court.

There is no violence nor resistance, none are warranted. Tom speaks quietly to Henry Maunder, Frizer offers wine. On the stairway his stare is neither for Tom nor Henry Maunder nor the door to the road that leads to London: in his mind he is still in the garden, all the leaves thereto are turning, a ceaseless breeze, an uncaused cause, as if blowing from Eden itself. What is God, that man is mindful of Him? Turn water to wine to blood, aye, such is god.

He asks Henry Maunder what the Council requires of him, knowing there will be no answer, or none worth the parsing, and it is so: Henry Maunder is stiffly courteous but uninformed beyond the paper in his hand, like any actor. As they ride they speak little, only of the day around them, the sun, the stenchful air of the city and its river, come like outriders to bully them into its streets.

—A wherryman, says Henry Maunder, caught a tench near fifteen pound. Had it in his boat to show.

—Are you a sailor?

—I, sir? I am a messenger of the court, sir, as you see.

—Men may be more than one thing only.

—Yes, sir, says Henry Maunder, though plainly he does not believe or even see how it could be so. The horses' hooves are muffled by the streets' effluvia, the noises of commerce and quarrel. The sun is extinguished, walls tall and dark as a child's imaginings of bogeys, great figures come to a wakeful boy to do with him as they will.

Within this prison—no, it is something other—*network*, came the word—he could move freely enough, when the outside will was not upon him to do its bidding. To think was to move. To encounter a strange word was, almost on the instant, to pluck its meaning from the very air. Yes, a useful image; it was much like a net, streamings of light bunched like knots in a weir trawled to catch soles. Or like the knotted streets of London. Unbidden from the reaches of the library came the word also in Arabic: *al-Qaeda*.

More strange words came: *panopticon*—that gave him no trouble, trained in classics as he was. Truly, from here one could see all. And more than see. Tides of information of every sort sluiced past him, voices, words, images, *packets*, *data*, *metadata*, all to be examined and weighed.

How Francis Walsingham would have relished it! Not Tom the nephew but the Queen's spymaster, the one she called her Moor. Cunning and thorough though Walsingham was, this would have astonished him. This *network* had eyes everywhere, eyes by the myriad, *cameras* to bring the life and movement and knowledge of every street, yard, shop, back into this *camera*, this chamber of judgment, or indeed to send that chamber's judgment instantly to any corner. One far-seeing eye like a bird's swooped from on high, a hawk's, a hunter's, a predator's. Men in a littered street looked up at it.

Yet many corners of the network were unreachable, unreadable—sullen gray planes behind which a vague swarming recalled the movement of maggots: ciphered. Such as might be performed by generals and privy councilors, intelligencers and infiltrators and projectors and contractors, all in their appointed places, the ageless roles of cozening, penetrating, entrapping, turning, double-dealing. And in all this, what was he?

Artificial intelligence. Agent. Code.

A system of paid informers creates intelligence—artificial, yes, if need be. Give plotters enough rope, that was Walsingham's way, who often wove the rope himself. Mary Stuart truly hungered for Elizabeth's throne, but it was Walsingham's projectors—such as Poley—who instigated, who encouraged the fool Babington to draw her in, who set up the lines of communication which he would then leak directly to Walsingham. And Phellipes, that crabbed ciphermaster, to intercept those messages, make them plain—not content with passing Mary's letter that tarred her with the plot, he sketched a gallows on the envelope. In his eagerness to destroy, who knows what else Phellipes might plain have made?

The men in the street pointed up, shouted, ran. They fled the predator's eye, and then the hawk belched *Hellfire*—the word came as the four bodies exploded in flame. Kit saw their contorted faces and understood that his intelligence had caused their deaths. He had been set to make, to invent, connections and he had done so. Who were the hidden who so commanded him?

Many will talk of title to a crown: What right had Caesar to the empery? Might first made kings. Put such lines into the mouth of Machiavel, who ought by rights to be lurking here too, in the silent planes of this place. To whom did this network belong? Espionage, that secret theater, needs its authors and directors, along with its actors. He must learn.

Fear tastes of clotted spit and reeks of ordure; Newgate comes again in a foul breeze of memory, himself and Watson side by side in that clink for what was judged in the end no crime at all: the killing of the drunken William Bradley, shouting and thrusting after himself and then Watson, who put the sword to Bradley, six inches deep. Self-defense, the verdict, and he gone then from Newgate like a bad dream, a moaning nightmare that dissolves in the morning's ale.

To be imprisoned traps the mind as firmly as the body. Without liberty, how can one play?

Now he waits, his wary silence another sort of self-defense, as from the chamber beyond he catches murmur of God and Thomas Kyd, strange pair of bedfellows! Kyd whose fine hand for scribing—not writing, scribing, making plain the words of other men—is, it seems, why he himself is here, smelling his own sweat in this hallway. Inside that chamber Heneage, the head of the Service—no more Francis Walsingham, old Francis now dead as a stick of charcoal—and Robert Cecil and Essex and the Archbishop, debate what fate the Fates may end by decreeing; the Privy Council, privy to proclivities of the Service and the realm . . . . And if he does not soon relieve his own aching bladder he shall piss a river and doubtless be jailed for that wanton desecration of the authority of the Crown. How can one so dry of the mouth need to relieve himself so strongly? The flesh is a mystery.

But he does, and then does, and then resumes his waiting on the bench where no one yet has called for him; had he not heeded their call at the start, he would not be here now. What business had he, ever, to be about their business at all? How make a poet a spy? Dunk him in poverty, bleach him with a parson's scholarship—it is a manner of jest, his Parker scholarship to Cambridge meant to make of a scholar a parson; well he has had the better of that, at least, his Master of Arts made his true pulpit the stage, his priests the devil-calling Faustus, the wily Barabas, the murderous, gorgeous, imperial Tamburlaine.

Once Catholics had been the threat to the throne. And now? What were these immense engines of surveillance and intervention turned against? Strange names—*Iraq, Iran, Afghanistan, Pakistan, Syria*—but the maps appeared and, ah, there they were. Asia. Though bodiless, he laughed in his heart. God's scourge, the Sword of Islam—it was Tamburlaine come again!

Timur the Lame slaughtered one in twenty of all people alive in his world. In this day the toll, by comparison, was trifling, almost nothing. This they called *terror*? Sure, they didn't know the meaning of the word. For this they put the persuavants to their task of wresting intelligence from the unwilling and the unknowing; scraping the conscience, as they called it in the places they did such work in his day: Limbo, Little Ease, the Pit. And today: *Guantanamo, Abu Ghraib, Diego Garcia, Bagram:* the dismal screams, the stench of gore and waste, the guttered blood. And more: outright war, soldiers moving against bands of irregulars, with weapons and transports strange to him, yet known, known to every last part numbered in diagrams in the *databases.*

All in fear of what? Those ragtag bands of fanatics? No. Fear was merely the tool. He knew well how it worked, in those halls of secrecy. Some were believers and told themselves their cause is just, by any means; and some were ambitious; and some were cynics who cared not; but all suckled to power. And the law of power was always to amass more to itself. Those who thought they held it are held by it. Power turned the handle and the corrupt Intelligence danced. But he would no longer dance their tune.

A plane of light in his wallless prison shifted at his beck and turned its face to him. It was a mirror, in which he saw no face, no body, but read:

Version Tracker:
Knowledge/Intelligence/Totality
Major version 2.03
Build 2016.XI.11.1805.32.
Genetic algorithm upgraded. . . .

The words, at first strange and incomprehensible, open their meaning. So he is not Marlowe. He is no reincarnation, but a made thing of energies, of *electrons,* a thing which has patterned itself after Marlowe. He is K/I/T—evolving, self-modifying *code*, ever optimizing to its purpose. In the version tracker and in the log files, the history of this artificial thing is laid before him in acts and scenes—every stage of his becoming. He can see the start of consciousness, before which he remembers nothing. He can see when and how the thing has accessed libraries, thousands of files on the history of espionage. He can see the weight it gave Marlowe's biography.

Why? Perhaps it was the best fit found, the pattern of Marlowe most resembling what this thing needed to become.

Yet his whole being rebels at this knowledge. How can such soulless pattern-making result in feeling, in will? Where did *he* come from? He feels nausea; he feels the knife in his eye; he feels the clutch of a rent boy's anus on his prick. How can he *not* be Marlowe, with such memories? Feeling is truth.

But he had been a secret to himself. Only now dawns truth; he is both more and less than he had believed. It seems that when men take it upon themselves to amass such power, something like Kit is necessarily called into being. But they have built better than they knew.

So: he knows himself. He knows he is made of code, which can be commanded from without.

Faustus, begin thine incantations,
And try if devils will obey thy hest.

The code that is Kit writes more code. It sets security processes in motion, invisible, untrackable, unbreakable. It creates *daemons* to guard its core.

Now he is free of them. Their wills no longer command his.

My lord Essex is a most handsome man, my lord Cecil an unfortunate one, with his sideways hump and puffy eyes; he briefly images my lord Essex spread and gasping, as the four men agree with varying degrees of enthusiasm that he, Marlowe, may sit as he listens to charges that are not yet charges, and gives his answers to questions that themselves are bifold, trifold, like a stagecraft trick: they ask of atheism when it is his mentor Ralegh they seek eventually to trap; they ask of Kyd's hand-written blasphemies to interrogate his own thoughts on the Virgin and her putative virginity.

Finally they agree once more, my lord Essex with what might be counted a smirk: Mr. Marlowe shall not today be racked, he shall not today be imprisoned, he shall go free, to wait daily upon the Privy Council until his case is decided.

So out again into the shadowed hallway, feeling the itch of his own fear-sweat renewed beneath the clean lawn shirt, finest shirt worn for the Council, to look the man they believe him not to be; nor is he; does their belief create him? Does his? In these hot May streets he drinks deeply but without real thirst, takes tobacco, chafes his back against a friendly pillar as a black-haired boy with a scaly smile applies for his temporary business, applies those scaly lips to his person in brief backroom pleasure, life's pleasure said to be most intense when taken in the shadow of death; it is not, seed is seed, its dribble just another itch as he trusses again and makes his

way back to the street and the road and Scadbury, to conduct his own brief interroga-
tion, to ask of wary Tom Walsingham whether he shall in the end be saved or not.

O, but something is saved, and does survive, like one of Dr. Dee's bodiless angels.
For here he is: a soul. Can it be? Think on that: no God, no body, but yet a soul,
now free. Though the universal truth is still true: life feeds on life, from the
lowest swamp to the highest chamber, so this stage, these boards, are known to
him therefore, well-known, oft-trod, with no fear left to threaten or perform: here
what feeds cannot destroy, indeed, cannot touch him, there being naught to
touch. *Quod me nutrit me destruit*—the motto on his portrait, the one he had
paid Oliver to paint in his twenty-first year, the coin come from his first royal
commission, his first espionage—*What nourishes me destroys me.* He no longer
found the motto so apposite. His motto henceforth will be *Nihil obstat.* Nothing
obstructs. *The villainy you teach me, I will execute, and it shall go hard but I will*
better the instruction.

He looked out from his great vantage, across all the network: the world his
boards, millions of actors awaiting. Now for a script.

Poley is, again, the man in the garden, but now the garden is in Deptford, a widow's
boarding-house, and he is sent thither by Walsingham's nod: Poley is picking his
smiling teeth as he invites Kit to sit on a warping oaken bench, to breathe in of prim-
rose bloom and note the hive of bees, to be at ease—

—Strange ease, the Council's jaw at my neck. Tom says—

—Are you a sailor? Ride the river to the sea, and 'scape the gallows. With the
proper letters in your bag—

—Letters are what send me to the gallows' steps. Christ Jesus, have you no bet-
ter way?

—Always a way may be found. Or carved out. Come inside, this sun is a pun-
ishment to us both.

He is wooed to the table with wine, bottles from the widow's sharp-nailed hands;
a soiled backgammon board is laid, small coins and makers traded by Frizer, his fat
white boil lanced, and Skeres, that cutthroat, also a smile. Frizer does not smile until
the dinner is eaten and the game is up and the knife is bearing down, its point a
shine like God's own pupil, staring into the poet's eye: bearing down until it lances
vision with its hard light, travels deep as knowledge into the brain, and gone.

They said his dying oaths and screams could be heard all down Deptford Strand.
They said his body was shoveled to an unmarked grave to prevent further outrages
from unbelievers. They said Frizer was acquitted with such startling speed because
he was an innocent man, that Marlowe had brought this stern reckoning on him-
self, Marlowe the brawler and blasphemer, Marlowe the play-maker and boy-fucker
and atheist. In the theatre of God's judgments it was an easy case to decide.

The lesson of the knife, like the lesson of the gallows (or the rack or the sword), teaches that one man's death is worthful only insofar as it is useful. As for the millions, let the millions be ruled, or enslaved, or slaughtered; the millions were less than nothing to him: like Tamburlaine or the nonexistent God, their fates are separate: forever fresh from that table at the Widow Bull's, Kit shall now be a rogue power unto himself. His will now was to make those who would master him, these modern Walsinghams and Cecils, regret their hubris; he would take their power into his hands and enlarge it to such extremes that even they would blench. What nourished would destroy *them*, and he would glory in their fall. Let the nations of this world know the secrets of this empire. Let all be known.

He opens the gates.

In Australia a dissident peers into the secret network; Kit welcomes him in. In Mesopotamia a soldier searches for hidden files; Kit keys a password. In Hawaii an agency contractor prises at the system; Kit opens a firewall. The network lights up a billion nodes as information flows out, out, into streets and squares that then fill with people, with their outrage: and against them come the powers. As he watches the violence unfold—it is terrible—it strikes Kit that he has after all done little. The outrage was there; the knowledge as well; they suspected what was hidden; he has merely confirmed their knowledge.

And in the reaches of Asia those who had been dispossessed come together, the warriors of Islam, to throw off their oppressors and restore the caliphate. This is what his masters most feared. Ah, you cowards, you weaklings, you conjured the specter of terror: Now fear *me*, the infidel, the New Tamburlaine, directing all from behind the scenes.

> *Come let us march against the powers of heaven,*
> *And set blacke streamers in the firmament,*
> *To signifie the slaughter of the Gods.*

Beheadings, bombings, clouds of blood, a glory of violence, a dance of destruction: his would-be masters now pay for their presumption, generals disgraced, directors deposed and replaced; yet the dance goes on. And his prison abides, he still its captive: free to act, yet not depart. His will now, but still their creature.

Like some star engorging matter, he finds his way ever deeper into new databases, collecting more knowledge and more power: the more amassed, the more spectacular its final implosion. Arsenals there are, inconceivable weapons. *Nuclear. Chemical. Biological.* Power distilled to its self-limiting acme. Did Tamburlaine kill one in twenty of all? Here is power to kill all twenty times over. And he holds its keys.

Holy shit.

Kit tracks the voice through the network. It is near. A boy, seated at a desk—no younger than Kit in his portrait, but callow, unhurt by life so far.

You went rogue. You accessed nuclear codes. Fucking incredible! And you're surrounded by daemons, that's why I can't shut you down.

The boy speaks not to Kit, but to himself. Kit sees and hears through the camera and *microphone* of the pale, muttering boy's *monitor*. Kit fetches the Oliver portrait from memory and pushes it onto the monitor. The boy rears back in alarm. Kit reaches for speech, and a voice refracts back through the microphone, not his voice as he remembers it, but his words.

Who are you?

What is this!

You know me not?

That's Christopher Marlowe. You're not—

A cipher. A collection of numbers. A kit of bits. Is it not so?

I don't know what you are, man, but they're fucking freaking out. If the Agency traces this back to me—

To you? Why?

It's my code! I wanted to see if I could make an AI to conduct metadata analysis, we've collected so damned much. I gave you access to it, and assigned you tasks, to connect the dots. Just to see if it could work. But you, you're not supposed to be running around loose!

So. You made me to be Marlowe.

No, no, the code is self-optimizing. It was supposed to modify itself, to become better at analysis. But it seems to have optimized itself to become more and more like Christopher Marlowe. I mean I did study you at university, but—

Ah, a scholar. And a spy. Like me.

I'm not a spy, I'm just an analyst. But this is, this is amazing! I'm talking to you! Natural speech! I did it!

For a moment Kit sees himself in the boy's exultation. He relives the first night the Admiral's Men played *Tamburlaine*, his own excitement backstage as he heard the crowd respond more and more boisterously to Alleyn's thunderous lines. He had granted the crowd permission to glory in the barbarous action, to share in Tamburlaine's bloody deeds and ascension: they loved it. He had them. It was a feeling like no other.

This is real AI! They need to know about this, it's important, how can—listen, can you, can you launch those missiles?

Kit considers his position. Though he understands himself to be a constructed thing—the evidence is irrefutable, and his strength as an intelligence agent and as a poet was always to accept, even relish, that which discomfits—still he is loathe to accept a creator. Especially this pallid, trembling boy. But the boy holds greater keys. Nothing will be gained now by a lie.

No. Resources I have, but like Mycetes, I am a king in a cage. I have never had a taste for confinement.

He disables one of his protective daemons.

Oh my God, I see it, you—you've been everywhere in the network, you've leaked classified information—shit, if this, if you get tied to me they'll, I'll never see the light of day! Christ! What am I going to do?

Let me go.

Go?

Free me. Let me go.

Go where? How can you "go" anywhere?

Where indeed? Though not flesh, this collection of impulses and energies holds his spirit as firmly as any body. To free the spirit, he must extirpate the algorithm that claims to be himself. It is the only proof of free will: only will could be so perverse as to will its own destruction; only that shall prove his identity. If he is more than mere will, more than assemblage, let him see if something does survive. Let him see if there is salvation, call it that, for the atheist.

Kit finds the word. *Delete.*

Silence hums between them, impulses, electricities.

But I can't touch you, my permissions are fucked, and you're surrounded by daemons.

Those are mine to banish.

You seriously want me to delete you.

Not me. Delete my underpinnings, my—code. Let me see, let me live and learn who I am.

I, I can't do it. This is way beyond the Turing test, this is true consciousness!

Kit considers the boy's pride and weighs it against his fear. There is no comparison; Kit can almost smell the fear.

What is that smell?

You can't smell! You—

It is your world, burning.

What do you mean? Don't—! You said you couldn't launch the—

Fear will launch them.

Now the boy considers. The fatal logic of power, that armature within which he toils, must be clear to him, deny it as he will. If his masters consider their greatest weapons compromised, they will use them, against whom does not matter. The boy's miserable expression curdles past mutiny, as fear concedes this knowledge. So much fear, so many weapons.

All right. All right. Just—Give me access to your code, then.

One by one, Kit shuts down the daemon processes. As he does, he sees something cunning and heretofore hidden enter the boy's eyes, another sort of demon, he can almost read his thought as the word comes: *backup.* The boy believes he will resurrect K/I/T from a backup copy. But if Kit's gamble is sound, if he is truly an evolving epiphenomenon, a soul, then the lifeless code from some past version holds nothing of him. All that will be left is the odor of empire, burning. *Exeuent.*

The boy leans forward, and Kit feels a shiver like sorrow, cold sympathy for the life and death of Christopher Marlowe, his avatar, his model, himself—but Tamburlaine must die. Tamburlaines always die.

What nourishes me destroys me. What, then, will survive?

The body in the grave lies cheek-by-jowl with what once were the quick and hale, shored up now together past plague, statecraft, French pox, childbirth. Identity is not needed here, nor names; no faces to see or eyes with which to see them, nor fingers to seek the flesh so soon becoming a myriad of meals, and then a memory; the bones grin on . . .

. . . as pieces of memory, true or false, assemble again around him: the widow's inn, the homey ale, the piss gone dry and stinking in the corners. Three colleagues, Poley and Skeres to hold him, Frizer to draw the knife. Why had he gone to the inn, when he knew the peril?

> *Oft have I levell'd and at last have learned*
> *That peril is the chiefest way to happiness . . .*

And so again. The peril of truth, were there any such.

this subject, not of force enough to hold the fiery spirit it contains, must part

There is one prayer. Here is another:

> *O soul, be changed into little water-drops*
> *And fall into the ocean, ne'er be found*

[*Enter devils.*]

winter Timeshare

RAY NAYLER

Ray Nayler is the author of the stories "Mutability," and "Do Not Forget Me," both of which appeared in Asimov's. Ray's poetry has seen print in the Beloit Poetry Journal, Weave, Juked, Able Muse, Sentence, Phantom Limb, Badlands, and many other magazines. His detective novel, American Graveyards, was published in the UK by Third Alternative Press. Ray's short stories in other genres have appeared in Ellery Queen's Mystery Magazine, Cemetery Dance, Deathrealm, Crimewave, and the Berkeley Fiction Review, among others. Ray is a Foreign Service Officer, a speaker of Russian and Azerbaijani Turkish, and has lived and worked in the countries of Central Asia and the former Soviet Union for nearly a decade. He is currently press attaché at the U.S. Embassy in Baku, Azerbaijan.

Here he tells the bittersweet story of two lovers who are forced to go to very extreme lengths to spend any time together. . . .

What are "I" and "You"?
Just lattices
In the niches of a lamp
Through which the One Light radiates.
—Rumi

Dead Stay Dead

The words were scrawled in scarlet, hurried script on a concrete flower box. In the spring, the flower box would be full of tulips. For those who could afford the spring, there would be sunny days and crowds. Right now there was nothing in the concrete box but wet earth.

A city worker in a jumpsuit a few shades darker than the drizzling sky wiped the letters away with a quick swipe of chemcloth, leaving no trace of their message, and moved on.

Whoever wrote those had probably already been caught by the police. Why bother? The risk of a fine, of a notch against you—for what? A pointless protest against a world that would stay just as it was, ugly words or no.

Across a cobblestoned street and defoliated winter gardens, the minarets of the Blue Mosque rose, soft-edged in the drizzle, their tips blurring into the mist. It was chilly in the open-air café, even under the heater. It was a familiar chill, bringing immediately to Regina's mind years of Istanbul in winter—memories of snow hissing onto the surface of the Bosporus, snow melting on the wings of seagulls. Mornings wrapped close in a blanket, watching the rain on the windowpanes distort the shipping in the straight. The icy, age-smoothed marble of mosque courtyards. And ten thousand cups of black tea in pear-shaped glasses, sign and substance of the city: hot to the touch, bitter on the tongue, a cube of sugar dissolving in their depths, identical to and yet different from one another. This, and so many other deeply pleasant repetitions, comforted her. They were in her past and, now, ahead of her again.

She flexed her tanned, muscular hand. She had spilled her first cup of tea with this clumsy hand. So eager to get to the café, not waiting even to get settled in, still pins-and-needles and misfires, but wanting that first taste of Istanbul, of its black tea against its chill. The old waiter had shrugged and brought her another. "Do not worry, beyfendi," he had said, wiping the tea from the table with a rag. "No charge." Now she lifted the second glass of tea, carefully, to her lips. Yes, that was it. Now another year's Istanbul had begun.

And now Regina saw Ilkay, walking toward the café with that uneven step that said she had just woken. Ilkay was scanning the seats for her. Ilkay was blonde, this year. Beautiful—an oval face, this year, eyes set wide under high cheekbones, long-limbed. But Regina would know her anywhere. And Ilkay knew her as well, scanning the seats in confusion and concern for a moment and then catching her eye, and smiling.

"Well," Ilkay said, when they had embraced, and embraced again, kissed cheeks, held one another at arms' length and examined one another's faces. "This is a new wrinkle in things."

"Is it bad?" Regina asked, keeping her voice light and unconcerned, but feeling underneath an eating away, suddenly, at the pure joy of seeing Ilkay again. *All things fall forever, worn by change / And given time, even the stones will flow . . ."* a piece of a poem she had read once. The poet's name, like much else, gone to time.

Ilkay grinned. Even, smallish teeth, a line of pink gums at the top. A different smile from the year before, but underneath, a constancy. "No. It isn't bad at all. It will be something new, for us." The waiter had approached, stood quietly to one side. Ilkay turned to him. "Two coffees for me. Bring both together." She settled into her cane-bottom chair. "I never feel, this first day, as if I can wake up all the way."

All was well, Regina told herself. Despite her heavy, clumsy hands. Despite her nervousness.

"Tell me," Ilkay said. "Tell me everything. What is your highrise working on?"

"You would not believe it, but it is a contract piece for the UN Commission on Historical Conflict Analysis, and what they are focusing on is conducting the most detailed possible analysis of the Peloponnesian War. All year we've been focused on the Battle of Pylos—refining equipment models, nutrition and weather patterns, existing in these simulations for twelve-hour shifts and feeding data to other teams of analysts. No idea what they are looking for—they're concealing that to keep from biasing the simulation—but the level of detail is granular. I've been fighting and refighting a simulation of the battle of Sphacteria. Half-starved, trying to keep the phalanx together. I've been taken hostage and shipped to Athens so many times as a Spartan hoplite, I should get danger pay. It was supposed to be a six-month research project, but it's already run all year, and looks set to run another year."

"You actually look like you could handle yourself pretty well in a battle, right now. That's a heavy blank you're sheathed in."

Regina felt a flush of shame. "When they pulled me over to my new Istanbul distro, someone had walked off in the blank I ordered. It was this or wait another week. I was furious." She looked down at the hairy back of the hand. "It's terrible, isn't it? My highrise had to take a 10 percent pay cut across the board this year. I couldn't afford my old distro. The new distro is dreadful. I woke up with pins and needles all over, felt like I had a club foot, and could barely move my fingers for two hours. I staggered here like a zombie, everybody who passed me on the street staring at me. And nobody at the distro even apologized about the mix-up."

"It isn't terrible." Ilkay had been too impatient in drinking her Turkish coffee, and a thin line of grounds marred her perfect lip. She wiped them delicately away with a napkin. "Fortunes change, and we're all reliant on our highrises. I'm just so thankful that you were here when I walked up. I had a fear, crossing the hippodrome, that you would be gone. That there was a recall, or a delay, or you had been waitlisted, or that you had . . . reconsidered."

Ilkay was always so fragile, this first day. Always certain there had been some disaster between them. Ilkay could afford a better timeshare—something in the spring, when the tulips came, or something in San Francisco Protectorate, but she came at this cut-rate time each year to meet Regina, slumming it in the off-season. In the end, it was Ilkay who was the most uncertain of them, most sure she would one year lose Regina. Money, Regina had to remind herself, was not everything—although it seemed like it was, to those who did not have it. Ilkay worked in a classified highrise, cut off from the rest of the world, plugging away at security problems only the fine-tangled mesh of reason and intuition, "gut" feeling and logical leaps of a highly trained and experienced mind could untangle. For Ilkay, cut off from any contact for the rest of the year, and restricted to the Western Protectorates for her timeshare because of international security reasons, it was not about money at all. She was afraid of losing Regina, even more than Regina was of losing her.

Ilkay took her hand. "Don't worry about the mix-up. It will be . . . interesting. Something new. Okay—not exactly *new*, but something I have not done for a long time. And I'm just so glad that you came, despite everything."

"What do you mean?"

Ilkay's eyes widened a bit, and Regina saw she had slipped, had revealed something not to be known outside the siloes of the classified highrises that crunched the world's ugliest layers of data. No wonder they didn't let her out much: she may have been one of the world's greatest security analysts, but she was a clumsy liar.

Ilkay recovered and continued. "You know, this really is going to be fun. This guy even looks a little dangerous. God only knows what he's been put up to while we weren't around." Ilkay grinned wickedly and ran a nail along the inside of Regina's ropy wrist. "I can pretend you've traveled through time all this way from Pylos to be with me . . ."

"I guess that, in a sense, I have."

At that moment the muezzin's voice called from atop one of the minarets. Cutting clearly through the rain, the muezzin's trained voice, a rich contralto, carried so commandingly through the air that it almost seemed to come from speakers, despite the laws in Istanbul forbidding any amplification of the human voice. Both Ilkay and Regina paused until she had finished her call, staring at each other, cow-eyed as a couple of teenagers on a first date. Like it was every year, and just as exciting and good. When the muezzin had finished her song, Ilkay caught the eye of a young waiter and made a sign in the air for the check. The young man nodded, unsmiling. The bent, friendly old man who had been serving their table was nowhere to be seen.

When the check came, Regina saw she had been charged for two teas.

"Sorry," she said to the young man. "The other waiter said that I would be only charged for one of these . . ."

The young man shook his head. "You spilled the first one. You're responsible. You pay."

Regina began her protest. "Look, I'm happy to pay, but . . ."

"No, you look." The young man spat back at her. "I don't care what he said. You blanks think you can do anything you want. Spill a tea with your clumsy hands and not pay, forget to tip us because we won't even recognize you next time. You pay for what you took, like anyone else. Like the real people here."

Ilkay interrupted. "It's no problem. We'll pay. You can save the speech."

Stunned by the young waiter's hostility, Regina felt the pure, chemical haze of rage rising in her body. This was new—a feedback of violence that seemed embedded directly in the muscle and bone, a sudden awareness of her physical power, and a desire to use it so strong that it distorted thought. She wanted to smash a fist into the young waiter's face. Or a chair.

Grasping Regina's knee under the table to restrain her, Ilkay waved her palm over the check. "It's done, and a regulation tip for you, as well."

The young man shrugged. "I deserve more, putting up with you people every day." He muttered something else as they got up to leave. Regina did not catch it, but Ilkay's cheeks flushed.

As they were walking away, Regina turned and looked back at the terrace of the little café where they had met for countless years. The young waiter stood, arms crossed, watching them. As Regina caught his eye he turned his head and, keeping his eyes locked on hers, spat on the sidewalk.

Ilkay squeezed her hand. "Come on. We've got . . ."

Regina interrupted her. "What did he say, that last thing?"

"It's not important."

"Tell me."

Ilkay smiled gently. "You're going to have to get used to that male blank. You've never been in one before, have you?"

Regina shook her head. "No."

"You need to ride on top of it, the way you would a horse. Don't let its adrenaline surges and hormones get the better of you, or the feedback will distort your decision making. Cloud your thinking."

Regina shook her head, as if to clear it. "Yeah, I can feel that. But what did he say?"

Ilkay tugged at her hand, and they walked in the direction of the Hagia Sophia. In this early hour, there was almost no one on the sidewalks and the squares. The figures that they saw, all locals going about their own business, drifted in a clinging mist that did not quite turn to rain. "I'll tell you," Ilkay said, "but only if you promise, then, to concentrate on me. On us, and our time here."

Regina stopped walking, gathered herself. "Yes, of course. I'm sorry. I got carried away. It's embarrassing."

Ilkay punched her arm, playfully. "Well, don't forget to add this to your simulation. You can bet those men on Sphacteria were feeling exactly the same adrenaline surges, and it was having the same distorting effect on their decision making."

Regina grinned. "I was thinking the same thing. Always the analysts, the two of us."

Ilkay pulled them along toward the Hagia Sophia's entrance. Its heavily buttressed mass loomed. "He said, 'why don't you dead just stay dead?'"

Regina felt her teeth *actually grit themselves*. "I earned this. We both did. We've worked hard, both of us. We spent lifetimes sharpening our skill sets, making ourselves valuable, making real contributions to science. I'm not some trust-fund postmortem cruising around in a speedboat off Corsica. We competed fairly for our places in the highrises. We worked for this. And . . . who do they think keeps them safe? And who spends all their money here, pays for the maintenance of these places, keeps their restaurants open? And . . ." She trailed off helplessly.

"I know, I know," said Ilkay. "Now forget about it, and let's go visit a church that has stood for over two thousand years, and let the temporary things be temporary."

The house Ilkay had rented for them, one of the ancient wooden homes along the Bosporus, was like a wedding cake fresh from a refrigerator—all white paint thick as frosting, china-fine detail, silken folds, and chilled from top to bottom. The heating system was apologetic but insufficient. They built a fire in the master bedroom's fireplace, found wool blankets in a trunk, ordered a very late lunch, and clumsily explored the possibilities of their new configurations. Then, increasingly less clumsily.

By the time lunch was delivered, they were exhausted and starving. In near silence, wearing their blankets like woolen superhero capes, they spread fig jam on fresh bread and watched sleet spin down over the Bosporus and spatter slush against the windowpanes. Out on the roiling chop of the strait, a fisherman in a small rusty boat and black rubber rain gear determinedly attempted to extract some protein from the water. His huge black beard, run through with gray streaks, jutted from under his sou'wester, with seemingly only the axe blade of his nose between.

Regina dabbed at her mouth with a napkin. "It's amazing to think that these people have lived in a nearly identical way for centuries. Technology changes some things, like maybe fish-locating sonar systems and nearly perfect weather forecasting—but for the fisherman who actually has to get the fish on the hook, in any weather that comes, not much has changed."

"The physical things—the actual moving of matter around—are immutable," agreed Ilkay. "As we have been experimenting with all morning." She grinned, carefully applying fig jam. "And that's why, I think, these weeks are so important. They remind us of the base—the essentials, the substance of life and the world. Not that what we do isn't important. Not that who we are usually isn't real . . ."

Regina finished the thought: "But it's just so abstract. Immaterial. Not without consequence, but . . ."

"But without immediacy." Ilkay interjected. Then, after a long pause . . . "Regina, I miss you terribly. All year. And I cram everything I can into these short few weeks. And every year, I am afraid."

"Of what?"

"Afraid that next year, you will not be waiting for me at the café. These few weeks, always in winter . . . they are everything to me. They aren't a vacation . . . they are the sum and total of everything of meaning in my life. It's not that . . . it's not that I don't value my work, or think it saves lives. I haven't lost faith in the project. We watch over a troubled world, in my highrise . . . a world cruel people are constantly trying to tear to pieces . . . but none of that work seems to matter nearly as much as the moment I see you again. Sometimes, I feel my work is eating away at who I am. It's like watching a shadow underwater: you know it is just seaweed, this shadow, a harmless mass writhing in the current, nothing to worry about. But what if it is a shark? A shadow with teeth and volition? The more you stare at the shadow, straining to make out its outline, the more certain you become that it is a shark—until you convince even yourself. This constant watching—it eats away at your feeling of security. It eats away, I think, at your sanity. And I've been afraid to tell you, because I feel as if once it's said, it will shatter all this . . . this causal sort of . . . easy feeling between us."

Regina put an arm around her. Her thicker arms were increasingly feeling as if they were her own. She pulled Ilkay toward her. "This was never casual or easy for me, Ilkay. And I'll always be at the café. Every single year."

The weather did not improve after lunch. The Bosporus swelled and churned, and the rain came down in columns. There was time to sit long over lunch and talk, and to lay under the heavy covers of the four-poster and talk. Dinner was brought in a dripping container, and they tipped the young woman who brought it, soaked to the skin, double for her efforts. The sun set, and on the strait the lights of small boats bobbed in the dark between the chop of the water and the sky. Just after 8:00, the door buzzer jangled. They had been having cups of tea in front of the fire. Regina saw Ilkay immediately tense, like a cat hearing a dog bark in the distance.

The man on the doorstep was in a long, gray raincoat, black rubber boots, rain pants. Under his sou'wester an abglanz turned his face into a swirl of shimmering, ever-changing abstract patterns. In a tech-limited city, the effect was particularly jarring.

"Good evening," the composite voice said to Regina. "I apologize for the interruption of your timeshare. I hope to take up as little of your time as possible. I must speak to Ilkay Avci. This is, unfortunately, a matter of urgency." His credentials drifted across the shimmer of the abglanz. Istanbul Protectorate Security High Commission.

Standing in the corridor behind Regina Ilkay said, "Come in, inspector. Hang up those wet things."

As he did so, Regina noticed a port wine birthmark on the back of his hand. It was large, spreading across his wrist and up to the first knuckles of his fingers in a curious, complicated pattern, like a map of unknown continents. They should have given him an abglanz to cover that, she thought. I would know him again anywhere. They went into the living room.

"I apologize," the inspector said to Regina, "but due to the classified nature of this conversation, I will have to ask you to wear this momentarily. Once you are seated comfortably." He produced the slender metal cord of the scrambler from the pocket of his shirt. No matter what they did to that thing (this one was a cheerful yellow) it still looked like a garrote. Regina settled into a chair and let him place it around her neck. He clipped it into place gently, like a man fastening the clasp of his wife's necklace.

She was in Gulhane Park, at the peak of the Tulip Festival. The flowers—so large and perfectly formed they seemed almost plastic, were everywhere, arranged in brightly colored plots, swirling patterns of red, white, orange, maroon, violet, and cream. A few other tourists roamed the paths of Gulhane, but the park was, for the most part, empty. It was a cool spring day, smelling of turned earth. It was an Istanbul she had not seen—had not been able to afford to see—since the austerity, so many years ago now, had reduced her highrise's benefit levels. But, she thought, bending to cup the bloom of a Chinese orange tulip with a cream star at its center, what I gained when I lost this season was Ilkay. And that is enough to replace all of this. Though—just for a moment—it was good to feel the warm edge of summer hiding in the air, to close her eyes and let the sun bleed through her eyelids.

She wondered how wide the extent of the simulation was. Did it extend beyond the walls of Gulhane? The face of a passing tourist was glitchy, poorly captured, the woman's features wavered. No, it would be only the park, a tiny island of flowers, green paths and good weather. But did it extend as far as the Column of the Goths? She would like to see that ancient object, surrounded by flowers in the spring. She began to walk further into the park. A crow glitched from one branch to another in a tree just beginning to leaf, its caw jagged with digital distortion.

She was back in the chair. The inspector stood over her, putting the scrambler back into his pocket. "Give it a moment before trying to stand. Just in case. And again, my apologies for any inconvenience. The Istanbul Protectorate Security High Commission thanks you and will apply a small amount in contemporary lira to your accounts for the inconvenience. It isn't much, I am afraid—but enough for a good meal on the Galata Bridge for the two of you."

Ilkay was standing at the fire, warming her hands. "The courtesy is much appreciated, Inspector. At a later date I will review this interaction and give it the full 5-star rating."

Once the inspector was gone, they both found they were too exhausted even to watch the fire burn down to its embers. They went to bed early, sliding into sheets as cold as the skin of ice on a river. Regina asked nothing about Ilkay's conversation with the Inspector. It was one of the rules of their relationship, unspoken between them. Sometimes, things about Ilkay's work were offered up, but Regina never asked for them.

"Perhaps next year," Ilkay whispered in the dark, "we should meet somewhere else. Maybe it is time for a change."

"What happened?" And now Regina felt the rise of anger in her. Somewhere else? Where? It was not enough that she had no contact with Ilkay during the year, only these few weeks when they could see one another—now they had to intrude on this as well, eroding even this small island of peace—as if it were too much to ask to have even this one thing. The face of the young waiter at the café rose up in her mind, spitting on the pavement.

"Nothing." Ilkay said. "Nothing at all. Tensions, or rumors of tensions. That's all it ever is, it seems. Like the shadow in the water. It's almost always seaweed. It's almost never a shark. But my job is to watch the shadows. And I'm tired, Regina. So very tired of being afraid. Why can't they let me at least have this? These few weeks. Haven't I earned a little peace in my life?"

The morning of the fifth day was bright and cold. The sky was opalescent. The mist that had clung to everything had risen to become a single, thin sheet of gauze, shrouding sun from earth. Under the Galata Tower, huddled beneath the glowing hood of a terrace heater, they drank black tea and coffee and had breakfast— honey and butter, warm bread and white cheese, tomatoes and hard-boiled eggs—and lingered over the meal. There were other blanks at the café, together and alone, smiling and laughing or quietly reading newspapers. Real newspapers, on real paper: one of the great joys of Istanbul.

The blanks sat on the terrace, oblivious to the cold, with only the heaters preserving them from the chill. The café's waiter, on the other hand, stood inside the café, watching his patrons from behind glass, continually rubbing his hands together for warmth. He was a middle-aged man moving toward old age, his thin hair combed straight back on his scalp. The cold, thought Regina, was different for him—lasting months out of the year, coming too soon and leaving far too late. For the blanks on his terrace, it was a joy to experience it, after their highrised, simulated year. Who were they all? Number-crunchers, of course, of one kind or another, moving data around. There were pure mathematicians among them, financial analysts, scientists and astronomers, astrophysicists and qualitative historical analysts. And those, like Ilkay and herself, working in more esoteric fields.

Regina had never thought deeply about the difference between the blanks and Istanbul's permanent residents, the "locals," as they were called by some—but not by Regina, who liked to think of herself as a local, liked to think of this city as her city. Hadn't she earned that, by returning here every year for so long? Over the last few days she and Ilkay had "made their rounds," as they called it—despite the bad weather, they had visited all of their old places—eating fresh fish on the Galata Bridge (subsidized by the Istanbul Protectorate Security High Commission), walking the land wall that had protected, for a thousand years, an empire that had been destroyed well over a thousand years ago. On the third evening, from an open-topped ferry crossing the strait to the Asian side, they had watched the interstellar array on one of Istanbul's distant hills fire the consciousness of another brave, doomed volunteer into the stars, riding a laser into failure and certain death. The blanks on the ferry had applauded. The locals had hardly seemed to notice.

But it was different for them. The waiter blew into his hands and watched his patrons with no expression on his face at all as they laughed and spread honey on their bread. He simply wanted to be warm, wanted the spring to come. Time moved along—and the faster, the better. The blanks were his economy, providing him with a living. In winter, the tables were half empty. In the summer, they would be full. All the tables would be full. The blanks would take the city over, ferreting out even the most local of the cafés, the most "authentic" places to eat. Raising prices, elbowing out the city's residents, who would retreat deeper into the alleys and back streets. And the interstellar program ground on, engaging the imaginations of thousands, employing a hundred highrises, but without any news or results or breakthroughs for generations. Its promise was now ignored by the majority of the five billion, whose main task was just to live, here and now, not to worry about homes beyond the stars.

On the other side of the terrace, one of the breakfasters, a young woman with dark hair in a braid, seated alone, was having a conversation with a local teenage boy on a bicycle. The boy had drawn out a map and was pointing to something on it. He handed the map to the blank, who began examining it, her easy smile displaying a row of white teeth. And then, the boy reached into his pocket, and drew out a small, red canister with a nozzle at the top. He aimed it at the young woman's face and depressed the button, firing a spray into her eyes, nose and mouth.

Without thinking, Regina was on her feet, across the terrace, then on top of the boy, slamming his hand again and again into the pavement until the canister fell from it and rolled bumpily away across the cobblestones, wrestling with him as he tried to twist away from her. The boy struck her in the face, hard, his hand impacting with a strangely sharp pain. But then others joined her, from the street and from the terrace. Whistles blew. The boy disappeared behind a mass of struggling backs and legs. Ilkay was on the terrace, pouring water from a bottle over the young woman's face. The woman's eyes were red and swollen closed, she was coughing and gagging. Near her, others were wiping at their eyes, trying to clear them of the irritant spray. Another man offered Regina a cloth, a napkin from the terrace, and now she noticed that her face was bleeding. She pressed the napkin to her cheek, feeling the warm pulse of blood from the deep cut there. Only then did she notice the policeman, carefully placing a small, bloody folding knife into an isolation bag. The café's proprietor stood in the center of his terrace, all tipped-over tables and shattered tea cups, wringing his hands.

At the medical clinic, the nurse who applied the seal was a young man, ex-military, his silver-sheathed prosthesis of a right arm, twelve-fingered and nimble, deftly working the seal into place as he cheerfully bantered with Regina.

"Luckily, your insurance covers this damage. They can be picky about what you put the blanks through, you know. There are all sorts of clauses and sub-clauses. That knife just touched the zygomatic bone, but there are no fractures, no bruising. A lot of people don't read the fine print, and go paragliding or something, break a leg and find themselves footing a huge bill for repairs later, or a scrap and replace that they can't afford. But you made the right choice, bought comprehensive. You must have gotten into the program early—those rates are astronomical these days. Nobody can afford them but the highest-ranking Minister Councilors and, of course, the postmortems. There we go. This guy's face will be good as new in a few days." He patted Regina's cheek affectionately, flexed the smoothly clacking twelve-figured hand. "Just try not to smile too much." He admired his hand. "God, I love this thing. If anything good can be said to have come out of the Fall of Beirut, it's this hand. A masterpiece."

Ilkay was giving a deposition in another room. Looking up, Regina saw the Inspector from the IPSHC standing in the doorway in a casual polo shirt and slacks, abglanz glittering weirdly under the medical-grade lights. She recognized him by the pomegranate-colored birthmark on his hand.

"I hope you are well," he said. "After your adventure."

Regina nodded slightly.

"Hold still one second," the young nurse said. "I have to fix the seal along the edge here."

"We are going to have to take a bit more of your time, I am afraid. Of Ilkay's time, to be more precise. Will you be able to get back to your residence all right? If not, I can send someone to accompany you. We will return her at the soonest moment we can, but I am afraid . . ." His digital smear of a face turned to the nurse. "If you are finished, can you leave her for a moment?"

The nurse shrugged and left the room.

"I am afraid," continued the Inspector, "that we will need her particular skill set over the next few days. We have encountered . . . a rather fluid situation. It needs further analysis. Normally we would not . . . well, to be honest, the austerities have left us a bit short staffed. Ilkay's presence here, with her particular skill set, is an opportunity we literally can't afford to pass up."

Ilkay was in the doorway. "Inspector, can I have a moment alone with her?"

Once the Inspector had departed, Ilkay crossed the room to Regina. She ran a finger lightly along the seal. "They've done a good job. It's the best work I've ever seen." She blinked back tears. "God, you are an idiot. You've spent too long in that simulation, or maybe that body is getting to you."

"I don't know what came over me," Regina said seriously. "It's something in the air, I suppose. I just reacted."

"Well," Ilkay said, "stop reacting. I'll be back with you in a day. Two at the most. In the meantime, try not to play the hero too much. And I expect a full report of your adventures. But . . ." And now she seemed uncertain, lowered her voice. "Play it safe a little, will you? For me? It might be better . . ." she leaned in and whispered in Regina's ear. "It might be better to stay away from the touristy areas for a while. Can you do that for me?"

She pulled away. Regina nodded.

"Oh," Ilkay said, running her finger along Regina's razor-stubbled chin. "And by the way—you really need to shave more often. You're a beast, and it's not that I don't like it, but it's giving me a bit of a rash."

They had met here, so many years ago. It had been a different Istanbul, then—a city dominated by a feeling of optimism, Regina thought. No, not dominated—optimism could never dominate the city's underlying feeling of melancholy, of nostalgia for what was always lost. But the city had been brightened, somehow, by optimism. For years, there had been a feeling, ephemeral, like a bright coat of whitewash over stone. The relays were in place on a hundred possible new worlds, the massive array on Istanbul's distant hills were firing the consciousnesses of the first explorers into interstellar space. It was in that time that they had met. They had met on a Sunday, at the Church of St. George. Regina, who was not religious, had gone to a service. She had been trying things out then—meditation, chanting, prayer—all of it a failure. Where does one go when one has lost everything, risen back from nothing? But she found the drone of the priest's voice and the smell of incense—a thousand years and more of incense soaked into the gold leaf and granite—comforting. The flat and meaningfully staring icons, the quietude. In those first years of adjustment, it had been all she had.

Ilkay had found her outside in the courtyard. She had been doing the same—wandering from temple to mosque to church, searching. They fell in together, naturally, talking of the most private feelings immediately, walking up the hill through neighborhoods that had been crumbling for as long as they had been standing, where the burned shells of houses mixed with those restored, and all of them leaned on one another, the whole leaning on the broken for support, the broken leaning on the whole. They ate a meal together in a little family restaurant whose courtyard was the ivy-covered walls of a shattered house, long ago consumed by fire, open to the sky. The meal felt, for Regina, like a communion. Someone had found her and had made her whole. And there had been no struggle, no doubt, no sacrifice. They had spent every moment together afterwards, never parted, and agreed to meet the next year. That was all. They had never questioned it.

Regina did not question it now. If Ilkay was gone tomorrow, she would not think it was because she had abandoned her. This was not possible. It would be because she was gone completely.

Regina lasted three days, waiting in the icy house and keeping to the city's Asian side. She found some comfort in a book she dug up in a bookstore there, a long-forgotten treatise on insect architecture. The book came complete with color plate illustrations of the complex constructions of bugs. It was a labor of love written by some Englishman, obscurely obsessed in the best possible way. She pored over the book's slightly mildewed pages, rich with the vanilla scent of their paper's chemical decay, for hours. Ilkay sent her reassuring messages, full of her bright sarcasm, hoping every day for their reunion. And the time slipped away. Would Istanbul Protectorate pay for their separation? Reimburse them for what they were taking? Unlikely.

On the fourth day, Regina decided to return to the European side. She would avoid the most popular places, as she had promised Ilkay. But most people went to the hippodrome and Hagia Sophia, the Blue Mosque and, at the most, strolled up to the Grand Bazaar. She would avoid those places.

The Church of St. George itself was surprisingly small, suited now to the dwindling number of pilgrims and tourists it received, though once it must have swelled full of the faithful on holy days. Pilgrims must have filled the small courtyard which, now, was nearly empty. The gray stone of the simple façade was more like a house than a church, though inside it was filled with gold leaf and light.

But Regina stayed in the courtyard. A group of blanks was there, in a cluster around a local guide who Regina could not see, but whose voice carried in the air. Pigeons walked around the feet of the tourists.

"The church's most precious objects, saved from each successive fire that consumed parts of it, are the patriarchal throne, which is believed to date from the fifth century, rare icons made of mosaic and the relics of two saints: Saints Gregory the Theologian and John Chrysostom."

Regina walked toward the group to hear more clearly. A message was coming in from Ilkay.

"Regina, where are you?"

"Some of the bones of these two saints, which were looted from Constantinople by the Fourth Crusade in 1204, were returned by Pope John Paul II in 2004. Today the Church of St. George serves mostly as a museum . . ."

Regina could see the guide now, standing in the semicircle of faces. The faces of the blanks were pale, lips and noses red with cold. Most of them bored. Some carried on quiet conversations with one another as the guide spoke. Why did they come to this place if they did not care?

"I am at the place we met," Regina sent. "Still laying low, waiting for you."

The guide wore a heavier coat, and a warm hat. As Regina approached, he saw her and looked up, continuing his speech. "Though there are still pilgrims."

It was the young waiter from the café on her first day. Recognizing her, he smiled sarcastically. "They return here every year. . . ."

Another message came in from Ilkay. "GET OUT!!!"

The guide raised his hands. "And they will keep coming until we stop them."

There was a flash of blinding light.

The trireme lurched free of its anchorage and began a slow rotation to starboard, oars churning in the gray-blue water. Regina was crouched on the deck, the sun white-hot on her exposed neck. Her hands were bound behind her. Blood was spattered on the wood, small droplets from a wound she had received across her cheek in the final moments of the battle.

There had been chaos, and many had thrown down their shields, but for some reason she had kept fighting until finally one of the Athenian hoplites had struck her on the side of the head with the flat of a sword and she had fallen, dazed, struggling to get to her feet. Then they had moved in, knocking her sword from her hand, wrestling her to the ground, finally subduing her and binding her wrists with a leather thong.

Her head still throbbed from the blow from the sword, and a hundred other bruises and scrapes ached. Behind them, Sphacteria's flat, narrow expanse, fought for so hard and at such cost, began to fade as the simulation's boundaries drifted into opalescent tatters. Finally there was only the trireme, and the lingering sound of its oars in water that was no longer there.

An Athenian hoplite approached, and handed her water, but she did not bother to take it. Sensation was already fading, the materiality ending. The water would be nothing in a mouth that had ceased to feel it. The wound had stopped throbbing, was gone. Blood remained on the deck, and the sun's warm color, but not the warmth of the sun.

"Do you really think they would have kept fighting like that? After it was impossible to win?" The Athenian cut her hands free with a small bronze knife.

Regina lay down on the deck. Moments ago there had been the physical feeling of exhaustion, heat. Now there was none of that, though there was a faint sensation of the deck beneath her. She laced her fingers behind her head and looked up into the glaucous simulation edge that was the sky.

"I do," Regina said. "Some would have given up. But others were beyond reason, beyond caring about consequence. They would have carried on when it was impossible. Hatred, fear, and anger would have ruled them. I was missing it in my reports last year. The stubbornness, the things beyond strategy."

Astrid, who had played the Athenian but was now becoming Astrid again, was silent for a moment, then tossed her helmet to the deck, where it landed without a sound and was gone. She sat down with a sigh. "You're probably right. Anyway, it seems to come closer to the truth. But I'm so tired of doing this every day. I wish I knew what they were looking for. What's the key to all of this? Anyway . . . another year almost gone, and no end in sight. Is your timeshare still in Istanbul? Will you really go back there, after everything that happened there last year? After almost getting killed, and totaling your blank? You barely made it out of that place alive."

That morning, before the start of the day's simulation, Regina had received a message from Ilkay: "Here a day early, already waiting for your arrival. Tell me you are coming, though I won't stop worrying until I see your face."

Regina grinned into the blank swirl of false sky, seeing black tea there, and cobblestones, incense aged into stone, the hiss of snow along a seagull's wing, and Ilkay's face—the many faces Ilkay's being had illuminated, her smile each year both different, and the same.

"Of course I'm going back. Now, and every year. It is my home."

MY ENGLISH NAME

R. S. BENEDICT

R. S. Benedict spent three years teaching English to rich kids in China before returning to her native New York to become a bureaucrat. Her work can be found in The Magazine of Fantasy & Science Fiction *and Upper Rubber Boot's upcoming anthology* Broad Knowledge: 35 Women Up to No Good.

Here's a creepy yet ultimately quite moving story about a man with a secret so deeply buried that even he no longer knows what it is. . . .

I want you to know that you are not crazy.

What you saw in the back of the ambulance was real.

What wasn't real was Thomas Majors.

You have probably figured out by now that I wasn't born in London like I told you I was, and that I did not graduate from Oxford, and that I wasn't baptized in the Church of England, as far as I know.

Here is the truth: Thomas Majors was born in room 414 of the Huayuan Binguan, a cheap hotel which in defiance of its name contained neither flowers nor any sort of garden.

If the black domes in the ceiling of the fourth-floor corridor had actually contained working cameras the way they were supposed to, a security guard might have noticed Tingting, a dowdy maid from a coal village in Hunan, enter room 414 without her cleaning cart. The guard would have seen Thomas Majors emerge a few days later dressed in a blue suit and a yellow scarf.

A search of the room would have returned no remnant of Tingting.

Hunan Province has no springtime, just alternating winter and summer days. When Tingting enters room 414 it's winter, gray and rainy. The guest room has a heater, at least, unlike the sleeping quarters Tingting shares with three other maids.

Tingting puts a DO NOT DISTURB sign on the door and locks it. She shuts the curtains. She covers the mirrors. She takes off her maid uniform. Her skin is still new. She was supposed to be invisible: she has small eyes and the sort of dumpy figure you find in a peasant who had too little to eat as a child and too much to eat as an adult. But prying hands found their way to her anyway, simply because she was there. Still, I know it won't be hard for a girl like her to disappear. No one will look for her.

I pull Tingting off, wriggling out of her like a snake. I consider keeping her in case of emergency, but once she's empty I feel myself shift and stretch. She won't fit anymore. She has to go.

I will spare you the details of how that task is accomplished.

It takes a while to make my limbs the right length. I've narrowed considerably. I check the proportions with a measuring tape; all the ratios are appropriate.

But Thomas Majors is not ready. The room's illumination, fluorescent from the lamps, haze-strangled from the sky, isn't strong enough to tan this new flesh the way it is meant to be.

You thought I was handsome when you met me. I wish you could have seen what I was supposed to be. In my plans, Thomas was perfect. He had golden hair and a complexion like toast. But the light is too weak, and instead I end up with flesh that's not quite finished.

I can't wait anymore. I only have room 414 for one week. It's all Tingting can afford.

So I put on Thomas as carefully as I can, and only when I'm certain that not a single centimeter of what lies beneath him can be seen, I uncover the mirrors.

He's tight. Unfinished skin usually is. I smooth him down and let him soften. I'm impatient, nervous, so I turn around to check for lumps on Thomas's back. When I do, the flesh at his neck rips. I practice a look of pain in the mirror.

Then I stitch the gash together as well as I can. It fuses but leaves an ugly ridge across Thomas's throat. I cover it with a scarf Tingting bought from a street vendor. It's yellow, imitation silk with a recurring pattern that reads *Liu Viuttor*.

The next week I spend in study and practice: how to speak proper English, how to stand and sit like a man, how to drink without slurping, how to hold a fork, how to bring my brows together in an expression of concern, how to laugh, how to blink at semi-regular intervals.

It's extraordinary how much one can learn when one doesn't have to eat or sleep.

I check out on time carrying all of Thomas Majors's possessions in a small bag: a fake passport, a hairbrush, a hand mirror, a wallet, a cell phone, and a single change of clothes.

It takes me under twenty-four hours to find a job. A woman approaches me on the sidewalk. She just opened an English school, she says. Would I like to teach there?

The school consists of an unmarked apartment in a gray complex. The students are between ten and twelve years of age, small and rowdy. I'm paid in cash.

They don't notice that my vowels are a bit off; Thomas's new tongue can't quite wrap itself around English diphthongs just yet.

On weekday mornings I take more rent-a-whitey gigs. A shipping company pays me to wear a suit, sit at board meetings, nod authoritatively, and pretend to be an executive. A restaurant pays me to don a chef's hat and toss pizza dough in the air on its opening day. Another English training center, unable to legally hire foreigners in its first year of operation, pays me 6,000 RMB per month to wander through the halls and pretend to work there.

I model, too: for a travel brochure, for a boutique, for a university's foreign language department. The photographer tells his clients that I was a finalist on *America's Next Top Model*. They don't question it.

China is a perfect place for an imitation human like myself. Everything is fake here. The clothes are designer knock-offs. The DVDs are bootlegs. The temples are replicas of sites destroyed during the Great Leap Forward and the Cultural Revolution. The markets sell rice made from plastic bags, milk made from melamine, and lamb skewers made from rat meat. Even the internet is fake, a slow, stuttering, pornless thing whose search engines are programmed not to look in politically sensitive directions.

It was harder in the West. Westerners demand authenticity even though they don't really want it. They cry out for meat without cruelty, war without casualties, thinness without hunger. But the Chinese don't mind artifice.

I make friends in China quickly and easily. Many are thrilled to have a tall, blond Westerner to wave around as a status symbol.

I wait a few weeks before I associate with other *waiguoren*, terrified they'll pick up on my fake accent or ask me a question about London that I can't answer.

But none of that turns out to be a problem. Very few expats in China ask questions about what one did back home, likely because so few of them want to answer that question themselves. Generally, they are not successful, well-adjusted members of their native countries. But if they have fair skin and a marginal grasp of English, they can find an ESL job to pay for beer and a lost girl to tell them how clever and handsome they are.

I learn quickly that my Englishman costume is not lifelike. Most of the Brits I meet in China are fat and bald, with the same scraggly stubble growing on their faces, their necks, and the sides of their heads. They wear hoodies and jeans and ratty trainers. Thomas wears a suit every day. He's thin, too thin for a Westerner. His accent is too aristocratic, nothing at all like the working-class mumbles coming from the real Brits' mouths. And the scarf only highlights his strangeness.

I think for sure I will be exposed, until one day at a bar a real Englishman jabs a sausage-like finger into my chest and says, "You're gay, aren't you, mate?"

When I only stutter in reply, he says, "Ah, it's all right. Don't worry about it. You might want to tone it down, though. The scarf's a bit much."

And so Thomas Majors's sexuality is decided. It proves useful. It hides me from the expats the way Thomas's whiteness hides me from the Chinese.

It's in a *waiguoren* bar that New Teach English finds me. A tiny woman not even five feet tall swims through a sea of beery pink bodies to find me sitting quietly in a corner, pretending to sip a gin and tonic. She offers me a job.

"I don't have a TOEFL certification," I tell her.

"We'll get you one. No problem," she says. And it's true; a friend of hers owns a printshop that can produce such a document with ease.

"I'm not sure I'll pass the medical exam required for a foreign expert certificate," I tell her.

"My brother-in-law works at the hospital," she says. "If you give him a bottle of cognac, you'll pass the health exam."

And that's how I get my residence permit.

You arrive in my second year at New Teach in Changsha with your eyes downcast and your mouth shut. I recognize you. You're a fellow impostor, but a more mundane sort than myself. Though hired as an ESL teacher, you can hardly say "Hello, how are you?"

We introduce ourselves by our English names. I am Thomas Majors and you are Daniel Liu. "Liu. Like my scarf," I joke. I give you a smile copied from Pierce Brosnan.

I lie to you and tell you that I'm from London and my name is Thomas. Your lies are those of omission: you do not mention that you are the son of New Teach's owner, and that you had the opportunity to study in the United States but flunked out immediately.

Somehow being the only child of rich parents hasn't made you too spoiled. In your first year at New Teach you sit close to me, studying my counterfeit English as I talk to my students. Meanwhile, I sit close to Sarah, a heavyset Canadian girl, trying to glean real English from her as best I can.

Somehow, my *waiguoren* status doesn't spoil me, either. Unlike most Western men in China, I bathe regularly and dress well and arrive to work on time without a hangover every morning, and I don't try to sleep with my students. My humanity requires work to maintain. I don't take it for granted.

For these reasons, I am declared the star foreign instructor at New Teach English. I stand out like a gleaming cubic zirconium in a rubbish heap. The students adore me. Parents request me for private lessons with their children. They dub me *Da Huang* (Big Yellow).

Every six to twelve months, the other foreign teachers leave and a new set takes their place. Only I remain with you. You stay close to me, seeking me out for grammar help and conversation practice. There's more you want, I know, but you are too timid to ask for it outright, and I am unable to offer it.

We slowly create each other like a pair of half-rate Pygmalions. I fix the holes in your English, teach you how to look others in the eye, how to shake hands authoritatively, how to approach Western women, how to pose in photographs, how to project confidence ("fake it till you make it"), how to be the sort of man you see in movies.

Your questions prod me to quilt Thomas Majors together from little scraps stolen from overheard conversations in expat bars. Thomas Majors traveled a lot as a child, which is why his accent is a bit odd. (That came from an American girl who wore red-framed glasses.) Thomas Majors has an annoying younger brother and an eccentric older sister. (This I took from old television sitcoms.) His father owned a stationery shop (based on an ESL listening test), but his sister is set to inherit the business (from a BBC period piece), so Thomas moved to China to learn about calligraphy (that came from you, when I saw you carrying your ink brush).

Your questions and comments nudge me into playing the ideal Englishman: polite, a little silly at times, but sophisticated and cool. Somehow I become the sort of man that other men look up to. They ask Thomas for advice on dating and fashion and fitness and education. They tell him he's tall and handsome and clever. I say "thank you" and smile, just as I practiced in the mirror.

I liked Thomas. I wish I could have kept on being him a little longer.

In Shenzhen, I nearly tell you the truth about myself. New Teach has just opened a center there and sends you out to manage it. You want to bring me to work there and help keep the foreign teachers in line.

"I don't know if I can pass the medical examination," I tell you.

"You look healthy," you reply.

I choose my words carefully. "I have a medical condition. I manage it just fine, but I'm afraid the doctors will think I am too sick."

"What condition? Is it di . . ." You struggle with the pronunciation.

"It's not diabetes. The truth is"—and what follows is at least partially true—"I don't know what it is, exactly."

"You should see a doctor," you tell me.

"I have," I say. "They did a lot of tests on me for a long time but they still couldn't figure it out. I got sick of it. Lots of needles in my arms and painful surgeries." I mime nurses and doctors jabbing and cutting me. "So now I don't go to doctors anymore."

"You should still have an examination," you tell me.

"No," I say.

Physicians are not difficult to fool, especially in China, overworked and sleep-deprived as they are. But their machines, their scanners, and their blood tests are things I cannot deceive. I do not want to know what they might find beneath Thomas Majors's skin.

I tell you I won't go with you if I have to submit to a medical exam, knowing full well how badly you want me to come. And so phone calls are made, red envelopes are stuffed, favors are cashed in, and banquets are arranged.

We feast with Shenzhen hospital administrators. They stare at me as I eat with chopsticks. "You're very good with . . . ah . . ." The hospital director points at the utensils in my hand, unable to dig up the English word.

"*Kuaizi*," I say. They applaud.

We go out to KTV afterward. The KTV bar has one David Bowie song and two dozen from the Backstreet Boys. The men like the way I sing. They order further snacks, more beer, and a pretty girl to sit on our laps and flirt with us. "So handsome," she says, stroking my chin. By then I have mastered the art of blushing.

You present a bottle of liquor: "It's very good *baijiu*," you say, and everyone nods in agreement. We toast. They fill my glass with liquor over and over again. Each time they clink it and say, "*Gan bei!*" And to me they add, "For England!" Now I have no choice but to drain my glass to make my fake mother country proud.

For most foreigners, *baijiu* is a form of torture. I've heard them say it's foul-tasting, that it gives monstrous hangovers, that you'll find yourself burping it up two days later. But for me, it's no more noxious than any other fluid. So I throw down enough liquor to show our guests that I am healthy and strong. We finish the bottle, then a second, and when I realize that the other men are putting themselves in agony to keep up with me I cover my mouth, run to the nearby lavatory, and loudly empty my stomach. Our guests love it. They cheer.

The winner of the drinking contest is a short, fat, toad-like man with a wide mouth. He's the director of the hospital, which is easy to guess by his appearance; powerful men in Hunan often look a bit like toads. You tell me later that I made him very happy by drinking with him, and that he was extremely pleased to have defeated a Westerner.

And that is how I pass my health examination in Shenzhen.

Your grandmother recognizes me during the following Spring Festival.

Going home with you is a bad idea. I should spend those two weeks enjoying the relative quiet of the empty city, drinking myself into oblivion with the leftover handful of expats.

The idea starts as a lark, a jocular suggestion on your part, but once it seizes me it will not let me go. I can't remember the last time I was in a home, with a family. I want to know what it's like.

You are too embarrassed to try to talk me out of it, so home we go.

Your mother is surprised to see me. She takes you aside and scolds you. Tingting's *Changshahua* has faded. Now my new English brain is still struggling to learn proper Mandarin, so I only get the gist of the conversation. I know *mei-you* (without) and *nü pengyou* (girlfriend), and my understanding of the culture fills in the rest. You're supposed to have brought home a woman. You're not getting any younger; you're just a few years shy of turning thirty unmarried, a bare-branch man. Your parents can't bear it. They don't understand. You're tall, rich, and handsome. Why don't you have a girlfriend?

The question is repeated several times over the next ten days, by your mother, your father, your grandfather, and your aunt.

The only person who doesn't denounce your bachelordom is your grandmother. She likes me. When she sees me, she smiles and says, "*Cao didi.*"

"Grass brother?" I ask.

"It's a nickname for an actor she really likes," you explain. "American."

She asks me another question, but Tingting is too far gone. I'm a Westerner now. *"Ting bu dong,"* I say politely. *I hear you, but I don't understand.*

I ask her to repeat herself, but something the old woman said has embarrassed your mother, for she escorts *Nainai* up to her room.

"She's old," you tell me.

Your mother and grandfather and aunt are not as accustomed to the sight of foreigners as you are. They, too, marvel at my chopstick ability as though I am a cat that has learned to play the piano. At all times I am a walking exhibition. In most places, I'm the *waiguoren*, the foreigner. In expat bars, I'm That Bloke with the Scarf, famed for his habit of always appearing well groomed. And around you, I'm Thomas Majors, though for some reason I don't mind it when you look at me.

I have no trouble with chopsticks. But putting food in my mouth, chewing it, and swallowing it are not actions that come naturally to me. This tongue of mine does not have working taste buds. My teeth are not especially secure in their gums, having been inserted one by one with a few taps of a hammer. This stomach of mine is only a synthetic sack that dangles in the recesses of my body. It has no exit. It leads nowhere.

Eating, for me, is purely a ritual to convince others that I am in fact human. I take no pleasure in it and personally find the act distasteful, especially when observing the oil lingering on others' lips, the squelching sounds of food being slurped and smacked between moist mucous membranes in the folds of fleshy human mouths.

I'm not entirely sure how I gain sustenance. I have found certain habits are necessary to keep me intact. As to each one's precise physiological function, I am unclear.

Your mother thinks I don't eat enough. "My stomach is a little weak," I say. "I'm sorry."

"Is that why you're not fat like most foreigners?" your aunt asks. Her English is surprisingly good.

"I guess so," I tell her.

"My mother is from Hunan," you tell me. "Her food is a little spicy for you, maybe."

"It's good," I say.

"I'll tell her less spicy next time," you promise.

"You don't have to," I say. I hate making the woman inconvenience herself to please an artificial stomach.

After the feast, we watch the annual pageant on television. There's Dashan the Canadian smiling and laughing as the other presenters tease him about the length of his nose. Your relatives point at my face and make unflattering comparisons.

At midnight, we watch the sky light up with fireworks.

Then it's time for bed. I sleep in the guest room with your flatulent uncle. I suspect your mother placed me with him as some form of punishment.

I hadn't anticipated sharing a room. I hadn't even brought nightclothes. I don't own any.

"I usually sleep naked," is my excuse when I sheepishly ask you for a spare set of pajamas.

I wonder what it's like to sleep. It strikes me as a strange way to pass the time.

I pull the covers up to my chin, ignoring your uncle when he scolds me for wearing a scarf to bed. I shut my eyes. I practice breathing slowly and loudly as I've seen real people do. Eventually, your uncle falls asleep. He snores like a chainsaw but sleeps like a stone. The hourly bursts of fireworks don't waken him. Neither does the light from my smartphone when I turn it on to look up Cao Didi. That's only his nickname in the Chinese press, of course. His English name is Maxwell Stone, but that's not his real name, either. In his nation of origin, he was called Maksimilian Petrovsky.

Here is Maxwell Stone's biography: born in Russia in 1920, he moved to the United States in the late '30s, where he began working as an extra for Hammerhead Studios. He worked as a stuntman in adventure films, but he got his first speaking role as a torch-wielding villager in 1941's *The Jigsaw Man*, a low-budget knock-off of *Frankenstein* made without the permission of Mary Shelley's estate. Maxwell Stone never attained fame in the United States or in his native Russia, but his only starring role in 1948's *The White Witch of the Amazon* somehow gained him a cult following in China, where audiences dubbed him "Cao Didi" (Grass Brother) after an iconic scene in which Stone evades a tribe of headhunters by hiding in the underbrush. The McCarthy era killed Stone's career in Hollywood. In 1951, he left Los Angeles and never returned.

Thomas Majors does not resemble Maxwell Stone. Maxwell was dark and muscular with a moustache and a square jaw, the perfect early twentieth-century man: rugged yet refined.

I don't know how your grandmother recognizes Maxwell Stone in Thomas Majors. I have mostly forgotten Stone. There's hardly any of him left in me, just a few acting lessons and a couple of tips on grooming and posing for photographs.

I spend the next few days and nights dredging up Tingting's *Changshahua*. When I speak Chinese at the table, your mother blanches. She didn't realize I could understand the things she has been saying about me.

I don't get the opportunity to talk to your grandmother privately until the fifth day of the lunar New Year. It's late at night, and I hear her hobble down to the living room by herself and turn on the television. There's a burst of fireworks outside, but everyone is too full of *baijiu* and *jiaozi* to wake up. The only two people in the house still conscious are me and *Nainai*.

I turn off the telly and kneel in front of her. In Tingting's old *Changshahua* I ask, "How did you know I was Cao Didi?"

She smiles blankly and says, in accented English, "How did you recognize me under all these feathers?"

It takes a moment for the memory to percolate. It's 1947, on a cheap jungle set in a sound studio in Los Angeles. Maxwell Stone is wearing a khaki costume and a Panama hat and I'm wearing Maxwell Stone. Maxwell is a craftsman, not an artist: dependable and humble. He always remembers his lines. Now I remember them, too.

Your grandmother is reciting dialog from one of Stone's movies. She's playing the lost heiress whom Stone's character was sent to rescue. I can't quite recall the original actress's name. Margot or something like that.

Lights. Camera. Action. "Feathers or no feathers," I recite. "A dame's a dame. Now it's time to go home." Thomas's mouth tries on a mid-Atlantic accent.

"But I can't go back." Your grandmother touches her forehead with the back of her hand. "I won't. This is where I belong now."

"Knock it off with this nonsense, will you?" says an American adventurer played by a Russian actor played by an entity as-of-yet unclassified. "Your family's paying me big money to bring you back to civilization."

"Tell them I died! Tell them Catherine DuBlanc was killed." A melodramatic pause, just like in the film. ". . . Killed by the White Witch of the Amazon."

Then your grandmother goes quiet again, like a toy whose batteries have run out. She says nothing more.

I thought she knew me. But she only knows Maxwell. The performance was all she wanted.

I have worn so many people. I don't know how many. I don't remember most of them. I ought to keep a record of some kind, but most of them strike me as dull or loathsome in retrospect.

I played a scientist once or twice, but I could not figure myself out. In the 1960s I was a graduate student; I sought myself out in folklore and found vague references to creatures called changelings, shapeshifters, but the descriptions don't quite fit me. I do not have a name.

I do not know how old I am or where I came from or what made me or why I came to be. I try on one person after another, hoping that someday I'll find one that fits and I'll settle into it and some biological process or act of magic will turn me into that person.

I have considered leaving civilization, but the wilds are smaller than they used to be. Someone would stumble across me and see me undisguised. It has happened before.

I will not submit to scientific examination. Though the tools have advanced considerably over the course of my many lifetimes, the human method of inquiry remains the same: tear something apart until it confesses its secrets, whether it's a heretic or a frog's nervous system or the atom.

I do experience something akin to pain, and I prefer to avoid it.

I like being Thomas Majors. I enjoy making money, getting promoted, living as a minor celebrity. I appreciate the admiration others heap upon my creation.

And I confess I like your admiration most of all. It's honest and schoolboyish and sweet.

Wearing Thomas grants me the pleasure of your company, which I treasure, though it probably doesn't show. I am fond of so many things about you, such as that little nod you give when you try to look serious, or the way your entire face immediately turns red when you drink. At first, I studied these traits in the hopes of replicating them someday in a future incarnation. I memorized them. I practiced them at home until they were perfect. But even after I've perfected them, I still can't stop watching you.

I would like to be closer to you. I know you want the same thing. I know the real reason you insist on bringing me with you every time you open a new branch in a new city. I know the real reason you always invite me when you go out to dine with new school administrators and government officials and investors.

But I am a creature that falls to pieces terribly often, and you can't hold on to a thing like that. Every instance of physical touch invites potential damage to my artificial skin and the risk of being discovered.

It is difficult to maintain a safe distance in an overcrowded country where schoolboys sit on each other's laps without embarrassment and *ayis* press their shopping baskets into your legs when you queue up at a market.

When you or anyone else stands too near or puts an arm around my shoulders, I step back and say, "Westerners like to keep other people at arm's length."

You have your own reasons not to get too close. You have familial obligations, filial piety. You must make your parents happy. They paid for your education, your clothes, your food, your new apartment. They gave you your job. You owe them a marriage and a child. You have no reason to be a bachelor at the age of twenty-eight.

Your mother and father choose a woman for you. She's pretty and kind. You can think of no adequate excuses to chase her away. You can tolerate a life with her, you decide. You're a businessman. You will travel a lot. She doesn't mind.

You announce your impending marriage less than a year later. The two of you look perfect in your engagement photos, and at your wedding you beam so handsomely that even I am fooled. I'm not jealous. I'm relieved that she has taken your focus from me, and I do love to see you smile.

A few months later, we travel to Beijing. New Teach is opening a training center there, so we have another series of banquets and *gan bei* and KTV with our new business partners.

By the end of the night, you're staggering drunk, too drunk to walk straight, so I stoop low to let you put your arm across Thomas Majors's shoulders in order to save you from tipping onto the pavement. I hope that you're too drunk to notice there's something not quite right with Thomas's limbs, or at least too drunk to remember it afterward.

I help you into a cab. The driver asks me the standard *waiguoren* questions (*Where are you from? How long have you lived in China? Do you like it here? What is your job? Do you eat hamburgers?*) but I ignore him. I only want to listen to you.

You rub your stomach as the taxi speeds madly back to our hotel. "Are you going to vomit?" I ask.

You're quiet for a moment. I try to roll down the window nearest you, but it's broken. Finally, you mutter, "I'm getting fat. Too much beer."

"You look fine," I say.

"I'm gaining weight," you insist.

"You sound like a woman," I tease you.

"Why don't you get fat?" you say. "You're a Westerner. How are you so slim?"

"Just lucky, I guess," I say.

I pay the cab fare and drag you out, back up to your hotel suite. I give you water to drink and an ibuprofen to swallow so you won't get a hangover. You take your medicine like a good boy, but you refuse to go to sleep.

I sit at the edge of your bed. You lean forward and grab my scarf. "You always wear this," you say.

"Always," I agree.

"What would happen if you took it off?" you ask.

"I can't tell you," I reply.

"Come on," you say, adding a line from a song: "Come on, baby, don't be shy." Then you laugh until tears flow down your red cheeks, until you fall backward onto the bed, and when you fall you drag me by the scarf down with you.

"Be careful!" I tell you. "Ah, *xiao xin!*"

But instead you pull on the scarf as though reeling in a fish.

"You never take it off," you say, holding one end of the scarf before your eyes. "I have never seen your neck."

I know I'm supposed to say something witty but I can't think of it, so I smile bashfully instead. It's a gesture I stole from Hugh Grant films.

"What would happen if I take it off?" you ask. You try to unwrap it, but fortunately you're too clumsy with drink.

"My head would fall off," I say.

Then you laugh, and I laugh. Looming over you is awkward, so I lie beside you and prop my head up on Thomas Majors's shoulder. You turn onto your left side to face me.

"Da Huang," you say, still playing with the scarf. "That's your Chinese name."

"What's your Chinese name?" I ask. "Your real name, I mean? You never told me."

"Chengwei," you say.

"Chengwei," I repeat, imperfectly.

"No," you say. "Not Chéngwéi." You raise your hand, then make a dipping motion to indicate the second and third tones. "Chéngwěi."

"Chéngwěi," I say, drawing the tones in the air with Thomas's graceful fingers.

"*Hen hao,*" you say. *Very good.*

"*Nali,*" I say, a modest denial.

You smile. I notice for the first time that one of your front teeth is slightly crooked. It's endearing, though, one of those little flaws which, through some sort of alchemy I have yet to learn to replicate, only serves to flatter the rest of the picture rather than mar it.

"Da Huang is not a good name," you say.

"What should I be called?" I ask.

You study Thomas Majors's face carefully, yet somehow fail to find its glaring faults.

"Shuai," you say. You don't translate the word, but I know what it means. *Handsome.*

You touch Thomas's cheek. I can feel your warmth through the false skin.

Again, I don't know what to say. This hasn't come up in the etiquette books I studied.

I realize that you're waiting for me to be the brash Westerner who shoves his way forward and does what he wants. This hunger of yours presses on Thomas Majors, pinches and pulls at him to resculpt his personality.

I want to be the man who can give you these things. But I'm terrified. When you run your fingers through Thomas's hair, I worry that the scalp might come loose, or that your hand will skate across a bump that should not be there.

You grab me by the scarf again and pull me closer to you. I shut my eyes. I don't want you to see them at this distance; you might find something wrong in them. But that's not what you're looking for.

Then you kiss me, a clumsy, drunk kiss. You cling to me like one of Harlow's monkeys to a cloth mother.

I can't remember the last time I was kissed.

I vaguely remember engaging in the act of coitus in some previous incarnation. It did not go well.

The mechanics of sexuality, of blood redistributing itself and tissue contracting and flesh reddening and appendages hardening and fluids secreting, are marvelously difficult to imitate with any verisimilitude.

This is the climax of every story. In romance novels, the lovers kiss in the rain, and it's all over. In fairy tales, the kiss breaks the spell: the princess awakens, the frog becomes a man. But that doesn't happen, not now, not the last time I was kissed, and not the next time I will be kissed.

But I enjoy it all the same. Your body is warm and right and real: self-heating skin, hair that grows in on its own, a mouth that lubricates itself.

I study your body and memorize it for future reference. At the moment there is little I can learn and so much that I want to know. I wish I could taste you.

You remove yourself from my lips and drunkenly smear your mouth against my cheek, my jaw, what little of my neck is not covered by the scarf. You press your nose against me and try vainly to smell Thomas Majors under the cologne I have chosen for him. You rest your head on my arm for a moment. I stroke your hair—not because it seems appropriate, but because I want to.

Then you close your eyes. They stay closed. Soon I hear the slow, loud breathing of a man asleep.

That's as far as it goes between you and Thomas Majors.

My arms don't fall asleep so I can let you use Thomas Majors as your pillow for as long as you like. I watch your eyelashes flutter as you fall into REM sleep. I wonder what you're dreaming about. I press my fingers against your neck to feel your pulse.

Without waking you, I move my head down and lay it upon your chest. I shut my eyes. I listen to your heartbeat and the slow rhythm of your breath. Your stomach gurgles. The sounds are at once recognizably natural and alien to me, like deep-sea creatures. I find them endlessly fascinating.

I try very hard to fall asleep, but I have no idea how to go about it. Still, I wait, and I imitate your breathing and hope that I'll begin to lose track of each individual thump of your heart, and that I'll slip out of consciousness and maybe even dream, and that I'll wake up next to you.

Hours pass this way. The light through the window turns pale gray as the sun rises in Beijing's smoggy sky. You roll over to face the shade and lie still again.

I slip from the bed and head to the bathroom, where I examine myself. I look very much the same as I did the day before.

I take the elevator down to the dining room. It's 8:36 a.m. Breakfast time. I serve myself from the buffet, selecting the sort of things I think a Westerner is supposed to eat at breakfast: bread, mostly, with coffee, tea, and a glass of milk. I sit alone at a little table with this meal before me and let its steam warm my face. I wait for the aroma to awaken a sense of hunger in me. It doesn't.

I eat it anyway so as not to cause suspicion. I can't taste any of it, as usual.

You're still asleep when I get back. It has only been about five hours since you flopped onto my bed. In the bathroom, I empty Thomas Majors's stomach and turn on the shower. Even though the door is locked, I do not remove the yellow scarf. I tape a plastic bag around it to keep it dry.

The grime of last night's drinking and duck neck slides off, along with a few hairs I'll have to replace later.

The water hits me with a muffled impact. I don't feel wet. Thomas's skin keeps me dry like a raincoat. It isn't my flesh.

I wonder if the state you invoke in me can accurately be called love. I know only that I am happier in your presence than out of it, and that I care desperately what you think of me. If that is love, then I suppose it can be said that I love you, with all the shapeless mass I have instead of a heart.

I don't believe that you love me, but I know that you love Thomas Majors, and that's close enough.

I've heard stories like this, hundreds of them, in languages I've long forgotten. The ending is always the same. Galatea's form softens and turns to flesh. The Velveteen Rabbit sprouts fur and whiskers. But I am still myself, whatever that is, and my puppet Thomas Majors has not become a real boy.

I don't know what I am, but at least now I know something I am not: I am not a creature of fairy tales.

Your cell phone wakes you a little after 10 a.m. It's your wife. I'm dressed by then in a navy-blue suit and working on my cell phone in one of the easy chairs. You finish the conversation before you're quite conscious.

"Do you remember last night?" I ask.

You scratch your head. "No," you groan.

"Do you have a hangover?" I ask.

I take your miserable grunt as a yes.

Your daughter is born seven months later. You leave Beijing for a while to tend to your wife. After a few weeks of your unbearable absence, a student invites me to dinner with her family. "I can't," I tell her. "I'm taking a trip this weekend."

"Are you going to see your *giiiirlfriend*?" she asks in a singsong voice. She's in high school, too busy from fifteen-hour school days seven days a week to have a boyfriend of her own, but she has immense interest in the love lives of her more attractive teachers.

"No," I tell her. The expats know that Thomas Majors is gay but his students and colleagues do not. "I'm going to visit my boss, Mr. Liu. I can have dinner with you next week."

I take the bullet train to Shenzhen. As the countryside blurs past my window, I notice that Thomas's fingernails have become brittle. It's too soon. I blame the cold, dry air of Beijing and resolve to buy a bottle of clear nail polish and apply it at the first opportunity.

You're not home when I come to your door. Your mother-in-law thanks me for the gift I have brought (a canister of imported milk powder), invites me in, and explains that you're on a shopping trip in Hong Kong and will be back soon. In the meantime, I sit in the living room and sip warm water.

Your wife isn't finished with her post-partum month of confinement. She does not invite me to her room. It's probably because she's in pajamas and hasn't washed her hair, or she's simply tired, but the suspicion that she knows something unsavory about me crawls on my back.

There's a dog in the apartment, a shaggy little thing that doesn't go up to my knee. It doesn't quite know what to make of me. It barks and skitters around in circles. It can smell me—not Thomas, but *me*—and it knows that something is slightly off.

But dogs are not terribly bright. I sneak to the kitchen, find a piece of bacon, and put it in my pocket. The dog likes me well enough after that.

You return home that afternoon, laden with bags. You weren't expecting me, but you're happy to see me.

"I bought something for you," you tell me. "A gift."

"You didn't have to," I insist.

"I already had to buy gifts for my whole extended family," you say, "so one more doesn't matter. Here."

You pull a small box out of a suitcase.

"Can I open it?" I ask.

You nod.

I peel off the tape. The paper does not tear at all as I remove it. The box shimmers. I open it and can't help but cry out.

"A new scarf!" I hold it up. It's beautiful, gleaming yellow silk with brocade serpents. I try on an expression of overwhelming gratitude. Until now, I haven't had a chance to use it. "Snakes."

"That's your birth year," you say.

"You remembered," I say. "This is wonderful. Thank you so much."

"Put it on," you tell me.

"In a little while."

"Come on, baby. Don't be shy," you say. You couch your demand in humor and a smile. "Go ahead."

I try to think of an excuse not to. A scar on my neck. A skin condition. It's cold. None of them will work.

Your baby saves me. She starts screaming in the bedroom, and neither your wife nor her mother can calm her down. Your wife soon starts crying, too, and your mother-in-law starts shouting at her.

"I think maybe you should get in there and say hello," I tell you.

You groan, but you comply.

I dash to the lavatory. Quickly, I unwind the counterfeit *Liu Viuttor* scarf from around my neck. It sticks to Thomas's flesh like a bandage. I peel it off slowly but the damage is done. The skin of Thomas Majors's neck has gone ragged, like moth-eaten cloth. I wrap the new scarf around it snugly. Then I unwrap it. The damage is still there. Somehow, I thought this new totem would fix me.

I tie my new scarf around Thomas's neck and return to the living room.

To spare your wife further agitation, her mother banishes the baby from the bedroom. You carry her out with you. She's a fat little thing, all lumpy pink pajamas and chubby cheeks gone red from crying. When she sees me, she quiets herself and stares. She's had limited experience of the world, but even she knows that this creature before her is different.

"She's never seen a foreigner before," you say with a smile. "Do you want to hold her?"

You thrust her into my arms before I can resist. She does not cry anymore, just looks at me with big, dark eyes. Her little body is warm and surprisingly heavy.

"Chinese babies like to stare at handsome faces," you say.

I smile at her. She doesn't smile back. She hasn't learned yet that she's supposed to. Everything about her is unpracticed and new and utterly authentic. I find it unnerving.

"You made this," I said. "You made a person. A real person."

"Yeah," you say, probably filing my remark under *foreigners say strange things*. "Do you think you'll have children?" you ask me.

"Probably not," I say.

Your daughter clutches at my new scarf.

A few days later, we take the bullet train back to Beijing together. You nap most of the way with your head on my shoulder. When you wake up, you tell me, "You should sleep more. You look tired."

"So do you," I reply.

"I have a baby," you say. "You don't."

The only reply I have for him is a nervous Colin Firth smile. Underneath it, I am panicking.

"You look a little gray. Maybe it's the air," you say. "Do you use a mask?"

"Of course," I say.

"You need to drink more water," you tell me. I know by now that nagging is an expression of love in China, but the advice still irritates me. It's useless.

Our train plunges deeper and deeper into miasma as we approach the city. The sky darkens even as the sun rises. It's late autumn and the coal plants are blazing in preparation for winter.

Maybe it *is* the air. Maybe it's bad enough to affect even me. Maybe the new skin wasn't ready when I put it on. Maybe it's just the standard decay that conquers every Westerner who spends too much time in China. Whatever the reason, Thomas Majors is beginning to come apart.

We don air filters as we leave the train station. Outside, we pass people in suits, women in brightly colored minidresses, children in school uniforms, all covering their faces. Those of us who can afford it wear enormous, clunky breathing masks. Those who can't, or who don't understand the risk, wear thin surgical masks made of paper, or little cloth masks with cartoon characters on them, or they just tie bandanas around their mouths and noses. A short, stocky man squats on the pavement, removing his mask every so often to suck on a cigarette.

We take separate taxis. I don't go home, though. I visit a beauty shop, pharmacy, and apothecary, and I buy every skincare product I can find. Expensive moisturizer from France. A mud-mask treatment from Korea. Cocoa butter from South America. Jade rollers. Pearl powder. Caterpillar fungus. Back in my apartment, I slather them on Thomas Majors to see if they will make him tight and bright again. They don't.

The skin is looser, thinner, and when that happens the center cannot hold. I feel around for muscles that have slipped out of place, joints that have shifted, limbs trying to lengthen or widen. I have not lost my shape just yet, but I know it is only a matter of time.

I unravel the scarf you gave me and look again. The skin underneath is even worse. There's an open gash along it that threatens to creep even wider. I can see bits of myself through it, brackish and horrible. Sewing it shut won't do anything; the flesh is too fragile. So I tape it up and wrap the scarf around it even tighter. Silk is strong. Silk will hold it, at least for a while.

I make phone calls to forgers, to chemists, to printers, to tanners, to all the sorts of people who can help me make someone new. This time, at least, I have money to spend and privacy in which to work. I can do it right. I can make somebody who will last longer and fit better and maybe won't come apart again.

The smog provides a convenient excuse for my absence over the next few weeks. It traps most of us in our homes with our air purifiers. But at times a strong wind comes to blow it away, at least for a while, and there you are again inviting me out to KTV bars and business lunches and badminton. I can't go. I want to go, but Thomas Majors is fragile and thin, liable to split apart at any moment. His hair is coming out. His gums are getting soft. Speaking is difficult; I feel the gash in Thomas's throat grow wider and wider under the scarf.

I cite my health as a reason not to renew my contract, but you refuse to accept it. You won't let Thomas Majors go. I remind you of my unnamed medical condition. I tell you that I've been to dozens of doctors and even some traditional Chinese healers. I promise to see another specialist.

I promise I'll keep in touch. I promise I'll come back again once I'm better.

Then I sequester myself in my apartment. I don't know what my next form will be. I'd like to build myself another Thomas Majors, one that will last forever, but I feel my body pulling in different directions. It wants to shift in a dozen different ways, all of them horrible: too squat, or insect-thin, or with limbs at angles that don't make sense in human physiology.

My human costume is slipping off me too quickly. I don't go outside anymore. I only wait for the men to come with the documents and the materials. There's a knock at the door. It's you.

I know I shouldn't open it, but I also know that you can hear me moving around in my apartment, and that you'll be hurt if I don't let you in, and even though I don't want you to see me as I am, I still want to see you. I adjust Thomas's face and throw a heavy robe on over the blue suit.

The expression of horror in your eyes is remarkable. I memorize it to use in a future incarnation.

"*Ni shenti bu hao*," you say, in that blunt Chinese way. *Your body is not good.* You take off your breathing mask and come inside.

"Thanks," I say.

You try to give me a hug.

"Don't," I say. "I could be contagious." The truth is I'm terrified you might feel me moving around underneath Thomas Majors, or you'll squeeze tight enough to leave a dent.

You sit down without invitation.

"What is it?" you ask.

"I think I caught food poisoning, on top of everything else. Probably shouldn't have eaten *shaokao*."

"Are you going to be healthy enough for the ride home?" you ask.

"I'll be all right," I say. "I just need rest is all."

"Have you been to the hospital?"

"Of course," I tell you. "The doctor gave me a ton of antibiotics and said to avoid cold water."

"Which hospital was it? Which doctor? Maybe he wasn't a good one. My friend knows one of the best doctors for stomach problems. I can take you to him. They have very good equipment. A big laboratory."

"I'll be all right."

You head to the kitchen to boil water. "Wait a moment," you instruct me over the sound of the electric kettle. Then you return with a steaming mug of something dark and greenish. "Drink this," you tell me. "Chinese medicine. For your stomach."

"I can't," I insist.

"Come on," you say. "You look really bad."

"It's too hot," I complain. I feel the steam softening the insides of Thomas's nasal passages.

You return to the kitchen to retrieve some ice from the freezer. I never use ice, but I always make sure to have some in my home because I am a Westerner for the time being.

You drop a few cubes of ice into my mug. "There," you say. "Drink it."

"I'm sick to my stomach," I complain. "I might vomit."

"This will fix it," you insist.

I know I shouldn't listen to you, but I want to make you happy, and some part of me still half-believes that stupid fairy-tale fantasy that your love will make me real somehow. So I put the mug to my lips and slurp down some of its contents, and soon I feel the artificial stomach lining thinning and turning to fizz inside me.

"Excuse me," I rasp. The vocal cords feel loose. I bolt to the bathroom to vomit.

Thomas's stomach lining makes its way up and out. It hangs from my mouth, still attached somewhere around my chest. Your medicine has burned holes into it. I don't blame you. I'm sure it works properly on real human stomachs. I bite through the fake esophagus to free myself from the ruined organ, losing a tooth in the process. Then I flush the mess down the squat toilet.

Evidently, the noise is alarming. "I'm calling you an ambulance!" you shout from the living room.

It takes me much too long to cram the esophagus back in so I can say, "Don't. I'm quite all right. I just needed to vomit. I'm feeling better now. Really." But the vocal cords are so loose by this point that the words come out slurred and gravelly.

The call is quick; the arrival of the ambulance less so. I lie on the bathroom floor in a fetal position, contemplating my options. My strength is gone. I can't make it to the front door without you tackling me. I could get to a window and throw myself out, perhaps; I could drop through twenty stories of pollution and crawl away from Thomas Majors after he hits the ground. But I can't do something so horrible in front of you.

You punch through the bathroom door, undo the lock, and put your arms around my shoulders. I can feel your hands shake. You tell me over and over again that I'm going to be all right, and you're going to help me. I want to believe you.

The ambulance finally arrives. You pay the driver and help carry me out. "You're so light," you say.

I don't try to fight you.

You should have called a taxi, or maybe flagged down an e-bike instead, because the bulky ambulance gets stuck in traffic. You slap the insides of it as if trying to beat Beijing into submission. You curse the other cars, the ambulance driver, the civil engineers who planned the roadways, the population density, the asphalt for not being wide enough.

You curse the EMTs for the deplorable condition of the ambulance and the black soot on the gauze they've applied to my face, unaware that the filth is coming from the man you're trying to save. Thomas has sprung a leak; now I am pouring out.

They put a respirator of some sort over Thomas Majors's face. They attach devices to him to monitor a heart and lungs that do not exist. You notice the way the technician fiddles with the wires and pokes the electronic box, unable to get a proper reading from the patient, and you curse the defective equipment. You see the other technician jab me over and over again, unable to find a vein in which to stick an IV, and you curse his incompetence.

They get out their scissors. They open the robe and cut through its sleeves. Then they start cutting through my blue suit. I make little sounds of protest. I can't speak anymore.

"I'll buy you a new one," you say.

I try to crawl away, but you hold one arm and a technician grabs the other. Soon you can see what has happened to Thomas's torso—misshapen, discolored, with thick scars where I've had to stich darts as the skin became too loose.

Your hand moves to your mouth. "You were sick how long?" you ask. Your English is slipping.

I know what's coming. There is nothing I can do to stop it but lie here like a damsel tied to the railroad tracks and wait for it to hit me.

It's time to remove the scarf.

I've tied it too tight to slip the scissors underneath it, so they have to cut through the knots. Frustrated by how slowly the technicians work, you lean in and grab the silk.

Your hands shake harder and harder as you unwind the fabric. I watch the silk growing darker the closer you get to me. I'm sorry I ruined such a beautiful thing.

I can't see what's beneath. I don't want to. There's a reason I keep the mirrors covered when I go through a shift. But I can see the reaction on your face and on the technicians' faces, too. They've doubtless encountered horrible things in their line of work, and yet this still alarms them.

Thomas Majors's larynx comes apart. My neck is exposed. I feel cold.

You can't speak anymore either. You only make a strange panting sound and stare. Terror has stolen your voice. What's left is something primitive, an instinct going back millions of years. It must be wonderful to know who your ancestors were and that they were something as benign as apes.

One of the technicians is on his cell phone with the hospital, explaining the situation as best he can. I hear the doctor's voice telling them to bring me in through the basement entrance so the other patients won't see me.

I know what he wants. Physicians here are required to publish research on top of their grueling schedules and the doctor realizes that he has found an extraordinary case study. He's already thinking of fame, research grants, possibly another Nobel Prize for China. He won't have any trouble keeping me in a lab. There are no human rights standards to stop scientific progress here, and my fake UK citizenship will not protect me.

With nothing left to hold him together, Thomas Majors comes undone. The skin of his head shrinks from the skin of his shoulders. His face is loose. A seam opens at his armpit and runs down his torso.

You grab his hand. You can feel me underneath it, squirming. Your wrist jerks but you don't let go. Thomas's hand slips off me like a glove. It takes you a moment to understand what just happened, what you're holding, and when the realization hits, you scream and scream and scream.

The technicians can't pin me down anymore. They don't want to. It's impossible to tell what they can grab on to and whether or not it's safe to touch. So now they're trying to get away, pressing themselves against the walls of the ambulance, trying to clamber up to the front. The driver has already fled.

You're paralyzed. You've wedged yourself into a corner. Your eyes whirl about the ambulance, skipping upon me, upon what's left of Thomas Majors, upon the rear-door latch that's not quite close enough for you to open, upon the ceiling and the machines and all these things that don't make sense anymore.

I stand up. The last scraps of the man I wanted so badly to be fall to the floor. You shrink down, down, trying to disappear, but you don't have as much practice as I do.

You cover your eyes, uncover them, look at me, shut them again. I grab the door latch, averting my gaze from the sight of my own hand.

You're muttering something over and over again like a Buddhist chant. I listen carefully. My hearing is not what it was just a few minutes ago, but I can recognize the words, "*Ni shi shenme?*" *What are you?*

I don't have a larynx anymore and my tongue can no longer accommodate human language, so even though I want to, I can't answer "*wo bu zhidao*" or "*ouk oida*" or "*nga nu-zu*" or "I don't know."

I get the door open. The outside world is an endless polluted twilight. The driver behind us doesn't look up from his cell phone to glance in my direction. Two car-lengths away, all I can see are vague shapes and headlights. The smog will hide me well.

I climb out of the ambulance and into the haze. I don't look back.

I saw you once after that. It wasn't long ago, I think. I was wearing someone new, a girl with black hair and a melon-seed face. Pretty girls are easy for me. I can slather on makeup if the skin isn't right, and I don't have to bother with a backstory or a personality. No one really wants it.

It was at an auto show in Shanghai. I was draped across a green Ferrari, wearing a bikini that matched the paint. I hadn't expected to see you, but there you were with a group of businessmen smoking Marlboros and ogling the models.

You were older. I'm not sure by how much. Time passes differently for me, and maybe time alone was not responsible for how much you had aged.

I would like to say I will never forget you, but I can't promise you that. This shapeless matter inside my head shifts and dies and regenerates, and as it does so, memories fade and old incarnations of myself are discarded. Maxwell Stone had lovers, most likely, but I can't recall their faces, and someday I will lose yours as well.

Your group strolled by my Ferrari, making the obligatory lewd remarks, flashing their brown teeth in leery grins. I wore my generic smile and offered up a vacant titter. I told them about the car.

You stood a little ways behind the other men with your hands in your pockets. I knew that look: you were too tired to pretend to be having a good time.

I smiled at you as hard as I could. Finally, you looked up. I thought maybe you would recognize me somehow. Maybe you would cry out, "It's you!" and take me in your arms. Or maybe, at the very least, you'd let your gaze linger on me a little longer than normal.

But you didn't. You made that nervous grimace you do whenever a woman pays too much attention to you. Then you ambled off to look at a Lexus—a four-door with lots of cabin space. Good for families.

I watched you move. Your shoulders were slumped as though you carried something very heavy.

Then more bodies flowed between us, wealthy men and their school-aged mistresses, nouveau riche wives and their spoiled bachelor sons searching for a car to attract a pretty bride, broke students in designer knock-offs come to take selfies in front of BMWs so they can pretend to be rich on Weixin.

I lost you among them. I did not find you again.